The Schreiber Chronicles Complete Collection

Echoes Of Dystopia

Broken Paths

Shattered Reflections

The Shadows of Redemption

Ethan Spadoni

CONTENTS

Echoes Of Dystopia

The Schieber Chronicles Part 1

Ethan Spadoni

Paperback: ISBN 978-1-0698501-0-2
Electronic book: ISBN 978-1-0698501-1-9

Contents

Hello everyone, I just wanted to thank some people before you get into the book itself. I want to thank both of my parents for their unending support, and my older brother Daniel for always being there for me. I really appreciate you guys and all you do for me. I'd also like to thank my cousin Jason Lavoie for providing his art experience in creating my cover art for this project. I couldn't have done this without you brother.

I'd also like to thank my writing mentor Susan Faw for teaching me how to self publish and for walking me through the entire process while helping me with the formatting challenges I encountered. Thanks again!

I'd also like to thank my professors Dr. Steve Jobbit and Dr. Ron Harpelle for guiding me on my academic journey and getting me into the Master's program at Lakehead; and for supporting me throughout that time period.

The next person I'd like to thank is my favourite librarian Trudy Russo for helping me with my research during my education career. My friends also deserve some thanks for not letting me give up on the series.

Finally, I'd like to thank all of you for deciding to take a chance on this project and reading my stories. I wouldn't be able to do any of this without your support. I have more to say at the end of the book but this is the gist of what I wanted to put out. I've been a writer all my life and have always wished to become an author. If you wish to contact me, feel free to email me at the email listed below.

I hope you all have a great time reading and I look forward to doing many more projects.

Cheers, Ethan Spadoni

espadoni@lakeheadu.ca

Prologue

The First Bite

As I SAT DOWN next to the person interviewing me, I couldn't help feeling nervous but excited as well. It's time to tell my story to the best of my ability. Many Years ago, a terrible calamity occurred within my hometown of Schreiber. Schreiber is a beautiful town in Canada but it met a horrific fate so long ago. There was once a humble man with generous intentions who wanted to make the world a better place for everyone. However, his haste and ambition overtook his kindness and he slowly transformed into a monster. No one truly knows when the change actually took place, but the kind man that once ran the water treatment plant became something completely unrecognizable.

This story takes place on June 25th 2015 at the very same water treatment plant in my hometown. It was at about 5 pm when the incident happened. It was a warm sunny evening and Doctor Jeb Winter-Fields walked into his office and began his work after taking a much-needed dinner break. Dr. Jeb was in charge of the entire treatment plant. He spent much of his time within his office filing paperwork and taking business calls but his true passion was working in his personal lab in the basement. Jeb had been working on a secret project that nobody else within the plant had any idea about whatsoever. It was meant to revolutionize the scientific community and change the way we looked at the world forever. As Jeb was spending one of his many late nights in the lab; June 25th would be the day that changed everything. While Jeb may have wanted to change things for the better, fate changed his course drastically.

The story opens while Dr. Jeb is working in his lab that very night. Jeb appears to be mixing various chemicals in his dark dingy lab while humming "staying alive" to himself. Just as he completed his work, he raised his hands in joyous jubilation. He was finally one step closer to achieving his goal. "Finally, my serum is going to be complete. Soon the world will be peaceful and there will be no more conflict", explained Jeb in exhilaration. His ultimate goal was to pacify the human race by curing all diseases and making them overall a friendlier and better species. As he was finishing up his experiment, something outside caught his eye. He looked outside his window and he saw some mushrooms glinting in the sunlight. These mushrooms were a sickly green and the smell alone was enough to make Jeb throw up. After some consideration, Jeb decided that these would be perfect to add to his serum. If he could extract the sickly cells from the mushrooms then he may be able to create immunities to any disease in the world. After putting the mushrooms into his vials, he put them into his machine that would allow him to analyze their molecular properties to ensure that the serum would work as intended. This machine was advanced but also very flimsy and it could take up to two weeks before the analysis was complete. Jeb finished up his work in the lab and departed in order to head home for the night.

After a couple of days things took a very dark turn for Jeb and his psyche. As a new day began on the horizon Dr. Jeb was sitting alone breathing heavily within his lab. "I'm getting impatient; I don't care about the analysis anymore", he said angrily. Just as he was getting prepared to remove the vials from the machine his assistant slowly walked in. "Sir what are you doing?" asked the assistant. "Nothing that concerns you; GET OUT!" yelled Jeb. The scared worker was concerned for his boss but he needed to make sure he was okay. "Sir you really should wait for the analysis to be complete, if you don't then this serum could kill you," said the assistant frightfully. The worker could see that Jeb was about to take the vial from his machine before it was finished being analyzed and tested properly. The assistant had no idea what was in the vial, but he knew it had to be important. Dr. Jeb was a genius and anything that he was going to make would be epic, as long as it didn't destroy himself first. The scientist was starting to get angry with his insolence and wanted him to leave. "Listen to me very carefully, I'm taking the serum and you can't stop me! Now leave me ALONE!" screamed Jeb. "Fine do what you want", said the assistant in fear.

The assistant was now terrified of his boss but he felt like it was his duty to make sure his mentor didn't accidentally kill himself. Still, there didn't seem to be anything the poor kid could do to help. As Dr. Jeb poured the vial into a syringe and injected it into his arm; he began to feel a tingling sensation around his legs and he started to feel amazing. Jeb felt better than he had ever felt in his life. With all this power coursing through his veins, he wanted to share this with the world. "DO you feel this power my assistant!" yelled

Jeb. The poor worker began to cower as a green hue covered the outline of Jeb's body. Jeb slowly advanced in a very threatening manner towards the scared assistant when Jeb finally began to feel faint. His throat burned and his eyes began to water profusely. He could still breathe but his breathing became shallow and uneven. His knees buckled and he collapsed into the arms of his helpless assistant while muttering things about ancient Egypt and five teenagers.

His brain felt like mush and he couldn't see clearly anymore as his eyes became foggy. By now the assistant had overcome his previous fear and held Jeb concerningly and tried to console his mentor. Soon Jeb realized that he couldn't think straight and started to feel very ill as memories long forgotten began to both stir and pass quickly. "Sir, are you okay, should I get some water?" he asked in a calming voice. Jeb's eyes fluttered open and he looked straight up at the ceiling in an attempt to get his bearings. "I...I...I don't feel well, I think that I should go home and rest", replied Jeb in a hoarse voice. "You do that sir," said the assistant softly. Jeb was able to regain his mobility and walked out of the lab in order to head home for some rest.

Nearly two weeks later things turned even darker for our favorite scientist. Dr. Jeb got out of bed feeling like he was going to throw up into the toilet bowl; which he ended up doing for several hours. He had spent nearly the last two weeks sick in bed and could barely move. His hair was greasy; his clothes were covered in vomit and his face looked very pale and clammy. By all means, someone of this condition should not be going anywhere but Jeb felt like he had to fulfill his duty and get back to work. "I have to finish what I've started", whispered Jeb to absolutely no one. Jeb forced himself to get out of bed and didn't even bother with changing his clothes. He had absolutely no energy to even do basic things but he still had to go into work. After a grueling ten-minute walk, Jeb went into work and headed straight to his office.

He didn't even give the other workers a second glance and trotted right to his desk. By the time he got to his desk he doubled over and struggled to breathe again. This had been happening for nearly two weeks but after taking slow breaths he was able to right himself again. Soon after Jeb regained some of his former strength, his unnamed assistant came in to check on him and see if he needed anything. Right when he entered the office, he could feel the air turn cold. "Sir you look awful, you shouldn't be here", he said defiantly. Jeb slowly looked over at him and asked, "Is the analysis ready yet?" in a weak voice. "I will check sir", said the assistant quietly. The worker went to check on the analysis but he saw that it wasn't ready yet. The machine stated it wouldn't be done for at least a few more minutes.

In order to preserve the work, he decided that he wanted to make a copy of the analysis when it was ready. This was an act of serious initiative on his part and he hoped that Jeb may actually pay him and not slap him this time. Dr. Jeb had become even more erratic since he got sick. Jeb was known to howl for no reason and laugh maniacally to himself while muttering things about Egypt and someone named Rathos. It was very unsettling honestly. The worker decided to search for a jump drive in Jeb's second office. He looked through some papers and found a dirty looking jump drive underneath them. This had only taken thirty seconds of searching so the assistant was extremely proud of it. It had a J on the jump drive. Since he had some time on his hands, he decided to look through it while he waited for the analysis to finish up. As he looked through the jump drive, he saw files that had parts of Jeb's past. Many of the files were redacted but the info he could access was very telling. To his horror, the assistant realized that Jeb may not be the person he thought he was. It was clear that someone typed this all up very quickly and rapidly recently. As he was skimming through the contents of the drive a ding from across the room could be heard. It was clear that the analysis was finished. Even though Jeb placed one of his vials into a machine in his lab, there were two other machines in both offices that would hold the same data. As the assistant went to read them, he heard Jeb call out "if the analysis is ready, I wish to read it first." The worker saved a copy of the analysis to the jump drive and put it in his pocket. He printed out the document and went to go see Jeb. Jeb's first office was extremely close to the second office so the worker knew he had to hurry. Jeb hated tardiness more than anything else.

As the assistant rushed in and caught his breath, he saw Jeb was sitting in the corner muttering to seemingly no one. As he went to go see him, he felt a twinge of fear in him. The air suddenly turned freezing and the assistant knew that his life was in danger. Still, he had to check and see if his boss was okay. "Sir, are you okay?" asked the assistant cautiously. Jeb looked at him slowly and his eyes became angry. His face that once held a hopeful and happy expression, now only held darkness and paranoia. "You see young man, I've made another serum. This serum will help me to equalize the world with me as its ruler. There will be no more wars, there will only be Jeb" he said with a smirk. The assistant looked away and said while quivering, "here...here...here is the analysis you asked for." Jeb snatched the paper away from him and tore it to shreds with his scaly long fingernails. Jeb turned back to his employee and said happily, "I don't need that analysis anymore because my plan progressed flawlessly." The assistant was starting to cry silently out of fear but managed to barely maintain his composure. "What plan sir, I thought you were going to try to end all wars within the world through creating peace?" asked the worker. "You won't live to see my plan unfold because I don't need you anymore. Goodbye old friend", said Dr. Jeb. Jeb's smile disappeared and all that was left was a cold expression on his face as his fists clenched.

Crippled by fear, the assistant knew that he had only seconds to live and bravely attempted to run towards the door to make a strategic escape. Before he could even take one step Jeb was already upon him like a vampire. It was as if Gollum had just found out that the assistant had the One ring and vaulted towards him. Jeb lunged at the assistant and pinned him to the ground. While Jeb looked old and feeble he always made a point to train during his downtime and whatever he ingested increased his existing power momentously.

The assistant tried to fight back with all his strength but struggled under Jeb's superior grip. Jeb grabbed his old friend by the neck and slammed him against the wall until audible cracks were heard. By the second hit the poor man was bleeding from his face and his thoughts drifted towards his pregnant fiancé waiting for him back at home. The third time had broken his jaw and he realized with growing pain and despair that he was never getting out of here. The fifth time Jeb fractured his skull and blood began to ooze from the assistant's head. By this point the man's final thoughts were of his home and how he was sorry he couldn't make it back to them. With surprising strength Jeb tossed him into the computer with only one hand.

The assistant's head went straight through the electronics and hit the wall with a horrible crunch that could be felt throughout the entire plant. The assistant's head exploded as he hit the wall and the existing white walls had now been covered with blood. All that was left of him were parts of his brain oozing out of his head, and the blood pouring out of his wounds. Jeb walked over to the body and quietly shed a few tears. Jeb knew this man from years ago and had helped put him through college. The assistant was a good friend to Jeb and was almost like a son to the old scientist. He almost felt ashamed that his old friend had died but he didn't really care. Even the most important people to Jeb were obstacles in his plans for world domination. As Dr. Jeb was beginning the process of eating the assistant's brains for science another employee came running into the room. The worker hummed a beautiful melody (this was a melody that he only hummed when he was upset) but his tongue got stuck in his throat when he saw the crescendo of blood that covered the walls.

The employee stared in shock as he saw the blood and seeing his boss standing over his colleague sent chills up his spine. Dr. Jeb stared at him with a cruel smile playing on his lips. Before the employee could react, Jeb rushed him and slammed him into the wall. Jeb bit his teeth into the employee's neck and sucked out his blood as the victim tried to scream for help. The employee weakly attempted to push Jeb off but Jeb bit deeper and deeper into his neck. Jeb absolutely loved this and his lower regions became wet as the employee screamed and flailed around. The screams only fueled Dr. Jeb's bloodlust and he never wanted this orchestra of pleasure to end. Jeb absolutely loved the taste of blood in his throat and each bite brought waves and waves of pleasure. Alas, the employee got a lucky hit to Jeb's temple and pushed him off but it was already too late. The unnamed employee's face started to become pale and clammy and he started to become hungry for brains and...other tastes. His skin turned a sickly green and his eyes became blood red. He looked up at the man who destroyed his life and he stalked toward him. A face of pure adoration and hatred broke out across the poor man's face as he seemed to be struggling between either attacking Jeb or bowing to him. Jeb looked absolutely thrilled at his new pet and named him Leo. As Leo stalked closer Jeb never broke eye contact and threw a spare vial of the serum into the water supply that was previously hidden through the well-placed grate from his office. The chemicals connected with the water supply and gushed through the entire town.

The First Death

Meanwhile, two long days had passed and no word came from the water treatment plant after Dr. Jeb put his plan into action. No one had heard anything about what had happened and life seemed to be continuing on as normal. At a house very far away from the plant lived a teenager named James. James lived on Manitoba Street which was on the complete other side of town from the plant. James was 17, over 6 ft tall, had short black hair, and was well built with green eyes to complete the picture. By all accounts, James was a very good-looking guy by society's standards. He lived with both of his parents and loved them dearly. James was considered very popular but he hangs around mostly with four other friends named Simon, Stacy, Christine, and Jake. These were his ultimate best friends and he couldn't imagine life without any of them. James typically spent most of his time either listening to music or playing video games when he wasn't reading philosophy or playing sports. James was in his room listening to some Rascal Flatts when he heard his parents call him from the next room. James' room has posters of Eminem and Ozzy Osborne all over the place. James couldn't quite hear them so he turned down his music and opened his door. "Son, we're still very sick, you shouldn't worry about us though, we're just going to get some sleep," said his mom calmly but with a slight wince. James frowned at this but replied. "Okay mom I'm going to go over to Jake's house for a little while", replied James. He put his hoodie on and walked to Jake's house. The crisp summer air felt good on James' skin. It had been really hot but now it was finally starting to cool down.

After about a ten-minute walk he finally made it to Jake's house. When he went up to the doorstep Jake suddenly came out and almost barreled into him. Jake seemed genuinely surprised to see him there. Jake was a somewhat tall 17-year-old, had blond hair and was well built but not as well built as James is. James and Jake had always been best friends since kindergarten and they were always competing. James was always better at sports and videogames than Jake and this caused Jake to become slightly jealous of his best friend's success. Nevertheless, the two were as thick as thieves and they had tons in common to keep themselves entertained for hours. Jake may have been jealous of his best friend but would never speak it out loud. He cared too much about James' friendship that he just swallowed his feelings and pretended that everything was okay when it really wasn't.

"James? What are you doing here man? I was just coming to see you", stated Jake in shock. "I was just coming to see you too Jake old friend, my parents have been sick for a few days", replied James. Jake seemed stunned after hearing this. "Shit man, my parents have been sick for a couple days too", said Jake quietly. James could tell that Jake was concerned even though Jake never seemed to care much about his family. Jake came from a very broken home and there were rumors that his parents had abused him daily. Jake never confessed anything but James could tell by the bruises on his face and neck that Jake was always in some sort of pain. "Something weird is going on; I think we should call the rest of the group. I'll call Stacy and Christine and you can call Simon," said James confidently. "Ok", replied Jake. As they called the rest of the group they decided to meet at the public school.

The public school was where they had all met as kids. The school was still in good condition but it wasn't used as much anymore. The dumpsters had flies swarming around them and it smelled like moldy cheese in there. While waiting for the rest of the group, James decided to talk about his favorite subject: philosophy. "Come on man, you know I don't understand any of that meaning of life crap," said Jake exasperatedly. "Look Jake, my oldest friend I know it can be difficult but philosophy can be very rewarding. I learned a lot about life from reading those books and Machiavelli sure makes things interesting. Because of Machiavelli's 'Art of War' I can apply new plays for the football team this year" said James confidently. Jake scoffed and looked away. Jake would never admit it but he tried out for years to get on the football team with no progress, but James was able to make it easily sophomore year and now he's the captain of the entire team. He tried to be happy for his friend but it became more and more difficult every year as James got better. Jake also couldn't wrap around why James found philosophy so interesting. "Look James; I hear ya. Philosophy can be useful at times but I don't think learning about the past is going to help us change the future. I know you disagree with me on this but that's how I feel. Also, did you hear about Donald Trump announcing he was going to be running for office? Now that's a man I can get behind", Jake said excitedly. James opened his mouth to respond when he heard footsteps crunching on the asphalt. Finally, the rest of the group was starting to arrive.

All three of them arrived so quickly it was as if they practiced this over a hundred times and they were going to perform this dance number on Broadway. The dance number would of course be called: "Walking". "Hey guys!" yelled Simon happily. Simon was by far the youngest of the group. Simon is 15 and quite short. While Jake and James are both over 6 foot, Simon stands at about five-ten. Simon has extremely short red hair in a buzz cut and wears glasses that hide his brown eyes. Simon is also short and skinny which means that he is not on the same level as James when it comes to sports. Simon never enjoyed sports except for Badminton which he excelled at. His favorite pastimes are coding and playing video games with James and the others. He also loved reading detective novels. Simon always looked up to James like an older brother and always gave him his support when needed.

Standing on his left side would be the beautiful Stacy. Stacy was tall and lean. She is 17 just like James and Jake; and she has long brown hair. Stacy is about six foot and is very athletic. Her main sport would be Track and Field because of all the running. She likes to jog during her free time but always makes time to hang with her group of friends. James was always the one she was closest to and everyone always wondered why they never dated. The main reason was because of Stacy's boyfriend. Gregory lived across the country but he and Stacy had been dating for two years. James always hated him but never let his feelings get in the way of Stacy's happiness. On the other hand, Jake loved him and always enjoyed beating Gregory at videogames on every occasion. Stacy gave a friendly nod to the rest of the group while her eyes lingered on James for just a minute too long before sitting next to him. Christine followed close behind before sitting next to Simon. Christine is 16 and is around five-eleven in height. She is fairly skinny like Simon and has long purple hair that extends to her shoulders. Out of the entire group she was always closest to Simon and Stacy. She typically never leaves Simon's side and is always playing video games with him on weekends whenever given the opportunity.

When the group finally settled into their respective benches on the playground, Stacy decided to kick things off. "My parents have been sick for the last couple days and it sounds like the same thing is happening to the rest of you if what James mentioned is any indication," she said slowly. James gave a quick nod as Simon perked up. "It's true. Mine and Chrstine's parents have been sick with flu-like symptoms. I don't know what could be causing it but their fever hasn't broken at all which worries me," he said with a concerned look. "Great so all of our families are sick; big fucking deal. What can we do about it anyway? It's not like my parents would care if I was hurting or anything," grumbled Jake. Everyone softened their gazes as they glanced at Jake. Jake looked away but you could see he was rubbing the back of his neck where a bruise usually was. James stood up from where he was sitting and addressed the group. "Guys, my friends, I think that we need to get medicine for our families. They need us and we owe it to them to help. I'm pretty sure Costa's has what we need. We should head there now before they close," he said confidently. The rest of the group seemed to agree and they all got up to go.

Jake wanted to reply but decided to push his feelings down and walked ahead without saying a word to anyone. Jake led the party and Simon and Christine followed behind. At the very end were James and Stacy walking casually while chatting animatedly about various things. From what Jake could hear, James was going out of his way to make Stacy laugh. Apparently, she and Gregory had been going through a rough patch with long distance and James was trying to be there for her. "I fucking wish I could be there for her", muttered Jake to himself. Jake always had a huge crush on Stacy but he never knew if it was because he actually liked her or if it was because she was in love with James. Either way, this little display of watching them flirt was making him sick. On the other hand, James was looking at this interaction in a completely different way. He and Stacy had been talking about new video games they wanted to try out and he knew that making her laugh would make her feel better about Gregory. All James wanted was to be there for her as a friend. He would never want to wreck that and he also wasn't ready to be in a relationship with anyone else.

His ex-girlfriend of one year had dumped him just before summer started and he had been trying to move on with his life. He loved his ex but never understood why she dumped him out of the blue like that. Talking to Stacy helped him forget that and he enjoyed their conversations. As the group continued onto their destination, they decided to take a peek into some of the houses in their neighborhood through the windows. They only chose to do this because there was absolutely nobody in sight and usually there was at least one ungrateful Karen walking the streets and bragging to everyone about how her new dog was going to be the best dog in the entire world or some crap like that. As the group passed each house; they saw that cars were still in their driveways and many people seemed to be sleeping on their living room couches. The mail seemed to be piling up after only a couple of days and the air didn't smell that great as they casually approached each house. Every person that was fast asleep on their couch had gray faces that looked extremely clammy and sickly. Vomit covered their clothes and it looked like the people hadn't moved in days. "It looks like everyone in town's fucking sick," muttered Jake. The rest of the group gained a new feeling of unease but they realized they had to move forward. Even the air began to feel cold as Christine shivered uncontrollably. The only thing left to do was just continue to press on.

After stopping and peeking into many more houses along the way, they soon saw the looming store in the distance. There wasn't a soul in sight as the urge to run away became even more difficult to defuse. The walls that once made the five friends feel so safe now loomed with danger. It's incredibly cliché but James was absolutely sure he saw a tumbleweed pass through town when they got to Costa's and saw it was abandoned. "What the hell do you mean you saw a tumble-weed pass by when we showed up James? This isn't a movie or videogame," said Jake indignantly. James looked taken aback by his behavior but responded in his normal calm voice. "I know how it sounds Jake, but I swear I saw one pass by. Either way it doesn't really matter. We need to go inside the store and find any type of medicine to help our families," said James reassuringly. The rest of the group agreed and even Jake gave a begrudging nod despite his hatred for his family.

While standing just outside the entrance everyone couldn't help but feel like something bad was going to happen if they entered that place. Each member looked at each other as they gained strength from their friends next to them. Just before they entered Stacy pulled James aside and out of earshot from the others. "Hey James, I wanted to ask you something quickly," said Stacy nervously. James' eyes softened as he took in her conflicted expression. "Of course, what can I do for you Stacy?" he asked calmly. Stacy steeled her resolve and without breaking eye contact asked: "What should I do about Gregory? I really like him but I don't think he and I are going to work out. We're just too different. I know this is a really bad time but I don't know what to do." James brought his hand to his chin and thought hard. He did have genuine feelings for her but he also didn't want to take advantage or lead her astray. He decided the only move was to be honest on what he truly thought. "Stacy, I can't tell you what to do. But what I can say is that if you aren't happy in the relationship then you should do what you feel is right. That's all I can say," he stated quietly. A genuine smile arched across Stacy's face. "Thanks James, I appreciate the advice. Now come on, let's go inside the store and get some medicine," said Stacy happily. The two of them returned to their friends and with one final breath, they pushed open the entrance and walked right into the store.

The moment the group of five entered the store, the smell of rotting meat invaded their nostrils and Simon fought the urge to throw up. There were no workers or customers anywhere in sight and the air felt even colder inside the store. As Simon ran to one of the nearby trash cans, Christine went up next to him and patted his shoulder as he threw his guts up. Simon always had a sensitive gag reflex and it was triggered so easily. Simon hadn't felt like this since Jake convinced him to intern at Costa's once as an assistant butcher. Suffice it to say...Simon was fired promptly and the entire butcher counter smelled like vomit for days. While Simon was reliving those great memories: James, Jake and Stacy decided to check the medicine aisle. Stacy and James began checking the containers to see if anything fit the symptoms that their parents were experiencing. Jake chose to use this opportunity to explore the rest of the store and see if he could find anyone.

Honestly, he didn't really care about what happened to his parents, he just wanted to get this over with. Jake liked hanging out with James but it always seemed to remind him of his shortcomings. Jake could feel the hatred burning in his heart but he still had to squash it. He didn't want to hate James, maybe once they found the medicine he could be honest about his feelings and maybe James could help him work through it. It couldn't hurt, but first he had to see if Dave was around. He never told anyone this, but Dave had a really potent supply of weed and coke that always gave Jake the perfect high to deal with his parents. Jake walked down every aisle and his unease finally started to show. He couldn't help but feel scared at not finding anyone. "Damn, I hope Dave's here. I really need my fix for the week," he muttered to himself. Jake turned the corner and finally came to the butcher counter. "Finally," said Jake quietly. He walked up to the counter and found someone with their back turned and swaying in front of the meat grinder.

Other than the occasional moan the man wasn't making any noise. Judging by the red x tattoo on the back of his neck, Jake knew this was Dave. "At least one person in this town isn't fucking sick," he muttered. Jake confidently walked up to the counter and rang the little bell. "Hey Dave, you got my fix this week?" Jake asked cheerfully. Dave lifted his head and slowly turned around to meet his favorite customer. Jake's smile turned to absolute horror as he saw Dave's gray and pale skin as he chomped on a severed leg. Dave happily chewed into his prize until he saw Jake. He spit the blood from his mouth and dropped his meat as he stalked toward him. Jake slowly backed towards the shelves and he knocked over a ton of metal cans. James and Stacy heard the commotion and came running. Jake was truly frozen in terror as Dave hopped over the counter and lunged at him.

James intercepted him and tackled him back over the meat counter. James was twice the size of Dave but now that Dave was sick; he was apparently granted extra strength and the two were now on equal footing. James punched and pummeled Dave but he just shook off all of his punches and nothing fazed him as he attacked James. James may have had Dave pinned but Dave turned things around and flung James off of him and into the meat freezer. Jake was truly frozen in terror but he also didn't mind seeing someone finally take James down a peg. A ghost of a smile appeared on Jake's face that vanished just as quickly as it came once Stacy rushed up next to him. "What's going on?" asked Stacy. Before Jake could explain they heard a sickening sound coming from the meat grinder. Stacy and Jake hopped the counter to see Dave squirming and writhing in the giant meat grinder. James was unsteady on his feet but managed to force Dave into it. They were frozen in shock as the machine sputtered until it finally pulled Dave completely into the machine and he was no more. Blood gushed out of the grinder and covered the entire room in blood which pushed James's back into the wall. The only thing that didn't go through the machine was Dave's head which was thrown high into the ceiling vents. Jake and Stacy found their courage and saw James shaking and covered in Dave's blood.

The Death Toll Rises

Simon and Christine finally caught up with the commotion and couldn't believe their eyes at the sight of the guts littering the room. Simon fought the urge to vomit once again. Once they recovered from their horror, they joined the rest of the group and ran to James to pull him into a deep group hug. The group was traumatized but they all knew they had to be there for James. James was frozen as they tried to hug him but he finally relented and pulled them all in as he broke out into sobs. He had never killed anyone before. After they each pulled away Christine began to cry as well. She couldn't help but look at the gruesome sight any longer. The room smelled completely of iron.

Judging by the context of the room and the fact that James was covered in blood, Christine and Simon quickly figured out what happened. "Why did this have to happen to Dave? He may have been troubled but he was still my friend," said Christine through tears. James walked over and tried to comfort her but she pushed him away. At the pure sight of him Christine's sadness turned to rage. "How could you kill him? He may have been sick but he was still a human being. He could have been helped! You didn't have to destroy him!" yelled Christine. James looked as if he had been slapped and backed off. Still, despite how bad he felt for her he still kept eye contact and held his ground.

Christine was his friend but he couldn't let this group fall apart during a crisis. "I didn't have a choice, Christine. I didn't want to kill him but he was attacking Jake and I. If I hadn't stepped in then we would have died. I'm sorry about your friend and I don't blame you; but I did what I had to do," he said quietly. James honestly looked defeated and Stacy knew she had to fix everything. Christine ran towards James and beat her fists against his chest in genuine anger. James did nothing but let her do as she wanted to get her emotions out. Even if he had to take the brunt of her anger, he would take it all for her sake. He and Christine were close in their own way.

James would comfort Christine after school sometimes when her anxiety and depression got really bad and he would be there for her. She spent many days crying into his shoulder and he always let her do it. He loved her like a sister and would do anything to protect her. He would take away all of her pain and put it on himself if he could. That was just the type of person James was. Stacy rushed forward and was able to come between them and pulled them apart. "Christine, don't blame James for this. He was only trying to protect us. James did us a favor by stepping in, we might be dead if it wasn't for him," said Stacy indignantly. Christine's anger began to dissipate and she lowered her head in shame. She turned to James and blubbered out: "I'm sorry James. I know you were only trying to protect us. Can you forgive me?" James' eyes softened and said softly: "Of course Christine my old friend. We've been friends for years. It's going to take much more than one fight to tear us apart." Christine finally smiled and rushed to hug James. He gladly accepted and they held each other for a few moments in each other's arms.

Christine finally let go and walked back to Simon who had recovered from his puke fest. Simon still looked sick but at least he didn't look as green as before. "Hey Simon, how are you feeling?" asked James concerningly. "Hey James, I'm feeling better. Sorry about that, I just have a really weak stomach," said Simon shamefully. "It's all good Simon, I'm just glad you're feeling better" replied James. The group suddenly felt exhausted and they all sat down in order to rest their bones and catch their breath. James sulked as he began to get lost in his own head while Stacy put her arm around him in order to comfort him. He instantly began to relax at her touch. James didn't consider Stacy to be his closest friend but she was still very important to him all the same. He knew he was in love with her but he had to look out for Jake as well. After taking a few moments to regain their faculties James stood up in order to address the group. "Okay guys, I know we're exhausted after this ordeal but I think we need to find those meds and bring them back to our folks. If Dave was any indication, then our families are in trouble too. We need to save them before it's too late. Even if we can't defeat this sickness then at least we can try and slow it down. Now who's with me?" asked James forcefully.

Everyone nodded in agreement and stood up. "Awesome, I think we should split up and then meet back at the school twenty minutes after we get the medications and help our parents," said James. At this, the air of confidence surrounding James began to disappear as nobody seemed to like that idea. "Um James, I don't think we should split up. If our families are hurt then we may not be able to face them alone. We should probably stay together," said Christine timidly. Jake rolled his eyes in response. "No way

Christine, I think we need to cover as much ground as possible and the only way to do that is to split up here and now," replied Jake with a snarl. "Are you serious!" yelled Christine.

At this the both of them began to devolve into a fighting fit until a shrill whistle broke them out of their trance. "Listen guys, we need to pick a plan and stick to it. I personally think we should stay together but James should have final say. What do you think we should do James?" asked Stacy. James tilted his chin for a moment before finally stringing his thoughts together. "I hear you guys so how about this? Since my house is the closest, why don't we stick together and head there first; after we determine if my parents are safe then we split up and check everyone else. If not then we stay together. After that we head back to school to regroup if needed. Does that sound fair?" asked James. The party nodded their heads in agreement and they raced towards the medicine aisle and grabbed as many pill bottles as they could. With that, they left the store and headed back to James' home. The entire walk was only about five minutes but it felt like an eternity. Each member was lost in their own thoughts. However, unlike everyone else Jake wasn't thinking at all about saving his parents. In truth, he was glad they were sick. At least then, they couldn't call him a failure or punch him anymore. He got the medication solely for himself since he needed something to help him sleep at night. Jake wanted to kill his parents if he could but he knew he would be broken if he did that. He had never killed anyone but he did almost kill James once a couple years ago.

Hostilities Flaring Up

It was during sophomore year and James had made the football team. James had been out celebrating with his teammates and got drunk at a party. James overindulged and ended up going off by himself to ride out the drunkenness.

One of James' favorite spots to frequent was the nearby cliffs where he would sit at the edge and look out over the town. It was a very quick walk up and the view was gorgeous. James knew the trail by heart so even when drunk he navigated with ease. At the time Jake had been walking by and had awful bruises throughout his face. He saw James head to the cliffs and decided to follow him. He wanted to confront James and explain how fucked up he felt but when he saw James sitting a rush of anger flooded through his veins. He ran towards him and before James could turn around to see what the sound was Jake flung him off the cliff and onto the ground below. James hit the ground with a sickening thud. For a moment Jake felt vindicated but then was overcome with remorse. He ran down the trail to where James landed and saw his oldest friend unconscious. Jake called an ambulance and James was taken to the hospital. James was incredibly lucky and the crunch Jake heard was the sound of James' beer bottle cracking near the crash site. James never knew what happened and Jake pretended to be a witness to an unfortunate accident. Ever since then James never goes to the cliffs while drunk anymore even though he never actually got hurt from the incident.

Despite that, Jake felt conflicted after the "accident". On the one hand, he felt awful and remorseful for letting his anger get the best of him; but on the other he felt so happy that someone finally proved that "perfect James" was just as mortal as the rest of us. During the walk back home, Jake spent time thinking over his friendship with James. The truth is, he always felt insecure around him. James was perfect but Jake truly didn't want to see him killed. He just wanted someone else to feel the same pain that he himself felt. The two were each other's first friends so it made sense why they would stick by each other's side. Jake and James had an unspoken understanding that if the other was in trouble they would do anything to help. However, Jake never felt like he could open up so the understanding always went unanswered despite James never giving up on him. To the rest of the group however, the friendship between the two was always a mystery. It was James that befriended the others and Jake was considered a package deal. To Stacy however, she always thought something was off about Jake.

For some reason, James was his oldest friend and they were best friends for years. The rest of the group didn't even want to include Jake in their party but James constantly vouched for him and never took no for an answer. Maybe he saw some good in him and at times Jake could be funny, but he just seemed like he never wanted to be around the group. From Stacy's field of vision; she could see James mentally try to defend him but he just seemed too tired to take any action. She felt for him, but there was nothing she could do. The group didn't often get into arguments but when they did, Jake would typically come off as cold towards James and try to ridicule him occasionally. Stacy hated that James always defended Jake but she knew that she couldn't do anything. She would never admit it but she was in love with James. She may have been dating Gregory but that was only because he was honest about his feelings right away. She wanted to be with James but he never seemed to be into her so she simply tried to forget about him though it was hard. Without the need to discuss anything between them the group decided to carry on until finally reaching their destination.

Once they finally crossed the street to James' house, the first thing the group noticed was that the front door was ajar. James had a sinking feeling and despite everyone else protesting, he burst into the house to see what was going on. Where the house was once clean and pristine was now trashed and walls scratched out. The entire house had been destroyed and it seemed like someone was trying to locate something within the walls. The white walls were now filled with holes and the foundation was completely shot. It was so bad that James couldn't even believe the house was still standing. Desk drawers had been pulled open and papers and files were thrown across the floor haphazardly. The entire house was in ruins but James didn't have time to digest any of this. He ran up the stairs and forced his way into his parents' bedroom. He was already sweating despite the entire trip taking less than a minute. The room was completely dark with one lamp on at the very back of the room...beside the bed. James saw both of his parents in their bed lying motionless, as if they were frozen in fear. James scurried toward his father's bedside and tried to shake them both. "Mom, dad you need to get up! Dad, please! Mom, I brought help! You guys can't be dead! PLEASE!" yelled James filled with sorrow. James couldn't feel any pulse and he knew they must have been dead for a while. He fell to his knees and broke down crying. He couldn't believe that the only parents he had ever known were dead. What was he supposed to do without them? As his entire body was shaking with grief something caught his eye and stopped him dead in his tracks. His father had risen from his bed and stared at his fallen son.

Before James could even react, his father threw himself off the bed and aimed for James' general direction. James' dad was on top of him in seconds and James immediately felt the pain of cold dead hands around his throat. Zombie dad was trying to choke James instead of biting him. James knew he had to act fast so with all of his strength he punched his father right into the eye. The blow itself did nothing to zombie dad but the force of the punch loosened his grip long enough for James to get out of there. James sprinted from the room as his parents gave chase. Apparently, his mom had been infected too and was beginning to close the gap as well. James found a wooden chair outside the room and pushed it against the door handle after slamming it shut behind his parents. They banged on the door while screaming his name. "JAMES! LET ME OUT OF HERE SON. WE JUST WANT TO TALK TO YOU!" his father shouted. This wasn't his parents anymore. The chair was wide enough to cover the entire door frame but it was loose. It wouldn't hold very long. James ran down the stairs in a panic with tears running down his eyes before running into his friends. "James what's going on? We heard a cry—" was all Simon could get out before James cut him off. "No time, my parents are zombies. Less talk, more running!" he quickly breathed out before pushing his friends out the door.

Christine however fought back and ran back into the house for something. Of course, nobody seemed to notice and they ran until they were directly across the street. The group of four sat down on the sidewalk to try and catch their breath. After about a minute Christine ran out of the house while clutching a thick manila folder to her chest. Christine plopped right next to Simon as she took the opportunity to catch her breath as well. She wanted to bring up the folder but then she saw the grief stricken look on James' face. The folder was casually hidden from view before anyone noticed. "I can't believe my parents are zombies. Damn it. What am I going to do?" asked James quietly. He put his head in his hands as Jake put his arm around him in an attempt to comfort him.

Jake may have hated James at times but they were still best friends. He really felt for his friend and wished that this didn't have to happen to him. He'd never admit it but despite the jealousy he felt he still considered James as his brother and would do whatever he could to help him through this. “Guys, if James’ parents are any indication, then the rest of our families are probably infected too. There’s nothing we can do,” said Jake sadly. The rest of the group sat in silence as his words began to sink in. What could they do? The five sat there while James sat crying his eyes and Jake continued to console him. The rest of the group bowed their heads in silence as they thought about how to move forward.

On the sidewalk they were sitting on, there was a pipe near a sewer grate that was leaking. Simon heard the leaking sound and scurried over to examine it while everyone else slowly followed behind. “Everyone, I think I know why our families are turning into zombies. Look.” Everyone glanced at the pipe and saw that the pipe was secreting a green unnatural liquid into the water lines. “I think someone tampered with the water lines. This looks like some sort of chemical. Maybe someone engineered a serum to turn everyone into these creatures, but I’m not a hundred percent sure,” said Simon doubtfully. Jake felt his anger boiling over and began to pace. He liked Simon but he never trusted the theories that came out of the brainiac’s mouth. “How is that even possible Simon? How could someone infect the entire town, and why aren't we infected? You are a complete idiot, Simon. We’ve been drinking the same water as everyone else!” shouted Jake. Everyone sat stunned at Jake’s outburst. Jake was always weird and could come off as cold or passive aggressive but very rarely ever lashed out like this. Simon was typically the quietest of the group but stood his ground. “I don’t know Jake! I don’t know. All I know is that someone must have been experimenting in the water treatment plant and somehow, we are immune to this. I don’t have all the answers, I just think this is the most logical conclusion”, huffed Simon. Jake seemed shocked that Simon was getting so frustrated with him. In one way he was proud of Simon since he wanted the nerd to stand up for himself. But now, he realized that he might have been losing his friends. If his friends ever saw the negative side of him or the cuts on his body, they would surely leave him.

Usually, James was the only one who ever stood up to him and Jake could live with that. But now, things were changing. Jake’s fear became very evident on his face. He was losing control of this group and he would lose them once they found out the truth. Little Simon fighting back was a surprise but Jake didn’t let it faze him. He knew better than to doubt his intelligence. If he wanted to stay in the group then he had to apologize. Almost as if in response, Christine got right up into Jake’s face like she was staring down the eyes of an angry god and said: “you need to apologize to him now Jake. Simon’s our friend and

I trust his judgment. If he thinks the water treatment plant is the cause of this then that must be the answer. He deserves your respect." She said harshly. Her eyes were brimming with tears. She rarely stood up for herself but she always stood up for Simon. She and Simon had much more in common than Jake thought. Jake realized he had fucked up and decided to try and make things right.

"I'm sorry guys. This whole situation has me really freaked out but that isn't an excuse. Can you guys forgive me for my outburst?" he asked quietly. "Yeah of course," replied Simon. After that everyone decided to drop it and Simon continued his explanation. "The water treatment plant has a sewer grate that connects to every house in town. That must be how the serum was deployed. The chemicals must have been synthesized since water's not typically this color. We need to go there and figure out what happened before this becomes even worse," said Simon confidently. Even though nobody truly wanted to put themselves in danger they couldn't argue with the logic. "I think that we should go to the water treatment plant and see if we can figure out what happened," spoke James. "That's a great idea," said Stacy. The rest of the group agreed with his idea. As they walked to the plant there seemed to be something wrong with Jake. "Hey are you okay Jake?" asked James. "I'm fine, I just need to think." "Alright," said James.

There was clearly more going on than Jake was letting on but James didn't understand why. Why is Jake acting like this? None of the friends knew. Soon Stacy came up beside James and pushed Jake out of the way. "Hey", said Stacy. "Hey", replied James. "Are you okay? It seems like something's on your mind." "I'm just confused about why Jake is acting so weird," said James. "He's probably just tired", replied Stacy. "Try not to worry about it if you can, okay?" After a long pause James finally commented "You're probably right." The two walked together in silence and Stacy resisted the urge to pull James close to her and tell him that everything was going to be okay. But she knew that she couldn't, she wasn't his girlfriend and he was still nursing a broken heart. She hadn't heard from Gregory in a few days. Maybe she should call him. She tried to call him on her cell but she couldn't get through. It was as if the phone lines had been tampered with but she wasn't sure. She asked Simon about it but he had no idea.

The Mystery Of The Plant

Twenty minutes later they finally made it to the plant. The plant looked completely normal from the outside but completely deserted. "Where is everyone?" Asked Jake. "Let's go inside, we might find more answers in the labs," said James. As they went inside, they saw that there weren't any zombies or anyone else around. As they went deeper into the plant, they saw that there was a lot of blood around. Blood was splattered in the walls and all over the floor. "There's a lot of blood," said Jake. "Yes, but where are all of the bodies?" Asked Simon. No one could answer that and they decided to continue to progress through the area without a word. They went through the rest of the plant until they came up to the main lab. All they saw was a dead man sprawled on the floor. "What happened to him?" Asked Christine tearfully. Christine broke down in tears and James comforted his friend while Simon took a closer look and examined the body. "It looked like he tried to run away from someone. He got to the door but someone pinned him down. He fought back but was overpowered. He got picked up and was hit against the wall numerous times and then finally was thrown through that computer which ultimately killed him," explained Simon. As the rest of the group stared dumbfounded Simon looked through the victim's pocket and found a jump drive with a J on it. Christine pulled herself together and huddled closer to Simon.

Simon then saw that a grate in the main lab was open. "This is where the serum was thrown into. This is how the water supply got infected," said Simon. Everyone knew Simon was at the top of his class but very few people knew how smart he truly was. Simon could easily be a detective with his skills at being able to understand a situation just by looking at the remains of a crime scene. He could easily make detective if he wanted to become a cop but Simon's passion was always in chemistry. "We need to look through this jump drive; it might have important information on it," said James. They went to an office that was nearby and logged onto the computer. They popped the jump drive in and were shocked to see the contents of the files. "Look at this newspaper article," said Simon. "Local scientist tries to destroy Lakehead University," read Jake. "Keep reading," replied Simon. "Local scientist Dr. Jeb Winter-Fields tries to blow up University after police found numerous students tied up and being experimented on in his underground lab. He tried to throw a chemical into the furnace to blow it up. Luckily a local student named James Adams caught the vial and threw it out the window before it went into the fire. The scientist has since disappeared. Published on July 21st 1965," read Jake. James took a closer look. "That student looks exactly like me but it isn't me, I wasn't even born yet", said James loudly. "Maybe it was one of your uncles who died before your time," said Stacy. "But my last name is Smith, not Adams," mentioned James confused. "James", voiced Christine softly. "What is it?" asked James. "I found this file on the floor of your house; I think you should look at it." James walked over to her and took the file. As he read it his palms began to sweat and his face paled as he skimmed through its contents. After a few moments the file dropped from his hands and he collapsed to the floor in shock. "James are you alright?" asked Stacy. James looked up at her and began to cry softly. He could feel her supportive gaze pierce into his bones and his emotions began to spill over. She reached out her hand and helped him up. Without a word he showed her the file.

The file had secrets regarding James' past. James said quietly through tears "A baby was found on the tracks in Schreiber. The Smith family found him and adopted him. There was a piece of paper on his blanket that he was wrapped in that said Adams." "James I'm so sorry," said Stacy. "I'm adopted. I can't believe that my parents never told me about this," said James. "That man in the paper must be your father or your uncle," replied Simon in response. James hugged Stacy close as he cried deeper into her shoulder. She grabbed him and comforted him in her embrace. The more she hugged him the more she wanted to break up with Gregory. She cared about him but Gregory didn't make her happy anymore like James could. While the touching moment was going on Simon looked through the jump drive some more and found a copy of the analysis for the serum. Simon printed it out and looked closer at it for further study. "This has everything that was used to create the serum. I might be able to make a cure for it," explained Simon.

Excitement washed over the group but their happiness soon turned into anxiety and fear as they remembered where they were. In the doorway growling could be heard from a distance. The five friends turned and saw one of the workers shuffling towards them. As James stood in fear, he instantly began to understand the situation and urged his friends to run out the other side of the room and into another hallway. James led the charge and everyone booked it out of the room. The five of them were panting but kept running as fast as they could through each hallway. The plant seemed really straight forward when they first entered but it soon became a labyrinth with every new twist and turn.

Turning one of the corners Jake accidentally slammed into the fire alarm and fell to his knees. Blood began to seep from his arm as he had gotten scraped by the impact. Before anyone could react, everyone covered their ears as a deafening sound roared from the speakers above. The fire alarm had been activated and suddenly the earlier growling and shuffling increased tenfold from seemingly everywhere at once. The entire group had become discombobulated by the sounds and Simon fell to his knees and almost began to sob. Simon has really bad anxiety so any loud noise that he wasn't expecting causes him to feel like he had been shocked twenty times to the gut. It was a very unpleasant feeling but an even worse sensation would be getting chomped at the bits by the living dead.

Christine ran over to Simon and grabbed his hand in hers and dragged him to his feet. The rest of the group shook off their shock and attempted to leave the area while Christine dragged Simon along behind her. After countless searching and much trial and error an exit was finally in sight. Ironically it was the fire exit but the group chose not to care about that at the moment as they threw open the door and ran onto the grass. The group kept running until they made it back into town. Twenty minutes of continuous running took its toll as Simon collapsed onto some grass and began to breathe heavily. Christine, also feeling drained, joined him and began to whisper comforting words to her friend until he calmed down. James, Jake and Stacy were out of breath but mostly unaffected as they were used to endurance sports. Jake clutched his arm as the pain began to return and grunted in anger. "What the fuck are we supposed to do!" yelled Jake. "Those demons are everywhere and our town is ruined!" Feeling an explosive anger Jake punched one of the nearby metal trash cans until it dented and was unrecognizable. Jake continued to punch until James caught his arm and pushed it down. James grabbed hold of Jake and held him in place to calm him down.

Jake struggled and tried to escape the grasp until he finally relented and quieted down. "I'm sorry", said Jake apologetically. James replied "It's fine, don't worry about it. We're all on edge, but we can't stay here." "Agreed, the town's in ruins. We need a safe place to try and lay low," said Stacy. "Wait guys, I have the perfect place in mind", said James excitedly. "There's an old house at the edge of town on the Western side. It's in good condition and hasn't been used in a few years. It's far from the plant and I still have the key to it." "That's awesome!" yelled Jake in response. By this time Simon had recovered from his ordeal and reunited with the others along with Christine. "I think that's a great idea," said Simon quietly. The others nodded their heads in agreement and Stacy looked at James with a proud smile on her face and adoration in her eyes. "It's about fifteen minutes away so we should head there as soon as possible." The group agreed and they began their trek to the new house.

Next Steps

The five friends ran to their hopefully new base of operations across town. When they arrived, they saw a two-story yellow house. The house was still standing and seemed to be in good condition despite obvious wear and tear but overall, it looked abandoned and hopefully safe. The house was promised to James as a graduation present and for when he wanted to move out. Since he got amazing grades and was doing great with the football team his family decided to give it to him early as a show of good faith though the house wasn't officially his yet and couldn't move out quite yet. He had just gotten it the other day and was so excited. As James pulled out his key and turned the lock the house looked well-furnished but needed fixing. The walls of the house were cracked a little and there was some mold growing around. "Well, this place looks like a fucking dump," said Jake. "Come on guys, I know it's not in the best condition but if we work together, we can restore it to its former glory" said James confidently. "I admit it's been a few years since I was here last but I think we can make it work." Everyone nodded their heads and Jake shut down his protests.

The group decided that they needed to fix it up as best they could while making sure they were well supplied for the next few weeks. Luckily James worked a lot of construction and knew how to make it pristine. Working together, it took a couple days to fix it up completely and have it look spotless. By the end of day two the entire group was dead tired but happy to finally have some relative safety and comfort. The house had five bedrooms, five bathrooms, an upstairs and a basement. The house was fully furnished and the heat and water were still working perfectly. Once the house was clean the group decided to secure it in case any stragglers decided to walk too close to the house in search of food or brains. The group spent another week building a fence around the property with wood and barbed wire along with boarding up the windows and doors. The house actually had a secret passage through the basement that led to a secret bunker near the property line as well.

The bunker was filled with many non-lethal weapons such as stun guns, batons, and more lethal ones such as knives and swords. James and Jake took to the wooden swords and knives and spent much of their downtime sparring with each other. Christine and Stacy used their time to work out and learn basic fighting techniques in case anyone tried to hurt them or the rest of the group. Simon found a significant amount of chemistry supplies in the basement and used the time to try and synthesize a cure to the plague. Soon the place was considered to be a pretty good base and all the doors and windows became sealed up except for the hidden entrance to the bunker that could lead them back to town. The group bonded really well during this period of isolation from the rest of the world and the old house began to feel like a real home. The electricity was working again and everyone had the time of their lives in their own space. They spent many days working hard and training and their nights were spent watching movies and playing video games on the giant flat screen tv in the den. The house belonged to James' family but they never used it. It was agreed that James would inherit the house once he graduated from university and got a job. Despite all the positives there was still a major problem that created a crisis after nearly two weeks of isolation.

"We're low on food." Said Christine. The group had nearly depleted the food reserves that they found in the cabinets and knew they couldn't last much longer without aid. "Let's go to the store and pick up all the food we can find then we go to the weapon store and find some weapons," said James. "Great idea, we can get coke on the way" said Stacy enthusiastically. "Yeah, that's a really fucking great idea" said Jake sarcastically. "What's your problem Jake?" Yelled Stacy. "I don't have a problem; I just don't know why James is in charge. Who voted him leader?" asked Jake. Jake didn't understand why he was feeling like this. He loved spending time with the group but at the end of the day he didn't want the plague to end. He was happy to be free from his parents and wanted to stay that way. He also didn't like that the rest of the group looked to James like he was their savior. The truth was that everyone loved Jake as well in their own way but he couldn't believe it. James sensed something more was wrong and decided he should take action. "You're right. Let's take a vote," said James. "Who thinks Jake should be leader?" asked James. No one put their hands up. "Who thinks I should be leader?" Everyone's hands shot up quickly except for Jake's. "Guess I'm the leader," said James. "Fine we'll go with your plan" uttered Jake begrudgingly. Jake felt immensely hurt that no one voted for him and he walked away without a word.

James wanted to run after him but knew that Jake had to work this out himself. After the food was completely depleted the next day, the group headed back to Costas and saw that it was still deserted. The mind-numbing task of going from aisle to aisle to get supplies took about thirty minutes and soon the entire store was picked clean of all the essentials that the group could carry. They took all of the food and headed back out in complete silence. The aura was still awkward but everyone knew the stakes. Food and weapons were essential. They went to the weapon store next and found that it was completely cleared out as well. "This is weird," said Simon. They decided to head back to the hideout and drop off their load.

As soon as the group got about five minutes away from the store, they realized that something was amiss. One of their group members was missing! "Hey what happened to Stacy?" asked Simon. They looked around and realized that Stacy was indeed missing. "We have to find her. She's one of us," said James. James started to freak out. His face became red; he started sweating and he had an awful pit in his stomach. "Dude, chill out," said Jake. "Stacy is missing and you want me to chill. Do you even care about her?!" yelled James. "I do care about her. Why the hell are you taking this so hard James?" asked Jake. "I'm in love with her, and I don't know what I'll do if I can't find her," said James sadly. Despite the shitty timing of the revelation nobody was surprised. They all knew James was in love with her but chose not to comment. Jake felt his anger boiling over at this confirmation and decided to give in despite wanting to swallow it down. Jake reared back his fist and punched James as hard as he could. James fell to the ground hard as Jake stood above him. "Screw you James, I know she's important to you but she has a boyfriend and she's our friend too." James stared in shock at the true anger in his friend before Jake finally calmed himself down. They needed to find their friend. Jake reached out a hand and pulled James up without saying a word before walking away. Everyone was completely stunned by Jake's behavior but nobody knew what to do about it. "We'll find her, James, I promise. Let's go back to the weapon store and see if she might be there," said Simon. They headed back to the store but they didn't see her there.

James looked around the back and saw the dumpster lid was ajar. Rushing forward, he tore open the lid and found Stacy beaten up and unconscious among the garbage. Her face was bruised and her arms and legs were scratched up and scarred. He fished her out and checked her pulse. "Thank goodness she's still breathing. Her pulse is low but at least she's alive," said James quietly to himself. He began to cry from relief and joy. "Guys get over here I found her." The others ran in his direction. They tried to revive her but nothing worked. Then James saw an old adrenaline shot on the ground. He picked it up and jabbed her with it after doing his best to make sure that it was clean enough. After two minutes of the shot and other attempted methods she finally woke up. "Stacy you're alive," said James. He cried as he cradled her close to him in arms. "James, thank you for saving me." He helped her up and then the entire group brought her back to the hideout. The journey was laborious but luckily there were no zombies in sight. She spent three days in bed recovering while everyone else took turns helping her until she felt well enough to walk on her own.

The group expended much of their medical supplies helping her heal. In addition, Simon spent further time creating the cure and felt like he was close to potentially succeeding. Along with the schematics for the cure Simon also managed to swipe a vial of the virus and completed rigorous testing to understand how it worked. Needless to say, Simon felt very overworked but increasingly confident that he could make a breakthrough. Christine spent time helping Simon with his work and being there on standby whenever he needed anything as often as she was able to. Jake took time caring for Stacy whenever necessary but he spent most of his time training in order to avoid the others. He still hadn't really apologized for hitting James. His anger was reaching a breaking point and Jake had no clue how long he could keep it from getting worse. As he punched one of the boxing bags, he suddenly pictured James' face. As his fist collided with the bag it fell apart and sand fell everywhere. Jake stared down at the spilled remains in both horror and pride. With a sadistic grin to himself he walked out of the room and decided to have a talk with James.

While Stacy was on bedrest James comforted her every moment that he could. On her last full day in bed James was holding her hand and stroking it. "I nearly lost you, and there are so many things I need to say. I love you, but I know you're with Gregory and I don't want to make things harder for you. If you don't feel the same I"–Stacy cut him off by holding her finger to his mouth. She pulled herself to him and kissed him deeply. She put her hands in his hair as James returned the kiss eagerly. He draped his arms around her waist as they kept kissing and kissing. After a couple minutes Stacy slowly pulled away as they breathed heavily. She rested her left hand on his cheek and said, "James, I've loved you since we met. But I know things are complicated with you and I. I need to break up with Gregory and I know you're dealing with so much. I will always be there but maybe we should press pause until the dust settles." James looked down at her and held her close. "I understand and I feel the same. Let's wait until things cool off." They nodded but continued to stay close to each other. He comforted her the rest of the day while Jake watched from the hallway. In Jake's right hand he held one of the wooden knives at his side. He was hoping to duel with James to let off some steam and to clear the air but after witnessing this exchange; his anger and sadness increased tenfold. Jake ran downstairs with tears in his eyes and headed for the basement to spar alone. He was in love with Stacy too and James stole her from him as well! Jake knew that he shouldn't blame James for this but he couldn't help it. He spent the rest of the day swinging the wooden knives against the concrete walls and enjoying the scraping sound they made. The weapons may end up getting damaged after this but he didn't care.

After she recovered Stacy gathered the strength to tell everyone what happened during her attack. Stacy always managed to heal quickly and could take a lot of punishment. But this was almost too much for her and she nearly died. "After we left the store, I thought I saw something that we missed so I went back in there. When I got there, I realized that what I had seen must have been a trick of the light. As I turned to leave two zombies appeared out of nowhere and grabbed me. They dragged me to the back of the store and they started to cut me with a knife and punched my entire body. I fell unconscious after the third punch and the knives began cutting up my legs and arms. It felt like they carved up my entire body. Finally, after a while they must have figured I was dead so they dumped me in the dumpster out back. The next thing I remember was James reviving me," said Stacy. "I'm just glad you are okay," replied James. The two looked at each other with love and adoration in their eyes. "Wait, you said the zombies were beating you up, right?" Asked Simon. "Yes," remarked Stacy. "Why?" "Zombies aren't supposed to be able to do that. They should only have the capacity for alleviating their hunger but without any rational thinking," said Simon. "Maybe something is controlling them" , affirmed Christine. "Perhaps." "I think that we should begin making the cure soon," said Jake. He may not have wanted his parents to survive but even Jake admitted he wanted life to return to normal if possible. "Maybe all the creatures are gone now from the plant. After we left, they could have cleared out and went elsewhere," suggested Christine. "We should check it out after Stacy has fully recovered," remarked James. "That's a good idea," said everyone but Jake.

The next night Stacy and Christine are talking. "Hey, how are you feeling?" asked Christine. "I'm alright, just a bit sore," said Stacy. "James is awake in his room if you want to see him." "I'm fine but thanks though," said Stacy. "Alright but James was really worried about you, he might want to see you. I'm going to go to bed, night," said Christine. "Night," said Stacy. After Christine left Stacy got up and headed to James' room. She went into his room and closed his door. "Hey James," said Stacy. "Hey," said James. "What are you doing up?" Asked James. "I couldn't sleep. Why are you still awake?" asked Stacy. "Can't turn my brain off," replied James with a chuckle. "I just wanted to come and see you for a minute before I went back to bed," talked Stacy. "I'm glad you did. Goodnight," said James. "Goodnight," affirmed Stacy. Even with those words Stacy didn't feel herself leaving. She walked towards James and began kissing him again. James happily returned it as they kissed long into the night. Despite their vow to cool things off they couldn't keep their hands off each other all night.

The next day Stacy felt a lot better and they decided to go to the treatment plant. Sleeping in James' bed did wonders to speed up her recovery process. Neither of them knew what to do about their relationship but they knew they loved each other and they didn't see that changing anytime soon. The two walked to the plant close to each other as they chatted about their favorite video games. As they walked closer to the plant, they never could have anticipated what they would see. As they climbed the hill overlooking the plant they saw that they weren't alone. Across the horizon zombies stood guarding the entrances to the plant with guns drawn. Some of the zombies had general hats on and seemed to be giving orders to the others. The generals were saying something and gesturing with their hands to the others. The lower ranked soldiers saluted their hands and went on their way. There had to be hundreds of them all over the place. They had made the plant into a giant fortress with the main labs near the top of the place. "I don't think we're getting into the plant any time soon," said Jake. "This can't be possible, zombies can't think," said Simon. James took a closer look at the plant; he always had really good vision and was sometimes called eagle eyes. "I have a plan on how we can get in there. First, we should go back to the hideout so they don't find us," said James. The others nodded and began to follow James back home. However, Jake decided to go his own way.

He still had the wooden knife from his training session. It was damaged but Jake had sharpened the end to a fine point. It was now a lethal weapon. He creeped towards the outskirts of the plant where he saw a cluster of zombies communicating to each other. Jake couldn't pick out what they were saying but he could tell that they were speaking English. He thought he heard one of them saying brains over and over again while the others hit him over the head claiming he was defective. Eventually the cluster began to move on one by one to their respective duties. Jake was hiding near the eastern wall in some bushes as he waited for all of the creatures to leave. Once the last one passed by his hiding spot Jake stealthily lunged out and pressed the tip of the wooden blade against the back of the zombie while using his other hand to cover his mouth.

A New Plan

Jake's hand stayed firm as he held the weapon against the zombie's back and whispered "if you make any moves, you're dead. You are coming with me and if you make any sound, I will kill you and it won't be pleasant" he snarled. The zombie seemed to nod in understanding as Jake led him away from the plant and out of sight back to the hideout. The creature smelled like literal death and while dangerous looking put up no resistance. The zombie even seemed to be slightly shaking in fear as it pissed itself. Jake could smell the urine and felt disgusted but vindicated as well. Jake knew this one was intelligent or at least had enough awareness to be of some use. Jake had been so angry at James lately that he hoped this might make a good peace offering. Jake removed his hand from the zombie's mouth but there was silence.

When the rest of the group returned to the hideout and took a moment to process what they saw, they reunited in the bunker. "Here's the plan, wait where's Jake?" asked James. As the rest of the group realized he was missing the door to the bunker opened. Jake strutted in guiding the zombie and then pushed him forward. The zombie fell towards James. Before James could react with lightning reflexes Jake sprinted forward and jabbed the hilt of the wooden sword against the creature's neck. The zombie collapsed to the ground unconscious. The rest of the group was shaking in shock after seeing an actual zombie in their home when Jake raised his arms in the air and proclaimed "I found the answer. A literal zombie from the plant and he was at least awareness about him. If we tie him up, we can find out more information about the plant and get some intel. What do you think James?" Jake asked while looking smug. Jake crossed his arms in satisfaction as James pulled himself together. "Jake, we need to talk about your destructive behavior but before then you're right. Let's get all the intel we can get." Everyone ran off to find rope and other supplies while Jake dragged their new friend into a nearby bedroom to begin the interrogation. Five hours later the victim was firmly tied up while the rest stood over him in the aftermath of Jake's playtime.

While everyone was getting supplies Jake restrained the zombie and began gouging out his eyes with a knife he hid on his person. The zombie was missing three fingers on each hand, his eyes were missing and was bleeding profusely from his sockets, and long gashes were present across his arms and legs. Jake was very thorough and by the time the rest came back the zombie was begging for mercy and was begging to be free while growling hysterically. After James pried Jake off the zombie and then tied the zombie to a desk chair; the zombie began crying as his wounds regenerated. "What the hell is wrong with you?" yelled James. "I was trying to get results and you just asking him nicely wasn't going to get us anywhere! The rest of you agree with me, right?" asked Jake. Stacy clung to James' side with a glare. Simon and Christine also glared and were clearly with James on this. "Fine, do what you want but I got him to beg for mercy. Let's see what he has to say now." The zombie began to cry even harder even though no more wounds were evident on him anymore. The serum must have given him that ability.

Jake advanced toward the zombie and the creature wailed "I'll tell you whatever you want. I know how to reverse the zombie epidemic and where to find Jeb. He's on the top floor of the water treatment plant and he controls each of us through a hive mind ability that he has. Many of us have sentience and are forced to obey while others are just dummies who don't know right from wrong. Dr. Jeb himself has been working on an even greater serum in order to expand his influence worldwide. I can tell you about the counter serum though, I was there when he created it. Jeb thought he killed me when he bashed my head in but some of the serum managed to infect me and my wounds regenerated. There is also a cannon set up so that he can distribute it more efficiently but if you put the counter serum in there, then maybe you can reverse the effects. I wrote the ingredients down, if you look in my right pocket you will find them all there." Simon came forward and searched his pocket. He pulled out a worn-out piece of paper and as Simon read, his eyes began to widen.

"He's right, if this is accurate, I can make a counter serum right here with household ingredients as substitutes. We can finally end this." James went to the zombie and let him out of his restraints. The zombie dropped down to his knees in fear and confusion. "Are you really just letting me go?" "Yes, you've helped us and you deserve your freedom." said James. Jake's face twitched in anger but he suppressed it. The zombie got up and quickly began to run out of the base. Before he could get far Jake grabbed him close. "If you try to warn Jeb before we come for him, I will kill you, do you understand" snarled Jake. "Yes, I swear I won't betray you. I can't stop him from reading my mind but I can try to shield it for as long as possible. You have my word." the zombie quivered. As the zombie left, the rest of the group decided to figure out what to do next. "I have a plan. Once Simon synthesizes the counter serum, I plan to sneak into the base myself. I'll take the serum with me and sneak across enemy lines. I won't kill anyone, but I will do whatever I can to ensure we are safe and that the town is free, however, I need a distraction. As much as I don't want to do this, I need you guys to use air horns and other means in order to lure Jeb's main forces here and fortify the base in order to give me as much time as possible." said James. Jake said in response, "I don't like you going off alone but I understand your plan. I'm with you until the end mate, you know that. I think there's a hidden room here with tranquilizers and other weapons we can use to aid you." said Jake confidently. "Thank you, Jake, I didn't expect you to be so helpful but I appreciate your support in this." said James genuinely. The other three looked on in agreement and were more than willing to stand with James in this plan.

In truth, Jake was conflicted but he didn't let it show. Jake disagreed with James' plan because he didn't want his friend to get hurt but he was also secretly happy with the fact that James may die from this excursion. He hated himself for that thought but it was the only way he felt he could support James in this endeavor. The group decided to search the house again and they found many hidden rooms filled with supplies. The house was a full two-story house but also had the bunker and was well built overall. A hidden button in the second story closet revealed baseball bats, tranquilizer guns, and tasers. Many non-lethal weapons and protective gear were available. James took a baseball bat, Simon and Christine took tranquilizer guns, and Stacy and Jake took taser batons. Each member took bullet proof vests as well and welding masks in order to protect their faces. The friends spent the rest of the day using wood and barbed wire they found to fortify the fence, windows, and doors around the base even further. Simon took his time analyzing the counter serum he was making in his makeshift lab in his room. He estimated it would take about two days to finish it using his intellect and own skills.

On the second day the group continued to train with their weapons that could be used for hand-to-hand combat. Baseball bats, wooden swords and wooden knives were what they decided to use along with the batons and tranquilizer guns. There were metal blades as well but they decided to avoid them for now. On the third day they found some air horns and alarm systems that could be used to lure the zombies to the hideout. By the fourth day everyone's anxiety levels were pretty high but they were ready. They spent the day resting up and then training. Simon had also finished the counter serum and presented it to James with a flourish in a special gaseous form that was to be administered by the cannon at the plant. James spent time training with the others to make sure they were up to snuff for the fight the next day. Overall, he decided that the group was ready and should be able to handle most minor threats at least and should be able to handle anything together.

By nightfall everyone was getting ready to go to sleep. "I'm going to go to sleep, night everyone." Said James. "Night," said everyone else. Later that night Jake went into Stacy's room to talk. "Stacy wake up, I need to talk to you," said Jake. Stacy woke up feeling startled and pissed. "Jake it's the middle of the night. What the hell do you want?" asked Stacy angrily. "I'm worried about James' plan; I think it will get all of us killed. I don't think James is meant to be our leader," said Jake. Jake still felt hurt about her and James getting close but he really didn't want to die tomorrow. Even though he wanted James to potentially die, he didn't want the rest of them to die in the onslaught. "I know it isn't the best plan but I trust James with my life," said Stacy. "I don't trust him; I think he may turn on us tomorrow," said Jake. Where the hell did that come from? Jake knew he hated James at times but he never questioned his loyalty like this. His hatred must be getting to him. "How could you say that; he's protected us since this outbreak started?" asked Stacy. "Look, I'm just telling you what I think. Let me ask you something, do you really trust James' plan or are you letting your personal feelings cloud your judgment?" asked Jake. He knew he was crossing a line but he had to get this out. "Just go to sleep Jake, we have a long day tomorrow," said Stacy. "Fine, just think about what I said," said Jake softly. Jake didn't know what he was feeling or doing. All he knew was that while he wanted to trust James he couldn't. He was losing his friends and James was the problem. He needed to think of something. Still though, he wanted James to live so that he could work out his issues with him. He also wanted to confess that he tried to kill him in the past but he didn't think anyone would accept him for that.

The next morning everyone got up at around 6am. The plan was that they would get their weapons and everything ready for 7 and then move out with the plan at 8. At 7:30 things weren't going as planned. "Everyone ready?" asked James. "I'm ready". yelled everyone except Jake. "I'm not ready," commented Jake. "What's the problem?" asked James. "My problem is you. You're going to get us all killed," said Jake. "I know the plan is risky but it's our only shot," said James. "What's been going on with you? You've been acting this way ever since the outbreak started," said James angrily. "I think I should be the leader," said Jake. "Guys can we talk about this later? We need to focus on the plan," uttered Stacy coldly. "Alright, we will talk about this later," said James." Looking forward to it," grunted Jake sarcastically. James didn't like that Jake challenged him so much and didn't appreciate how inconsistent he could be. He knew Jake had some issues but none of that justified his treatment of the group.

James got his gear and started to head to the plant. "I'm going to head to the plant, fire the air horns in 25 minutes." said James. "We will," said Jake. "Good luck," said Simon and Christine. "James, be careful," said Stacy concerned. "I'll be fine. Good luck to the four of you," said James. James gave everyone a tight hug and wished them luck one more time. James started walking to the plant and noticed that the path to the plant was eerily silent. There were no enemies in sight and the air smelled like blood and rust. Once he finally got there, he decided to begin scouting the zombies and area in order to gain some intel. Suddenly he could hear talking from close by. James dove into a bush and began to listen from his vantage point.

Three zombies began to come into view as they walked past his hiding spot. "I can't believe those kids didn't get infected," said Zombie #1. "Yeah, I was sure the serum would work," said Zombie #2. "The boss isn't going to want to know that they're still alive," said Zombie #1. "I think he already knows," replied Zombie #2. "Hey guys," said Zombie #3. "What's up dude?" asked Zombie #1. "Not much except that you better get to the bathrooms, boss needs you to clean them," said Zombie #3. "I just cleaned them," commented Zombie #1. "Yeah, but Zombie #8 had too many brains and had the runs. The whole bathroom stinks," said Zombie #3. "Damn it, the last time this happened he farted over some gas he spilled," said Zombie #1. "He nearly burned down the west wing," said Zombie #2. "Well, you better get to the bathroom or else the boss will chop off your leg, again," said Zombie #3. "Alright I'll go do it," said Zombie #1. He ran off to clean the bathrooms. "What are you still doing here; this is a two-person job," said Zombie #3. "Fine, I'll take care of it," said Zombie #2. He ran off to join his colleague. Zombie #3 walked off and started barking orders to the other zombies. "Pick up the pace you lazy bitch. Do I have to cut off another offending body part?" The offending zombie ran away in terror as Zombie #3 grabbed his sword and began chasing them. James watched all of this in horror. "I still can't believe they can talk and that they can be so cruel to each other," whispered James.

After a few minutes he heard the sound of an air horn and alarms blaring in the distance. All of the zombies turned their heads and surged towards the source of the sound. James could feel their saliva as they salivated at the thought of fresh meat. There had to be hundreds of them, maybe thousands of them running out of the plant. After the coast cleared up James walked slowly towards the entrance. Still no other enemies were coming out of the plant so it must be clear enough. Breathing in deep and working out the nerves, James slowly entered the plant.

A Clash of Enemies

After he snuck in through the front door James realized that there were still a ton of zombies left. "I wonder what that sound was," said Zombie #5. "I don't know," said Zombie #6. The interior of the plant was dirty and ruined. There were cracks in the walls and there were lots of mold growing everywhere. The air felt suffocating and hard to breathe but James held his composure. There was no point in letting his nerves destroy him now. He had to protect himself and the people he cared about. "What are you two doing here?" barked Zombie #8. "We were just hanging around," said Zombie #5. "Get back to work!" yelled Zombie #8. The two zombies ran off to the west wing. "Lazy dicks. They just hang around all day and expect to get a full day's pay," grumbled Zombie #8. After the zombie had left James continued his quest to find the main labs. He saw a map on the wall that showed he was on the ground floor and that the labs were on the 10th floor. "It's going to be a long way to the top," said James. James quickly ran around the corner and dashed up the first set of stairs.

Meanwhile back at the hideout things weren't going very well. The zombies were coming in from all directions and were destroying everything in their path. The group members were terrified. They needed a leader and weren't unified without James. Many of the zombies were stopped by the barbed wire but were still fighting through it in order to push through. "Look I know that I'm not James but in his absence, I think that I should take over as leader for now," said Jake. "No, James is our leader." Affirmed Christine. "James left us. He is probably dead," said Jake. "No, James isn't dead; he'll be back for us," said Stacy confidently. "I think I should take over as leader for the moment," said Stacy. "Great idea," said Simon and Christine. "Fine," said Jake. Stacy was the closest to James overall and knew how he thought despite him potentially disagreeing with that statement.

Stacy also had great leadership skills from her time as an athlete. Stacy started giving orders and the team was finally working together. Simon and Christine would take the bottom level of the house. Jake would take the second floor and Stacy took the roof herself. There weren't nearly enough people to cover every area effectively but they did the best they could with what they had. It was known that there were many enemies from the plant but no one knew just how many there were. Even though each member had decent fighting skills, they still weren't a match for the sheer number of enemies. Jake took great glee in using his stun batons and wooden swords to hit enemies that breached the second floor. He finally had an outlet for all of his anger towards James and was very effective in battle but was still a hothead. While Jake and Stacy were handling themselves as well, Simon and Christine weren't faring so well.

Simon's anxiety began to take over and he had a panic attack and nervous breakdown in the middle of the fight. "We are going to die here," wailed Simon. Christine ran up to him after using a dart to knock out a couple zombies trying to break in through a nearby window and tried to comfort him. She looked at him and said "Simon we can do this; we may be outnumbered but we can hold them off long enough for James to distribute the cure." Simon looked at her and realized that she was right. "How are you so calm during this?" asked Simon. "I'm calm because I have a reason to fight; I am fighting for my friends." said Christine calmly. "You're right, we can do this." said Simon. She gave him a quick hug and then they started fighting again.

Simon knew that Christine was someone he trusted unconditionally and knew that he had to survive in order to keep her safe. Even if they never became more than friends, he was going to do whatever he could to ensure her happiness. Back at the plant James had managed to get up to the fourth floor unnoticed but it was getting harder. Each floor James went up more zombies appeared on the next floor. "There has to be a quicker way to the top." muttered James under his breath. Finally, he noticed an elevator. The relief was evident on his face as he stared at the godsend of the elevator. He went inside it and saw that it only went up to the 9th floor. As he stepped in the elevator abruptly stopped near the eighth floor. "What happened?" asked James aloud. James was very confused by this. He opened up the top of the elevator and climbed out. He started to climb the shaft up to the eighth floor. Just as he got there, he heard voices nearby. "What happened to the elevator?" asked Zombie. "I don't know but I know that if we don't fix it then the boss will chop off both of our faces," said Zombie #10. "Your right, we better get on it," said Zombie. James hid in a closet that was close to the shaft. He heard the two zombies go by and waited for them to go down the shaft. After 10 minutes they finally went down the shaft and began working. James slipped out and went around the corner. He knew that Dr. Jeb had to be at the very top and he would do nothing else until Jeb was dealt with.

Meanwhile the others were starting to get the hang of things for a brief moment back at base. Then just as they were starting to get into the rhythm of things; things took a turn for the worse. Simon and Christine tried to fight off some zombies on the ground floor but they managed to break through the defenses. The windows and door broke and the zombies swarmed through. Simon and Christine ran upstairs to where Jake was. "Jake the zombies broke through our defenses, we can't hold them off any more," said Christine. "Oh, so now you need my help. I'd love to help but I'm a little busy at the moment." Jake was fighting off 5 zombies with a bat. His batons and knives had gotten lost in the fight. Simon and Christine decided to stay on the second floor and help Jake. Stacy was having trouble on the roof. About 15 zombies had started to fire bullets in her direction. She managed to tranquilize a couple of them but it wasn't enough. A zombie adjusted the angle of the gun and fired right at Stacy. The bullet had managed to pierce through her armor and went right into her shoulder. She fell down to the ground and started to bleed. "James, where are you?" asked Stacy quietly.

Back at the plant James had just got to the staircase that would lead him to the 9th floor. Up at the top he saw a zombie. "I can't wait any longer, I'm going in," said James. He quietly crept up the staircase to where the zombie was facing opposite of him. He took his bat and slammed it against his head. He hadn't killed anyone but right now he had to eliminate any threats in his way. James realized that if Jeb were to call for reinforcements he would be overwhelmed and needed to neutralize any in his way. Blood fell everywhere. He looked at the body and the sight he saw destroyed a part of him. His eyes became red and started watering up. He realized that this zombie was his ex-girlfriend Sam. "I can't believe she got infected too," said James softly. "I knew she volunteered here but I thought she was out of town. Now she's dead because of me," cried James. James knelt down beside her and held her. He lifted his head and had anger in his eyes. James knew that this death was his fault and that he would always carry a part of it with him forever. However, he could deal with his emotions later. This had to end. Trauma and guilt could come later.

He had to stop this once and for all before more people died. He ran up to the 9th floor and redrew his bat. He saw that there were 20 zombies down the hall. He ran in at full speed and started hitting all of them with the bat. All of them were now unconscious. “Clean up on Aisle 9,” said James angrily. He then ran around the corner and into a few more rooms knocking out any zombie in sight. Finally, he had found the final staircase and ran up to the 10th floor. He ran into the next room and made it to the main labs. James took out the serum and started to set it up before he went to the cannon. Just as he was finishing up; he heard a voice behind him. “It’s been so long James,” said an unknown voice. James turned and saw that it was the one person he never wanted to see.

Meanwhile back at the hideout Stacy is still on the roof bleeding. After a little while she ripped off a piece of her shirt to cover the wound. Then she got up and started to fire tranquilizer darts at all the zombies. She had managed to get 13 zombies. She then heard footsteps coming up the stairs. She saw it was the others. “There are too many zombies down there so we came up here,” said Jake. They soon realized that zombies were coming in from all directions. Even more were beginning to stream through the grounds and into the house. Everyone was feeling terrified but they were united. “If we have to die then we shall die fighting,” said Stacy. They got ready to fight as the zombies came closer to them.

Meanwhile back at the plant. James realized that the person was Dr. Jeb. “No, how is this possible? You look exactly the same as you did in that newspaper article.” Said James. “Yes, I suppose you’re right,” said Jeb. “How are you doing all of this?” asked James. “Well, first I created a serum that would allow me to turn everyone in town into slaves. Then I created another serum to put them under my control,” said Jeb. “I drank the water; how am I not infected?” asked James. “I’m not sure. It may have to with Egypt though,” said Jeb. Jeb maintained clear eye contact with James. James felt confusion overcome his features but couldn’t get the words out to ask him what he meant by that.

Dr. Jeb stared at James with cold dead eyes. His appearance hadn’t changed much except that he is much paler and slightly older. James felt fear in his heart but he knew he had to stop this madness. “Who was that person that stopped you all those years ago? Was it my father?” asked James. Jeb grinned at him and said nothing. “TELL ME!” yelled James. “My boy this is so much bigger than you realize. But I will tell you one thing, your father is dead,” said Jeb. "You're lying," said James. "No, I'm not," replied Jeb coldly. "Did you kill him?" asked James. "I was involved but I didn't do it alone. My son pulled it off," said Jeb. "Who is your son?" asked James angrily. "I would tell you but it isn't worth it. After all, you won't survive long enough to figure out his identity anyway. By the way it is good to see you again James after so many long years," said Dr. Jeb. A look of shock and terror came over James' face. Jeb grinned even more. He then muttered calmly "goodbye James."

Jeb lunged at James and pinned him to the ground. James tried to fight back but Jeb overpowered him. Because of the serum the scientist had gained super strength and agility. James knew he was going to die. Suddenly he thought of someone important to him. He thought of his friends and how they were going to die without him. He used every ounce of strength in him and pushed Jeb off of him. He then grabbed his bat and hit Jeb with full force against his skull. Jeb was crying out in pain and was walking close to the window. James took a step back and ran forward at top speed. He kicked Jeb with all of his momentum and knocked Jeb through the window. Jeb fell to the ground. James looked down at his mangled body. Dr. Jeb had scratches all over his body and his face was destroyed by the glass. "That was for my father," said James coldly. James quickly went back to the cure and finished his prep. Suddenly he saw the cannon and figured he could use that to finish this. He loaded it up and shot the vial near the town.

Back at the hideout everyone was beaten up and were about to die. "We can't take much more of this," said Christine. "I don't think James succeeded," said Jake. Suddenly a vial landed near the hideout and it exploded upon impact. A blue gas erupted from the vial and covered the whole town. It even made it all the way back to the plant. James saw the gas and knew that he succeeded. "It's over," said James. As he went back down, he saw that people were turning back to normal. When he got to the bottom, he noticed Jeb's body was gone. All that was left were traces of blood. He hurried back to the hideout and saw everyone was returning to normal. He ran to the top of the hideout and saw his friends wounded and close to death. When they saw him, they got excited. "James, you did it," said Simon. "You survived," said Christine happily with tears in her eyes. "Good to see you man," said Jake. "I knew you could do it," said Stacy. Everyone finally realized what had happened and knew that these teenagers saved them all. Some doctors quickly came and brought James' friends to the emergency room.

Peace?

A FEW DAYS LATER everyone was released and they decided to meet up at the public school. James was the first to arrive and then soon came Stacy. "Hey," said Stacy. "Hey," said James quietly. "Are you okay?" asked Stacy. "I'm fine but there is something I need to tell you," said James. "What is it?" asked Stacy with concern. "It's about what I saw in the labs. I saw Dr. Jeb in there. He looked exactly the way he did in 1965. He told me that he controlled the zombies because of a serum he took and then gave the town a different serum to turn them into those things," said James. "Wow, I didn't think anyone was capable of that," said Stacy. "I didn't think so either," said James. "He must have been powerful. How did you get rid of him?" asked Stacy. "I fought him and when I thought I was going to die I used the strength inside me and I managed to kill him, I think," said James. "Wow you must be pretty powerful too," said Stacy. "I don't know, maybe I caught him off guard," replied James. "Why aren't you sure that he is dead?" asked Stacy. "When I released the gas on the town I went down to the bottom of the plant and his body was gone. He may still be alive," said James. "Don't worry about it. Also, even if he does come back, we stopped him once so we could do it again," said Stacy. "At least it's over for now," muttered James. Soon after the others started to arrive and they all began talking. James told them everything except about what had happened to his father. He planned on telling them later. "We should get going to the ceremony," said James. "Yeah, your right," said Simon.

The town was giving them an award for saving the town. They headed to the ceremony. At the ceremony Mr. Jameson came up to the stage. "I would like to thank these teenagers for saving our town," said Mr. Jameson. "First, I would like to present this award to someone who showed true intelligence during all of this. I present this award to Simon the intelligent," said Mr. Jameson. Everyone cheered for him as Simon received the medal.

Simon had always been incredibly smart and everyone thought he would be either a great detective or scientist. He definitely earned this award. "Next, I would like to give this award to someone who showed great courage during this. I present this award to Christine the courageous." The crowd cheered loudly. Christine was always someone who was afraid of getting close to others but she was always stronger than she thought and I'm happy that the rest of the town can see that as well. "Next I would like to present this award to someone who would rather work alone. I present this award to Jake the loner." People cheered for him but not as loudly this time. Jake enjoyed hanging out with us but he never really liked opening up. This award definitely reflected those sentiments. "Next, I would like to present this award to someone who was almost unstoppable no matter how wounded they were, they still fought hard. I present this award to Stacy the Unstoppable." Everyone cheered very loudly for Stacy. Without Stacy's indomitable will we would have lost this fight. "Finally, I would like to present this award to someone who was a true leader and who cared more about his friends than himself. I present this award to James the strong." Everyone cheered at the top of their lungs for James. As the mayor put the medal across his neck James felt a surge of pride.

After the ceremony ended Jake walked off alone to the woods. James pulled Stacy aside and told her about his father and his ex. "James I'm so sorry." She pulled him into her arms and they hugged for a while. Meanwhile a dark figure climbed out from under the plant. It was Dr. Jeb. Jeb was completely cured and had no influence anymore. "I can't believe I lost my powers. James is more powerful than I thought. I can't believe my own son conspired against me. It won't matter soon because the end is near." Jeb looked up to the sky menacingly. "Ha, ha, ha, ha, ha."

Jake walked into the woods to get some air and then headed back home. His parents were weak but managed to recover from the illness. Jake returned home and felt nothing but anger towards them. He could only see red as his heart beat faster and faster. They were both lying in their beds and were breathing shallowly. Jake ran up to them and pulled their pillows over both their faces. Both his parents tried to struggle and fight back but ultimately nothing could withstand Jake's death grip on them. Their breathing slowed until it completely stopped and Jake slumped down to the ground. He knew that he would get away with this since many people died during the attacks. No one had to know that Jake killed the monsters that were his parents himself. Outside of town Jeb hobbled his way to a jet he stashed away and looked at the contents as he flew to Arizona. The boxes and crates within the place looked like blue corpses and looked almost alien. Jeb smiled in response as he saw one of the aliens' hands began to twitch and Jeb clasped its hand with his own and said, "You are going to love Schreiber my new friend. Soon you will help bring the world to its knees," he said menacingly.

Two months later:

Our story continues two months after the events of the zombie outbreak. The five heroes have always stuck together but now their bond would soon be tested. The age of peace would also soon be over. On August 27th 2015 James went to meet Stacy at the Voyageur to talk. James walked into the restaurant and headed to a booth. The smell of food filled his senses. There are lots of people talking and laughing. A few minutes later Stacy walked in cheerfully. She scanned the restaurant until she sees James. Ever since James found out he was adopted he has been trying to find information about his father. Stacy walked up to the booth and sat across from him. "Hey James," said Stacy. "Hey Stacy, good to see you." Stacy looked closely at James and saw that something was bothering him. "Are you okay?" asked Stacy. "Yeah, I'm alright. I just haven't had much luck in finding my father." "You'll find him. Do you need any help?" asked Stacy. "No thanks, I need to do this myself," okay," said Stacy. Stacy knew how hard this summer had been for James. All she wanted was to be able to help him. James looked at his watch and said "I should get going," "ok," said Stacy.

As James got up to leave Stacy quickly grabbed his arm. James seemed to like the feeling but he knew he had to get going. "Do you have any plans tonight?" asked Stacy. James looked her in the eye and said "No, I don't have anything going on tonight." "Do you want to come over to my house? No one'll be there and I'd like to have some company," said Stacy. James looked unsure at first but then he decided maybe he should spend more time with Stacy. "Sure, I'd like that. Should I come by around seven?" asked James. "Yeah, sevens good." James walked out of the restaurant and Stacy was thrilled. James and Stacy got really close during the outbreak. Stacy broke up with Gregory and she and James were more than friends but not quite a couple yet. James wanted more than anything to be with her but he knew he had to figure out what happened with his family before he could focus on a relationship with the person, he loved the most.

She was still sitting down when Jake came in. He had changed a lot since the outbreak. He had become cockier and he seemed to hate James even more. He even confessed his love to Stacy after the zombie attack but she rejected him. Things were very awkward between them now. Jake had created a new look for himself. He was wearing a ripped-up skull t-shirt and he had blue jeans that were also completely ripped up. He didn't have much hair anymore either. All he had was a thin blond sheet of hair on the top of his head. His face had become dry and he smelled so bad that you could smell him a mile away. The only thing that stayed the same is his unbelievable hatred towards James. He seemed to like James isolating himself from everyone. He saw Stacy sitting down and he slid into the booth. Stacy smiled at him but she didn't like seeing Jake this way. "Hey Jake. How have you been?" asked Stacy. Jake looked at her. She could tell he had been using drugs and that he had been drinking last night. "I'm alright. Did I just see James step out of here? asked Jake. He had anger in his eyes. "Yes, James and I were talking," said Stacy. "James is pathetic. You shouldn't be talking to him," said Jake. "James is a great guy. Why do you hate him so much? The two of you used to be best friends," said Stacy. "James and I have just grown apart," said Jake calmly. "I just don't want you to put your trust into someone who will eventually abandon you." "James won't abandon me," replied Stacy. Jake looked her right in the eye and asked her as calmly as he could "do you have a thing for James?" "What are you talking about? Me and James are just really good friends," said Stacy shakily. "Right," uttered Jake sarcastically. Jake rose up from the booth and took one last look at Stacy. "Don't let your personal feelings cloud your judgment," said Jake. Jake walked away and Stacy wasn't sure what to think now.

Jake admitted in his mind that he still wanted James dead but also wanted to ask him for help. His parents died right after the outbreak. Nobody knew what happened and it looked like they died from overdosing due to the needles being located nearby. But Jake knew the truth, he always knew. He knew that he made it look like they overdosed in order to get rid of the abuse. In truth he suffocated them, but nobody else needed to know that part. He currently lived with his aunt who didn't mind him crashing there. She never really talked to him so he could do whatever he wanted essentially. While he was free from his family's abuse, he still hated himself and hated James.

The New Threat:

MEANWHILE, IN AN UNDERGROUND lab near Arizona someone was busy at work. The underground lab was filled with chemicals and lots of high-tech equipment. In the very center of the lab was none other than Doctor Jeb. Dr. Jeb is a tall man with white frizzy hair that had been cut short and a pointy nose. He also wears a set of glasses. Jeb was pacing around the room trying to think of what his next plan should be. The serum he had drank to become stronger had worn off and was now cured of all of his powers but not his memories. After James kicked him out the window, he used all of his strength to crawl away and heal up. Jeb looked at pictures of the five teenagers. Whenever he looked at them, he got extremely angry. He looked at closely at them and said “one day my son, you will come to your senses and align with me.” Jeb looked the other way and started to mix more chemicals.

Finally, he had finished his serum. He went into another room and started to pull out bodies that were strapped to gurneys. The bodies weren’t human though. The bodies were aliens. He poured his new serum on the bodies and they started to shake. Their cold deteriorating bodies had sprung to life and began walking around. Their bodies were light blue and just under 6 ft tall. Their faces are round with black eyes and somewhat long and thin arms. Dr. Jeb took out another serum he had created and he drank it. When he drank it, he felt a nice tingling feeling. He then felt a sharp pain in his stomach and he fell back. His throat began to close up and his vision began to blur before a feeling of relief and peace overcame him. The negative symptoms faded and he felt stronger than ever. He got up slowly. The serum had changed him. Now he felt even stronger and faster than before.

Because of the serum he was now able to communicate with the aliens. He only had 10 of them but then he saw that the aliens were starting to lay eggs. After 10 minutes there were thousands of aliens occupying the space of the laboratory. Jeb ordered them to stop laying eggs and they slowly stopped as if they were robots. Their obedience was second to none. Jeb also ordered them to create vehicles that could be used to destroy the world. The aliens began to work and after many hours they had built hundreds of advanced vehicles that mankind could only dream of creating. Many flying cars with laser guns were only part of the weapons they created. Needless to say, Jeb was very impressed. Next Jeb decided to train them. Weapons like guns and swords were used, along with hand-to-hand combat were the main bases covered. He trained with them for a few more hours until they had become elite warriors. The aliens only needed that many hours in order to attain their full potential. The aliens are also very smart and could make quick decisions. Dr. Jeb realized that he would have to get rid of the teenagers before he could do anything. And the aliens were the perfect weapons in order to do just that.

Meanwhile at Stacy's house she was getting everything ready for when James came over. Stacy was getting out lots of food and drinks. At James' house James was looking through some old family albums. His mother came up to him and asked with concern "are you okay honey?" James looked up at her. His mother couldn't see happiness or joy in his eyes. All she saw was a shadow of what her son used to be. She sat next to him and gave him a hug. After the hug James looked at his watch and saw it was ten to seven. He got up and said "I'm going to Stacy's place; I'll be back later. His mother said "okay, have fun." She looked at her son and saw that there was a flicker of joy in his eyes. She knew that there was still hope for him. James headed out and started walking to Stacy's house. He liked feeling the hot summer air. He hadn't gotten to spend a lot of time with Stacy or any of his other friends. He only bumped into Jake a couple times and he had only seen Simon and Christine around town a few times. Stacy had been the most persistent in trying to spend time with him. After about ten minutes he saw Stacy's house. He walked up casually to the door and knocked a few times. He waited and then Stacy opened the door. They said hi to each other and then Stacy grabbed his arm and she led him inside. They went into the living room and sat down on the couch.

They started to reminisce about things they used to do and old memories. They were having a good time. "I'm glad we are hanging out again," said Stacy. "We've hung out before," said James. "I know but the last few times we've hung out you've been isolating yourself and not letting yourself have a good time," replied Stacy. James moved closer to Stacy and gave her a big hug. "What is this for?" asked Stacy. "It's for standing by me even when I was in a dark place," said James as he let go of Stacy. As Stacy looked at James, she heard someone knocking at the door. "Be right back James." She got up to get the door. As she walked, she kept thinking about how she had finally broken through the barrier that James had put up to keep his friends out. When she got to the door, she opened it up to see the one person she really didn't want to see.

Jake was standing at the door. He was in his ripped-up skull t-shirt and he had shaved his head completely. He had self-inflicted scars on his arms and chest. He was wavering while standing so it was obvious he was drunk. "Heeey Stacy. What's up," said Jake drunkenly. "Are you alright?" asked Stacy. Jake stumbled in and said "I'm worthless." Stacy grabbed him and brought him to the second couch to relax. Jake saw James and yelled "WHY IS HE HERE?" James came up to Jake and asked "what's wrong with him." "He's been drinking", said Stacy. Jake seemed to get upset with James in the room so Stacy asked him if he could leave her and Jake alone. James agreed. As he walked out Stacy called "wait, after I'm done with Jake can we talk later?" "Sure," said James. James walked out and Stacy felt happy because of how close she and James were. When James left the room Jake started to calm down and he felt happy to be with Stacy. "Thank you for watching over me," said Jake. "No problem. "We may not be as close but you are still my friend," replied Stacy.

A few minutes later there was a knocking at the door. James heard it and told Stacy he would get it. When he opened the door, he saw that it was Christine and Simon. "Hey guys, it's good to see you," commented James. Simon looked surprised to see him but happy nonetheless. "Hey James, it's been a long time, how have you been?" asked Simon. "I'm doing better. I think you're going to see me a lot more around town," said James. "That's really great to hear," said Christine. "By the way what are you guys doing here?" asked James. "Jake texted us to come," said Christine. "He said he was drunk and he wanted us to come see him," said Simon. James stood aside and Simon and Christine came in. They went to the living room and saw Jake curled up on the couch next to Stacy. Simon and Christine went to go see him and Jake seemed really happy to see all of them. A few minutes later they heard a rumbling sound coming from outside. The ground then started to shake and then something tore the roof off of Stacy's house as her place was exposed to the elements. A rush of wind overcame the friends and they all shivered and braced themselves for what was to come.

Things Change

Everyone was horrified by what was happening. They looked up and saw what appeared to be blue aliens. Aliens were flying above her house in their sleek metal hovercraft. The aliens turned on a machine on their vehicle and they pointed it at the five friends. Suddenly everyone realized that they couldn't move their bodies at all as a blue laser fired at them. They were feeling an intense feeling of tightness within them and that feeling kept getting tighter and tighter. Eventually the feeling caused them so much pain they slowly fell unconscious. The aliens used their machine to pick up the five friends using telekinesis and then threw them across the town in five different directions. With the teenagers out of the way Dr. Jeb used the time to take over the entire town without much resistance. An era of darkness and blood was about to overcome the town that nobody was ready for.

5 days later James awoke in a ditch in the outskirts of town. He felt disoriented until he quickly came to his senses. The first thing he realized was his hunger and thirst. Through sheer luck he managed to find some crackers in his pocket and a bottle of water nearby. He ate them and drank the water greedily until he managed to feel some semblance of normality. He smelt blood and war in the air and the town was in complete ruins. He looked around but he didn't see anyone. He walked around a bit until he came closer to town. He noticed the sky was grey and the buildings were abandoned and some of them destroyed. After a few minutes he made it to the main part of town and he was horrified by what he saw. Buildings had collapsed in on themselves and his favorite store from when he was a kid had been completely vaporized. He also saw a giant statue of Jeb in the center. He saw some aliens flying overhead and he quickly ducked into an alley to hide from them. As he was hiding someone was coming up behind him. As the person

got closer, they said "James?" James quickly looked around and was surprised by what he saw.

Meanwhile At the public-school Simon woke up on the roof and soon realized what was going on. He saw some posters with Jeb's face on it. They depicted him stomping on everyone else in the world with his alien army. He quickly jumped off the roof and heard something in the dumpster. He looked and he saw Christine was thrown in there. He picked her up and they hid behind the school. He tried to do everything to get her to awake. "Christine, please you have to wake up. You are my best friend. I don't know what I would do if you weren't around." He started to sob. Finally, Christine started to stir. Simon looked and saw that Christine was waking up. He went up to her and gave her a big hug. "Thanks Simon. I understand." He realized that she had heard everything he had said. "You are my best friend too." Simon helped her up and then they started to walk away from the school. They could see the burnt buildings and all the destruction. They realized that it was happening again. Suddenly some aliens were riding above them so they ran for a few minutes until they made it to the restaurant the Voyageur. They quickly took refuge in there to hide from the chaos.

Meanwhile James looked behind him and was surprised to see who was standing there. It was Stacy. James ran up to her and they hugged. He held her in his arms for a long time. "I'm so glad you are okay," said James. Stacy pulled away and asked "what's going on here." They looked around and Stacy saw the giant statue. "Looks like you were right. Dr. Jeb is back," said Stacy. "He said he killed my father. Now I might be able to finally get some answers." James looked at Jeb's statue and started feel angry. His face started to become red and he was using every ounce of his energy to keep himself from exploding. Stacy came up to him and grabbed his shoulder. She looked him in the eye and he slowly started to calm down. "Everything's going to be okay. We stopped him once and we will do it again," said Stacy. James knew she was right. He gently pulled away and said "we need to find the others." They looked around and they decided to head to the ballpark.

They walked up the road until they could see the entire ballpark. "I don't see anyone," said Stacy. "Wait, look," said James. Stacy looked and she saw two aliens carrying a body around the ballpark. They soon realized it was Jake. They ran down the hill and they hid behind the bleachers. The aliens carried the body near the bleachers and then they dropped it. "I'm tired." said alien 1. "Me too. Let's take a break," replied alien 2. James and Stacy were shocked that they were able to talk. "I want to but we can't. We need to keep moving and bring Jake to the dr. If we don't the boss will hang our heads in the center of town," said Alien 1. "Right, I forgot about that. Do you remember what happened to Jared?" asked alien 2. "Yeah, when he didn't clean Jeb's bathroom correctly, he shaved all his hair from his body. He was in a lot of pain for a few days," said alien 1. "I don't want that. Let's keep moving," said Alien 1. They picked up the body and started to walk away. James knew he had to strike so he snuck up on the aliens and he jumped them. The aliens were completely caught off guard. James shifted his weight into one of them and then Stacy came and tackled the other one to the ground. They fought the aliens until they gave up.

The two aliens ran away and left Jake on the ground. James and Stacy got up. They both noticed that they only had minor injuries from the brawl. James went to go pick Jake up and he hid him behind the bleachers. Stacy knew that reinforcements would come so they hauled Jake up together and decided to head to the voyageur instead. For some reason James felt stronger than ever. He had more strength and more energy. They quickly ran away from the field and decided to get out of sight. James felt like even his injuries were beginning to heal faster than he expected. He had no idea what was going on but he was happy with the results.

Meanwhile at the voyageur Simon and Christine were hiding out in the restaurant part of it. The area used to be a convenience store, gas station, and restaurant all in once. The Voyageur looked like it was in ruins from the outside but most of it was intact on the inside. They were hiding behind the counter. Simon felt happy to be with Christine and she also felt happy to be with him. Christine looked away from Simon and started to feel upset. She had a bad pit in her stomach and her eyes began to become wet with tears. Simon noticed and he asked "what's wrong?" She replied "I'm really worried about the others." Simon went closer to her and he put his arm over her shoulder to comfort her. She started to feel a little better. Simon started to lean closer but he suddenly felt really weird. His head had a screeching pain and he doubled back. He was lying on the floor screaming out in pain. He had never felt anything like this before. Suddenly an image started to pop into his mind.

He saw James and Stacy running into the Voyageur while carrying Jake. That image then started to slip away and another one popped into place. He saw two best friends fighting each other. One friend is covered in light whereas the other one is covered in darkness. The faces of these two individuals are unknown. The image slowly slipped away and Simon started to come back to reality. When he lost the image, he immediately gasped for breath. He was lying on the floor feeling weak. Christine rushed over to him.

She picked him up and brought him back behind the counter. He slowly got up and said that he was fine. He just has to rest a little. When Christine tried to ask him what happened but he said that whatever it was it's over now. At the moment that was good enough for Christine.

After a few minutes Simon decided to tell her what had happened. She knew he would tell her eventually once he was ready. He told her about the two visions and she was shocked top say the least. At first, she didn't think it meant anything but then she saw James and Stacy run into the restaurant while carrying Jake. She looked at Simon and said "we'll talk about this later." She and Simon got up to greet them. "You guys are ok," remarked Stacy excitedly. Stacy and James ran up to hug Simon and Christine. After that they all picked up Jake and brought him behind the counter. For some reason Jake just wasn't waking up. They all tried to talk to him to wake him up. After a while Jake finally woke up. Jake was very happy to see everyone... except for James. "What is he doing here!" yelled Jake. James looked at Stacy and said "maybe I should wait outside." James started to walk out when Stacy took his hand and said "wait, you don't need to leave." She looked at Jake and felt angry. Jake said "what are you doing? You know I don't like James." Stacy got closer to Jake and got even more angry. "JAMES JUST SAVED YOUR FUCKING LIFE! YOU HAVE NO RIGHT TO TREAT HIM LIKE CRAP! IF IT WASN'T FOR HIM, YOU WOULD BE DEAD!" yelled Stacy. Jake slowly looked from Stacy to James and said "James I'm sorry. Stacy is right you don't deserve to be treated this way." "It's okay Jake," said James. James helped him up and Jake looked around the restaurant. Jake asked "what's going on here?" Everyone gathered around Jake and they told him everything they went through. "Holy crap. I can't believe Dr. Jeb's back," said Jake. No one knew what to do now.

James was wondering what they should do when he got an idea. "I think we should go back to our old hideout on the other side of town." said James. "That's a great idea," said everyone. They left the Voy and they headed there. After about a half an hour of hiding from the aliens and trying to get to the hideout they finally made it there. Simon was the first person to see what had happened. The house was in ruins. Simon started to feel a bad pit in his stomach. His face became red and he started to break down crying. This was one of the few places he truly felt at home with his friends and now it was gone. Christine and Stacy went over to him to console him. After a few minutes Simon started to feel better. "Thank you." said Simon to Stacy and Christine. They helped him up.

James said "I think we should explore the house to see if there is anything that we can use." Everyone agreed.

James led the way inside. When they went inside, they were immediately hit with the smell of destruction. They searched the place but they found nothing of use. Even the bunker underneath was destroyed. They were about to give up when Simon noticed something amiss. "There's a shadow over there," said Simon. James went to get a closer look and he heard a groaning sound. "Groan, help meeee." said an unknown voice. James crept closer and he saw an old man impaled with a wooden spike. The old man looked about 70 with wrinkles all over his face and his clothes were torn and ripped up. James ran up to him and asked "what happened?" The man looked up at him and uttered "James, I haven't seen you since you were a baby." James looked at him funny but he knew the man didn't have a lot of time. "Hang on I'll get help." said James. James got up but the old man grabbed his arm. "No, I don't have much time left. You need to listen to my words," said the old man. James knelt back down to listen to the old man's final words. "There is an underground lab just ten miles outside of Arizona. Dr. Jeb was holed up there for a while. You may be able to get the answers you are looking for," said the old man. His voice was starting to get weaker and weaker as he said each word. James knelt closer to him. "James, you need to lead your friends down the right path. You and your friends have a destiny that will decide the fate of the world," said the old man. "One more thing, the secret of your father will be revealed to you soon." James looked at the old man with shock. "I can feel my spirit passing on. Before I die you must beware the darkness for it will try to destroy you or it will lead you down the wrong ... path," said the old man quietly. The old man had lowered his eyes and died peacefully. Despite the pain from the wooden spike the old man had a serene expression on his face. James knelt over the old man and he started to cry.

He felt close to this man for some reason but for the life of him couldn't explain why. James slowly looked up and his eyes became red with anger. He realized that he had to figure out this man's name. He found his wallet. The old man's name is Elijah. "I feel like I know him from somewhere," said James. Christine came up and tried to comfort him. James accepted her comfort and hugged her back. He noticed that she seemed to linger a bit longer than expected but he still appreciated the support. After a few moments he walked away from her and went to the other members of the group. "What should we do now?" asked Jake. "I think that we should go to the lab near Arizona," said James. Everyone agreed with the idea... even Jake. Before they made a plan James decided that

Elijah deserved to have a proper burial. Everyone picked up his body and they trudged a few miles to get to the graveyard. It was night fall when they reached the graveyard.

The Depths of Despair

James picked up a shovel and he dug a hole for Elijah. After the hole was dug Jake and James gently put Elijah into the hole. Simon found a stone and decided that they should put an engraving on it. Jake took out a knife and gave it to James to use for the engraving. James carved into the stone *Here lies Elijah. A great and wise man*. James put the stone near where Elijah was buried. Suddenly a hover car showed up with four aliens riding in it. The second they saw the group they parked the car near them. The aliens looked at them and noticed that they were the teens Jeb is looking for. "We have been looking all over for you," said Alien 3. James and Stacy looked closer at the aliens and they gasped in horror when they saw that two of the aliens were the ones who they fought in the ball park. "Those are the two teens who kicked our butts in the field," said Aliens 1 and 2. Alien three looked at Aliens 1 and 2 and said "are you sure? I know you two probably would remember but do you remember when you got into that fight with the old lady? She kept beating the two of you with her purse and then walked off." "I don't remember that." said alien 1 in a huffed tone. "You know what, I do remember that. I remember because you two had a few broken bones after the first swing. She really beat the crap out of you," said alien 4. "NO that didn't happen!" yelled Aliens 1 and 2. All four aliens were arguing and the teens had no idea what to do. Suddenly alien 1 yelled out "EVERYONE STOP!" The other aliens quickly stopped and looked at him. Alien 1's face was bright red. The other aliens seemed to fear him.

He slowly came closer to alien four. His body started to shake. His arms and legs suddenly became long and thick, large muscles took the place of his thin body, his hands became long sharp claws and he grew to the height of 12 ft. He raised his claw high into the air and he struck Alien 4 right in his chest. Alien 4 fell down clutching his stomach. He was wincing at the pain. 1 came closer and closer until he was right in his face. He grabbed alien 4's stomach and slowly started to pull him apart. Alien 4's face was starting to grow a dark shade of blue. Alien 4 only managed to utter "...sorry." Alien 1 let go of his stomach and kicked him hard in the chest. He then leaned over him and said "if you ever cross me again you will regret it." Alien 4 laid down on the ground for a few seconds before getting up. The teens were scared because of what they had just seen. Alien 1 looked at the other aliens and said "if anyone steps out of line, I will release my fury upon you tenfold." The other aliens bowed down in front of him. Alien 1 turned to face the teens. He walked closer to them and said with an evil grin "I'm going to have a lot of fun kicking your teeth in." Christine slowly became scared and backed up behind the others.

James knew that his friends needed a leader and he knew he had to step up. James turned to the group and said "I know this seems bad but we've dealt with bad situations before. This is just another one of those. If we stand together then we can do anything." The group started to get their bravery back and even Christine stepped forward. They all turned to face the aliens. James started to suggest a plan which was "I think if we sneak around alien 1 and hit him from behind that may knock him over." Jake quickly joined in and said "good plan but I think it is crap. I say we attack it from the front." Jake quickly ran forward before the others could stop him. Jake used all of his momentum to jump and kick him in the head. He did kick him but the blow seemed to have no effect. "That won't work," said alien 1 cruelly. Alien 1 grabbed him and threw him into a rock. Jake managed to get up and felt really dazed. He realized that his reflexes were still weakened because of all the drinking and drugs. Alien 1 came up to him to finish him off. "Wait. You can't kill him; Dr. Jeb needs him alive," said Alien 2. Alien 1 looked at him and sneered while saying "I'm not going to kill him but I am going to do the next best thing." Alien 1 raised his foot as if to cave Jake's head in.

Alien 2 said "I can't help you do this. They are just kids; they don't deserve to go through this." Alien 1 quickly ran over to Alien 2 and raised his claws and then dug them into his head. Alien 2's head started bleeding and pieces of brain were slowly oozing out. James quickly ran to Alien 1 and he jumped and punched him in the head. Alien 1 fell over but James wasn't finished. He kept kicking him in the head numerous times. Eventually the other aliens tried to help but Stacy, Simon and Christine fought them off. After a few minutes all three aliens were defeated. Alien 1 quickly kicked James off of him and he grabbed Aliens 3 and 4. They quickly jumped in their hover car and flew off.

James quickly ran over to Alien 2 and he knelt beside him. He asked "why did you help us? You could have let him defeat us," said James.

Alien 2 slowly turned his head to James and said "you kids don't deserve to go through this. Dr. Jeb needs to go down. I have another hover car stashed in a field two miles from here. Take these keys and you will be able to use the car to get to Arizona." James grabbed the keys and said "Thank you for your help. You don't deserve to die like this let me help you." Alien 2 said "that's okay I have helped you and that is all that matters. One more thing, beware the dark entity in your group. Simon can tell you more about it. He is a good and very smart son." Simon quickly ran over to him and stuttered "d... d... Dad?" "Yes, my son, I am sorry that it had to end this way." Simon's eyes became watery and his face became tense. “Listen to me Simon, you have a gift and you can use this gift to help your friends. But in order to do so you must open up to them about what you saw at the Voyageur.” said Simon’s dad weakly. Simon was trying to fight back his tears but he was starting to become overcome by emotion.

He held it together and looked at his father and asked “how did you know I saw something?” “I know because I have the gift of foresight. Your gift on the other hand is much stronger than mine.” Simon couldn’t control his emotions anymore. He broke down crying next to his father. Simon decided that if this was the end he needed some answers. He wiped away his tears and asked “dad what happened here and how much time has passed?”

His father looked to his side and said “Five days ago aliens started to attack the town. Many of us stood our ground and fought but the aliens were too strong. They easily captured us and they executed some of the ones who resisted. I tried to fight but I got captured as well. We were taken to labs and we were experimented on. Some of us died from the experiments but others were transformed into aliens. We are all being controlled by a man named Dr. Jeb. After Schreiber fell, we took control of the rest of the world. We torched the buildings and we killed all members of the government. Civilization has been destroyed.” His voice slowly began to get weaker but he continued talking. “I am ashamed of what I did but now there is hope. You must go to Arizona." Simon looked at his father and asked sadly “Is this truly the end?” His father looked at him and said “I don’t think so. If you can defeat Jeb and cure everyone then I might be able to come back.” Simon stood up and said confidently “I won’t let you down.” His father grew weaker and weaker. His eyes began to close and his chest stopped rising.

After a few moments he was gone. Simon looked over his father's body and started to cry again. Stacy and Christine went to comfort him and James and Jake hung back because they knew Simon wanted to be with just the girls for now. After a few minutes James and Jake took over and Christine and Stacy hung back. After a few more minutes Simon decided he was ready to tell the group about what he had saw. "I saw two visions while in the Voy. One already happened but the other one hasn't yet." Simon told everyone about the visions and they were shocked. "Wow that's amazing," said James. Everyone was amazed but then they soon became frightened. "Who are the two friends who are destined to fight each other?" asked Jake. No one knew who it could be. "I think I know who was covered in light," said Simon. Everyone came closer to him. "I think it's James," replied Simon confidently. "He is the strongest one of the five of us," said Christine. "I don't know. It's always possible," said James.

James knew he and Jake had a very strained friendship and he didn't want to strain it any further. "It could be you," said Jake to James. Jake seemed ok but there was anger and jealousy in his eyes though no one noticed. James realized that they had to find that hover car now. Everyone got up and they started the 2-mile-long walk. After a long trek they finally made it to the spot. The hover car was covered in bushes but they could easily see it. The hover car was in perfect condition. It was white and it was fairly big. James waited for everyone to get inside before he jumped in. James pushed a red button on the center of the control board and it started up. James casually pulled the lever near the button up which caused the hover car to rise. James felt really comfortable with this. A weird feeling went through him. He felt a sort of power in his fingertips. He figured he was just very comfortable with it. James pushed the lever forward and they sped off towards Arizona.

The Trek To Arizona

THEY ZOOMED ACROSS THE sky and they felt free. The wind whipped past their hair and the five felt the best they had ever been in a long time. Suddenly they saw all the destruction that the aliens had caused. The rivers and lakes were drained and all the trees were burned down. Only a small amount of vegetation remained. The rest of the land was scarred and wounded. They continued to fly until they were ten miles outside of Arizona. The whole drive took about five hours. When they got there, they parked their hover car. They all got out and they tried to look for the lab. After a half hour of trying, they realized they weren't going to find it anytime soon. Suddenly James had an idea. "Simon, I know this is the last thing you want to do but maybe you could use your gift to locate the lab." The group looked at Simon. Simon looked around nervously and said "I only experienced it once. I don't know if I can control it." James came over to him and said reassuringly "It's okay. You don't have to do this if you don't want to."

Simon started to say something but suddenly he had a screeching pain in his head and he doubled back. "It's happening." said Simon in a pained voice. Simon grabbed his head as blood began to pour from his nose. Everyone rushed over to him. Simon was wincing at the pain. Suddenly an image started to enter his mind. It was really blurry but from what he could tell there was a hidden metal hatch underneath a big rock. The image started to slowly fade away and he returned to his friends. He immediately gasped for breath and he coughed on the ground. He even threw up. His friends helped him up. He looked at the vomit and said "I don't remember eating fish." He then realized he had to focus and he told his friends what he saw. Everyone was searching under every rock they could find. When James looked at a fairly big boulder, he noticed something wasn't right. He turned it over and he found the hatch.

He called to the others and they came to see him. James quickly opened up the hatch and they saw a ladder heading down. Everyone looked into the hole of darkness. "This is it. We finally made it to his hideout." James looked down at the hole and said "you'll finally get what is coming to you Jeb." James looked at the others and said "we don't know what could be down there. There may be more to face than just Jeb. If any of you want to back out, I understand." Everyone looked at him. Simon came up to him and said "we are with you to the end. We will always stand by you, big brother." Everyone else nodded in agreement. James and Simon saw each other as siblings even though they weren't blood related. James knew he had built a strong trust with his friends that could never be broken. James went down the ladder first and everyone else followed.

When they got down the room was in complete darkness. James felt for a light switch. Finally, he found one. When he turned it on the room became flooded with light. The group looked around. The room was white and in ruins. The walls were cracked and there were cracked beakers all around the lab. Even down here they could still smell the blood and death but it wasn't as bad here. Christine looked around and she saw that the computer had been destroyed and that most of the records on paper were destroyed as well. She then saw five pictures. She realized they were of her and her friends. She looked closely at one of them. She felt a twinge of fear when she saw an inscription on it. It reads "my only son. Someday you will be aligned with me." She was shocked to see this inscription on her friend's photo. She quickly erased the inscription and then left the pictures alone. She saw her friends were still looking around and it seems like they didn't see the pictures. She went over to Jeb's desk and she opened the drawers. She realized that one drawer didn't look right.

She felt her hand against the bottom and she realized it was false. She opened up the bottom and she found a secret file. She took it out and she called the others. "Hey, guys get over here. I found something." The others quickly ran over to her and they looked at the file. It was filled with pictures of ancient tombs in Egypt. They looked closely at the tombs. They realized that someone had used red marker to put an X on each tomb. Each tomb had an X except for an unmarked tomb. "I wonder why this one wasn't crossed off," said Christine. James looked closer at it. He said "I don't think Jeb made it to this one yet." Stacy looked at him and asked "James what are you talking about?" James looked away from the folder and started to pace slowly in front of his friends. James always used to pace whenever he was nervous or had to think. It helped him to focus and everyone knew it.

They all looked at him. "I think that Jeb is looking for something. He tried looking in all the other tombs but whatever it is he's looking for it wasn't in there. I think we need to go to Egypt and see if we can locate the item before he does." Everyone realized that this was their best lead. "I agree with you," said Stacy. Simon and Christine said "we agree with you too." Jake looked away and said "this is bullshit." Jake turned to the group and said "Jeb probably got to the tomb and destroyed it already." James walked up to him and said "listen Jake, I know that the tomb may be destroyed but going there may give us some answers." Jake looked him dead in the eye. Their eyes locked.

Jake felt ready to punch James out. He looked at the rest of the group and he knew that they would retaliate. He slowly looked back at James and said through gritted teeth "fine." Jake turned away and said "let's get moving." He started to head up the ladder but he realized that the rest of the group wasn't following. He uttered angrily "come on, we need to get moving." The rest of the group looked really exhausted. Their eyes had become red and their muscles ached. James looked at the rest of the group and said calmly "I think we should set up camp down here for the night. It's been a long night." Jake didn't seem too happy about this but he agreed along with the others.

James stood against one of the walls when he felt something shift under his weight. He realized the wall was opening up. The group looked in the hidden room and they were ecstatic by what they saw. They saw a large room with couches, chairs and a flat screen TV. The room was connected by six other rooms. One room was the kitchen with a stove, fully stocked fridge and a dishwasher. The other five rooms were the bedrooms which had a king size bed, one-bathroom, mini fridge and a smaller flat screen TV. Everyone was so excited to finally be able to relax. The place no longer smelt like blood and death. Instead, it smelled like air freshener and cleanliness. Everyone quickly sat on two of the couches and turned on the TV. James and Simon were sitting together and Jake was sitting with Stacy and Christine. They were watching Harry Potter and The Philosopher's Stone. James felt pretty relaxed on the couch.

He would rather be sitting with Stacy but he liked Simon. Simons a good kid. Simon liked sitting with James but he would also rather be sitting with Christine. Jake on the other hand felt completely content. He felt this was the best option for him. James got up and said "I'll be right back." James casually walked into the kitchen leaving his four friends there. Jake got up without saying a word and followed James into the kitchen. Jake saw James cutting up some meat with a very sharp knife for a snack for the rest of the group. Jake eyes gleamed when he saw the knife. He knew he could kill James with that knife if he wanted to. After a moment he decided that he was still human and that he couldn't kill him. James set down the knife and went to put the meat on a plate. Jake came up to him and said "hey." James was slightly startled but then he calmed down as he said "hey Jake, what's up?" Jake looked at him and said "not much just sitting with your girlfriend." James looked confused but then he asked "do you mean Stacy?" Jake said "Of course I'm talking about Stacy you idiot." James casually replied "Stacy and I aren't dating. We are just really good friends." Jake came closer to him and said cruelly "don't lie to me. Everyone knows you two have feelings for each other." James wanted to deny it but he didn't want to lie about his feelings for Stacy. He decided to say "she and I are just friends right now."

Jake walked even closer to him. Jake raised his hands above his face and he pushed James onto the floor. Jake then knelt down and he punched James in the eye. James grunted in pain. James asked "what are you doing man?" Jake looked at him and grinned. He then said coldly "finally doing what's right." Jake tried to kick him in the face but James was too quick. He got up before the kick hit his face. James quickly grabbed Jake's arm and pushed him to the ground. Jake accidently bumped into the counter and knocked a plate on the ground as he fell. Jake couldn't take it anymore. He yelled "YOU ARE DEAD TO ME JAMES!" The others heard him yelling and they quickly ran into the kitchen.

They saw Jake laying on the ground and James leaning against a wall so he wouldn't fall down after releasing Jake. Everyone quickly asked "what happened?" Jake said "well I came into the kitchen to talk to James and he just started to beat me up. I fought back to defend myself but he's crazy." Everyone looked at James. James said "me and Jake were talking and he got angry at me for some reason. He pushed me to the ground and we got into a bit of a struggle." James looked at Jake and asked "what is your problem with me? We used to be like brothers." said James. Jake glared at James.

Jake looked at the rest of the group and said calmly "I don't think James's can be leader. I think he is too unstable and he could put us into harm's way." Simon said "Jake, James is our friend. He is our leader and he is one of us." Christine said "James would never do anything like this. James is our ally." Jake looked to Stacy and said "please get rid of James." Stacy came closer to Jake. She knelt down and kicked him really hard in his privates. "OW!" yelled Jake as he crumpled to the ground in pain. Christine looked at Jake and said "you need to get yourself under control. We are never going to be able to defeat Dr. Jeb like this if we aren't a team." Jake got himself up and said "whatever. I'm going to my room." Jake left the room and went upstairs. Jake felt a familiar sensation of killing an older man that looked a bit like James but he couldn't recall the situation. He then cleared his head and continued to skulk out of the room. Stacy went to James and she grabbed his arm. Simon grabbed his other arm.

They helped him walk to his room. Stacy set him on the bed. Stacy looked at Simon and said "I'm going to clean his wound. Why don't you go and finish the movie with Christine?" Simon agreed and he went downstairs. Stacy closed the door behind him and she took out some gauze for his eye. Stacy asked "why did Jake do this to you?" James said "I don't know. It just seems like he has some vendetta against me." Stacy said "he could be jealous of you." James said "maybe but I don't think so. I'm really nothing special." Stacy removed the gauze and said "yes you are. You are the nicest, funniest and greatest guy I know." She then said "I think we should kick Jake out of the group. He is very unstable and I don't think he can be trusted." James wanted to agree but he didn't think it would be right. He said instead "I think we should give him another chance. Maybe if he and I can bond then maybe we can get back to what we used be." Stacy didn't think it was a good idea but she did want to have Jake back as a friend. "Alright I trust your judgement, James." James stretched out his arms and he pulled her into a hug. Stacy liked being in James' arms. She felt safe with him. "What's this for?" asked Stacy. James let her go and said "for helping me and standing by me. Even when it looked like I was the one who hurt Jake." Stacy said "I know you would never hurt him unless you were defending yourself." James was starting to get sleepy.

Stacy could see his eyes getting red. James laid in the bed and started to go to sleep. Stacy crawled into his bed with him and she put her head on his chest. She knew she would be safe with him. James didn't comment on what she was doing. They just drifted off to sleep. Meanwhile Jake was in his room. He felt really shitty. He had left his door open. Simon and Christine came in and found him sitting cross legged on his bed. Simon couldn't hold in his anger anymore. "WHY WOULD YOU HURT HIM! HE IS OUR FRIEND AND YOU GAVE HIM A BLACK EYE!" yelled Simon. Christine held her hand on Simon's shoulder in comfort and to make sure his anger wouldn't spiral.

Jake looked at them and sighed. "I guess I was sick of James getting everything. I just wanted to prove I could beat him at something." He got up and said "look I know I really messed up but I am truly sorry and I really do regret what I did." Simon and Christine said "don't apologize to us, apologize to James." Jake said "okay I will head up to his room." Simon quickly blocked his path. "You might not want to go in there. James is asleep and Stacy is sleeping next to him." Jake wanted to punch a wall but instead he said in a really calm voice "alright, I will talk to him tomorrow." He headed back to his bed and he slammed his door in Simon and Christine's face. Jake walked back and slumped back on his bed. He had a really big pit in his stomach.

He didn't know how he felt. He felt a bit of remorse but he also wished he had been able to hurt James more. He said aloud "I wish James would leave the group." He laid his head on his pillow and slowly drifted off to sleep. Later that night Jake heard someone walking outside his door. He then heard someone knocking on his door. "Come in." The door opened and Stacy appeared. "Hey." said Stacy. Jake turned away and said "hey." Stacy absolutely hated what Jake did to James but she wanted to know why he did it. "Can we talk for a second?" asked Stacy. Jake turned to her and said "alright." Stacy walked over to Jake and sat on the bed. She asked him calmly "why did you try to hurt James?" Jake knew this was coming. "I don't know." said Jake quietly. Stacy asked again "why did you hurt James? I want a real answer this time." said Stacy a little louder. Jake sat up and said "I did it because everything comes so easy to him. He is so popular and everyone loves him. He gets all the respect in this group and I get none."

Stacy looked at him and said loudly "well maybe if you tried giving James some respect then maybe others would respect you to. Respect is something that has to be earned and James has earned that in spades unlike you. James has done everything to protect us and to help us. All you have ever done is try to get James out of here. In spite of all that he still thinks that there is hope for you to go back to the way you were." Jake knew that he had to get back on the group's good side. He said "you're right. I shouldn't have treated him like that. I promise I will try to get along with him." Stacy looked satisfied and said "okay good." She got up to leave and said "night Jake." She left the room without another word while still mulling over her doubts about Jake and his mental health. While she worried about him his behavior couldn’t be justified.

Fractures

Jake really didn't want to work with James but he knew that they had to work together to defeat Jeb. He laid back down on his bed. The next morning James woke up. He noticed Stacy wasn't with him. "She probably got up already." said James aloud. He got out of bed and went to the closet. He found lots of old looking clothes. He knew they belonged to Jeb. After he searched through them, he found a red t-shirt that was about his size. He tried it on and it fit perfectly. He then searched through some drawers and he found a pair underwear, a pair of socks and some blue jeans that fit perfectly. James figured these were his son's clothing. James didn't think about it too much and he left the room.

He went into the kitchen and found that he was alone. He heard someone coming and he saw Christine, walk into the kitchen. "Morning." said James. Christine noticed James and said enthusiastically "morning James." James walked up to Christine and asked "Christine, I was just wondering. Do you know why Stacy stayed with me last night?" Christine seemed a little surprised that he was asking this but she still said "she probably wanted to watch over you and make sure you were okay." James looked satisfied with the answer. "I figured but I just wanted to make sure." James walked to the coffee machine and started to make a cup. He looked back at Christine and asked "do you want some?" She said "sure." After a few minutes Simon entered the kitchen and Stacy came in soon after. Everyone felt relaxed and they seemed to enjoy staying here. Meanwhile Jake was still asleep in his room. He woke up when he smelled coffee in the air. He sluggishly got up out of bed. He didn't bother to change his clothes at all. He just got up and headed to the kitchen.

When he got there, he saw that everyone was here. They didn't seem to notice him. He walked in and casually said "morning everyone." Everyone looked at him. He could sense the tension in the air. He knew that they still hadn't forgiven him. He walked up to James and said "James I'm so sorry about what I did to you. I guess I was jealous and I went too far. Can you ever forgive me man?" James maintained eye contact and said "of course brother." James pulled him into a hug and Jake accepted the hug. Everyone was glad to see that they were starting to get along again. James walked to the center of the room and said "everyone, I know this is a good hideaway and it's relaxing but we still have a mission. I think that after we get cleaned up, we should head off to Egypt and keep moving." Everyone agreed with James' idea. After they had eggs and bacon they cleaned up and when into their bathrooms. They each had a long shower and they did their laundry. James changed back into his old clothes and he put the new ones back where he found them. They got into their hover car and then sped off to Egypt. It was a 12-hour journey to Egypt. They had to stop frequently because of bathroom breaks and to eat. When they got there, they searched for the tomb.

Simon had always dreamed of coming to Egypt. He wanted to see the amazing architecture and read up on the history. He never imagined to see it like this. The pyramids were in ruins. Everything was destroyed. All of Egypt was pretty much deserted. Finally, after ten minutes of flying they found the tomb. The outside was completely destroyed. The door leading into the tomb is sealed shut by a big piece of broken architecture. They saw the destruction. James looked around and said "we were too late." He kicked a rock near the tomb to the side. "Damn it, Jeb beat us again." He said in frustration. He eventually calmed down and turned to face the group.

Everyone looked worried about him but they knew he was strong. "I say we look around and try to find any answers." Everyone decided that was a good idea. They all started to look around. James went to a part of the wall that had some writing on it. He instantly knew it was Hieroglyphics. He couldn't understand it at first but then the text started to make sense. It read "those who wish to see the king must repeat this ancient phrase. The five have returned." James read the text out loud. At first nothing happened but then a secret door appeared. Everyone noticed what was going on so they joined up with him. They all slowly walked down into the tomb. The room was in complete darkness. It seemed though that as the five of them continued down the path they were able to slowly see ahead of them.

Their eye sight had become much stronger in the dark then it used to be. After a few minutes of walking, they were able to see perfectly. Finally, they saw a light. They headed towards the light and they found themselves in a large room. When they got there their eyes instantly adjusted to the light. They saw the room in perfect condition. There wasn't much in there. There were four pillars which were used to keep the room stable and there was a set of stairs that lead up to a golden coffin. There were also bodies of other people who were presumably servants to the pharaoh. They were sent to serve the pharaoh in the afterlife. They all walked slowly up to the coffin. James touched the coffin and it started to glow. James immediately took his hand off. The coffin glowed brighter and brighter. Soon the top of the coffin came out and a ghostly figure appeared before them. He was a somewhat short man. He wore silk robes and he carried a sword with him. A black hood covered his face. Jake immediately drew his fists but James put his hand up to stop him. He went up to the ghost and asked "are you the keeper of this tomb?" The ghost stared deep into James' eyes. The ghost had a very grim expression on his face that could be seen through his hood.

He seemed intrigued by James though. He answered "yes I am the keeper of this tomb. My name is Rathos I was the king of Egypt from 1329-1324. I believe you are the one called James." James was shocked that he knew his name. Rathos saw the shock on his face and said "don't be shocked my boy. I know who all of you are." Everyone became surprised at that. King Rathos knew he had a lot of explaining to do. "I watched all of you grow up. I know who you are. I know who your families are. I also know who your enemies are." said King Rathos. James figured he should ask about Dr. Jeb. "We have come across some files that our enemy left behind. They contain information on every tomb within Egypt. Can you explain what it is that Jeb wants from your tomb?" asked James politely. King Rathos decided that it was time they learned.

He stepped closer to them. He decided to begin by saying "I shall tell you but you need to hear my tale from the beginning." Everyone decided that that was fair. King Rathos came to them and explained his tale. "My tale begins on the day I was born. I was born exactly three years before my brother King Tutankhamun was born. When I was born, I was considered imperfect by my parents. They didn't want anyone to know but they wanted a perfect son. I have a birthmark that covers my eye. The birthmark looks like my eye has become incredibly scarred. Because of that my family decided to try once more to get a perfect son. Three years later my brother was born and he had a perfect face. My parents considered him the perfect child. They didn't want the kingdom to see that they were imperfect so they kept me in the dark from everyone. My brother had become king when our parents were murdered. After three years he realized that he wasn't cut out to rule. I told him that this was what our father would've wanted. He didn't agree with me but after a while he relented.

"I studied him while he was ruling and I knew he was miserable. I decided to cut a deal with him. He would be king but I would really be in control. I would give all the orders and he would take credit for it. He decided that was a fair deal. I was 15 when I had taken control. It wasn't until two years later (1327) when I realized something was wrong in the world. My brother had found a rare stone in the desert. The guards didn't know what it was so they put it in the artifact room of the palace. I looked at the stone for hours. I sensed a weird aura coming from within the stone. A few days later a weird man had come to the door. He claimed to be a medic. I believe he said his name was Jeb. My brother felt he was alright. I didn't know it at the time but he was about to be a big threat to Egypt. While he was here, I noticed him staring at the stone a few times. I wanted to get him away but I couldn't show him who I was. One day I noticed him admiring the stone for a long time.

"I was about to intervene when he touched the stone. I saw his body glow. I could tell that the stone was giving him power. I rushed to tell my brother. He quickly brought the guards when he saw the man start to disappear. The guards didn't believe that the man did anything wrong however. My brother believed me though. I was glad that someone was on my side. I noticed that the stone was still in its place. I wanted to take some power from the stone to combat Jeb but I knew that I couldn't do it alone. Me and my brother needed soldiers. We knew the guards wouldn't help. We had to be cautious with who we brought into this. I went into the city one day. I used an alias so no one would know that I was from the palace. I met up with five teenagers doing some work. I called them over to me. I talked with them and I realized they looked strong enough. I soon noticed that they were probably starving. I asked them to come with me. They decided I was cool so they came with me.

"I snuck them into the palace when the guards were switching out. I took them to see my brother who was in the artifact room. He and I explained what was going on and that they might be the champions we need. They decided that it couldn't hurt to try. They all touched the stone at once. All five of them began to glow brightly. They were absorbing the power. When they had absorbed all that they could, they took their hands off the stone. They knew they had gained new powers. I decided that they had to train their new powers quickly. I brought them to the training grounds. After a few days they had managed to develop their powers to their full extent. They were ready to destroy Jeb.

That following day my brother received a letter from Jeb. We hadn't seen him since he disappeared. The letter was a warning. It said that he will declare war on Egypt unless we give him the stone. We had 24 hours to meet him far outside of the city to present the stone to him. We weren't sure of what we should do. My brother decided that we should go across the Nile. I reluctantly agreed with him. The next day we set out for it. I wasn't going to let Jeb have the stone so we came up with a plan.

"We would let our champions present the stone to him and then they would toss it to us and we would take the stone back to the city while our heroes fought Jeb. Soon the plan was underway. We got to the area and Jeb appeared to collect the stone. The champions were about to toss it back but Jeb quickly snatched it before they could even blink. Jeb had known what we had planned. He took the stone and he took everything he could from it. Suddenly the ground began to shake. Out from the sand arose a large army of warriors. They were covered from head to toe in thick black armor. My brother quickly ran back to the city to alert the guards. He ran back towards the Nile and jumped back in to head back to the city. The five friends tried desperately to hold off the soldiers. Jeb thanked us for giving him the stone but because we tried to trick him, he was still going to declare war on Egypt. Luckily my brother had managed to warn the guards. They rushed to the Nile and they saw what was going on. They couldn't believe their eyes. They realized that we are now at war.

"They didn't want the citizens to get worried so we tried to keep it a secret. Jeb took the stone and created a fortress close to the Nile to house his armies. The five friends tried to stop him but they were soon overpowered. For a year we tried desperately to cross the river and invade the fortress but every group would be destroyed before we could even touch the ground. The five friends spent that year practicing and training hard. Jeb's forces weren't doing anything. All they tried to do was protect their fortress when we tried to attack. I realized that Jeb must have wanted our numbers to dwindle so he could easily take Egypt and break our spirits. I decided that the five friends were our only hope. I sent them across to fight the armies. After the year of training, they had become much stronger. Each one had a different ability. One was extremely strong and was a natural born leader. One had strong will power and is able to get through anything. One has great courage and is able to turn invisible at will but it doesn't last long. One is very smart and has telekinesis as well as telepathy. He has also had the ability of foresight. Finally, the last one has extreme strength but he was fueled by anger and hatred.

"He is very strong on his own but he relies on his anger to give him strength. His heart is also darker than the other's hearts. The five of them came up with a plan to retrieve the stone. They knew that that was the only way to defeat the armies. One used their power to turn invisible so she could sneak across the river. Another used telekinesis to lift some architecture to damage the fortress. Two of the heroes used their strength to lift up heavier pieces of architecture to try to damage it as well. The last one used her will to fight her way across the river. Four of the heroes were trying to distract Jeb's line of sight so that the other could sneak in. After hours of battle, she finally managed to sneak into the fortress. She snuck around hundreds of guards and she was almost seen by them multiple times. It took her a long time to get to the top floor but she eventually made it.

"She was really nervous when she saw Jeb. He had the stone on a pedestal next to him. She managed to retrieve the stone from Jeb's pedestal. The second she took it he instantly knew someone was there. She ran quickly downstairs and tried her best to evade him. She barely managed to get out of there. She was sweating hard because the soldiers had seen her once or twice as she was escaping. She felt so tired but she knew she had to get the stone back. She quickly threw it to me and I used its power to strengthen the five friends. With their combined energy they managed to steal Jeb's power from him and they sealed the dark army deep beneath the sands of Egypt so they could never harm anyone again.

"The five of them went to Jeb and used the power of the stone to destroy him forever. After Jeb was destroyed the stone started to shake violently. It then shot out a large beam of light. The light covered all of Egypt. It seemed to have been getting rid of any evidence of Jeb and his armies. It also erased the event from everyone's minds except for mine, my brother's and the five heroes. The stone also resurrected all of the fallen soldiers. I finally thought there was going to peace. It seemed that I was wrong. Two years later something happened. I had decided to keep the stone with me because I wanted to keep it protected. I soon realized that Jeb wasn't completely dead. His body was destroyed but his spirit still lived on. He quickly inhabited the stone and used the last of his power to destroy me and the five heroes. A few hours later we all died of heart attacks that day. My brother was stricken with grief. He found the stone and he made a wish. He wished that the five teenagers would be reincarnated so that if Jeb came back, he wouldn't win. He also wished that I could come back. The stone granted him both wishes. I soon appeared before his very eyes. We were happy to see each other but I told him I couldn't stay.

"I knew my duty would be able to watch over him and to watch over the five heroes when they returned. He was saddened by my news but he understood. I made one last request to him. I asked him to break the stone in half and to scatter the pieces. He agreed to what I wanted. I then told him to let me go and he let me pass on. To this day I have watched over all of you. You five are the reincarnations of the heroes from long ago."

The friends were shocked by this news. James was about to ask something but Rathos interrupted. "Before you ask, yes the Dr. Jeb from back then is the same Jeb now. He has regained his memories and he is plotting to get the stone first." James came forward and asked "how do you know that we are the five?" Rathos walked towards a darkened wall and he beckoned them to follow him. They followed close behind him. He snapped his finger and the darkness lifted from the wall. On it they saw pictures depicting an ancient prophecy. He lifted his hand and slowly guided them through the pictures. "These images depict five heroes shall come forth. Five heroes shall vanquish the darkness that plagues their town. Five heroes shall face the darkness once more using the power of the sacred stone." Jake looked through it and he noticed that part of the wall was still dark. He turned to Rathos and asked "hey, why is that part still dark?" Rathos said to him "that is another story. I don't wish to get into that one yet. You five have too much on your shoulders right now. That story has not yet come to pass and hopefully never will." Jake seemed confused and angered by this but he slowly let it go. He knew Jeb had to go down. "You five have very special abilities that I'm sure you must have noticed by now." said Rathos. The others knew that they had been experiencing weird abnormalities within themselves. They nodded. "You will start to develop your powers further and eventually you will remember your past." Said Rathos. James knew he had to ask him about something Jeb had left behind two months ago.

James stepped forward and said "My lord, two months ago I found a newspaper article that mentioned a story about a student that had foiled Jeb's plans in 1965. The student was named James Adams and he looked exactly like me. What I'm asking it was that man my father?" asked James. Rathos said "that man wasn't your father. That man was you, James." James was extremely shocked by this. He didn't understand. Rathos sensed his confusion. "You and your friends were supposed to be reincarnated together. It seems though that you were actually reincarnated by yourself. That means you are very special." said Rathos calmly. Everyone was surprised by this news. Jake seemed very upset by this but he tried to suppress it, for now. James had more questions. "How many times have I been reincarnated and how many times has Jeb been reincarnated." He asked quickly. Rathos said "you both have been reincarnated three times and your friends have only been reincarnated two times. James wondered if he had any special connection to Jeb. He suddenly had a horrifying thought. He asked "who is my father?" Rathos looked closely at him without taking off his hood. He said quietly "you will find out in time. It is not my place to tell you." James decided that the only other question he can ask is "who is Elijah?" Rathos knew he had to tread carefully with his answer. "Elijah is an old friend of yours. You met him in another life. No, he isn't your father but he is your cousin." James fell to his knees.

He was saddened to think his cousin was dead. He didn't really remember him but he knew he was a good friend. Stacy and Christine wanted to comfort James. He had lost so much and they didn't like seeing him in pain. James wasn't sure what to do anymore. He had lost so much. James looked back at his friends. He saw the sadness in their eyes. He knew that his friends needed him. He decided to turn off his grief and turn it into determination. He was devoted to his friends and he wasn't going to abandon them. He slowly stood and faced King Rathos. "What can we do to stop Dr. Jeb?" asked James. Rathos turned away from James and led the five friends to a pedestal that wasn't in the room before. Rathos put his hand onto the pedestal and waved his hand slowly over top of it. A shining blue stone materialized on top of the pedestal. Rathos beckoned the group to come before the stone. James led his friends to the stone. The friends felt something emanating from it. They knew this stone had immense power within it. They felt drawn to it like moths to a flame. Rathos observed their behavior. Rathos snapped his fingers and all of a sudden James and the others became aware of their surroundings.

For some reason Simon felt very unsure about something. Rathos seemed to sense it. He went closer to Simon and said quietly "you seem very confused about something my friend." Simon decided to say what was on his mind. "I am just confused. I thought that there were two pieces of the stone. I only see one here." said Simon. the others seemed to realize this as well. The room was suddenly filled with confusion. Rathos explained "this is only the first part of the stone. When you find the second part the two shall merge together to become the stone of legends." The confusion that was in the air started to drift away. Rathos said calmly "there is a legend that goes with this stone. When one becomes two the power will be split. When one is found it shall lead you to its other half. When they are together two shall become one and the power shall be restored." James immediately understood the message. Jake seemed even more confused than ever. "I don't get it." said Jake angrily. James came forward and tried to explain it to him. James started "the passage means that—" "ENOUGH." yelled Jake. "I DON"T CARE ABOUT

WHAT YOU HAVE TO SAY JAMES. I'VE HAD ENOUGH OF YOU BEING THE SUPERIOR ONE." Everyone was shocked at this behavior.

Jake felt angrier than he had ever felt before. His face was completely red and he was breathing heavily. James has always been calm with Jake but this time he had had enough. James stepped forward slowly because he knew he had to deal with him... again. Jake and James walked towards each other until they were five steps away from each other. Simon, Christine, and Stacy wanted to protect James. They ran towards Jake and James but Rathos stood in their way. He raised his hand to signal them to stop. Almost as if they were under a spell the three friends stopped abruptly in their tracks. Rathos calmly said "this is James' fight. He needs to fight his own battles." His friends reluctantly understood but they still wanted to help. Stacy felt very worried. She knew what happened to James the last time Jake came at him. She tried to feel calm but she couldn't help but start to sweat heavily. She could feel the sweat go down her forehead onto her face. Jake raised his fists above his face. James raised his fists but he immediately put them down. He wanted to try one last time to calm Jake down. He said "Jake, don't do this. You and I used to be like brothers' man." This wasn't going to change anything thought Jake. "We need to be united in order to take down Jeb" said James calmly. Jake didn't seem to want to listen to any of this but he did look like he was calming down.

Jake came forward and said in a peaceful tone "you could be right James." James seemed happy that Jake had calmed himself. "I'm sorry James." said Jake. Everyone seemed surprised by how easily Jake gave in but Rathos wasn't too sure. Jake came closer and a bit louder he said "I'm sorry that I wasn't able to scar you back at the hideout or kill you when you fell off that cliff years ago." James' smile had slowly vanished. Jake raised his fist and lunged his fist at his face. James tried to dodge it but Jake was too quick. Jake plunged his fist right into James' left temple. James fell backwards and hit the ground hard. He had fallen unconscious. Jake seemed really happy with himself. He continued to kick at James until he was bloodied and his breathing became shallow. He threw his fists into the air and yelled out "FINALLY I TOOK CARE OF JAMES." The rest of the group were horrified by what they saw. Stacy immediately ran over to James to try to revive him. Simon and Christine ran to Jake and pushed him hard in the chest. "What the hell Jake," said Simon assertively. Jake turned to look at James lying on the ground. He then looked to Stacy who was very scared but then she quickly turned angry. She was really pissed at him. Her heart was racing and her adrenaline was pumping. She had never been so pissed at Jake. She got right in his face and said loudly "JAKE, HOW COULD YOU

DO THIS TO HIM! HE WAS YOUR BEST FRIEND! HE DID EVERYTHING TO PROTECT YOU AND YOU REPAY HIM BY NEARLY KILLING HIM!" Jake's newfound happiness soon disappeared. He saw James lying limp on the ground and he knew he could die.

Jake felt a bit of remorse and he felt ashamed for what he has done. "Look I'm obviously really sorry for what I did to James." Said Jake apologetically. The group didn't seem to believe him. It had come off as sarcastic this time. This has happened way too much. "I don't believe you." said Christine. Jake noticed that his friends were starting to get into a fighter's formation. He knew they had turned against him. He had lost his friends. "I'm sorry." Said Jake. His friends started to slowly come forward with pure hatred in their eyes. Even Rathos seemed to have turned against him. Jake couldn't see his eyes but Rathos was slowly drawing his sword. Jake quickly ran out of the temple saying "I'm really sorry" as he left. Stacy ran back to James and knelt beside him. His heart rate was decreasing. Simon and Christine ran to James and they tried to pump air into him by giving him CPR. Stacy tried it as well but nothing was working. Stacy tearfully asked Rathos "please, isn't there anything you can do? He is my best friend. I won't survive without him." She pleaded with him but Rathos grimly said "there is nothing I can do." Rathos turned to the stone and said "there might be one way to save your friend. But it's risky." Everyone's eyes lit up at the thought that James could be saved. "How can we save him?" asked Christine. Rathos picked up the stone and held it out to Simon.

He said to him "when you find one of the pieces of the stone the stone shall shine and a beacon of light shall lead you towards the next piece." Rathos extended his hand to Simon and Simon slowly took the stone into his hands. He felt the immense power within it. "When you connect the two pieces you will be able to do anything with it. You may even be able to help your friend. But you must be careful the journey could be perilous to the next piece. Once you leave this temple the stone shall guide you to its counterpart." Explained Rathos.

Simon nodded at this. Stacy wanted to go with them but she felt that she should stay with James. "I think I should stay back and look after James." Said Stacy. Simon and Christine agreed. "That's a good idea. James will need someone to watch over him." murmured Rathos. Stacy knelt beside James and said "good luck guys," to her friends. Simon and Christine nodded in response and they went through the passageway to get back outside. Their eyes immediately adjusted to the darkness. They figured this was their powers starting to kick in. After a while of walking, they managed to get out of the tomb.

The stone started to shine brightly. A beam of light shone from the stone and it created a beacon about 5 miles away. Simon and Christine saw that the hover car was still where they left it. They quickly climbed into it and they flew off to the location of the stone. Meanwhile about four miles away Jake was running through Egypt. He felt really ashamed of what he did. Eventually he stopped running to catch his breath for a moment. He could hear something inside his head. "You hurt your best friend. You need to make it up to your friends," said an unknown voice. Suddenly another voice came into play. "What you did was right. James deserved everything that happened to him," said the darker voice. Jake didn't know what he should do. He felt so angry but he also felt really upset and happy. Maybe he was going crazy. He didn't know for sure of anything anymore.

Suddenly a hover car flew over him. He hid behind one of the old architectures to avoid being seen. He then saw a large beacon of light that was about a mile away from him. "That could be important." Said Jake under his breath. He felt drawn to the light. He ran towards the light to see where it led. Back at the hover car Simon and Christine were closing in on the beacon. The beacon shone its light on a small crack in the earth. They landed the hover car on the ground. Simon and Christine walked over to the crack in the earth. Simon looked down it and he thought he could see a shining light coming from the crack. He tried to stick his hand in the crack but the crack was too small. Simon began to feel very frustrated. He kicked at the sand multiple times. Christine hated seeing him like this. Simon yelled out "WE CAME SO FAR. THIS IS THE KEY TO SAVE JAMES AND WE CAN'T EVEN GET TO IT!" Christine ran up to Simon and pulled him into a hug. She wanted to comfort him. Simon steadily began to calm down. She soon released him from the hug and Simon began to think more clearly. Suddenly he felt a sharp pain in his side. He fell down clutching it and began to groan. Christine became concerned and wanted to help but Simon signaled her to stay back. An image began to appear in his mind. He saw the crack in the earth opening up. He also saw himself standing near it chanting an incantation. Usually, his visions have been kind of blurry at times but this one was as clear as crystal. He heard himself say "spirits of the earth, give me your power, give me your strength, let me become the master of the earth". After the incantation had ended, he saw himself grab the stone from the earth. The image began to slowly fade and he slowly returned to reality.

He woke up gasping for breath. He felt so sick. He wanted to vomit but he barely managed to hold it back. Christine went over to help him up. She realized that he had seen something. Simon had to rest for a few minutes. After a few minutes Simon told Christine about what he had seen. "Wow that's great." Said Christine. Simon led Christine over to the crack and he began the incantation. "Spirits of the earth, give me your power, give me your strength, let me become the master of the earth." He chanted loudly. Suddenly the crack began to expand. It grew and grew. After a few moments the crack had opened up enough so the stone could be extracted safely. Simon reached down into the crevice and managed to recover the stone safely. Just as he took the stone out it started to shine brightly. The two pieces of the stone seemed to start flashing in perfect sync and began to spin around Simon and Christine. The two pieces came together perfectly and created the stone of legends. It seemed though that things were about to take a turn for the worse. Suddenly eight hover cars flew overhead and they landed next to the two teens. They saw a familiar face come out of one of the hover cars. "Well, well it seems you have recovered the stone for us." said the familiar voice.

James?

Meanwhile back at the tomb James was in critical condition. Stacy was getting really worried. "James please wake up. You are my best friend and I need you. Please wake up," said Stacy worriedly. James was completely unconscious but he was having a dream. He dreamed he was walking through the forest. He felt completely alone. The sky was clear. It was full of stars that stretched out across the sky. James felt almost at peace here but he couldn't help but feel that there was something watching him. All of his memories of the last few years were gone and he simply existed in this space. He heard the leaves rustle. He also thought he saw a shadow move behind the trees. He now knew someone was watching him. He saw an old man come forward. He didn't have much hair on his head and he walked with a cane. The old man had torn clothes and he had been wounded. His arm was covered in blood. James knew the man was in danger so he ran up to him and asked "excuse me sir do you need help?" The old man looked curiously at James and said "thank you, young lad." James went beside the man and he grabbed his arm. "My house is about a mile walk from here." James agreed to help him and they slowly began the mile walk to his house.

On the way James felt like he knew him from somewhere. He felt close to him but he didn't know why. After a long walk they came across a wooden cabin. James helped the old man inside and he laid him down on the couch. James helped to bandage the old man's wound and he offered to make him soup. The old man declined his offer for soup. He wasn't very hungry. "Why don't you sit here on the couch?" asked the old man. James decided to sit with the old man. The old man slowly got up and headed to the kitchen. James got up to stop him but the old man didn't require his help. "I'm going to make us some green tea. Is that ok?" asked the old man. James was surprised and concerned but he decided to let the old man do as he wishes. "Sure, that would be great. Thank you." said James. The man walked to the kitchen and began making the tea. After a few minutes he returned with two cups full of piping hot tea. He gave one cup to James and sat down next to him.

The old man started to drink the tea. James took a sip of the tea and it immediately burned his tongue. He screamed out in pain. The old man looked curiously at James and said casually "hot tea I guess." James was surprised at his reaction but he kept his cool and stayed calm. He knew the old man deserved to have respect. The old man said "I knew you would find that tea hot. Only someone who is strong can handle the tea." The old man continued to drink his piping hot tea as if nothing had fazed him. James didn't understand what was going on. The old man got up and beckoned for James to follow him. The old man walked outside and motioned for James to stay back and observe. The old man dropped his cane and began to stand normally instead of his earlier hunched appearance. He jumped high in the air and landed on a very high, very thin branch hanging from a tree. James was completely shocked to see this. The old man then jumped down from the tree and landed safely on the ground. He kicked the tree trunk very lightly and the tree came crashing down beside the house.

James was in awe of what the old man was capable of. The old man then returned to the house and asked "do you still not know who I am James?" James looked at the old man and he began to think hard. He felt like he was remembering something. He soon realized that he had in fact met this old man before and it was recently. His memories began to rush back in an instant. The old man bowed and said "my name is Elijah." James couldn't believe it. He had been reunited with his cousin. Suddenly his happiness became sadness because he knew that Elijah was dead. "How can I see you? You're dead." said James sadly.

Elijah said grimly "you and I are connected. I am dead but you are not. At least not yet. You are in critical condition and that is why you and I can communicate." James was horrified to hear this. He didn't want to die yet. Elijah said "if you were to become strong then you could get through this without the help of your friends." James wanted to be able escape this. He wanted to do this himself. He knew it was the only way. He turned to Elijah and said "I want to be able to become strong. Can you train me?" Elijah agreed with a smile on his face. "We shall start training now." replied Elijah. James felt ready to train with him. For months they trained to increase James' endurance, physical strength, strength of mind, the five senses, and his spirit. For his endurance Elijah forced him to run around the entire forest for days on end without stopping. He often had to stop and rest. He had little to no sleep.

After days of training, he was able to run around the entire forest without stopping or getting tired. Next, they trained his physical strength. Elijah kept forcing him to kick at the trees until they came down. After weeks of training, he was able to bring them down in one kick. Next, they trained the strength of his mind. James trained by meditating for weeks until he was able to keep his mind calm and collected. Next, he was trained to use his five senses properly. It involved lots of meditation and being able to learn how to feel everything in the forest. After a while he was able to hear and feel everything that happened around him. Finally, he was training his spirit. He learned to be able to control his power. After a month he was able to kick down trees with very little effort. He also learned to communicate with spirits without being close to death. After his training was completed, he had become a master. He then started to remember past memories. One of his final tests was to confront the thing he was most afraid of and he realized what that was. He was terrified of Jeb but he was also afraid of letting his friends down. They meant everything to him and he needed to remember their past lives together.

He remembered him and Elijah taking down Jeb decades ago. Elijah had assisted him in getting rid of the serum and saving the other students that were trapped underneath the university. James started to cry at remembering these memories. He knew him and Elijah were really close back then. Elijah came up to him and put his hand on his shoulder. He said "I will always be with you James. You can call on me to assist you in times of need." James gave Elijah a hug and thanked him for everything. After the hug Elijah felt he needed to tell him something crucial. "During your time in here only a few minutes have passed in the real world." James felt glad to hear that. He didn't want to be out for months.

James now had to figure out how he was going to break through the barrier that prevented him from returning him to his own body. He chose to meditate on this. After hours of meditating, he thought he could hear a soothing voice from afar. It said "James, please wake up." After hearing it for a few more minutes James knew the voice belonged to Stacy. He kept on meditating. Soon he could feel himself leaving the dream world and returning to his body. The next thing he felt was him gasping for breath in his own body. He had finally been reunited with his body.

Stacy noticed he had awoken and rushed to see him. She gave him a big hug and held him for a long time. James felt so happy to be reunited with his best friend. After a while

Stacy let go of him and James got up. He felt so much stronger. His muscles ached but they felt better. He knew that the training had been real. He hadn't dreamed any of it. James explained to Stacy what had happened and she was amazed and happy that he got to see Elijah again. "I'm really glad you're okay." said Stacy. James pulled her into a hug and they embraced each other. James leaned over and gave Stacy a kiss on the cheek. Stacy was shocked but very happy that he did that. "What was that for?" asked Stacy. James said "the reason why I came to was because I heard your voice. It gave me the strength to escape." Stacy smiled at him and felt very happy.

She knew that her feelings for James were real and now she knew in her heart that the feeling was mutual. Despite their moments together she still had lingering doubts about his feelings. James knew that they had to get to the location of the stone. He led Stacy outside and after a little while they made it outside. James saw the beacon of light. Stacy knew that the area looked about 5 miles away. He then came up with an interesting idea. "Get on my back." said James. Stacy didn't know what he had in mind but she did it anyway. This intrigued her. James stated "during my training I focused on endurance and I have developed a lot of strength and speed. I am going to run to the beacon of light and I am going to carry you so we will get there faster together." Stacy agreed that this was a good idea. She mostly liked it because she would get to climb on James' back.

James started to run towards the beacon of light in hopes of helping his friends. Meanwhile Simon and Christine were scared of the man they saw come out of the hover car. He was their greatest enemy. Out came Dr. Jeb. Jeb activated a machine and he used it to pull the stone out of their hands and into his arms. Jeb took the stone and he started to absorb the power within it. Simon and Christine watched in horror as Jeb took everything the stone had in it. After a few moments Jeb started to glow brightly. Suddenly he had a revelation. He has regained all of his memories from his past lives and not just his first life. He looked at Simon and Christine and asked coldly "where is my son?" Simon and Christine didn't know how to respond to this. Simon didn't want Jeb to know they were terrified so he said bravely "we don't know who your son is and even if we did, we wouldn't tell you anything." Jeb looked to Christine and said "she knows who my son is. She saw his picture at my bunker."

Simon and Christine were shocked that he knew this. "Don't be so shocked you two. I am Jeb the immortal titan. And you two shall be nothing but skeletons by the time I'm done with you." Simon and Christine readied themselves to fight. The hover car that Jeb came out housed four aliens and the other seven cars housed five aliens each. Simon and Christine knew that they weren't going to survive this fight but they weren't going to go down without a fight. The aliens had created a fighting formation where they would come at the two friends from all directions. Suddenly two figures came running through the horde of aliens and they stopped at Simon and Christine. It was Stacy and James. Simon and Christine were shocked to see James alive but they were so overjoyed to see their friends. "It's really good to see you guys." said Simon and Christine.

They then realized that the prophecy foretold that five heroes were to stop Jeb but there were only four here. "We can't stop Jeb on our own. Only all five of us can stop Jeb," said Christine. James looked to everyone and said "we are severely outnumbered and even though there is only four of us we can still win this. Jeb may be stronger than all of us but we can take him down. We fought him before and we can do it again." The group regained their courage and they decided to fight back. "My alien army. Destroy them all and rid our world of pathetic children." The aliens said in unison "yes sir!" One of the aliens started to come forward but a bullet came out of nowhere and hit him right in the heart.

Aliens are very powerful but a hit in the heart was fatal to them. The alien fell down to the ground dead. Dr. Jeb became enraged by this. Then he saw that rushing forward was none other than Jake. He jumped forward and he kicked Jeb right in the face. He then grabbed the stone and threw it to James. James caught it and was surprised by what just happened. Jake said "I know you can never forgive me for what I did but can we at least put our differences aside to defeat Jeb." The group reluctantly agreed. James said "thanks for coming back." Jake smiled at James. The group was still pissed but they decided the mission was more important. James took the stone and he noticed a small flicker of light. He made a wish. "I wish that we would have all the power." The stone used its last bit of light to take back Jeb's power and transfer it to the five friends. The five friends rose up into the air and began to receive their gifts. They all started to regain some of their lost memories and they remembered what happened back in Egypt and Rathos but not much else. James also remembered that Jake had killed his father in an accident back in Egypt but that didn't answer the question of where his real father is now. The stone had increased their power and gave them their abilities.

With their powers combined they fought through the aliens and defeated them quickly. Jeb didn't seem afraid though. All he had was a smirk on his face. Jeb looked at the group and said "my you five have grown so powerful. Especially you, my son. You have gotten so much stronger." Said Jeb with an evil grin. No one knew what to say.

Simon and Jake didn't know that Jeb had a son. No one knew who it was except for Christine. Jeb said "I'm glad you are doing well, James." James was completely shocked but he couldn't believe what he was hearing. Jeb liked seeing them in complete shock and denial.

The entire group was trying to deny what they have heard, except for Christine. Christine came forward and said "liar", to Dr. Jeb. She turned to her friends and said "James isn't Jeb's son." She looked back at Jeb and said loudly "your son is Jake." Jake came over to her and asked "how do you know this, Christine?" Christine looked down and said "back at Jeb's lab I found pictures of all of us and one picture had written on it "my only son, someday you will be aligned with me." Jake couldn't believe this. He wanted to help his friends but he didn't want to kill his own father.

Jeb came forward and said "my son, I'm sorry that I couldn't tell you sooner. I wanted you to became strong enough to face me and now you are." Jake looked at his father and then he looked back at his friends. He didn't know who he should align with. His father said "if you join me, you will be able to get rid of James completely. You will finally be free." Jake's eyes gleamed at this thought. He glared back at James and suddenly he started to feel his hatred returning. He desperately tried to suppress it. The two voices came back into play. "Join your father and you can kill James. You will be able to get everything you've always wanted." said the darker voice. "No, Jake don't do it. Stay with your friends. Dr. Jeb may be your father but he abandoned you when you were young. Your friends are your true family." said the lighter voice. "Stop feeding nonsense into his mind." said the dark voice. "Nonsense? I'm not feeding him nonsense. I'm trying to help him. You on the other hand are feeding him nonsense." said the lighter voice.

The dark voice was starting to become angrier. "This reminds me of that other boy you 'tried to 'help'," said the lighter voice. "Don't you dare go there," said the darker voice. "Oh, I'm going to go there. You were feeding him so much nonsense it scared him so much that he jumped off a cliff," said the lighter voice. The dark voice was starting to become really angry. "That was an accident and you know it. That could've happened to any male." "Yeah, except that male was a mouse. I've never seen that happen before. I know you hate that you did that to a poor defenseless animal," said the lighter voice. "WHY DON'T YOU JUST GO JUMP OFF A CLIFF? yelled the dark voice. "HONESTLY ANYTHING IS BETTER THAN BEING HERE WITH YOU! yelled the lighter voice. The two voices eventually stopped trying to tell Jake what to do because they were so upset with each other. Jake had no idea how he should react to what just happened within his mind. His mind was in pieces and he felt like he was coming apart. He wanted to scrub his head clean of the voices but didn't know how. Soon after he had made his decision.

He picked up the stone from James and he brought it to Jeb. Jeb was delighted to see his son chose him. "Good choice son. You won't regret it." Jake muttered "I know." Jeb reached out to take the stone but Jake pulled the stone away from him. He made a wish that shocked everyone. He wished that Jeb would be destroyed and that the alien army would be turned back into humans. The stone started to flash brilliantly and every single one of the aliens became human again and even the dead ones became resurrected and turned back to normal. Jeb noticed his body started to crack. His body was starting to fall apart. He ran towards Jake to steal the stone back but James jumped in front of him and kicked Jeb's body which caused him to crumble completely. Dr. Jeb was dead. The group saw that the stone began to flash bright for a moment before fading. They didn't know what it was but they didn't think anything of it.

The stone began to glow and it rose into the air. The stone's light began to shine on everything which would bring it back to life. The stone was undoing all the damage. After a few moments the world was completely revitalized. All the former aliens began to cheer in their honor. Rathos appeared before the five friends and said "you have done it. I am so proud of all of you." He then had to explain something that was very crucial. "I think it's time you have learned about how the stone works. The stone does allow you to reach your full potential but it only allows you to reach your full potential based on what you have learned. If you were to train for years and then use the stone then you would become that much more powerful. There are still many more abilities that you have to relearn and new abilities that you will learn as well."

The group was glad to hear this. It would help them to know that they still have to train to become stronger. Rathos kept his hood over his head as he spoke. He still felt ashamed about his face. Rathos bade them goodbye and took the stone back to his tomb. The five friends took one of the hover cars and they flew back to their hometown. A couple days later. The five friends were eating at the voyageur. The day before was their award ceremony where they were given medals and $900,000 each. The friends decided to enjoy their victory by eating at the Voyageur. Simon got up from the booth and left. "I have to use the restroom quickly." said Simon. The others said "ok." Simon left to use the bathroom. After he finished and he was just washing his hands he had a sharp pain in his back. He fell and hit his head on the sink.

He was having a vision. It was really blurry but it looked like something was coming out of the sand. He didn't know what it was but he saw it come out. The image then faded abruptly. Simon woke up with a really bad head pain and he threw up in the toilet for a few minutes. He recovered quickly but he became scared of what he saw. He ran back into the restaurant to tell his friends. The group heard what he had to say but they didn't think it was a big deal. "It probably isn't anything to worry about." said Jake. "I agree with him." said Christine. Simon decided it wasn't anything he should think about.

A few minutes later James got up but he didn't say anything. He walked outside and laid against the wall. Stacy came out soon after. "Hey, are you okay?" Asked Stacy. James looked at her and said "I don't know anymore. I thought that confronting Jeb would get me answers but I still have so many questions. Stacy came up beside him and she grabbed his arm. "It's going to be ok. I'll help you get your answers but I don't think you should worry about that now. You should just enjoy this time with your friends." James knew she was right. He looked into her eyes and said "yeah, you're right." She let go of his arm and he led her back inside the Voyageur. They sat back down and began talking again about their victory. But then James had a thought. "Didn't Jeb raise an army from the sand in Egypt many millenniums ago?" asked James. Everyone realized that he did but he is dead so he can't do anything about that. "I'm sure we don't have to worry about it. Dr. Jeb is dead." said Jake.

Meanwhile back in Egypt the stone of legends which was sitting on an altar next to Rathos' coffin started to flash briefly. The stone was actually home to Jeb's spirit. Jeb had snuck into the stone just after he died and his spirit bonded with the stone and its powers. Jeb started to smile as he made a wish. Outside of the tomb in the sand a hand covered in black armor rose out of the sand. It started to claw its way out. The horrors that the teens have faced had only just begun.

One Month Later

THIS PART OF THE story takes place another month after Dr. Jeb's "death". It is September 26, 2015 at 3:00 PM. At Lake Superior High School James was just getting out of his history class and was getting ready to head home. James has changed a bit in the last month. Now he was letting his hair grow out and he dyed it brown. He has gotten a lot more muscular and is more relaxed now. He has been hanging out with his friends more and he isn't as focused on finding his father. He has gotten a bit taller as well. He grabbed his books and starts to head out of class. He is the last one to go. As he exits the classroom, he accidently bumped into someone on his way out. James and the unknown figure fell to the ground and James dropped his books. "Watch it dude." said the unknown figure coldly. James said in response "sorry." James looked at the figure and he saw Jake. Jake realized it was him and he said nicely "no it was my fault. Don't worry about it." Jake helped James up and he helped him gather his books. Jake had changed a lot as well. He has stopped the drinking and he is trying to get along with James more. The group seems to have let him back in after he redeemed himself by betraying his father and confessing what he did about trying to kill James. James became more aware of Jake's issues and instead of turning on him decided to try and help him through them instead.

Jake has been letting his blond hair grow out a bit as well. He had also gotten much stronger and somewhat taller but not as much as James has gotten. Jake has also let go of his two voices and was making decisions for himself. Jake and James decided to walk down the hall to their lockers. The school was somewhat small. Their lockers were a couple hallways away from them. Jake and James have been starting to become best friends again and James felt like he could tell Jake anything. Jake felt the same way about James. As they were turning around the corner which would lead them to their lockers, they saw Stacy go to her locker. Stacy was very slim, attractive, had long brown hair and was a very good athlete. She was almost as strong as James and is only a month younger than he is. James saw Stacy first and started to walk towards her. Her locker was right next to his.

Jake grabbed his shoulder and gave him a pat on his back. Jake knew James wanted to talk to her so he gave him a nod which James knew he understood to leave the room. Jake left and James headed over to his locker. He felt really good when he was with her. She had helped him through so much and she always stood by him. He went to his locker and he said "hey." to Stacy. Stacy looked at him and her eyes lit up. She liked being around him and felt like she could trust him with her life. She said to him "hey." "How are your classes, James?" asked Stacy. James said "they are going good, how about you?" "I like them." said Stacy. Stacy always worried about James because he had gone through so much and she didn't want to lose him. "How have you been doing with everything?" asked Stacy with concern. James knew she was going to ask him this. He was depressed for a couple weeks after Jeb's death but he was starting to accept that maybe it was best that he doesn't find out about his father. "I've been doing pretty good lately. I haven't been stressing out as much anymore and Jake and I have been getting along really well." said James. Stacy was really happy to hear this. "I'm glad you are doing so well." said Stacy. James said "I think I'm going to head home. Would you like a ride?" asked James. Stacy desperately wanted to accept but she had to decline. "I really appreciate your offer but I have to stay here and finish some work." said Stacy. James was going to leave but he had an idea. "How about you finish up your work and I'll hang back here as well. I have some work I can probably finish up too. I can give you a ride when you finish up." said James. Stacy replied "thanks, I would really like that, thanks." James said "anytime." Stacy walked off and headed to the library. Jake noticed Stacy had left so he went to his locker which was on the right side of Stacy's whereas James' locker was on the left. Jake went to his locker and said "hey James." James turned around and said "oh, hey Jake what's up?" Jake asked "hey are you heading out soon? I was wondering if I could get a ride with you." James replied "sorry Jake but I'm going to give Stacy a ride home when she is finished with her school work." Jake looked down and said "oh ok I guess I'll see you later then." Jake walked away and headed outside the school. James decided to walk to the library to hang out with Stacy.

Things Change

Meanwhile back in Egypt a dark figure had managed to completely rise out of the sand. He was 7 feet tall and he was covered from head to toe in black armor. He bore the letter J on his left arm. He also had the letter G on his chest which meant he was a general. He was second in command of his army. He also carried a large black sword and his eyes were red. He looked down at the sand and he knew his brothers were trapped beneath the sand. He then saw Rathos' tomb near him and he could feel the presence of the stone coming from there. He ran into the tomb and he went through the tomb until he came across Rathos' coffin. The stone of legends was gleaming on a pedestal near the coffin. The general ran to the stone and he made a wish. "I wish for my master Jeb to be alive once more," said the general. Secretly the general always hated Jeb and wanted the army to himself. The stone flashed and it set Jeb free. Jeb was back from the dead. Jeb felt all of his joints and he could also feel his heartbeat. Jeb said "thank you my general. Now give the stone to your master now." The general considered it but he had a different agenda. He wanted to give Jeb false hope by bringing him back to life and then striking him down when he least expected it.

Instead, he took the stone and he absorbed its power. The general drew his sword and he cut the coffin in half. Rathos managed to dodge the blade just in time. He saw the general and for once Rathos feared for his life. The general tried to kill Dr. Jeb with his sword but Jeb dodged it. He didn't die but the blade did cut through his chest. He was losing lots of blood and fast. Rathos used his power and he transported Jeb and himself away from the bloodthirsty general. The general tried to stop them from leaving but they had already escaped. The general didn't seem to worry. "He was pathetic. All humans are pathetic." Said the general aloud. The general left the tomb and walked back to where he freed himself. He made one more wish with the stone. "I wish for my army to be free from their eternal slumber beneath the sands." The stone obeyed his command. After a few seconds thousands of warriors had risen from the sand and were prepared to do anything to remain free.

The general used the power of the stone and rose into the air. The army bowed down to their leader. The general said "today my brothers we fight for our freedom. Too long have we been oppressed by these pathetic humans. The time has come for us to put them in their place. With the power of this stone, we can take this world for ourselves." The army became pumped and ready for battle. They cheered for their leader. One soldier came forward because he was confused. "General, what happened to our leader Jeb?" The general said loudly "our leader has been murdered. These humans got to him. They earned his trust and then they destroyed him!" The army was saddened by their leader's death but they turned their grief into anger. The army was starting to become bloodthirsty just like their new leader. The general yelled at the top of his lungs "I AM GENERAL BASILISK AND WE SHALL SPILL HUMAN BLOOD TONIGHT!" The army cheered for him and they were willing to fight for him. Basilisk felt that as long as no one knew that he had usurped Jeb's throne then his men would remain loyal. He said to himself "Jeb may have been bad. He may have brought the world to its knees before but I am ten times more the tyrant then he ever was." Basilisk dropped down to the ground and he absorbed the power of the stone until it had almost nothing left within it. The stone now had no light, no nothing. The stone was useless to him and Basilisk knew it. He then gave some of his men his power so that they would become even stronger. They had extreme speed and strength. Basilisk summoned a black horse and he led his men in the direction of Schreiber, Ontario at super speed.

Meanwhile back at the high school. Stacy was finishing up some of her math homework but she was struggling with it. James was working on some history beside her. He heard her sigh and he knew she was having a hard time. He came over to her and he sat beside her. She looked at him and said "hey James what's up." James replied "I saw you were having a hard time and I wanted to help you." Stacy smiled and said "that's very sweet, thanks." James took his pencil and looked at her textbook. He was always very good at math and he was a very good tutor. He noticed that she was studying parabolas and he was good with those. He showed her how to solve them and he gave her a couple examples to try on her own. She followed his advice on everything and she managed to understand it all on her own. "Thank you so much James. I get it now." she said excitedly. She gave him a big hug and held him for awhile. He was glad he could help because he did care about her a lot. After a little bit she let him go but she still looked at him. She had beautiful blue eyes which James really liked.

She really liked looking into his mysterious green eyes. She leaned closer to him and he did the same. She felt an attraction to him and she wanted to tell him again how she feels. She had tried to tell him a few times but they always got interrupted or they decided to put things on pause. Suddenly Jake came in and Stacy noticed him. She quickly let James go because she didn't want to cause any tension between him and Jake. Jake came forward and said "hey guys." They both said "hey Jake," in response. Simon and Christine came in soon after. Simon had gotten taller and much stronger in a month.

He kept his red hair somewhat long and he felt much more confident with his abilities. Christine wasn't as afraid as she used to be now. Her hair is still long and purple. She is slim and very attractive. She is still a bit stronger and taller than Simon. Simon and Christine said in unison "Hey guys, good to see you." They have been doing that a lot lately. Stacy and James felt awkward but they tried not to show it. James figured Jake would have gone home by now. "Jake, I thought you went home already old friend," said James. Jake replied "I was going to but I ran into Simon and Christine. They had some work to catch up on and I know that I'm behind in a couple subjects so I decided to come here and get some work done too. "Is that ok?" asked Jake sincerely. James wanted to say no but he didn't want to cause any problems. He said "sure that's fine with me I guess." James looked at Stacy and she understood why he said ok. She said "yeah that's fine." Jake, Simon and Christine sat next to them and all five of them began to finish their work. Suddenly they saw a flash of light appearing in the room.

Enemies Reunited

They saw Rathos and they were horrified to see who was with him. It was Dr. Jeb. Jake immediately jumped up and he ran to Jeb. He didn't know how he survived but he wanted to make his death more permanent. Rathos blocked Jake's path and said "no we need him alive. He has information that is vital." Jake said "no I don't want anything to do with my father. He tried to kill us." James ran over and grabbed Jake's arm. "Just relax Jake, everything will be okay. Let's hear what he has to say." Jake started to calm down quickly. He nodded in agreement but he really didn't want to hear anything Jeb had to say. He felt so much hatred within himself and seeing Jeb again brought all of his negative feelings rushing back like a whirlwind. The other three came forward and they saw Jeb was injured. Rathos waved his hand over Jeb's wound and he managed to repair the wound. Dr. Jeb decided to explain what happened but he had to start from the very beginning.

He explained "back in Egypt I had come across a secret cave that was filled with ancient statues. As I came closer to them, I realized they weren't statues. There was an inscription on the wall that said 'Here lie the ancient warriors. They have met a terrible fate. Recite this spell to reawaken them.' I chose to recite the ancient spell in order to get everything I could ever want. Back then I was looking for power but I still didn't believe that this army was real. I recited 'I am your master now, I am your leader, I shall reawaken you and you shall be bound to me. Rise my warriors.' The statues began to shift and then the inscription faded. I had given them back their life. The leader of them came forward and bowed to me. He thanked me for saving the lives of him and his warriors. They decided that they would serve me and become my soldiers. It was after that I heard about the stone of legends. I felt that it would be the perfect opportunity to achieve ultimate power. Over time my warriors had become very loyal to me and they started to trust me over their general. When Rathos sealed my warriors away and I had died I vowed to bring them back. When you had killed me Jake, I transferred my spirit into the stone and I wished that I could remain in there until someone freed me. I also wished that my warriors would be resurrected. It seems that only the general had come back to life. He freed me but he didn't plan on serving me. He took his sword and he slashed me. He also took the stone and tried to destroy Rathos. Rathos used his power to transport us out of there. I owe him my life. The reason why Rathos was in danger is because the sword he possesses is called the Ulto Blade. It allows you to destroy anything, even ghosts. If he were to destroy Rathos then he would be out of existence. That treacherous warrior tried to kill me and now he is going to come here and kill you." The five friends knew that he was right despite not wanting to believe him or his story.

They didn't want to believe him but they trusted Rathos and he nodded in agreement with Jeb. Dr. Jeb said "I am going to help you take down my general. General Basilisk is a tyrant. He believes all humans are weak and that genocide is the right thing to do." The group was horrified by this. They had faced difficult threats before but they sensed Basilisk was far more powerful. Rathos said "I sense that Basilisk has absorbed everything from the stone and that he knows it is useless. If he destroys it then the entire world will fall out of balance. We have to retrieve that stone back." The group agreed with what he was saying.

They had to prevent the world from falling out of balance. For the first time Jeb was on their side...he wanted to get rid of Basilisk as much as they wanted to. Just as they were talking the ground began to shake. They also noticed the school was starting to crumble. "WE HAVE TO GET OUT OF HERE!" yelled Jake. The group ran out of the school and just barely managed to escape before the school came crashing down. They then saw the worst sight imaginable. All of Schrieber was coming apart. All the buildings were crashing down for no reason. They then saw an army of black armored soldiers with red eyes coming towards the town. James noticed that the stone was cracked into two pieces. They knew the world was falling out of balance. "We are too late." said Simon. James saw this horrible sight but he couldn't let this stop them. He turned to face his friends. "We can do this. We didn't think we were able to defeat Jeb but we did. We can stop him too. Are you with me?" The group was really unsure. His pep talk didn't seem to help. I think it was because for the first time his fear was starting to show through. He saw a tall and powerful warrior slaughtering all of the humans in town. James realized that this threat is way too powerful and that they weren't strong enough. "Actually, I don't think fighting him head on is a good idea. I think we should flee and live to fight another day." said James. Everyone agreed with him. They saw Basilisk throw the stone into a pit. Simon knew he needed the stone so he ran after it and he used his telekinesis to lift the pieces out of the pit. Their powers had gotten much stronger. Simon threw the pieces to James and Rathos waved his hand and he transported the group back to his tomb. Rathos beckoned the group to a darkened wall. He snapped his fingers and the darkened part of the wall lit up like a lighthouse.

They saw another prophecy. The prophecy read "the five heroes shall reunite with their old adversary. They shall work together to bring new light back to the world. The heroes shall use the two stones of legend to dethrone the new tyrant." Everyone was surprised. They didn't know there was a second stone. "Where is the second stone?" asked Christine. "The stone is in the past. It would be located in Medieval times. The stone was destroyed because the people couldn't trust it's power. Luckily the stone had a brother so the world didn't shift out of balance. Also in that time period is a sacred pool that will bring the broken stone back to life." Simon asked "how can we get to the stone?" Rathos replied "I can send you back in time. I may be a ghost but I am still very powerful. Before I do though I want to say that you five are the people that I trust the most. I want to show you who I really am." He slowly removed the hood from his face. His face had a bad burn mark on his eye. It was a birthmark but it looked like a scar. Rathos looked very Egyptian and regal despite looking youthful. He had clearly been through many hardships despite his young age. Everyone saw the mark and were shocked. They were surprised but they felt that he was honourable for showing them his mark. "This is the last time that I shall be able to assist you." James and his friends were saddened to hear this news. James came forward and asked him "will we ever see you again?" Rathos said grimly "Perhaps our paths may cross again." Everyone figured that they probably wouldn't see him again after this. Rathos said seriously "it is time to begin the ritual. Step next to my coffin." The six stepped onto the coffin. Rathos was about to do the ritual when A loud voice came from outside the tomb. "OH JAMES. WHERE ARE YOU!" The others started giggling because they knew who this was. "Man, how did she find me all the way out here?"

A woman came running into the tomb. She was a somewhat tall woman in her early forties. She had red curly hair and she carried a purse on her shoulder. She was wearing a red shirt and blue jeans. James was not happy to see her. "Hi aunty Janice." Aunty Janice rushed in and gave him a really big hug. She squeezed him so hard that his face began to turn blue. After a few moments she let him go and James was able to catch his breath.

She then said "I know you are going on a long journey so you need to be really careful out there. If anything goes wrong just come home and I'll give you the biggest hug ever to comfort you."

The others were trying really hard not to laugh. Even Rathos was covering his mouth with his hand. James said "don't worry I will be fine." She then said "ok but I need to give you something before you go. Take this beer. They come all the way from British Columbia." She gave him two six packs of beer. James accepted them and he thanked her for the beer. She then gave him a really big hug and she kept saying "I'm going to miss you so much." She said that multiple times. The others couldn't hold it in anymore. They burst out laughing. She let him go and said "goodbye James." James bade her goodbye and he got back on near the coffin. Before Rathos began James bowed to him and said "thank you Lord Rathos, you have helped us in so many ways. We consider you to be a true friend." Rathos nodded in agreement before waving his hands near them. Suddenly the six people started to feel themselves being taken away from this place. They then began to travel through time and space. They landed in front of a large castle. They realized they were in front of a giant castle straight out of a book.

They soon realized this was Camelot. There were knights walking around and there were lots of horses. James started to walk around when two knights came up to them. They said in unison "Halt." They drew their swords and threatened to kill James right there, right then. James put his hands up and said "we aren't here to cause you any trouble. We just want to locate a sacred stone. We aren't from around here." The guards noticed his clothes and said "yeah, no kidding." The guards ordered everyone to come with them. The other five had no choice. They had to obey. The guards took them inside the castle. The castle inside was pretty big. The interior was in good shape and it was covered in banners. It was the symbol of Camelot. After a short walk through the castle, they ended up in the throne room. There they saw King Arthur.

He greeted them with a "welcome to Camelot." The guards kicked the group to their knees. Jake wanted to bite their heads off for the mistreatment and being treated like a dog but James calmed him down with a look. James looked up at the king and said "your majesty, we are looking for a sacred stone that your people may be afraid of. It is vital to our journey that we acquire it." King Arthur rubbed his chin. He was thinking really hard about this.

He called his advisor to see him. "Skragg, I need to speak with you," said King Arthur. A somewhat old man came walking through the castle. He was very thin and bony. His eyes were bloodshot and he had rotten teeth. Jake looked closer at him and he realized that this was a much older and much uglier version of Jeb. This was his ancestor or descendant depending on how you looked at it. He quietly told the others and they were surprised. Even Jeb was shocked to see his relative. Skragg thought hard and then he came to a decision. "I say that they should be executed." King Arthur agreed with this idea. "Throw them in the dungeon. We shall execute them in the morning." The guards started to take them away but James wasn't going down without a fight.

He broke free from the guard that was holding him and he kicked him hard in the chest. All the other guards started to go after him but James was too quick and too strong. He kicked them hard and he started running out of the castle. There were tons of guards but James managed to evade all of them and he ran out. The rest of the guards quickly pressed hard against the other five so they couldn't break free. The guards took the prisoners to the dungeons and they kept them there. Stacy was scared but all she could think about was James.

Clashes in Camelot

Meanwhile James was trying to escape the guards when someone grabbed his hand and pulled him behind a hut nearby. James waited for the guards to pass before he could see who helped him. After a few minutes the guards were out of sight. He turned to thank his rescuer but he was kind of shocked by what he saw. It was a very pretty girl. She looked about 18. She had long black hair and she had white skin. She was pretty slim and very attractive. James instantly felt an attraction to her. For the first time in his life, he suddenly felt nervous. "Th, th, thank you." he muttered. The girl smiled at James. She said "I have a safe place from these people. Come with me if you want to be safe." James instantly trusted her and he nodded. She took him by the hand and she led him to a nearby cave and they took shelter in there. In the cave James came across a pool of water and he felt a connection to it. He figured this was the sacred pool that would repair the stone. He was about to put the stone into the pool but the mystery girl grabbed his arm and she pulled him close to her. He thought she was very pretty but he liked someone else. The mystery girl finally decided to introduce herself. "My name is Caroline. What is yours?" asked Caroline. "My name is James." Caroline looked him over and she said "you aren't from around here, are you?" James said "I'm from far away. Really far away." Caroline seemed very intrigued by this new guy and she wanted to get to know him better. She said seductively "do you have a girlfriend, James?" James looked at her said "I do, sort of. I mean I really like her but we aren't dating at all." Caroline seemed somewhat sad about this. She let him go and she turned away from him.

She really liked him but she didn't want to interfere. James sensed she was upset and he put his arm around her. She felt happy to have him close by. She said to him "I'm sorry I shouldn't have been trying to flirt with you. It's just that I really like you but you belong to someone else. No one would go for a girl like me." James came closer to her and said "you are very attractive. If I didn't like Stacy, I would want to be with you." This seemed to cheer her up. She looked at him and said "thanks James, you're sweet." James sat closer to her and she looked him in his eyes. She felt entranced. She pulled him close and she started to kiss him.

He pulled away at first but then he leaned in and kissed her back. They started to kiss for a long time. She pushed him lightly to the ground and she started to kiss him while being on top of him. James really liked Caroline. He still really liked Stacy but he wanted to try it with Caroline for a moment since he and Stacy technically weren't dating yet. She started to pull his shirt off. She liked seeing how muscular he was. She also pulled off her own shirt. He felt even more attracted to her now. This is the farthest he has ever gotten with a girl. She leaned down and she started to kiss his neck. He had no options to get back into the castle for now until things calmed down so he figured he may as well enjoy this while he could.

Meanwhile back at the dungeons everyone wasn't sure what they could do. All Stacy could think about was James and how much she wanted to be with him right now. They tried to kick the door down but the cell they were in was very sturdy. The group spent a long-time pacing and thinking but nothing came to mind. They figured their best shot would be to wait for James. They knew James wasn't going to let them down. Meanwhile back at the cave. James and Caroline were making out on the cave floor. They hadn't taken anything else off but they really liked being with each other. James wasn't thinking about this at the moment but he only had a physical attraction to her. There wasn't an emotional connection. With Stacy he had both.

Abruptly he let go of Caroline. He sat back up and he quickly put on his shirt. Caroline felt uncomfortable. She thought that she did something wrong. James knew something was wrong. He reassured her that it wasn't her fault. "I have to save my friends. They are going to be executed tomorrow and I have to save them." he said seriously. Caroline understood and she wanted to help him save them. She said to him" I know how to get to where they are going to be executed. The North East wall is unguarded during execution time. You can climb over the wall and you can sneak behind the guards. When you climb the wall, you will be facing the guards and they will be positioned the other way." James was eternally grateful for this information. She wanted to help him out more though. She suggested "I want to come with you to save your friends. I might not look strong but I have a lot of experience with fighting the guards. I can help you save your friends." James was glad to have her support but he had to ask her something else. "Do you know where King Arthur would keep a sacred stone. I know that it has great power and that it is feared throughout the land. I also know that King Arthur will want to destroy it but I can't let that happen. It is very crucial that I retrieve it." Caroline thought hard for a second. She had a thought. "I think that he would keep it in his throne room. It would be on a pedestal next to it." James thanked her for the information. He took the broken stone out of his pocket and he dropped it into the sacred pool. The stone automatically sprung to life and it mended its cracks together to create the stone of legends once more. James decided to rest here because it was starting to get dark out and he didn't have to be at the wall until morning. Before James went to sleep, he found a sword that had been wedged into the cave wall. James grabbed the sword and it came out easily. He figured this sword would come in handy against the guards tomorrow.

He thought about the legend of King Arthur. He said under his breath "I pulled the sword from the stone huh. Guess I'm the new king of Camelot", he said sarcastically. He then laid down on the ground and he slowly drifted off to sleep. Twelve hours later. At the dungeons the guards kicked the group awake. "Ow." yelled Jake to the guards. Everyone was really pissed off to be woken up like this but they knew that it was execution day. The guards opened up their cell and they dragged the prisoners out. The guards took them out to the courtyard and they lined them up one by one. Simon was first, then Christine, then Jake then Jeb and then Stacy. There were other prisoners that were lined up next to them. There were four other prisoners. One was an old man. He was completely bald and he had many scars on his face.

He was partially blind in one eye and his left hand been mutilated. Another prisoner was a young woman. She was about 26. She had somewhat short black hair and she was very slim. Part of her leg was wounded but she could still walk fine. Her face was covered in dirt. Another prisoner was a young man. He was in his mid forties. He had a bit of hair on his head and he had scars on his legs. They were possibly self inflicted from being in the prison for a long period of time. The final prisoner was just a kid. He was about 14 years old. He had lost one arm completely but he didn't seem to pay mind to it. He seemed to be very depressed. If he was in the prison any longer, he probably would've committed suicide. The guards started to call the prisoners to come to the stand.

The prisoners would have to lay on a box and the executioner would cut off their head into a crate. "Dean, front and center." The old man stumbled over to the box. He laid his head on the box and waited for the axe. The executioner slowly raised his axe into the air and he brought it down really quickly. His head came off and fell right into the box. Blood splattered everywhere. Pieces of his neck were coming off and falling to the ground. The guards just shrugged it off and said "NEXT! Judith you're next." The twenty-six-year-old came forward. She laid down on the box and she prepared to die. She began to cry as she thought of her dead family. The executioner raised his axe into the air. He was about to bring it down when out of nowhere an arrow came and pierced him in the back of his head. The executioner fell to the ground and he dropped the axe. Pieces of his brain were oozing out and blood was spilling out quickly. The executioner was dead. Judith quickly raised her head and she saw two people on the North East wall. It was James and Caroline. They jumped off the wall and began to run to the prisoners. Caroline was firing arrows at the guards and James would beat them up at close range. James ran towards the prisoners and he began freeing their hands. The guards had bound their hands together.

Stacy gave him a big hug after she was free. He liked her hugging him but he felt guilty about what he did with in the cave with Caroline. He freed the other prisoners and they all decided to work together. The others didn't want to be here. James told them the plan and they headed into the castle to find the stone. Caroline followed close behind while firing arrows at the oncoming guards. James led the way into the castle and they headed towards the throne room. After awhile they found the throne room and they barricaded both doors so guards couldn't get in. James searched the throne room until he saw a blue stone sticking out of the throne. He took it out and he felt the power in the stone. Just as everyone was celebrating a dark figure snuck into the room and they snatched the stone from James. James looked to see it was none other than Jeb's ancestor Skragg. He admired the stone and he lit up at the sight of it. Jake ran forward and he tried to punch Skragg in his chin. Skragg dodged it and he kicked Jake right into the wall.

James drew his sword and he pointed it in the direction of Skragg. "I challenge you to a sword fight." said James. Skragg thought about it. He said in response "Alright I accept your challenge. First blood it is." James agreed. Skragg drew his sword and came forward. They bowed to each other and then they pointed their swords at each other. James tried to slash Skragg from the side but Skragg was too quick and he blocked it easily. James tried to do it from a couple other directions but nothing seemed to work. Skragg seemed to enjoy seeing James try and fail. Skragg was in no rush to win this battle. James decided to do two attacks at once. He took a step back and he jumped up high into the air. He then aimed his sword above Skragg's head. He looked like he was going to try an aerial attack. That was only part of his plan though. When he was only a few inches from Skragg's head James threw the sword at his head and then he jumped to the side while Skragg blocked the sword. James took the opportunity and he kicked Skragg in his side which caused him to fall down. James quickly picked up his sword and he scratched his cheek. Skragg had lost the sword fight. James threatened to kill him if he didn't give up the stone even though he really wouldn't have killed him unless he had to. Skragg raised his hands into the air to show he surrendered.

He handed them the stone and then he ran off. Skragg was much more of a coward then Jeb was. James felt happy that he won the fight. The group cheered for him. They were all really proud of him. Even Dr. Jeb was pretty impressed. "Not bad James." said Jeb casually. James looked around and he saw that Skragg had dropped a piece of paper. James grabbed it and he unfolded it. The paper was a very old map. It showed a circular platform that was three miles away. It also mentions that when you go to the platform and you raise the two stones above it then the platform will glow and it will send you to any desired time period. James felt excited and he showed the map to everyone. Everyone was ecstatic because now they could return home. The other three prisoners wanted to escape this world as well. James walked over to them and he said "would you like to come with us? We would really like it if you would come with us". The three prisoners said "we would very much like to come with you please." James nodded and told everyone "We need to get to the platform before the guards get to us. We have to work together if we want to survive. Are you with me?" Everyone felt pumped up and they wanted to follow James. James slowly removed the pillars that they were using to barricade the doors. The second they did that the guards burst in through the door. James led the others through a window and they tried to escape from the castle. There were guards everywhere which took up a lot of time. The entire group combined was strong enough to hold their own against the guards. Everyone was punching and kicking the guards out of the way. Caroline was shooting arrows at all the guards. Everyone felt nervous about getting out but they were confident enough that they could win.

After a long trek through the castle, they managed to escape and James suggested while running "I found a cave that we'll be able to lie low in." Everyone agreed with his idea. The group headed off to the cave. The cave had cracked walls and water dripped from the ceiling sometimes but it was big and hidden. James looked at the spot where he and Caroline were making out and this caused him to feel very guilty. He now knew that Stacy was the only one he wanted. Caroline came up to him and she grabbed his arm. James let go and said "I like someone else Caroline. I'm sorry." Caroline understood. James and Caroline walked to the far side of the cave so they could talk in private. Caroline said "she is very beautiful. I can see why you like Stacy so much." James felt happy that Caroline understood. He gave her a hug and then they walked back to the group. They stayed in the cave for awhile. The guards were sniffing around the area but they never found the cave.

When it was nightfall, the group decided to get some sleep. Just as the group was starting to lie down a loud and very familiar voice came from outside the cave. "JAMES! IT'S YOUR AUNTY JANICE!" James' friends were trying hard not to laugh and even the prisoners were starting to grin. Caroline chuckled a bit and Jeb grinned at James. A figure ran into the cave and James realized that it really was his aunty, Janice. "Aunty Janice, I'm glad to see you but how did you find us?" asked James. His aunt ran over to him and squeezed him with a big hug. She said while hugging him "I missed you so much. An aunt always knows how to find her nephew." James uttered "losing light, room getting dark." His aunt let him go and said "wow James, I haven't seen you in so long." James replied "you saw me a couple days ago." Aunty Janice said "oh I know but I always need to see you. Oh, by the way I brought you more beer. I love beer. Don't you love beer, it's the absolute best isn't it?" James said "thank you." She gave him two more six packs. She even gave him a bag that he could use to carry all of his beer while she was prattling on and on about how great beer was and how much she loved James while he looked down embarrassed.

She then said "I have to go but James don't you dare do anything too dangerous. Goodbye." said Aunty Janice as she ran off. James stood there completely stunned. "How the hell did she find me here?" asked James aloud. Everyone was laughing so hard now because they couldn't hold it in. James said loudly "not one word." The group stopped laughing and James walked outside the cave for a moment. After he left the cave, the group started laughing at the top of their lungs once more. Somehow all that chaos and laughter never attracted any of the guards to their location.

A couple hours later everyone else had fallen asleep except for Jake. He felt really alone. He knew his father was near but he couldn't trust him and even though he has his friends he still thinks he's missing something. He had a bad pit in his stomach and his head hurt. He heard someone walk behind him and sit next to him; it was Jeb. Jeb looked at his son and said sincerely "listen Jake I know that I have done some bad things but I am still your father. Please listen to me son." Jake really didn't want to listen but Jeb was still his father. He turned to face Jeb. He said coldly "I'm listening." Jeb said to him "I think I should explain why I left you. When I met your mother, I was extremely happy. She made me feel like I could be anyone. Before I met your mother, I was severely depressed. I wanted to commit suicide but your mother helped pull me out of my depression. When I found out she was pregnant with you I couldn't have been happier. I was excited to be a father but I also had a lust for power. It was that lust that made me pick obtaining more power over my own son. That has always been my biggest regret." Jake turned away from him. A tear shed down Jake's cheek. He felt so upset by this. Jeb put his hand on his son's shoulder. "I wish I could change everything. I want to have you back in my life. I don't want to be your enemy." Jake knew he was sincere but he just couldn't seem to trust him. Jake took his father's hand off his shoulder and he said "I hear what you are saying but I just can't trust you Jeb." Jake got up and left. Jeb seemed heartbroken.

He laid his head down in shame. After a few hours James returned and everyone had fallen asleep. James walked over to where Stacy was sleeping and he laid down next to her. He wrapped his arm over her and he fell asleep. 12 hours later. Stacy woke up and she noticed James' arm was around her. She playfully punched him in the arm to wake him up. He awoke with a start. "What was that for?" he asked jokingly. "You were fast asleep. As much as I liked seeing you asleep, I thought you should get up. This is my way of waking you up." James rubbed his arm and said sarcastically "well in that case, thank you so much for waking me up really early." Stacy giggled at James. He got up and she got up as well. James walked over to the cave entrance and he saw the sun was coming up. The morning dew was just coming out on the rocks. James woke everyone else up and they sluggishly got up. They decided to leave for the platform now. It was a few miles away. They spent a couple hours trying to evade the guards and trying to get there as quick as possible. Eventually they made it to the platform. James gestured for the group to stand on the platform. He noticed two pillars, one on each side of the platform.

Homecoming At Long Last

James put one stone in each pillar. He went to the center and he wished that "I wish that we would all be sent to my own time." The stones obeyed James' command. The stones began to glow and everyone else began to see the platform was glowing as well. The entire group began to feel like they were being taken away from here. The next thing they remembered was the entire group ending up in King Rathos' tomb. James knew the world was out of balance and he didn't want the three former prisoners to have to deal with this. He said "I think you should stay here until I return. The world we are in now has problems that only me and my group can fix." The former prisoners understood and they agreed to let them deal with it. Caroline offered to help as well. James' group liked the way she fights and they know she is capable. Simon said "we would really appreciate your help." Caroline was delighted that she could help out. She, James, Jake, Dr. Jeb, Simon, Stacy and Christine left the tomb and walked outside. Caroline was completely horrified to see what had happened. Everything was completely out of balance. The pyramids were destroyed and the sphinx's face had been cut out and replaced with Basilisk's helmet with his red eyes. James quickly explained the situation to her. He mentioned everything Jeb did and how Jake is his son. He then mentioned Basilisk's rise to power and how he needs to be stopped. Caroline understood the situation completely.

It was a lot for her to take in but she knew that she had to help, now more than ever. She said "wow a lot has happened here." Parts of the earth were also opened up and everything was scarred. Christine wanted to know where Basilisk was. She wanted to put him in his place. Simon could hear what Christine said about Basilisk. He said to her "I'll try to find out where Basilisk is Christine." Christine looked at him but she was really surprised. She said "I never said anything about Basilisk. I was thinking about how I want to know where he is though." Simon realized that he had read her mind. The group were amazed by this. Simon has been getting stronger. He suddenly had a really sharp pain in his forehead. He fell backwards and he hit his head on the ground. Simon began to have another vision. He saw Schreiber. He saw everything coming apart. He then saw that Basilisk was oppressing the remaining humans. All the live ones are being forced to work in internment camps. Basilisk's army bowed down to him. He also saw that the army was getting rid of the humans because the army believes that they killed their former master Jeb. Their banner also says Down with the humans, down with the oppression and down with the death.

Finally, it showed Basilisk hiding inside a giant castle. The castle was really big. It had cannons connected to the walls. It also had giant metallic walls. It also has a gigantic gate which only opens once every two days to allow the soldiers to collect food and taxes. The image slowly started to fade and Simon started to regain consciousness. He started to gasp for breath heavily. His group came to see him and he explained what he saw. Jake came up with a suggestion. He suggested "I think we should attack the castle head on." James considered the idea but he said "I see your point but I don't think we would be able to attack the fortress. The fortress is impenetrable from the outside." The group bowed their heads. They couldn't think of anything else to do. James had a thought. He said "the fortress may be impenetrable from the outside but not from the inside." The group started to perk up. James continued. "The gate opens every two days. If we can get in then we can destroy Basilisk from the inside. I have a plan for it. First, we should show the soldiers Dr. Jeb. If they realize that Basilisk was lying then they may side with us. If they don't then we sneak onto one of the soldier's vehicles and let them take us in. Then we navigate the castle and use the two stones to overpower Basilisk and then force him to expose his treason. He will lose the respect of his followers and they will turn against him." Everyone seemed to like the idea. Caroline said "that's a good plan James." Simon thought something was off with Caroline. She seemed to really feel close to James as she was hanging off his every word and hanging near him constantly.

He stared into her eyes and he was able to read part of her mind. Most of what he saw was James and Caroline making out in the cave when the others were trapped in prison. Simon felt really angry at this. He decided he wanted to try to send James a message through his mind. He stared into James eyes and he sent the message "I know what you did with Caroline." James received the message and he instantly became nervous. He was able to hide his nervousness well but he knew Simon was really pissed at him. Simon wasn't as interested in James' plan anymore but he knew that this was the best plan. He knew that if Jake was going to try to mess with James, he wasn't going to stand by James anymore. James betrayed everyone to have a hookup with some random girl he just met. He could have been using that time to break us out of prison thought Simon. James asked everyone "everyone ready." The others replied "yes." James made a wish on the two stones and the stones glowed together.

The two stones slowly merged into one to make one ultimate stone. Everyone started to glow and they felt themselves being pulled to Schreiber. When Schreiber came into view it was completely destroyed. All the buildings were torn apart and they were replaced with concentration camps and worker camps. The trapped humans are being forced to dig in the mines for jewels for their leader. The humans were also being forced to do manual labor to power all the generators in the town. The town is filled with posters of Basilisk crushing pathetic humans. There is also a giant statue of Basilisk in the middle of the town. It doesn't even look like a town anymore. It looks more like a prison. Near the group are the remains of the Cenotaph. On the ground near the remains are a tattered Canadian flag covered in dirt. Christine ran over to the flag and she started to cry. This clearly meant the loss of humanity. Her eyes began to burn because of all the tears. After a few moments her expression shifted from grief to anger. She wanted revenge against the beings that caused her and her friends so much pain. She yelled out "YOU'RE DEAD BASILISK!" The feeling in the air was a scared and angry sensation. Simon walked over to Christine and he put his hands on her shoulders. He started to massage her neck. Christine liked the feeling of Simon's hands on her. Christine then started to hear a voice in her head. The voice said "It'll be okay Christine. We will take out Basilisk." The voice was Simon's. She loved that he could read and send messages into people's minds. Simon eventually let go when Christine started to feel comfortable. Suddenly when James turned to his left, he saw the gigantic castle before him.

It was extremely huge. Looks like the plan was going to have to begin now. Soon the rest of the group saw the huge castle and they became even more determined to see those giant metallic walls fall. James turned to the group and asked "is everyone ready?" The group nodded in agreement. Jeb went first and he ran up to the large gate. He began banging on it but no one was around. Simon ran up to the gate and he used his abilities to look through the wall by creating a small portal. He realized that there wasn't anyone behind the gate. A machine is used to open the gate and it only activates when soldiers are coming through. James turned to the group and said "I suppose our only plan is to sneak on a caravan when it comes through." Everyone agreed with his idea. Suddenly the sound of a vehicle was in the air. A caravan was coming right towards them but the driver didn't notice the group. Christine waved her hands in the air and everyone turned invisible. Everyone was completely shocked by this but then they became ecstatic. They could now sneak onto the caravan. As the caravan came closer the group jumped onto the sides of the caravan. They were holding onto some handles that were attached to the sides. The caravan stopped at the gate.

The gate started to open and the caravan went inside. The interior was really impressive. the castle went up thirty floors and there were guards everywhere. There were signs that lead to prisons, break rooms, execution room, armory and the throne room which is at the very top. the group jumped off the caravan and they headed up the stairs that led to the thirtieth floor. They went up floor after floor which took hours. Finally, after a long time they finally made it...they made it at least to the fourth floor. The floors were gigantic and Christine can't hold the invisibility for a long period of time so she has to keep dropping it and they have to take cover from oncoming guards. Jake was getting really fed up but not at James oddly enough. He grabbed the stone from James' pocket and he made a wish. "I wish we would be taken to Basilisk." The stone shined and the group was being whisked away to Basilisk's throne room. The group appeared in front of him and Caroline asked "why didn't we just do that earlier?" The group was now muttering "yeah why didn't we just do that." The group then noticed Basilisk sitting on his golden throne. Jeb came forward and said "you tried to kill me Basilisk but you failed." Basilisk stood up and came forward and he started to laugh cruelly. "You are weak Jeb. I didn't need to kill you to take back my followers." Basilisk drew his blade and pointed it at the group. Jeb could feel the hatred emanating from him. That and his indomitable will caused Jeb to double over in shock and awe at the power coming from him. Jake threw the stone back to James.

James made a wish to the stone. "I wish that me and my group could absorb your power." The stone did what he wanted. James, Stacy, Christine, Jake, Simon, Jeb and Caroline absorbed all of the power. They all ran forward and they kicked Basilisk in his chest. This attack caused him to go flying into his throne and denting it. Basilisk got up and he ran towards Jake. Basilisk's sword was drawn and the power of this sword would tear Jake to pieces. Jeb sensed the danger so he threw himself in between Jake and Basilisk.

The sword went into Jeb's heart, killing him instantly. Basilisk picked up his sword and he threw him out the window. Jake immediately fell to his knees. No matter how powerful his hatred was for Jeb, he was still his father. Jake rose to his knees. He lunged at Basilisk and he knocked his sword out of his hand. He then picked up his sword and he quickly cut off Basilisk's head. Basilisk's head rolled off his body. Blood splattered everywhere. Jake felt powerful. He yelled at the top of his lungs "DEATH TO TYRANTS." James quickly came over and he held Jake's arm. Jake stared at James but it wasn't in hatred. He was finally starting to truly like James. James didn't like that Jake killed him in anger but he was glad that Basilisk is dead. The stone started to glow brightly. A ball of light shone down outside on Jeb's body. The light carried him back up to the castle and it resurrected him. Jeb's eyes came open and he felt so free. He felt like he was a 19-year-old again. Jake ran over to him and he hugged him hard. Jeb had done some really bad things but Jake still really cared about him. The group seemed somewhat happy to see Jeb alive because they knew Jake still really loved him.

The happiness in the room came to an abrupt end because Basilisk's head had fallen out the window and the guards noticed. Soldiers were busting in through the doors with swords and axes drawn. They were out for blood. One guard started to come forward until he saw Jeb "Master?" asked the guard quietly. The other soldiers started to notice Jeb and all of them muttered "master." They bowed down to him. Dr. Jeb came forward and said "my soldiers. I am alive. Basilisk lied to you. It wasn't the humans who tried to kill me; it was Basilisk himself. He usurped my throne and he turned all of you against the human race." The soldiers felt remorse for what they have done. They thought that genocide was the only way to avenge their master but he wasn't even dead. Suddenly Basilisk's body started to glow. The power that Basilisk had absorbed from the stone is now being released from him and is trying to find a place to go. The power is deciding to go into the direction of James.

With the power coming towards him James turned to his side with his arms out on each side and he turned his head in the direction of the power. James absorbed the power into his fingertips and he started to channel the power through him. It is going in through his fingertips, through his chest and out his other arm. James released the power out the window. The energy wasn't just going to stay in the air. It was actually heading outside the earth's atmosphere and it was now creating a barrier around the earth in order to protect it. James then put the stone into a pedestal that was close to Basilisk's throne. The stone shined together and the world was now starting to regain its balance. All of the buildings were starting to be rebuilt and all the humans that were dead were being resurrected. Jeb said to his soldiers "humans are our friends and our two groups can live together in harmony." The soldiers decided to befriend the humans and live in peace together. A few days later the prisoners from medieval times showed up in Schreiber and they ran into James and his friends. Caroline was now a permanent friend of theirs. Judith came up to James and she said "thanks for saving us from the execution block." James replied "no problem. I'm glad I was able to help out." Judith turned to her friends and she decided to introduce them. First, she introduced the 14-year-old. "James this is Ian." Ian waved to the group with his good arm. Next Judith introduced the forty-year-old man. "This is Walter." Walter said "hello." James said "nice to meet you both." Over the last few days Jake has been hanging out with his father a lot and he has been neglecting his friends.

He seemed to be really happy when he was his father. Everyone decided to head to the Recreation centre to get some food once things settled down. There was a barbecue going on. On the way there Jake started to hear the two voices again. The light voice said "you shouldn't be spending time with Jeb. He may be your father but he can't be trusted." Next the darker voice showed up and said "Jeb is the only one you can trust now. You need to stay with him." Jake decided to do what he wanted now. He blocked one of the voices from his head and he only listened to one now. "That was a really good choice, Jake." said the darker voice. An evil grin spread across Jake's face.

Meanwhile:

□James and Stacy were talking at her place alone at last. James turned to her and said "listen Stacy, me and Caroline had a moment when I couldn't get back into the prison to save you guys right away. I really am sorry, but I realized you are the only one I want." Stacy tilted her head to her side and said "that's it James? You and I weren't even dating at that point so that's fine. I'm just glad you didn't abandon us after the fact." James smiled and kissed her deeply. "I'm glad we are finally dating." Stacy beamed and said "me too. Want to head to my room?" James nodded and they began kissing all the way up the stairs until finally landing on her bed. They were finally at peace; but somewhere across town Simon was watching them with his powers. He was angry that Stacy forgave him so easily and dialed his phone. He had allies to call.

One year later:

A year ago, a warrior named Basilisk tried to enslave the world with his armies. He spread darkness across the world and he threw the world out of balance. It seemed like there was no hope to save the world. Then out of nowhere seven warriors appeared. They faced Basilisk head on within his palace. Together they overthrew him and brought light back to the world. After this event, Doctor. Jeb who had been trying to kill James and his friends for months, decided to side with them and take care of Jake, his son. He also told Basilisk's armies who are now his armies to stand down. Now his men live in peace with the humans and they accept each other. Dr. Jeb is a tall man with a pointy nose, white frizzy hair that's been cut short, and grey eyes. After that the group parted ways and they had lost contact with each other.

James and Stacy were currently attending Lakehead University while dating and studying philosophy, Jake was living with his true father and was also attending Yale, Simon and Christine are still in high school, and Caroline was living in Kingston, Ontario and she was working at Green Earth. As for the three prisoners from medieval times, they have changed since they came to the real world. They were starting to adapt to the real world...well sort of. Walter has been really enjoying his life. He is starting to get a fair amount of hair on his head and he has many self-inflicted scars on his legs that are slowly beginning to heal and fade. His hair is black and he has blue eyes. He is about 5 1/2 ft tall. He realized that he absolutely loves the food industry and he feels that he has the best job ever. He is working at...Macdonald's.

He loves the hamburgers and he is excited to be working the grill all day long for low pay. He loves living in Thunder Bay. Judith on the other hand has been living a good life. Judith is a young 27-year-old woman. She has long black hair and she is pretty slim. Her left leg used to be badly wounded but now it is as good as new. She has bright blue eyes and she has nice white skin. She is living in Calgary and is a best-selling author. She has just recently published her third book. Ian has lived an alright life. He was very depressed for the duration of five months after he came to the real world. He received therapy and he is doing a lot better now. He is now 15 and he is attending Lake Superior High School. He has short black hair and he has hazel eyes. His left arm was cut off but now has a prosthetic arm. He never used to want to talk to anyone but now once he starts, he can't stop talking. He can talk for long periods of time without getting tired. People still do like him but they find him kind of annoying. Out of the three prisoners Judith is doing the best in the real world so far.

Meanwhile Simon and Christine are enjoying the peace throughout the world. They are also enjoying the glory that has come from them saving the world. The entire town treats them like celebrities. They are extremely popular and they get lots of respect from everyone. Christine is close to 6ft tall. She has long purple hair and bright blue eyes. Her skin is white and she is more confident with herself. She is 17. Simon is somewhat tall. He is about 5/11. He has brown eyes and long red hair. His skin is white and he is 16. The story begins at Lake head University.

James is sitting alone in his trashed dorm. There are books scattered everywhere, the walls are cracked and James' picture of him with his friends is broken and laying by his bed. He knows that what he did was a mistake. The air was filled with regret and sadness. He wished he could go back in time and prevent it from happening. Suddenly a blue light appeared in front of him. Startled, James sat up and he walked near the light. The light seemed to form something. As he got closer, he saw a face that looked very familiar to him. He soon was standing only inches away from the light and he looked at the person standing there. He tried to speak but couldn't. He was filled with so much emotion. He hadn't seen this person in what felt like a long time. He finally uttered the word "mom?"

A week earlier. On September 29th James is sitting in his business classroom listening to his professor. James is a 6ft man with green eyes and white skin. He has somewhat long brown hair and he is 18. Sitting next to him is his best friend and girlfriend Stacy. She is very slim and tall. She is slightly shorter than James. She has green eyes and has white skin. She has long brown hair and she is also 18. They are listening to their professor who is giving a lecture on accounting. The bell rings soon after and James and Stacy are free to go. This was their last course for today and they are heading to a Tim Horton's to grab some coffee. Stacy follows James out of the classroom and to his Green with black stripes Corvette. It is a nice warm day outside and the air feels good. Stacy gets into James' car with him and they drive off.

After a short drive they get to the nearest Tim Horton's and they order two coffees. James pays for both of them and they sit at the nearest table. Stacy says "so how are your courses going?" James replies "pretty good I guess." Stacy knows something is bothering him. She grabs his hand and she asks "what's wrong?" James says softly "I'm upset that I can't find my father. I know that I will probably never get the answers I am looking for but I still want closure." Stacy nods in agreement with him. She knows that this is a very sensitive topic and that she needs to tread lightly on it. At that very moment a worker comes up to their table and says "here is your French vanilla Capuchino." She hands the drink to James. James says "I never ordered this." the worker says "I know but that gentleman over there ordered it for you." She points to a very tall man with a large grey trench coat. He had his hood on so his face isn't visible. The man soon decided to get up and head outside.

James decided to thank the worker and starts to drink his coffee. He looks closer at the cup and scrawled in black marker is written very lightly "Adams." James quickly shot out of his seat and he ran outside. He tried to look for the man but he was nowhere to be seen. The air started to feel cold. Grey clouds began to block the sky. Soon it started to rain. James felt so lost. A feeling of depression and anger took over him. He slowly sunk to his knees. Stacy looked out the window and she saw him. She jumped out of her seat and raced outside. She ran over to him and she put her hand on his shoulder. "What's wrong James?" James slowly raised his head. His eyes had become red. There was lots of strain in his muscles and stress. She could see that in his eyes he only feels pain. James said quietly "I think I saw my father." Stacy couldn't believe what he had just said. There was a lot of tension in the cold air. Stacy grabbed his arm and said "let's go back inside. It's cold out here." James picked himself up and he led her back inside. They didn't say anything the whole way in.

The Start Of Something Awful

Meanwhile in Schreiber Ontario, Simon and Christine are just getting out of their Psychology course. The last class of the day has just ended. A feeling of happiness dawns on the entire school. They can't wait to get out of here. Simon was throwing a party at his camp. Everyone was incredibly pumped to go. Simon left the classroom and he headed to his locker. On the way there he gets tons of high fives and chest bumps. He has become increasingly popular.

Christine follows close behind and she gets tons of high fives as well. Christine's locker is ten lockers down from Simon's. Simon goes to his locker and he opens it. He grabs all of his books and then walks with Christine to his car outside. As they walk Christine asks "you ready for tonight?" Simon replies "I think so. I have everything I need for the party." Christine says "that's good. Oh, hey by the way I talked to Jake and he said that he might be able to come down for the party tonight." Simon said "sweet, it'll be good to see him again." Suddenly a loud vibrating sound came from Christine's pocket. She felt around in her pocket until she fished out a small black cell phone. She flipped it open and she noticed a notification saying she got a text. She read the text and her face brightened up. She said excitedly "I just got a text from Caroline. She said that she is coming down and that she is going to come to your party." Simon's face tensed up. He did not like this news. He tried to hide it by saying "great." He didn't mean it though. He has been really pissed at Caroline since James screwed his friends over during Medieval times and made out with her.

If he hadn't screwed them over then maybe they could've avoided the execution bloc k... wow that isn't something you hear every day. Simon has been holding onto this little tidbit of information for a long time. He really wants to tell everyone but he is waiting for the right moment. He didn't trust James anymore. Whenever he tried to get in touch with Simon, he always ignored both his and Caroline's calls. Simon got into his car with Christine and they drove off towards Simon's house to prepare for the party. James and Stacy were also planning on coming down for the party. He hated that but knew he had to keep the peace with everyone. Lately he and Jake had been closer than ever and would vent to each other about their dislike towards James. Jake finally got himself clean from the drugs and drinking and is doing a lot better. He now has short blonde hair and is quite lean. Simon still had his typical short red hair but was loving it regardless. He's 5 11 and was proud of his height. Christine kept her look and has long purple hair. She's 6ft and is considered very attractive by the rest of her classmates. Simon always wanted to ask her out but decided they were better off as friends. Simon decided to head up to his camp with Christine in tow after school let out.

As they arrived to the camp at Walker's Lake, the wooden exterior looked amazing as always. The camp had a big deck jutting out from the main floor and had a basement that could be accessed through the use of swirling wooden stairs that branched off from the main floor. The basement had a big space down there enough for multiple people to play games on a big tv while the main floor had more than enough room for games like beer pong or card games. Simon couldn't wait for everyone to get here. He was so proud of Jake for kicking his bad habits and gained a lot of muscle mass. Jake was probably on par with James now physically. Simon hadn't been to the camp in a while so he made sure to do some light cleaning while Christine helped set up decorations to make the place look nicer. Christine may not have had romantic feelings for Simon anymore but she was going to do everything she could in order to make sure the party was a success.

Soon after all the prep was done, students began to pile in a couple hours later as the sun was beginning to set. As everyone came in, they greeted Simon and Christine with fist bumps and hugs. Both Simon and Christine were so happy to see everyone and were eager to party all night. Eventually Jake came in and Simon and Christine rushed forward to hug him. "Jake! You're here!" yelled Simon as he wrapped Jake in a bear hug. Christine rushed him from the other side with just as much enthusiasm. Jake while surprised happily reciprocated. "Good to see you too guys" he said happily. Soon after James and Stacy came in along with Caroline. James did have a small fling with Caroline but he was completely over that now and Caroline was the same.

Stacy and James were holding hands as Christine rushed over to hug them both. While that happened Simon went over to Caroline and gave her a fist bump. "Hey Caroline glad you could make it" Simon said fake happily. Caroline smiled in response. "Right back at ya man." Simon handed her a drink of beer and then grabbed drinks for James and Stacy as well. Simon got into brewing as a hobby and with the help of his earth spirit he has been able to make contact with the other three elements. Together he made the best beer around. He circulated the beer around until everyone and then he proposed a toast. "Hey everyone, I would like to say a toast. I'm happy everyone's here and that we can chill together again. To friends! Old and new!" said Simon happily as he raised his cup in the air. Everyone else did the same as they sipped the best brew they ever had. After that, everything went black.

The First Trial

JAMES AWOKE WITH A start in a dark hallway. His right foot was chained to the wall and he couldn't pry it off no matter hard he tried. James took a moment to examine his surroundings. The hallway was pretty narrow, only big enough for him to fit in comfortably. There seemed to be doors on either side and the rug and walls were a dark red. Any light he saw were from the use of torches that flickered in the night. James had no idea how much time had passed but he felt tired and hungry. It must have been days at least. The area around him was pristine but he had no idea how he even got here. The last thing he remembered was drinking with his friends at Simon's party and then he must have blacked out. James examined the chain again and saw that it looked secure except at the very edge. With all of his strength he pulled and managed to pull the chain out of the wall. Then it was quick work to pry it off of his leg. James decided to keep the chain though since it could be used as a decent weapon if needed. James kept the chain on his arm. Since James awakened his powers, he didn't need to eat or drink as much as he used to.

James crept forward and went to the door to his left to see if he could make sense of where he was. The door looked beautiful and wooden with a red and black finish and an ornate doorknob. James pushed the door open and saw a giant tablet in the middle of an otherwise empty room. A second glance revealed a chest in front of the tablet but nothing else in the room. James walked towards the plaque and saw that an ancient inscription could be found on it but he could understand it. He who is the chosen one can wield this weapon and shall be bathed in golden light read the text. With all of James' training he knew that could outrun anything and was one of the strongest people in existence so he knew from a fighting standpoint he could handle most things that came up against him; but from a mental standpoint he was in trouble. He wished Simon was here to help him.

He knew that Simon held a grudge since he didn't immediately go to rescue them back in medieval times but he did the best he could. Caroline was great but she just a fling and he'd never do anything with her now. He told Stacy about it of course and Christine found out. Neither of them cared and both knew that James couldn't rush into save them right away due to timing and circumstances. They later forgave him but Simon and Jake both don't talk to him much lately. James was hoping that this party could be a way to help mend fences but that apparently wasn't going to happen anytime soon. James examined the chest and decided to open it. Pushing the lid was easy and once it ripped open with a crack; James was able to see what was inside. It was a beautiful one-handed sword with an ornate hilt. The beauty of the sword reminded him of the Master Sword from Legend of Zelda. Of course, the sword here was completely different, the radiance of it brought a tear to James' eye as he had nostalgic thoughts of playing Legend of Zelda with his friends. Overcome with awe, James gingerly picked up the blade with respect and it fit perfectly in his left hand.

The moment his grip was adjusted correctly, he could feel a peaceful sensation coming over him and the sword began to glow with golden light. James instantly knew that he could control the light and shoot it as beams. And he also realized that he had a mastery over weapons like this. He may not have remembered all the details of his previous reincarnations, but he knew that he fought against Dr. Jeb in every one with allies. And that he was always close with his friends which would never change. Putting his arm to the side while pointing the sword downwards; he decided to explore the rest of the area in order to figure out how to leave. Heading into the next room revealed that the room matched the same theme except this one was occupied. James was over 6 ft but the opponent in front of him stood over ten ft tall and nearly touched the ceiling. The enemy before him was a startlingly tall silver armored knight with horns on his helmet and red eyes could be seen from the hilt of his helmet. The knight drew a beautiful black sword that singed with the power of blood. James could smell the copper in the air. Other than drawing his weapon, the knight did nothing as if waiting for something.

James not knowing what else to do decided to walk forward. James kept his sword drawn but knelt to one knee in order to show respect for his foe. The knight in response also knelt to one knee to show respect. This man was clearly a man who appreciated the ancient customs. Once the kneel was over both warriors stood up and the knight slashed towards James. James ducked and barley managed to get his sword up enough to grind against the enemy's. James tried to stab towards the knight's midsection but with surprising speed the knight bounced away and leaned forward while holding his sword pointed behind him as if he wanted to run with it. James took the opportunity to jump as high as he could and slash his weapon towards the knight's head.

As the knight moved to block James faked him out and actually aimed the sword towards his arm. James' blow connected and he cut off the knight's right arm which held the sword. The black sword clattered to the ground as the knight clutched the stump where his arm used to be. James backed up in order to do another lunge when the knight began to screech. "EEEEEEEEEEEEEEEEEE" yelled the knight as his armor began to come off in waves as the person underneath turned out not to be a person at all. It was Jeb but with the features of a wolf. The Jeb creature dropped to four legs and began to lunge toward James. "I regained my memories when I took the first serum James, I knew that you would lie dead at my feet regardless of what you did." James took his sword and tried the jumping maneuver again but Jeb dodged it and scratched James in the back with his razer sharp claws. "AHHHHH"! screamed James as he fell to the ground. He could feel poisonous blood rushing into his veins and he screamed in agony. Jeb smiled through his wolfish teeth and rushed James again.

This time James strained to use aim his sword towards Jeb and then stabbed into the ground with all of his might. What James had been unknowingly been doing was collecting golden energy from the blood magic Jeb was using and sent it back towards Jeb in constant waves until James passed out from exhaustion. The golden power healed all of James' wounds and he woke up soon after. James saw that Jeb was disintegrating into nothing and then vanishing into the wind. "Well, you passed the test James. But how will you fare against me?" said a voice coming from everywhere. The voice was deep and familiar but James couldn't place it.

The voice was also laced with hatred and venom so he had no idea who hated him so much. Dust from everywhere began to circulate and collect at the entrance to the room. A figure in a black cloak stepped forward and drew a sword made of pure darkness. "Know this James, I won't be as forgiving or go easy on you like my father did," said the voice. James instantly knew it was Jake and redrew his sword. James and Jake rushed forward and their swords clashed at the same time. "Jake, ugh, why are you doing this?" asked James. "Why else, to finish what I started of course," Jake bitterly replied. The light and darkness of the swords clashed as each side tried to gain an edge over the other but nothing worked. Both were exactly even as Jake and James tried to push but neither could break the stalemate.

At this point, it was a war of attrition unless James could find a way to break the deadlock between the swords. As James tried to backpedal to create space Jake took control of the attempt and forced James's back against the wall. Jake kept pushing and pushing until James' golden light went out and was snuffed out by the darkness.

The darkness also infected James and he began to suffocate as darkness went through his mouth and throughout his bloodstream. Jake sheathed his sword and picked James up by the neck and began to squeeze. James tried to struggle but all he saw was the dead cold look in Jake's eyes and a cruel smile forming. James nearly passed out from the pain when the golden light suddenly re-engaged and pushed Jake back similar to Dr. Jeb. The light didn't kill Jake though, all it did was cut up his arms and body as blood began to flow like a geyser. James struggling to stand up took the opportunity to re-ignite his sword and plunge it deep into Jake's chest. "I'm so sorry Jake, but you gave me no other choice." Jake said nothing as he crumbled into darkness. As the darkness whooshed out of the room James could hear a voice from the entrance once again. "Well done, James, you managed to live up to my expectations at last." "Who, who are you?" gasped James as he doubled over. The figure came towards him and James could see that the man was about fifty years old but there was no doubt about who it was. This man was James's father. "It is good to see you my son" the voice boomed. The man embraced James tightly as both men cried tears of joy at the sight of one another.

James held his father as the golden light continued to heal his wounds and regain his energy. James let go his father and asked, "what happened to you? Jeb told me Jake killed you, and was that you at the coffee place back in Thunder Bay?" Asked James quickly. The man had scars all across his face and he looked battle hardened. Despite that though, his eyes held a kind soul and James could see the affection he had in his eyes. "My son, the truth is that I neutralized Jeb long ago but he didn't defeat me. The man from the newspapers you found wasn't you, it was me. You do have memories from that time and that is accurate but the truth is, I call you my son but you are not. You are actually a clone I created long ago. You are me and I am you. The Smith family are your real parents but I always saw you as a son. I had to leave because you would be in danger if I stayed. Jake never killed me, Jeb wanted to manipulate you and your power to join his side so he could use you as a pawn. He also never loved Jake; he just wants to torture everyone even without his power. I always loved you though my son and I watched over you from a distance. I may have my strength but my power has waned significantly", said older

James. Older James looked strong physically but also with a hint of weakness that was threatening to overtake him.

James took a moment to process his words. "Dad, me, you're saying you left to protect me from Jeb so I could do what you could not. Then why did you make contact at the coffee place then?" wailed James. "My son, I did that because I felt you were ready to know the truth. This reality you are trapped in, you must break out. I am able to communicate with you just like how Elijah contacted you the first time. I know with your power; you can call on any of us whenever you want now. I do not know why you are here, but I came to this place to help you," said older James. "How can you help me?" "I can help you by giving you, my power. It isn't much but it will aid you when you need it most. To do this, you must kill me, and my power will transfer into you. My time is almost up anyway; Jeb inflicted a powerful disease on me that has lessened my lifeforce. I only have a few more days to live; but you need this power son. My strength let me live and age slower well beyond my means but the disease is catching up to me. If you take my power, then you will be strong enough in case the disease infects you as well," said Older James. "Dad, I can't kill you. I don't care if I'm a clone of yours, you're still my dad and I refuse to end your life," wailed James. The man put his hand on James' shoulder and calmly said "I am already dead my son. I have days left at most, and you need my power. I give you my consent to end my life." James began to cry uncontrollably. He wanted to know his dad but he never wanted it to end like this.

He knew in his heart he had to but that didn't make it any easier. "Okay dad, I'll do it." James clutched his sword with a white-knuckle grip and plunged it into his father's chest. Older James looked down at his son with a smile and disappeared into golden light that was absorbed into James' chest. James broke down crying in despair at what he had done and the next place he ended up at was his dorm in Lakehead University. James saw all of his stuff around and he began to destroy it. With his super strength he destroyed the entire room in a manner of seconds and there was nothing left but his bed and a pile of rubble at his feet. The wall had also been destroyed and all that lay outside was a black void of nothingness. James continued to cry as he held his knees to his face. James lost someone else he cared about and never got the chance to say how much the man meant to him.

James cried out in pure agony as the weight of everyone he lost came rushing back. He wanted to summon Elijah's and his dad's spirits but his heart was too fractured in sadness. Suddenly, a blue light materialized and a woman's shape began to take shape. "James, honey, I'm here," the soft voice said. James looked up and said through tears "mom?" The blue spiritual woman smiled softly and replied "No James, it's your aunty Janice. I promise you aren't alone and you will make it out of this illusion. You have spent many days here, but you are not the only one being tested." "What do you mean?" "The truth is, you and the rest of your friends are in training to increase and manifest your powers. Everything that happens here is a part of that trial and the powers you gain will transfer once you complete the journey." James' aunt lifted her hands and materialized a swirling vortex and at the center of it were the other four friends undergoing their own trials.

The Remaining Trials

Stacy woke up covered in sweat and her arms were chained together in a hallway. She broke free of them and quickly grabbed her weapon of choice, a golden bow and arrows. This combined with her endurance and agility made her the perfect choice for her trial. She needed to be able to hit all of the targets at the far end of the room which was the size of a football field. She also had to deal with fireballs being thrown at her and other enemies shooting arrows. If she got hit it could throw her aim off and she had to keep moving to avoid spike ceilings and spike traps jutting up from the floor. Every second she spent waiting meant her death and she couldn't take that chance. She needed to get back to James and their life together.

James watched her with adoration and love as he saw the love of his life battling golems and other enemies as she tried to shoot her arrows at the impossibly far targets. It was clear that the point of this trial was for her to last as long as possible and if she didn't survive long enough, she would die. A few times Stacy got hit with arrows right in her heart but her strength allowed her to shake them off and keep going. Her wounds were healing quickly but she wouldn't be able to last forever. She was stronger than most but not even she could handle this indefinitely.

James kept watch but then realized he could see the others as well. Christine woke up dangling over a pit of lava and had to use her reflexes to get out before she sank. She grabbed her weapons which to her and James' surprise were two obsidian daggers. Christine wasn't much of a dagger wielder but with her powers she could use them flawlessly. That combined with her power of invisibility made her the perfect assassin. With all of her training she could also run quietly so she didn't always have to go slowly if she didn't want to. Christine had overcome a lot since her powers awakened. Her confidence increased significantly and she could do most things now that she couldn't do before like being open with her feelings. After Stacy and James got together, she confessed her feelings to James. James let her down gently and they stayed best friends. Christine was okay with that and decided to stay single to enjoy her life.

Christine's trial was to stand her ground against the things she was afraid of by using her powers offensively instead of just to hide or get away from the enemy. Monsters of different kinds came after Christine but with her daggers and powers was able to cut their throats with ease and monster after monster laid at her feet as she reveled in the bloodlust. She was definitely changing but it was hard to say if it was for the better or not. After the first wave ended Christine deactivated her powers and yelled "Is that all you've got you fuckers!" She then put one of her daggers to her mouth and began to lick the blood clean off it. She then laughed maniacally at the power she was gaining and how strong she was. When the second wave came the monsters were a lot more afraid of her but still kept on charging forward. Christine killed one after the other until there were hundreds if not thousands of corpses dead.

James looked away as he couldn't watch her anymore. He was super proud of her for standing strong but wasn't sure if he liked the new her honestly. He decided to check out his other friends. The next one was Jake and Jake was essentially growling angrily at every single monster in his path like an animal. The monsters also resembled James and Jake wielded a sword made of darkness. To say that this disturbed James was the understatement of the century. Turning away from that happy image, James decided to check on Simon. Simon's trial looked very different than everyone else's. Simon was equipped with a magical staff and had a book of spells with him. Instead of trying to kill monsters, Simon was summoning them as people clad in black and shadow tried to kill him. Some of the monsters he was summoning were disturbing to say the least. Many of them looked like the monsters from the other trials like James' knight, Stacy's golems, and even the James faced monsters. James couldn't see how many shadows were trying to attack Simon but it couldn't have been that many. Under five for sure.

Either way, Simon was also summoning many other monsters as well. It became clear that Simon managed to make contracts with the other three elemental spirits as he was summoning dragons, elves, and water demons. It's quite clear that Simon is incredibly powerful now with his upgrade and training and that he is not someone to be underestimated. Simon was casting spell after spell and while was physically weak his mind was his true weapon. There were a few other shadows that managed to make it towards him but Simon dealt with them swiftly. To James' shock, Simon used his telekinesis to blow one person's brains up, cause one person to have a heart attack, and restrain another person while his elemental beasts devoured the poor soul. James threw up after witnessing this. He had no idea Simon was so angry and powerful. He definitely had to make things right with him before Simon decides to use his powers against James. James had seen enough and backed away from the portals. James knew he had to get out of here. "Aunty, can you help me get out of here?" "Of course, my nephew, you have passed your trials and you have seen the threats your friends pose to you. You must go and save them." She used her abilities to create another portal and this one James could interact with. He stepped through it quickly ready to help save his friends from their tr ials.

The End Of James

JAMES GASPED FOR BREATH as he awoke and realized that he was restrained to an altar. He looked around and saw that he was in an ancient temple of some kind, actually he was in Rathos' temple. He saw the bloodied corpses of Caroline and Rathos lay permanently dead on the floor as well. James felt a pang in his heart at the thoughts of two of his closest friends being murdered so brutally. Caroline had her head caved in and her eyes had been gouged out. Rathos had been stabbed with an ornate sword and it looked like part of him had been devoured by...something that James couldn't identify. There were other corpses as well and it looked like their throats had been slit but he couldn't be sure. One person even looked like she had killed herself by cutting her wrists and bleeding out. All of these corpses were around James in a full circle and he couldn't help but stare into the eyes of every person that was dead. James tried to move but he was being restrained by something he couldn't see. He could hear Jake laughing as Stacy and Christine begged him not to do something he'd regret.

Dr. Jeb appeared standing over James with a new look. His hair had been cut shorter and his face was covered in scars. Jeb smiled happily as he gloated to James. "Well, well, well, looks like I finally have the upper hand. Jake and Simon have joined my side and we are going to finish you off for good this time. Hahaha, I never thought that my own enemies would become some of my strongest allies." James couldn't believe what he was hearing. Jeb removed his hand from his left pocket and cut it with his right hand. The blood flowed but before it could drop Jeb halted it and pulled it back into his bloodstream. The blood swirled around Jeb and it looked like he had gotten an upgrade. "Hehe he James, I've learned a few tricks since I saw you last." Jeb happily licked up the rest of the blood into his mouth and felt euphoric. James couldn't even speak and began to cry inside.

He turned and saw Simon was glaring daggers at him while stretching his hand out towards him. Simon refused to speak and James could feel the invisible restraints closing around him. Jake walked into view and said "alright dad, now it's my turn." Dr. Jeb nodded and backed away with the same smile on his face. Jake kneeled over James and whispered "I always hated you, and I never regretted trying to kill you. I wanted you to be my safe space, but I think I really just wanted control. And now with Simon and Jeb on my side I can do anything." Jake picked up James and began to squeeze his neck as hard as he could. James gasped for breath but couldn't move. No air was coming and he was stuck.

James tried to regain his breath and the golden light began to build up inside of him again. He tried to use it to free himself but he couldn't focus on one target and the energy dissipated. "Looks like your power's failed you, James. Is this really how you want to spend your final moments? Very well then, allow me to finally end this once and for all. Goodbye James, I wish we could have been friends, but killing you is so much sweeter," said Jake. Jake grabbed tighter as Simon chimed in. "Stop enjoying yourself so much Jake, it's taking a toll keeping both James and the girls at bay," he said gruffly. Simon's nose began to bleed from overexertion but he didn't seem that worried or fazed about it. More of an inconvenience apparently. James could only look at Jake and couldn't even say goodbye to Stacy or Christine. James' last thought was of Stacy and how much he loved her. Jake then snapped James' neck and his head popped like a tomato and landed at Jake's feet. Jake released James' body and began to cry. He wept for James but then started to laugh. "HAHAHAHAHAHA, I WON I WON I WON!!!" yelled Jake. He jumped high in the air and did a jig over James' lifeless bloodied corpse. "I wish I still had a rival but I can finally say I put you down for good. I'll miss killing you again but the first time was so satisfying." Jake took James' head and began to kick it like a soccer ball against the wall. Stacy and Christine began to sob in despair at their best friend. "Please you have to stop it"! screamed Stacy. Jake paused his game and said "As you wish" before kicking the head at Stacy's face and ricocheted back to James' body. Stacy was in horror seeing James' lifeless eyes up close as his blood got in her mouth.

She sobbed and screamed as Christine screamed as well. They both loved James in their own ways and wanted him back more than anything. Simon released Stacy and Christine from their confinement and they both ran up to James. Stacy ran to his left side and began to cradle and hold him while Christine took his right side but couldn't touch him. She didn't think badly of Stacy at all for clutching her lover but she herself couldn't touch

James like this. The thought was too saddening and she couldn't remember James like that. She loved him too much as a friend to let Jake and Simon disrespect him anymore than they had already. Jake and Jeb began to leave without saying a word but Simon decided to stay. He walked towards them and said calmly "James is dead, and the rest of the world will be too. If you join me though, I can spare you from the cataclysm if you wish." Simon extended his hand to them. Stacy began to bawl but she wiped her tears and glared at Simon. "No way in hell Simon, I'd never join someone who could do this to one of their oldest friends" she said defiantly. Simon didn't even flinch and turned to Christine. "What about you? I've always loved you Christine and I think you feel the same. Will you join me or will you burn like Stacy and James?" Christine slowly began to stop crying and said "I'm sorry Simon but I can't. I've always loved you too but I can't side with someone who killed James like this. James was our leader and he deserved respect" she said through sniffles. Simon's calm demeanor vanished and a look of anger replaced his expression. "Fine then, you'll both regret this as I murder you myself when I destroy everything else." Simon whistled with his fingers and a giant red dragon flew through the temple. Simon jumped on it and flew it out of the temple forever. Christine sat scared but turned back to Stacy. Stacy grabbed Christine's hands and said "We have to bring James back at any cost." Christine gave a resolute nod and replied "We will. We'll bring him back and take Simon down."

Stacy and Christine looked at where the dragon left through and resolved that no matter what they would bring their friend back and bring peace back to the world.

Immediately after:

James' death took a toll on each member of the group in their own way. Jake took immense glee in watching the life leave James' eyes and was happy to be the one to finally do it. Simon was also happy with James dead but also felt pangs of regret that would get to him at times. Weeks before his party, Doctor Jeb and Jake came up with an idea to eliminate the other members of the group. They needed Simon's help to do it though. Simon refused but agreed to help them kill James on the condition that each member of the group had the option to train in order to become powerful in their own right including James and themselves. Jake disagreed but ultimately went along with it since he wanted to become stronger. Jake and Jeb convinced Simon that the best way to get revenge would be to kill James and then use his abilities to destroy the entire world and remake it in a peaceful and happy image. Simon truly believed this was the best call so he had no qualms against hurting innocent people if he could bring them back using all of their powers anyway. Jeb had also managed to steal the stone back and gave it to Simon so their plan could commence.

Simon decided that he wanted everyone to suffer in some way while also becoming stronger so he created trials for everyone. The trials would involve them killing monsters and other people in order to become more powerful and in tune with their abilities. The monsters would be created by Simon himself and the entire world constructed would be his to control. It would be a good test ground for when he tried to take over the world. He gave Jake an outlet to vent his frustrations, and Simon used his powers to test Christine, Stacy, and James with tough and even heartbreaking things. The spirits James encountered were real and so were the threats. If James had died then he would have died in real life as well. The weapons and power they gained were also real and would be transferred to their real-world counterparts. When the party came Simon drugged everyone and then teleported them to Rathos' temple in Egypt. Dr. Jeb also reclaimed Basilisk's sword and used it to kill Rathos and then Jake killed the rest of the party guests including Caroline. Simon then used his telekinesis in order to manipulate Christine into killing her other classmates while she was in the trial. When she was killing monsters, she was actually killing her former friends.

He also used the trial to twist her mind so that she might be more open to joining him when the time came. The guests were all arranged in front of the altar as a sacrifice and James was placed on the altar itself. Once James awoke and died, Simon would absorb the magical energy into his staff and use it to bring about the end of the world. His version of the end of the world was to summon monsters and demons in order to kill everyone and Jeb and Jake would help kill any stragglers. Simon would then use everyone's powers combined to create a new world with him, Jake, and Jeb as its rulers. After James died and Stacy and Christine rejected his offer, he now stood alone at the top of his obsidian fortress sitting on his throne with Jake and Jeb by his side. Simon still wasn't completely sure if he wants to continue doing this but he knows the time to turn back has already passed and he has to move forward or die trying. Simon clutched his staff and chanted "Gods of the earth hear my plea, lend me your strength and your power. Allow me to be your vessel and end this world! Cleanse it of humanity and let the three of us control you. Slaughter everyone in your path and bring about a new age!" Simon chanted this at the top of his lungs and an earth-shattering crack was heard. Coming out of the woodworks were millions of dragons, demons, elemental monsters, dinosaurs, skeletons, zombies and aliens. And at the helm were the four ultimate elemental gods that served only Simon.

Jake and Jeb each took a dragon with them and began to lead their respective armies across the world to exterminate everyone. This was going to be an amazing genocide and Simon would have a front row seat to it happening. The armies would flatten and crush the entire world from all directions. No one would be safe from his genocide.

The Beginning Of The End

Stacy and Christine were still grieving James' death and both were holding him and crying. The trials each took their toll on both of them as well. Stacy came out of it with many cuts and bruises but they have since healed. Christine also came out with blood covering her and her hair turning a mix between purple and red. Her eyes also turned a sharp red and they looked almost demonic. She looked very goth and Stacy admitted she liked the look. Christine got up first and helped Stacy to her feet. "We have to find help. I think maybe if we can summon Elijah like James could then maybe he could help us," said Christine. Stacy sniffled and quietly said "yeah...you're right. If anyone can help us it would be him." The two of them had no idea how to bring him forth but they figured that maybe meditating would be a good place to start at least. Both of them sat cross legged and tried to focus their minds. They also decided to focus solely on James. Christine thought of all the times that he was there for her and how much she valued being his friend. While she may have been in love with him at one point in time, she had moved on and only saw him as her best friend. She thought of all the times she felt miserable after school and he would stop by and cheer her up. She and Simon were like siblings but James was the one she felt the closest to even if they didn't interact as much. She promised to herself that she would do whatever she could to bring her friend back and make sure he gets to live a long happy life. She focused her meditation on happy thoughts and a hope for the future.

Stacy on the other hand thought about James but in a different way. She thought of each of the intimate moments they shared together and how much she valued him as her partner and friend. She was in love with him for as long as she could remember even when she dated Gregory. She cared for Gregory and truly wanted to be with him, but she was just settling for him and she could finally admit that to herself. James was the only one that she wanted and she was truly happy when she finally got together with him. He was the love of her life and she needed him back. She doesn't know how to live without him. Her thoughts related to solely James and tried to figure out how to summon his relatives.

After what felt like hours of meditating, Elijah finally appeared in front of both Christine and Stacy. Another man also appeared; neither of them knew who he was but based on his appearance they realized it must have been James' father though they had no idea how they managed to summon him. Stacy and Christine bowed reverently to them and said in unison "please help us bring James back. If you both care about him you'll do everything in your power to help us." Elijah and presumably James' father looked at each other and walked towards James' body to examine him. Elijah put his hand out on James' head and said "I'm afraid it's beyond our power to bring him back permanently. But there might be something we can do." James' father nodded his head and said "with our power we can bring him back but only for seventy-two hours. If James can defeat the threat and get the stone back in that time then maybe he can come back permanently. James has a strong soul, if anyone can do it; it would be him" he said sagely. Stacy and Christine clasped their hands together in pure happiness.

James' Final Hours

Elijah and James' father began to chant and their spirits began to disappear into James part by part until only James remained. "Please take care of him" said Elijah quietly as he faded away. At first nothing happened; but then a golden light appeared out of nowhere and James' head began to re-attach to his body. There was a sickening crunch but the transfer was complete and James opened his eyes. His eyes had a golden glow to them but it was still him. Christine ran over to hug him tightly and he reciprocated. "Oh James, I thought we lost you for good there. I'm so glad you're back," said Christine happily. James hugged her back but then he saw Stacy standing nearby crying happy tears. Christine let go of James as he rushed over to Stacy. The couple embraced and happily kissed over and over. "I love you, James." "I love you too Stacy." The two of them held each other but then James slowly let go. "I know the stakes; I only have seventy-two hours until I die again. I can't believe Jake and Simon betrayed us, but we can neutralize them together!" James yelled. Christine and Stacy cheered in agreement and they decided they had to find a way out of there. James smirked and said "When I died, I actually managed to learn a new trick in the afterlife. Check this out." James put both of his hands out and seemed to be muttering something under his breath.

Suddenly a deafening roar could be heard as the beating of wings could be heard entering the temple. A beautiful gigantic golden dragon appeared and bowed to James. "This is my animal companion; he's agreed to help us and is loyal exclusively to me." Stacy and Christine were in awe as James climbed on like a pro and they soon followed suit. Once they were all top of the dragon James pulled off and they flew away. Christine held onto the saddle for dear life while Stacy clung to James as they flew out of the temple and into the night sky. In the distance they could see a rising structure that was pure obsidian and looked like a giant castle. "That must be Simon's fortress. We've got to head there," said James. James flew as fast as he could and landed on the ground by the fortress. James considered using his dragon to fly overhead but the dragon seemed hesitant and James didn't want to push his luck. James and the girls hopped off at the entrance and James turned to his new friend. "Thank you." The dragon smiled and said in a deep ancient voice "you're welcome, it is nice to be reunited with you, old friend. I see many of my dragon brethren from Egypt are here. I was known as the king of dragons back then until my rival took that position from me. That black and red dragon is him. I will go and try to stop him myself and hopefully turn the tide. If we don't meet again, farewell my friends." The dragon flew away and began heading South of where they were. James, Stacy, and Christine all took a deep breath and headed inside the towering fortress.

Father And Son

Meanwhile, on the other side of Egypt. Jake and Dr. Jeb were both standing at a craggy old altar that hadn't been used in eons. "Look at this my son, we can use this altar in order to multiply the power of the stone by infinite. We can truly rule everything and have each of our desires granted forever!" said Jeb maniacally. Jake examined the altar and asked, "how do we do this?" "We need a sacrifice; someone has to act as a conduit so that even if Simon falls, we can still continue the plan. The altar was meant for Simon but we can make do. Would you like to volunteer my son?" asked Jeb with a cold smile. Jake's blood ran cold at that statement. He knew that the true plan was to lead Simon to the altar once he outlived his usefulness in order to gain control of the monsters themselves. Jake had hoped that he and Jeb would rule like father and son, but deep down, Jake knew that it would always end like this and that Jeb didn't care about anyone except himself. Jake also knew that while Jeb claimed that he was abandoned in order to be protected; Jake found out in the trial that Jeb killed his mother and left him with addicts in order to torture him and turn him against James. Jake still took the opportunity to kill James since that was all he wanted but he didn't want to be a pawn in Jeb's games anymore.

Jake turned to Dr. Jeb and said "I won't serve you anymore. We were supposed to be a team but I know you abandoned me because you wanted my powers. I don't regret killing James and I believe you were a good man once; but the greed and the memories from Egypt have twisted your psyche into something awful. We could have been family once; but you made that impossible. It's time to die father." Jake drew his dark sword and lunged towards Jeb. Jeb smirked and sidestepped the blow before extending his hand towards Jake's face. Jeb's blood extended from his hand and held Jake in place.

Dr. Jeb had gained control of Jake's blood now and began to manipulate his movements towards the altar. "My dear boy, did you really think you could overtake me? I am your father and I have learned many more tricks than you could ever imagine. Now go into that altar and be my conduit or I will torture you until you beg me to end your miserable life. I brought you into this world and I will remove you just as easily," said Jeb. Jake tried to fight back against the manipulation but he couldn't help but watch his movements jerkily head to the altar. Jake decided that the only way out was to use his lifeforce ability that he learned during the trial. He meditated as he moved and disconnected his mind form his body. He then patched into his lifeforce and weakened it significantly. He could feel the dizziness getting to him but he pressed on. Eventually he took enough life force and put it into his right hand.

His hand was free and then he materialized a sword of darkness made out of the same lifeforce and threw it at Jeb with surprising accuracy considering the rest of his body wasn't even facing him. The sword swept through the air and skewered Jeb straight through the heart. Jake felt immense relief as Jeb's manipulation left his body and Jake collapsed to his knees. He then used more of his lifeforce to pick Jeb up and force him onto the altar. Jeb coughed up blood in shock at how fast Jake got the upper hand. Jeb collapsed onto the altar and began to wheeze. He knew this was the end and he decided to accept his fate just this one time. He never wanted to be a conduit but maybe he could help his son attain world domination this way. Jeb smiled cruelly at the thought of Jake surpassing him in terms of cruelty as the darkness left his eyes and he took his last breaths.

Jake's Heart

Jake couldn't even put his thoughts into words. For much of his life he had two different voices trying to guide him and they final quieted when he embraced his darkness and his father. But now that he killed his dad, both voices were booming against the inside of his skull. A massive headache overtook his head and he had no clue what to do. Jake was having a crisis of morality and wanted to rid the pain at any cost. It felt like Jake was being split in two and he couldn't help but feel regret for killing his father and for murdering James. He knew both were justified but he couldn't tell which side to give in to. Jake loved violence and embracing his darkness allowed him to do that; but on the other hand, he didn't want to rule a destroyed world but he also didn't want all of this to be for nothing. "What am I supposed to do!!!" yelled Jake to the heavens. Of course, no one had the answer. Jake had to come to terms with this himself. Jake rested a while on the ground and his lifeforce became restored. With powers like these he and his former friends could have reigned as gods and essentially be immortal. But of course, James would never have wanted that. He would have rather given the power to be used by the people and freedom. In fact, that's exactly what he did after Basilisk; then how did Jeb get the stone back? Did he go back in time and find another one? Knowing Jeb that wouldn't be much of a surprise. The magic of the original stone, that can't return since it was given to the people of earth and space. But that doesn't matter. This stone could make things right; but maybe it's best to just let the world burn.

Meanwhile back in Simon's fortress. Simon continued to send out dragons and demons to protect his castle while James, Stacy and Christine fought through each one floor by floor in order to make it to the end. Each floor was filled with unimaginable monsters but James led the charge by killing them all with his sword and absorbing their magic into his weapon. Stacy used her bow so kill off any stragglers and be the ultimate shield when necessary. Stacy's endurance and resistance to damage allowed her to be shot and stabbed through the heart multiple times and still be able to keep on going. She was the ultimate warrior and James was happy to have her by his side. Christine used her stealth to get behind the enemy and cut their throats as they were approaching James and Stacy so they would have less enemies to deal with. The more enemies Christine killed, the more she seemed to revel in the bloodlust. At first, she just seemed to smile more but now she seemed to be gleefully laughing every time she takes a life. Regardless, the three were quite an effective team and the entire castle seemed endless as they went up floor by floor.

Eventually around the twentieth floor the three had to take a break. Christine used her invisibility powers to mask them and they made camp in a minor hallway. They needed to sleep so they set up a small tent in a nearby room and slept while one person would take guard duty. Christine took first watch and while she was waiting in the hallway Simon appeared in front of her. "Hey, please don't shout or try to kill me. I just want to talk" said Simon hastily after seeing her draw her daggers. She lowered her daggers and asked him "what do you want?" Simon gestured towards her with his staff and spoke, "I want you to join me. I know that when I had you kill your classmates in the trial you weren't aware of that but I controlled everything you all went through. I gave you your weapons and I made you a mass murderer. I also put in a slight magic spell into your head that when I appear before you next you would be completely under my command," said Simon slowly. Christine began to shake and held her head in her hands as she began to scream silently. Her insides felt like they were being twisted and she was coming apart at the seams.

It felt like she was being rebuilt atom by atom until she became something completely unrecognizable. Blood began to spurt from her eyes as she tried to resist the urge to go with Simon and follow his commands. She loved Simon sure but she would never betray her friends. Her friends are the ones she cares for and Simon was no friend to her anymore. But on the other hand, James did reject her for another woman. She thought to herself even Caroline got to be with him briefly, why not me? And Stacy that lying bitch already had a boyfriend. There was no need for her to steal James as well. Simon always comforted me when I needed it and Simon was always there for me.

Eventually the blood began to receded and stop flowing as much. Perhaps Simon really knows what he's doing. Maybe I should just give in to what he wants. Life would be a lot easier without constantly worrying about everything. It's obvious that Simon's going to win since he has the armies and the power. He has everything he could ever want except me. He and I would rule over this broken world and rebuild it to create peace. As the thoughts overwhelmed her, she began to stop fighting as heavily.

Her original friendship with Simon seemed to win out and she finally stopped resisting. She dropped her hands and adopted a cold and blank expression as she turned to regard Simon. "What would you have me do master?" she asked. Simon smiled and said "I want you to kill James and Stacy. Sneak into their tent in the other room and cut their throats. Do this and I will reward you greatly my love." Christine smiled happily and nodded eagerly at the chance to serve her new lord. She bowed and drew her daggers. Simon teleported away as she crept up to the tent that housed Stacy and James. She snuck in and looked over at them. James was sleeping soundly and Stacy was sleeping right next to him with her arm around him. Christine put her daggers by Stacy's neck and slashed.

Betrayal And Doubts

Simon returned to his rooftop throne room and felt disgusted with himself. He didn't want to have to do that to her but he needs James and Stacy out of the way. If he can remove them from the chess board then he will be able to take over the world and then bring them back once everything is anew. He would be able to bring back their friendship and he could learn to forgive James. Simon thought to himself at the heart of my core I know that James did the best that he could given that situation. But being near the executioner's block really traumatized me and I feel so weak. I may be able to summon powerful creatures now but back then I couldn't do anything even close to that. I still feel angry that he wasn't doing what I wanted him to do. But in the end, I get that he's human and he did the best he could given the situation he was in. Maybe if he ever comes to confront me maybe I'll try to forgive him. I don't want to have to fight him again. Doing it the first time made me sick, but I felt like it was necessary at the time. I could stop my monsters from spawning but I still need to destroy this world. I could create more but I think I'll hold off. I hope Christine at least kills them quick but I also hope on some level that she manages to fail. I was able to see her because of my magic, and I imagine James will be able to see her as well. Simon was pondering all of this to himself when he heard a deafening explosion of emotion from across Egypt.

He then realized that Dr. Jeb did in fact try to betray him but it seems like Jake managed to get the upper hand. Simon realized it was time to protect himself against Jake decided to take him out as well. Simon extended his hands and summoned the four elemental gods from the four corners of the earth and brought them back to his fortress. He also decided to summon even more enemies in order to keep the fortress secure from Jake or any other enemies that dare to invade him. The smell of death permeated his nostrils and he could hear the screams of people getting squished. The cracking of bones almost became too much to bear and Simon threw up. He couldn't believe he had become this monster. He never wanted to be. But he had to be able to protect himself.

If Jake was willing to kill his father, then Simon himself would definitely be someone who would quickly become a target in the way of power. Now that Jeb's dead it was as if Simon came out of a haze. Now he wasn't sure what he even wanted to do. Does he try to defend himself against any enemy, or does he let his enemies come for him and kill him? One thing's for sure, that black dragon coming towards his fortress is definitely not a friend. Jake and Jeb's armies were still marching despite Jake returning and Jeb nowhere to be seen. Simon was still controlling them. He could pull his forces back but they have to continue the genocide. The world is rotten and it needs to be rebuilt and restored.

Back in the tent, Christine put her dagger to Stacy's neck and slashed. Blood gushed out and Stacy awoke. She grabbed for her neck as the blood continued to flow. James awoke at an instant and tackled Christine to the ground. Christine growled and thrashed like a wild animal while James held her wrists. Christine's daggers flew to the ground and out of reach. Stacy continued to hold her bleeding neck and tried to keep herself steady while her regeneration abilities kicked in. While she was shocked at the initial attack, she had seen it coming. She heard from James how she had acted during her trial and had seen for herself how much she loved killing all the monsters.

James continued to fight with Christine until finally he slammed her head hard on the ground. Christine instantly fell unconscious as blood gushed from her head and onto the floor like a geyser. James knew she wouldn't be out for long but maybe whatever curse she was under would wear off by the time she woke up. James ran to Stacy and held her while examining her neck. "Stacy, are you alright?" he asked worriedly. Stacy gurgled a bit but managed to get out "I'm okay James, just hurts to talk but I'll be fine. I can feel the wound closing up as we speak" she said through a hoarse voice. James kissed her in relief that she was okay and she reciprocated. They both knew they only had a few days to get this done so they poured all of their emotions into the kiss. Grief, happiness, sorrow, frustration, and sadness all in one. After many moments they both pulled back and by that time Stacy's wound had fully healed around her neck and she could keep going. "What do we do about Christine?" asked Stacy. James looked down at her body and said, "we should leave her here for now. I suspect Simon did something to make her turn against us and he won't harm her. She's safest here than she is with us unfortunately" he said sadly. Stacy nodded and they decided to keep going. By now the invisibility had worn off of them both so they knew they had to be ready for a fight. They left the room and dashed up to the next floor in hopes of ending this quickly.

As the two of them ran forward they stuck dead in their tracks when they heard the four elemental gods screeching in pain. It was a loud bellowing sound and the two of them instantly knew Simon was fighting someone dangerous. They heard the beating of wings but couldn't pin point what exactly was going on. Maybe some of the monsters had turned on Simon, or maybe Jeb and Jake had turned against him. They had no idea but they knew that they had to hurry. When James came back to life, he was given a special enchantment around his neck and it would flare with pain as the time limit grew closer. Right now, it had been about twelve hours out of the seventy-two and it was starting to flare up a bit. Not enough to interfere with his fights but enough that it felt like something was slowly closing around his neck and burning it. James clenched his neck briefly and Stacy didn't notice as she was staring out one of the nearby windows. They saw Jake riding a giant black dragon fighting off both their golden dragon friend and the wind elemental Nera who looked like a gigantic blue eagle with tornadoes for wings. Nera slashed at Jake but his dragon kept him upright as his dragon blew out fires tainted with darkness back at both of them. Nera got burned badly across her chest and she fell to the ground and writhed. The darkness was overtaking her as she screeched in pain. Jake's dragon then flew towards the golden one and bit through their friend's chest. The dragon that James had known during his past life had his heart ripped out and was quickly beginning to descent.

Before he could die however, the golden dragon flew up one last time and chomped his teeth against Jake's dragon's head and ripped it clean off. Both dragons descended from the heavens and hit the ground in an explosion of light and darkness. Jake was nowhere to be seen but his dragon was gone and James' friend was lost forever. James knelt to his knees and wept. He was losing everyone from his past lives and he didn't know how he could live with himself. Stacy wrapped her arms around him in a comforting manner and he began to calm down. By now all of Simon's monsters had been redirected from going after James and Stacy and were being used against Jake as he fought to survive. Stacy could see Jake on the horizon decapitating monsters left and right while attempting to goad the other elemental gods to challenge him as noted by his very vulgar and crude gestures towards Nera's corpse. Jake next fought against the fire god Fyra; a giant humanoid figure made of flames.

Fyra conjured a gigantic fireball and threw it at Jake. Jake dodged it and ran up Fyra's body. His dark sword apparently protected him and gave him fire immunity from Fyra's essence. Even from a significant distance away Stacy and James could feel Fyra's power and it slowly burned them. Not enough to kill but enough to know that someone powerful was nearby. Jake continued to run up the fire god's body until finally approaching his head. Jake leaped up and used his sword to completely brutalize Fyra by slashing across his face over and over again until finally the fire god collapsed completely from his wounds and burned out entirely. With two of the gods dying chaos began to run rampant across the world. Nera's influence over wind ended and tornadoes were running rampant everywhere. Fyra's control over fire was destroyed as well and fires began to spread and scorch the earth.

As the gods fell, the world was beginning to die even faster. Simon may have had contracts with the gods but he had no idea this would happen. James and Stacy watched on in horror as Jake went up against the water and earth gods together. The earth god Erai was a gigantic elephant completely made of rock; and the water god Nerefa was a gigantic snake made of water. Both were very dangerous and known for their high durability and defense. They wouldn't be going down easy. James and Stacy decided to keep moving forward and they realized they probably had many more floors to go. Simon's fortress seemed to be infinitely massive and they felt exhausted just thinking about how high it must go. They pressed on and continued to slay monster after monster that managed to get in their way though it was few at most. As they kept going, they could hear the gods' cries of pain as Jake managed to land blow after blow against them. It sounded like Jake was goading each god into accidently hurling their attacks at each other whenever they tried a pincer attack and that was witling down their defenses judging by the sounds that could be heard.

James and Stacy hurried even more and finally managed to close in on the top. When they got to the second last floor, they were horrified by what they saw. Jake had managed to take control of the water god and was using her to fight the earth god. The siblings were both forced to fight each other until both gods eventually died from their wounds. The earth and water gods let out deafening and heartbreaking death cries as they passed away with wounds covering every inch of their bodies as Jake stared on smirking at their deaths. As the two collapsed their control over their respective elements completely vanished.

Earthquakes and tsunamis devastated the entire world and it became clear that Simon was losing control of his monsters as many of them were turning away from Jake and going against Simon. Jake leapt away from the carcasses and landed on the roof of the fortress. James and Stacy ran to catch up. Running as fast as they could they finally managed to make it to the top and saw Jake sauntering over to Simon as Simon was losing control of his magic. All of Simon's monsters were disappearing and he tried to reign them back in; his magic was working against him and began to burn his hands. Simon dropped his staff and book in despair as they turned to ash before his eyes. Simon looked desperately at Jake and attempted to bind him with telekinesis but the backlash of the magic made his power unpredictable and he ended up only hurting himself. Simon's hands continued to sizzle as he ran to the edge trying to get away from Jake. Jake summoned a fireball that he took from the fire god and summoned a gigantic wall of fire between him and James. Jake looked back and said "don't worry James, I'll be right with you. I just got to finish off the leach first," said Jake cockily. James and Stacy couldn't breach the fire and all they could do was watch.

Simon continued to crawl away backwards while Jake sauntered towards him and put his foot on Simon's neck and began to press down. "Please Jake, don't kill me. I'll do whatever you want. I'll give you power, riches, anything! We promised to make the world peaceful again, not destroy it beyond recognition" Simon wheezed out. Jake smiled and pressed down slightly more as Simon gasped for air. "I don't want anything from you, except your death. Once you die, I'll finally have everything. I've absorbed the power of the dead gods and Dr. Jeb's power through the conduit. All I need are your powers and then James and Stacy will be next," said Jake. Jake stomped hard down on Simon's neck and with a sickening crack, Simon ceased to exist. His eyes looked regretful but mostly terrified as he died. "NO! SIMON!" yelled Stacy. Despite him betraying them they still didn't want Simon to die. James felt immense grief but also anger. He pulled Stacy to him and said "I know you love me and you've got my back, but I need to do this alone. Go check on Christine downstairs, I'll hold off Jake," said James confidently but earnestly. Stacy wanted to protest but she could see the look in his eyes that he was determined and wasn't going to be talked out of this. Stacy grabbed him and kissed him quickly and said "be safe" before running off back down. Jake extinguished the flames and turned to James. "You want to fight me alone? That's unwise." He said cockily. James stomped forward with hatred burning in heart and said "enough talk, I hate you Jake and it's time to end this once and for all. You killed someone I cared about, and you killed me as well! It's time to die!" yelled James. James rushed Jake and they both pulled out their respective swords in unison. They clashed again and again as they each tried to get a hit on the other. Now with James at full strength despite the burning sensation in his neck; he and Jake were an equal match and this fight wasn't going to be an easy one for anyone involved. Jake gained nothing from James' first death but he still had enough strength to hold James at bay.

An Emotional Reunion

STACY RAN BACK DOWNSTAIRS as she could hear Jake and James continuing to fight. It was like a whirlwind of slashes and the noises echoed even many floors down. She was deathly worried about James but she knew that he could handle himself. She wished that Simon didn't have to die but she had to hope that his influence over Christine had finally died out. She managed to make it down to where Christine was in record time and Christine was still unconscious. Stacy desperately woke Christine up and awareness began to return to Christine's red eyes. Christine sat up while holding her head and uttered "Stacy? What happened?" Stacy said nothing and wrapped Christine in her arms. "It doesn't matter. I'm just so glad you're okay." Said Stacy through tears. Christine laughed and said "I have no idea what's going on but I'm happy to see you." They continued to hold each other for many minutes until Christine let go. She looked at Stacy sadly and said "Simon died, didn't he?" Stacy nodded with tears threatening to spill over once again. Christine sighed and said "I realize that I attacked you and James while under his influence. I'm beginning to remember everything. Once he died, I could feel his influence fade. I don't know how I knew but I know he passed brutally." Stacy nodded again. Suddenly Christine began to tear up again and said softly "I am so sorry Stacy for everything. I would never want to hurt you both; if you need to kill me, I would understand." Christine stood up and picked up her daggers. "Perhaps my death will take away your pain. I really am sorry and I will miss you and James. Goodbye Stacy" said Christine while smiling through tears. Stacy jumped up and wrapped Christine in an embrace.

The embrace was so sudden that her daggers clattered to the ground harmlessly. Stacy had no words to describe her feelings so she poured every ounce of her emotions into the hug. Stacy cried deeply in despair and grief for Christine's attempted suicide and needed her to know that she was wanted. Christine stood in complete shock before returning the hug. "I understand, and thank you" she said softly. Christine brought her lips up to Stacy's ear and whispered "I want you to know, that you and our friends saved me. I considered suicide long ago." Stacy tensed up at this. "I was so sick of living everyday and I wanted to end it all. Every day felt like a burden and it felt like all my parents did was fight over me and use me as a tool to complete their chores when they didn't want to do them or couldn't. I felt like their weapon and that if I wasn't on top of everything then I was useless to them. I also loved strategy guides and it became my passion and obsession in order to escape those feelings. I knew my parents truly loved me and were just trying to teach me the only way they knew how; but it still caused me so much pain. And yet, I was always worried about putting my parents into debt with my interests and I considered killing myself in order to ease them of that burden. I never saw my life as much worth other than to give it up for someone else. But then I met you and the others. You all taught me that life was worth living and you especially loved hearing me talk about my strategy guides." Christine and Stacy both began to tear up and they held each other tighter.

They had come to a mutual understanding that neither would abandon the other and they together they would help Christine to overcome her self-doubt and other issues. They both reluctantly pulled away when they heard a gigantic boom coming from outside. "James is holding off Jake, we need to help him," said Stacy. Christine nodded with a determined expression and started running back to the rooftop in order to help James. They ran and ran until finally they made it to the top and they saw the fight was now at its peak.

Clash Of The Warriors

James was on top of a tornado/geyser of pure golden light and Jake was the on a dark filled geyser as they fought in the air. Their swords continued to clash until both men began to pant in midair. *Pant pant,* "This isn't getting us anywhere," said Jake. *Pant,* "Agreed," said James. "How about we settle this hand to hand?" Jake smiled in response and said "Let's do it." Both straightened up and tossed their swords to the ground. Using the power of their respective geysers they pushed towards each other and grappled. Jake punched James in the face while James bit into Jake's neck and kneed him in the groin. The both of them clashed and clashed as their wounds opened up with blood and then quickly re-healed before any permanent damage could be done. Christine and Stacy knew that there wasn't much they could do they but just watch and hope for the best. After what felt hours of grueling hand to hand Jake finally got the upper hand and slammed his foot into James' groin. James yelled out in pain as Jake winded up his arm and brutally punched his head in and sent James falling to the ground.

James fell out of the sky and fell deep onto the roof of the fortress. James was still alive and conscious but was dazed. James felt like his bones were on fire from the fight and the burning sensation on his neck was only getting worse and worse. James fought through the pain and lunged through the sky and delivered a brutal sucker punch to Jake which also knocked him out of the sky. The two continued to grapple on the ground and even resorted to biting when necessary. Finally, James had reached his breaking point and yelled "ENOUGH!" James delivered a strong punch to Jake's temple and managed to knock him to the ground. James continued to beat the shit out of Jake and just kept punching until Jake was a bloody stump on the ground and his healing wasn't working fast enough. James kept punching and punching until Jake finally fell unconscious. James then stomped on both of Jake's legs so that even if he did wake up, he wouldn't be able to move. James vented all of his anger on Jake's body until he finally had enough. Jake was still alive but barely. Jake's nose was broken and his eyes had been punched out. All of his ribs were cracked and his arms were scratched up and finished. Jake's breathing had become ragged and many of his teeth had become shattered from the fight.

James panted and stared at his bloody knuckles. James knew in his heart that his rivalry with Jake had finally come to an end. James re-summoned his sword and stared daggers at Jake's body. "I'm sorry my old friend. I wish things could have been different. At the end of the day, you and I are not the same and we will never be able to reconcile our differences. I loved you like a brother and I think you felt the same at one point. But this is goodbye." He said sadly. James teared up and Jake groaned.

Jake couldn't see James but seemed to be saying silently that it was okay. And that he was sorry. James accepted his apology and silent words. He raised his sword in the air and plunged it deep into Jake's chest. Jake groaned and accepted his death. James then removed the sword and decapitated Jake's head. As much as he was going to grieve his former friend; he knew that this was the right thing. Jake also felt immense relief that this was finally over. James turned towards Stacy and Chrstine and said "It's done," before collapsing to his knees.

Christine and Stacy both ran up to him and comforted him. James saw that Christine had been freed from Simon's influence and hugger her happily. All three of them were happy but then...the world was still in ruins. The monsters hadn't been destroyed and were actually multiplying. "ROAR" bellowed a terrifyingly powerful sound came from the other side of Egypt. James grabbed Christine and Stacy and used his powers to fly over to where the sound was coming from. Stacy climbed on James' back and Christine grabbed James' right hand as they flew overhead. After what felt like an eternity, they finally managed to come across the altar that Simon had created. Jeb's corpse was still bleeding out into the altar but a giant black dragon appeared and it wore parts of Jeb's face on it. Apparently, even with Simon's death as long as someone or something acted as a conduit to the power, the monsters could still spawn and end the world. And this dragon seemed to be the manifestation of that power. James tried to fly closer to get a better look when the dragon turned and blew fire that was mixed with all the other elements. It hit James square in the chest and him, Stacy and Christine all began to fall. They hit the ground hard and blacked out.

The End Of Times

"Cough, where am I" asked James as he woke up in a daze. James woke in a nice cool and dark forest and standing in the distance was Elijah. "Elijah?" James asked incredulously and ran to embrace him. Elijah did so as well and said "It's good to see you cousin." The two stayed like that for a while and felt at ease. James also saw the spirits of his father and even saw Jake and Simon there as well. "Am I dead?" James asked. James' father replied "no son, you're not dead. But you're nearly there. If you want to win this fight you need all our help." James looked at Jake and Simon and said angrily "Why the hell did you cause all of this chaos? Was it just to kill me for being better than you? Or for not saving you the moment you needed me when there was nothing I could do! The two of you are pathetic." Jake and Simon both had the good nature to at least appear embarrassed.

Simon spoke first "I can't explain why I did what I did. I was so angry with you; I think Dr. Jeb infected me with something that amplified my greed but I'm not sure. Still though, that's not an excuse for doing what I did. I'm really sorry James." Simon bowed to the ground and put his head in the dirt to show just how sorry he was. He seemed to be truly remorseful. Jake came forward and said "I did always hate you; that's true. My dad didn't have to manipulate me to help him but I do regret how far things went. We were like brothers and when you killed me; you freed me from my darkness. I really am sorry James and I don't expect your forgiveness. But I will help you and make things right if you will allow me and Simon to." Jake also bowed to the ground and started crying. James sighed and said "I can't forgive you both for what you did, but if you really want to make things right then I could use your aid in this." Jake and Simon smiled and stood up. "We won't let you down" they said in unison. James turned back to Elijah and his dad and said "thank you all, for everything." He hugged them both tightly and then began to meditate.

After many hours of meditating James finally awoke next to Stacy and Christine. All three of them were injured but alive. Then ghostly figures of Simon and Jake appeared. Stacy and Christine instantly knew what happened and grinned in anticipation. "Let's do this," said James. James gave a rallying cry and all five of them used their respective powers to fly towards the dragon. The dragon smirked as he saw the five of them approaching. "Well look who it is; the five teenagers reunited at last. This shall be the last time we fight; it is time for you to die permanently" the dragon bellowed. He breathed in and blew out many streams of different elemental blasts aimed at the five friends. They all dodged them and Simon used his telekinesis to help bind the dragon in place. Stacy used her endurance to take any major hits as a human shield.

Christine used her stealth in order to slash at the dragon from all sides and avoid the major blasts. James and Jake used their swords and super strength in order to decimate the dragon's arms, legs, wings, and then head. The dragon began to fall out of the sky and Stacy continued to fire arrows out of her golden bow. The dragon landed with a thud and the five friends landed next to the dragon and surrounded it. The dragon wasn't dead and continued to fire blast after blast that the friends continued to dodge. Many blasts nearly hit James and he could feel the intensity but didn't buckle under the pressure. One particularly nasty blast scarred his cheeks but he kept moving forward.

James and his friends used a coordinated attack where Simon would use his magic to explode the dragon's eyes while the others took pot shots at his other weak points like his neck and belly. The dragon's eyes exploded in a cacophony of blood and gore that streamed over the group. The group kept on fighting though until finally the dragon breathed its last. "You will pay for this, I will return," said the dragon hoarsely. Jake and James walked up together; drew their swords and stabbed the dragon in the head and decapacitated it. Jake took hold of the head and ensured his demise by stomping on it. The dragon let out one final wheeze and then died for good. The dragon Jeb was no more. James went to the stone still in the altar and decided to use its power one last time. "I wish to undo the damage that this world has been through." James said loudly as he commanded the stone. The stone glowed brightly granting his wish. Everyone that was dead had been restored back to life and when the disasters were averted the elemental gods were brought back to life and made their home back in their respective elemental planes of existence. The world was beginning to heal again. Even Rathos reverted to his ghostly form and decided to move onto the afterlife in order to be reunited with his family.

The only ones that didn't come back to life were Jeb, Simon, and Jake. Simon and Jake remained in their ghostly forms. Simon turned to his friends and said "thank you for letting me make things right. I can't forgive myself for what I've done. I felt your desire to bring me back but I've decided to stay dead for now. I can't come back to life until I've made amends." James looked sadly at his friend and said "please Simon, you deserve another chance." The stone glowed again and this time Simon accepted the gift.

He returned to his former condition and all of the darkness that surrounded his heart was now gone. "I feel free James, thank you once again. But I must leave you guys though. I think I need to go on a solo journey to try to redeem myself. I will return someday when I feel I've proved myself" said Simon calmly. James and the girls hugged him tightly and said "good luck old friend, I hope you can forgive me someday for my part," said James. Simon looked at James and said "oh James, I already did." Before Simon left though, James gave Simon the stone and said "take care of it, be it's guardian for me." Simon cried upon hearing those words and quietly uttered "I will." Right after, everyone saw Jake and realized he was still in his ghostly form. "Yeah, I ain't coming back to life. James, I may be free of my darkness but I tried to kill you many times over the course of our friendship. You and I can't co-exist in this world. One of us has to die. I also know that you still have a time limit around your neck. Allow me to remove that for you," said Jake. The burning around James' neck cut off instantly and it spread to Jake. Jake fell down in pain. "Geez man, I don't know how you put up with this for so long. I think it's best I take your place and go to the afterlife. I'll be okay, and I know I don't deserve forgiveness but I need you to know something. Thank you, guys, for everything," said Jake. James hugged him tightly and said "thank you brother, I forgive you." The others echoed that sentiment and Jake peacefully let the time limit run out before dying for the last time.

James reverted back to normal as well and was free from his bonds. James hugged everyone and felt completely at ease with everything despite his mounting sadness for Jake's death. Jake may have hurt them each but he was still someone that they cared about at one point or another. The four mourned their friend but decided to move forward.

Epilogue

The powers of the stones had granted James and his friends a form of immortality. They could still be critically injured but they could live for millennia and age much slower than the average human. Perhaps it was a gift from the gods, that James and his allies had earned through their trials. James and Stacy finished off their years at Lakehead and eventually got married and had a kid after settling down. The family loved each other and they remained at peace for many years. Jake's spirit passed on but continued to watch over his friends as they lived their lives. Jake knew that his and James' values would never match up and could never be reconciled, but he was happy seeing his friends be at ease. Simon journeyed to many different places and spent many years trying to make things right and atone for his sins. Overuse of the stone could destroy him in the long run if he used it frivolously but he did everything he could to ensure his friends could live in peace. He even visited parallel universes in order to help out different versions of his friends. Christine missed Simon but she ended up getting married to a man in New York when she went there to revitalize the strategy guide industry. She's really happy and so is the rest of the group. Before they all got to live peacefully the group got to go on one final adventure a year after this one, but that's a story for another day.

I finished up my interview with the chronicler and headed out of his office for the night. We had been talking for many hours and he told me that someone with journal entries was coming in next to discuss his tale. I bade him goodbye and left.

Final Thoughts

Hey! It's the author here. I wanted to thank everyone for making it this far and joining me on this journey. I am also working on the sequels to this series such as Broken Paths and my Shattered Reflections collection. By the time this gets published I may even be finished with those stories but who knows? The plan is to write one more tale bringing everyone together for one last run and I hope that's come to pass. This story has been haunting me for over a decade since I started writing this before high school and I'm almost thirty. Writer's block can be really tough but it can be important to work through. As well as dealing with life stresses and my masters it's been a long time since I've been able to dedicate time to writing like this. As an author and as a person, I myself have struggled with many mental health issues and many of these scenes have been both cathartic and emotional to write even if they aren't one hundred percent the extent I dealt with them.

Writing that scene with Christine and Stacy crying in despair over James' death was very emotional and important to me especially. That was one of the first scenes I imagined while writing this and waited years to bring it to reality. I feel I can connect with all the characters and I hope you can as well. To me, that scene was the by product of many years of editing and dreaming until finally I could make it right. I wanted to write Jake as someone who had many issues that people could sympathize with but that he really shouldn't be redeemed due to everything he did until the very end. He was a conflicted character by nature and was definitely the most fun character to write at times due to his dark nature and foil to James. And when Christine wanted to kill herself in order to atone for her misdeeds, that scene was really hard to write but felt necessary in order to show the depth of mental issues and how hidden they can be until they are forced out into the world. I also always wanted one of the main characters to die and I went back and forth on which it should be.

I figured the one that did would carry the most emotional weight to the group dynamic and decided that Jake was the best option for permanent death since James had already died once and that with the two's rocky relationship; there would never be peace if both were alive. At the end of the day, this story was about friendship and the trials they face. . I once considered making James the bad guy at times and making him be corrupted by darkness but decided Jake would be a better fit. As you can tell by the additional scenes down below, this story may have taken many different directions.

At the end of the day, this story was about friendship and the trials they face. Writing this collection many years later reminds me of my life long friends that I used to spend my days with. I used to feel very lonely during that time of my life but I have come into my own since then and have gained much more confidence than I had back then. My friend group wasn't as chaotic as James and his friends are but we had our moments that I remember fondly. Nowadays I am more open with my struggles and I have found a way to fall back and get help so I can finally make my mark on the world and get out of this crippling fear and depression that I have dealt with throughout my whole life. When I first started writing this story in, I want to say grade 8 I did plenty of research on ancient Egypt in order to write Rathos' story accurately and ensure not to mess with history. I wanted to write Rathos as someone who acted behind the scenes but was able to preserve the timeline of actual history in the end. As for the medieval arc, I wrote that entire story in a day and then spent much time tinkering with it in order to make it into the arc that it is today. I am very proud of the way the scenes turned out and I am content with how it went.

Some Additional Scenes:

Here are some additional scenes that never made the cut in the original story but I thought were still relevant in order to make this story feel more complete. They are some short scenes but should provide more context into what I was thinking during my years of writing this tale.

Scene 1: James is lying dead while Christine and Stacy comfort each other and cry in despair. Simon comes up to them and says "James' time has ended. Join me and I shall spare you from the cataclysm I shall force unto the world." Christine looked at Simon and began to laugh hysterically. "Hahahahaha, you just killed the love of my life and you expect me to join you. You know what, maybe it's time for the world to burn. If I couldn't have James, at least Stacy can't have him either. Sorry Stacy, it's time to move on," she said sharply. Christine stood up and walked over to Simon hungrily. She kissed him passionately as they reveled in each other. Simon was always second best to James but now he was dead and Simon seemed that much more appealing. Her mind had felt like it fractured after his death but seeing Simon standing there got her heart beating faster once again. She both loved and hated him for what he did. Simon took Christine by the waist and hopped on his dragon as they left Stacy crying alone for James.

After James was brought back to life, he and Stacy went throughout the temple in order to confront the others and they fought against Christine, Jake, Dr. Jeb, and Simon all at once. Stacy and James fell to their combined strength and Christine took great pleasure in killing them both. She and Simon embraced and used their collective abilities to kill Jake and Dr. Jeb next. They took over the world and ruled together as its god and goddess. The two remade the world in their image and spent their anniversaries destroying it once it had time to thrive in order to rebuild once again. They were happy together even though Christine still missed James in some cases. But Simon had twisted her mind so much that she really only had eyes for him. Someday she would kill him and bring James back to be her lover but that day was a long time away.

Scene 2: Christine and James sat together outside of the school where they grew up and Stacy had continued to date Gregory despite wanting to dump him many times. James approached Christine timidly and gently took her hands in his. "Christine, for the longest time I've always had feelings for you. I used to think that I was in love with Stacy but I realized that you were the one I always wanted. If you don't feel the same, I understand but I still felt the need to tell you on the off chance that you felt the same about me," James said calmly but timidly. Christine had tears running down her face as she grabbed him and kissed him softly. She wanted James to be hers for as along as she knew him and she finally had him. They kissed over and over while Stacy watched sadly from a distance.

She ended up breaking up with Gregory later that night and went to Jake for comfort. The two talked long into the night and eventually their feelings of friendship developed into something rougher. They kissed and eventually had long and rough sex. Jake finally got someone that James didn't and Stacy let out her feelings of frustration and longing into her sex with Jake. There wasn't love between them, there was just frustration and longing between them both and their feelings finally reached a boiling point. They went at it long and hard into the night while Simon was angry that Christine had chosen James instead of himself.

Fast forward to James' death and Christine held her lover while Stacy looked triumphantly over his death. She had thrown in with the ranks of Simon and Jake in order to get revenge on him. After being with Jake, she realized how awful James was and how selfish he was and how he needed to be taken down a peg or two. Dr. Jeb was horrified by what he had seen and after the others left Christine had managed to convince him to help her bring James back to life. He agreed and the three of them confronted Jake, Simon and Stacy. Dr. Jeb was disappointed in how far Jake had fallen. His humanity had come back and felt the only way to save Jake's soul was to kill him. The six collided and after a long and heavy battle the six of them were dead and gone for good. No more reincarnation cycle, no more magic involved. The six of them were finally dead and the world was in ruins.

No one would ever rise up again in order to save or destroy the world since everyone was dead. Even the few that managed to avoid getting their bones crushed or getting devoured were forced to live in a world with no one left and that wasn't sustainable for anyone. The remaining humans killed themselves in despair and the world fell apart. The animals that survived retook the world and it became a paradise for animals to thrive once the enemies finally disappeared once their work was done. This was an ending that no one wanted, but it was the ending that they got. Did they deserve it? Who's to say?

Scene 3: Christine sat alone with her thoughts at James and Stacy getting together and her trying to kill them. Simon had also left and Christine didn't feel like her life was worth living any further. She took her obsidian daggers and she cut her own wrists. She continued to cut until she couldn't heal any further and she died. Her parents were the ones who found her and they were devastated at her death. She was unappreciated by her parents but they still loved her more than anything. They may have misunderstood her struggles and didn't know how to help her but they never wanted to make her conditions worse. They never understood the depth of her depression and anxiety. They cried at her funeral and Simon and the rest of their friends cried as well. Simon wanted to bring her back to life but her last note said that she didn't want to be brought back to life again. She wanted to stop being a burden to her parents and her friends.

Her love for strategy guides made her afraid of constantly bankrupting her parents and she was too nervous about getting a job. The graphic nature of her death showed that she really hated herself and felt ashamed of herself. Her parents cried at her funeral and they apologized profusely at her grave. If they could have her back, they would have bought her any guide she wanted and would have bankrolled her forever if that was what it took. They never said it out loud but they were really proud of her for everything she had accomplished and they were so rough on her because they believed their parenting techniques were making her stronger instead of weaker.

Scene 4: During the fight for peace James became corrupted by Jeb's influence and joined him willingly. He used his super strength in order to break all of Jake's limbs and then pry them off him until he was nothing except a head. James then took the head and waved it around to his former friends. Many of them tried to appeal to him but he used his sword in order to slaughter them all and embraced Jeb as his adoptive father. Jeb was so proud of him and embraced him back. James would soon be disposed of but that would come another day. James lapped up the blood of his former friends and felt at ease with the world. Jeb stared happily and grinning at his new student and how far he had fallen.

Intermission:

Some of these scenes but they are potential endings for each character that I had considered during the writing process. I considered Christine betraying James and Stacy permanently and I even considered her being with James romantically at times. I also considered one of the characters killing themselves but decided it would be better just to show the attempt rather than the graphic death itself. I always knew I wanted the book to end with James and Jake facing off and that James had to die at least once. I went back and forth on which one should die before ultimately deciding that Jake should die permanently. I never really thought that the two could co-exist in any meaningful way so I always planned on one of them biting the bullet and dying for good but I never knew which one of them was going to do it. As for Christine, I initially wanted her to end up with Simon before deciding that it would be better if they stayed friends.

Jake and Stacy were also an option but their relationship never really worked in my mind. So far, I'm happy with the way things turned out and I hope you feel the same. Initially this book was meant to be five parts long and an entire series on its own. However, the entries ended up being far too short for that so I decided to compile them into one solid mass. My dream was always to have a collection of my stories published and released to the public so this worked out in my favor anyway. This collection will be my true magnum opus and a testament to all the years I put work into this thing. I hope you all enjoy it as much as I did. Now, it's time to continue on with the story. How shall Darwin Fitzgerald fare with his trials? Read on and see.

Chapter 33: The Beginning of the End/Broken Paths

These are a series of journal entries that detail the struggles of a young man named Darwin Fitzgerald. Were his struggles genuine, or was he in denial from mental illness and delusions? You decide. As I passed this series of entries of to the chronicler, I wonder what he'll think of the contents. He nods in my direction as I leave him to his work. He pores over them intently and decides what to do next with them. Edward will accept anything that comes across his desk, it's only natural. He is a chronicler after all.

I'd also like to thank my mom, dad, and brother for supporting me on this endeavor. And for any lovely fans of the series, I am indebted to you. I'd also like to thank my mentors Susan and Trudy for helping me start this journey and my friends for not letting me give up when I needed that most. My pets also deserve a thank you for providing their unending support as well. And finally, last but not least Id like to provide a special thank you to my cousin and artist Jason Lavoie for providing the cover art for my work. I hope to write more continuations in the future but for now this is the end of the story until I write the next part. I'm currently working on parts 2 and 3 of Schreiber Chronicles and once that's finished, I will write my finale to the entire franchise. It will be a collection of many stories I have written over the years and I hope you will all still enjoy it. It will provide a conclusion to the end of the franchise.

I hope to see all of you in the next volume!

Cheers, Ethan Spadoni

Broken Paths

The Schrieber Chronicles Book Two

Ethan Spadoni

Contents

Preface and Acknowledgement:

Message from the Author:

Hey! It's the author and I wanted to thank everyone who took the time to read this from beginning to end. I understand that many of my stories involve heavy issues like mental health problems and suicidal tendencies; but I appreciate everyone who decided to bear through it. I myself have dealt with many variations of mental health issues and writing and video games were coping mechanisms to help me deal with my own trauma. I also loved Philosophy classes so much and in them I learned about many different projects such as the Stanford Prison Experiment, the Stanley Milgrim Experiments, and MK Ultra. If my stories are even able to reach one person who dealt with similar issues, then I have done my job as an author. I want to thank my family like my mom, dad and brother for encouraging me to finish this gargantuan project and move forward with my life.

There are many people I wanted to thank last volume but didn't get the chance to. I would like to once again thank my friends and mentor Susan for helping me get this out to the world and Trudy for helping me get through university when it mattered most. I'd also like to give a huge thanks out to my cousin Jason Lavoie for his incredible artistry in creating the cover art for me. I couldn't have done this without you cousin or my other friends and family. I'd also like to thank my professors for instilling a love of Philosophy and History into me and my writing. My former boss Dr. Nathan Hatton also deserves a thank you for mentoring me during my Master's. The History and Philosophy departments deserve a thank you for allowing my love of history and philosophy to thrive and survive even to this day.

Writing many of the scenes below were quite cathartic but also hard to write in some cases. If you are someone who cannot handle graphic scenes of psychological horror than let this serve as a warning to you before you cross the threshold into psychological horror. Below is many years' worth of writing and mental illness converging into one beautiful piece of work (at least I think so). Once again, thank you so much for making it this far and reading through my ramblings ha-ha. I'm currently working on part 3 of my Schreiber Chronicles series and hopefully that will be finished soon. I hope to see you all in the next volume! For business inquiries or just wanting to chat more about the story please contact me at the email listed down below:

espadoni@lakeheadu.ca

Cheers,

Ethan Spadoni

The Beginning Of The End

Entry 1

Name: Darwin Fitzgerald

Date: March 14th 2016 9:39 PM

I guess I should start off by explaining my situation but before I get into that I think you should know a bit about me.

My name is Darwin Fitzgerald and I am a freshman at Lakehead University in Thunder Bay Ontario. I was born on June 19th 1997 in Kingston, Ontario. As for what I look like, I'm 19 years old with freckles on my face and green eyes with light brown hair. I also have a tattoo on my left arm of a dragon to symbolize my freedom. I got it after I graduated high school. The pain hurt differently than the pain I experienced throughout my life and it reminded me that I was alive. It felt good and liberating. The pain felt like I was shedding part of my weak old self and becoming something entirely new.

What you need to understand about me is that I had to escape Kingston. There is nothing left for me there. Through all the blood and suffering I was finally able to make my escape. My time at Lakehead has been good to me and writing in this journal has helped me to cope with all that I have been through.

I am also writing this so that if anything were to happen to me then people could know me for who I truly am and not the image my parents have tried to turn me into. I suppose I should get some rest since I have a big day tomorrow.

The other day I was walking around the Agora Building when I saw this very tanned man handing out flyers. He had a badge that said he was from the LU Board. This man looked to be about 26 with blond spiky hair. His face looked tanned but it might have just been dirty. He looked like the kind of guy that had very rich parents but didn't give a shit about his appearance and didn't take anything too seriously. Every fiber in my body was telling me to avoid this guy and move on. He seemed creepy with his wide grin and his somewhat threatening looking eyes.

I still felt curious and was drawn to him though for some unexplained reason so I walked towards him and he handed me a form. He explained that if I wanted to participate in a study that could change the world then I should fill out the form and hand it back. The bottom of the form had a brief summary of the experiment which said "If you wish to change the world then you should join up with Piece for Peace, the world's leading corporation in helping people with amputations. This study has to do with the effects on people that are thrust into various roles. This may sound similar to the disastrous Stanford Prison Experiment but we at the LU Board assure you that this study is completely safe. If you wish to leave at any time, you may.

"There will be no penalty for those who wish to leave early but we encourage you to see the study through. You shall be paid very well to do this. If you are accepted into the study then you shall get an email tomorrow afternoon with the date of the experiment. On the day in question one of our employees shall come to pick you up at the address you have stated above. They will take you to the site and you will be staying there for two weeks. You will also be paid $20 an hour for your services. We encourage you to please join us and you shall be making the world a better place. Sincerely, Dr. N. F." I got chills coming from this paper. It felt sort of familiar somehow. I looked over the form and decided that I didn't have anything to lose. It could be exciting and since people are being paid 20$ an hour to do it I guess I may as well give it a shot. I ended up getting accepted into the experiment and the study is scheduled for the next day.

I admit I'm extremely nervous about the experiment. I've had a pretty tough life so I'm hoping this can be a good change for me but I'm not sure to be honest. Something about the vibe I got from the spiky haired guy really threw me for a loop but the money and experience seem too enticing to me. I've also tried to join many clubs since I've been here as well. I'm currently part of the Anime Club and the Badminton Club.

I even started dating someone. Her name's Angela and she's a freshman at LU with me as well. We just started dating and it's been great so far. Her major is in business and mine is a double major in history and philosophy. I admit that I don't have a lot of interest in history but I was told that it could help lead me down the path of teaching. One thing I always enjoyed that may surprise people is museums. I always liked museums even though they are filled with history. Something about being in a museum always made me feel connected to the world in a way I can't explain. Philosophy is my true passion and I love everything about it though. I've always wanted to teach philosophy and I think having a history degree under my belt wouldn't hurt either. I've always wanted to teach at the University level and I'm prepared to do whatever it takes to get there. Someday I'll get my PHD as well and I'll be successful in my field of choice.

Right now, I'm happy despite my past which I'll get into later. My therapist says that journaling is a good outlet and writing has always been fun for me. Someday I'll teach philosophy to anyone who will listen and I will be successful in it. I get a lump in my throat whenever I think about that potential future. It's a future I never would have thought was possible if I had stayed in Kingston. I remember I had this one friend named Leonardo who became a close friend of mine but when I tried to confide in him about my parents and my problems he laughed in my face and told the entire school some pretty deep stuff I told him. It took me a long time to trust anyone after that.

I also think I'm being stalked right now. I keep seeing someone following me out of the corner of my eye and I tried to tell the RA about it but they couldn't find anyone. The police also aren't much help. I can't do much about it but I'm still scared. Is it even real? Hopefully it'll die down soon and I can get some sleep. I've had nightmares about it and I can barely rest. Right now, one of my best friends is Jared who's been there for me during all of this. I credit him with saving my life as well. Anyway, I think that's enough for now. Tomorrow is the big day so I think I will leave you all here for now.

--Darwin signing off.

Entry 2

Name Darwin Fitzgerald

Date: March 15th 2016 7:57 PM

Holy shit, this is not what I signed up for. This morning a police officer just came to my dormitory and arrested me in front of my housemates. I was dragged all the way to the police station for booking but then they blindfolded me and took me somewhere else. When I was in the car, I felt my breath catch in my throat and I almost gagged from the fear. I wanted to throw up but one of the officers kept yelling at me to shut up and to not puke! It really was terrifying and they clearly had no patience for me. I've suffered from panic attacks my whole life and this was definitely one of the days I had one. Fortunately, or maybe unfortunately, I can't seem to remember much from the incident. I think I passed out after booking. All I remember is that the police dragged me into this warehouse and I am now in my own cell with 11 other prisoners in their own individual cells next to mine. The air smells like shit and I think someone literally took a shit in here at some point because I can still smell it. The funny thing though is that I know all of these people. They are all in my classes this year. I also see 12 other students dressed as prison guards. I guess this must have to do with the study. This reminds me of the Stanford Prison Experiment.

The study focused on obedience and it was eerily similar to this one. People were allowed to leave though but despite that some of the guards became sadistic and some of the prisoners had mental breakdowns and the experiment was shut down after six days. The study had many ethical complications and the overseer was not known for being neutral and wanted to continue the experiment at all costs. This also reminds me of the Stanley Milgrim experiment. In that experiment, subjects were brought into a room and were told to administer electric shocks to someone on the other side of the room. The overseer would tell the participant to continue to increase the shock levels even though the participant could hear the person being shocked and crying out in pain. Sometimes even the victim on the other side would claim to have a heart condition and that they couldn't take much more of this.

The overseer would eagerly encourage the participant to keep on administering shocks despite the cries of the victim and sometimes people would continue until the max limit. What they didn't know was that the victim on the other side wasn't actually being shocked and he was just pretending to be shocked. In reality the victim was perfectly fine but the participants were not made aware of this. They essentially held the life of someone else's in their hands and many consented to administer torture on another human being just because an authority figure told them to. Some people really are fucked up. Not just the scientists in charge of these things, but the people who willingly consent to torturing innocent people. The reason I bring this up is because I see the looks of the prisoners and that of the guards. The prisoners look terrified and the guards look nervous but smug as well behind their shades.

I fear that instead of just pretending to play these roles, we may just become them. I can also see someone in the shadows who seems to be giving orders to the guards. I can't see his face but there seems to be an authoritarian vibe emanating from him. Now that I think about it, I can't see any defining features. He seems to be just a shadow on the wall. If I had to guess I would assume he is the overseer of this study. When I was brought in here or should I say dragged in like a marionette, the guards stripped me of all my personal belongings which really bites. Luckily, I was able to convince them to let me keep my journal. One of the guards is one of my closest friends and he is one of the few people who know what happened to me in Kingston.

I guess I should be lucky he is sympathetic to what I have dealt with, it might make my time here easier but who knows. It's Jared and we went to high school together. He is one of my closest friends but I really hope his psyche does not become morphed by this study. I have heard that these studies can have long term psychological and neurological effects. I never believed it but now I can see why. As for where I am, I am in a dark grey room with 12 individual cells side by side in it. My cell is number 11. I feel like I am in a cage...literally and figuratively. I feel trapped, but I know I can do this. I have to. I need to ignore the buildup of tension in my chest, the sweat on my brow, the bile in my throat, and the unforgivable odor of what also appears to be death. Wait, DEATH? What the hell is going on in this place?

I can see blood and what appear to be markings on the walls. It looks like there are 14 lines etched in the wall. Maybe that is how long someone was kept here. It looks like there is something faded on the floor of my cell. It must have been written in blood. The message says "get out while you can". I am officially freaked out. Wait, maybe I can get out. We all had to sign contracts and consent to this. Maybe if I can get Jared's attention, he can help me convince the other guards and the overseer to let me out. It looks like one of the prisoners is trying to summon one of the guards. Shit, I couldn't make out everything the prisoner said but it sounded like he was asking to leave. This might be my chance to get out of here. Instead of responding the guard just punched him in the face through the bars. I guess this isn't my chance after all. Fuck. The prisoner is bleeding pretty badly. I think it's safe to assume that I am not leaving anytime soon. What the hell can I do? But the contract did say this study only lasts two weeks, maybe I can survive that long. I hear one of the guards saying that 8:00 PM is lights out and I think the clock says 8 now, I guess I should put this down. I really need to get some sleep but I want to keep on writing for as long as I can. This is a form of therapy for me and they can't take that away from me. What am I going to do? Please help me. I don't want to die in here. I miss you, Angela. Goodnight.

Darwin signing off.

Things Take A Turn For The Worse

Entry 3

Name Darwin Fitzgerald

Date March 16th 2016 7:36PM

Today has been interesting. Today was in fact one of the most memorable days of my life. It was so amazing that I want to beat my head into the wall over and over until I can't remember the amazing experience that I just had. My day began at 5:00 AM. I and the other prisoners were awoken by a loud alarm that kept blaring until each of us was able to stand up. The ringing jolted me awake and the ringing continued in my ears for hours after the fact. It took all of us a good 30 seconds or so to finally get up and get ready. It may not seem that long to those who might read this but it felt like an eternity to me and those around me. One of the guards said that if it takes us longer than a minute to be ready then the entire cell block will be punished. I honestly don't know how things could get worse. Once we were considered ready, we were forced to endure countless exercises for an hour. We had to do pushups, jumping jacks and then burpees. The human body can't sustain exercise for that long and the recommended amount is thirty minutes five times a week I believe. Definitely not for an hour every day.

Miraculously I was able to last the hour but I had to keep stopping. The guards urged us to keep going but at least they allowed us to rest for a few minutes at a time if we needed to and trust me, we all needed to. My muscles ached really badly after that and my breathing came out really hard and it took me forever to catch my breath and stop being tired. I hadn't done exercises like that since high school and they were hell on earth. My gym teacher used to shout at us to go faster and would verbally abuse any students who weren't up to his standards. I suppose that in his mind he believed he was trying to help us reach our potential but it just felt like abuse to me. This reminds me of that honestly. Someone is really trying to get me to remember my hellish high school experiences. Maybe it's just a coincidence but I don't know anymore. I just need to survive this; it's only been a day.

After the wake-up call and exercises each of us were given pails and toothbrushes and ordered to clean our cells. Each of our cells has tons of dirt on the floor and faint traces of blood everywhere. Clearly, we weren't the first occupants in these cells. Did someone actually die in here I wonder? I tried to ask one of the guards about that and he just spit in my face and slapped his baton on my left hand hard. It really hurt but I don't think it's broken. Luckily, I'm ambidextrous so it's not too much of a hassle to write with my right hand. When we were nearly finished cleaning out all the dirt the guards would come and pour more dirt in our cells or they would come and piss in them. They were starting to act cruel even though it was less than a day at this point. I noticed the overseer kept egging on the guards to be even crueler from his office doorway.

Some of the guards were very hesitant to continue but the overseer would explain over an intercom that any guards who committed these cruel acts would get a bonus and extra credit for their studies. Many of the students jumped on that and eagerly acted worse towards us. The same thing happened during the Stanford Prison Experiment but that happened much later in the study. I believe at least one of the prisoners tried to rebel in that study by placing a mattress by their doors to block the guards but I'm not a hundred percent sure. I could be very wrong about that and I probably am. Anyway, the guards who pissed in our cells were rewarded greatly apparently. Whenever we tried to protest, they'd always say "clean it or sleep in it". Man, I hate this place. They kept us cleaning for two hours. Finally, at 8am we were given breakfast. The only way for me to describe what was given to me is by saying what the guards called it. They call it mystery meat. It smells like my gym socks and sweat.

The worst part about it though is that I can see it move occasionally. I really don't want to eat this but it's either this or starve to death. I was somehow able to eat some of it but I constantly wanted to puke. That is how bad it was. I thought Aramark food was bad. This is clearly much worse. At Lakehead University Aramark has a reputation for not being very great with their food. The food was always sanitary and cooked properly but it never tasted very good. At least that's what me and my friends thought. After an hour for breakfast, we were left to do nothing. The boredom is very unbearable. This lasted until 12pm when we are served; you guessed it, mystery meat again. After an hour of that we are left to be bored once again. The only thing I seem to be able to do is counting the cracks in the wall all cross the cell block. I feel so bored and I don't know how to continue this. I have counted three hundred and two apparently. I did this until about three when things took a turn for the worse.

The prisoner in the first cell started to beckon the guards. He pleaded with them to provide better food. The guards of course refused but number one kept on asking and asking until finally the guard took out his baton and wacked him in the forehead with it. Number one fell flat on his face as the blood from the hit gushed everywhere. The poor kid was bleeding badly and I couldn't even recognize him much after that first hit. There was so much blood. I've heard that head and face wounds bleed much more than wounds on other parts of the body.

The look on the guard's face was one of horror but the face quickly reverted to one of indifference. After that all twelve guards surrounded the cell and the overseer came from a nearby door at the end of the hall. I still couldn't see any defining features as it was just a shadow or maybe he was dressed in black and using a smoke machine to make himself look like a shadow but I can't tell. There also seems to be someone there with weird blue eyes and the plainest face I have ever seen. From the figure I could see a hand extending and a finger pointing at One's cell. The guards quickly unlocked it and dragged the prisoner to the room that the overseer had just come out of. It wasn't until 5pm when he was being escorted out of the room with two guards supporting his weight on either side. One had a look of pure terror on his face. His eyes were bulging and I could see a vein by his forehead pulsing. What have they done to him?

When the guards left One just stayed curled up in his cell rocking back and forth for an hour. It wasn't until after he stopped rocking that the guards came and brought "dinner"/mystery meat again. I ate for an hour and then spent the next bit trying to figure out what happened to One. I guess since he misbehaved the overseer wanted him punished or something. Why do I keep calling him One? He has a name but for some reason I can't remember it. What's going on? Am I beginning to lose it? I really need to try to lay low here or I might be next. As I said before today was interesting and one of the absolute worst days of my life. The clock says it's about eight so I guess I should close this journal and try to sleep. I may be calm right now but my mind is racing. I just hope I can get some sleep.

Goodnight, all.

Darwin signing off.

Entry 4

Name Darwin Fitzgerald

Date: March 17th 2016 7:00 pm.

I decided that I will only write at the end of the day when everything is finished. Today was surprisingly uneventful. We all managed to get up in time and no one was taken into the unknown room today. I guess we are at a temporary peace for today but who knows if it will last. I am usually a very optimistic person but I feel kind of negative. I miss Angela so much and I really want to go on a date with her again. I am just waiting for the next prisoner to slip up and get us all in trouble. I am bored as hell but I think I should finally talk about what happened to me back at Kingston. Not even Angela knows this much about my past. I had to escape because my parents were abusive. My mother was always putting me down by calling me pathetic and worthless. My father has a drinking problem and he liked to physically abuse me whenever he got upset. My older brother was my only safe haven until he moved out when he was 16 and didn't take me with him.

I have always been angry at my brother for that. I was 12 when he left and forced to endure it until I turned 18 and came to LU. I haven't talked to him since he left. He has written me letters and attempted to see me but I don't want anything to do with him. The letters are just piling up in my dorm room. I don't know how to feel about him anymore honestly. He was a good brother and I know he never intended to abandon me; but he left me with my parents and they made my life my own personal hell. My father always liked to beat me until I bruised or until I couldn't get up. He would laugh at me if I begged him to stop and would yell at me for being weak if I cried. He truly loved hurting me and I don't think he wanted me to survive into my adulthood. One time my dad took a knife towards me and slashed up my hands and arms really bad.

He called it character building but I called it pure and unadulterated violence. He made me feel physically helpless and I remember crying myself to sleep after I would bandage myself up. He would never hurt me enough to get stitches or to have to go to the hospital but he would leave marks. My mother on the other hand would always berate me and make me feel like I was worthless. She told me to kill myself every day because I reminded her too much of my brother who abandoned the family. Whenever I tried to talk back or beg her to stop, she would shout at me and get my father to lock me up in the basement in the tool room. They never cared about me and I think they were so angry at my brother for leaving that they took it out on me. They were abusive to him as well and to me when we were younger but after he left that amplified their torture against me.

I had tried to tell others about the abuse but I was always too afraid to come forward. I was very depressed and anxious for a long time. I used to wake up and have anxiety attacks. For those that don't know what I'm talking about; an anxiety attack in my case is tension and looped thinking. For more details, when I would wake up my face would feel tight and my head would feel tired and tight as well. My ears would feel tension as well and it would feel like air was leaking out of them. My ears have always felt plugged but the anxiety attacks make them feel worse as well. My thinking would become looped and I couldn't break out of my thought process. I would think about the worst moments of my life or how worried I was about something specific and it would be on constant repeat in my head. I still get those attacks at times but not as frequently than when I was with my parents. All throughout high school I would lay in bed for hours when my parents weren't home and just stew. For a long time, I wanted to end it all. I truly believed that ending my own life was the only option and the thoughts in my head were booming at me to kill myself.

I tried to use my father's gun to end it when I was a sophomore but I was too much of a coward to do it. I put the gun up to my mouth and I was crying through it all. Tears blurred my vision and I sobbed for hours as I held the gun to my head. I also considered aiming it at my parents but I knew I would get in so much trouble if I did that. My parents might have actually killed me if I stood up for myself like that. I was too afraid to use the gun in the end and I dropped it harmlessly to the ground. After that event a year later, I tried to cut myself when I was a junior but I just couldn't do it either. I took a steak knife from the knife drawer and put it up right to my wrists. I pushed down with enough pressure for a small amount of blood to come out but I couldn't go any further than that. I was such a pathetic weakling for not being able to kill myself that time.

The third time I tried to cut myself again was when my best friend Jared walked in on me when I was in the janitor's closet alone. I had a pocket knife stashed in my locker for protection even though it was against school policy but I didn't care. I was bullied mercilessly and having the knife made me feel slightly better even if I never had any intention on using it against my bullies. I had a really bad day that day and my parents had hurt me badly before school and my teachers were yelling at me for not being a perfect student.

Whenever I would go for a short walk around the school to center myself, they would act like I was killing someone or if I took slightly too long in the bathroom, they would always comment on it. Eventually I just shut down and never spoke to them. The moment I saw Jared I dropped my pocket knife and I broke down in front of him. Tears were flowing for what felt like hours and he was stunned but he just hugged me tightly and listened to everything I had to say. He brought me to the principal and I told them everything. This was when I was just beginning my senior year of high school.

My parents were locked up for the abuse and violence and I was allowed to live with Jared and his parents since I had no other family or home to go back to. Eventually I started seeing a therapist and got some meds that helped immensely. Before I move on, I need to talk about my former boss. He was also a factor in why I wanted to kill myself. I don't want to mention where I worked because that would be too obvious to who I'm talking about but I worked for my supervisor with cleaning and customer service duties. I loved my job and even though I sucked at the cleaning I excelled with customer service surprisingly. That place was where I could finally be me and I felt myself becoming even more confident; at least on the surface. I began to trust my boss like a father figure and we would talk about my dreams of getting into LU and wanting to become a teacher. He supported me in his own way and despite being gruff and judgmental at times I got the feeling that he cared to some extent. I felt safe with him but that ended up being a mistake.

He never hit me or anything but he began to become verbally abusive when I began to fail at my cleaning duties and eventually the customer service I had excelled at began to decrease since I started hating the job. In the beginning I felt so happy to be working but then I started to hate myself and I felt empty all the time while I was working. Gone were the genuine smiles and the light in my eyes. All that was left was darkness and nothingness. I never intend to lie unless I believed that the truth could hurt someone more; but I would lie to protect myself at times when my parents would ask me why my grades were so low or why I was late. I would lie about the cleaning to my boss but he would set traps to see if I was lying like putting feathers in doorways to see if I had opened them recently like the storage room or the room where we kept other supplies. He would also take the checklist of duties right on the computer monitor in my office so that I would be forced to look at it and it would interfere with my archival work. He finally called me out on one of my lies and he told me I didn't deserve to work there.

He said I was pathetic and worthless and he laughed as I broke down crying. He was one of the vilest human beings I had ever met by that point and he had turned on me. He said I made him look bad by sucking at my job. I wanted to kill him like I wanted to kill my parents, but I couldn't. I ended up running away crying and then I quit. My superiors tried to comfort me and asked what I wanted to do. I wanted them to handle it internally but they ended up pushing it under the rug despite promising results. I don't know what ended up happening to him after I left. I heard he transferred to a small town called Schreiber in order to run some sort of business there. I don't know. All I know is I'm never going anywhere near him even though Schreiber sounds like my kind of place to settle down and have a family.

He became one of my greatest enemies and was just as bad as my parents in some cases. Instead of trying to teach me and guide me he used draconian measures in order to keep me in my place. If I fucked up anything on my list, he would staple it right near my face by my workstation so I would always see it and it would interfere with my other duties. He really was a dick. I don't care what happens to him anymore. I wish he died but honestly, it's just wasted energy thinking about that stuff. I don't wish him well and I hope he rots in whatever kind of hell he makes for himself.

I still have nightmares of those experiences and I still wasn't fully stable but at least I felt better and I had no intention of trying to take my own life by the time Jared helped me get help. The scars my parents and boss left me were finally beginning to fade when a few days before my graduation I got a letter from my parents. They said that they were going to make me wish I had killed myself. I told the police this and they ceased all communication between me and my parents. I found out they weren't going to be released for a long time so I'm hoping that was all just talk. After high school I decided to go to Lakehead with Jared and try to forget the past. Up until now I had been feeling pretty good but since this study I have been having nightmares about my parents again. I keep waking up in sweat and I can't seem to relax. I have to try to calm down. I can see it is close to eight and I should get some sleep. If I can, that is.

Goodnight

Darwin signing off

Entry 5

Name: Darwin Fitzgerald

Date: March 18th 2016 7:30pm

The guards are getting worse. Each morning the guards shuffle out of the room at the end of the hall one by one until they are facing our cells. For the last few days, they have only had a look of indifference. Now it seems like they are becoming harsher. I can't see their eyes due to them all having sunglasses but their smiles have a sadistic sense to them. Even Jared seems to have that smile now. The guards also shuffle out of the room like trained soldiers and they act like they are in the military. Also, at the beginning of each morning they are now only giving us 30 seconds to get up and be standing. I found out the hard way what happens if we aren't all ready to go. The guards will leave the room and then they will return brandishing water guns. As one they would aim at us and fire. The problem with this is that it isn't water, its piss. It was really disgusting and I can only imagine how and where they got so much piss to fill twelve water guns.

I and the other prisoners attempted to duck and cover our faces but the piss just got everywhere. Some of the piss even got into my mouth and I gagged on the floor for what felt like hours. We also aren't allowed to use the sink we have in our cells to clean ourselves up. As punishment we can't use the sink for the entire day. Our water privileges were also cut off so we couldn't even use drinking water to clean ourselves. I thought this would be the worst part of my day but it only got worse. I saw two prisoners try to use the sink even for a second but the guards unlocked their cells and hit them both in the forehead with their batons twice. I don't even know what to say. All of our meals were also cancelled for today and we don't get any water at all throughout the entire day as I said earlier. I am currently lying on my cell floor covered in piss and feeling weak and hungry. I don't know how much cough, cough, cough, more of this I can take. The lights are starting to go off; I guess all I can do is sleep. I hate myself so much for getting into this situation. Maybe my boss was right, I was pathetic and I didn't deserve to breathe the same air that he did.

Entry 6 (I think)

Date: March 19th 2016

Name: ?...?

I am still reeling from the effects of yesterday. We all managed to get up on time so we got to use the sinks and we got to eat and drink finally. I still feel a bit dizzy but I feel a bit better, I guess. The guards also took the clock down so I have no idea what time it is. I think they did it as some sort of psychological torture so we wouldn't know how much time has passed or something. They really are sadistic bastards. They laughed as they did it too so they knew exactly what they were doing. Jared looked at me with something that resembled sadness before erupting into laughter at seeing my despair. I've always loved the concept of time and I typically wear a wrist watch on my hand. I also have an antique pocket watch that my grandfather left for me. He was the only one who encouraged me to pursue teaching but he died when I was really young. My parents never let me go to the funeral and I couldn't even say goodbye.

As for the time, all I know is that it is after 5 since that was when I had my last meal. The prisoners seem to be on edge but I think the person doing the worst is One. Now that I look at him, I think his name was Joey. Yeah, he's Joey. I am pretty sure he was in my psychology class last term. He was a pretty good-looking guy I guess, blond hair, green eyes, strong build. He could easily get a girlfriend if he wanted to but now, I hardly recognize him. His body is sagged and I can see his long hair getting messy. There is dirt all over his face and he still looks like he is in pain from his hit. The other prisoners who were hit worse seem to be recovering but Joey doesn't seem to be. I pity him. I don't really have any more to say so I guess I will call it quits and count the cracks in the wall again.

My hand also doesn't seem to be healing well. It's all bruised and I'm afraid there's something wrong with it. Anytime I try to get the guards attention they either ignore me or spit in my face. Luckily, they don't beat me much but it still hurts. I'm also someone who constantly worries about their health and am always worried about getting cancer and stuff like diabetes or other diseases. I can't think straight anymore. The journal helps me to keep my thoughts together but everything feels scattered. Did I mention my boss, he verbally abused me for not picking up the slack with cleaning when I had depressive episodes. Oh wait, I did mention him already. Fuck, I'm such a stupid idiot. I need to get some sleep or something. I haven't slept well in days.

Entry 777777...

Date: March 22nd 2016

Name: Darwin Fitz...

...I ... I... I have a lot to say. I don't know what kind of place this is. I have been stuck in an isolation chamber for three days. On the 20th I received my food and I ate it lovingly but I had made the mistake of taking the time to berate Jared for not talking to me for days. He has just completely ignored me like all the guards do. Normally I wouldn't do anything but I was tired and hungry and my tolerance is very low. He is my best friend so he should still talk to me or at least not just ignore me. He kept telling me to back down but I didn't. I felt so mad that I actually chucked the plate at him and a piece of it scratched his face just below his eye. Right after that all the guards surrounded my cell and I saw the overseer shadows and all approach me.

He pointed at my cell and the guards dragged me out of it while Jared was being tended to. The guards took me through the door and I saw that there were three doorways. One said overseer's office. One said guard barracks and the final door said isolation chamber. Of course, I was pushed through there and unceremoniously thrown to the floor. I hurt my knee when they dropped me but that was the least of my problems at the moment. The door was sealed shut as soon as I was in. The entire room was white and I saw a camera at the far end of the room. Before I could do anything there was this loud alarm that blared through the room. It was even louder than the alarm played at the beginning of the mornings. It was so intense that I actually had to drop to the ground and cover my ears but it didn't help much. This voice kept saying you are worthless, end it all.

The voices kept repeating it over and over and eventually I saw words appear on the far wall that said submit or end it. These words eventually began to appear all across the walls, the ceiling and even the floor. The voices on the intercom changed to saying submit to the overseer. That in combination with the alarm caused me to panic and no matter that I did I couldn't drown it out. This reminded me of my anxiety attacks and it felt like air was leaking from my ears again. I was afraid of going deaf but it wasn't loud enough to damage my hearing thank God.

I almost considered hitting my head on the walls until I realized that the walls weren't thick enough for me to hurt myself but too strong to be broken. This kept up for what felt like an eternity and no matter what I did I could not sleep. I am already very sleep deprived. My thoughts had become so disconnected and disjointed that I didn't know what was real anymore. I even thought I saw pictures of my parents and former boss on the walls telling me to kill myself and bow to the overseer. I don't know for sure if what I saw real or not but it still haunts me to this day. When I was released, I guess I was shaking. I was told that it was two in the afternoon of the 22nd of March. I eventually slept for what felt like a few hours until I woke up and decided to write this. I can still see the images flashing in my brain and I can't even think straight. I don't know how I am able to write this I am.........I can't seem to.... Help me please....... Mom, Dad, help......I miss you...I love you...I miss the father son time where you'd do character building with me and your switchblade...anything's better than this...can you please kill me? I don't want to live in this hell anymore. Sob, sob, sob, sob. I want to die.

Entry 8

March 23rd 2016

I was told that I had slept for twelve hours straight. I don't even know what to believe anymore. All throughout today I have seen more and more prisoners being forced into the isolation room and every day I see more and more prisoners getting hit with a police baton, myself included in that last part. I honestly don't know what the point of all this is anymore. I guess I should just, Oh crap. The guards are beginning to surround my cell. Please no, not the chamber! Anything but the chamber!

I can't seem to stop shaking. I have spent the last two hours in there I think but I don't know. I want to end it all. I want to end it all I want to end it all I want to end it all I want to end it all I want to end it all I want to end it all I want to end it all I want to end it all. Please kill me. Please kill me. Take away the pain. Take away the pain. Take away the pain. Why are you doing this to me? Why are you doing this to me? Why are you doing this to me? Just let me die. Just let me die. Just let me die. Please. I don't want to live here anymore. I miss my cat Sophie so much. She was the only one that loved me after my grandfather died. Not even Jared loves me anymore. He wants me dead, I know it. He's going to kill me soon, I think. The guards are always whacking their batons and scraping them against the cell walls in order to rattle us. It's working.

Entry 9

March 24th 2016

Jared has officially turned on me. Now whenever he comes to my cell, he spits on me and then kicks me or grabs me through the bars if he can. If he can reach me, he will crack the baton on the crown of my head which hurts like hell by the way. If not then he will just bang on the bars which is honestly very terrifying. I thought I was afraid of my parents. This is way worse. I can also see that he has a bandage just below his right eye. I see that the plate nailed him pretty good. I don't even know what time it is anymore. I am always so terrified every second that I can't relax. I see that One has just fallen into despair and won't stop crying. I can't even remember my own name or his. Was it Jenna, Jayne, Joseph? Who am I? Tom, Leon, Stacy, I don't even know anymore! I am only known as 11 now. I am 11 I am 11 I have no identity; I have no identity. I must submit to survive. I must submit to survive. I must submit to survive. I must submit to survive. Submitting is the only way to survive this hell. Also screw you to anyone who thinks my journal entries are too short. You try to come up with scenes and dialogue to write over and over again. It's hard work. Who am I even talking to???? Who the hell am I? I'll never submit. I never will. I will retain my sanity for as long as it takes. I will survive this!

Entry 10

March 25th 2016

My name is Darwin Fitzgerald. My name is Darwin Fitzgerald My name is Darwin Fitzgerald. My name is Darwin Fitzgerald My name is Darwin Fitzgerald My name is Darwin Fitzgerald My name is Darwin Fitzgerald. .... My name is Darwin my name is Darwin My name is Darwin My name is Darwin, oh my god, I can't remember my own last name. Darwin 11, no, no, that isn't it. What is it? I have been racking my brain for what feels like hours and for the love of God I can't remember my true last name. I am losing my mind.

Entry 11

March 26th 2016

What is real and what isn't? I have been back and forth through that isolation chamber and I just barely have enough strength to write this. I can actually feel my life force seeping out of me. The only thing that is keeping me going is that tomorrow will be the 14th day that I have been here meaning I can finally get out of this forsaken place. I can hardly wait.

These entries may be short but I have little strength to write anything anymore. This is all I have left. If anyone sees this, please help me. I...I.... I...I want to die please. I submit to the overseer. I submit! Anything's better than this.

Entry 12

March 27th 2016

I have finally done it. I have survived today. I wasn't taken to the isolation chamber thank goodness and I was able to avoid all encounters with the guards. I feel so amazing to see that I should be released today. I see the overseer walking into the room. I can see his shadows starting to whisp away as he comes closer to my cell. He is nearly here. He is now facing me and his shadows have revealed that he is...wait is that? ...

The End?

Entry 13

March 28th 2016

Name Darwin Fitzgerald

I wish I could forget everything that has just happened. I am told that it is 4:30 pm but I don't know for sure. I saw the overseer of the prison. It was my cousin Nathaniel. I remember him from a few years ago. He and I were in grade 9 together. I always thought there was something off about him but it wasn't until I saw him beating up Jared in an alley that I knew he needed help. When I approached them, I saw Jared was left within an inch of his life and Nathaniel had this weird look in his eyes. It was almost sadistic like he enjoyed inflicting pain on others. I had already called the police by this point and they arrested my cousin. Nathaniel always swore that he would make me pay but I haven't heard from him in years.

It wasn't until I saw his face at the prison that I recognized him but then everything went black. I think someone hit me on the head with a baton. I then found myself waking up in my dorm room with chip bags littered everywhere and take out boxes. I went to my computer to check the date and I saw that the date said it was two weeks since I left to do the study. I also noticed that there were a bunch of emails. I also checked my sent ones and I noticed that apparently, I sent a couple emails to Jared's family saying not to bother me.

Apparently, I was working on a very important project. There were also emails to my professors and friends saying that I was dealing with a family tragedy and that I needed some time alone. This is crazy. I also saw a bunch of texts with people checking up on me and messages of me replying to them saying all was well. I know that none of this happened but I can't explain any of it. I also checked the very first email since I did the study and it was from the LU board. It said that they were sorry to inform me that the study had been cancelled due to budgetary concerns and ethical concerns and that they were sorry for any inconvenience. If, the LU board didn't do the study, then who did? I'll admit I was pretty freaked out when I first read this email. I read it over countless times but I have no explanations for this. The first thing I did was call up Jared. Despite what went down between us he is still my best friend. I won't give up on him. To some extent I owe him my life.

I tried calling him but when he answered he was really weird. He said that he had no memory of the last two weeks. Apparently, he also sent out emails to his professors and family giving excuses for why he can't call or show up anywhere for two weeks. I tried calling up Joey and some of the others but they all said the same thing. I sadly found out that Joey was taken to the ICU after trying to kill himself due to having a psychotic break and he didn't make it through the night. I never knew him long but I really liked the kid.

It seems that I am the only one who can remember the event but I don't know what that means. It was at this time that I decided to leave my dorm and drive to the police station. I don't know why I didn't just call. I guess I just thought I needed to do something. I am not crazy but who knows what really happened during all that time? I just felt so helpless and scared I wasn't thinking straight. My entire body was spasming and I was constantly sweating.

I opened the door to my room when I saw none other than Nathaniel walking down the hall of my building. He looked at me and said "Darwin, is that you? I haven't seen you in years". At this point I couldn't believe my eyes. If everything was real then he had taken a big risk in coming here. He seemed to not know what happened in the last two weeks and he also seemed to forget the grudge he held onto for years against me. He had a welcoming smile on his face as he saw me. I felt adrenaline flow through me and I practically ran into him and tackled him to the ground.

I punched him in the face and kicked. He kept begging me to stop but I didn't care. I needed to make him pay for all the misery he put me through. I am still a little fuzzy on what happened next. I think that when I went to punch him a fifth time, he moved his head out of the way and he landed one on me right into my temple. I guess I fell to the ground after that. The next thing I remember was feeling restrained and him talking to someone. I couldn't hear everything but as I struggled to open my eyes and lift my head, I thought I heard him say the words 'attacked' and 'needs help'. After that I felt myself being dragged and put in some type of cell. When I finally regained consciousness, I realized that I had been admitted into a mental hospital by none other than my beloved cousin.

I tried to explain what happened but my body hurt so much. It hurt even to speak. I realized no one would listen and I heard Nathaniel say something along the lines of that this is the best place for me and that this is for my own protection or some BS. I am currently writing in this journal trying to figure out if I am crazy or not. Maybe the doctors are right and that I had a mental break and that I built up this irrational thought that my cousin actually was going to torture me for getting him sent away. I can see him talking to the doctors. I guess I am about to take my pills now. I could really use some sleep.

This place is the perfect...wait I see Nathaniel has finished talking to the doctors. He just handed a large envelope to one of the doctors who seem to have a sadistic glint in his eye. I can also see Nathaniel is smiling a little as he takes one last look at me. That doctor was with me in the prison I just didn't know it. There was always someone who accompanied the overseer but I thought it was just another guard. This one had his face partially covered and it looked like I could only see his eyes. This doctor has the exact same eyes. Piercing blue eyes that look like they could peer into your soul and rip it to shreds belong to him.

I guess I never noticed it because I only ever focused on the overseer and my former friends. How come I never saw him before yet I can perfectly recognize him now? Why am I the only one to remember the events of the last two weeks? Was this Nathaniel's master plan? I have no idea but I do know one thing, I need to get out of here. I promise that I will make Nathaniel pay for what he did to me, even if I have to wait decades for it to be complete. I'll regain my sanity and my freedom.

The Prison Experiment: Darwin's Last Stand Part 2:

The First Six Months

It's been months but I'm finally done writing journal entries for good, I think. After many months I can officially say that I have no idea what to do with myself anymore. My physical injuries have since healed but my mental issues have only increased. I wish I knew what was right and wrong anymore. I have no perception of anything and I wish I was dead. I have been on so many meds that I can't even tell what is real or not. I have just decided to shut down and not say anything. I have made myself a victim for the last six months. Maybe someone will come by and finally end my misery for good. Even though I haven't seen Nathaniel since I was checked in, I know that he is still involved. He has won. I have been in this institution for far too long. All these meds, I can't even think straight anymore.

In the beginning I had tons of visitors. I almost always saw Jared and his family along with some of my other friends. None of them seem to remember the last two weeks and they don't seem to believe me when I tell them what we all went through. Maybe they just don't want to remember. Ignorance is bliss, or so they say at least. Angela also broke up with me. She said she couldn't date someone who was crazy like me and she shut me down when I tried to beg her to take me back. After two weeks of that I think everyone just got sick of me and they just left me to rot in here until I could "come to my senses". I have been questioning if that study was real or not constantly. I still see the "doctor" with the piercing blue eyes occasionally. If I had to guess, I would say that that is Nathaniel's right-hand man. He always wears a surgical mask so I can't see his face fully. I need to get out of here.

I've stopped taking my meds slowly and I've been regaining my faculties. I pretend to take them whenever the doctors come in and force me to swallow them. They never know that I'm faking it every time now. I am officially done playing the victim. I made a promise and I intend on slaying Nathaniel. Then I will go after every single person that was involved in torturing all 24 of us until everyone is either behind bars or six feet under. First though, I need to get out of here. I am stuck in a white room with each of the walls white except for one. One is transparent and that is where my door is. I can see everyone who comes in and out before they even enter the room. Maybe I could smash the wall. No, that probably won't work and even if it did, I still have security to deal with and of course Nathaniel's influence. I saw the cover of a newspaper yesterday as someone was reading it while walking past my cell.

It seems that Nathaniel has invested money into this mental facility and he is currently on the board of directors. It's only a matter of time until he owns the entire building. I need to escape before he can torment me any further. It's the morning right now. I can see the sunlight coming from my locked window on the left-hand side of the room. I can just see it peering in and it is beautiful. I haven't felt the sun in six months and just the sight of it makes me want to cry. No, no. Even just a glimpse is enough to give the courage to escape. I need to be strong and make it out of this. I can see an air vent on the ceiling. The room is about 7 feet tall and I am just above 6 ft. During my stay I have been able to learn that for 30 seconds the cameras turn off for maintenance at midnight every Thursday. It just so happens to be Thursday today.

Many hours later. It is finally time for me to make my escape from this godforsaken place. I can feel my lungs breathing against my chest. Every fiber of my body is telling me not to jump and grab the air vent but I so don't care anymore. I am so full of adrenaline and I need to get out of here. I see the red glow from the camera facing my room shut off. Most people don't even know the cameras turn off. I just happen to be a very keen observer of things. Now, time to jump. I try three times but the grate just seems way too high. Finally, I use every ounce of strength and soul and I jump. The only problem is that I jump too hard and I hit my head on the grate. My head rings as I struggle to clamber inside the vent.

Currently my head and torso's in the vent with a slight dent on the top where my head hit but my legs are dangling from the opening. I quickly crawl further into the vent and then re-secure the grate so nothing looks amiss despite the dent. This place is really falling apart. I mean come on, who in their right mind would actually turn every single camera off for maintenance while there are still prisoners? Whatever, sometimes it feels like everything is preplanned for me. It is almost like I am just some character in a story.

I wonder if anyone has ever felt like that before. Well, no time to dwell on who or what may or may not be controlling my every thought and action. I need to get out of here.

I begin to crawl for what seems like hours. I realize though that it has probably only been a half hour or so. Right after I managed to get a few feet between me and the opening, I hear this loud alarm go off. I guess someone found out that I had made my daring escape. Fucking great. The only problem is that I have absolutely no idea on where to go. I can only hope that one of these vents will lead me to the garbage chute or something. Whenever I pass a room that is occupied, I always try to be as quiet as possible. I looked through the various grates I passed by. Some were occupied with other patients and some were occupied with guards searching.

One of the rooms was filled with prisoners in cages similar to mine from the study and they all looked miserable. I took a moment to observe them and I desperately wanted to free them. I couldn't though, I needed to get out of here. Many of the guards had their batons out and were threatening to hurt any of the patients who were being too loud. What the hell is this place? The other rooms had guards searching through them and guard dogs were being used to try and track me. Luckily my scent threw them off and they never thought to look up here. I can't explain why. The dogs would perk up if I was near but then they would go back to searching. The guards would look at the mutts confused but they would continue their search with no questions or complications. The air felt stale in the vents and I constantly wanted to cough but I held it in in order to not be caught. I also had to be very quiet while going through the vents. If any of the doctors or guards hear a creak coming from the vents they would know I'm there.

I saw another room that had doctors conducting tests on people and they looked very much like torture. People were being force fed their medications and some looked like they wanted to gag. I've still been taking my anti-anxiety and anti-depressant medications and they make me want to throw up half the time. They are the only meds I've been taking routinely because they helped me to feel at least somewhat normal while my mind was fractured. Now my mind has been slowly repairing itself since the effects of the other meds have worn off. The trek through the vents was exhausting and there were so many rooms that I wanted to intervene and save everyone but it was out of the question. I needed to focus on myself and get the hell out of here.

I saw one room that was particularly interesting. It was honestly a sight that I had never seen in my entire life. There were various people with lab coats on running frantically and screaming. I realized that my escape and the alarms must be stressing out the patients which in turn will make it harder for the doctors to do their work. I see some lab coats carrying papers and frantically signing them as they run. There is one person just banging his head against his keyboard. I could also see someone injecting himself with some sort of sedative to try to calm down. I have seen self-medicating before but that seems to be going too far.

Despite the stressful sight in front of me I found myself smiling very sadistically. It felt really good to know that my actions are really taking its toll on the people in this facility. I get that some of these people have no mal intent and that they are just trying to do their jobs but at this point I don't care. Nathaniel practically runs this place and if I can knock him down a peg or two in any way, I am going to take it and savor it. I quickly shake my head of all those thoughts and just decide to keep moving on.

I quickly pass through the vents when I finally come across one vent and the room seems to be unoccupied. I didn't really think to wait and listen before jumping right in but I was too energized and thrilled to find a seemingly empty room to think rationally. Once I descend into the room it soon becomes apparent that this room is completely empty. I see that there is a big computer screen with a ton of functions. Wait a minute, this place is much underfunded. It doesn't matter if Nathaniel put funds into it. This computer is very high tech. There are flashing lights on the keyboard and a ton of circuits and stuff all throughout the room. I realize that I don't have time to think about it.

I just run right up to the giant-sized computer and I push a button that seems to lead to a map. I pull if up and I see that of the three doors in this room only one of them leads to an exit and it is actually the door to the back of this room. Under normal circumstances I would have probably just bolted out the right then and there but my curiosity got the better of me. You know what they say, curiosity killed the cat. I tried looking through a few more folders. Most of it was junk except one. One folder said the name Nathaniel. I clicked on it and it was a profile of him. He was 19 years old and was in jail until three years ago. I go through some of the info but just before I can get to some of the probably more important stuff, I saw a folder that said my name. I clicked on it and I saw photos. Photos of me. There are photos of me when I am asleep, photos of me when I am with Jared and photos of me before and after I got into Lakehead University.

I was in so much shock that I vaguely heard the door open behind me. I turned around when I came face to face with the most terrifying person I have ever seen. It is Nathaniel's right-hand man. Up until this point I only saw his eyes but now his entire face is exposed and I finally get a good look at him. His entire face is deathly pale. His mouth is curved and cracked, his nose is full of nose hairs and pointed slightly, the rest of his face looks stressed and tired but the second we lock eyes his mouth turns from a look of tiredness and turns into one of delight. I dare myself to look into his piercing blue eyes again and I instantly realize it is a mistake. I feel so much shock that I can barely get my words out. "IIIIII, IIIIII, III." He cuts me off by holding up his right hand and I am instantly silenced. His hand looks so bony. His entire body looks thin but he also seems lean. His head is covered with black hair. I have a feeling that he is much stronger than he looks and a chill runs down my spine.

Normally I would think he could be a good-looking dude if he wasn't terrifying me so much or so bony. He comes closer but then turns away from me and I can only see his back. I instantly feel myself being able to calm down and think normally. I hear him speak and his voice could cut the air like it was nothing. "It has been a while, hasn't it Darwin." I can hear the way he says my name. It is almost like it was laced with venom. I finally regain my courage and I say loudly "where is Nathaniel".

He doesn't say anything but I soon hear him laughing hard. I can't tell why he is laughing but the laugh almost sounds evil. He says to me quietly "you have no idea what is coming Darwin. And you probably never will. Him funding this asylum was only the first step of his plan." Before I can say anything else he continues "we were supposed to update the cameras and the entire tech so escape would be impossible but you managed to escape before we could implement the new changes. You have been a real thorn in my side, ever since that study. You have no idea how beautiful it was to see Nathaniel's work. Seeing you and all those others begging for your families was oh so satisfying. It was like a piece of art that I just wanted to keep painting and morphing until it was finally complete. I think that I and Nathaniel are nearly there. Soon the world will fall to its knees once things finally change. One day, the world will know who we are. They shall bow down in fear and admiration under the name of Raphael Fitzgerald."

"Raphael?" I utter in disbelief. I can't believe this. It feels as if the world has finally caved in on me. I sink to my knees as I process this realization. I feel tears welling up in my eyes as I realize that Nathaniel isn't the only family member that tore me apart. I also have to face my older brother. Raphael turns to me and smiles with delight at my reaction. "What's the matter, Darwin? Don't you recognize your big brother? I understand my appearance is quite disturbing but you are to blame for it, as you are the one to blame for everything else." He said sickeningly sweet and quiet. I can tell he is enjoying seeing me suffer. "Why are you doing this brother? What did I ever do to you?" I ask quietly. Raphael seems to ponder this for a moment.

He stares back at me and says "It began when we were young. You and I used to be close but that changed once I turned 14 and you were 10. Due to our treatment from our parents, you and I just tried to survive. When I turned 16, I ran away from home. I wanted to live on my own. I planned on getting a job so I could make money and come back for you to live with me away from our family but something happened. One night in my apartment someone broke in. I couldn't see who it was since they had a mask on. I think it was one of a decapitated goat head. I stepped up to fight him but he caught me off guard when he put some rag over my head. I tried to fight it but I soon my felt my body weakening and after a few moments I went completely limp. I woke up in a cell just like the one you were put in at the beginning of your study. I spent months being punished and being tortured until one day Nathaniel revealed himself to me in private in his office. He made me an offer.

"I could either continue to be tortured for another year and never see you again, or I could become his right-hand man and torture others. My only thought was of getting back to you so I made my choice and agreed to his offer. For a year I abused the other prisoners. I hated it at first but then I started to love it. It became the reason I woke up in the morning. I became so engrossed in it that Nathaniel told me of his plan to take control of the world with this experiment. I loved it so much I helped him set everything up. Some of the trials lasted for over a year until we managed to fine tune it to two weeks for everything to take effect. Despite this I still wanted to see you so I sent you various letters and emails. I even tried coming to your home but you were either not there or you just didn't want to see me and you shooed me away without actually seeing my face. Eventually I started to get it in my head that you were to blame for the reason that the world is the way it is. I also heard Nathaniel's plan of making you pay for what you did to him and I finally gave him the green light to go through with it. You deserve all of the pain that you received and you deserve even more. I blame you for everything that has happened and I have Nathaniel to thank for showing me the light. You are the true enemy and I am going to enjoy delivering you to him so that he can finally squish you like the insignificant insect that you always have been."

The only thing I can do is just stare at him in shock. Before I can even blink, he lunges towards me and tackles me into the ground. I then feel his hands wrapping around my throat. It really hurts as I feel my life fading. I try to push him off but his grip is far too strong. I begin to see spots in my vision and I can feel my mind closing and dying. The oxygen must be leaving my brain. I can't breathe. I start to feel limp but I get my second wind. Until now I have been trying to pry his hand off of me. I instead go for his eye.

Luckily my index finger nail is somewhat long and I jam it into his left eye as he slowly moves his face closer to mine. He screams out in pain but I keep my nail in there until finally I feel his grip loosen and I pry it off with my left hand. He stumbles back while clutching his eye. I take the moment to breathe and feel my bruised throat. Then before Raphael can recover, I lunge into him and I knock him into some of the tech scattered around the room. He lands on one of the generators and I right hook him right in his right temple. He collapsed immediately. He fell back onto the floor and I can hear him breathing but shallowly.

My eyes see that he has a pocket knife in his front left pocket. I take it out and I see that it is a Spadoni Motors pocket knife, one of the newer ones. It is red and with a lot of utility tools. I look at my fallen brother and I think that it would be so easy. I want to lunge it into his chest before I realize that he is still my brother. I decide to head to the door that leads outside and I take one last look at my brother before I go. All I can feel is pity.

Meanwhile:

As Darwin makes his escape Raphael lies there bloody and broken. Guards come rushing through the office and find Raphael unconscious. They decide to stop tailing Darwin in order to help Raphael. They help him up and put him on a stretcher. They bring him to the medical ward and they patch him up. His eye is damaged beyond repair so the doctors there fix him up the best they could and then put a bandage over his eye. They then use adrenaline to force him to wake him up. Raphael awakes with a start and sees Nathaniel sitting there at his bedside; but his expression doesn't appear friendly at all. The two talk and the conversations ends with Nathaniel beating the crap out of Raphael.

Raphael begs him to stop but Nathaniel keeps whaling on him until finally enough punishment has been given out. Raphael had to be punished for letting Darwin escape. Raphael shakily gets to his feet and the two head out of the room together. Raphael appears nervous in front of Nathaniel and is starting to feel bad about he's done to Darwin. Raphael had been told numerous times that Darwin is the enemy and for a long time he truly believed that. But seeing Darwin again cracked something inside of him. It wouldn't be enough to dissuade him from killing Darwin for Nathaniel but something has shifted and he wouldn't be the same. Nathaniel decides to head for Lakehead to see the status of some of his soldiers on guard there. On the way-out Nathaniel swipes a syringe of something from the hospital to potentially use against Darwin.

Outside

Back to Darwin's perspective:

The second I step outside I am greeted by the warm rush of a summer's wind. The only thing I feel when it hits is euphoria. I let the wind go through every ounce of my body. It isn't until after this that I realize I am still in the clothes from the hospital. I find a plastic bag near the entrance and I see that it has some clothes that are pretty close to my size. I see a bright green t-shirt and some blue jeans. I also find a black hoodie that is a size 10, same as me. I stuff it on and I throw the hood over my face as I see that some of the guards from the facility are starting to search outside. I duck into a nearby alley and I head through the alley and into the city of Thunder Bay. I just kept running and running until I finally made it to LU.

I was about to head inside Bartley residence to look for Jared since he is an RA there, but when my hand reached the door handle, I froze. I saw leaning against another building a few meters away was Nathaniel. He seemed to be having a smoke. I pulled my hood up more over my face and I slowly walked towards him when I saw a couple guys with masks on approach him. Nathaniel was wearing a black skull t-shirt and his comrades both had on green hoodies and both had goat masks on. I crept closer as I saw them start walking left into the streets. I stalked them for about thirty minutes when they came across this old abandoned building. It had no windows and it seemed to be falling apart. I saw Nathaniel take out an old-fashioned key and unlock the wooden door. There were cracks in the walls all across the building. This place was definitely on its last legs. I waited about five minutes and then I crept inside the building behind them.

It soon became apparent that this was someone's house. The walls were gray and all of the lights were off. I slowly crept down a hallway until I saw there was one room illuminated with light. I dared to peer my head into it and I saw Nathaniel sitting on a La-Z-Boy brown chair smoking a pipe while the two masked men sat on the brown couch in the middle of the room. Neither of them was facing my direction but to be safe I crouched behind the wall and kept my ear near the doorway to be able to listen in.

After a few painful moments I finally heard Nathaniel speak in his calm cold voice. "We have a serious problem Jorgen." It sounded like someone was shaking, I couldn't tell for sure but I was guessing that Jorgen was shaking slightly. Someone else spoke; his voice was deep and rough but with a hint of fear. He said "I know Nathaniel. I am sorry that we let the prisoner escape. We should've been keeping closer tabs on the control room and we should've had more guards situated around the perimeter. I am sorry." Nathaniel replied "Don't worry about it, Jorgen. These things happen." His voice seemed almost kind but then I heard his voice become lower and colder. He commanded "But make no mistake; a second offence will not be tolerated. Do you understand me?" The one who I suppose was Jorgen spoke through his mask quickly. "Yes sir, I understand perfectly." I heard Nathaniel sigh. He then said "good. Glad we finally understand each other. However, I must ensure that this does not happen again. I will let you live but I need to give you something to remember this day." Before anyone could say anything, I thought I heard someone pulling out a gun and then I heard a shot fire.

I nearly screamed due to the sound. I also heard the sound of someone collapsing. I heard the sound of someone dropping to their knees and whimpering. I realize that Nathaniel must have fired the shot because he said very coldly "Do not worry Mateo, your friend will survive. I only shot him in the side. I don't think I hit any major organs. Now, let this be a lesson to you both. If you do exactly as I say then the world will be yours for the taking. Go against me and you will suffer. Next time I won't be so lenient."

I heard Nathaniel begin to walk in my direction so I quietly stood up and raced to the exit at the end of the hall. I threw open the door and raced into a nearby corner where I could still see the entrance to the house. My body was really sweating. The only thing I can think of is that Nathaniel actually had a gun. I looked at the entrance and I saw the two masked men walking and limping out of the building. I saw that one of them had a lot of blood coming from his side and I realize that must have been Jorgen. I saw a black sedan pull up and I saw Jorgen and Mateo (I assume) climb into the sedan and then it sped off as soon as it came.

I Saw Nathaniel stare into the distance as the car left and then I saw him walk towards the corner I was by. I didn't exactly think it would go down like this but maybe with my black hoodie I can sink into the shadows behind the streetlight and ambush him before he got the chance to shoot again. I saw him walk towards me but since I situated myself into a very dark corner, he seemingly passed right by me without noticing me.

He stopped about ten feet in front of me and I swore I heard him say "thank you my god." I desperately wanted to ambush him right there since he seemed so vulnerable but there was something holding me back. I realized that if I just killed him right now, I might never know the true reason behind my capture and why so many people have lost their memories. I also wasn't sure if I could take him down since he had the gun and was pretty strong. I decided that until I had a better plan, I would let him live for now. No need to rush things, I just need to bide my time and take everything he has before he dies. Nathaniel then starts to walk away but I see something drop from his pocket.

Once he is out of earshot I dash up to the item and I see it is a business card. It talks about a property nearby and how much it costs and who to contact. I see though that the card was created last year and that the building was probably bought by now. I don't really know what this means but I am curious to see where this leads. I wonder if I actually am being controlled to some extent. Am I just some puppet and someone else is pulling the strings? It really is a scary thought but I can't worry about this right now.

I need to get to 421 Fake Street. I personally have never heard of it and it seems pretty unnerving but it's the only lead I have. But before that I decide to head back to the house that Nathaniel was in initially. I double back and I go through the front door. I peer around but it's clear that no one is here. I explore the main room and the upstairs but nothing can be found. I almost give up before I see the basement. I rush to it and I fling the door open before peering down. The way down is dark but I fumble for the light switch and light my way down. I go down and the moment I see what lays before me I feel lightheaded and I retch on the floor. The last thing I remember is the world fading black as I fall directly into my vomit and hit my head on the hardwood floor.

I wake up panting for breath only to realize that I'm back in the cell and Nathaniel is peering over me with a blowtorch in one hand. He looks like a demon with glowing red eyes and lights the torch up and pushes it against my face. The searing hot burns my flesh as he laughs maniacally. I finally woke up with a start and realize that the last part was a dream. I'm still panicking as I take in the room before me in the basement but I manage to catch my breath and wipe the vomit off my face. The room I'm in is cold and dark but I can still see what's inside. It's a makeshift dungeon and I can see cells that looked exactly like mine. I knew the study was real and that I really was kept in a cell for weeks.

I hyperventilate as I remember everything; I went through but I manage to calm myself down by taking deep breaths.

I quickly scan the room but other than shackles and chains there isn't anything here to indicate where I should go next. It looks more archaic than the one I was kept in but maybe this was a prototype of the study. Who knows anymore? I decide to leave the house and go back to the street corner where I last saw Nathaniel. The warm air feels nice on my skin once again. I felt something in my left hoodie pocket. I open it up and I see it is a schematic of the city Thunder Bay. I look for Fake Street (I know right) and I see that it is actually on the corner of Balmoral Street. I run as fast as I can and I finally make it to Balmoral and I see there is a very long alley that is obscured by everything the street offers.

I carefully tread down the alley until I see there is this building that is pressed against another building that says Piece for Peace that can only be seen from the original street. Piece for Peace is a corporation that supplies prosthetic limbs to amputees and provides support for them. I know they are a very profitable company but I wonder if it could be a front for something. I thought I heard Nathaniel was somehow involved in it but I can't be sure.

The Truth Revealed

I DECIDE TO JUST head into the building and not dwell on any thoughts. I look inside the building and I see that it is dark. I open the door and I see that it is huge on the inside. The walls are gray and there are multiple doors at every end of the giant room but other than that there is nothing here. The walls seem to be aging rapidly but it just looks dark except for a swinging lamp on the ceiling. I decide to go through the door on the left. I feel my hands going numb as I reach for the handle but I push it quietly anyway. I cannot believe what I am seeing. I see a room labeled prisoners ahead and to my right I see three doors. One says Overseer's office, the other says guard barracks and the third one says Isolation chamber. I feel my heart begin to beat rapidly. I am back in the study. I fall to my knees while clutching my heart. I think I am going to die. I am too young to die in this place. My breathing is quickening and quickening until I finally realize that this might be a good thing. Maybe I can finally get some answers.

I realize that it must be 10 at night or something so I know that everyone must be asleep. I see that there is a camera looking straight at me but maybe the guard is asleep. I also see another room that says control room. I creep up to the room and I peer inside. I can see a typical setup of computer monitors analyzing the various rooms and I can see that there is also an audio feed. The man I see slumped against his chair must be in his late 50s. His hair line is beginning to recede, his pants are dirty and his white shirt is covered in dirt as well. I can't see his face but due to the way his chest is rising and falling I think it's safe to assume that the guard is fast asleep.

I leave the room and I decide to creep over to the guard barracks. When I step into the room, I immediately have to creep back out of the room to avoid being seen. I did manage to catch a glimpse of what was going on though. I don't really know what I was expecting to see but it sure as hell wasn't this. In the room I saw there to be about 12 people lying down with metal helmets and a bunch of wires attached to them. I saw various monitors showing brain wave activity and multiple people in lab coats observing their vitals and adjusting certain chemicals. I saw where certain parts of the brain were isolated and how some parts were functionally differently than other parts.

I decide to risk peeking in again. This time the doctors are facing away from me so I know that they can't see me. I can hear a bit of what they are saying and I realize that it isn't anything good. "Oh! Oh! Oh! Look at this doctor, look at subject number 7. He is doing so admirably. His brain waves are off the charts. It truly is beautiful" said this seemingly male doctor with an unusually high voice. The other doctor replied "Not now Marshall! We need to isolate these subjects' brains. We need to make sure that they are getting the correct dosage of drugs so that they will do what we ask without question. The prisoners are always getting their meds from their food.

"Little do they know is that their mystery meat is laced with a very specific drug to lull them to sleep at 8 and to slowly eat away at their memories until we pull them off the drug. Once that happens, we can store their memories farther into their brains so they don't have easy access to them. By using our machines and the drug we can make the process easier. As for our pets in this room, we need to be sure that their dosage is correct as well. If we can store their memories elsewhere using our equipment and the new drug we developed, Apitonin, then we can imprint a number on their brains and when we say it then they will remember their sadistic tendencies and be perfect soldiers. Now shut up and get back to work."

"Geez, okay lay off dad. I am just trying to have a little fun and all. I am just so excited. We never get to work on live subjects and Nathaniel's plan is absolutely perfect." said Marshall. The gruff doctor replied "yes, I know, this is a very invigorating experience for all of us. Nathaniel is currently in a meeting in his office working out the matters with our employers. Nathaniel may very well be able to bring the world to its knees." Marshall replied "I am aware. But you know just as well as I do that, I am not following Nathaniel for his ideals like you are. I am only interested in fulfilling my own agenda but since we have similar passions then I will happily go along with whatever Nathaniel wants. By the way, did you hear about what happened to Raphael? I think he's in trouble." He said in a sing song voice.

The gruff doctor said quietly "yeah, I heard about what happened. Darwin escaped and left him within an inch of his life. I don't know how Nathaniel will take that but at least someone finally knocked Raphael down a peg or two. I guess the stress and work that Raphael did to himself in the past caused him to look the way he is but still. He doesn't seem fit to lead. With Darwin escaping and our plan approaching completion I have no idea what Nathaniel is thinking about. I guess that's what the meeting with the council is about."

It would appear that Nathaniel is in fact here. I need to find out what his plans are but first, I need to take care of the guard manning the computers. He is probably still asleep but I need to make sure. I slowly crept out of this room and crept back into the control room. The guard was still asleep but I decided to take some action to ensure I was uninterrupted. I snuck up behind his chair until I was able to latch my arms around his neck and pull as hard as I could. He awoke with a start but he wasn't able to fight me off since I had the advantage of surprise. He attempted to struggle but after a while he went limp and fell unconscious. I stared at him as he fell to the floor and his chair fell to the side and made a lot of noise. I waited for a moment but no one seemed to notice the noise coming from this room. I didn't know what to feel. I didn't kill him but I did incapacitate him for the time being. I guess I shouldn't worry about it. I realize that I have a belt on so I decide to bind his hands and stick him in the corner behind some of the excess equipment. I also position his head so he is pressed against some machinery and he can't call for help since he is trapped. I will admit it will take some time for him to be discovered and free but no matter.

It is time to eavesdrop on Nathaniel. I press my ear against the doorframe and I can't really hear anything. Wait, I can hear Nathaniel yelling in there. Something about not getting enough troops in time I think I heard. I am really not sure honestly. I hear footsteps coming from the office so I duck into the control room until I hear the footsteps head out the door that leads to outside. I can hear angry muttering but I can't make out much of it. After a moment I creep back to Nathaniel's office and I can't hear anything. I take a step inside and I see that the office is pretty plain. Nice large wooden desk, nice black Asus laptop and a few picture frames on the desk. There doesn't seem to be anything else in here. I head to the desk and I see that there are no photos in the frames. That's really weird and eerie. I then activate his laptop and I see that it is password protected. I try putting his name in and of course Nathaniel would be the password.

The computer is unlocked and I start going through all of his files. I come across one that the second I open it chills me to the bone. I scroll through it and I finally see why this project exists. Nathaniel is actually a pretty high-ranking member of the group **Piece for Peace.** Nathaniel is currently 19 years old and he left to join the company when he was 16 after he was released from jail. He joined because he didn't know what to do and he wanted to see if they could help him get revenge on me and the government for what happened to him. While he was there, he started to morph their ideals and wanted them to help him take the world. He seemed to turn them from a company dedicated to helping people into one with more seemingly anarchist views.

It seems that Nathaniel pitched the idea of using a simulation of a prison to create more soldiers to the cause and to punish those that do not believe in the cause. As the idea grew and grew, some of the scientists working for Piece for Peace created a new drug called Apitonin and it is supposed to allow the brain functions to imprint a number on it so that past memories and feelings can be retrieved at any time. The drug also helps isolate certain memories and keep them out of the way until they need to be awakened. It seems that after many tests the project was deemed worthy and a success and Nathaniel; I guess took control over his own facility where he could do what he wished so long as he kept getting the results he and some council who put up extra funding wanted.

That's why no one remembers. The realization hit me like a ton of bricks and I feel myself backing away from the desk in fear. When the time comes the guards can be awoken and they will fight for Piece for Peace. This is much worse than I thought. I need to get out of here. I need to warn the police. Just as I am getting up to leave, I see the door opening. In comes Nathaniel wielding a 44 magnum and Raphael with a nasty bandage over his eye comes in with a 38 pistol. "Well, well, well. It's been a long time hasn't it been Darwin. I haven't seen you since I put you in that mental institution. I would ask how you liked it but since you escaped, I guess that answers the question itself." Nathaniel said cruelly. I stand my ground and utter "Nathaniel, why?"

The smile that Nathaniel had on quickly vanished and he said loudly "you actually want to know why I did this. I did this because you deserved it. You and I used to be friends and then you got me locked up. Jared got what he deserved and now he is my mind slave. You deserve everything that you got and you deserve even more after what you did to Raphael and you always trying to get in my way." I never took my eyes off of Nathaniel. I didn't feel scared that he had a gun pointed in my direction. I was more afraid of how he would torture me if given the chance. I should've killed Nathaniel in the alley when I got the chance. "Why would you work for Piece for Peace, is that how you got all this money?" I ask loudly. Nathaniel smirks and says coyly, "but of course my dear Darwin. What else do you think I would've done? You should know that I can hold a grudge for a very long time and Piece for Peace was the best way to help me deal with my anger. I was finally apart of a group that I could influence and that was forced to understand me. I bring in what we all want and they supply me with riches and anything else that I could ever want."

As he is talking, I see two masked people walking in. I see that one is limping and I realize that this must've been Jorgen. I turn to him and say "Jorgen." The man turns to me in surprise but before he can react, I continue "why are you working with Nathaniel? I saw the way he punished you. You don't deserve it." Jorgen stares at me through his mask and says quietly "this is the only life I have ever known. My family died at the hands of a murderer. My family did nothing wrong. They paid their bills and lived their lives but one day from out of nowhere this man in a black hoodie descended upon our house and he slaughtered my wife and two kids that were only 6 and 9 years old. When the suspect was caught, I guess that the evidence had been tampered with. Apparently, the leader of Canada and his government believed that this man couldn't be convicted and they let him off.

"He gets to go free while I am alone with no one and every member of my family is in the damn ground. The man also tried to kill me as well but I leapt out the window after he managed to shoot me in the knee and tried to run until I tripped on the sidewalk near my 'ome. Nathaniel happened to be walking by and he took me to the hospital. When he found out my family was murdered, he stayed with me and tried to help me get back on my feet. He made me an offer. I was a very good gunman in the army long ago and if I work for Nathaniel then he would help me bring the country to its knees. I never trusted our leader and I wanted to be a part of anything that tears this world apart. That is the answer to your question. I am still alive because of Nathaniel and I intend on working with him until I can be free from this burden." Before I could say anything, Nathaniel ordered Mateo and Jorgen to take me away. They each grabbed one of my arms and started to drag me out of the office. I guess I am going to be executed in front of the cell block or something. I don't really know anymore. I don't care honestly. I can finally prove that I am not crazy. I feel tired now. I want to sleep now and forever.

Revenge

As I am being dragged out, I am still in a daze when I hear a shot ring out. I hear Jorgen falling to his knees but my arm is still gripped tight. I try to figure out what happened when I see another two shots ring out. Jorgen got two in the gut (ouch) and Mateo got one right in the head. Blood from both victims sprays all over my face and as they fall to the ground I fall flat on my face. I have no idea what just happened but I can't even think straight. I hear Nathaniel shooting but I happen to see a shot hit him right in the foot and Raphael dropping his weapon to try to support him. I feel strong gruff hands pulling me up and running out of the hall just before Nathaniel can recover.

When we left the hall and start to head back to where I came when I entered this place, I finally take a look at my savior and I see that it's Jared. Jared has many more scars than I remembered and his beard has grown but I can still tell it's him. When we finally get outside me and Jared run to the nearby alley and we hide in the shadows to calm down. I see Nathaniel and his guards running past us and out the other side of the alley. My heart is racing and I sink to my knees. I can't believe what just happened. I turn to see Jared who has changed dramatically. His hair is much longer and he has grown a brown beard that is covering his neck slightly. I see his brown eyes haven't changed but he looked slightly older then when I last saw him six months ago. He looks very tired and on edge. We both knew that this probably the stupidest place to hide since we are so close to the facility but I don't care. I need to rest.

He turns to me and he whispers "I'm sorry. I'm sorry for everything that happened. I should have stood by you when you were admitted. I guess I just didn't want to remember what happened because I was afraid of what I might see. It all came back to me the other night. I was trying to sleep when I had this terrible nightmare about torturing you and being probed. I also saw myself being pumped with drugs and I thought I saw this number being imprinted on my brain or something. I can't explain it, I just remember seeing this number appear in my head over and over again. I don't know why I am remembering now or why I still feel like myself but that doesn't matter right now. I have no excuse for my actions toward you or the others. I saw Nathaniel tonight and I wanted to see where he was going. I followed him here when I saw you go in after him. I decided to follow you and when I saw you getting dragged away; I quickly drew the gun I stole from the barracks and I fired. I killed two people. I murdered them in cold blood but I had to. I had to rescue my best friend. I don't know if I can live with what I did but I had to at least try to make up for my past mistakes. I don't expect you to forgive me. In fact, I wouldn't be surprised if you turned me into the police for my crimes or killed me right here and now. I am truly sorry."

Jared sunk to his knees and silently wept. I just sat there and listened. After a few minutes I grabbed him and hugged him tightly. He appeared to be shocked but I spoke before he could react. "It's ok Jared. I understand, you never wanted to be used as a tool in Nathaniel's game. You are a good person and I know that you might never forgive yourself but I will help you cope with it buddy. You are still my friend." I said softly. I let go of him but I still saw the pained look in his eyes. He looked away and said quietly "I know that Nathaniel is planning on unleashing his soldiers for Piece for Peace all across the world to fight in their name. The facility here is one of many. There are hundreds of thousands of these places all across the globe and they are only getting bigger and bigger. Nathaniel and some of the other leaders are planning on broadcasting their message across the world to bring their soldiers alive."

I want to butt in when I hear footsteps coming from the head of the alley. I turn to look but I see Jared's gun flying from his hand. Someone had shot the gun away. I turned around and we both saw the smug faces of Nathaniel and Raphael. Both armed with their weapons. Jared looked ready to fight but we all knew that without his weapon he would lose instantly. Nathaniel and Raphael both walked towards us slowly but Jared reacted without thinking. Jared ran towards Nathaniel when he very calmly aimed his gun and fired.

I couldn't believe my eyes. I saw Jared lying on the ground in a pool of his own blood. I felt numb. I realized that there was nothing I could do. Jared was dead. I felt tears well up in my eyes when I saw Raphael walk to Jared and pick him up. Jared's eyes were open and he was still breathing. The shot only caught him on his right shoulder. I felt relieved until I saw what Nathaniel did next. He walked to face Jared and said "Subject 343, it is time to arise. Dinner is ready." I saw Jared begin to stand up without Raphael's help and he said monotone "of course my master. I only live to serve Piece for Peace." Admitting that I was very shocked would be an understatement. I realize that the power over Jared's mind is so powerful that his body will fight no matter how much pain he is in.

Nathaniel then says "turn and face your opponent. The time has come to face your final test. If you succeed in killing him then you will be my new left-hand man." I see Jared turn to face me and all I can see is the sadistic glint in his eyes and his smile as he realizes that he finally gets to murder me. I know that I have lost my best friend all over again. I see Nathaniel handing him another gun but then I see Jared toss it to the side and then bow to me. I see that he also wants me to do the same so I follow suit and then we rise at the same time. I guess Jared wants this to be a fair fight and face me one on one. As Voldemort would say "the niceties must be observed." At least I have a chance to win. I feel the sweat dropping down my brow and my back. I can feel my heart pumping as much oxygen and blood into my system as possible. I know that I am going to need every last shred of power and courage that I have left.

Jared quickly rushes towards me and tackles me onto the dirty ground. Before I can counter Jared brings his fist and hits me in the face over and over. I can feel warm blood coming from my nose and my mouth. I can feel my bones and veins struggling to remain intact as each hit becomes more and more intense. I can actually feel my body leaving this earth after each hit. My vision is becoming more and more blurry as each hit lands its mark. I don't want to die here like this. Please God, help give me the strength to survive this. The next thing I know is that I feel Jared's hands around my throat but I don't worry about dying. For some reason my rational thought seems to kick in. I can only seem to think about what is going on right now.

I take my left hand and I hit against his hands until his grip loosens and I can drag them off. Jared stumbles away and I take the opportunity to lunge toward him. I tackle him and his head hits the ground hard. I back away quickly when I realize that his head is seriously bleeding. I see that his eyes are hollow just before he closes them and that he can barely move. The last thing I hear him say is "Hail Nathaniel." And then he goes still, seemingly never moving again. I can feel the tears welling up in my eyes but I just stare at the lifeless body in shock. I just killed someone and my best friend no less.

I overhear Nathaniel snickering and saying "well I admit I wasn't expecting this at all. I figured Jared would come out the victor but clearly Darwin here is the stronger of the two." Nathaniel comes slightly closer and says "I was going to kill you but you have proven yourself to be quite the fighter. If you were to join us then you could help rebuild the world. You also wouldn't have to feel so much pain at the loss of your friend." I think over his words for the briefest of moments but I catch that there is a bit of slight glee at Jared's death from Nathaniel and I yell "I WILL NEVER JOIN YOU NATHANIEL!" He looks me once over and sighs. He then says "very well then. Raphael, dispose of him for me." Nathaniel walks away back to the lab and Raphael aims his gun at my chest. I decide that maybe I should welcome death. Before I can even comprehend what is going on I see Jared rise up and block Raphael's gun.

Raphael had been able to fire but due to Jared's intervention the shot missed my body by an inch and landed harmlessly on the ground. I don't even know how he is still standing but he knocks the gun out of the way and Jared quickly tosses me his gun that he had. Apparently, Jared managed to pick up the gun he tossed aside moments ago. I can see that Jared doesn't have much life left but I also see that the hollowness in his eyes seems to have disappeared. He seems to be whole again. He says in a weak voice "I know that I will die on this night but I will not die as a puppet. I will die fighting for what is right." Raphael appears to be stunned throughout this whole ordeal but he quickly recovers and tries to lunge for his gun on the ground. I manage to grab it first and I aim the 38. at Raphael's forehead and I fire. I find myself lying on the ground in shock until I can pull myself up and I drop the 38. in terror.

Raphael's head opened up like a water balloon. Blood went everywhere. I rushed to my brother and I saw that he was barely alive. Most of his forehead was gone and I saw brain and blood oozing out of him. It reminded me of the inside of a watermelon or a pumpkin. His face still seemed to be mostly intact though. He grabbed my arm and said weakly "I am so sorry Darwin. I should never have abandoned you and I shouldn't have gone along with our cousin's plan. If Nathaniel succeeds then the entire world will fall. I was too weak to stop it but maybe you can Darwin. I don't expect your forgiveness after all the heinous things I have done. I just want you to know that I always tried to care about you, even when I was lost. You brought me back little brother. My loyalty is to you and only you. Thank you." I see a tear fall from his right eye and then he goes still. I can't stop the flow of tears from coming out. I never wanted to kill my brother. "I forgive you Raphael." I say quietly. I then see Jared fall to the ground as his head wound is still bleeding. He tells me "He's right. You need to go on by yourself but be careful. Nathaniel has a lot of tricks up his sleeve. Go to his office, he will be waiting for you there. In the meantime, I will head to the hospital to get my injuries assessed. Goodbye Darwin." I gave him one last hug and I said "I understand. I will see you on the other side man." He flashed me a thumbs up and hobbled to the nearest hospital.

I pocketed the gun Jared gave me and I headed back to the labs. It isn't a long distance but it feels like an eternity walking all the way there. My heart is racing so fast I am surprised that I haven't had a heart attack yet. I don't know what to expect. I just know that I need to end this once and for all. My steps begin to feel heavy as I get closer and closer to the office. I can feel the sweat dropping from my brow. Despite this I know I must press on. I need to face my demons. Before I can really contemplate what is going on I find myself at the door to Nathaniel's office. I see guards come out from nowhere and I see that they are beginning to block every exit. There truly is no going back. I breathe in deeply into my chest and I push the door open and step inside. I see Nathaniel standing behind his desk facing me with a silent expression. I can't really tell what he is feeling but then he says "I can't believe Raphael is dead. He was a good cousin. Perhaps he didn't deserve to die like he did." Before I can respond he mutters "he was a better man than you ever were Darwin." He raises his gun at me and I follow suit.

Nathaniel lowers his gun slightly and fires a shot. The shot seemed to miss me until I realized that he shot the gun out of my hand and onto the floor in pieces. He smirks and then puts his gun back inside his desk. He then takes out two antique swords that are hanging on his wall. One sheath is black and the other is red. He takes the sword from the red sheath and I see it is a beautiful blade. Nice silver blade with a curved tip and the hilt is short but dark red. He tosses the other blade towards me and says "pick it up." I do as I'm told and I see that this blade is more or less the same except with a black hilt. I am left-handed but for sports I tend to rely on my right hand so I place this blade in my right and he does the same. He says to me "you have proven yourself to be a very powerful opponent. I wish to see how you fair in a one-on-one fight with the best. Can you do it Darwin? Can you best the new god of this world? Only time will tell." He is about 30 feet away from me but I see him slowly advance towards me. Nathaniel's family has always been involved in sword fighting so I'm not surprised that he practices as well. I have a little bit of experience from my grandfather's side of the family but not much. I just hope that it's enough to best a real master like Nathaniel. My palms begin to sweat as I think about Nathaniel thrusting his sword into my chest but I hold it together.

He raises his sword and I lunge towards him but he casually blocks my weapon. I advance faster again and he blocks the other side. He seems to be very calm and advancing slowly which I don't seem to get. I try again and he blocks it. I tried horizontal slices, vertical slices and even diagonal slices. I just can't seem to get a hit on him. I decide to move my hand to my right side and I see him slowly move his blade as if to block. I move slowly as well and just as I try the slice; I quickly move my hand to my left side and catch him off guard. I end up slicing his cheek and he falls back slightly. He wasn't expecting that. "Well, well, seems like someone has some decent skill. That may have helped you thus far but you will need much more than that to best me in combat." He advances faster this time and it takes everything I have to block my left side from being hit.

He seems to try to hit me from any angle that he can think of and it takes every ounce of my skill to barely block it. I want to counter but every time I do, he just blocks and pushes me back. This time I see that he is moving faster and faster and then it dawns on me. Nathaniel has been playing me this entire time. He has been moving slow so as to conserve his energy and then will steadily move faster to try to throw me off. He really is the best swordsman I have ever seen.

I need to beat him though. I am already beginning to lose my breath. My lungs are burning. Nathaniel doesn't seem to have broken a sweat. I finally make one last ditch effort to take him head on and he blocks it but doesn't push back. Instead, we are both in a bind. It's sword pressing against sword. I am trying to stay strong to push him back but I can feel my knees buckling. I try to fight but he just keeps pushing me down and down until he pushes my sword to my left side and brings his sword down right onto my right hand. I scream out in pain as my right hand comes flying off as the blood begins to gush out of my arm like a dam exploded. I am lying on my back as the blood rushes out and I feel my body burning. Nathaniel stood atop me smiling with glee and says "I should have known. There is no way that some insignificant insect like you would be able to destroy the almighty god of this world. I should put you out of your misery but you deserve this." He then kicks me in the chin and walks away while taking his sword with him. My jaw rattles and I can feel blood flowing from the inside of my mouth. My chin and face hurts but it is nothing compared to the pain my arm is in.

I see him head to his computer and upload a jump drive. I see though he is not completely facing me. I am not in front or behind him. I am closer to his side but maybe I can finish this. I slowly crawl to my knees and I try to cover my hand with my shirt to try to stop the bleeding. With great effort and a lot of strain I somehow manage to tie the arm hole around my stub to try to stop the bleeding. I then take my left hand and I grab the sword out of my dismembered right hand. The thought of my hand lying motionless on the ground was enough for me to throw up but I hold it down. I move my body so

I am more behind Nathaniel and then I finally begin to stand. Slowly but surely, I walk to where Nathaniel is and I raise my blade in the air. My left hand feels weaker with the sword but hopefully my aim will be true. I bring the sword down and into Nathaniel. I managed to slash a huge horizontal gash across his back.

It went very deep. I heard his knees buckle and he falls onto his desk and hits his head before falling onto his back and onto the ground. He looks up at me and for once I see the look of horror on his face. He looks shocked but says "I honestly didn't think you could do it. You cut me." I see him try to get up and in retaliation I use all my effort to push my sword into his chest. He tries to grab the blade with his blood-soaked hands but fails and says "nice work Darwin. First you murder your only brother and then you murder your cousin. How can you live with yourself?" I look down at him and say very coldly "I can't." He seems surprised until I pull the sword out and I slash his neck. More blood seems to gush out of him and I see that he is still horrified. He clearly thought that he would win. I honestly don't know how I feel. I felt almost sad at first that I had beaten him but then I just felt angry. I had to slash him. I had to torture him like he tortured me for all that time. I can see him choking on his own blood. I revel in it. He deserves this. He suddenly drops something out of his pocket. I take a glance at it and realize it's a syringe full of poison. Of what kind I can't tell but I'm certain he meant to poison me as a last resort. Clearly, he failed.

I just decide to leave him to it and with the last of my strength I see what he uploaded to the computer. It has all the information about the leaders of the group and their plans. I guess that each of the leaders wanted to broadcast a message across their own area to reawaken their soldiers. The drive also shows a list of every soldier that was experimented on and every casualty. The casualty rate is extremely high. "I thought 9/11 was bad" I mutter to myself. I also see that each leader is meant to broadcast their message fifteen minutes after the previous leader did their message. I guess instead of everyone broadcasting it at the same time I guess they want to awaken some soldiers and then if one wave begins to falter then another wave will be awoken to try to overwhelm the police and military presence. I guess that once the police are slaughtered and when most of the people have been massacred then I suppose Nathaniel and the group will rise from the ashes and repopulate the world in their name.

The group will truly become the leaders of the new world. I need to prevent this and I see that Nathaniel uploaded a tape that is meant to be broadcasted within ten minutes. I assume he is the first to spread the message. I can feel my strength waning so I send an email to a guy I know in the city who is also a cop that says that Nathaniel is dead and that I am holed up here. I also say that this file must be stopped immediately and then I press send. I can feel my strength dying but I don't care. After everything I don't feel anything anymore. I fall to my knees and I decide to die on my own terms. I eventually fall onto my back and not unlike some of my previous brushes with death I decide to welcome it with open arms. I close my eyes as I feel my spirit being taken far away from here. I don't know how much time has passed but I can vaguely hear footsteps running into the building and I hear ambulance and police sirens. Everything went black after that.

Peace At Last?

...What the hell? I can't see anything. Am I alive? I try to open my eyes but I can't. I try again and again until finally I can feel my eyes opening and my vision immediately becomes blinded by the light. I slowly open them again and I realize that I am in a hospital room. I can hear the heart monitor and I see that I am hooked up to an IV machine. "Good, you're awake," says a voice from across the room. I look and I see what appears to be the doctor. He is an old looking man with white hair and round glasses but his expression seems friendly enough. He comes to me and says "you have been through a lot my friend. You are lucky to be alive." I have no idea what he is talking about until everything comes rushing back. My heart rate begins to increase and I can feel myself panicking until I see the doctor summoning a nurse or something and they inject me with probably morphine. I begin to calm down slowly and I ask him "what happened?"

The doctor goes on to explain that once the police found my file they looked into the group and they quickly used their best IT teams to stop the videos from being uploaded. They found each leader hiding out in various places but eventually everyone was caught and each of the people that were affected had been brought into various hospitals to receive treatment. All of the leaders admitted to their wrong doings and the grunts admitted the same as well. Without Nathaniel to lead them all I guess no one saw the point of keeping quiet anymore. Many of the subjects that were brainwashed have had the drugs pumped out of them and the numbers are no longer imprinted in their brains. I also heard that Nathaniel was in charge of his own Swat team. He had money invested in various companies. Jared and the other guards remembered their ordeals so as punishment they are sentenced to community service for six months and a little bit of jail time with the stipulation that they must see a psychologist to deal with their demons. The doctor told me that I had fallen into a coma for eighteen days. They were also able to repair my right hand and I should be able to get at least 95% functionality from it in time.

When I was finally released from the hospital I was given my sentence. For the murders of Nathaniel and Raphael, I have to stay seven months in jail. Since I helped the police crackdown on Piece for Peace I am given my own cell away from general population. Honestly for the first time I feel at ease here. I don't need to worry about being killed here and I have a psychologist that I can talk to whenever I need to. I still have nightmares but I feel at peace here in jail. I know that I am kept here for my own protection and so that I don't lash out at any of the other prisoners. I still have outbursts and sometimes I still think I see Nathaniel but the doctors say that I am just dealing with post-traumatic stress disorder. I don't know for sure. I honestly don't know if I can ever function properly after this again. I don't know for sure but I think I miss Nathaniel. I miss him and my brother. I want to believe that everything will be okay but who knows for sure? Sometimes I think that it could be just someone in a Nathaniel mask trying to taunt me but I guess I will never know. I can actually see the hallucination. He has a mask that resembles Nathaniel and is holding a knife. Guess I better just head to sleep. Hopefully it will all be over soon. I don't care if the courts told me that I'm innocent, or that I didn't do anything wrong. I know that I deserve to be in prison for what I did. I will remain in here until I'm either dead or I feel ready to go back home.

One Hour before...

In an apartment building not too far away from the Thunder Bay jail there is a lone man drinking some bourbon. He is located on the third floor of his building and he seems to have a beautiful view of the city of Thunder Bay. This man is in his late sixties possibly. He has a white beard and white hair. He has a pair of glasses on and he is wearing a nice and elegant black suit with black dress pants. He has white socks on and black shiny shoes with pointed tips. He seems to be deep in thought when a knock on the door is heard. "Come in" he says absent mindlessly. The door opens and it appears to be Marshall from the labs. "Sir, I must inform you that the decoys that Nathaniel planted in the file worked. All of the other leaders are safe from harm." The old man says quietly "good work Marshall. It is now time for the next phase." He turns towards Marshall and he pulls out something from his sleeve and tosses it to Marshall. Marshall creeps towards it and the man says "put it on." Marshall puts the mask over his face. It is a mask resembling Nathaniel.

The old man chuckled quietly and says "that mask suits you, Marshall. Now it is time for our men to rise. What the world is in the dark about is that Nathaniel stashed away a very large number of men and women who are devoted to his cause. Now that Nathaniel is dead the masses shall rise up to avenge him." Marshall says nervously through his mask "that sounds great sir but what about you and the other council members? I know that you were just elevated without Nathaniel's complete knowledge but still the others have accepted you. What will you do?" The man stroked his chin and said "we shall play a less active role this time around. I will be along the sidelines while all of this is going on. Now no more questions leave me." Marshall bowed to him and left without another word. The lone man went back to his bourbon and mutters quietly "you have failed me my son. You always fail me, even after what you did to your own mother" as he stares off towards the jail that currently houses Darwin Fitzgerald. "You will pay for what you did Darwin. Our conflict isn't over," he said quietly.

Interlude: The Prison Experiment: The Origin of Nathaniel Fitzgerald

I am sure many of you are wondering who I am. I am known by many names but most of you should know me as Nathaniel Fitzgerald. Many of you must be curious as to why I put Darwin through so much grief and why he needs to be punished. I will get to that in a moment but I will admit that due to my actions I am sure that many people want my head on a stick. Perhaps one day I shall be slain but until then I want you to know why I have done the things that I have done.

Before I get to that I must tell all of you about a group I know. It is a group called Piece for Peace and it is a very charitable group. The group started out as two brothers named Dylan and Mathew Tallen. They are originally from a small town in Saskatchewan. These two brothers worked together right after they graduated from high school and they tried to found their own company. It was 2006 when they started to create their company. They wanted to help people so they would always give food and clothes to the homeless and they attempted to create programs that would help them get back on their feet. This went well but in 2008 despite their best efforts the homeless population began to rise once more and their programs were too small to be able to properly accommodate them. They decided to scrap the idea and they started anew in 2009.

They used all of their money to purchase a small building for rent and they tried to create a program that would help amputees. This began to work out well and any amputated soldiers that passed through the town were able to get some relief and they were given prosthetic arms and legs. Both of the brothers were very good at building good functional prosthetic limbs. Eventually they began to hire more and more people and the company began to expand. By 2012 they had multiple buildings across Saskatchewan. By

2014 they had buildings across Canada and by 2015 they had buildings all across the US as well.

I had joined the company in 2013 which was right after I was released from Juvenile detention. They need more workers so they let me on despite me being a convicted criminal. I proved my worth and eventually I was able to work my way up through the ranks until by 2014 I was a shareholder. The company had very few people to make decisions so they elevated multiple seemingly trustworthy people to be able to provide insight on how the company should be run. When I was elevated, there were only 5 people. By 2015 there were 10 people on the council.

In 2014 I tried to propose that our views should change and that the only way to help the world is to become anarchists. The two brothers didn't like the idea and they persuaded the other members to veto the idea. Unfortunately, soon after this event Dylan went bungee jumping when the line snapped. He fell to his death and the bungee jumping facility got shut down. It was a real tragedy but kind of funny if you think about it. Hahahahahaha, it is such a funny thought. Anyway, once Dylan died Mathew elevated another council member and gave his shares to that person.

Mathew attempted to prove I did it but there was no proof. It was just an unfortunate "accident". Eventually with Dylan out of the way I began to sway the other council members and I forced Mathew to agree with me or else something bad might happen to him or the other workers. Mathew was an honorable man and he truly cared about his workers and he was smart enough to know that if he went to the police with only suspicion then he would lose all of his credibility. It would look like Mathew is just trying to discredit another shareholder in order to gain more influence in the company. Or that he was just grieving his dead brother and was jumping at shadows with no proof.

I kept him on entirely and I eventually was given authority to handpick certain council members. I picked members that were loyal to Mathew but ones that could easily be influenced. The company's ad campaign always stated that for every dollar you donate, 75 cents would be donated to our personal amputee research. We fixed the books to make it seem legitimate but really, we were only giving 35 cents. The rest of it was going to company wages and the research for the new prison facilities for my various subjects.

By 2015 the group was beginning to take off and I personally hired various philanthropists and celebrities like Damian Markson and John Smith to endorse my company. With all of these respected celebrities and philanthropist's donations profits went through the roof. In case we are ever targeted for messing with our books I have a personal treasury full of money that only I know about so I can tip the odds in my favor if anyone asks. I have bribed various politicians to keep quiet about this and various workers to remain silent about my true activities. I decided to hire various scientists who approved of my plan to rebuild the world in my image. I eventually built up quite a large number of followers. Many of them don't know the true reason behind my actions though. Some want to be a part of helping amputees and some want to be a part of tearing the world apart.

This was when Mathew began to become a serious problem. I needed him so I always bribed him and threatened him but by now he just couldn't take it anymore. He confronted me in my office after hours alone and we got into a very heated debate. He threatened to go to the police unless I put my plan to a halt and I actually try to help people with amputees. Of course, I couldn't do it so this time I decided to threaten his family. I threatened to murder his beautiful fiancé and his two sons if he did not comply. I had always been bribing him with sums of $5000 payments to keep him quiet so this time I decided to sweeten the deal and bribe him with $15,000 since the money could be put to good use for his family. I could tell that this was tearing him apart but honestly, I didn't care. He knew that he couldn't go to the cops because he didn't have any actual evidence. He only has what I have told him but even then, I know how to cover my tracks. He doesn't know anything about the prison facilities. About half of the council knows about my true plans for the prison facilities but Mathew and the other half think it might have to do with amputees but Mathew knows something more sinister is going on. I have been bribing him to keep quiet about Dylan and about messing with the books. He doesn't know where the money is even going though. Finally, he took the money and he left my office.

About 6:00 am the next morning I drove over to his place. With the money his brother left him and the money that he gets from the company, not to mention the checks I have given him, it has helped him to pay for this beautiful two-story house. Including the $15,000 I gave him last night all of the checks should add up to about $35,000 in total. He also gets a tenth of all the profits that the shareholders receive. His house is made out of plaster of course and it is white with two windows in the front. He also has a nice rose garden in the front. The door is brown but it complements the place nicely.

I exit my car and creep up to the doorknob. I pulled out my personal bobby pin and I unlocked the door. I crept inside and the house was dark but the morning light illuminated parts of the house so the lights did not need to be turned on to see. To my right would be the living room with a television and two brown couches along with a brown chair. The living room also has many trophies related to soccer and basket ball which probably belong to his kids. There is also a nice lava lamp beside the couches which seems to be deactivated for the time being. Straight ahead would be the dining room with a beautiful brown oak table with a kitchen leading from there. To my left are a flight of stairs that lead to the bedrooms and the bathroom. There is also a basement that I may use for my own personal amusement and his family but that will come later.

I slowly sneak up the stairs feeling exhilarated. When I get to the top, I head to my left which is where Mathew and his fiancé are sleeping. I creep ever so closely and I put a chloroformed rag on Mathew's face. He tries to struggle but after a few moments he went limp. He never saw me. I pull him out of the bed and I slowly drag him back to my car. I also leave a note that I typed out that says he went into work early.

I drag him into the trunk of my red convertible and I drive to an abandoned warehouse that I secretly bought with my own funds. I lead him through the building which is very empty. There is no furniture or anything. The only thing here is just walls and doors. I lead him into one particular room where there is one lone chair. I sit him in it and I tie him up with a lot of rope. I tie up his entire body except for his head. The rope is tight enough that it will feel like hell but not enough to restrict his airways. I pull up another chair I had stashed in a closet nearby and I sit facing him as I wait for him to wake up. I also took the liberty of placing a chip inside his fiancé's cell phone so that anyone she tried to call would be put through to my own number. It is just a precaution in case she happens to figure out what I know but I doubt I will need it. Once I am done with Mathew, I will just destroy my phone and the chip will automatically deactivate. I just can't afford to let anyone disturb us and our "talk."

We always meet in the conference room at 10:00 o'clock each morning to discuss where we stand. It is about 8:15 when Mathew finally decides to wake up. He seems very disoriented until he sees that he is tied up. I see him trying to break free and I almost laugh at his misery. The second he realizes I am in his presence I think I actually heard his heart stop. I should mention that Mathew is an attractive young man. He is about 5ft11 with short brown hair and a round face with dimples and brown eyes. He is in his very late 20s but the second he sees my eyes his entire face turns white. He begins to panic until I say quietly "shh." He quiets down but stutters "N, N, Nathaniel, what is going on here?" I stand up and say "Mathew Tallen, it is so good to see you. I was hoping you and I could have a little chat about your standing within this company. I can see that you have left your shares to your family if something should happen to you. That is very noble of you but I think you should transfer them to me. Don't you think that would be wise?" The look on his face is one of astonishment. He says loudly "the company is mine Nathaniel. You may have gotten my brother out of the way but you won't get rid of me so easily. If anything happens to me, I rigged my phone to send out a distress to my fiancé if I don't open my phone within 24 hours. You will never get my company from me."

I can see the determination in his eyes but by now I have had enough. I need to break his spirit. I say coldly "do you mean this phone?" I take his phone out of his pocket and show it to him. I also open up the phone and rip the memory card out. I show it to his face before I throw it on the ground and step on it. I can see the determined look on his face begin to fade away. I also show him various bank statements that I have made in his name that show that I have already transferred every one of his shares to me and that his family will get nothing. I also listed statements regarding how his fiancé and his two sons (aged 12 and 14) won't be able to keep the house if he dies and that they will have nothing. Mathew begins to struggle even more and say "that's how you want to play it. You want to drag my family into this." I can see his eyes begin to tear up a little. I haven't experienced such great joy in a while. He says quietly while maintaining eye contact "what is it that you want?" My smile gets even wider as I pull out my trusty hatchet. I can see the fear in his eyes begin to widen. I step closer and closer as he tries to free himself from the restraints. I put my right hand on his shoulder to prevent him from moving and then I raise my other hand into the sky and I swing towards him. My aim remains true and the hatchet hits the restraints and misses his body by centimeters.

The ropes fall harmlessly onto the floor. He had closed his eyes but opens them when he realizes that I just freed him. I say "I got what I wanted. You can go now." All I wanted was to mentally fuck with him one last time. I walk out of the room and then exit the building. I can only assume that he was still in shock because he didn't find his way out until a few minutes later. I look at him and say "I will see you in hell Mathew." I walk away and I can hear him trying to run towards me. I walk for about 5 seconds when I hear the fateful sound of a transport hitting something. I turn around and I see that Mathew had been hit by the transport and was killed instantly. I donned my goat mask when I left the building and I walked down the street to my company. I removed the mask before I entered the building of course.

When I made it to my conference meeting, I heard that an hour ago Mathew had been killed and that his shares were transferred to me. I then used those shares to exert more influence and spread my facilities around the globe. If there were any council members that didn't agree with me; I caused them to disappear and no one would ever know what happened to them. I also realized that Mathew had kept his $35,000 a secret from his family and he left them that along with an additional $500,000 in an insurance plan to give them. I clearly missed a document but no matter. At least the family got something. I also used some of my own money to invest in various businesses. I later kept the family in prison within their own basement and tortured them for months for fun. It was truly amazing watching their spirits break as I took everything from them.

I got Mathew killed in March 2015. I found out about my cousin Raphael Fitzgerald in April and I took him into one of my prototype facilities. I tortured him the same way I did to Darwin and I twisted his mind so heavily that he only became loyal to me. I offered him a place on my team and he agreed. I tortured him for months and then when Darwin cut him off, he decided to agree with my plan to make him crazy and keep him institutionalized. Raphael is an interesting right-hand man. I didn't hate him the way I hated Darwin and eventually I began to see him as an older brother to me as well. Raphael is of course expendable and I will kill him if necessary but I don't mind him. He is a good man to have around I suppose.

I also met Jorgen in May. I heard he was a war veteran so I figured his skills might be of some use to me. I sent an unnamed assassin to slaughter his entire family and to make it seem like Jorgen was also a target. I was watching the whole thing while smiling from ear to ear. I saw him get shot in the knee and him trying to run away. He tripped of course and I just so happened to be walking by and brought him to the hospital. I spent days comforting my new "friend" and trying to help him. When the suspect was caught, I tampered with the evidence to get him off. Jorgen was infuriated when he heard the news that his family's killer had gotten off unscathed. Because of that I convinced him to assist me in getting revenge on this country that let the monster that slaughtered his family walk away. I eventually twisted his mind so heavily that he did everything I said without question. I even think he began to love me. He is such a useful tool.

Once I got my assassin out from prison I toasted with him at my apartment. The beautiful thing is that I laced his bourbon with Cyanide. He died a very painful death and then I burned his body so no one would ever know who he was. His brother is still looking for him but who cares. I had to get my assassin out of the way since he had been ID'd. I had also spent all of 2015 perfecting my facilities and perfecting my new drug Apitonin which would be vital to my plan.

By the end of 2015 I had been finally able to sway every council member so that they were only loyal to me. I never explicitly said I was in charge as this is a council but they know that my opinion carries the most weight. In about March 2016, I was finally able to get my hands on Darwin. I saw him struggling in the prison and it brought me great joy to see him squirm. It was even better to see him remember everything and see him lose his mind. I have just finished talking to the doctors and to Raphael who will oversee this place. Darwin has been locked up and I will soon rule within seven months time.

The thing I love about Raphael is that his skin is so pale that he looks terrifying. He also got these contacts that make his blue eyes look like they are almost glowing. He also has short black hair. Before the study Darwin had light brown hair with green eyes and was about 6ft. He has nice round eyes and a fair build. He never had a beard but it seems like that during his time in the institution his hair had become more and more disheveled and his face became dirtier and more stressed. He also had a bit of stubble growing under his neck.

I am sure many of you are wondering what I must look like. I have dark brown hair with piercing green eyes. I have a very strong build and am just over 6 ft tall. I can finally have my revenge against Darwin for getting me locked up. Jared deserved what he got. Now I am pretty sure that most of the people reading this want me to die but you know what, I don't really care. Even if in some way I do end up dying then I for sure will not let Darwin be free. He will always be haunted by his demons and he will never live a normal life. I guarantee he will never be the same after this. Perhaps one day I will also be able to please my father.

Before I end this, I will tell you about my past. I love murdering animals. I loved killing any insects I found and I loved torturing them so. I brought back dead bunnies with gouged eyes out and I brought back beaten animals to the house and I would drown them or bury them while they were still alive. My father beat me heavily for that when he found out so I did it in secret. I really wanted to increase my kills so I went to humans. I Beat Jared within an inch of his life when my faithful cousin Darwin got me sent to Juvie. While there I heard about various terrorist attacks on the world and I realized that I wanted to shape the world in my image. I wanted to torture people and make them pay for everything that has happened to me. When I was finally released, I returned home to see my mother on the couch. She and I got into this heated argument about what I did to Jared and the fighting kept heating up until I snapped. I had never killed a human before but this time I felt the urge swell up inside of me like a drug. I brandished the pocket knife

I found on the ground on the way back home and I thrust it into my mother's heart. She looked up at me in shock and I could see she was terrified. I had to kill her because she didn't come see me once while I was imprisoned and now, she seems to hate me after what I did to my cousin's stupid friend. She thinks I am crazy and maybe I am. All I know that killing my mother felt amazing but it seemed that my dad wasn't home. I think I will let him live while punishing him. I moved my mother's body and I put her on the cream-colored couch in my living room and I positioned her so it seemed like she was sleeping. I also put this dirty brown blanket over top of her. I cleaned up the blood and I wiped my fingerprints and any DNA from the area. I also cleaned the pocket knife and I placed it in my pocket.

I left the house that day and I have never looked back. Now I am the leader of Piece for Peace and perhaps my father will figure out what I did. I never went to the funeral and I have dodged all of his phone calls. I don't think he suspects me but thinks that I am angry. He is half right. I also heard that someone new has been making waves and rising up inside my council. Perhaps it's my father or maybe it isn't. If it is him, I will show him the true meaning of fear.

One hundred years later:

"There once was a man named Darwin Fitzgerald. He was known as a very honorable man back in his day. He started out as a normal person trying to live his best life until eventually his achievements became legendary once he became a hero. It started when he got the monster Nathaniel locked up for punishing his best friend, Jared. While Darwin attempted to deal with his own demons Nathaniel bided his time while waiting for the opportune time to strike. He took control of a company called Piece for Peace which originally was used to help amputees. Due to Nathaniel's influence the darkness of his heart spread throughout the company and eventually he was in full control. He used his newfound influence to try to brainwash scores of innocent people to do his bidding when the time came. He used various makeshift prisons in order to accomplish this. He also used the same prisons to kidnap the great Darwin and torture him until his soul became broken. Once Darwin was released, he began to question his sanity as he was the only one who remembered the monster's actions.

"Eventually he broke through Nathaniel's illusion and he went after him. Darwin fought against Nathaniel in his own base of operations. After losing his hand Darwin used the last of his strength to slay the god and prevent Nathaniel's soldiers from being awoken. Darwin became a hero that day. Nathaniel had finally been slain. But, despite

Nathaniel's death his influence was spread too far and the darkness began to take over the entire world. Many people have forgotten about the noble Darwin but Nathaniel's legacy still lives on. No one really knows what happened to Darwin. Some say he died in prison, others say he lived a full life before succumbing to illness. Others say that he was assassinated. It has been 100 years since Nathaniel's death. Still, the darkness that once corrupted his heart has now corrupted many others who have taken on the bitter task of completing his work."-An unnamed historian whose name has been lost throughout history

The Next Generation

I GUESS YOU ARE wondering what ever happened to Darwin Fitzgerald huh? I've been wondering the same thing myself for a while now. My name is Aaron Jacobson and I am a survivor. One hundred years have passed since that fateful night. The night that Nathaniel was slain was supposed to bring peace but it only brought more bloodshed. It seems that Nathaniel was the only leader that was taken out. All those names on his file were decoys. All nine of the other council members went into hiding. There they decided to formally recognize Nathaniel as their faithful leader and their god, I guess. I can only imagine what happened because after that tons of people started appearing all around the world wearing Nathaniel masks. At first, they didn't do much. They just stood around and watched people, but then the attacks started happening. They would break into people's houses and murder them in their sleep. Then they would attack hospitals and police stations. Eventually these attacks became so widespread so fast that the police were not able to contain everything. It was a long and brutal war between the police and Nathaniel's former men. At one point the police were able to get the upper hand for a moment and push some of the attacks back but then the bombings began.

Every military caravan, every squad car, even every military base was being bombed one after the other and the group's numbers began to increase as many pledged their allegiance to Nathaniel's spirit. Eventually the group was able to secure every major city in Canada and the US. The US President and Vice president were all assassinated and the Canadian Prime Minister was barely able to escape into hiding. Even places like Korea and Russia fell to the group. This happened over the last hundred years. The attacks stopped twenty-five years after Nathaniel's death. Now every major country is under their control and nearly every city and town has either been bombed or taken over. I am currently residing in the very small town of Schreiber Ontario. I am 17 years old. I have somewhat long brown hair with blue eyes and a fair build.

I am 6ft and I have a scar on my left arm from an accident that happened two years ago. I am wearing my favorite Kiss t-shirt and I have a pair of blue jeans on. I also got lucky to be able to wear contacts. I used to need glasses but now I can see clearly without them. I am hiding out in my childhood home with my younger brother Sam who is 15 and my older brother James who is 18. Sam has short red hair and has a bit of acne around his face. It isn't too noticeable but it is still there. He has brown eyes and a fair complexion. He is wearing a ripped Mario brothers t-shirt and has ripped blue jeans on. Sam has been suffering from epilepsy and my older brother suffers from depression. James has short black hair with piercing green eyes. He has a strong build and has a very clear face. He has perfect vision and has a very nice complexion. He has a few scars up and down his arms from when he used to cut himself. He is currently wearing a casual black shirt and blue jeans. We all suffer from something. I currently suffer from anxiety. My parents are both still alive and they are here with us. My mom is in her early forties and she has a nice complexion with brown hair and brown eyes. My dad has black hair with a black beard and blue eyes.

Our house is somehow still mostly intact but a lot of the other buildings have been destroyed. There are two other families that are still in this town. That would be the Johnson's and the Spadoni's. They are the only three normal buildings still somewhat intact and they all currently live on our street, Manitoba Street. My dad and James both have to go to work every night from 7pm-7am at the local factory. Basically, they go and they help to produce more pulp and plastic and other stuff. I don't really know much about it I just know that when I turn 18, I will have to do it as well.

The only reason my mom doesn't have to work with them is because she is a woman. I don't have anything against gender equality or anything but apparently this group only wants men to come into work for very low pay and since they work then they will get food delivered to us. The food is very shitty like very stale bread or canned stuff but I am okay with whatever I can get. I haven't known any other life. I actually turn 18 tomorrow. I am not looking forward to this but at least I can stay home with mom and Sam until the leader calls upon me. During the day we are allowed to go outside to do some shopping from the market. It's usually pretty crappy stuff like moldy fruit or vegetables but sometimes it will be somewhat fresh. It is quite expensive, it is 5$ for a piece of fruit. My brother and father each get paid 5 cents an hour which equals to them bringing a total of $1.20 every night. At least the food they bring home is free and sometimes we might get a couple pills which are very valuable. If we are good on food, we will always try to find Sam's epilepsy pills at the market but if there aren't any then we might get some Tylenol or Ibuprofen which we desperately need.

Due to the strains of the work my family does they get frequent headaches. Luckily, I get headaches rarely and when I do get them, they are usually pretty mild. It looks like it is 7pm right now and I can see my father and James heading out to work. My father leans in and gives my mother a kiss and then gives a hug to me and my brother. James doesn't say anything he just gives us each a nod. I always worry about my family because my dad and James always seem stressed before they go into work and I never know if I will see them in the morning or not. I give my brother a nod in return and they leave out the door to work in the Factory of Nathaniel.

There is also Nathaniel's Food Market and the Township of Nathaniel. There are always guards with Nathaniel masks on guarding the three houses at night to be sure none of us leave after 7pm. 7pm is a curfew for women and any man under 18. The old Township Office on the south side of town is supposed to be the home base of the leader in charge of this town. I think his name is Damien but I am not sure. I can feel someone approach me and I turn around to see it is only Sam. I wish I could fight back against the guards. They are organized and have all sorts of weapons. I see Sam walk past me and just look out the window. The Factory or whatever is in the place of the former restaurant the Voyageur. I want to talk to Sam to see how he is doing but I know not to. When he gets like this it is best to leave him alone. He doesn't like to talk to anyone when he gets stressed about dad. I guess all I can do is go to sleep. Mom is fast asleep in the chair in here (the living room) but I see that the couch is unoccupied. I think I will sleep there tonight. I have a bed but I feel so tired I don't want to make the trek upstairs. I slowly walk to the couch and just collapse. Sleep completely overtakes me.

I think that I am dreaming. I am sitting in my home with my family and for once we are happy. There are no worries, we are just watching a TV program about a chemistry teacher who is making meth to support his family. It is awesome. Everything is good except that the scene has changed. My family is dead. Sam had a seizure and hit his head on the ground. Mom died of food poisoning. James is choking on the ground and dad is coughing up blood. I want to rush over and help them but my feet are glued to the ground. I am hyperventilating. My breathing is quickening and my heart is beating so fast I think I am going to faint. I don't know what to do. Help me. Help me. Help me. Help me. HELP ME

HELP ME HELP ME HELP ME HELP ME HELP ME HELP ME. That is all I can think. I feel totally helpless. Suddenly I feel something pierce through my chest. I see that someone stabbed me with a sword. As I fall to the ground I see the smiling face of Damien. Long red hair, cheeky grin, 5ft12 Damien.

I awake with a start. I am covered in sweat and I am breathing so fast I am surprised my heart hasn't given out. As I try to calm down is see my brothers both slumped on the other couch and I see my father has passed out in a different chair. Phew, my family is still alive and I see that it is only 8am. I see James begin to wake up and I see him trying to rub his eyes when he finally opens them, he catches me staring and says gruffly "what's up?" I shrug and ask "how was work?" He begins to get up and says "I don't want to talk about it." He then walks upstairs to get a new change of clothes. I know better than to press him because he and my dad both say the same thing each time they are asked and I know that James will shut down and not say anything if I press him too much. I sit down for a few minutes to try to properly wake up and then I head upstairs to get some clean clothes. I head up the stairs to my room which is straight ahead but to the left of James'.

I pull out a green t-shirt that has a clover on it and says in the middle "drink up fuckers". I might not be allowed to do much but at least I have somewhat okay clothing. I also change into a different pair of blue jeans and I change my socks and underwear as well. After that I strip down and head into my private bathroom for a quick shower to clean myself up. The hot water is quite relaxing. I can feel my troubles slipping away. Once that is done, I change back into today's clothes and I exit my room. As I pass James' room, I can see that he is shooting himself up with Morphine. I see the look on his face as he injects himself with the poison. His face is one of euphoria. I turn on my heels and head back down the stairs away from the sight. James has been dealing with a tough time. He had a beautiful girlfriend named Stacy. She had long brown hair and smoldering brown eyes.

She always had her hair in a ponytail and she was very athletic. There is a school here for some of the kids and we go from Tuesday to Saturday. The school goes on until 8am to 4pm with one 10-minute break for food. There is only one teacher and they mostly teach us about Nathaniel's history and about how he was a true god and he could do absolutely anything. We are meant to hail Nathaniel but none of us do. At the time there were many of us at the school. There was me, Sam, James, Stacy Johnson, Grant Spadoni who is James' age, Sean Johnson who is 15, and Caroline Spadoni who is 18. James had met Stacy when he was 17 and she was 16. They clicked easily and they dated for six months. It had all gone to shit when Sam's epilepsy medication began running out. James pleaded to Damien and his men to provide them with a little more so they could help him. Damien just laughed in his face and began to leave the Factory.

From what I heard is that James tried to grab Damien but one of his guards Tazed him three times. The guard wanted to arrest him but Damien decided that the Tazing is enough for now. Stacy ran into him the next day and he explained what happened. I know that Stacy truly loves James so it didn't surprise me that she did what she did. In the Township Office on the other side of the town there is a storage room that has boxes and boxes of pills. I guess she managed to grab a box when she got caught. I don't know the details but all I know that the next day James found Stacy's body outside his house. When he left for school, he saw her limp body on his doorstep. I was right next to him and I saw James fall to his knees and cradle her lifeless body. There was a note on her body that said what has had died of. The note read "here lies Stacy Johnson, she has been convicted of stealing the drug (epilepsy meds) and as punishment she has been pumped with lethal doses of the drug. We hope you have a Nathaniel day"—from the Republic of Nathaniel. James knew that this was a personal attack on him.

I comforted him all the way to school and I tried to keep him calm. He turned 18 two weeks after that and he was elevated to the Factory. According to him he can get access to small bits of morphine and heroin and he has been using that to help him cope with Stacy's death. He has been using for three months. I feel for him. I never told him this but I actually used to be in love with Stacy for a long time. She was my age and we did click. I had planned to ask her out when she met James. I saw the connection they had and it was instant. I knew in my heart that I didn't have a chance after that. By now James, Grant and Caroline have all graduated and are stuck working in the Factory. Caroline may be a woman but her intelligence was enough for Damian to take notice and make an exception for her to work in the Factory as well.

The only time I see them is if I run into them in the market. I want to help James but I don't know how. He truly loved Stacy. I see Sam sitting on the couch and trying to take his epilepsy medication. Today is Sunday so we have today off. I see dad is passed out in the chair still and I see mom has left to go to the market. I head over to Sam when I hear a knock on a door. I head to the door and open it. Standing on my doorstep is Damien with two of his guards. Damien has a pair of shades and says "hello Aaron. May I come in?" I give him a nod and he walks in right past me and into the living room. Damian can do whatever he wants so my resistance wouldn't mean anything in the grand scheme of things. I see Sam starting to back away and Damien says "don't worry I am not here for you or for your father. I am here for Aaron here." He turns to me and flashes his famous cocky grin. He says "I have come to congratulate you on the fact that you have officially turned 18 and are now eligible to work at the Factory. Your first shift begins tomorrow at 7pm. Do not be late." I hear the way he said that last sentence. It was almost laced with venom.

I can see he is about to leave when I hear James coming down the stairs. I realize what he is about to do and I yell "JAMES NO!" I am too late though. When James sees Damien, he takes out his pocket knife that he inherited from our father and lunges down the stairs. Damien's cronies are both wearing Nathaniel masks but since he is the leader of the town he does not need to. James is high on Morphine so he isn't as fast as he usually is. Damien just grins and pulls out his revolver. He fires two shots at James. One into his left leg and one into his right arm. James drops the knife and falls down the stairs. Luckily though the shots aren't lethal and he didn't hit his head or neck at the bottom of the stairs. My father woke up at this moment but before he could act one of the guards pulled his gun out and used it to keep us from interfering. Damien went to James and picked him up. He handed him to the two guards and said "take him away." The guards dragged him out of the house while aiming their guns at us to keep us at bay. They went into this long black limo (the only limo or car in this town) and drove off.

Sadness

No one said anything but we all knew where James had been taken. This was a serious offence and he had been taken to the township office to be executed slowly. I knew that there was a way to get him out but it would cost $5000. This was impossible for anyone in this town to get even close to that amount. Dad could try to appeal to Damien to get a lighter sentence but I doubt it. Damien doesn't care about anyone but himself and this is a very serious offence. The only thing I can do is go to work and hopefully we can save up enough to bribe someone to let him out. The only thing me and my family feel is despair. I have truly lost my older brother. I know that the rest of my family wants to comfort me or me to comfort them but I can't right now. I run upstairs as fast as I can and run into James' room. I look under his mattress and I see various syringes under there. I feel the urge to take something to make myself feel better. I pick up the small syringe that says "Morphine" and I bring it close to my vein on my left arm. I want to plunge it into my arm and forget everything but I can't. I just can't and I don't know why.

Maybe it's because I know that I have to go to work in a few hours. Maybe it's also because I know that we have a month until James' execution. I just have to bide my time and get him out. I decide to head downstairs and I see my mother being comforted in my father's arms. She must have just came home from the market. I see she packed the food away already. We have a small cooler in our dining room which has a table and five chairs. I go to the cooler and I see a carrot with little mold. I pluck the green parts away and I eat the rest. We barely get any food so I know to expect to not eat much. I snack on the carrot and then I head back to James' room. I feel shitty being in here but this is the only way I can feel close to my brother; even if he is far away. I should be with my family but I just can't. I don't deal with grief well and I prefer to do it alone. I see it is 2:30 so I decide to fall asleep. The next thing I know is someone shaking my shoulder gently in order to wake me up. I slowly open my eyes and I see my father is standing over me. He says quietly "time to go to work." He doesn't say anything else after that. I follow him downstairs and I see that he is hugging my mother and my brother.

I reluctantly come down and I give my mother a hug and then I give my brother a bigger one. I know that he is going to need me in this difficult time but I don't know how much help I will be. We let go and me and my dad begin to walk to the Voyageur. The air feels cold against my skin. My father isn't saying anything the entire way. I feel completely on edge but I am afraid to say anything. The Factory is coming into sight and I see that it looks like a generic pulp mill. Before we enter, I can feel my dad pushing me to the side. He whispers "be careful my son. This place is mandatory but very dangerous." I turn to him and ask "what goes on in this place?" He looks at me regretfully and says nearly sobbing "I can't remember." Before I can question him, he puts his hand on my back and lightly pushes me inside the Factory. I try to see what is going on but I just see this mist. I venture inside but the next thing I know is that I am lying on the couch in my house. What the fuck just happened?

I awake in a haze. All I feel is pain. My entire body aches and I have a throbbing headache. I try to sit up but I can feel the pain shoot up my body and I fall back onto the couch. I hear someone faintly say "don't move. It always hurts the first time around." I look in the direction of the voice and I see my father sitting on the chair staring at me. He comes closer and he touches my head. I am shocked to say the least when he rubs my temples to try to comfort me. I can feel the headache easing up slightly. He hasn't been this kind in a long time. I know that he cares about us but he is always so tired from work that he can never spend any time with us. I look at him and ask "why can't I remember anything?" He replies with a hint of sadness "I don't know. I can't remember anything either. I don't think anyone does." We take a moment to regard each other and I just get this bad feeling. My thoughts turn to James. I hope he is alright.

Memories

Meanwhile…

"Get me out of here! My name is James; you can't do this!" I don't know what the fuck is going on. All I know is that I am trapped in a rusty cell and all I see is grey walls and a desk on the other side. There isn't anyone here. Someone is probably watching but I don't see anyone. I need to get out of here. My energy is nearly exhausted but I don't care. I need to get my drugs. I can't think straight without the drugs. Please, someone help. I don't know what to do. I need Stacy, the only woman I have truly loved. Damien needs to die for what he has done. He will…wait…wait…oh god. Please no. In the factory, what happened in there! I couldn't have, no way. I loved her, what could force me to do that… "WHAT HAVE I DONE!" I'm in the fetal position now. I don't know what to do. All I feel is agony and heartache. I deserve to die. I killed Stacy. Damien aimed the gun but I pulled the trigger. God help me.

Meanwhile…

I am still laying in the bed. I know I have work again tonight but I am so tired. My father brought me some bread and tea which helped. I have to go back to work in six hours. My father has told me stories about how he has slept for hours after the first shift. According to him it does get easier. I hope it does. All I feel is pain and sadness. I can't remember what I have done. Everything is a haze. I can feel my dad nudging me awake to give me food every so often and I eat as best I can. My mind is spinning and I only get up a couple times in order to take a piss or shit. After that my mind just shuts down and I go back to bed. I can feel Sam trying to nudge me to check on me but I can't deal with him right now. I love him to death and I know he needs me but how am I supposed to be strong for him when I can't even take care of myself? James is still alive but I don't know what to do. I keep waking up and falling asleep every few hours. I feel my father nudging me quicker than usual so I know what that could mean. I look up at my father slowly and he says solemnly "time for work." He extends his hand and I take it as he pulls me up. We silently regard each other as I see my father hug my brother and mother goodbye.

I walk over to my mother and I give her a tight hug. I then see my brother who looks like he is about to cry but he is trying to stay strong. I run to him and we embrace as tight as possible. He knows that I am in pain and he wants to help. I reluctantly let go and me and father leave once more. We walk down the road and silence looms between us. I really want to talk but I don't know what to say. We finally get to the entrance of the Factory when my father pulls me aside. He looks at me with eyes of regret and he says softly "I am so sorry my son for what has happened. I never wanted this life for you." I see a tear drop down his face. He then grabs my hand softly and pulls me inside. I see the gas in the building and I am met with the smell of death. I can feel myself beginning to black out but before I do I see a twenty-dollar bill on the floor. I know that I could be executed for just holding it but I grab it and pocket it before I the darkness overtakes me.

I awake once more in a haze. I can't remember anything. My head is throbbing like crazy. I can feel my father standing over me. I try to open my eyes but it hurts to even do that. I do though and I see my father looking at me with a sad look. He hands me some tea and bread and doesn't say another word. I slowly eat my meal and then something comes back to me. I remember picking up a twenty-dollar bill at the entrance. I check my pocket and it is still here. I slowly stand up and I walk from the couch to my room. I glance at the clock and see it is 8:30 am. I slip the twenty under my mattress to keep it safe. I begin to head to the stairs when I fall to my knees in agony. I can feel the agony as my body splits apart at the seams. I feel my head ringing and my entire body feels like it is on fire. I...I...I...don't know what is going on.

I can see an image surface. I don't know what it is but I see people surrounding a gurney. I see a purple haired girl strapped and trying to break free. I then see someone that looks like...no...good god...what is happening. I see myself come toward her with a syringe filled with an unknown liquid. I then see myself forcing it into her left arm as the other people surround her. ...What is going on? This can't be a dream but it also can't be real. I would never harm that girl. I know her but I can't remember from where. Wait...I think I went to school with her before she graduated. She was best friends with Stacy until her death. Her name was...it was...Caroline Spadoni! We were friends once. Come to think of it, I haven't seen her since she graduated. I saw her once at the market but she looked utterly terrified. I never knew why because she wouldn't tell me. Did I hallucinate this, or did this really happen?

I can feel the pain beginning to lessen and lessen. I am able to open my eyes and I see Sam looking over me in horror. I guess I was loud because he ran up to me and hugged me. I never enjoyed being around my family but at this moment all I want to do is hold my brother. After he lets me go, I decide to use the bathroom and then go see my brother in his cell. Damien doesn't like it when people come to see the prisoners but we are allowed to come in for free but we only have an hour alone with them. After my shit I went out and began the long 10-minute walk to the Township of Nathaniel. I can see many guards along the way and I see a few people browsing the market stalls on main street. The stalls are very close to the statue of Nathaniel in the town square. Basically, it's just a statue of someone who might have been Nathaniel holding a torch. I guess people are trying to say he was fighting for liberty or something but who the fuck cares. I am sick of seeing all this Nathaniel shit and I am sick of Damien walking around like he owns the fucking place. After a long uneventful walk, I make it to the township and I walk in the door. The township is nothing special.

Most of it is just various doors leading to offices and storage. The walls and floors are painted gray and there are golden signs on the doors. I see one that says Damien's office. I ignore that one and head into the door that says holding cells. I walk in and I can't believe my sight. I see James eyes that were once piercing green are now red from exhaustion. I walk over to his cell and I see only mania in his eyes. His hands are shaking against the bars and he looks like he has lost all of his sanity. I know that there are cameras in here but I don't know where. I say softly "James?" He turns to me and it seems like he is looking right through me. I say "James, it's me Aaron." "What has happened to you?" James just stares at me and says hoarsely "Aaron?" I run to his cell and say "yes, it's me." James stares at me and says "I missed you little brother." I reply "I missed you too man." James then looks away from me and it looks like he is ashamed. I know that I need to ask him about his time at the Factory but I see something sharp by his finger. I try to see what it is when I realize it is a razor blade. James turns to me and says "I'm sorry, but I can't take the guilt anymore. I can't do it." He then takes the blade and slashes his wrists. The only thing I can do is scream at the top of my lungs as the blood leaves his body. We share one last look and then everything went black.

I don't know what's going on. Where am I? I can hear voices coming from all around me but I cannot open my eyes. Everything is black. I see what looks like a shape in the darkness but I am not sure. I run towards the shape and it slowly gets closer and closer. I reach out to it and I see its James. I try to put my hand on him but it goes through him. What is going on? I do not think I am awake. I think I am dreaming. This cannot be James. He looks grey, and ethereal. He looks haunted, and tortured. He looks dead. I am trying to look into his eyes but his eyes are downcast. Whenever I try to look at them his eyes turn away from mine. Why does he look dead? I do not know what is going on. Why does my brother look dead? Where is he? This is not James! James is alive! He has to be!

I can feel hot tears streaming down my face as I fall to my knees. I sink my head into my knees to try to find some comfort. As I am crying, I can feel warm arms wrapping around my shoulders. I look up and I see James as he was. He looks kind and happy. He is serene. I want to tell him how much I need him but I cannot get the words out. He looks at me with his kind eyes and whispers: "I am sorry my brother. I wish things could have been different. I know what I have done. I murdered Stacy in that factory. I may not remember it but I still did it. I wish I could take it back but I cannot. I can finally find my redemption in the afterlife. Take care of yourself Aaron and do what I could not do. Remember the Factory." He slowly begins to disappear as I try to grab him. He looks back at me one time with a smile on his face and says: "I believe in you little bro." It is like I am watching him die again. I can feel the raw emotion surging through me as I feel crushed once more. I can see something in the darkness again. I see that it is not a shape. Instead, it is light. The darkness around is me starting to fade. The light keeps getting brighter and brighter. I think I am waking up. I can feel everything around me fading. Everything is crumbling around me. What am I supposed to do! HELP ME JAMES! COME BACK, DON'T LEAVE! I know my screams are in vain as the dark room is now flooded with light and I know I am being dragged away.

My eyes feel heavy. I wake up back at home and my family's clearly devastated from James' death. They knew he was suffering but they never expected him to take his own life like that. I wake up again on the couch. Dad's standing over me and says "I have this for you son." He handed me a pill and said "it will help you retain your memories in there. I only have the one and I feel you should have it. Please my boy, free us all," he said sadly. He then went upstairs to cry and I pocketed the pill. The next day that I was scheduled for work I took the pill before we headed off. I walked into the haze of the Factory and realized what was actually going on. The place was even more dangerous than expected.

The Factory

We weren't doing anything with pulp; we were torturing people. Every night we would be pumped with drugs and essentially acted as drones and assassins when needed. I saw my dad kill a former soldier that tried to act out against Damian with surprising efficiency. I also saw that sometimes we broke into people's houses and stole people who were close to turning 18 and forced to kill people they cared about just to torture them. That must have been what happened to James. And I...I...I killed Caroline. I injected her drugs until she died screaming. Luckily this time I wasn't called onto do anything serious. I just had to check drug production. I could tell that even though my dad had done these awful things with no memory of them, he still felt flashes of them in his dreams.

We are supposed to be the perfect assassins and yet I have my memories. I need to be able to blend in or else I won't be able to survive here. I did hear from one of the other workers that if I really want to discover a secret about Damian, I can pay a guard 20$ and he will let me into his office when Damian's not around. I pretend to be the perfect drone for the next few hours when me and the rest of the workers are ushered out at the end of the night and sent back home. I walked back home and crashed on the couch. I woke up to my mother screaming. I jumped off the couch and saw that my father had been murdered. He had cuts all across his body and I instantly knew what it meant. He must have slipped James the razor blade and allowed him to take his own way out of the chaos. There was no note, no public declaration. Just Damian gloating over his dead body before walking out with his guards. I must have blacked out and fell asleep back on the couch. When I woke up, I headed into work like normal. I had no pills so I allowed my memories to be taken from me as time went on. After many weeks of this I decided to make my move.

I went to the Nathaniel Town House when I knew Damian would be presiding over an execution. I walked up to the guard and with the twenty dollar bill I had I gave it to him in order to let me inside. He examined the bill and without questioning he said "have a Nathaniel day!" cheerily as he stepped aside. I walked in and saw that his office was just like any other office. There were some knick knacks on the desk and a computer. I turned on the computer and found that there was a secret passage in this office. I activated it and a hidden door at the back of the office opened up. What I didn't realize was that by doing that I had triggered a silent alarm. I walked down to stairs to a dark room and turned the lights on. There I saw it; there was Nathaniel's dead body preserved in a machine despite his injuries. He was still breathing but unconscious. I saw various charts and realized that Damian was actually Nathaniel's father.

He had been leeching on his son's life force in order to retain his youth. There were other files that showed that the council Nathaniel's dad led had used the Nathaniel cult to take power over a hundred years ago and he then wiped them out when he got what he wanted. His ultimate plan was to drain Nathaniel's life force into him so that he would be Nathaniel and then do battle against someone who would represent Darwin Fitzgerald in order to solidify his identity as the god Nathaniel. As I began to feel anger boiling up inside of me at this, I suddenly felt a sharp pain in my chest and I could see a giant sword pushing through my heart. I collapsed and coughed up blood as I lay dying. Damian stood over me and smirked at my defeat. I cried out in agony to try to tell him off but only gurgles came out of my mouth. I collapsed in a heap of my own blood. As I lay dying, I saw him go to his machine and begin to suck out Nathaniel's life force into his own. I blacked out soon after. *You can't give up yet Aaron.*

The End Of Aaron

"HAHAHAHAHAHAHAHAHA" cackled Damian. I lay there dying as he absorbed Nathan's life force and began to turn into him. Damian then activated another machine and out came another body. The person in stasis must have been Darwin Fitzgerald. I could hear an otherworldly voice communicating with me but I couldn't make the words out. The next thing I knew I woke up in an unfamiliar body. Ugh, where am I? The last thing I remember was going to sleep in my prison cell...wait I was never in prison. Am I Darwin now? Or have he and I merged somehow. It's hard to tell, but I somehow feel more powerful than I used to. Damian's gone from his office, I guess he assumed I died and didn't feel the need to check. I can't seem to communicate with Darwin but I feel at peace being connected with him. It's like we have reached an understanding or something. We grabbed a beautiful looking sword laying against the wall. I grabbed it and it felt perfectly in my hand. I could tell that Darwin had experience using this sword so he and I wielded it together. We left the office and saw that Damian was giving a press conference where he was proclaiming to be the new god. The audience was eating it up and everyone was bowing.

We dashed out and jumped up on stage. We yelled out "Nathaniel! It's time to end this." Damian looked back at us with shock and then smirked. He drew his sword and we clashed. We fought back and forth and I figured that if I could kill him in front of everyone then that would prove that he wasn't a god and my family and friends could rise up. We fought and continued to slash at each other. It's clear that Damian in his youth was an amazing swordsman and now that he's merged with Nathaniel, he's even more powerful. But with me and Darwin combined I know he doesn't stand a chance. We went back and forth as we each tried to find an opening until finally Damian slipped up and I stabbed him right in the chest. Damian gurgled and then fell to the ground dead.

I stood up to the crowd and said "here lies your beloved god, dead and broken. If you wish to serve a dead man that's fine with me but if you want to move forward; join me and let's rebuild this land in peace!" I admit I couldn't have said that without Darwin's confidence. The guards all looked at each other and at the crowd. They had drawn their weapons and then they dropped them at their feet in surrender. They clapped and the crowd followed suit. We were finally on the way to happiness.

Epilogue

It took a long time for us to get to where we needed to be but it worked out eventually. Together we tore down the Nathaniel buildings and we began to dismantle all of the cults around the world. It took many years but we were able to get things back to the way they used to be and relations with the rest of the world improved significantly. Me and Darwin also got separated and we became fast friends. I decided that if he needed my help, I would come with him. It was with the help of a kind wizard named Simon who had helped us and even restored my family and other friends back to life.

I hugged James happily and he and Stacy got back together almost instantly. Simon teared up when he saw the two together. He must have known people like James and Stacy in his world and felt a kinship with them. Either way, the Factory was no more and the MK Ultra like experiment was finally finished. Nathaniel's influence had been destroyed from the world and we could live in peace. I decided to give this compilation to my friend Edward, a mysterious scholar from across the multiverse in order to publish this work. He told me there are other tales to come as well and this won't be the final one. Perhaps I shall live to see that day. He also told me had been on many adventures and I would love to listen to them sometime. Maybe one day I shall.

I also heard that he has an office in a little town called Schreiber that is different from our counterpart and Darwin said he would like to visit someday. Simon says he's been there and that we'd enjoy it. Perhaps I'll go there as well. Edward went on about his adventures with his relatives and said his heritage was filled with chaos and war but also with light and peace. Edward and Simon decide to leave to explore worlds and I decide to go with them. Darwin and I decide that our first stop is Schreiber so Simon sends us there and we end up meeting up with so many new friends. I meet an alternate version of James and Stacy, and I meet a friend named Christine. I realize that this must be the

Schreiber of an alternate universe but I don't care. Darwin and I settle in and we find new jobs.

It was hard leaving my family but the James and Stacy of this world embraced me with open arms and it feels like I have a real family once again. Darwin also realizes that his previous boss doesn't exist in this world and he's able to finally find peace here. Darwin told me about his experiences with bosses and how he sometimes got angry emails from people who didn't understand him even when he was doing everything right. Darwin found a new job working at the Schreiber Rail Museum and he ended up running the place in a matter of years. The original caretaker had been looking for someone with his gumption and was more than happy to pass on his legacy to Darwin Fitzgerald.

Darwin ended up bringing relics back from his world that Simon helped him get and they displayed them in the museum for all time. I ended up helping him as well and became his assistant. He said that someday he might consider leaving the museum to me if I choose to work in the field full time. I still have a lot of learning to do and I'm planning on going to Lakehead University once I'm old enough. Darwin had a lot of demons but through therapy and his love of badminton and sword fighting he was able to slowly let go of his demons.

I also believe that since he and I were merged he was able to find someone who truly understood what he went through. Me and Darwin found a new family here and Edward set up a new office here. He told us to come visit him in his hometown of Linia someday. I'd certainly like to see his world and culture. Christine, James and Stacy end up leaving for their own reasons but we all find the time to meet back up again whenever time permits. They have also told me that me and Darwin are allowed to contact them anytime we wish. I think Darwin has something he'd like to say as well.

Shifting to Darwin's perspective:

I never knew what it felt like to be truly happy at times. Ever since Nathaniel tortured me and tried to kill me, I've been haunted by so many memories and the blood flowing still gets to me at times. I've found a new therapist here and I've finally found a family of people who understand me through and through.

I miss Raphael and I know he never meant to truly hurt me. He was manipulated by Nathaniel and I can forgive him for his past transgressions. I do miss him but I believe things turned out for the best. I think at the end of the day he wanted to be free from his burdens and demons and I was finally able to give him that. I may have failed him in the past but I didn't fail him in the end. Nathaniel on the other hand was truly monstrous and got what he deserved.

I don't regret killing him, but I do feel guilty that I had to end a life. But then I remember that countless people would have been killed if I hadn't done what I did. And when Aaron and I merged together I feel like I was able to let go of my past. I forgave my previous bosses and I forgave my parents for everything they did. Forgiveness isn't about letting the other person off the hook; it's about giving yourself the peace and mind that you need to be able to move on. I may never get closure from them on their side but that doesn't matter. I can get closure on my own terms through my own actions and feelings.

Simon began to age slightly before he left us but he seemed okay. I wondered if the stone he was using to help everyone was beginning to take its toll. God, I hope not, he's a good guy and this is his home. He deserves to be among friends. Anyway, I got a job at the museum as Aaron had said earlier and I'm really happy here.

I still have nightmares but I learned that it's okay to forgive the past since it made me into who I am. Nathaniel is finally out of my head and I got some peace at last. Of course, that was before the rumbling began. As me, Aaron, James, Stacy, and Christine were having lunch with other friends we heard a distinct sound like a rumbling. It didn't seem like an earthquake but then we saw it. From all the way across the world was a gigantic purple mass destroying everything in its path. What was that monstrosity? Is this the end of days?

The end for now...

Find out in the next volume!

Some thoughts:

Hey everyone, this is the author again. I thought I'd interrupt your pleasant reading in order to provide some words of wisdom before we get into the next part. Writing the story related to the Stanford Experiment was very exciting for me especially. I have always been fascinated with experiments like this and felt interested in it from a young age. Studying conspiracy theories in my philosophy classes also allowed me to delve deeper into similar stories and to learn how cruel the world could be. As for why Darwin ended up in prison? I felt that he should be punished in some sort of way in order to atone for his sins even though he wasn't a bad person and only did what he thought was right.

The murders were done in self-defense and he definitely didn't deserve to be locked away forever but, in his mind, he felt that he needed to pay for his crimes since they felt like they were done in cold blood. Once he had gotten the help that he needed he would have been let go immediately. I see a lot of myself in all of my characters and each character has traces of my personality or my life in some capacity even if its exaggerated or amplified. I see a lot of myself in Darwin especially and I have dealt with guilt for things that I wasn't at fault for. I may not have tried to kill myself like Darwin did but I can understand and empathize why some people would feel that way. Writing Darwin was cathartic and very fun to write since I got to delve deep into mental issues in order to write him perfectly in my mind. I'd say James and Darwin are two of my favorite characters and I wanted to do them justice.

As for what I was thinking during this whole thing. When I was writing this story, I initially wanted it to end at the end of the first experiment and make everyone wonder whether Darwin was crazy or not. I felt that was a fitting end to the story but I felt inspired to continue the story with him trying to repair his fractured psyche and getting revenge on those who wronged him. My original intent was to have the scene where Darwin was in prison and then have more prisons around the world be opened as someone announced that it was time for the real work to begin. I never wrote that scene since I felt satisfied with Nathaniel's father swearing revenge on Darwin but it always clung to my mind even years later. It felt right to discuss that scene now in order to say goodbye to the franchise for good. End of intermission.

A New Tale/Shattered Reflections

After hearing the accounts of Darwin, Nathaniel, and Aaron, Edward began to feel exhausted but excited for the future. He wanted to capture everyone's stories and release them as individual books. Next two were someone who lived in a Medieval World and someone from far into the distant future.

Shattered Reflections

The Schreiber Chronicles - Part Three

Ethan Spadoni

Contents

Preface and Acknowledgements:

Hello all, it's the author here.

I wanted to say thank you for everyone who decided to take a chance on this series. I hope you enjoyed the previous entries in this series and I'm so excited for what is to come.

This will be my third book out of five and I hope you enjoy this in the same vein as you enjoyed the others. This will be a collection of two novellas combined into one book.

I would like to thank my parents for encouraging me to pursue my passions and I would like to thank my brother for giving me his support as well.

I'd also like to thank my mentor Susan for helping me with the logistics of this process and my favourite librarian Trudy for helping me during my undergrad and graduate years at Lakehead University.

I've been a writer all throughout my life but I've never had the courage to take the plunge and try to get things published if not for my friends in the writing field. I appreciate each and every one of you who encouraged and helped me along this journey.

I couldn't have done any of this without you.

I'd also like to thank my friends for inspiring me to write again and for not letting me give up on it. My buddies Travis and Doug deserve a thank you as well. My friend Shawn also deserves a thank you for helping bring this project to life.

I'd also like to thank my cousins Jeffery and Jillian for supporting me during this time.

I'll have more to say throughout the book but this is all I wish to say currently. I hope you enjoy this third installment and read on! If you wish to contact me further, please email me at espadoni@lakeheadu.ca. I'm someone who has suffered from mental illness throughout his whole life and many of my works reflect that. It's important to find something that helps you through it whether that's therapy, medication, or anything else that brings you joy and doesn't cause harm to you or the people around you.

Cheers,

Ethan Spadoni

Prologue

Have you ever felt content with your life? Have you ever enjoyed your life fully but still felt like something was missing? Have you ever tried to find meaning in your existence?

If you or a loved one has ever felt like this then perhaps you need to play this new medieval simulation game created and published by the Videogame Corporation. Newest programmer Elias gets promoted to head game designer for this project and gets his own press conference to discuss the game.

Join Elias as he demos his new game with the help of his company backing him and the general publics allowed to join in on the fun.

Humble Beginnings

I woke up from my dream and leaned over groggily to my alarm clock. It read 6:30 AM. It would appear I woke up just before the alarm at 7:00 AM. That was a good dream but I can't do much more right now. I feel too awake so I may as well shower. My name is Elias Thompson and I'm a 24-year-old who lives in Vancouver, British Columbia of Canada. The date is November 4, 2025 and I groggily get up to have my shower for the day. I'm 6 feet tall and I have a slight muscular build. I'm Caucasian and I have glasses with bright blue eyes and some dimples and freckles across my face. Overall, I look fairly attractive to people who pass me by and I sometimes get compliments on my appearance from strangers. I finish up my shower and get a quick breakfast of scrambled eggs and toast before work.

I have a bit of fat on my belly but most of it is muscle as I've been working out lots in my spare time. I'm not a gym junkie or anything, but I enjoy it from time to time. I also eat relatively healthy but sometimes I splurge on junk things. I eat some junk everyday but not an unhealthy amount and I'm happy with myself. I love playing videogames in my spare time and I love to read and write whenever I can. My favourite things to read and write are medieval fantasies and my favourite games to play are role playing games. I'm also an avid Dungeon and Dragon's nerd and I love to read comics and graphic novels about all the geeky things I enjoy.

I grew up in Kingston. Ontario and have a loving relationship with my parents. They love me dearly and always supported my dreams. I also suffer from anxiety and depression at times and they helped me to get on the medication that helped me so much. I also went to therapy for many years but I don't need that as much these days. I use cognitive behavioural techniques as taught by my doctor and psychologist in order to help me better take apart what I'm actually suffering from and how to better deal with it. My hobbies help me as a form of therapy these days and I no longer have deep depressing thoughts or want to end my own life. While I never wanted to kill myself genuinely the thought has crossed my mind and I realized something. There really isn't an easy and painless way to guarantee death. If I took pills, I could have a bad reaction to it and it wouldn't be peaceful. I could try jumping off a building but there's always the chance I land the wrong way and end up surviving and being paralyzed for the rest of my days which wouldn't be much of an existence at all for me. I think I'd want to die peacefully in my sleep from old age. That would be the best way to go about it. I also always loved sword fighting and I've been learning from an instructor here in Vancouver. So far that's been one of my favourite hobbies.

I also work as a videogame programmer and coder for one of the biggest companies in British Columbia. I spend my days working on various projects in order to get them ready for release on time. At times I only get to work on minor projects with small teams but I recently got the opportunity to join a larger team to work on a much bigger project. One day I hope to be able to create my own videogames and tell my own stories but for now I settle for telling other people's stories. I live alone but I also have a girlfriend who lives nearby. Her name is Maria and she's gorgeous. She's 22 and just graduated university for engineering. She's very smart and athletic. Like me she's also Caucasian and works at a company near my office. She's tall but still shorter than me by a bit and she has long brown hair that she keeps in a ponytail. Her face is absolutely flawless to me but she isn't a porcelain doll. She has some blemishes that make her look even more beautiful to me.

We always get drinks after work and sometimes she comes over to my place to watch me play videogames and sometimes she'll join in with me. We have been dating for 2 years and I haven't been happier. My parents love her and I adore her family. I don't have any siblings except for an older brother and she has fun with my friend group. I hang out with five people from the office and I have two lifelong friends who sometimes come into town from Kingston to visit me. Maria's friends with all of them and we always have a blast when we hang out together. Her interests are things like rock climbing and board games but we get along so well. She loves playing videogames with me and enjoys watching from the sidelines while cuddling with me on the couch. I think I want to marry her someday but she and I are still young. We have time to figure out all those details and I don't want to move too fast. I fire off a quick good morning text as she's probably awake already and then I finish getting ready for work. Work starts at 8 for me and it's about a five-minute drive from my place of residence. I live in a small two-story house that my parents helped to pay for and I love it. It's cozy and the living room is perfect for my gaming setup.

I play games on my Xbox Series X and sometimes on my PlayStation 5. I also have a Nintendo switch and multiple handhelds from my childhood that I still use to this day. I also have an old Wii that I enjoy playing classic games on. In my home office I have a PC that I built myself that I use for work and to play other online games with my friends. Sometimes when I'm coding at home, I take a break and play a small game to unwind and it tends to help my productivity. I don't get to do that at work of course but I always get my projects done on time and my bosses are always impressed with my work ethic. My bosses are super nice people who understand that we have lives outside of work and despite crunch time in certain situations they are usually very lenient and understanding with us and don't make us work too hard if they can avoid it. My two supervisors have always been good to me and they always treated me and my work with respect. We always have a good dialogue and love talking about classic videogames during our breaks. One of my favourite games of all time is Final Fantasy IX. Something about the medieval fantasy elements mixed with the charming characters and amazing world building made it into a masterpiece for sure. My dream would be to work on a potential remake of that game but I know that'll never happen. Square Enix is very particular about their projects and they don't like to be told what to do. My company is much smaller but we release some fairly big games at times. We have never won any major awards but the reviews and profits are more than enough to keep our business afloat for the time being and we are all happy.

I would love to be project lead on a big assignment someday but I accept that won't be the case for a long time. I've been at my company for the last two years and I've loved every second of it. My bosses told me that I could start leading my own teams in a couple years if I keep my progress up. I love my company and want more than anything to stay involved for as long as I can. My parents are insanely proud of me and they always call to check on me. I appreciate that and love them dearly. After my breakfast I play a quick round of whatever game I'm playing at the time and then head off to work. Since I woke up earlier than usual, I play fallout New Vegas a lot longer than usual.

The Fallout franchise is also one of my favourites and I have always loved the work that Bethesda and Obsidian put out. After my round and chatting with some of my online friends I pack up my work stuff and head out for the day. When I get to the office, I sit next to my coworker Connor as he and I work on the latest project *Elder Dragon VS. the Wizard of Agony.* Connor is about my height and also Caucasian. He has dark green eyes and is one of my closest friends at the office. He and I always hang out after work with Maria at times and he's really fun to be around. The game we are working on is a medieval strategy game where you play as either the Elder Dragon or the Wizard of Agony and you move units on a small grid. The combat is real time based so you don't have much time to work out your next play.

My job is to focus on the troop movements while Connor focuses on the abilities that each side uses. We have multiple people working on similar elements and the job is hard but fun. After many hours of work and our breaks we decide to head home for the day at 6:00 PM. Maria meets me outside of my office and we kiss and get into our respective cars and head to my house for the night. We order pizza and play Mario Kart Double Dash on my Wii for hours and we have a couple drinks to unwind. We end up getting comfortable on the couch together after that and we put a movie on. I feel so happy and I love Maria so much. I won't tell her that until I feel ready but I feel so content with her and never want these moments to end.

Tomorrow is the start of the weekend so we have days to ourselves. She's planning on visiting her parents for a couple days so I probably won't see much of her. That's okay, I appreciate her and trust her completely to take care of herself. Her parents live pretty close to her place so it will be a fun time to visit them for a few days. She hardly ever gets to see them due to her work schedule and social life. I'm truly happy for her. I fall asleep on the couch and I have a nice dream. The details are fuzzy but it was really nice while it lasted. At least until I woke up.

The True Start Of It All

I WAKE UP IN the middle of a field...wait a field. I notice that my usual alarm didn't go off like normal and I groggily sit up. The sun's in my eyes so clearly, I'm outside. What the hell? I look around and realize that I am in fact outside and in the middle of nowhere. The air feels crisp and fresh. A hell of a lot fresher than normal. I stand up and see I'm still wearing my usual clothes of a red t-shirt and black shorts. Have I been kidnapped and left in the middle of nowhere? I don't know anymore. What the hell happened to me? I don't typically panic but I can feel myself having a mental breakdown. I start to breathe heavily and I feel like I'm about to throw up. I also notice that Maria isn't with me. I need to calm down though. I begin to slow my breathing and calm myself using the techniques I was taught. I close my eyes to center myself and begin to relax. I can't control what's going on, but I can control how I react and how to get out of this situation. I open my eyes and begin to feel more at ease.

The first thing I need to do is try to get my bearings and figure out what's going on. I don't feel drugged or anything, and it appears to be morning. I feel like I slept soundly so my sleep wasn't disturbed or anything. And yet the dirt that's creeped up into my clothes tells a different story. Clearly, I've been here for a while. I see that the fields seem endless and I decide to trek North for the time being. Maybe there's a town nearby. I feel so disoriented. Am I even in Vancouver anymore? And if I'm not then how did I get here? I check my pockets and see that my cellphone isn't there, of course its charging by my bed right now. I also have no cash or anything in my pockets. I decide to keep walking and finally I see what appears to be a small village.

Hang on? This place seems familiar. When I was a kid, I used to dream of a medieval village and I always told myself that I would make a videogame about it someday. This can't be that village, can it? I always dreamed of going to that village and going to the castle that lay at the Northernmost plane. I need to explore this place and find out how to get back home.

I continue into the village and see there are two people working the fields. The fields look like garlic. I go up to them while raising my hands up to my chest in a motion of surrender and yell out "excuse me! Can you please help me? I seem to be lost?" I realize that the words coming out of my mouth feel foreign to me but yet it feels like I've known them forever. The two villagers drop what they are doing and at the sight of my clothes they run up to me and brandish their pitchforks at me. I yelp and keep my hands just level with my chest. "Who are ye? What are you doing in our fields?" bellowed the male villager. He looked to be a very muscular fellow and appeared to be very strong. I knew that if I ever got into a fistfight with him, I would surely lose. The woman next to him looks frail but stands firm. I guess that these two must be married due to the matching rings on their fingers. The rings look like copper and very cheap but very well loved.

I sputter out my reply "please, I mean you no harm. I don't know what's happened to me. I just woke up in the fields South of here and I need help returning to Vancouver. Can you please help me get out of here? If you can then I'll get out of your hair and leave you alone." I plead with them and the two look at each other in confusion.

"You speak our language, but what is this Vancouver you are going on about? You are in the Linia Empire and we don't look fondly upon trespassers. The only two kingdoms near here are the Xatish Empire which borders us to the South and the Selitus Kingdom which borders us to the East and West. We control the Northernmost Plains and are surrounded by enemies."

I stare dumbfounded at them. Have I been teleported to medieval times or something? But that's impossible, the kingdoms don't sound familiar to me at all. Am I in a parallel universe or something and if so, how did I get here? I need to get home. I stare back at the couple with the most confused and kindest expression I can think of and say "Look, I really don't understand what's going on and I'm sorry for trespassing onto your lands. If you two could help me I would be grateful. I promise no harm will come to you or your own. Please help me."

They finally seem to relent and they let down their pitchforks. They say in unison "welcome to our home." The man says "this way traveller" with a small smile on his face.

I have no idea what's going on but I follow the rough but nice-looking couple into their home.

Their home is small and shabby but it feels like home to a certain extent. I feel at ease here for some reason. The couple isn't familiar to me at all but the landscape is for some reason. I need to get out of here. The man offers me some tea and I graciously accept. They also give me some of their finest bread and soup for breakfast and we eat in silence. The husband looks at me and says "what happened to ye traveller?" with a sad look on his face. I know that I can't tell them about my world if this is some parallel world but I realize that I need to be honest in order to get their help.

"This might sound strange but the last thing I remember is spending time at home with my girlfriend and then I woke up here. I know my name is Elias and I remember my past but I don't have any idea how I got here." I say honestly. The husband looks down at his food and seems to be judging if whether or not he can believe me. Eventually he must have decided that he could believe because me smiles and says "I'm sorry about what you've been through traveller. How about you stay with me and me wife at our home for the night? We can help you with your travels and maybe get you back to this so-called Vancouver place."

I say graciously "thank you so much. Any help you can provide would be greatly appreciated." We finish up our meal and then the couple led me to a room in order to get a change of clothes since my clothes were all dirty. I end up wearing a navy-blue tunic with short pants of a matching color and the outfit seems to fit me perfectly. It really does feel as if I've been here before but I know that can't be true.

I must be going insane. I need to figure out how to get home.

The First Day Of Your New Life

After I change, I decide to help out the couple with their daily chores. They tell me their names are Lisa and Danny. First, I help out with tilling the fields and picking the garlic. I really love garlic and eating fresh garlic is truly the best. Their farm isn't that big so the chores don't take too long and we decide to talk while we work. Especially with three of us the work goes by fast. I ask them questions about the kingdom we're in and about our neighbours. Lisa looks at me and says "well lad, I'll tell you everything we know about the kingdoms. The Linia Empire is where we currently are and we live under the rule of King Linus. He rules our world peacefully but we have our own problems here. There is a giant dragon that lives near our borders and he frequently asks for tributes in order to avoid razing the kingdom to the ground.

"He's a monstrous beast that has killed armies and King Linus has had no choice but to bow to it. He frequently posts ads for adventurers to try and take out the dragon but so far not enough people have signed up. We have considered asking the other kingdoms for aid but they refuse to help us. That dragon is ruining our time of peace and many people have been conscripted into the army in order to help fight off the dragon. So far no one has succeeded in taking out that beast. We really need help or else our son who's off travelling might be conscripted as well."

Lisa broke down in sobs as Danny comforted her by putting his arm around her and holding her tightly. "The truth is lad we are in a bit of a bind. And you remind us of our son so that's why we decided to take you in. We will help you get home if that's possible. You might want to go speak to the mayor of our town. Perhaps he can help you more than we can. In the meantime, I'll tell you more about our kingdom. Our main trade source is garlic but the dragon has a taste for it and is always taking our crops to feed his ego. If this keeps up our kingdom won't be able to survive for much longer. King Linus cares deeply for his people but there's only so much he can do. We aren't a rich country and the other countries are willing to let us starve or get destroyed in order to get our garlic and money.

"I'm afraid I don't know much about the other kingdoms except that war is always threatening to break out over land disputes and the abundance of resources we have. We have garlic but we also have small gold mines that help keep us afloat but that won't last forever. The gold is slowly running out and the iron and steel we have are limited and all of it goes to the war effort in order to better equip our knights and soldiers."

Danny holds his darling wife and I feel sad for these people. I wish I could help them but I don't know how. I can use a sword but not particularly well. I'm also rubbish in a fight and won't be much use against trained knights or a living breathing dragon. I can't do this. I get up and say "I promise I'll do whatever I can to help you with my limited resources." The couple smiled and replied "thank you son."

My heart swelled at them calling me that. I know they don't think of me as their son but it still reminds me of my own parents. I want to help them, but first I need to get back home. I spend the rest of the day helping out the couple with their chores and then I go to sleep for the night. I have peaceful dreams and I dream of going back home. I wake up still in the Medieval World but I feel slightly at peace here. I help the couple again with their chores and then I decide to head to the nearby town for help.

Township Complications

I HEAD INTO TOWN and I breathe in the fresh crisp air. My back still hurts from all the back breaking work the couple had me doing but that's okay. I definitely want to find my way back but I'm happy I could help them in any small capacity. I head to the mayor's office when I see a small woman with tribal tattoos all over her body and she looks black. The woman comes over to me and says coldly "who is ye? What brings ye here stranger?"

The accent sounds unrecognizable and yet I feel as if I've heard it many times before throughout my whole life. I can't explain it. I try my best to respond clearly "I come from a land called Vancouver. I woke up in the fields outside your lovely town and I have no memory of how I got here. Can you please help me my lady?"

The woman seems amused and says "my name is Linda, who are you?"

I reply "my name is Elias." The woman stares at me and beckons me to come inside of her house. Her house is slightly bigger than Lisa and Danny's home but not by much. I breathe in the stale air of her home and sit down on a dusty chair. She sits in the master chair and appraises me from a distance.

"Do you know much about the gods of this realm stranger?" I shake my head no. She sighs and continues. "There are many gods in this world and they go by many names. Some of them are Riquarim, Magna, and Titus. These are the three main gods and they are always competing with each other. We believe that the dragon threatening our kingdom is a test from the gods to prove if we are worthy in order to ascend into the heavens once we die. I don't know for sure though stranger. All I know is that the gods have given us nothing but trouble. There are also rumors of gods taking travellers from their homes and dropping them in the middle of nowhere with no memory of how they got there. Perhaps that's what happened to you" she said quietly. She seemed almost sad at the prospect as if it's happened before.

However, she then rose to her feet and her gaze turned icy cold. "Or perhaps you are an infiltrator from one of the nearby kingdoms and the gods have sent you to lead us to our ruin. I'm sorry but I can't trust ye stranger. Guards! Arrest this man and throw him into the dungeons!" she bellowed. Her tiny frame screeched that out and it's any wonder how she managed to get that loud of a volume.

I cover my ears at her words due to how loud she is but then guards come rushing into the home with swords drawn. The knights' armor looked hobbled together with mixes of leather and steel but they still look formidable to someone like me who doesn't have any experience fighting against real people to the death. I drop to my knees and let them drag me away. There's nothing I can do and they drag me against my will to the nearby dungeon. The dungeon is actually quite large and I see many other criminals lounging around in there as I get escorted to my cell. I'm then thrown unceremoniously into my cell and the guards kick me from behind when I tried to get up. Their kicks hurt like hell and I fall back to the ground in pain with my breath knocked out of me.

I decide to pace my cell while I catch my breath after I recover and I hear rumors about prisoners getting executed the next day. I start to panic but I try to calm myself down. Clearly this new world is very brutal and I need to calm down. I always found that snapping my fingers can calm me down at times. I try snapping my fingers but it doesn't help. Suddenly many hours later some of the other prisoners try to talk to me but I ignore them. Many of them utter disgusting phrases about what they would like to do to me and I can't bear to think about those vile things. I need to get out of here. I try to pry the bars and pick the lock with a hairpin I found but nothing works. The only way out is either with the guards help or when I get dragged out of here for my execution. I eventually decide to fall asleep for the time being. I try to snap my fingers to calm me down but the prisoners begin to yell at me to shut up! I can't do this anymore. Finally, I fall asleep and I dream of going back home. I remember picturing my apartment and then snapping along to the beat of a song only I can hear.

Suddenly I wake up back in my apartment. I don't know how I got back but I feel relieved at being home once again. Maybe it was all a bad dream. I really don't know. I pace around my apartment and see that it's Monday morning at 6:30 AM. I really don't feel like going into work but I know that I have to. I check my phone and see that no one has messaged me in the last two days which is pretty typical. I tend to be the one who makes all the plans anyway so I don't worry about sleeping for two days. However, the aches in my back feel real so I don't know what happened to me. I get back to work and continue working on the medieval game project like always. I love my job but the work seems rather boring now compared to my dream. I wish it were more exciting. I've always wanted to start my own company and create my own games but I don't have the experience or the know how to do that yet. I just keep up with my work and fix any bugs that come up in the system which they always do. Man, I'm feeling down. I wish I could go back to that Medieval World. After work I decide to call Maria but she isn't answering. I realize she wasn't at work today so I decide to go to her place to check up on her. I also realize that Connor wasn't seen at work but I don't understand what that means. Could they both have gotten sick on the same day? I'll check on him later.

I head to her apartment and I hear laughing coming from the inside. I have her spare key so I decide to go inside and I see her and Connor having sex on the couch and kissing passionately! I watch them for a second in complete shock as she says "Fuck me, Connor! Fuck me harder than my boyfriend ever could!" She yelled that so loudly that the entire complex could hear. That does it for me. I rush into the apartment and I punch Connor in the back of the head. He falls off of Maria and I beat the shit out of him. He tries to fight back and say "Dude I can explain." But I don't listen to him. I hear Maria screaming at me to stop but I tune her out. Since Connor decided to let his dick do the talking, I kick him really hard in his privates in order to teach him a lesson. I also punch a few teeth out of his mouth and they go flying. I also break his nose and his mouth begins to bleed. It feels like magic is flooding through my veins and amplifying my strength. I keep on punching and kicking until I hear bones beginning to break and blood coming from his genital area.

Lightning arced all across the room as well and my eyes apparently began to glow as I stared Connor down. I eventually stop and look at the carnage. There's blood all over the apartment and I see Maria trembling. The lightning dies down and my eyes stop their glowing. I stare at her and say "we're done Maria. Don't ever contact me again. And Connor, if you ever show your face at the office again, I'll kill you." Connor trembles as well and cowers on the floor. He's in awe of my skill and is afraid of my apparent magic. I don't know how I managed to pull that off but I think Connor and Maria are smart enough to leave me alone. I leave the apartment and rush away before the police get called. Despite how heinous the crime was the police never get called on me. I think Connor and Maria were too scared to think rationally and I got away with it. I don't know I managed to summon lightning but it's cool as hell. I'll need to take some time and figure out how to train that ability so I can do it again.

Connor never came back to work and he ended up moving to another province with Maria. It was a scandal in our friend group that they ran away together. My friends were shocked and comforted me but they didn't know the entire story. I spent the rest of that week getting caught up on work and drinking myself into a stupor whenever I could. My work performance never suffered and I never came into the office hung over or drunk which was a good thing. I think back to the Medieval World and still wish I could go back but I haven't dreamt of it in a few days now. After the week was over, I head back home and drink myself to sleep. Apparently, Connor needed reconstruction surgery on both his face and his teeth. It cost him a pretty penny but he deserved it. I go back to my drinking and for the first time in a little while I dreamt of the Medieval World. I wake up back in that world in my prison. Despite the shitty circumstances I smile as the guards' stare at me dumbfounded. "How did you get back here? You just appeared out of nowhere! Warlock! He must me a wizard of some kind!" The guards yelled and ran away calling for backup while tripping over each other on the way out.

I spend the rest of the day in my cell sleeping while guards slowly begin to surround my cell. Eventually when I wake up and feel less groggy and hungover the guards yank me out of the cell. "If you really are a warlock then you shall prove yourself to the gods," one of them said sharply. The guards dragged me outside of the jail and into a nearby courtyard. They pushed me onto some sort of stage looking thing and then blocked the exits with their swords and spears. I raised my hands and backed away further onto the stage. The elder rose to her feet after catching sight of me and said to the gathered crowd "this man has been accused of being a warlock. He shall prove himself worthy of being in our home or he shall die. The gods themselves shall decide his fate during a duel to the death!" I stand there dumfounded as I see my opponent rising to the stage as well. He's covered completely in leather armor and draws a two-handed longsword that he carries in one hand. He must be very strong and the man is huge. Over 8 feet tall and built like a mountain. I see to my left that there are many swords and maces in a sort of armory so I go over to grab something. The guards let me pass to it and I grab two short swords. That was always how I trained so I figure this might be the best bet. I really don't know how I'm going to get out of this situation but it's going to take all of my skill and power just to survive.

A Duel For The Ages

I DRAW MY TWO swords and he draws his steel longsword. My blades seem also to be made of steel. I hope they'll be enough. The man looks like a guard captain. He chuckles to himself and says "ye pipsqueak think you can take out the great Godfrey the Giant! We shall see insect." He bows to me and I follow suit. He then readies his sword and I ready mine. I see the elder presiding over the duel out of the corner of my eye and she yells out "LET THE DUEL BEGIN!" Godfrey alters his stance and charges me. I race up to him and we clash our weapons for a brief moment. For that brief moment I can feel his overpowering strength as his sword nearly slices through my blades and cleaves me in two.

I struggle against his superior strength and I have to retreat in order to avoid losing my grip on my swords. I try to put all of my strength into my left hand as that's my dominant hand and slice towards him but he casually blocks and pushes me back. I try with my right hand and the exact same thing happens. Our swords keep connecting and nothing I try works. I try to use both of my swords to gain some leverage over him but his superior grip and technique always overshadow me. I can hear the crowd cheering as our swords clash again and Godfrey leans closer to me and whispers "you've done well kid. Most opponents don't last this long against me. If you surrender now, I'll end your life quickly and peacefully. You won't even feel it." I stare him down and through gritted teeth I get out "not on your life. This isn't over." He smirks and pushes my swords away.

I immediately get disarmed and my swords fall to the ground near me and wedge themselves in the wooden boards of the stage. Godfrey stands tall over me and raised his longsword above me. Before he can finish me off, I gather my courage and I run away. His sword crashes down just inches where my head used to be. I run to where my swords are and I yank them out. The crowd seems to cheer at me not giving up and trying to fight back. They know it's in vain but some even seem to be coming around to my side as well. I throw my left sword at him and he blocks it casually with his blade. For that brief moment while I'm out of sight I rush him with my other sword and I manage to slip through his defense and I cut off two of his fingers on his other hand. He screams in pain and I take the opportunity to cut off his hand holding his sword. He bleeds out and he cries out in pain as he falls to his knees in shock.

The crowd is completely silent at this point. I take my swords and I jam them by his neck. I say "Yield, and I will spare your life. No one has to die here today. I decide my own fate and if the gods disagree with me then let them strike me down right here and now!" I pause for dramatic effect and wait for a moment. Nothing happens and the older opponent bows his head and utters "I surrender." I look to the crowd and say "get this man some help. He's been a loyal guardsman to you for how long? Heal him and get him back on his feet. He deserves your respect!" Once the people realize that the god's aren't striking me down and that I'm not rushing to kill everyone they start to applaud and they hurry Godfrey off the stage and into what I presume is the medical bay. I sheath my two swords and I approach the elder. She eyes me curiously and I bow to her. "I am no threat to you, my lady. Please help me with getting back home. I have genuinely no idea what's happened to me." I plead with her and her features turn from that of an old lady to a slightly younger woman with a genuine smile on her face and her features light up.

"You've proven yourself well lad. Perhaps we can help each other. Since you spared my guard captain which is against our traditions, I shall grant you a pardon. You may not be a warlock but you are clearly a very powerful individual. Come with me, we shall commune with the gods and perhaps they can teach you." She begins to lead me away from the stage and I follow close behind her. She has guards accompanying her but they don't seem to be paying me any mind anymore. Even the ones that were increasingly hostile towards me seem to have changed into one that of slight respect and admiration for sparing their captain.

As we walk towards where we can commune with the gods, I explain that I truly have no idea what's going on and that I wish to be able to control whatever's happening to me. The elder agreed and she decides to guide me to some stones where the gods are closest to the Human Realm. After many hours we make it to the stones and it appears to be midday now. She sits down cross-legged and not even out of breath and I follow suit while trying to catch my breath. How can someone so old and short be in such great shape? Damn. I sit down next to her and the guards stand a little distance away watching the perimeter and making sure I don't do anything funny. The elder turns to me and says "my name is Eloise and I shall teach you how to commune with the gods. Perhaps they can teach you how to control your circumstances better."

I nod in respect and she begins to chant. I don't understand the chanting but I decide to close my eyes and follow suit. The rest of the guards also chant judging by the sounds I can hear in the background. After many hours of meditation and my back beginning to kill me, I see a vision in my mind's eye. I see myself becoming a very powerful warrior with a sword and transporting myself back and forth between the Modern World and this Fantasy World. I can't see how I do it though. I just see a vision of my future. I awake with a start to the elder looking up at me with awe and reverence in her gaze. "You've spoken to them, haven't you? They've shown you visions. What did you see?" she asks excitedly. "I...I...I don't know exactly what I saw. It was very fuzzy but it looks like I saw myself becoming very powerful and fighting alongside many guards and knights in order to protect this kingdom." I say this all quietly but loud enough for her to hear me. She nods her head and beckons me to follow her.

A Legend For The Ages

She leads me a little way to a grove sitting nearby with a beautiful black sword lodged within a stone. The elder turns to me and says "you have received a vision of your future. Perhaps you are meant to be our saviour yet. Now lad, this sword was used by the first person ever to use magic in our world and fought an elder dragon with it. That dragon was defeated and in retaliation it burned the sword to a crisp. However, in recent years the sword has never lost its power and has marinated in the power of the dragon's heat and has been waiting for a worthy successor. Magic has long been a myth but our village has been tasked with safeguarding this sword for its master to return. Perhaps you are the one destined to wield this blade." She said gravely.

I can tell that she hasn't felt this much hope in such a long time and really wants me to help her slay the dragon that threatens the world. I breathe in deeply and slowly approach the sword. I take my right hand and put it on the hilt of the black sword. The sword looks damaged but still looks incredibly beautiful. The blade itself is particularly striking. I grab the hilt and I slowly begin to pull. At first nothing happens but then eventually my mind becomes overwhelmed with visions and I feel sick. I fall to my knees and begin to gag but I continue to hold onto the sword. I keep pulling and pulling and it feels like burning red hot hands are grabbing me. I keep pulling and I see visions of me trying to make it back home but then I realize that I had travelled back to the present and the Medieval World in my sleep. If I can replicate that then perhaps, I can gain control over my life.

I let go of the sword and I gasp for breath. The elder comes over with a disappointed look on her face and she comforts me by tapping my shoulder and laying her wrinkled old hand on top of it. She gives me an affectionate squeeze and says "perhaps you aren't ready yet. That's okay. If you are the chosen one then you shall reveal your power in time. For now, you should rest lad. Come back with me, there's an inn you can stay at for the time being." I gasp for breath and my breath slowly begins to slow down and I can feel myself calming down. The burning in my hand disappears and I slowly rise to my feet. I look back at the blade and mutter "I'll be back for you."

I follow the elder out of the grove and back to town. By the time we make it back it's nearly nighttime and she insists I join her for dinner in her home. We have fresh garlic and it's delicious with potatoes and steak. It's the most delicious meal I've ever had. When I get back to the inn with a full stomach, I take my twin blades and put them near my bed before I go to sleep. Before I try to sleep though I decide to try to figure out how to go back home. I try out many hand gestures and chants in order to try to figure it out but nothing works. I need to figure out how to make this work for me. Suddenly I get a very vivid image of home and I decide to snap my fingers in order to feel myself become centered. The moment I snap my fingers I feel myself being taken far away and my body feels like it's being taken apart atom by atom. I cry out in pain as blinding light overtakes me.

Homecoming At Long Last

Once the blinding light fades, I slowly open my eyes and I realize I'm back in my house. Huh, so snapping my fingers and having a vivid image in my mind triggers it. Good to know. My bed is the same as it was since I left it and I feel so happy. I sink back into my bed and feel at ease. I hear my phone go off and I check it. I see about 50 text messages from Maria and I ignore them all. I then block her and block Connor as well. I don't need those two in my life. I realize that if I want to get into the good graces of the townspeople, I can help out old Godfrey and maybe return him to his former glory. I go to my doctor friend the next day after sleeping for many hours and he manages to get me a bunch of supplies in order to fix a dismembered hand. I thank him profusely without giving him any significant explanations and I head back to the Medieval World. I go to my bed and I grip the supplies in a white-knuckle grip while thinking vividly about the Medieval World. I think long and hard about the inn until I can picture it perfectly in my head. After I snap the next thing I remember, is a slightly less blinding light and I feel myself being pulled back there.

I open my eyes and I'm back at the inn. I collapse into the bed happily as I feel more at ease here than in the real world. I take the supplies to the medieval doctors as they tend to Godfrey's wounds. I explain to them the supplies I have and that they can help him. They find his hand and they manage to re-attach it using the diagrams and supplies I gave them. They also use the morphine to dull his pain and after many hours of surgery he passes out from exhaustion and the doctor slumps in his seat. "I've done all I can do, it's in the hands of the gods now," said the doctor gravely.

I nod and I leave the room for the night. I decide to spend my time with Lisa and Danny and we work the fields once again and I help with their daily chores. There's also a travelling swordsman that travels through the village once a year and he agrees to teach me for free. I even manage to meet Danny's son before he heads out to war against the dragon. Apparently, King Linus has been increasing his efforts to conscript any able-bodied people to help out in the fight against the dragon. Before he heads out, I decide to ask him about the other kingdoms since he has done so much travelling. "Well Elias, I can't tell you much. I can say that the other two kingdoms are very rich and are willing to sit idly by while we destroy ourselves from either the dragon or our own political issues. We need help friend, I need help," he says sadly. I grip his arm in a soldier's embrace and I comfort him. He smiles weakly at me and then he parts ways. He's heading to the capital in order to start his new duties and it's clear he won't be coming back alive.

I wish I could help them. Eventually Godfrey manages to survive the procedure and he thanks me profusely for both sparing his life and for saving his knight ship. I nod in response and we spar together. My style involves using two swords while he uses one big sword. We learn lots from each other and the travelling swordsman also teaches me much whenever he's in town. I spend the next few months travelling back and forth between both worlds. I continue to learn from my master in the Modern World and he teaches me to incorporate this new medieval style I've picked up with more modern techniques. After many months of training; he believes that I could be a better swordsman than him in time. I also use my medieval experiences in order to make better game designs and my bosses have been noticing. My ex-friend Connor was up for a major promotion while he was still here but since he quit, I got the promotion and am now in charge of my own gaming development team.

We made a new medieval style RPG game and it became a massive hit! It won so many awards and it raised the profile of our company. I also got some gold from helping the medieval people and I used that money in order to fund and create my own videogame company. Many of my coworkers and bosses came with me to the new company and we created massive games. I feel so happy and have been interviewed many times about my inspiration and games. Thanks to the gold and the success from the gaming development side I am very wealthy. I moved out of my small house into a much bigger house on the nice side of town. My parents are insanely proud of me and the people in the Medieval World are always grateful to me providing medical aid to them and showing off delicacies from my world. They also introduced me to the finest and purest alcohol I have ever tasted. Me and the elder drank tons of it one night and we had long talked into the night about our lives and I gave her some insight into my home world.

She asked me if I ever wanted to stay here permanently and I genuinely thought about it. I truly wasn't sure but I did feel at home here. The elder even gave me my own house here for free that they have kept maintained for many years and it's a pretty nice place. Not as nice as my home back in Vancouver but still nice enough. I spend five days of the week in the Modern World and then spend the weekends in the Medieval Fantasy World. I finally feel like I've found the world of my dreams but I haven't seen the castle yet. If I were to go to the capital city then perhaps, I would see the castle of my dreams that has haunted me for years. It's a good haunting but I still wish to see and find that castle for my own self satisfaction.

Two Years Later

TWO YEARS OF LIVING in the Medieval world and the Modern World have passed and I have built up quite a lot of muscle and feel very healthy. I'm now twenty-six and feel the freest I've ever felt. I have a girlfriend in the Fantasy World and we are very happy together. We have been together for two years and it's been great. I'm still not planning on rushing into anything and sometimes she comes with me to the Modern World in order to see the wonders of my home and to get the finest medical care and even finer luxury items. Her name is Caroline and she's the love of my life. My swordsmanship has improved and I'm now considered a master across the realms. Anyone who has ever sparred with me has lost miserably and they have always accepted the loss with honor.

I now teach swordsmanship in both worlds and am quite successful in those side endeavors. My friends don't know anything about the Fantasy World but they've met Caroline and are very in awe of her worldly charm and her fun-loving personality. She also loves videogames and we play together all the time in the Modern World. I also pray at the statues every so often and I gain more visions of my future. Sometimes I see myself wielding fire and ice and other times I see myself leading others into battle. It really is amazing what can be seen. The gods have never talked with me directly but I can sense their intent in wanting me to be stronger before I can wield that blackened sword. I never forgot about the sword and I don't think I ever will. I also have some news on the Maria and Connor front. Connor got into a really bad car accident and he's fell into a coma. He will probably never wake up and Maria doesn't have the heart to leave him since he's hurt. She really wants to but is afraid of what people will think of her. She really was a vain person and I don't feel bad for her. I do feel bad for Connor since nobody deserves to go through that but I also don't feel much sympathy for him. I've moved on with my own life. I just feel bad for their five children that they had together. Apparently, they weren't smart enough to use protection and they kept having kids. Maria never wanted to be a mother but I don't feel bad for her. She got what she deserved when she decided Connor was a better man than me.

News in the Medieval Fantasy World isn't going particularly well however. The dragon has begun to roost right on our borders and the tributes have increased. Whenever a tribute is late the dragon has razed some of the nearby villages to the ground and has burned them until there's nothing left but ashes. I've been training my swordsmanship in preparation of going to the capital in order to finally face the dragon in combat. I wish to use all of my skill to be able to defeat it. Before I do though I need to claim the dark sword as my own and then purify it in the spring of wisdom. I decide today's the day to finally take my rightful place as warrior of the town. I go to the grove and I find the sword. I reach down and feel the heat burning my fingertips again as I try to lift it out of the ground. I end up falling to my knees and just before I pass out from the pain the sword miraculously comes free. I nearly drop the sword in shock but I manage to wield it perfectly as if it were meant for me. As soon as I get my bearings, I feel another vision overcome me. I see past people using this blade and all of their memories and their skills gets transferred to me as if it was all muscle memory. After the vision ends, I take some experimental swings and I feel like a master. I'm now able to do strikes that I would have never thought possible and I no longer use two swords. I use one long sword in one hand just like Godfrey. He taught me how to use his sword effectively and I helped him through his physical rehab using advice from my doctor friend who knew what he was talking about.

The dragon is dark red almost black and can breathe fire. He may very well be the descendant of the dragon who first fought against this sword. I can't wait to be able to plunge my sword into his heart and kill him for good. I decide to go to the spring of wisdom next and I plunge the sword into the spring. The spring is beautiful and the cool wind rushes through my hair. I feel the wind pick up as the sword bathes in the beautiful water. The water is so blue and clear I can see the bottom of the spring easily. The sword begins to glow and I see all of the dark markings leave and it becomes a blade of pure obsidian. It's truly a beautiful blade and one of the most powerful weapons of this lifetime. I take my blade and decide that it's finally time to head to the capital. I don't want to join the army; I want to be a champion who they hire so to prove myself I need to win the swordsmanship festival they have every year. The festival begins in two months and it will take about three weeks to get there. I kiss Caroline goodbye and I take some time off work and leave one of my former bosses in charge for the time being while I work on personal stuff. They were more than happy to help and promised to keep the company in safe hands until my return. I pay off all of my debt and ensure that everything in the Modern World is secure and paid off until I'm ready to return.

I take my trusty horse Ghostlight a beautiful black and white steed who almost glows in the night like a ghost hence the name and we head off to the capital. I do plenty of research on dragons and sword festivals before departing from the real world in order to better prepare myself for the long journey ahead. I went to the local library and took out every book there was about dragons and sword festivals and I used the internet extensively in order to find out everything I could about their potential weaknesses and how to use their own pride and arrogance against them. I ride the night after I made all my preparations and I head off. I make camp at many safe areas and I hide from any soldiers or bandits who happen to make camp nearby as well. I really don't want to get into any fights with the army if I can avoid it and bandits are just trouble. The more of them I can avoid the better. I do fight off many bandits though since they can't help but admire my new sword and yet they all fall to my blade one way or another. I try not to fight them if I can dodge it but if they start the fight, I make sure they all walk away from the encounter dead and six feet under. No one survives an encounter with me unless I believe they deserve it. I continue on my journey and I leave my cell phone in the Modern World since I don't need it here. Caroline loves her world but also loves to visit the Modern World with me sometimes.

The journey stretches for many miles and I make camp at various sites in order to get some rest. The festival awaits and it'll allow me to prove myself in front of the king. I may even run into Lisa and Danny's son since he went to the capital in order to enlist. That dragon has been asking for even more tributes and I believe that he could come to my village soon enough if something doesn't get done. What we need is a coalition of knights from each of the kingdoms in order to oppose the dragon. The other kingdoms might be content to watch this world die but eventually they will have to deal with the dragon one way or another. Perhaps if I win the tournament, I can gain an audience with each of the leaders since they shall all be in attendance at the yearly festival.

After making camp for the last time, I can finally see the capital in the distance. The castle overhead looks magnificent and I can see spires coming up from it and a drawbridge. It truly looks like the castle from my dreams. Until this mission is over, I have no desire or inkling to return to the Modern World. I consider the kingdom of Linia to be my home now. I wish to protect it and save my people from the onslaught of the dragon Cronus. I nearly fall asleep by my campfire when I hear the sound of footsteps crunching under the gravel near my tent. I awake with a start and grab my sword. I also have my own leather armor given to me by the elder. It's the finest set she has ever made and it fits my fighting style perfectly. Heavy armor doesn't work with my style as much. I look up to see there are three people in mismatched armor with weapons drawn and staring daggers at me. The three chuckle at me and the leader steps forward with his hand hanging lazily around his sword. "Heh, hey there tough guy. You want to give us all your valuables stranger and we'll leave you alone ha-ha?" he asked mockingly. I responded by gripping the hilt of my sword tighter and drawing it. The leader smiled even further at my stance and replied "the fun way it is then. Get him boys!"

The three rush at me but they aren't even close to being a match for me. I disarm the first two with a quick strike of my sword and I slice clean through their hands. They both fall to the ground in pain and then I advance on the leader. He looks afraid but holds his ground. I commend anyone who's willing to stand and fight against their enemies. He and I square off and I twirl my sword mockingly in order to enrage him and it works. He growls and runs forward. He tries a jump attack where he jumps in the air and aims his sword for my head but instead of dodging, I rush to block him and meet him in battle. His maneuvers don't scare me. My strength is also superior to his and with all of my strength I push forward and decide to end this. I hit him over and over with my sword until his sword finally breaks and I take his hands. I then take my sword and execute the three of them with quick strikes to the neck. They don't deserve mercy or a quick death. They can choke on their own blood for all I care.

I scavenge their pockets and find some gold coins for the taking and decide to pocket them. They won't be needing them anymore anyway. I take their waterskins and their flasks as well. I see one coin in particular they have is stamped with a red skull. I wonder what it means. The regular currency in this world has the face of King Linus on it with two swords crossed on the other side. This is very peculiar. I pocket the coin and decide to get some sleep. I move the bodies far from camp and then lie down in my sleeping bag in front of my fire and fall asleep. The next morning, I wake up and decide to head out once again. After another day's ride I finally set my eyes on the capital.

I breathe in the brisk air and ride towards the gates. The castle's enormous and it's just like the castle in my dreams. I remember visiting there when I was a child and it feels the exact same as it did back then. Two guards the drawbridge and at my approach they cross their spears in front of it. “Halt! Who goes there in this time of night?” The first guard yelled out. I remove my hood from my head and say “I’m a simple traveller hoping to enlist in King Linus’s army through his annual tournament. Please let me come in and rest my weary bones after this long journey.” The guards look at each other and then they tap their spears on the ground in unison as the drawbridge begins to lower. They uncross their spears and gesture into the capital. I bow my heads to them and ride my horse into the city. A new adventure finally awaits me and I can’t wait to see what’s next.

The Capital City At Long Last

As soon as I get into the city, I put my horse in the nearby stable and head to the nearest inn in order to get some much-needed rest. Luckily, I have more than enough coin that if I wanted to, I could live quite a wealthy life back in the village and at least a somewhat modest life in the capital. But, that's neither here nor there. I go into the inn and pay the merchant for breakfast in the morning and one of the finest rooms. He happily accepts my coin and I pass out as soon as my head hits the pillow. I wake up the next day and immediately I register for the festival. They accept my application and my gear so I am good to go. I decide to spend the next month training, working odd jobs for the mercenary's guild, and even sightseeing when I have the time. I wrote letters to my girlfriend all the time and she often wrote back. One of my favourite jobs for the guild was the escort jobs. It allowed me to see the rest of the kingdom as I escorted rich nobles to their estates outside of the capital city. I also learned as much as I could about King Linus. He was a good man who did everything he thought was right in the beginning. But now with the threats of the other kingdoms and the dragons looming over him he's been forced to make some hard decisions like conscripting his citizens in order to get enough numbers to hold off the dragon. So far nothing he's done has worked well in the long run and the people are starting to lose their faith in him. Perhaps if he could defeat the dragon then the people would follow his rule one again.

It was told that whoever would win in this festival would be considered a champion of the people and could fight alongside the army as a leader. That was a privilege I wanted desperately. I would also get an audience with the king and the neighbouring nobles as well. I trained hard and decided that my choice of weapon would be my legendary blade that I pulled from the stone so long ago. The glowing magic resonated with me and I'm sure that the people of the kingdom would be shocked to see its raw power in battle. I could also shoot beams of light from the blade that could cut through any type of armor. I also learned how to summon the four elements with my sword and I could even attach the elemental powers to my blade itself to use in battle. I also mastered my lightning abilities through meditation and communing with the gods at various statues. I can now arc the lightning from my fingertips or concentrate into a small ball in the palm of my hand and then toss it wherever I wish.

No one else in the world has ever seen magic like this before so they will be in for quite a surprise. I can also now teleport between the Modern World and this world with simply a thought. I can't seem to teleport anywhere else but I wonder if I could improve that skill through training. I found if I used my magic too much at the beginning, I would get a nosebleed and my head would gain a splitting headache. If I persisted in using my abilities I would eventually pass out and be left vulnerable to an enemy attack. Luckily with all my training those episodes are few and far between now. I trained long and hard and the warriors who would train with me were very impressed with my skill. After over a month of preparations it was time for the tournament.

I took my magical sword with me and entered into the barracks. I saw many of the other entrants training and I silently observed them for a moment before heading further into the tent to the registration area. The receptionist was very kind and helpful and she led me to the waiting area. I saw that my number was twenty out of one hundred so I realized I would be waiting for quite a while. I decided to take the time to train while I waited my turn. If I didn't get to fight that day I could sleep in the barracks with the others if I so chose. I also decided to talk with some of the other combatants and they all complimented my sword while also telling me all about the rules of the festival. The main ones were that the bouts weren't to the death and only went on until the other opponent either yielded or couldn't continue. I liked those rules since I didn't have to kill anyone and I managed to spar with some of the other entrants. I bonded with many of them and they all thought my sword skills were impeccable. I enjoyed my time with them and we swapped stories about our lives and what our plans were.

Finally, after many hours of waiting I was called in for my first fight. My opponent was a large man with heavy iron armor and a giant great axe. I could tell that the strength behind his swings could cut a man's head off and that I could be dead within one hit. He grunts when he sees me and bows while holding onto his axe with one hand. I bow as well and he nods in respect. The bearded man hefts his great axe and starts lumbering towards me. I rush to meet him and I use my sword to block his axe. The force of his axe and his strength combined sent an earth-shattering crack as he pushes against my sword. My grip holds even as the force reverberates and hurts my hands badly. I still manage to hold on however and I push forth. I soon realize that my sword strength alone isn't enough to break his hold so I decide to back off and re-evaluate. I quickly catch my breath after that exhausting ordeal and decide to try a different tactic. The bearded man hefts his axe and runs towards me while I dash underneath his legs and I aim my sword at his crotch area. My sword punctures through his crotch and blood gushes everywhere. I see that his penis has fallen onto the grounds nearby and he cries out in pain. He drops his axe and falls to the ground. He cries out and tries desperately to re-attach his penis to no avail. I also learned some healing magic throughout my training and I walk over to him and I re-attach his penis with magic. He looks at me in shock and with approval and he says "I yield to your magic and mercy, thank you." He grabs his axe and bows to me as the crowd cheers. I feel overwhelmed by the sheer number of the crowd but I bask in my glory for a short time.

I catch my breath and walk away. The fight was very short but it was effective. The other combatants looked at me with a mix of awe and fear. Some congratulate me on my bout and my abilities but others cower away and some apparently chose to drop out of the tournament right then and there. After another few hours I'm up again and I see a man about my age with a bunch of weapons on him. I can tell that he has daggers, a shield, multiple swords and twin axes. As soon as he sees me and my sword; he discards all but most of his weapons in order to make it fair. He bows to me with a smirk and I bow back. All that's left on him is a typical sword and shield. I rush him and he meets me with his sword and shield. He catches my sword with his shield and tries to slash at my arms with his blade. I double back and manage to dodge his sword just before it catches my arms. I run backwards as I try to figure out how to proceed. He isn't very heavily armored and he's clearly guarding his crotch area when he sees me eyeing it. Also doing that again wouldn't be honourable. I want to win this fight fair and square.

I push a bit of lightning into my sword and I dig it into the ground. I only put a little bit of magic in it and it spreads all across the battlefield. It catches his armor and electrocutes him. He drops to the ground and discards his metal shield and sword. He decides that the only other way is to beat me hand to hand so he bows and readies his fists. I discard my sword and follow suit. We rush each other and meet in a flurry of punches and kicks.

With magic augmenting my strength I used the power of lightning to also enhance my punches and hit his armor with all of my might. After many hits I manage to dent his armor significantly and then push him to the ground. I jump on top of him and angle my hands above his throat in a threatening manner. "Do you yield?" I say quickly. The man looks at me and nods. He yells out that he yields and we stand up. I use some of my magic to repair some of his armor using a mix of magic and skills from the Modern World. We grip each other's hands as brothers in arms and we bow to each other once again. I meet up with him afterwards and he congratulates me on my victory. I have many more bouts like that and I find that using my fists can be just as effective as the sword if I use them correctly. After a significant number of fights, I make it to the finals after five days of fighting.

The only ones left are me and a tiny guy who's known to be very quick with a dagger. I decide that the best way to fight is with my fists so I pump some fire into them and use it to coat my fists in a protective barrier. I wait for him to come to me and we meet each other in battle. The sweat coming off my face is significant but I also never felt more alive. He's extremely quick with his little dagger and is leaving tons of tiny cuts all over my body. I can feel myself slowing down as my blood begins to seep out quickly and I have to use magic in order to keep my body together. I can't lose like this. Eventually I decide on a risky play. Out of breath and my chest heaving I decide to play dead. I fall to the ground as he puts the dagger to my throat. He asks me if I yield and as I catch my breath, I grab the dagger and I rip it out of his hands. I grab blade first and manage to cut my hands pretty heavily before being able to flip the blade into my left hand. I then draw my sword and dual wield that and the dagger. The opponent begins to run away but I'm too quick this time. Even with my injuries and without the use of his dagger I quickly catch up to him and stab him multiple times in the legs and back in order to incapacitate him. I also realize that whenever I hold the dagger time seems to slow down and I become much faster. I wonder if there are magical artifacts in this world. I pin his legs down like a pincushion and then I get on top of him. I grab his head and I put the dagger right by his neck and whisper into his ear "where did you get this? Tell me and I won't make a rug out of your vocal cords." He begins to cry and tells me through tears "it's...it's from the land of the Giants. If you win this tournament you're allowed to go there and pick an artifact for yourself. I won the last tournament and was able to get that beautiful dagger. I thought that if I won again, I could get something even better but this isn't worth it. I yield!" he screams out sadly. He cries out desperately and I remove the weapons from him. I then hand back his dagger and he grabs it gratefully. I offer to heal his wounds but he shakes his head and runs as fast as he can (which isn't very fast with his injuries) and exits the grounds for good.

I throw my arms into the air as the crowd booms for my victory over every other combatant. The announcer announces that I am the champion of the kingdom and am asked to go and greet King Linus up the nearby stairs. I sheath my sword and I go up to him. I see a kind old king who looks weathered by stress and bad experiences but who still holds a fondness for his land and people. I can tell that despite his negative calls he truly wants to help the kingdom prosper in any way possible. I kneel to him and the king chuckles. "Rise sir Elias, you need not bow here. You have proven yourself worthy of my favor," he says gently. He has a booming laugh and seems like a great guy for a king. I rise to my feet and say "My liege, thank you for honouring me with an audience. I live for nothing more than to help our kingdom become even stronger than it is and to be able to push that dragon back" I say sincerely. The king nods and replies "thank you for your service. I appreciate your eagerness to help our kingdom. It's unfortunate that our kingdom has fallen on such dark times with the dragon and the neighbouring kingdoms threatening war. I had hoped this festival and the threat of the dragon would create peace but alas, that has not come to pass. I have a task for you, my knight. Use the portal in the basement of the castle, and travel to the land of the Giants. You shall gain a magical artifact to aid you in your fight against the dragon once the meet the priest there. He shall help you on your way. Do you accept this task?" I nod my head and say "yes my king, I shall accomplish this for you." The king smiles even further and then beckons me to the castle.

I follow with my heart feeling heavy and willing to undergo whatever is needed of me. I want to save this land and its people if I can. As we walk to the castle I'm overcome with feelings of nostalgia as the castle seems so familiar to me. I feel completely at ease as if I had come home from a long journey. I'm certain I've never been here before but I still feel like this is my home. I follow the king into the castle and we head into the basement. I put my hand on a giant statue and it looks like a marble cut out of a gigantic man wearing a suit of leather armor and a giant broadsword. I stare at the statue in awe before the king beckons me to touch it with his left hand. I touch the statue and I feel myself being torn apart in a blinding light. I can tell that I'm being teleported as I can feel the familiar ringing of my ears and the dryness in my mouth. The next thing I remember is screaming into the void as my body feels like its being broken piece by piece.

The Land Of The Giants

I WAKE UP ON the stone floor as I throw up on the cold stone floor. I vomit my guts out and I retch for what feels like hours as I hear people coming and going around me. They don't seem to be paying me any mind. I guess they are used to people retching on the floor when they first arrive. I get to my feet and stare at the room around me. I'm in a small room with a giant statue behind me and a big door in front of me. The people seem to be around my size and I decide to leave the room. After dry heaving I drag myself out of the room and I see tons of people walking throughout a giant city that stretches as far as the eye can see. I can see buildings higher than anything I have ever seen and I feel like I'm moving. I hold myself onto a pillar as I get used to the constant movement and rumbling beneath my feet. My equilibrium feels out of whack. No one else seems to notice it and are just living their lives. I flag someone down to tell me where the priests are. The generic citizen tells me where to go and I follow the road South. The road is paved with marble and the buildings look pristine and everyone looks really happy. I feel at ease among these people but none of them are Giants. I wonder where they are. I keep on walking until I manage to find the church. There are priests standing outside and I reach out to them to get their attention. "Hi, can you help me? I'm looking for the head priest." I say softly and the priests look at each other. They respond in unison "follow us." Their voices sound exactly the same. They're high pitched and wear purple robes. The priests guide me to a large room with a gigantic statue with two great axes and a man with his back to me and wearing a golden robe with the hood covering his face.

He turns towards me and I see that the hood is covering his face except for his mouth but his mouth turns from a neutral expression to a warm smile. "Welcome my child, it is wonderful to see you. Another acolyte from King Linus' kingdom I presume," he says softly. I nod in response and he takes his hood off. He reveals himself to be an old man with youthful green eyes that shine in recognition at seeing my face and black hair. He has scars all across his face and I can tell that he has been in many battles. "My friend, I welcome you to the land of the Giants. It is wonderful to see someone like you again. Or perhaps you are his descendant. Do you have any questions for me?" He asks sincerely. "Father, where are all of the Giants? All I see are happy people and this constant rumbling and moving beneath my feet. What is going on here? And why does it seem like you know me?" The man eyes me with a smile and beckons me to a plaque near him. "I shall explain all to you, but first I shall translate this plaque in Giantese to you. It tells of the legend of our people." I nod and follow him towards the plaque. He puts one hand on the plaque and it looks old and worn but still seems like there's power emanating from it. He keeps his hand on it and then puts a hand on my shoulder. I then see a vision as he speaks to me in my mind.

"Eons ago, this land was riddled with chaos. Humans fought against the Giants but they were no match for their superior strength. Humans lived on the surface while the Giants walked the surface in search of a new home for themselves while crushing any Human that got in their way. Humans created technology using magic and put them into artifacts in order to counter the Giant threat and both sides were at a standstill. Many Humans and Giants fell during the long war and neither side was willing to gain ground. The smell of blood was in the air constantly and no one could live in safety while the war was being waged. It's unclear who started the war; but it's believed that a giant accidently stepped on a Human king and flattened his kingdom to the ground. Once that happened the Humans began killing any Giant that got in their way. Both sides fought on for many years until finally a truce was forced. Mythical beasts that resemble alligators crawled out of the earth and began to walk on land. They were humanoid as well and could walk on two legs. They were about 10 feet tall each and were very fast. The Humans were quickly becoming overwhelmed until the Giants decided to intervene and killed many of the beasts that ravaged the land. Both sides worked together to take out the new threat since the beasts were also hurting the Giants as well.

"The Giants and Humans came to an agreement to stop fighting and they combined their technology and strength in order to counter the beasts. The creatures could also run and walk on four legs but many walked on two. They were very deadly but were no match for the combined efforts of Humans and Giants. Eventually the Giants decided to apologize for their transgressions and the Humans bowed their heads in shame for all the Giant blood that was spilled. The Giants agreed to help the Humans protect themselves in exchange for the Humans promising to never kill another Giant again. The Humans agreed but eventually the beasts were too much for both of them. The beasts took over the surface world and the Humans nearly became extinct; until the Giants came up with a plan. They decided to build cities on their backs in order to house the Humans and protect them. The first Humans agreed and they started building together. Eventually the Giants would walk all across this earth destroying everything in their path which included the beasts. The Giants are about ten thousand meters tall and crushed anything in their way like ants. Even the tallest buildings fell to their touch. The Humans and Giants co existed for many years and we Humans live in relative peace. However, there are problems with this method. Giants can live for millions of years but eventually they can die from either old age or from the wounds inflicted on them by the Beasts. The Beasts may reach up to the Giants' feet but they can still cause damage over many years. Some even crawl up them before the Giants catch them and stomp on them. No creature has ever made it into the cities as the Giants are now our sworn protectors.

"Us Humans have become accustomed to the movement of the Giants and they are constantly on the move in order to protect themselves from the beasts catching up to them. They are also searching for something at the edge of the world. It will take them many years to get there but when they do, it's believed that there will be peace for both Giants and Humans forever. The beasts will no longer be a problem if we can make it there. But alas, that might be beyond my lifetime. Oh well. I'm content with my life. I used to fight against the beasts in my younger days. The beasts have never made it to the cities but on the outskirts, there are Human warriors perched in order to defend the cities as well in case the Giants miss any. I have been in many battles with them and I don't regret any part of my life but I am happy with my current position as grandmaster of the church. As for why I seem to know you; I shall show you. In the basement are statues of some of our greatest heroes, both Humans and Giants alike. As for you, I believe one of your ancestors was one of the most legendary warriors who facilitated the peace between our two races. Instead of fighting the Giants he worked to befriend them and actually managed to make peace with them before other Humans even tried. His name was Eli and we are proud to have him in our history. Now my child does this provide you with the answers that you seek?" He asked calmly. While he was talking, I could see visions of Humans vs. Giants as they fought seemingly endlessly for years. The Humans gained much ground when they started using magical infused artifacts in order to give them super powers but the Giants always held on and never gave more than an inch at the end of the day .

The smell of blood in the air overtook my nostrils and I could feel the war in the air. The wave of it all almost made me double over in pain due to wanting to throw up. I then saw the horrifying beasts that attacked both Human and Giants alike. The two then worked together to take out the threat. I saw someone who looked starkly like me working with the Giants in order to attain peace. He and a few others worked together with the Giants in order to become friends and their efforts paid off. I then saw a statue of that ancestor in this very church and he looked exactly like me. I felt a sense of pride swell up in me as I saw his face and knew that we were related. I also saw that the artifacts were stored down there as well. I then realized something horrifying. Once a Giant's life ended, they would crumble to the ground and beats would then overtake its corpse. The Humans on the cities on their backs would then either be crushed by the fall or devoured by the beasts. It's truly a horrific sight seeing their limbs getting crushed by impact and hearing the bones crack. I could also feel their fear as some of the "lucky" ones managed to survive the fall and become eaten alive by the beasts. The priest took his hand away from me and awareness came back to me. I doubled over in pain as the weight of everything threatened to overtake me. So much history transferred throughout my body like a program being uploaded to a computer felt overwhelming but eventually the ringing in my head began to settle and I felt slightly better. I stood up to face the head priest and he took my hand in a comforting gesture. I accepted it and I instantly began to feel better.

The priest looked at me with kind but sympathetic eyes. "My child, I'm sorry for the strain that put on you. I felt it was important to show you our history but the strain isn't easy to handle for everyone. Are you alright my friend?" He asked sincerely. I slowly removed my hand from his and nodded my head. His face lit up and clasped his hands together. I realized something that I had to ask. "Is there a way for me to talk to the Giants? I wish to speak with their leaders if possible." The old man's eyes narrowed slightly but he nodded and said "you can speak with them, but it will not be an easy task. You must go to the temple and enter the portal in order to meet them. You will have to pass a trial of their choosing in order to prove your worth in meeting them. I will not be able to help you in this endeavor." He said solemnly. I nodded and said "I shall prepare for the journey then. Is there any assistance you can provide me though?" The old man put his hand to his head and then nodded. He beckoned for me to follow him and I did.

He took me to the hall of artifacts and gave me a map to where the temple would be. It actually wasn't too far from here. It was just a few miles south of here through some dark forest. I see that there are many different artifacts I can choose from. There are weapons, jewelry, and even suits of armor and other outfits. The possibilities are limitless. The head priest came to me and said sagely "choose the option that best suits you, you may even take two if you wish. The right object shall call out to you and you shall know its heart." I nodded and replies "yes father." He smiled at me and let me pick.

I pored over every option until I began to hear whispering. I couldn't make out any words but it seemed like they were saying garbled and different things. Many of the voices sounded frantic and some sounded calm and terrifying. I didn't like the feelings I got from either of them honestly. The voices eventually began to get so overwhelming I could feel my ears beginning to bleed and my eyes began to water. My vision started blurring and I passed out. The priests apparently had intervened because I woke up a moment later with their hands on my shoulders as they pulled me up. The voices were still there but their volume had decreased significantly. I decided to block out those voices until I felt a steady ba-bump coming from an ornate golden looking sword and a necklace that appeared to be made of both light and darkness. Both objects seemed to resonate safety and stability and there weren't any terrifying voices. The voices had been drawn out completely by the steady thumping sound coming from these two items. I picked up the sword and it felt perfectly in my hand. It would go perfectly with my sword made out of pure obsidian. I had training in dual wielding blades so this would work for me. I also picked up the necklace and the two black and white orbs almost seemed to flash in sync with my heartbeat. I put the necklace on and I instantly developed a massive headache as it felt like my head was splitting open.

The pain was unbearable but I managed to hold my ground and become attuned to the object. I felt like it was trying to tell me something. I then saw visions of me getting stabbed and the necklace intervening in order to protect me from getting hurt. Apparently, the necklace would allow me to create a small shield every once in a while, to protect myself against a fatal blow. Apparently, the necklace was rather arrogant and wouldn't react unless the blow was lethal. Not particularly useful in some cases but being able to survive a fatal hit would give me options in the fight ahead. The pain died down and the necklace burst into a million pieces and absorbed itself into my chest. The feeling was painless surprisingly and felt extremely intimate in the best way. I felt like I was finally reunited with my other half. I put my two swords together and did some experimental swings in order to get used to their weight and balance. Both swords felt like home within my grips and the weight felt heavy and perfect for my style of fighting. I never liked light weapons so the heavier the better in my opinion. Both swords felt like they represented light and darkness. I know that as a Human I have both light and darkness inside of myself. I've learned many things from being in this crazy new world. Everyday I may have the potential to be either good or bad but it isn't that simple. Human beings are complicated and there are many people who do good things for the wrong reasons and there are those who do bad things for good reasons. The truth isn't black and white and it's very difficult to discern what the best call is to make for every situation. When I beat the crap out of my ex best friend, I disfigured him and brutally hurt him. That was wrong but I don't regret it. I know that I have the potential to go down a dark path but my friends and family keep me grounded. I have the resolve to fight the dragon because it's the right thing to do and I wish to get the Giant's help in this long fight. I don't know if it'll work, but I have to try.

If I can save the Giants and the Humans here from the beasts then perhaps, I can bring peace to all the realms. The head priest nods happily at my choices and I then head out into the forest. With my swords cutting through the overbrush it's easy and my advanced sight due to my magic allows me to see through the darkness. It's dark by the time I head out into the woods and I feel ready to find this temple. I travel for some time before finally making it there. The sound of silence reverberates throughout the entire forest and there aren't even any animals or insects making any noises. Clearly even the animals are afraid to come here. I wonder why. I finally make it to the temple and I take a drink from my canteen filled with water and take a bite of my sandwich before finally heading inside. Within this temple, I will find the answers that I seek.

The Temple Of The Giants

THE MOMENT I ENTER the temple I feel cold. The outside air had been warm and comforting despite the eerie silence but the inside feels like a snowstorm has hit. I shiver a bit uncontrollably before I managed to calm myself down. My internal magic abilities allow me to also keep my body temperature at the optimal temperature wherever I end up going. I really love magic and I seem to be the only person able to use this ability among my other ones. Perhaps I will try to give the gift of magic back to the world since they haven't seen any trace of it for millennia except for the odd magical artifacts from the land of the Giants. I peer further into the temple and I manage to warm myself up. I keep walking and my magic eventually makes my eyesight crystal clear enough to see in the darkness. I move on and I see an altar in the center of the room that seems to be bathed in darkness. Even with my magically enhanced eyesight I can't see through it; I just see more darkness. It feels almost suffocating and the closer I get the more I feel my throat begin to close up and my breath becoming really heavy.

The darkness must be magical in nature. I advance closer and closer slowly as my breath begins to fail me. By the time I get to the altar I'm on my knees wheezing and this doesn't feel right; but I don't see any other option however. There aren't any other doors or entryways to move forward within the temple. Finally with the last of my strength, I pull myself up to the craggy altar and I put my hands on top it. Suddenly I see a blinding darkness and then I can't see anything at all. I scream into the void but the darkness suffocates me and I feel myself falling to the ground and coughing. My hands are still stuck to the altar and I feel myself being split apart once again. It's like my entire body is reforming itself elsewhere. Finally, I wake up and take a large breath as my breathing finally returns to me. I woke up on the floor of the temple and there finally seems to be a doorway opening up for me to advance forward. I stand up shakily and walk towards the door. I go through it and I see what looks to be a cave. I go forward into it when the door slams shut. I can't get back out and I feel myself begin to panic. I manage to push my fears down slightly but it isn't enough to get rid of them completely.

I reach for my swords when I realize to my horror that my swords are missing. Not only that, but my rations and water canteen are also missing. Did someone steal them when I was knocked out? What the hell happened to me? I walk further into the room and I see that there is a canteen of fresh water on the top of a pedestal in the center of the room. I examine it closely to make sure there aren't any traps connected to it and when I realize there aren't any, I take the canteen and I examine it to make sure the water is fresh. It is so at least I have water. I decide not to drink from it yet. I look to the wall and see that the wall is actually glowing. There are letters forming in the temple walls. I look closely and realize that it's saying "Survive for the next three days and you shall prove your worth." I guess I have to survive for three days or something. Huh. This water doesn't look like enough to hold out for three days so I'll have to ration it. I look around the room and see that there isn't anything else of note. The exit is completely sealed but there aren't any other doors anywhere. The room is completely dark except for some lit torches that flicker. There isn't any wind so I wonder what's causing that. Whatever, I can worry about such musing later. First, I have to survive the next three days. I feel like boredom is going to be the worst part of all.

I decide to use some of my excess energy and work out for the time being. I work out by doing push ups and jumping jacks until I can't feel my muscles anymore. I take small sips of water in order to conserve my energy and then I spend some time sleeping. Eventually I feel too weak to move but I still force myself to do sparring drills in order to keep myself in tip top shape. I can feel the hunger and thirst knowing at me but I decide to fight through it. When I feel tired, I sleep and when I feel thirsty, I drink slowly from the canteen just enough to quench it partly so I can sleep. The hunger pains are the worst but there isn't anything I can do about that yet.

After a couple days of this I assume I begin to hallucinate. I can't keep track of time in here and eventually I stop exercising completely. It's too much to bear so I just sleep. When I'm awake, I see visions of my girlfriend offering me food and water but I reject them since I know they aren't real. My girlfriend loves me but she would never come here. She's back home in the village safe with the others. After what feels like hours I finally manage to sleep again and I dream of her once again. I really do love my girlfriend and my adoptive parents in this world. Lisa and Dan mean a lot to me and I will do whatever I can do to protect them from the dragon's wrath. I can't tell if I'm going crazy or what. All I know is that I have to endure this.

After what feels like days a door at the other end of the room manages to open. The glowing words disappear as the door opens and I see blinding light coming from the way forward. I shield my eyes and slowly push myself up. I down the rest of the canteen that I had been saving and press on. I walk through the door and I see a beautiful looking forest in the daytime. This is clearly a different forest than the one I was in previously. What is this place? As I consider these things I don't notice someone creeping up behind me and I definitely don't notice the heavy object being raised until it smashes me in the back of my head. I feel my head tingle and my vision beginning to blur again as I'm overcome with pain and I feel blood coming from the back of my head.

After I fall to the ground the pain finally registers and I can hear a bone splitting crack as I hit my head on the ground. I black out instantly and have no recollection of what happened next. The next moment I can recall is waking up being strapped to a wooden table. There is rope binding my arms and legs and I can't move. The rope is encircling my entire body and I can't move no matter how much I try. I also can't focus on summoning my magic since the rope is restricting my muscles and I can barely breathe. There is also rope around my neck that's is getting tighter and tighter as I slowly begin to pass out again. Eventually I hear what sounds like a foreign voice and they scream frantically at someone to stop choking me and then the ropes begin to recede. I open my eyes and see a monstrous figure that looks like a giant pig demon with boar tusks. He looms over me with dead eyes staring me down and he starts speaking in some garbled tongue. I can't understand anything he's trying to say and the only thing I can do is stare blankly at him. That's all I can do with my fear. I also think I pissed my pants the moment I saw him.

Despite saving my life I don't think his intentions are pure. He sees me misunderstanding so he changes his approach and attempts to adopt a soothing tone as he says "does this tongue work for you?" I nod weakly and his dead eyes light up slightly. "Good, I have need of you, my prisoner. Can you tell me where those pesky Giants are? Me and my people have been trapped in this temple because of them and you freed us! However, we cannot leave yet until we find those awful Giants and tear them limb from limb. Surely you can help me?" he says gruffly but as gently as he can. I see that there's something sinister behind his eyes and I don't think I can trust him. I haven't met the Giants yet but

I have learned about their history. They seem like good people and I don't want to betray them. If I do then the Humans could also be massacred by these things. They don't look very big compared to the Giants but I wonder if they could act like parasites. I can't take that chance. I shake my head as much as I can with the ropes restricting my movement. The creature looks almost disappointed and walks away with a sigh.

"We could have done this the easy way, I would have let you go...but now I can't. Time to be punished," he says quietly to himself. The ropes binding me begin to constrict even further as creature I hadn't seen prior are holding the ropes to me and are pulling them into me. I scream as loud as I can and blood begins to pour out of me. After an eternity of this the pressure stops and the ropes go slack. I'm still bound but I'm not bleeding anymore and I can breathe deeply. I see the same creature coming again and he brings forth a bunch of medical instruments that look terrifying to me. I see scalpels, saws, scoopers, grabbers, and many other things that look like torture devices. I still keep silent as he plucks on of them out seemingly at random in a sing song voice that sounds unsettlingly deep.

He holds the scalpel threateningly above my right eye and says "Are you sure this is the route you wish to go?" I honestly don't know what to say so I don't say anything. He sighs through his tusks and then plunges the scalpel into my eye. I scream out in pain as he digs around in there until he then uses a scooper to scoop out my eye and presents it to me. He then stuffs the eye into my mouth and forces me to swallow it. I choke on it and begin to gag but one of the other creatures forces me to keep it down and eventually the eye goes down my throat. It feels like the absolute worst thing I've ever tasted and my remaining eye is tearing up in fear. I can feel the stinging pain of the scalpel still as he cut through the optical nerves and severed them enough in order to remove the eye. I can't breathe anymore as I begin to hyper ventilate. I slowly pass out until I feel someone injecting me with something. My good eye bursts open as the creature stares at me with a chuckle and laughs deeply. Clearly, he's not going to let me pass out while he's having his fun. It must have been adrenaline or something similar to that effect.

He then takes his bloody scalpel and uses it on my other eye. I feel an even more intense burst of pain as he severs the nerves and forces my other eye out of its socket. I can't see anything anymore and I just scream and scream until my lungs give out. At this point I feel ready to tell them anything just to get the pain to end but I have to protect my friends. They don't deserve to die and I need the Giants. The artifacts won't be enough to win this war. I spit in the creature's face I assume by the sound of him retching in disgust. I then feel rough hands gripping my tongue and he then sawing it off. I can't scream anymore but the pain becomes unbearable and I begin to cry through my empty eye holes. I scream internally and I slowly fall asleep. Apparently, the adrenaline isn't enough to keep me up and they finish their work until I woke up again. This continued for what felt like an eternity.

Not to go into graphic details but I essentially lost my fingers, my toes, my arms, my legs, and my genitalia. My thoughts are so distorted I can't even think straight anymore. Who am I? What am I? Am I even a person or am I an object of epic proportions. Should I just die? I think I should maybe just die. Please kill me. Please kill me. Please kill me. Please kill me. Please kill me. Please kill me. As I feel my life force finally begin to die out, I hear a sagely voice whispering in my ears. "Congratulations, you have passed the test." I feel everything that I lost beginning to grow back and I feel the blood making its way back into my body. I feel my wounds stitching themselves together and I feel my strength returning. I feel better than ever but I'm afraid to open my eyes. I also feel my mind begin to repair itself and I no longer want to kill myself or end my life. "It's okay, you can open your eyes. You don't have to be afraid of us Elias." The voice says softly. I slowly open my eyes and see what looks like a bunch of ethereal Giants standing around at podiums. There looks to be around ten of them and they seem to be quite old. Like millions of years old and yet they appear to be quite strong. They all have beards and are quite muscular. These must be the Giant's leaders. I can tell they saved my life so I bow in supplication. At this point I'm just happy to have my body parts back and be healed so I will agree to anything at this point. However, I then realize that these Giants must have put me through that torture intentionally. I bite my tongue and know that I have to show some respect since these are elders and they clearly have more power than I could ever have.

I bite my tongue until it starts to bleed internally and I say "with all due respect, why would you put me through that? What test are you talking about? What's the point of all this and why do you hate me so much?" I ask desperately. At this point I start to sob from all the pain I endured and I feel both relief at being healed but also hopelessness at not understanding what's going on. The Giants wait for me to stop crying and then finally they speak as one. "We are the council of Giants. We have brought you here to test if you are worthy of asking us for help. We put you through that torture in order to test your endurance and your will to survive. We made those creatures up in order to terrify you and test your spirit. We thought that if we could break your spirit then you wouldn't be worthy of our aid. Others before you have come before us and they have misused the Giant's help. While we are sorry for putting you through such extreme methods, we had to be sure as you understand. We are honored to say that you have passed the test." They speak so sincerely all at once that I can't help but believe them. I can see that the Giants have many wounds inflicted on them and they must have been through many battles. My anger slowly begins to fade and I feel myself feeling at home in this calming place. I can tell that this place is sacred to both Giants and Humans. I see there are many other podiums but only ten of them are occupied currently. This place looks like it could hold thousands or maybe even millions of people.

"You have been tested and you have passed we shall help you if you wish. Any questions you have, now is the time to ask." They all say in unison. I rack my brain for all the questions I want to ask but my mind feels muddled. Finally, I ask the question I've been wanting to ask more than anything. I get on my knees and put my hands together and beg. "Please my lords, please help me fight against this dragon that has terrorized my land. If this dragon can't be contained then he will unleash his wrath on my friends. Can you please help me with this task?" I plead as much as I possibly can as I'm so desperate. One of the Giants come forward and says "Of course, we shall help you. You protected us by not giving away our location to the creatures and you protected the Humans who would have been slaughtered as well. You have earned our trust and we shall help you in any way we can. I shall assign you ten of our finest and youngest warriors. They are young Giants as they are only a few hundred years old but they shall be as tall as skyscrapers in your world and are very eager to prove themselves in battle. I only ask that you please bring them back safely," he said cautiously. I nodded my head in agreement as relief flooded through me at the thought of finally being able to help my friends.

The Giants also explain that while they are long dead they can commune with people through their temples and sometimes, they test people who are looking for aid like my case. I also realized that Humans who have gained the favor of the Giants are also allowed to come here and my ancestor is also here. I didn't get the chance to meet him but I felt honored to be in such a holy place. The afterlife essentially acts as a meeting place for Giants, philosophers, and Humans to live in harmony and debate amongst themselves in friendly banter. It sounds like a philosopher's dream. I wonder if Immanuel Kant made it into here, but who knows. After our conversation they snap their fingers and send me back into the temple. I have my gear and rations back and I head back into the main city. By now I've gotten used to the rumbling of the Giant moving and I feel at ease with it. Once I leave the Land of the Giants, I can open a summoning portal with a special stone that will allow ten of the Giants to come forward and help me. I hope that if these Giants can co-exist with Humans without flattening them then perhaps other Humans and Giants can live in peace here. I doubt it but you never know! Anyway. I decide to move on. I head back to where the priest is and he gives me food and water as I've run out of it on the way back. They are proud of what I've accomplished after I tell them everything and they feel happy for me. They are also happy I didn't end up getting killed or failing the test. If I had failed, I might have died as others had previously done and by tradition, they were honor bound not to say any of this to me. I understand to some extent so I have no ill will towards the priest or his followers.

I take my blades and the summoning stone and head back through the portal back to the kingdom. I see King Linus and I decide to ask him about my ancestor. "If he's who I think he is, then he's the one who first founded this kingdom. If you manage to slay the dragon then I shall name you my successor in his name!" He says happily. I feel honored and overwhelmed by his great honor and I heartily accept. I would love to be a king and to rule this land. Me and the king go over final details about the Giants and we decide to summon them on the outskirts of the kingdom near the dragon's home. We shall invade his home in two days time once we get our forces together. I will essentially be leading the army of twenty thousand strong and with the aid of the ten Giants hopefully that will be enough. One day later me and the king head to the outskirts and we open up the summoning portal. Ten Giants walk through as promised and they brought thousands of Humans in order to help out as well. Apparently, they are a package deal and we now have ten Giants and another ten thousand Humans willing to fight with us. They join the ranks of the other Humans and we spend the next day planning our formations and getting everyone up to speed. I will lead the Human forces through the base of the mountain while the Giants will take the other side and we will meet the dragon in a pincer attack. Hopefully our combined forces will be able to push the dragon back and slay him for good.

The Dragon Arc

I REST IN THE barracks with the other knights and we head out the next day. The Giants go to the Northern side of the mountain while we head to the southern side. As we begin the trek up the mountain, we realize something we hadn't anticipated. It's not just one dragon living here, it's an entire nest or hive of them. Dragons operate under a strict hierarchy you see. Elder dragons take the top ranks while middle aged dragons are next, then its young adult dragons which are smaller, and finally child dragons which are still much bigger than Humans and are only a few hundred years old. Typically, an elder dragon will leave his nest once he becomes too old in order to die with dignity but this one didn't appear to operate that way. This is even more dangerous than we thought but we decide to keep moving on.

I lead the Humans up the mountain and some baby dragons come out to greet us. I also run into Lisa and Dan's son and we talk about how we can't wait to go back home. I find out his name is Jason. As the baby dragons begin their attack most of our forces raise up their shields to block the flames and me and Jason run towards a nearby cave in order to avoid the heat. As we adjust to the darkness, we both see that there's another baby dragon inside the cave waiting for us with its jaw outstretched. I see an orange glow emanating from its mouth but I decide to run forward and then dash to the side at the last second. Jason followed my strategy and managed to dodge to the other side. The flames just missed us both by an inch and this cave is really small and narrow. I managed to dodge the dragon's claws and I plunge my swords into his neck. The dragon jerks back as he's struck but I keep digging and digging my blades in deeper and deeper as blood begins to seep into the cave floor. Eventually I manage to decapitate the dragon and me and Jason fall to our knees in exhaustion.

This was just the first dragon and there were countless more to deal with. We quickly rush out of the cave to see that the army managed to deal with the dragon with no casualties. Me and the commander talk and we decide that we have to split up. Me and Jason will attempt to climb the cliff face and make it to the elder dragon while the army and the Giants fight off the rest of the dragons and cause a diversion so we can make it through unseen. I don't like this plan but I know that fighting every single dragon on the way up will be exhausting and time consuming. This really is the best option so I ultimately agree. Jason decided to come with me because he knows me and because he really wants to help and make his parents proud. I promise to look after him and we head off.

I happen to have some climbing gear just in case we needed it and me and Jason attach the gear to our belts and head up. I hear the boom and pounding of the Giants as they fight against the dragons. Their skin is rock hard and resistant to flame which makes them perfect for fighting them. The ten of them are making quick progress and are already scaling part of the mountain while taking many dragons with them. I continue my agonizing climb until me and Jason manage to make it to a cliff face that edges out slightly. We pull ourselves up and decide to rest here for a bit. The army is also making quick progress and I believe they should make it to the young adult dragons soon if things go smoothly. God I really hope things go smoothly.

Me and Jason decide to catch our breath and we decide to talk things out. He looks exactly like his parents with his father's jaw line and his mother's eyes. We talk about our past and our futures while we wait for our breath to come back and our muscles to ease up slightly. Eventually the tension settles and we decide to keep moving forward.

Meanwhile from the perspective of the army, "Move forward people! We need to keep these dragons off our allies!" The commander yelled out harshly. The rest of the men replied "SIR YES SIR!" The commander was an older man in his mid thirties and was almost ready to retire from his service and be with his family. But once he heard about the upcoming dragon op, he knew that he had to be apart of it. Once he had done twenty years, he was eligible for retirement but he decided to postpone it. He's got a pregnant wife at home and will do anything to get back to her. He personally doesn't believe that he can take out an elder dragon so he hopes that those two young warriors will be able to do it. He knew that going on this mission might be a death sentence and that he was risking leaving his family for good but he knew that if the dragon ran rampant then he would destroy his family anyway. In his eyes, the choice was more than clear. He would die fighting if he had to. On this day the dragon threat would come to an end. So far, he and his army had been able to get rid of most of the baby dragons while some of the others managed to fly away presumable to warn their elders about the attack.

The army had minor burns on their bodies but their armor and shields had held and kept them together. The commander's leadership was also keeping morale up. The commander knew they could win if everything went well but he also knew that in war nothing ever rarely went perfectly. The men didn't have to know that however. As long as they continued to fight then they could at least put a dent in the hive and that would be a great service to the kingdom. Many of these people were peasants and farmers who had no formal training but the commander had whipped them into shape with his training techniques. It was all he could do in the grand scheme of things. But he hoped it would be enough. They hadn't expected to be an entire hive here; they thought it would only be one dragon. Luckily the Giants had been making great strides and were already on the middle-aged dragons on their side. They couldn't let the Giants show them up so they kept on moving. The young adult dragons would be next for them. Hopefully the armor will be able to hold up for this. If not, they were completely screwed and would be dead by morning. The commander took off his helmet for the first time and his scarred face was visible for everyone to see. He had deep scratches on his face and had wounds everywhere else across his body.

He was ready to fight for his men and his kingdom. "Move forward men!" He bellowed and the rest followed suit. Meanwhile on the other side of the mountain the Giants were crushing puny dragons beneath their feet and were grabbing them before they could fly away in cowardice. The Giants were having the time of their lives as they never had the opportunity to fight monsters such as these. Some of the Giants were injured as their rock-hard skin could only take so much punishment but all ten of them were still standing. Their skin was tougher than rocks and steel but the dragon's breath was tougher than they thought. Their pride however wouldn't let them back down. They would fight until the end and would gladly put their lives at risk if that's what it took. Eventually the army had managed to fight through the young adult dragons and the middle-aged ones were next. There were some casualties but not many luckily. They could mourn their losses later. They had to keep moving.

Meanwhile, me and Jason on the other hand had managed to bypass most of the dragons and made it to the giant castle that laid on top of the mountain. How had no one seen this? I guess the castle had been hidden behind the mountains and hills. Anyway. It was time to go on. Jason had sustained some injuries after falling and hurting his ankle but he could still fight. I however was in tip top condition and was able to keep going as well. We fought many older dragons around the castle and they were tough but the Giants had also made it to the castle and were helping us beat them back by keeping them distracted. Me and Jason took the opportunity to sneak into the castle and avoid any dragons still lingering in there. Some of the dragons were simply doing nothing and looked very bored. One of them even had a book in his claw and was reading it happily to himself. I think it was The Schreiber Chronicles Echoes of Dystopia by Ethan Spadoni but I'm not sure. I also think I heard the dragon say "I hope the sequel is just as good. I wonder if it'll be shorter or not." He said to himself. I saw someone sitting in cage typing on his laptop that seemed to be Ethan Spadoni. Me and Jason scurried past them and we made it to another floor. Some of the dragons were not even remotely concerned about the invasion and were even drinking tea and having crumpets. One of them was even building Legos and some were playing Yugioh and Magic the Gathering. I have no idea what's going on honestly. But whatever. We keep on going until we make it to the throne room.

There the Elder dragon is and me and Jason breathe in deeply and ready ourselves before walking in. As soon as we walk in, we see the largest dragon we had ever seen. He was gigantic and took over the entire size of the room. He was even bigger than Bonetail from the Pit of One Hundred Trials in Paper Mario the Thousand Year Door. Me and my brother would play drinking games every Christmas and we would play through that game and see who could handle the most liquor. It was always a fun time. Anyway, Jason and I face the dragon down and he looks almost bored. "Sigh, another meal comes in for the snacking. I wanted to go on a diet but I guess if the gods want me to keep eating then I shall eat. Prepare yourselves my meal, this will not be pleasant for you." He said sharply. He raised his claws to the sky and slammed them down on the ground. Me and Jason had just managed to avoid the claws and we barely made it out of the way in time.

Me and Jason continued to dodge the dragon's claws and even his fire breath. His fire breath was difficult to dodge but didn't feel as tough as the middle-aged dragons. This dragon seemed much weaker than them but I can't figure out why. The elder seems to be tired and bored like he's just playing with his food. My swords aren't strong enough to pierce his hide so I'll have to aim for his belly where it's slightly softer. I rush towards the belly and I ignite both of my blades with water and turn them into ice. I plunge them deep into his belly and I begin to twist. The dragon bellows in pain and his fire breath goes everywhere as he screams. He roars out in pain as I cut through his belly and into his gigantic stomach. His intestines spill out everywhere as he struggles to keep himself alive. I see the fire in his eyes but there's nothing he can do about it. I ignite both of my swords with a combination of light and darkness and I aim them towards his open mouth. As his fire breath nearly escape his mouth my magic chokes it back into him and it destroys his insides. The elder falls to the ground and lays his head down for the last time. "It is your time my child, finish them." He says weakly to himself.

I have no idea what he meant by that. I go to Jason to give him a high five when I see him slumped on the ground. He had gotten hit by one of the dragon's claws and was bleeding profusely while slumped against a pillar. I run over to him and I put my hands on his body. I guess I never noticed him go down during the initial struggle. I heal his wounds and eventually he wakes up. He says weakly "thank you friend." He clasps my hand in his and I help him up. As we make our way out, we hear a roaring coming from the other side of the cavern. Coming from a room above us a golden dragon dives down and tries to devour us whole. We both manage to dodge just in the nick of time. I stare in awe at the dragon as he flies around. He must be a young adult but he seems much faster and stronger than the others combined. The elder must have been at the end of his life which was why he was so weak. And this dragon is in the prime of his life. I've heard golden dragons are exceedingly rare and this must be the last one in existence. The Giants and the army manage to make their way into the throne room as well and they stare in awe at the golden dragon descending upon them. The Giants get ready to protect their Human friends and try to grab the dragon out of the air. The golden one swiftly evades their attack and bites one of the giant's head off him.

That Giant slumps to the ground dead and everyone begins to scream. People begin running around in horror and the Giants mourn their friend. I go to the commander and I slap him hard as he's beginning to succumb to panic. I slap him again until he finally turns to me and nods at me. He yells at the top of his lungs "LISTEN UP, THIS IS JUST ANOTHER FIGHT WE HAVE TO WIN! ARE YOU WITH ME?!" The crowd roars in response and they are unified once again. The Giants try to create a shield around the Humans while the army uses bows in order to try and hit the golden dragon from the ground. Eventually the dragon comes to the ground and we all rush in in order to overwhelm it. The dragon bats us back with his claws and many Humans lose their lives. I rush in and manage to get a solid hit on his eye with my swords. I summoned lightning and aimed it at his right eye. His eye popped out with a crack and he cried out in pain. I told the army to aim their bows at his other eye and they did just that. Eventually they managed to fell his other eye and we all cheered...until his eyes began to grow back. Clearly this dragon had regenerative abilities. The dragon opened its mouth and golden flames burst out! They rained down on us and many people's armors melted like butter with them still inside of it.

They screamed in agony as their faces melted and their organs collapsed in on themselves. The bodies slumped to the ground but people still kept on fighting. There were still thousands of us left but we wouldn't last long at this rate. I decided that I had to do a risky play. When the dragon opened his mouth to devour someone else, I pushed that person out of the way and let myself be devoured. The dragon tried to snap his teeth closed but my swords kept his mouth open. I strained my muscles as I worked my way down to where his stomach was. Eventually his mouth snapped shut and I used my blades to cut him through his stomach. I continued to cut and cut as dragon blood gushed out before slowly regenerating itself. I could tell that the dragon was just going to mend itself unless I could put him down permanently. I avoided the stomach acid and I made my way down to where his heart was. I found my way there and the stench of Human and decomposing bodies along with dragon overwhelmed my nostrils. The acid nearly melted me many times but I always dodged it.

Once I saw his giant golden beating heart, I knew this was where I needed to be. I infused my swords with light and darkness and I plunged them deep into his heart. The heart cleaved in two and the light and darkness spread all throughout his body. The magic eventually made its way out and he coughed it and myself up before dying. I then quickly took my swords and decapitated him before he could recover. I held the dragon head at the army and yelled "WE DID IT GUYS!" Everyone cheered and the commander looked relieved. Jason also looked happy before passing out again. I knew he would be okay though so I wasn't too concerned.

The End Of The Dragons?

Many of the dragons that managed to survive flew away and promised never to invade our lands again. We made an agreement not to hunt them and they flew off. Jason got medical attention and the commander officially retired. I decided to head back to the Modern World in order to check on things and to say hello to my friends again. We had become quite rich so I bought a mansion with my money and I sold the company for a huge profit. Me and the other employees are very well off and are quite happy with our lives. After making sure everything was set, I headed back to the Fantasy World where I saw a statue of my ancestor in the basement of the castle and I realized that I must have been seeing his memories in my dreams. That was why this place seemed so familiar to me. He had been sharing them with me and he had granted me the power to come here through the help of the gods. He was the first person to ever be blessed with magic and he came to the Modern World just before he died and that was how his line had started.

I even managed to commune with him and he was very proud of me for all that I had accomplished. After that we had mass funerals for the people we had lost. We lost about half of our forces and the Giants lost five of theirs and about five thousand of their Human warriors. The Humans decided to stay here and the Giants returned to the Giant's realm. They promised to do everything they could to smooth things over with the elders. They held no ill will towards us but the elders would be furious at losing many of their famed warriors in a fight that had nothing to do with them. I really hope we don't have to deal with war against the Giants as well. Anyway, the king kept his promise and he crowned me the new king of the kingdom. I inherited all the wealth and also the problems of the kingdom. I now had to negotiate with the other kingdoms in order to avoid direct war which was problematic to say the least. I ended up marrying my girlfriend and we decided to settle down in the Fantasy World for good while visiting the Modern World occasionally for holidays and to check on things there. I never used magic in the Modern World again after what happened with my ex-friend as I wanted to live a normal life there with my wife at times.

I had heard that there was a dangerous prisoner in one of the nearby kingdoms that couldn't be killed. He was imprisoned in a giant dungeon down underground because they didn't know what to do with him. I knew that he would be a problem in the future but I would deal with him later. I also learned how to pass on my power to others that I had chosen. I passed the power to my wife and any of our future children would also gain that ability. I also gave the power to Jason who became my top lieutenant and partner during the Dragon War and I got to see Lisa and Dan again. They wanted to stay in the village but they managed to thrive there since the dragon was no longer causing trouble for them there. I finally had the chance to say that I was happy and I was with the love of my life and my future children. I ruled for many years until another calamity happened but that's a tale for another time.

The Escaped Prisoner

You've all heard of the tale of Elias the Great, the successor to King Linus of his territory. He reigned for many years and I knew of him as well. He and I were friends once; but that was a long time ago. For the time being, I will tell you about myself and my story. I was born in the Modern World, where Elias was born as well. I came from Eli's line and had children of my own in the Modern World. When I was in my twenties I transported to the Fantasy World for the first time. I ended up in the Selitus Kingdom which was known for their gold and iron mines. The Selitus Kingdom was very rich during those days and is still rich to this day. The Xatish Empire was one of our main allies but we all knew that we would turn on them in time. The Xatish was known for their navy and ship production so they were a force to be reckoned with on the seas, but on land they were vulnerable. I was born hundreds of years before Elias and made a living as a woodcutter in the empire and also worked in the mines. I met a lovely young woman and we became married. I never did get to see my family back in the Modern World again and I could never figure out how to get back home. I ended up having two children with my beautiful wife Grace here in the Selitus Kingdom. We had a small and modest life but we were happy.

I ended up forgetting about the Modern World and decided to stay with my new family. Eventually I learned that I had been blessed with magic from the gods. It was that same magic that brought me here in the first place but once I got there it ran out since the magical quality was so low in this world. I ended up praying to many statues in order to find solace and I rediscovered my magical abilities. By then enough time had passed that I had no intention of ever returning to the Modern World and my family might have been dead for all I knew. All that mattered was my current wife and two kids. Unfortunately, the magic had corrupted me and made me invulnerable to attacks and made me immortal. At the beginning me and my family were blessed and they trusted me completely. However, the good times began to change when bandits invaded our village. They tried to attack us and I used my magic in order to subdue them. I took many hits with arrows and swords but never went down. The townspeople had seen me take so many hits and became afraid. I woke up the next morning to smoke and realized my home was ablaze. I realized the townspeople must have tried to eradicate me with fire; the powers of the demons. I found my poor wife and children burned alive in the blaze and I held their charred bodies as I cried. The fire burned around me for many days as I held them crying. Eventually the blaze had run its course and the smoke began to clear. I know now that it was my magic that had acted unpredictably and killed my poor family. But at the time I had no way of knowing that to be the case and I used my abilities to raze the entire village to the ground. My anger and hatred were overwhelming and I believed I was doing a good thing by purging it from the world.

I went on a rampage and slaughtered many villages and cities in order to prove my point. This world had given me magic and they took my family away. They all deserved to die. I massacred so many people I've lost count of the atrocities I committed. I joined a mercenary group for the Xatish Empire and I defected to their side in order to kill off the entirety of the Selitus Kingdom. I earned many riches for my service but it was all for nought. Eventually the Xatish King turned me over to the Selitus King and I was arrested for treason and crimes against the kingdom. I was betrayed because the alliance was still strong at the time and both weren't planning on betraying each other yet. The neighbouring kingdom was still a threat.

The king tried to execute me but nothing took. He tried taking my head but it would grow back soon after. He would also try to cut off all my limbs and even poison me but nothing worked. Each time hurt like hell but nothing compared to the burning hatred I felt in my heart. I accepted my fate each time they tried but nothing stuck. Eventually the kingdom constructed a gigantic labyrinth of a prison that would become my cage that couldn't be broken out. I was bound in chains and raised in the air with chains covering my entire body. My arms and legs were splayed out in an x and my torso was covered in chains as well. It was painful but not restricting. The king had told his people that I had been trapped there in order to serve my life sentence but in truth he and the others were afraid of me and didn't know what else to do. They figured that if they couldn't kill me then they could contain me at least. During this time the magic in my veins allowed me to age slowly and despite growing a beard and wrinkles I didn't look much different from my young adult self. I felt weak and hollow but had no motivation to break out of prison.

The prison acted as a labyrinth and people only ventured down in order to check on me and give me food. I still had rights after all. There were guards everywhere and you had to go through multiple checkpoints in order to gain access to where I was. The only people allowed down there were the elite guard, the servant who brought me my food, and the nobles. No one else could even get close to me even if they could get into the labyrinth at all. The inquisitor would come in at all hours in order to torture and try to get answers to my immortality and regenerative abilities. He took out my eyes and fed me them. They were disgusting but I couldn't do much about it. The magic keeping me alive slowly began to burn out each time it brought me back and eventually it could only just barely keep me alive. I lost my genitals more time than I could count and my tongue and teeth were sawed and pried off so many times. My mouth became a mountain of blood as I cried myself to sleep. I spent hundreds of years in prison paying for my sins. I never tried to break out because I hoped that someday the inquisitor would actually be able to kill me. I had given up on genocide and only wanted to die. After many centuries I had become a hobble old man who barely had enough strength to speak.

Once Elias had become king he decided to come visit me on a diplomatic mission. The first time he visited me I was surprised to see the sheer power in his eyes. He was someone who could probably kill me but he chose not to even try. He and I talked for many hours and he began trying to rehabilitating me while trying more humane ways to try to end my immortality. Every time he showed up the residual magic would end up absorbing into myself and I could feel my strength slowly returning. I never told him this however, he didn't need to know. We talked about our old lives and I told him about my family. He couldn't understand what I was going through but he never judged me for my actions. He really was trying to help me and was a truly good friend. Relations between each of the other kingdoms was stronger than ever since everyone else was afraid of Elias and his magic. Even the Land of the Giants stayed allies despite losing some of their members in the Dragon War. Elias talked about the Modern World and we realized that I was his relative. The magic from our ancestors must have gotten twisted and made it unpredictable when it was within me. I can't explain it. We spent many years talking and we even played a version of chess. A servant had to stand in for me but we played constantly whenever he wasn't busy with other matters.

For the first time I felt at ease. Unfortunately, he told me that he couldn't keep visiting me anymore. He had to focus on his kingdom and maintain relations with everyone else first. I understood and we parted ways as friends. Whenever Elias wasn't around the inquisitor would try and torture me but he got nothing out of me. I finally realized that Elias would be a strong opponent and could finally end my life. I had asked him many times during our conversations to kill me but he always refused. He wanted me to be able to serve my sentence and then once I was punished enough, he would remove the immortality from me if he could. The idea was that I would lose all of my magic and I would then crumble into dust peacefully. I was alright with that at the beginning but now I want something more. He never kept his promise to me.

After about fifty years of his reign, he still looked the same age but slightly older with a beard as well. The magic was also sustaining him but not to the extent it was sustaining me. The time had come to finally take my vengeance on him. He betrayed me by not helping me as much as he could. When the servant brought me my food, I took the opportunity to use my reserve magic to break out of the chains and then use them to strangle her. I strangled her from behind and she choked to death very quickly before I snapped her neck. I took the chains with me as weapons and used them as whips. I also had significant training with a sword before I was imprisoned but my sword had been destroyed many years prior. I would need a new one. The magic had also made me younger again and was back to my young self. I used my chains to strangle all of the guards and I used them as human shields when it became necessary. I was going to slaughter everyone in my path to Elias and I would make him suffer just like I had. I worked my way through the cold labyrinth and killed every guard in my way. The cook was one of the last people to die and I stuffed him in his own oven. His face burned off and the sight of it was glorious. The stale air began to become suffocating and the moment I broke through the exit doors felt amazing.

With all of the magic coursing through my veins I wondered why I had ever stopped trying to kill people. Murder is so much fun and the magic makes me feel so powerful. Now that I'm back to my young self, I feel amazing. I see one guard is trying to crawl away and I see that the prison is overlooking a gigantic cliff. I pick up the poor pathetic guard with my hand and dangle him over the edge. He pleads for me to let him go and I oblige. I break his neck with a satisfying snap and then drop his body off the cliff and onto the ground far below. I breathe in the fresh night air and stare up at the moon. It's felt like an eternity since I felt the moon on my skin. I forgot how much I missed the moon and the sun. I finally take a look at my reflection in some water nearby. I look great and rough at the same time. I have long blonde hair and piercing green eyes. I have a beard but I'll get rid of that soon enough. The world shall fear my name once more. I am Leon the conqueror! The first thing I'm going to do is go get a drink and then head to where King Elias is in his kingdom. We shall meet there.

The Woes Of King Elias

I SIT ALONE IN my throne room while my queen is off getting our children to safety. They each have the ability to travel to the Modern World and will be safe there. I got word that Leon had escaped his prison and is heading this way. I have about one hundred warriors infused with my magic and I sent half of them to the Modern World to protect my family. I shall stay here with the other fifty and guard my kingdom. I'll meet Leon head on and try to reason with him. I'll prepare my guards and get ready for his arrival. The last thing I want is my people to get caught in the crossfire. I still have time before he arrives but who knows how long it'll actually take for him to arrive here. I believed that I could help Leon but I appear to have failed him. He may be invulnerable to my attacks but I believe that I can give him what he wants and end his life for good. I don't want to but I believe it's the only option at this point.

I rest my hand on my throne as I think things through. I decide to send my guards to protect the people first. Even if I die, I can hold my own against him by myself. I don't need my guards but my people do. I'm about seventy-six years old now but I look like I'm in my twenties. My magic allows me to age much more slowly than most people. I draw my swords and begin training in anticipation for his arrival. This will be a hard fight, but I believe I can win. Jasons agreed to stay with me as my bodyguard. I appreciate that kind of loyalty from him. I miss my wife and children but I know that they are safe wherever they are in the Modern World. I also ready my soldiers to be able to counter this threat as best as we possibly can.

Chapter 16: Leon's Journey

□I Leon make my way closer and closer to King Elias. He has sent some of his personal guard after me but I kill them with ease. Every time I kill a magic user, I absorb their magic into my own personal arsenal and become that much stronger. So far, I've killed many of his assassins and my magic has increased tenfold. I can augment my fists with magic and set my chains ablaze with fire and lightning. I have many of the same abilities as Elias except I don't use swords and I can't teleport between realms. I've slaughtered the Selitus army and they no longer send forces after me. I walk through the countryside in peace as everyone's too afraid of me to confront me. I take whatever I want and I get whatever sleeping arrangements I desire. Life is great. I decide not to kill anyone I don't have to since it's unnecessary. I make my way through the cities as well and take all the gear I feel I'll need. After many weeks of walking, I finally make it to the Linia Empire.

As soon as I get there, I see assassins and guards coming for me. I crack my knuckles in preparation and then light my chain on fire. I slash my chain at the nearest guards and they incinerate instantly as their armor becomes red hot. They scream in agony as they fall to the ground. I then use the power of ice to freeze some more of them as they freeze in place in shock. I also use my chains to strangle many of the guards at once and they fall to the ground dead. The magic users come and they also attacked me with weapons of their own such as swords. I dodged all of them deftly and used my magic to counter them. They were no match for me. I also made my way through this little village that I believe Elias once made his home. I saw the villagers brandish pitchforks. None of these people had magic so they weren't a threat. Suddenly I felt someone stab me from behind and decapitate me. I saw my own head fall to the ground in shock as I see someone with fire brimming from their fingertips yell out "Lisa, get the others out of here." I admit he caught me off guard. I respect anyone who is willing to stand their ground against their enemies.

My head re-attaches itself onto me and I stare him dead in the eyes. I take my chain and I whip it at him quickly. He blocks with his sword and I rip the sword from his hands. I then take the chain and strangle him. I take his sword and I stab him once in the heart. He dies quickly. I then absorb his power and burn the entire village to the ground. The townspeople were running away once my head hit the floor but they weren't quick enough to escape my wrath. I killed everyone in that village and then left their heads on pikes in order to send a message. No one messes with me and my mission. Elias shall fall. I continue to walk through the kingdom until finally making it to the capital city. The greatest influx of guards and magic users will be here but they won't be enough. Elias must have wanted to protect the people of the capital city the most. Who knows? Not me. I progress through the city and many users come at me brandishing swords and spears in order to try and slow me down. None of them succeed and I make my way through them all. I've also decided to leave a record of my journey through so I am writing a book about my experiences. Elias also told me he was writing a book about his life so perhaps I shall combine them both into one main account once I mount his head on my trophy wall. After many hours of slogging through guards and their pathetic magic users I finally make it to the castle.

I use my fire and I set the entire capital ablaze except for the castle. I enter the castle and head for the throne room. In there, Elias sits waiting for me on his throne. He regards me as I approach him. "So, you finally made it here. I knew it was only a matter of time before you reached me. My family is safe from the likes of you now. I wish I could have helped you, Leon. You deserved better. I'm sorry for failing you my old friend. Shall we get this over with?" he asks solemnly. "It's time." I say gruffly. I draw my chains and he draws his two swords. I then use my magic to trans mutate my chains into a powerful new sword. The sword is blood red with skulls covering it and is ready for action. We cross swords almost instantly and we both fight for dominance in this fight. I use my fire to augment my sword and he uses water and ice in order to augment both of his weapons along with light and dark magic. We clash and clash and it's like clash of the titans up here. He slashes right and I block both of his swords in mine and we constantly lock swords. We stare daggers at each other and part of me can't help but feel pity. He's a good man Elias but he should have helped me instead of his people first. They didn't deserve his kindness. I did. We go back and forth and it's like a whirlwind of blades. No matter where I slash, he catches my blade in his and we become locked once again.

Our fighting ended up with the castle crumbling all around us and us fighting in the ruins of nothingness. We both pant as we look at the carnage around us. "Is this what you wanted? To destroy everything around us?" He asks incredulously. I glare at him and respond "you should have killed me when you had the chance." He stares at me and nods. Clearly fighting with swords isn't getting us anywhere. We decide to settle this hand to hand. I drop my sword and he drops his two swords. I use fire combined with lightning and coat my hands in those elements while he does the same with water, ice, and earth. We run towards each other and punch and kick each other as hard as we can. We already have tons of tiny cuts each from the swords but in my case they already healed. We punch each other until our teeth get knocked out and I manage to grab him into a headlock.

"You did well but I'm afraid this is the end. Goodbye old friend." I say quietly. Before he can respond I pry his head apart in my hands and then I yank the bloody remains of his head and I kick it off a nearby cliff. I admit I thought I'd feel better at the death of him. Perhaps what I really wanted was to die myself. Suicide never worked for me since I always came back to life. Suddenly Elias' body disappeared into shimmering magic and I absorbed all of it. The absorption hurt like hell as it pierced into me and I saw all of Elias' memories. He really did want to help me but his people needed his help first since they were afraid of the other kingdoms and the Giants.

I feel a tear fall down from my eyes as I see his memories and his life. I can tell that some of the happiest times of his life were talking to me in that cold, dark cell. The magic eventually faded but I saw a vision of something. Some future that I could influence. I must bring that future to fruition. I saw the world burning and me finally long dead. If I have to die then I will bring everyone down with me. I go into a nearby temple and I put as much magic as I possibly can into the basin nearby. This site is sacred and is a bastion of magic since Elias took control. My fingers burn as I push all of my magic into the basin and then...everything goes to black. In that moment, all of the enemies' rush into to attack the Linia Empire and even the Giants get involved. War has officially begun.

This story has been lost to time. The fragments have been scattered but there are rumors of someone going off on a quest in order to reconnect with their heritage and to bring magic back to the world. The only question is, was he able to complete that quest?

The Story Of Edward

Five hundred years later:

The history of Linia has always been a dark and dangerous one. The kingdom of Linia was the target of many enemies for as long as time began. Whenever enemies dared to fight against the kingdom like dragons there was always a hero to step in and stop the threat. One of the most notable and recent ones was Elias. There was also the story of Leon who was known for being a dishonorable person but still managed to be friends with Elias for a time. However, it has come to light that the Linia History Society has come across transcripts of what really happened during Elias and his reign. Elias wrote an account of what happened in secret and he left the journals with his family for protection. And yet, it appeared that Leon had destroyed the world with his magic and caused a catastrophic war. However, we are at peace which still eludes me. If Leon destroyed the world, then why are we at peace and still here? It has been five hundred years since either Elias or Leon had been seen in this kingdom. After Elias' death there hasn't been any mention of either of the two in our history books.

The kingdom has changed much in the last few centuries. The monarchy has been abolished, and we have evolved. We are now governed by a council of representatives from every race and major business in the world. It isn't a perfect system by any means but it allows everyone to have a voice and we all must be in agreement before we can make any decisions of importance. We now use former magic users as our bodyguards in our corporations. They have been freed from their magical capabilities and potential corruption and wish only to serve the people of Linia and there are much stronger safeguards in place to prevent them from defecting. We still use swords and shields but we have added much more powerful enhancements to them. There have been talks of people on other continents using weapons called guns but we have no need for such archaic technology. Instead of writing letters, we have smart phones and computers that we use to gather our information. We have access to the internet and we are capable of finding anything with the click of a few keys. However, we don't use our technology for every aspect of our life. We still have to go into stores to buy things and talking on our phones isn't the same as talking in person. We are social creatures and we have made it easier to travel to and from various places so that we can see our neighbors all over Linia.

We no longer need magic to protect the world from threats. We have our own technology if needed, but we are at peace for now. For some reason, the gods are no longer being mentioned and that ended up being for the best. Whenever I would search the archives to find more information about the history from the last five hundred years, it's been destroyed.

Nobody seems to understand what happened during the transition between Elias's reign and our current era of peace. The history of Elias and Leon is incomplete. I was hoping that Elias's and Leon's journals would have been able to provide some insight but the pages have been ripped out and lost to time. We don't know what happened after he tried to create chaos in the world. Many traces from the old world have now disappeared. For those of you who don't know me, my name is Edward and I am a young scholar in my early twenties for the Museum of National History. For those who are wondering, I was born and raised in Central Linia. I was born here but my bloodline extends to every race across Linia. My ancestors were very well travelled and I have learned about all of their cultures through their journals. I yearn to learn more about my life but for the time being I am content to learn about the mystery that is Elias and Leon. I've always been interested in seeking out the truth and I was astonished when I found the journal entries written by them. If we can find the rest of the pages, then we can complete the history and I will be able to put my mind to rest about who Elias and Leon really were. I was the one who found the original journal, and now I'm going to head to the same spot to see if there are any clues as to what happened to the rest.

Because of my find, there have been many debates circulating about who Elias really was. There are many statues of Elias that predate Leon but also many that were quite recent. Politicians around the world are debating on whether these statues should be torn down or left standing. The truth deserves to be heard and that is exactly what I'm going to find. The site where the book was found was in an old house in an abandoned village. The area is in ruins, but the major structures still seem to be intact. This must be Taryn Village. It's believed that Elias used to live here while he was resting during his adventures. The journal was found underneath the bed in one house that may have been Elias's house. He must have lived here during his lifetime. Hang on; there is something in the distance. That's interesting; I can see an old man walking towards me and my team. Civilians aren't supposed to be here so I should get rid of him.

I can't believe it; this man had the remaining pages of the journals. He heard about the find online and he came to the site to locate us. He handed me the tattered remains of the journal and he said that he was a descendant of a close friend of Elias' from back then. He wouldn't tell me his name or who he was descended from, but the man seemed to love the color blue. Perhaps he was also a fan of Elias as well. Either way, he gave me the journal and he asked me to compile an entire history of what happened to Elias during his conflict with Leon. He didn't want money; he just wanted us to know the truth. The man seemed vaguely familiar to me even though we had never met before. He had such kind eyes and I could tell he was very experienced from the scars on his face. Naturally I was excited to meet him. I happily took the journal and began translating it. The language that the journal is written in is ancient French. We now have an evolved form of the French language but it is still similar to the old ways.

At last, the translation is finally done! I have compiled the entire history into one and I am ready to give it to my supervisor. He is waiting for me in his office to present my findings. Once my meeting is done, I am planning on leaking this to the public on my online blog and writing a book about my discoveries. Oh yes! I am so excited to tell everyone what I have discovered. The contents of the journal do explain a lot of what happened during the last few centuries. In fact, it could change the way we look at history as we know it. Here is what is left of the second half of these journals. Get some popcorn and find a nice comfy seat to read this in boys and girls! It's time for the show to begin!

The Story Of Leon Continued

After putting all of my magic into the pillar I caused rifts to open between the Giant Lands and the Fantasy World. Giants came out rumbling and began stomping on everything since Elias was the only one keeping them in check. The kingdoms of Xatish and Selitus began rallying their armies and began destroying what was left of the Linia Kingdom. I felt so happy to see everything coming into chaos and eventually the whole world had caught on fire. I avoided the onslaught and retreated to a nearby cliff as the Giants began destroying everything in their path. They even fought against the Xatish and the Selitus Armies but they were like fleas to them. I used my magic to open a portal into the Giant Lands and to give everyone the power of magic. Now that much of my magic is gone, I feel hollow and empty on the inside. What have I done? Did I really want to kill everyone? What was the point of all this? Can I finally die? I pick up my sword and try to stab myself but of course it heals instantly. Guess I still got a lot of residual magic within me keeping me together.

I need to make amends for what I've done. I need to get out of here. I find a nearby cave and decide to spend my life there in solitude. I block off the entrance so I'm the only person capable of getting in or out. This is what I need to do for the time being. I need to reflect upon my actions.

Three hundred years later:

I've become old and craggy but I still yet live. I'm not sure how long it's been since I first came in here. I still use my magic to see what's going on outside of this cave and it isn't good. The Selitus Kingdom managed to unite all of the kingdoms under their banner by killing most of their opposition and even the land of the Giants came to heel. The Selitus Kingdom managed to make the most of their new magical warriors and used them to slaughter everyone in their path. They mastered their new gifts rather quickly compared to the others and that was why they were able to launch a deadly first strike on the other nations. Even the Giants were no match for their combined strength. I think it's time to leave this cave. I heard rumors of a temple where I can purify my spirit and regain my emotions. While I may want to make amends, I don't feel that I can do that while the magic is still suppressing my emotions save for my anger. I need to become human again, or at least as close to human as I can. I break out of the cave and decide to head to the temple. It's a temple of darkness that can be bathed in golden light if I complete all of their puzzles.

I enter the temple and the feeling of darkness overwhelms me. It infects my nostrils and goes down my throat and into my body. I cough on the ground as the darkness swirls around me and threatens to blind me. I manage to push through it however and force myself into the next room. The room is filled with statues in no particular order. One of them resembles a gargoyle and the other three resemble knights. The door on the other side is sealed so I assume I have to put them in the right order. After messing with them for a while I finally manage to get the correct order and the door opens. I go into the next room and see a beautiful light orb after completing many puzzles. I touch the orb and feel myself get transported to another world. The temple fills to the brim with light and I find myself standing in the middle of a beautiful field. There I see the personification of many goddesses and gods as they stand before me. I kneel before them and start to cry. I can feel my emotions returning to me and I'm horrified at everything I've done. I fall to my knees as memories of everything comes rushing back. All I wanted was to finally die and see my family again. I also see that I was the one who killed my family in the first place. It was my fire magic that burned them alive. I can still smell their charred burning flesh and it makes me feel sick.

I can't believe I did so many horrible things. I feel sick to my stomach and the gods and goddesses come forward and comfort me. "It's alright my child, you're safe now. You need to forgive yourself for everything you've done." They say softly. "But my gods and goddesses, how can I forgive myself after everything I did? All the people I killed, and the people I gave magic to in order to bring chaos to this world. I don't deserve to live! Please kill me!" I plead in front of them. They softly cry in unison and they comfort me further by putting their hands on me. "Don't cry my child, it's okay. We shall lift your curse but first you must make amends for everything you did. We forgive you but you must learn to forgive yourself. We believe that we can help you with that." I stop crying at this point ant stare at them. They all look like ethereal shadows but I can feel them and I can see smiles on their faces. "How can you help me?" I ask almost pleading. They continue to smile and the lead shadow puts their hand on my forehead. Once we make contact, I see visions of a Modern World where I see a familiar figure living happily with his family. It's Elias! He's alive! I heard his artifact was powerful so he must have used it to teleport just before he died or maybe the artifact brought him back to life in the Modern World. I wonder if he has any magic on him. I need to get to him! I also see a grove filled with statues that seem to lead to the Modern World.

The goddess releases her hands and I say "thank you." They nod in response and I feel myself being teleported back to the temple of light. The temple is overflowing with beautiful light and I feel at ease for the first time in a long time. I take my sword and leave the temple for good. I need to find a way to the Modern World. My own magic won't allow me to get there but perhaps the statues of the gods can. Perhaps if I pray to them, I can make my way back home. I begin a long and excruciating journey to the grove in the village where Elias found his sword. I find the statues and I pray to them. I pray for what feels like many hours until I see a portal open up. One of my old gods that I bowed to was Riquarim the God of Rogues. He granted me a vision of a potential future and even gave me a glimpse into his life. Before the connection was severed, I thought I heard Riquarim say something like "YES! MURDER! MURDER! Get him Magna. The rest of the group is waiting for us back at the guild hall." After that the voice disappeared and I was left with my own thoughts. Riquarim sounds completely insane, but at least he has friends who are just as crazy as him in the afterlife. I wonder if I'll ever meet them.

I actually see many portals open. I decide to peer into some of them while I wait to go to the Modern World and try to find Elias. He must be in one of these portals. The first portal opened and I could see everything going on inside but I couldn't enter it. At first glance I couldn't tell exactly what was going on but I felt sad for some reason. I looked closer at the scene and I saw two people were trapped in what looked like tubes with liquid in them. It didn't look anything like either of the worlds I knew so it may have been another dimension or timeline. I could see the name of the first person trapped in the tube. It said Darwin Fitzgerald. I saw another name but it had been scratched off. The two people looked about the same age but one appeared to be mortally wounded. I don't know who any of these people were but they seemed to be important somehow. I hope they are going to be okay in the end.

I walked up to the second light beam and I peered into it with mild curiosity. In it I saw a lone man walking through the abandoned ruins of some town. The sky was dark and I could feel the cold chill from the wind emanating from the dimension. There seemed to be an electronic field that covered the entire town so I'm wondering if he was trapped inside with no way out. Just before I was about to leave, I saw hideous creatures walking around in the distance. It looked like people with fangs sucking the life out of any innocent people that couldn't escape in time and wolves running throughout the fields tearing limbs from any unfortunate bystanders that happened to get in their way. As soon as I left, I couldn't help but feel unsettled. What was that place? It looked like it was called Schreiber but I can't be certain. It looked like such a weird place.

Looking into the portals was beginning to take their toll on me but I had to keep going. I needed to find any more information if possible before I went to find Elias. I approached the third pillar of light and I forced my way into it to see get a better view of what was inside. I admit I didn't expect to see what I saw in there. There were five teenagers fighting against what appeared to be a mad scientist using magic. The five young teens seemed to be wielding supernatural powers that were not unlike the abilities the gods had given us. I wonder if they are some of the heroes incarnate. I don't know but I feel better knowing that there are other heroes out there in the world. I also don't feel the need to kill any of them. Finally, all of the portals vanish except for one. I look into it and see Elias with his wife and two kids. They look happy where they are but I need to speak to them. I walk through the portal and I end up on a beach. The town sign says Terrace Bay Beach. I must be near a small town or something. Elias is gently throwing one of his kids up in the air and when he sees me his eyes turn cold. He gently puts his son down and turns to me. He turns to his wife and beckons her to take the children away. I understand their trepidation.

Elias comes towards me and draws his two swords and points them right at my chest. "I knew you'd find me one day. What, finally trying to take the only piece of happiness I have left away from me. Well, my friend it won't work. You'll die here even if I have to die again in order to accomplish that." He said harshly. I noticed his wife and kids vanish in front of my eyes so they must have teleported back home. He must have had his swords with him at all times in order to protect himself in case I ever returned. Elias looks younger again like he was back in his twenties and he spits in my face. I let him do it and I put up no resistance. I raise my hands slowly in a show of surrender and then I say "I'm sorry for everything. Can you please hear me out?" His eyes narrow but he gently points his swords downward. "Speak," he says quickly. I gulp and explain everything. I explain that I regret everything I did, that I don't care about dying anymore, I just want to help the world I destroyed. I beg him to help me right the world.

Elias doesn't say anything. He just sheaths his swords and thinks things through. I can tell he's trying to figure out if I'm being sincere or not. Eventually he nods to himself and takes my hand. I feel us teleporting somewhere and I realize that we are in a small house. Elias's wife and kids cower in the next room and he puts a hand out to calm them before they go upstairs. Elias explains to me that after I killed him the amulet brought him back to life in an alternate universe and his wife and children came to find him after they heard about his death. He managed to retain his young self and the magic he gave his family granted them immortality but they could die whenever they wanted. Elias agreed to help me right the world back since he wanted to help his former people but he didn't forgive me for any of it. I understood and acknowledged his pain. I apologized for killing everyone and for killing him. I apologized for every single thing I did but it didn't seem to make a dent. That's okay, I'll prove to him I'm on his side in time.

Elias's Perspective Once Again

I don't know what to believe anymore. Leon came out of nowhere and told me that he has changed but I can't completely believe him. If what he said is true then he caused a lot of problems for the Fantasy World. I need to help them though. I'll work with him and perhaps we can make a difference in the world. We decide to head back to the world and he's right. The Medieval World is in complete chaos. The Selitus Empire has completely taken over everything and are the one ruling body throughout the entire world. Apparently every one of their citizens has magic and they are the most powerful force in the universe. I can't believe that but I know I need to stop them.

Leon and I infiltrate their main castle and see tons of guards throwing magic at each other for sparring purposes and I see some of the weaker citizens being whipped for not serving the elite guards fast enough. I shudder and continue sneaking past the other guards. We manage to make it to the throne room surprisingly easy and see a bunch of pillars surrounding the throne. The scent of magic overwhelms my lungs and my face and palms begin to sweat but I push through it. I see who I describe as a skeletal king sitting on the throne absorbing all of the power from the pillars and cackling madly. He turns to look at us and I can tell he's an elder lich. Someone who has managed to transcend the barrier between life and death is immortal in a sense. He never kept his good looks though which is unfortunate. Anyway, me and Leon draw our swords and we engage the lich in combat. He draws two broadswords and he blocks both of our attacks. He locks swords with us both and it takes everything we have to keep him from pushing us off our feet and stabbing us with his dangerous weapons.

We go back and forth like any other sword fight and eventually my swords go flying from my hands. The magic in the amulet ran out so I can't take another critical hit or I'll die for sure. The lich is about to stab me when Leon pushes me out of the way and takes the hit. The lich stabs Leon with his two blades and impales him to the wall. Leon grunts in pain and gurgles some blood before reaching for his sword and impaling the lich right back. I take the opportunity to behead the Lich and stomp on his skull so he can't get back up. The lich ends up dissolving into dust and finally dies. Leon drops to his feet as his body heals himself. I go up to him to check on him and he says he's okay. He gestures that he's fine and tells me to venture onto the throne. I do so and see the pillars glowing once again. They are arranged in a circle around the throne. I go to touch one when I can feel the all-powerful magic emanating from it. Clearly this is something I need to deal with. Leon joins me after wiping some blood from his mouth.

We both examine the pillars and Leon eventually comes to a realization. "I caused you so much pain Elias, but I don't think we can stay here. We need to leave this place and go elsewhere. If we want this to end peacefully, we have to leave this Fantasy World forever." I looked at him in shock but let him continue. "Elias, we need to bring magic to another world. What good has it done to us here? The people live in poverty and I know you wanted your people in the desert to get better healthcare and better conditions." I remember the harsh wind tearing apart my skin and the heat draining my throat of all its fluids that it needed to survive. The first time I went to the desert to appeal for their rights I nearly died even with my magic. I realize that he's right. We need to leave. Leon grabs my hand and we both put our hands on the pillars. It's time to take the magic back!

Leon and I suck up the magic and we both double over in pain while still holding onto the pillars as the magic overwhelms us. I can feel the magic attempting to corrupt me and I feel for the first time the pain Leon must have went through and not being able to die. I feel pity for him and I think I can finally forgive him. Before I can say anything, Leon looks over at me with a genuine smile and we both disappear in a burst of light.

I wake up on Terrace Bay Beach surrounded by my family and I see Leon on the ground puking his guts up. I'm glad he's okay. We decide to give the magic to the people of Terrace Bay and create a safe haven for people. We blast the magic into the sky and everything changes.

The End

We have finally completed our mission to the promise land. We have each found a new home within Terrace Bay. It has been decided that the Fantasy World should be left to its own devices so it can recover on its own terms. I and Leon relinquish our magic to the gods above in order to repair itself. Terrace Bay is a peaceful land that is filled with some chaos and strife and bad weather conditions at times. By giving up our magic we can heal the land and make it something worthy of its former greatness. We no longer have full access to our powers but the residual light of the combined Goddess Magic has bathed Terrace Bay in its golden light and has offered its protection. The people of Terrace Bay have now been blessed with immortality.

Anyone who lives here shall live forever and they will stay the same age that they currently are forever. The exception seems to be with children. They will continue to grow until they turn roughly twenty-five and then will remain that age. The way to counter this is to leave. It seems that if you stay for years and then leave you will then continue to age normally. If you leave for decades and then return you will return to your original age when you first left. This seems to only happen once but you can still age normally and live the rest of your day's travelling the world if you are so inclined. I have remained here for what seems like forever and their culture has evolved.

They now offer travel opportunities for young men to leave Terrace Bay and go onward to other parts of the world for experience and work. My wife and I are happy here with our two children. I wasn't able to return to the Fantasy World initially because of my shame in failing but I'm glad that I could make things right. I am planning on travelling myself to see what the world outside has become. I am curious to see what has happened to Linia in my absence. I am still in possession of the swords and I can still use their abilities. Perhaps it was a gift from the gods but I am not certain. My wife has enjoyed her time here greatly and she and Leon are leading figures in politics. They are on opposing sides of course but they are civil and can agree on certain things. We are finally at peace here and I hope that these journals can explain what happened during the reign of me. This is the end of my tale, and this journal shall be the only record of this journey.

Meanwhile in the Linia History Society Centre main offices:

I can't believe that I, Edward have been able to compile an entire history of what Leon's life was like during the reign of Elias. It turns out that he actually was the Hero of this tale and that he brought balance back to Linia and restored our lands. I believe that after they left the people of Linia came together and created their own society and political system. The Giants who once terrorized our kingdom have become our guardians and are elite mercenaries who protect us from outside threats. We are finally at peace and I think it is for the best that magic is no longer in our kingdom. Because of the success from the journal entries, I finally got a promotion at my job. When my boss retires, he is planning on leaving me in charge of the entire museum within the next five years. It's all I ever wanted. He finally recognized all my hard work here and dedication to the society. In fact, the mysterious man who gave me the final set of journal entries has agreed to meet with me for coffee. I need to properly thank him for everything he did for me.

Well, it turns out that my connection with history is actually much more strange and obscure than I ever could have imagined. This will be my final blog post unfortunately. I have decided to take a leave of absence from the Linia Historical Society and am planning on travelling. My boss will keep my position open for me until I am ready to return. You see, that man in blue who gave me the final set of journal entries was actually Elias himself. He had grown old and decided to travel the world before returning to Terrace Bay once again. According to him, he has made many travels throughout the last two hundred years and I am his direct descendant. I know right; totally amazing! But still, I never thought that I would be related to the man I worshipped so reverently. He explained to me in great detail that my lineage can be traced to him and Leon. My bloodline started with Elias' ancestor but it didn't end there. The bloodlines converged and become one complete genetic line itself. This means that I am the only person in existence that can wield all aspects of magic without needing to be blessed by the goddesses. Elias has offered to take me to Terrace Bay to learn about my history and to travel a new land with my ancestors. I can't wait.

It was a crisp summer evening and young Edward was completing his final blog post as he left his new office with his meager bag of belongings to begin his new life on the road. Outside there was an old man dressed in blue who was eager to teach him new things about life. As Edward happily left his building after saying goodbye to all of his friends of course, he embraced his relative with a hug. "I can't wait to meet everyone Elias. Do you think they will like me?" asked Edward nervously. "Ha, of course they will Edward. You are family. I wish Jason had been able to meet you but you will get to see Leon and everyone else at least." said Elias sadly. Edward gave a sad nod just as Elias pulled out a magic crystal. He crushed it with his hands and a portal to Terrace Bay opened up beneath their feet. Elias and Edward held onto each other tightly and jumped into their new adventure with hearts full of excitement and hope. Isn't always the goal of human beings to try to attain happiness? Well, I can't say for certain but at least for these two characters; they will finally find happiness within...Terrace Bay.

In Terrace Bay Edward met with Leon and learned swordsmanship from him and Elias. He also got to meet James, Stacy, Christine, and Simon in Schreiber which was a community about ten minutes away from Terrace Bay. It was after hearing James' accounts of what happened to them in their universe that inspired Edward to chronicle everyone's stories. First, he sat down with James, and then sat down with the rest of his friends and then met with Darwin and Aaron and was able to collect their stories. Edward was also able to meet with Elias and Leon in order to get more details on their respective stories and Edward finally met with his relatives. Edward found a true family and dedicated the rest of his life to travelling the multiverse in order to find more stories and release them to the public with his friends' consent of course.

Everyone loves the idea of spreading their tales far and wide and they don't trust anyone more than Edward to be able to make that happen. Edward also met with many random people in order to get additional details about what's happened in the universes and he compiled everything into his journals. Edward also learned how to manipulate lightning and the entirety of the four elements while also being able to summon a sword out of thin air. Edward even learned about telekinesis from Simon and how to manipulate the air around him. Edward was truly happy and he established many offices around the multiverse in order to properly catalogue everyone's stories that he came across. Edward was finally at peace and was enjoying lunch with Darwin, Leon, Elias, Stacy, Christine, Aaron and James when he saw a gigantic purple mass far in the distance. It appeared to be humanoid and was stomping and devouring everything in its path. What could this new threat be? Edward knew that he had to do everything he could to find out and stop this new enemy! He had a new family and his old family to protect. He couldn't afford to die just yet.

The End!

Meanwhile, there are rumors of chaos happening in another universe very similar to this one. In an alternate universe there exists a world born out of science fiction and Medieval Fantasy combined. What's going on in that universe? Read on to find out!

After Edward finished up hearing Elias' and Leon's perspectives, he heard the tale of someone coming from the distant future with a heartbreaking tale of six families vying for control of the universe

INTERMISSION:

HELLO ALL, IT'S THE author here. I just thought I'd write a few notes here about what I was thinking during the writing process of this project. I was inspired to write this after talking to one of my cousins and I wanted to write a major fantasy story. I had hoped the project would be exceedingly long but I'm very happy with the length so far. I appreciate anyone who made it this far and I look forward to seeing you in the next part. As for how I came up with the storylines, videogames such as God of War inspired me heavily like with Cronos being forced to carry things on his back as punishment and many anime inspired the idea of teleportation between worlds.

I tend to write short stories as they are easier for me rather than long projects so it may get done relatively quickly or may take a long time. It'll all depend on so many things. Anyway, I hope you all enjoyed what you have read thus far and if you'll indulge me, I'd like to end on a different note. Never let anyone who doesn't understand you tell you what to do and forge your own path if you aren't happy with your current life. That's not to say you should do anything drastic or disobey the laws of society; but there's nothing wrong with living your own life on your terms if that's what you wish. I'm trying to figure out what I want to do with my life and writing has been a good outlet for that so far. Please forgive me for rambling so much, there is so much I'd like to say but I will end with this. Enjoy your life and treat the people you care about with respect. They deserve that just as much as you deserve to live your own life.

Greed:

A Tale of Six Families and Their Stories

By Ethan Spadoni

Preface and Acknowledgements:

Hey! It's Ethan here. I wanted to thank you so much for reading up until this point. If you have read any of my other works then you are aware of how dark my writing can get. If so then I appreciate even more how many of you managed to make it this far. This whole thing may have been my friend's idea, but I'm the one who brought it into existence and did the writing portions. That's not to say that his contributions were nothing or minimal; I couldn't have done it without him and he advised me on many major plot points that I ended up including in some capacity. This story truly wouldn't exist without him and I'm genuinely happy to write this with him.

I will always be grateful to my mentors Susan and Trudy for helping me throughout school and this journey to self publish; I would also like to thank Shawn for giving me the idea to write this with his consent. I would also like to thank my family and friends for supporting me on this as well. Finally, I would like to thank you all for making it this far and taking a chance on a young guy from a small town with a big dream of becoming an author. Even if I never make it big and this tale reaches one person, then I have done my job effectively.

Cheers,

Ethan Spadoni

Prologue

People thought that science fiction was just a pipe dream. That's the same thing people said about going to the moon. In the twenty-first century people play games like Warhammer 40,000 and Final Fantasy IX. These are two of the most popular games of all time and scientists and engineers used their talents and dreams in order to make those fantasies a reality. In the year 4500 people are using airships right out of Warhammer and Final Fantasy in order to travel with ease throughout the Universe. The rich people of the Aquila Family and the solar system use the Warhammer ships with Cathedrals placed on top of them.

The cathedrals were built for worship and for status. Only the Aquila Family and their citizens were allowed these great gifts. The other people in the world were able to use airships with glass plating on the outer deck so that people could survive the cold vacuum of space. The galaxy is governed by six Families and they have been at peace for 500 years. They had spent over a thousand years fighting until the Aquila Family forced peace through ending the conflict. How they ended the conflict; nobody can remember. The six Families are the Aquila Family, the Delphinus Family, the Ursa Family, The Cepheus Family, the Ophiuchus Family, and the Serpens Family.

This story shall focus on the six Families and their origins and motivations. The six Families meet every year on a council location that's about twenty lightyears (twenty days) away from each of their territories. Technology has also extended people's quality of life and lifespans significantly longer. People can live as young adults up until they turn one hundred at least and then start to become middle aged by two hundred, and then decrepit well after three hundred and approaching four hundred. The galaxy lives in relative peace and enjoys a golden age of space technological advancement but there are rumors of even greater treasure at the center of the universe. What lies at the center?

No one truly knows. But each family secretly covets the long-forgotten treasure at the center and are all willing to do anything to get it. Will alliances be betrayed in search of the relics? Read on dear reader and find out!

The Origins Of The Aquila Family

The origins of the Aquila Family start during the twenty-first century. They were some of the first investors in Warhammer and Final Fantasy IX technology and built their fortune through that and inheriting much of their wealth from their long family line. They never had to work very hard for their wealth and had almost limitless wealth before space tech took off. Once they took to the stars the Aquila's were able to exert their wealth onto the world and took control of many planets and solar systems under their own. They ruled over most of the galaxy but ended up having to share the rulership with the other five Families.

The Aquila fought with the other five initially but using their wealth and advanced technology they neutralized the other five into submission. As part of the exchange the other five had to treat them like an equal in all trade disputes and the Aquila's would part with some of their technology in order to level the playing field. The Aquila's agreed to part with some of their lower tier ships which were still much higher advanced than what the other families were using up until that point. What no one knows is that the Aquila's secretly took out loans from the Delphinus Family in order to finance their war and Delphinus wanted a piece of the action. Delphinus was elevated to the table along with the rest and now they're at relative peace with each other. Now, the Aquila are just finishing up a meeting with the other families, while their children are in the waiting area discussing next steps.

The meeting room is an open cavern on the planet of neutrality where all issues can be brought up in neutral ground. On the planet is a gigantic fortress that is filled with rooms and hallways enough to fit thousands of people easily. The colors of the fortress are decorated in the colors of the six Families as well. Blue for the Aquila's and the others for the rest. Inside on the main hallways are several chairs which is just enough to fit each of the representatives from the six Families. Representing the Aquila's are Sirius the patriarch of the family. A portly 246-year-old man with blue hair and blue eyes. He looks middle aged and not in the best shape. Sitting to his right is his beloved wife, Ursa. She's a 256 shrewd old woman who looks far older than she really is but isn't decrepit. She also has blue hair and blue eyes and is considered a very ugly woman by many. Despite this, her intellect goes hand in hand with Sirius' ambitions. The two are the head of the most powerful family for that reason. Everyone believes that their wealth came from their wealth from thousands of years ago but that's a lie.

Their true wealth comes from their secret slave labor mines. Slavery is against the law but with help from the Delphinus Family, plus many bribes the Aquila's are able to get away with much. Sirius waits with bated breath as he and his wife plan their next move and hopefully the end of this meeting. "In conclusion, this is why I believe that the Aquila's should give us more of their ships in order to close the gap between us. The Aquila's have so much and even if they were to sacrifice one of their many ships it would be a great boon to the rest of the families. What say you?" spoke the representative of the Ophiuchus Family.

Arcturus is the head of the Ophiuchus's and despite being unmarried and a widower is able to hold his own in meetings even though he is alone. Arcturus' orange hair makes him stand out against the pale blue and white background of the meeting hall. The rest of the families look on bored as they had heard these arguments before. Arcturus always considered himself a rival to the Aquila's and for good reasons. He may have inherited his wealth but he also worked hard to quintuple his wealth in order to be on par with the Aquila's. Arcturus may have been 250 and looked middle aged but still looked quite attractive considering his age and physique.

Sirius did respect Arcturus for all of his achievements alone and considered him a worthy rival. However. That still didn't stop him from looking down on him and the other four for their insolence to even try and ask them for things. Sirius stood up before any of the other families could agree or disagree. He approached the neutral podium and spoke: "Good points Arcturus, but as much as I would love to give you all my ships, I fear I must disappoint you. I only have a small number available and they are in use by my family and my rich friends. We are in no position to make any more ships or give them away so frivolously. Besides in order to get the cores you ask for requires a substantial number of diamonds that frankly the Aquila's do not have," he said haughtily. Ursa murmured in agreement. The rest of the families agreed and so they all voted to deny Arcturus' proposal.

Arcturus sat down in anger but accepted the agreement. He would have to try again next year. Sirius and Ursa looked smug as they were able to keep the secret of their wealth concealed and that they didn't have to give up any of their valuable ships. They were in desperate need of diamonds but were hoping that the slave mines would be able to produce more soon. If not, then they would have to take out a loan from the others and they didn't want to do that at any cost. Sirius wanted the center of the universe in order to attain the ultimate treasure and stay on top for the rest of their lives. They forced a peace before and they would do whatever it took in order to achieve that goal. Meanwhile in one of the main waiting rooms waited Sirius and Ursa's children.

As they waited for their parents to adjourn the meeting Altair and Lyra waited patiently while discussing their own boredom and restlessness at having to wait for these meetings all the time. Altair is the heir to the Aquila fortune and is privy to the secret of the slave mines. His blue hair shone brightly in a long cut that matched his piercing blue eyes. He may have only been twenty seven but he had ambitions well beyond his years. He wanted the treasure at the center of the universe more than anything and would even kill another person in order to accomplish that.

Altair also looked quite attractive given his age and had killed many rivals in order to get to where he was today. He wanted the power that came with being the head of the Aquila Family and wanted his parents to give up and die already so that he could take power himself. Of course, killing another person violates the accords that each family must follow but what the others don't know can't hurt Altair. Lyra on the other hand was very different. At the age of twenty five she is unaware of the darker aspects of her family history and simply believes that her family earned their wealth by inheriting it from other people who did the hard work themselves.

All she wanted was to spend time with her many boytoys and spend her family's money recklessly. She has no interest in familial politics and just wants her money now. Lyra is also considered very young and beautiful for her age. Her long blue hair and blue eyes allowed her to get many different lovers every week and she was happy to string them along for as long as she was entertained by them. Her face looked like a porcelain doll which was very enticing to many prospective bachelors in search of a beautiful wife. Lyra had no interest in marriage however. All she wanted was to have as much fun as possible for as long as possible.

Altair and Lyra always got along despite their differing views. Altair always cared about his sister in a way, like a pet that he enjoyed spending time with. If he could care genuinely about anyone, it would be her. He doesn't use her like his other pawns in order to get ahead. If anything happened to her, he would feel sad and foolish since someone took something precious from him. The two waited patiently while Lyra went on and on about the money she wanted to spend and the trips she wanted to go on when their trek to this shitty planet was over while Altair was thinking more about what was going on with the familial politics and how he could maneuver things in order to get his family ahead even further. The first goal he was focused on was the diamond cores. They needed those in order to power their new ships effectively and to provide armor plating against threats that may come their way.

When the meeting was finally over Altair embraced his father while Lyra hugged her mother and took her wallet in order to buy some nice shoes she saw on spacezon. The family got into their luxurious cathedral looking ship and began the twenty-day trek home. While on the ship they discussed all about what was going on and how the other families were trying to resist the new accords that the Aquila's had been putting in place.

The current accords were that:

1. 1. No murder shall occur throughout the galaxy,

2. 2. No illegal activities such as slavery shall be permitted throughout the galaxy,

3. 3. No cannibalism allowed,

4. 4. No one family shall have more power than the council.

The final accord states that no one family shall harm the other. The council is what governs the galaxy and the Aquila's own many planets under them. The accords are what bind the council and galaxy together.

The families are also forbidden from committing acts of treason against each other such as robbery. The Aquila's want to break free of the accords so they can rule openly and without fear of retaliation. Their brand of justice is that they can do whatever they want, commit whatever atrocities they want, and that no one can stop them. Bribes and other aspects of the accord allow some robbery and exceptions can be made but the council must agree to them. The Serpens are the only ones allowed to rob each of the other families but they are bound by the accord to only do so when it would cause ineligible harm to the family or if they look the other way in some cases.

It will involve a lot of hard work in order to make progress on each of their goals but the family is more than willing to do whatever it takes to achieve their goal of ultimate domination and spending all of their money in the case of Lyra. On the way back home, Altair practiced his sword fighting while Lyra practiced her archery. Despite both being raised rich; they were both very capable of protecting themselves and were proficient in hand-to-hand fighting and ranged maneuvers. Altair thought long and hard about the other families. He always felt closest to the Delphinus Family due to their mysteriousness and awe-inspiring power. However, not even that would stop him from burning them alive in his quest for strength.

The Origins Of The Delphinus Family

The Delphinus Family are a very prestigious family that come from a long line of investing and banking. Back in the twenty-first century they controlled the banks and investing firms throughout North America. They invested heavily into airships and space flight in order to guarantee a seat in space. The Delphinus were so influential that when regular spaceflight became a thing they gained control of the largest banks in the galaxy and now everyone has to come to them for loans and favors. When the six Families were at war the Delphinus secretly sided with the Aquila's in order to attain more influence by them owing many favors and much more money.

The Delphinus provided the Aquila's with significant tech and money in order to win the war and the Aquila's still owe a significant sum of money in return. The Delphinus never owned the ships but they owned the plans on how to make them and that allowed the Aquila's to become the master of space flight and the most powerful family in the galaxy. The Delphinus' prefer to stay neutral in most affairs but will side with anyone as long as it benefits them in some capacity. They would like the treasure at the center of the universe in order to maintain their neutrality and power but they are in no rush to attain it. Their ambitions are merely to be in the same position they have always been and that they hold all the power even if they aren't at the top of the food chain.

They have a surplus number of diamonds that they are willing to keep in reserve until they decide to best make use them and their engineers and builders are always building on their ships; and are in secret possession of many of the same type of ships that they gave to the Aquila's hundreds of years ago and they have a significant amount of diamond cores. Their engineers are always secretly making improvements to those ships in order to guarantee the safety of their military and their people on their territory's planets. At the meeting hall while Arcturus is making his proclamations for everyone to get more aid from Aquila; the two representatives from the Delphinus Family are waiting for their turn to speak.

Cygnus is the patriarch and everything beyond his hair and eye color is unknown to everyone at the meeting hall save for his wife Carina and their kids. Their green and hair color is dark green and they wear neutral looking white masks that cover their faces. It's clear that both Carina and Cygnus are adults but no one knows how old they truly are. They could be young adults or they could be decrepit but no one would ever know based on how well they carry themselves physically and in political gatherings and meetings. Even when the other families go to their banks for aid and loans the masks are still being worn so no one knows who they truly are or what they look like.

Once Aquila stepped in and rejected the notion Cygnus takes his turn to speak after the fact. "I concur, if we were grant everyone a ship like that at this juncture then the Aquila's would surely lose their position as head of this council." Cygnus said seriously. The Aquila representatives tried to rebuttal but the rest of the council began to murmur amongst themselves. The council went on discussing matters of importance that didn't affect the Delphinus much. During the meeting Carina didn't speak once; instead opting to let her husband speak for them both. There were times where her head would twitch in annoyance or she would laugh at inappropriate times but due to her mysteriousness and wealth nobody paid it any mind. While the meeting was ongoing the children of Cygnus and Carina are waiting in their respective waiting room drinking champagne.

Vega and Cassiopia (the son and daughter respectively) of the Delphinus Family continued to wear their masks even though nobody would ever see them in the waiting room except for their family. The two spent their days managing the family business and training in aerial combat. Their ships were outfitted with powerful cannons and cannonballs that could decimate enemy soldiers. The other families' ships have cannons as well but they aren't as powerful. Once the proceedings were over the family reunited with each other and they all boarded their ship to go home. It would take about 20 days to reach home but their new advanced ships would be able to make the trip in half the time once they were finished.

Perhaps next year they could debut their new starships but they probably wouldn't. While they all appreciated status, they preferred to ensure the people under their control were happy first. While they may have been benevolent to their subjects and did everything they could to protect them; they were ruthless against their enemies and would play the long game in order to completely destroy them and make them suffer. Vega and Cassiopia were exactly the same as their parents down to their hair and eye color and were capable of working in tandem in order to achieve their goals for their family. Vega and Altair were somewhat close but Vega truly didn't trust him or any other family. The only family they respected truly and didn't fully distrust was the Ursa Family.

The Origins Of The Ursa Family

THE URSA FAMILY ARE quite a bit different from the other five families. While they have respect in their own right due to their large mining colony, they only run their planet and territory. They don't own any of it. In the twenty-first century they ran many mines and worked in tandem with who would become the Cepheus Family. The Cepheus Family owned a large mining corporation and bought out the Ursa Family business for a lump sum and job protection. The Ursa's felt grateful to their new benefactors but soon became to resent their new overlords for not letting them have any independence or sovereignty.

As spacecraft evolved and humanity moved to space the Ursa's followed the Cepheus' into space in order to continue to receive their protection and influence. The Ursa's eventually built up enough influence to run their own mining colony and planet but still owed their allegiance and tithes to the Cepheus'. In public the Ursa's were overly polite and grateful to the Cepheus' for their protection but behind closed doors they plotted a way to gain their independence back and their sovereignty. That's why they want the secrets at the center of the universe in order to gain their independence and power back and to prove to everyone that they could stand on their own against the Cepheus Family.

In the meeting room Taurus, the Family patriarch waits for his turn to speak next to his decrepit wife Gemini. Taurus has red hair that is balding with red eyes and looks very middle aged but also very muscular and still young looking for his age. He works out a lot and injects himself with stimulants in order to keep his body young. His wife however is three hundred and seventy eight and has sworn off all those stimulants and refuses to work out. She loves her family and husband but has essentially given up on life and appears much older than she should. Her hair is also red and still attractive looking despite looking disgusting. She is resentful of the position her family is in and doesn't know how to make it any better. She knows that if the Cepheus Family were to ever go to war, they would be conscripted into helping them out.

On the other hand, Taurus was very optimistic about his position and believed that he would be able to negotiate a better settlement offer for him and his family so that they could stand on their own. Taurus hopes that at another meeting they can renegotiate their standing and try to break away while still receiving some of their protections and money payments. The meetings happen every year and their position becomes stronger each year. Each year they try to bring up gradual separation but the Cepheus Family always gently shuts them down and Taurus never fights them on it lest he invoke their wrath.

In the meeting room are the two children of Taurus and Gemini. Leo, aged twenty-four, and his twin sister Aries sit in the room drinking wine and going over the adventures they hope to have someday. Their mines are plentiful of diamonds but they lack the technology to make the proper diamond cores. They also have to give up every single one of their diamonds to the Cepheus Family which makes them feel resentful and trapped. Both have red hair and are very attractive looking for their age. Both have had many suitors for their age but decided not to date until they were older and their station was much more secure. The twins are extremely close and will always support each other. They were always happier with each other rather than with their respective lovers.

Leo dreams of being his own captain someday and exploring the universe by himself, his sister and a loyal crew. Leo already has his captain's license and a good starter ship to get from territory to territory but not one that is strong enough to make it across the universe. Leo doesn't care much for familial politics, but he does love his family and wants the treasure at the center in order to help them get out of the situation that they found themselves in centuries ago.

Aries is somewhat timid at times but always stands up for her brother whenever he gets bullied or messed with by the other families. She only dreams of spending her life alongside her brother in a purely platonic way and out of sibling love. Aries and Leo hold no romantic feelings for each other and are just happy to have found a best friend in each other. Aries also loves adventure and would love to be part of a crew led by Leo and explore the cosmos. Leo and Aries are both considered good people and they act as each other's moral compass. They keep each other grounded and on the path of adventure and goodness. "Hey Aries, what do you think I should name my ship when I get one for myself?" Leo asked happily.

Aries thought to herself and replied "I think you should name it the Leo Enterprise. What do you think?" Leo thought long and hard but it didn't feel quite right. "I like the name but I don't know. What about something like freedom?" Aries could tell that this was the name her brother really wanted to choose right from the start but was too embarrassed to say out loud right away. "I think that's a great name!" she shrieked happily. She hugged him in celebration and he felt happy having such a great sister with him. After the meeting their parents came to collect them and they began their trek home. Taurus told his son and daughter that their pleas for separation were rejected once again. Leo comforted his father and said "you will get him next time dad. You always make a great case for separation and someday they will see that." His father smiled and said "thanks son, you always know how to make me feel better." The father and son hugged each other and Leo vowed to do everything he could to help his family and their station.

Leo had heard rumors that the Aquila Family worked with slaves but could never prove it. He always thought that if he could prove them wrong then maybe the Aquila would lose their influence and the Ursa's could increase their standing. Leo's been thinking of travelling into Aquila territory in order to find evidence about their potential corruption and illegal activities and to be able to steal a powerful ship that could cross the universe. Leo may have had an aversion to stealing and immoral things but he knew that his family could never afford a ship like the rich people use in Aquila territory. They also don't have much that they can offer in way of an exchange with the Delphinus Family. The Cepheus Family was always dangerous to the Ursa's due to their dependence on their wealth but the Aquila are much worse criminals.

The Origins Of The Cepheus Family

The Cepheus Family started out in the twenty-first century as a mining conglomerate who bought out smaller business that were struggling and gave them job security and massive paychecks in order to stay loyal to the company. The company treated each of their business equally and with genuine loyalty. They have them bonuses, paid vacations and sick days, and even allowed them to renegotiate their original deals if after a few years the smaller businesses were unhappy with the arrangements. One such family business was the Ursa Mining Family who became the Ursa Family.

The Ursa Mining Family was struggling to make ends meet so the Cepheus Corporation stepped in and saved them from bankruptcy. In exchange for saving them they wanted absolute loyalty to the company and they would gain some of their independence back once they could stand on their own. For many years this arrangement worked out quite well for everyone. The Cepheus Corporation got many businesses under their thumb and was able to generate a bunch of passive income from the remaining businesses that were reinvested into making the overall company structure that much stronger. The Ursa Mining Family also gained the protections of the Cepheus Corporation and gained significant bonuses and leeway in how they conducted their business. All they had to do was donate much of their resources to their superiors and to remain absolutely loyal to them.

Once both entities went to space, the Cepheus Family fought in a war against the other families. Despite not initially wanting to the Ursa Family followed them into battle and proved their absolute loyalty by fighting alongside them. Once the war was over the Ursa

Family was elevated to being one of the six council representatives who would act as an extra vote for the Cepheus Family.

During the council meeting in 4500 representatives from the Ursa Family wanted to stray from the Cepheus Family and wanted their own independence to grow and prosper while still retaining much of their protection and benefits. The Cepheus Family kindly rejected those offers because they would not be able to offer the same level of protection and benefits if they strayed. Perhaps if they proved they were better off being on their own then the Cepheus Family would reconsider their position. However, doing so would incur a large penalty of money and resources since the Cepheus Family would lose a valuable vassal state.

The Cepheus Family aren't tyrants; they give freedom to those who prove their worth but otherwise don't interfere in how their vassals live their lives or their business. The only thing they care about is the allocation of resources and loyalty. Right now, they have a large collection of diamonds and cores but they lack the engine and ship power required to use them effectively. The diamonds may get allocated by the vassal states but the Family pays a hefty amount of money in exchange so it isn't a complete loss. The representatives of the Family are Cancer who is 198 and looks somewhat middle aged but still youngish. His signature purple hair stands out against a sea of colours that covers the entire room.

His younger brother Capricorn is also in attendance. The man one hundred and ninety six and only looks slightly younger than his brother. The two work hand in hand in order to lead the Family and company effectively. Since Cancer adopted his two children and never married; his brother stepped up and became the second representative in order to support him. The two of them have turned their conglomerate into a very powerful and strong family business. The Family may not be the most respected because of how they got their wealth but their goods and services provide them with a place at the table and begrudging respect from the others. Cancer's children are also waiting in their respective waiting room for the meeting to come to an end.

Canis is the older sibling at seventeen and she loves her brother dearly. Her youthful face and somewhat long purple hair made her stand out against her younger brother Canes. Her brother Canes may have been young at sixteen but stood at about six feet tall which is about the height of the other children from the other families. Canis has a very innocent personality and loves everyone in her family. Canes on the other hand does not. His purple hair and purple eyes hide a very sinister personality that he keeps hidden behind a happy smile and strong wit. Canes has always hated his siter and always felt that she had everything that was supposed to be his even though she would disagree with that statement.

Secretly he always wanted to kill her. He would love to have her blood on his hands but he knows his family would murder him if he did that. While they wait, he spins his makeshift knife in his hands and he tosses it up in the air and then catching it with the other hand. He's normally left-handed but is also considered ambidextrous. A feat which he is very proud of. While he's tossing his knife in the air Canis is texting her friends on her phone about how proud she is of her brother and how much she wants to be a part of the family politics in the future.

As the family come into the room Canes tries to stab his father with his knife. Hs father catches his right hand and then puts in behind his back as the knife clatters to the ground. Cancer pins Canes to the ground and says "well done, you've gotten faster." He releases Canes and Canes nods in gratitude. These two have been training like this for a long time. Canes always wanted to know how to fight and Cancer was always happy to teach his youngest how to be a warrior. Canis had no interest in being a fighter and always felt closer to her uncle Capricorn who treated her kindly and with respect. Cancer loved his daughter dearly but just felt like he connected with his son more. As the two wrestled on the ground Capricorn took his niece to the ship and they bonded over board games and other fun stuff. While the family was on board the ship heading back home Canes was plotting on how to kill his sister and get away with it. He considered framing his uncle for the murder and sexual assault but knew that no one would ever believe that. He thought of the other families and the Ophiuchus Family always came to mind for their strength and wealth.

The Origins Of The Ophiuchus Family

THE OPHIUCHUS FAMILY ARE one of the wealthiest families in the galaxy and are on par with the Aquila's. They invested heavily into spacecraft and Warhammer in order to gain riches and to be in one of the top spots. Once they made it to space, they continued to invest heavily into space technology and became one of the most powerful families in the galaxy. They worked hard for their money and inherited a significant amount of funds that allowed them to gain respect.

The Aquila's are their only main rival and are on good terms with the other families except for the Serpens. The Ophiuchus would like the treasure at the center of the universe so they could finally prove their superiority over the Aquila's and turn the council into a dictatorship. Their version of justice is punishing the Aquila's for merely acting as their equal and to provide kindness to the other families that prove loyal to them. They could arguably be worse than the Aquila's in many cases except there are no allegations of corruption or slave trading against them. At the council meeting Arcturus stands down after trying to get more aid for the rest of the families. The main reason for him doing this is to weaken the Aquila's and to get access to the premium space flight technology.

Arcturus isn't happy that his proposal got turned down but was happy that the other families seemed to be discontented with the Aquila's so that's a victory in his book. Arcturus sits at the meetings alone without a wife since his last wife died many years prior and he's been alone ever since. His wife died under mysterious circumstances that even he can't explain. She was stabbed with a sword in the middle of their territory in broad daylight but no one could figure out who the culprit was. Arcturus is certain that it's the Aquila's who killed his wife and wants justice but he lacks any strong evidence against them. The only thing he knows for sure is that one of Aquila's ships was seen speeding away from the area around the time of the murder. Even if it kills Arcturus, he will prove that the Aquila's did it and will strip them of their council seat and prestige. His three children are awaiting in their respective waiting room for the meeting to finish as well.

Scorpius the youngest son at aged twenty-eight is considered very attractive with his orange hair and orange eyes along with his tattoos and piercings all across his body. Standing next to him is his older sister Virgo. Virgo has long orange hair and is considered very attractive at twenty-nine. She is well aware of the family business but nobody listens to her because everyone thinks she isn't as smart or clever as she actually is. She's constantly frustrated by this. His oldest sister Libra sports many designer earrings and necklaces that complement her orange hair and orange eyes quite nicely.

Libra is very vain and only cares about spending her money and getting everything she wants. She has no interest in the family business and just wants to be happy on her own terms which doesn't include anyone else standing in the way of her happiness. Scorpius on the other hand doesn't care about the family business either and only cares about mischief making. He loves to play pranks on his dad and his sisters when he gets bored which he is a lot of the time. His favourite pranks are swapping his dad's blood pressure pills with sugar pills. Just a small dose but enough to cause quite a scare. Now his dad always checks every pill before he ingests it. Scorpius is very proud of that fact. As their dad returns Scorpius tries to get his dad to sit on a whoopie cushion but it fails as his dad is too smart for that. The four travel back to their territory and think on what they should do next. They see the other families leaving as well and fear a twinge of fear when they see the Serpens Family.

The Origins Of The Serpens Family

The Serpens Family are quite different from the other families. Both in their origins and how they portray themselves. The Serpens Family love snakes and back in the twenty-first century they were pirates and marauders. They would steal gold from merchant ships and from other pirates. There was no order or code of honor that they lived by. They just wanted everything that they could get their hands on that wasn't nailed down. When space flight became a thing, they cemented their legacy by stealing any craft they could and used their weapons against the other families.

During the war they fought against everyone and used their own tech against them at times in order to become more powerful. When the dreaded peace was formed the Serpens were merely tolerated and given a place at the table since it was easier to keep them on a leash instead of making them a full out enemy. The current era of the Serpens is that they are mercenaries and still pirates at heart. The center of the universe is about 300 lightyears away and the Serpens want the treasure there as well. They merely want it because they believe it will be the greatest heist of all time and they want the freedom to do whatever they want. Right now, they have the freedom to rob anyone they choose but they can only do so as long as it doesn't have a large impact on the other families. Bribes and threats work to help the other families look the other way but if the Serpens go too far then the other five could turn on them. The Serpens are still constricted and they resent having that noose around their necks. They want the freedom to steal everything they could ever want and kill anyone they so choose. If they got the treasure, they would use it to destroy everyone and create a dark period of anarchy for everyone involved.

In the meeting room their opinion isn't really considered much unless they cause a big enough fuss. The two representatives of the family are Ophidian who is 200 years old with black hair and black eyes. He looks somewhat middle aged but still very young looking. His wife and partner are Hex. She's 250 years old and looks very middle aged. The two considered making a fuss during the meeting but after seeing the meeting go the way it did, they decided it wasn't worth it this time. Their children were waiting in the ship awaiting the okay to go back home for the night and they didn't want to delay their journey any further.

The two siblings are Asmodeus and Basilisk. Asmodeus is the younger brother with a ruthless personality at 37 years old. Basilisk on the other hand is the elder brother at 75 years old and is quite similar to his younger brother. Both are ruthless when it comes to business and they've already personally robbed many merchant ships from each of the other families. The two brothers are discussing who to attack next and are thinking the Aquila's since they could afford to lose a bit of their wealth. The parents return to the ship and they head off back home.

The Power Of The Aquila's

Two months after the meeting the Aquila's are back home on their home planet and are happy to be back in business and thriving. They may be missing diamonds due to their slaves not working hard enough in the mines but their advanced ship schematics are coming along nicely. They have also nearly completed paying off their debts to the Delphinus Family. Perhaps once their new ships are completed, they won't even need the diamond cores. The new ships are designed to be able to work without them or diamond plating. The Aquila's have had some contact with the other families but not much has happened between them lately.

Altair and Lyra practiced their fighting skills with each other during their down time in between meetings. The next meeting wouldn't occur for another ten months so they had lots of downtime on their hands. Sirius and Ursa aren't in the best health so Altair has been taking over more and more responsibility. It will be many years until his parents die and he's ready to take over their seat on the council but it's still important to get him ready just in case. He is the heir after all and Lyra would be the next in line if anything happened to him. Altair was quite proficient in the use of swords and other hand to hand combat while Lyra was more experienced with utilizing bows and arrows and other ranged weapons.

When space flight took off many years ago; the evolution of guns evolved into more steampunk versions of bows and arrows and swords gained the ability to shoot beams of fire through technology. Bows and arrows and other medieval weapons with a technological twist became on the rise and things like guns and lasers became obsolete. Cannons became the most powerful weapon to be used on ships so every ship was created with that in mind. They used diamonds and other ores in order to fly through the stars or their home planets. The ships could fly across the sea and the skies.

It was the Aquila's who invested heavily into those weapons when guns and other ones began to fall apart in the early twenty-second century. For some reason, the materials used in making guns would melt when exposed to space and many other weapons became obsolete due to these reasons. No one was able to figure out exactly why but people evolved and worked around those conditions in order to make the weapons we know and love today. Vega had been by the Aquila's every now and then. Altair appreciated their friendship but wanted nothing more than to kill him in order to weaken the other families. The Aquila's felt that if they went to war against the other Five, they wouldn't win without incurring heavy costs. And even then, that might not be enough to win. This is why they want the long-lost treasure at the center of the universe. They want to ensure their victory for generations to come and to make sure that no one could ever oppose them anymore.

The Aquila's also have secret access to a stash of nuclear missiles. If war ever comes about that will be their trump card. Of course, the downside of using them is that if the other Families caught wind they would work to come up with a counter weapon. That's why the Aquila's keep this a secret from everyone except the people within their own family. Altair recently learned the truth about the nukes and was in awe of their raw and destructive power. He realized that they had access to exactly one hundred and twenty missiles and that could be enough to devastate the entire galaxy for years to come.

The Aquila's other secret is that they did in fact murder Arcturus' wife because she was closing in on figuring out the secret to their wealth and their secret nuclear option along with their new ship schematics. They murdered her in order to preserve their secret and bribing the right people allowed the case to go away and get dropped right away. That didn't stop Arcturus from snooping around however. He may have not entered their territory in years but has still been studying them from a distance. Right now, he's a threat but one best kept under wraps. Unless he becomes a major threat, there is no need to kill him yet.

The other problem is the Serpens Family. They have been stealing shipments from each of the other Families including the Aquila's and it's become quite an inconvenience. In the long run no permanent damage will happen but it's still a problem. Diamonds have also been a part of those shipments and they can't afford to lose any more. Diamonds used to be so plentiful that everyone could use them easily but now there are significant shortages all across the galaxy.

There have also been scary rumors of deals being made between the others. Deals themselves aren't that important and can happen all the time but if they turn out to be much bigger than usual than the other Families could either be gearing up for another war or trying to weaken the Aquila's at their critical moment. The Family may be thriving in many areas but they are struggling in others and it isn't good. The Aquila's must never show weakness and must never shame themselves. They will never fall onto their sword and will go out fighting when necessary. Their warehouses are very secure and are heavily protected against any forms of attack or infiltration. Perhaps it's necessary to make another deal with the Banks. They might be able to help them even further.

The Glory Of The Delphinus Family

The Delphinus Family are as mysterious as ever. Their masks are worn at all times except for when the bathe. That's the only time that they ever show any weakness and vulnerability. The family is close with each other and they are open about their emotional problems when the situation arises. But beyond that, they are emotionless in public and no one truly knows who they are behind those masks of emotion and their literal ones.

Even when Vega goes over to Altair's place, he keeps his mask and emotions tight lipped. The family has been described as mysterious and off and that is no surprise to themselves. They are intentionally mysterious in order to cause their opponents to underestimate them. Carina always played the oddball in public so that no one would think twice about her as being intelligent but she is the true driving force behind the family ambitions and power. Cygnus was also very intelligent but was able to pretend to be the smartest in order to lull the other Families into a false sense of security that he was the most intelligent one in the family. Vega and Cassiopia are also quite smart and after the yearly meetings they discuss things themselves in order to figure out the best way to move forward.

That includes figuring out what deals to make next and with whom. The Aquila's had approached them for another deal about diamonds but the Delphinus' rejected them. The Aquila's hadn't finished paying off their first loan yet and the banks don't make deals with people with outstanding debts. The Delphinus' decided to pay off the Serpens in order to protect their shipments and even hired them as bodyguards in some cases. Better to keep them on the payroll so that they don't rob them significantly next time. The contracts the Delphinus Family make are also binding through a mix of technology and both sides must adhere to the terms or consequences will happen. This is part of the reason why the Aquila's had been eager to pay off their debts so that they could remove the noose around their necks.

If the Delphinus' ever did make deal with others about the center of the universe; they would stipulate that a percentage of the profits would go to them and that the winning family would owe them a significant favor. They haven't made this type of deal with any of the other families yet but they have toiled around with the idea of working with the Ursa Family if they could prove themselves ruthless enough to try and pull it off. The Ursa's would have to show that they were willing to cut ties with the Cepheus Family and show their independence in order to gain the trust of the Delphinus'. The other Families would have to show other forms of treachery and willingness to break the accords in order to gain their favor in such a way as well. They love being the ones in control and don't care much for even more riches. All they want is power and controlling the banks is the best way that has worked for them for centuries. Even controlling the center of the universe wouldn't satisfy them, they'd rather the family who gets there first owe them heavily instead. That's what would give them the greatest amount of satisfaction and gratification.

The Sorrows Of The Ursa Family

THE URSA FAMILY HAS been through a lot. No one else may believe it, but they have been enslaved by the Cepheus Family. The other families don't see it that way, and even the Cepheus' probably don't see it that way either. The Ursa Family owes much to them, but they want their independence as well. They have gained security and protection with the Cepheus' and gained a significant amount of money and jobs in exchange for an allocation of resources and absolute loyalty. That arrangement however doesn't work for the Ursa's anymore.

Taurus is still very muscular with all the ointments and stimulants he takes despite his age but his wife is becoming very decrepit. She is very smart and polite but people tend to leave her alone due to her advanced age and slight senility outbursts. She is slowly losing her mind but when lucid she's quick witted and very intelligent. She's resentful of their situation and wishes Taurus would do more to change their station. This has led to friction in their marriage and the two aren't speaking much anymore except for when its necessary.

Leo and Aries are both at a loss for what they can do to help their family. They have attempted entering deals with other families but no one else wants to aid them. The Ursa's are quite rich in their own right but they can't afford to leave the imposing thumb of the Cepheus' and no one wants to cross another family; at least not openly. If they are ever going to free themselves, Leo and Aries are going to have to take drastic measures. They have been scoping out the Aquila' territories and are planning a heist to steal one of their prized ships. That combined with diamond cores would allow them to cross to the center of the universe and finally free themselves from their station. And Leo and Aries want to go on a major adventure anyway.

Since they were kids, they wanted to travel the cosmos and see what the world had to offer them. They have always wanted to meet new people and see new things. Going on an adventure would also get them free of their parents fighting and maybe give them some space. Leo loves using his steel sword with his upgraded tech. His sword allows him to shoot fire from it and he can ignite the entire blade if he wants.

Aries loves her bow that allows her to shoot fire and ice from her arrows. Her archery talents are her favourite thing about herself and loves to train with them any chance she can get. Her and Leo always love to spar as well and Leo always wins when it comes to swordsmanship or hand-to-hand combat. But when it comes to archery Aries always wins and Leo is always happy for her. They love each other deeply and would do anything to protect each other and the rest of the family. Right now, though, they have to find a way to get the necessary fuel and ships in order to get to the Aquila's territory. Leo and Aries have decided to start hiding some of the diamonds they collect from the Cepheus' and use those to make diamond cores. It may not be much but it might be enough to power one of the high tech ships the Aquila's own.

The tricky part is making sure the Cepheus Family doesn't catch on. They have to make sure their quotas aren't off by even a slight amount and they need to be able to explain away any losses that occur. This will take a lot of planning and timing but it can work. Leo and Aries just have to be very careful. If they can pull this off then they will be able to make history. The trick is that they have to be able to frame another family as well. That way they won't get blamed.

They also have to make sure the Cepheus' don't find out or they will be killed and their territory will be re-absorbed into their conglomerate. There are other vassal states that want to rebel. If Leo and Aries can prove that it can be done then perhaps the others will follow their example. If they get all the vassals to rebel then they will equal to about half of the Cepheus' resources and military. It may still not be enough but it'll still deal a massive blow to that Family and their armies.

It's time to begin planning. Leo and Aries pore over documents and schematics and decide on their first steps. They need enough diamonds to make diamond cores; they also need to find a loyal crew and a ship fast and discreet enough to be able to sneak into Aquila's territory. They will also need the support of another family once this is done to provide them military might since they aren't strong enough on their own. That can come later however. First things first are getting the diamonds.

The Wrath Of The Cepheus'

Te Cepheus Family is not one to be messed with. People tend to underestimate them because they are merely a mining colony but they are actually quite dangerous to the unobservant. They have hundreds of planets acting as their vassal systems and funneling their resources to them. In exchange for that and absolute loyalty; the Cepheus Family provide their vassals with money, job security, and protection. It's perfectly legal and the vassals are always grateful for them being saved by the bigger Family. However, the Cepheus' are actually enslaving them and slowly tightening the noose until the vassals have no choice but to obey or forfeit their rights and freedoms.

The Family doesn't care what their citizens do during their daily lives; so long as their quotas are up that's all they care about. But if they start to want independence or want more freedoms; then that's when the cruelty behind closed doors begins. It might be something like cutting off their access to food and water for a day saying that there's a shortage; or imprisoning innocent people for a few days for seemingly no reason or miniscule reasons. If the rebellion continues then their rights and freedoms continue to get less and less until they are begging to be reinstated back into the Cepheus Conglomerate Family. In public they are kind people who saved many families from gong out in the cold, but behind closed doors they are cruel tyrants who will stop at nothing to protect their assets. They have a significant number of diamonds and other cores for fuel but they lack the required engine power and ships to be able to utilize them effectively.

The Ursa Family are troublesome ones however. They are always appealing to the council in order to be granted their freedom and are always making stronger and stronger cases for why they should be allowed to be free. Maybe it'll be time to start cutting wages so they will lose some of their wealth and not be able to afford the penalty fee for leaving. The penalty fee for leaving the protection of the Cepheus Family is two hundred million gold coins and a significant number of resources.

If the vassal state can afford both fees and prove that they are strong enough to be independent then they will be let go but this has never happened in the history of the Cepheus Family. They have always used threats, bribery, and manipulation in order to keep the other vassals in line and so far, none of them have ever shown genuine signs of rebellion or discontent. If they believe that they are happy then they must be happy. The Ursa's will be taken care of in time but for now they are worth the trouble and the investments.

The other vassal states are compliant and have been grateful for the benevolence and kindness of the Cepheus Family. In terms of each family's net worth; last time they checked their own net worth was eigh hundred million gold coins. The Aquila's had five hundred billion gold coins and the Delphinus Family had about twice as that with their banks and their government contracts with the other families. The Ursa's net worth was about four hundred million gold coins. The Ophiuchus Family has about the same as the Aquila's and are equal.

The Serpens net worth is unknown since they are constantly stealing and blowing all their money on fun times and new upgrades. They spend lots of times in the stripper zone and constantly upgrading their ships to be top of the line. They are very dangerous but for now they can be bought off so they are more of an inconvenience best left alone until an opportune opportunity comes up to get rid of them.

As for the family dynamic, Canes and Canis are fighting again. Canis loves her brother and never understands why they are always fighting; but Canes understands. He always hated her and never wanted her around. She's the reason that mom died since she went out to get Canis' favourite snack from the market and died right in the market. Of course, he doesn't know that her death wasn't her fault but that's a fact he doesn't need to know in order for his hatred towards his sister to fester. His mother was killed because of the result of a mugging gone wrong. To him, Canis was always the perfect one. Their uncle (Capricorn) loves both children but was always closer to Canis and Canes was always resentful of that fact. Their father also loves both but is so busy doing political stuff and running the household that he doesn't always get time to spend with them. The most time he gets is when he spars with Canes in order to train him.

Cancer believes that Canes wants to learn how to fight to be strong enough to defend the household and maybe even join the army but Canes has other ideas. He wants to use his fists in order to drain the life out of her and leave her for dead. He loves the idea of killing her and even fantasizes about doing it whenever he has restless nights. The day when she finally dies by his hand will be the greatest day of his life and he will do whatever it takes to make that dream a reality. It will be the most glorious thing in the entire world.

The State Of Affairs Of The Ophiuchus Family

In reality, there isn't much to say here. The Ophiuchus Family is doing quite well for themselves. They are still in competition with the Aquila's to become the next top family but other than that they are doing great overall. Their ship and ore research are both going well and are trying to find an alternative to the diamond cores for the high tech ships the Aquila's have. The Aquila's are geniuses though and nobody has been able to replicate their technology without their help. The only options are either one of the Aquila's would share their tech with other families or one of them offered to help build one for them. Neither of those are likely to happen however. Also, in case anyone was wondering; the Families each have many members of their unit.

If all four of the Aquila's were to die for example; there would be hundreds of family members next in line to take the power for themselves and start attending the meetings. The Aquila's are vast and have hundreds of planets and family members under their control. The Ophiuchus Family also has many family members under their control as well. The only ones who don't would be the Ursa Family. Once those four are dead there is no one else except crew members to take over as the heads of the Family.

The Ophiuchus' have tried to assassinate members of the Aquila and the Serpens Family many times in secret but all attempts have failed. Both Families are too powerful for that kind of thing to work. The Ophiuchus Family are planning on making deals with other families in order to try and get rid of the Aquila's and Serpens but those deals aren't likely to go through. Most of the other Families are too afraid or unwilling to go to war without some sort of incentive other than money. If either side lost the war, then the winning side would enforce heavy penalties for the rebellion and the losing Families would be severely punished. Despite the Ophiuchus' making the deals, they genuinely don't expect to go to war until someone proves themselves willing to openly break the accords. The Serpens would be willing to break the accords if they didn't have to worry about punishment or retaliation. The other Families are very scary for different reasons and no one wants to mess with any of them. There are other smaller families under the control of the main Families but they are of no consequence.

The Mercenary Life Of The Serpens Family

THE SERPENS FAMILY HAVE a big goal in mind for the year. They want to steal as much shit as possible and make as much money as they can. Okay, that's their goal every year but they really want to increase their returns this year. By the next meeting they want to steal more high-end cargo and maybe even destroy a ship or two. Of course, that's against the accords but the Serpens are starting to become restless.

They also want to start killing people again. They used to be full blown marauders and would murder anyone that came across their way back in the twenty-first century but have since been chained and locked away metaphorically by the accords and other Families. Perhaps the Ursa Family should be the ones to fall first. They are the weakest and least defensible currently. But they are under the protection of the Cepheus Family so that might be a problem. Ophidian and Hex's marriage has been great and their sons Asmodeus and Basilisk have been getting along swimmingly. Asmodeus has been getting more and more involved with the family business and Basilisk has been helping him.

The two brothers are planning on becoming pirates together and committing their own heists once they get a crew separate from their parents. They want to rob everyone blind and prove to their parents that they are worthy successors to their family projects. Once they prove themselves, they will be given the secrets of the Family and so much more. Asmodeus has been planning a heist on the Aquila's Family as well after many failed heists to figure out what their secrets are.

The Bad Luck Of The Aquila's

The Aquila's have had a lot of bad luck lately. They don't know how to explain it but it hasn't been good. Another meeting has come and gone and the Aquila's are losing votes. Many new accords they wanted to pass got shot down by the other families and they are losing influence. The allegations against them about using slaves have also become more and more prominent. There have also been rumors of collusion between the other families and the Aquila's are afraid that their secrets are going to be found out and that another war is bound to break out.

Heists have also been attempted and their ship technology has nearly been stolen many times. Luckily all attempts have failed but the Aquila's have been beefing up security in light of this. They don't want anyone stealing their technology. They have also made arrangements to finally pay off their debts with the Delphinus Family. Hopefully once that debt is finally paid off, they can start making deals with them again.

By next year the debt should finally be paid off. The Delphinus have been rejecting deals left and right since no other family has what they want but the Aquila's are sure that they would want some of their shit technology in exchange for some diamond cores. The deal should be going down next year and both families should come out of happy. The Delphinus Family clearly don't care about anyone except themselves and are so mysterious and off that they should be easy to swindle.

The Good Luck Of The Delphinus Family

The Delphinus Family really has been blessed as of late. Some of their extended relatives are having a baby and the core four are so happy to hear about that. The entire extended family wear masks when they get together at family reunions and only a select few actually know what each family member looks like. The Family also got new and updated white masks in order to fit their mystique and hidden power. They have also made a deal with the Ursa Family. If the Ursa Family is able to follow through with their end of the bargain, then they will help free them from the Cepheus Family. They will also help them stay free and the favor they do in exchange will count for the money provided to set them free so the Ursa Family won't have to pay any fees or interest back.

The Delphinus' are very excited about this deal and are hoping that this will shake things up. The family reunion also went well and the extended family learned that Vega and Cassiopia have finished business school a long time ago and are working extensively with the family business. They are both set to take control of the family once their parents retire or die and the entire family is excited for the new blood when it comes. The entire Family is mysterious but they are all very close even though they only get to meet up every ten years or so. They are all extremely proud of each other and are happy to be working together. The Family business is extremely vast.

There are banks all over the galaxy and even banks in the other Family's territories. The Delphinus' may not be the ones in full control but they have power everywhere and have an even greater reach than the Aquila's in some cases. Cygnus and Carina aren't ready to retire and won't be ready for quite a while. They are happy though to have their children joining the Family business and they can be taught everything about banking and how to make the best deals possible.

Vega and Cassiopia have already made small deals with other families and have been successful in helping out their people. They are aware that the Aquila's use slave labor and that the Cepheus Family uses slave tactics in order to keep their vassals in line. They don't know for sure but based on the data they've discovered they are well aware that they are acting like they are above the law.

This type of behaviour is unacceptable and the Delphinus Family are planning on taking swift action once they get the evidence that they need to destroy both families. Once those families are defeated, the Serpens will be the next family to go since they are slowly beginning to get out of control. Eventually they will slip up and get themselves in trouble with the accords. Once that happens the Delphinus' will be there to stop them and make sure that they face justice. It would be easiest if the Delphinus Family ran everything but they prefer to be in second place and have full control through favors by the ones in power. Hopefully the next few deals will go out without a hitch. These deals could shape the balance of the universe and may even speed up the secret race to the center of the universe.

The Troubles Of The Ursa Family

The Ursa's are in big trouble. They have finally found a crew loyal to only them and have been in contact with the other vassal states. If the Ursa's do something then the other vassals have agreed to aid them in any way they can. Leo and Aries found a ship that was discreet and neutral enough to blend in with the Aquila's poorer ships and it's even painted in their territories' colors so no one will think twice when they see them. The Aquila's territory is by far the most secure in the entire galaxy and the most dangerous overall. It'll take a lot of skill and a lot of luck to break in and steal one of their new ships.

That's the plan, Leo, Aries and their crew are going to sneak into their territory and use their diamond cores in order to steal and power one of the high-tech ships that Aquila keeps hidden and are exclusive for the rich and powerful. Sneaking in won't be difficult, the checkpoints are usually easy to pass. It's getting back out that's going to be tough. The Aquila's are already on high alert because people have already tried to steal from them and they are going to be on the lookout for people acting suspiciously in their territory.

Their crew is filled with three other people that they can trust completely and are like family to them. Despite the risks, Leo's very excited to be going on this adventure and Aries is looking forward to be going with him on this trek as well. The other three are completely trustworthy and loyal to Leo and Aries exclusively. They served with their dad many years ago and are willing to serve with Leo as well. Leo's been practicing with his sword in case he comes face to face with any Aquila guards and Aries has been training with her bow as well. Leo also upgraded his sword so that it can switch back and forth between fire and ice at will. He's very pleased with the upgrade. As the ship gets closer to the first checkpoint of Aquila territory the entire ship is filled with tension. Leo's guiding the helmsman and other pilot but he's sweating. His throat is beginning to close up and his insides feel like they are on fire until Aries grabs his arm.

He jerks away and looks at her. She says softly "don't worry, this is going to be fine." Leo nodded and instantly felt better. He guided the pilot into the checkpoint and despite the tension they eased into it easily. They had all the fake permits they needed and the guard let them through without a second glance. That was the easy part. Now they just had to make sure their clearance would hold up as they get to the more secure checkpoints. Leo guided them through the other checkpoints with ease as having Aries with him restored his confidence.

They continued and finally they were in Aquila territory. A vast array of planets laid out before them and Leo was in awe of just how vast their world really was. He wanted to explore every inch of the cosmos and wanted to see it all with Aries. Aries held onto his arm and gave him a happy smile as they were both seeing such wonder. They had never been to Aquila territory before so this was very surreal for them. They continued until finally hitting the last checkpoint which was just before the planet that held all the ships. They managed to clear it albeit just barely with their credentials and continued on. They were planning on abandoning this ship once they got what they needed so they didn't care too much about what happened to it in the long run. They landed on the planet and dyed their hair blue so as to blend in better with the citizens. Their red hair would stick out too much on this planet of blue haired people.

They left the ship and headed for the ship depot. There were guards but Leo was able to knock them out with ease with the hilt of his sword. His crew members ran into the depot while Leo and Aries managed to hide the bodies in a nearby bush. Ursa territory was very beautiful with caves everywhere for mining. Mining was their whole world so they were happy with it initially. But being here in Aquila territory where everything is like a forest it's overwhelming to say the least. Leo headed into the depot with Aries and they saw thousands of high-tech ships on display.

The Aquila's had tons of them. Many of them looked new and some looked like prototypes. Leo went down the line until he found the perfect ship. It's high-tech and not necessarily new but it hasn't fazed out of the diamond cores yet and it runs quite well and is stable according to the charts. Leo considered stealing a prototype ship but he wasn't sure if he would be able to fly it honestly. He needed to be able to fly something effectively so he picked the one that stood out to him the most. It was a beautiful ship and quite gigantic. It was a steampunk ship made out of steel alloy and had a giant cathedral on the top of it. The diamond cores would be perfect for it. Leo got into the ship and began firing it up. He knew that they would have to get out quickly. While he and the rest of the crew was working Aries thought she saw something odd a few aisles down and decided to go check it out.

While she was doing that Leo continued to fire up the ship with his crew and opened the hanger doors so they could fly out. Luckily no one seemed to be in sight despite how big the place was so Leo kept on working. Suddenly, there was a scream in the air. The scream pierced through the air like a knife and Leo felt like he had been punched in the gut. Leo ran towards the sound and saw Aries crouched on the ground with an arrow straight through her heart. Leo ran towards her and drew his sword as he faced off against her attackers. There were five of them and they all had black hair. The Serpens Family! They were here too? Why? Leo didn't have time to ponder these questions. Aries fell to the ground and hit her head hard on the ground.

Leo ignited his sword with fire and ice and faced off against the other Family. It was five against one but Leo managed to hold his own as he locked swords with them. His arms got all cut up and his legs began to bleed heavily. Leo fell to one knee and tried to shield Aries from the blows. He ignited his sword with just fire and thrust it into the ground. Fire erupted all over the place and the five attackers got incinerated alive in the flames. Leo smiled in satisfaction before he saw Aries stir. He doused the flames with his sword and then grabbed Aries and ran back up to the ship. By now, alarms were blaring and Leo was hurrying up with his preparations. He put Aries in the medical bay and the crew finished with what they needed to do. The ship eventually whirred to life and the diamond cores synced perfectly. Leo saw guards coming from all directions so he loaded up the cannons and fired. Many dead Aquila agents laid dead at his feet and he smiled in satisfaction at the blood and gore that spurted all around him. One guy lost his testicles in the fight and they were flopping around in the wind. Another got his head caved in by the cannons and another lost half of his body on impact. Many of them died instantly; at least the lucky ones did. Others had life threatening injuries and were maimed permanently but were still alive unfortunately.

Leo chose not to put them out of their misery. They got what they deserved and were no longer a threat. He and the crew piloted the ship and suddenly they were off and back into space. With all of the chaos no one knew for sure what had happened and they snuck through the remaining checkpoints. As they were flying away, they heard an ear shattering BOOM! The entire planet had blown up and there was nothing but a crater where the planet once stood. Leo fell to the ground in shock as the rest of the crew continued to pilot the ship out of there. Leo slowly recovered from his shock and said softly to himself "how the hell did that happen? Was that the Serpens agents?" He didn't know for sure. He ran to the medical bay and saw Aries was still in the pod. He held her hand as he cried. Leo apologized profusely for everything that had happened and he never got to tell her how much he appreciated her friendship and support during trying times.

He looked at the doctor and the doctor explained that she had sustained life threatening injuries and brain damage. She would take a long time to recover and for now she would have to recover in a coma until she was ready to wake up. If she ever woke up, that is. Leo was devastated by the news but knew that he had to be strong for her. He realized that he had completed his end of the deal with the Delphinus Family. Hopefully they would pay up now and they could move on with their lives. One of his crew members came up to Leo and asked "should we continue? We completed the mission but it doesn't feel worth it. What do you think captain?" Leo thought long and hard and decided that they had to move on.

"We move forward with the plan. Aries would want us to finish the mission and get to the center of the universe," he said sharply. The crew member nodded his head and walked off. Leo continued to hold Aries hand for many hours and cry while his crew flew the ship without his guidance. "I hope you'll be okay Aries. I'd never forgive myself if you didn't make it," he said softly. Leo didn't care about vengeance but he did feel a burning hatred for the Serpens Family. If they hadn't been there at the same time then perhaps Aries would still be okay. He loved her as his sister and best friend and would do whatever it took to bring her back and avenge her. First though, he had to free his family from the bonds of the Cepheus Family. He sent a message to the Delphinus' and they sent a reply. They told him they'd have an agent ready near their home so Leo headed back to his home planet. It was time for this to finally end

The Rage Of The Cepheus Family

ALL CANCER WANTS IS to figure out what happened to his wife; but now he also has to figure out what happened to his children. To start, Canis was found dead in the living room. Her throat had been ripped out by an animal and blood was everywhere. Her eyes had been gouged out and there was barely enough of her face to be recognizable. Her purple dress and hair were the main way people were able to figure out who she was. Also, DNA evidence proved it was her. The blood and gore were insurmountable and Canes also went missing soon after the act. Cancer was heartbroken and ended up in the hospital due to stress and a broken heart. He couldn't believe that his only son would do that to his beloved sister. He knew that his son had problems but he never thought Canes would be capable of doing something like this.

Cancer later died on the operating table and was buried next to Canis. His brother Capricorn took control of the Family business and took over his vassals. Canes went missing soon after the murder and no one ever saw him again. Capricorn later legitimized some of his bastard children in order to take the place of his dead family. Capricorn showed intense cruelty towards his vassals and this only created more rebellion and discord between them. He started cutting food and water privileges and started slashing bonuses so the vassals couldn't support themselves.

This led the council to investigating and allegations of corruption and slavery methods were thrown against him. Nothing was proven in court but it was enough to draw the attention of people who Capricorn didn't want sniffing around his business. He also got evidence from an anonymous source that the Aquila's were behind the murder of Arcturus Ophiuchus' wife and proof that they were using slave labor. Capricorn didn't know who sent him the information but decided to send it to the Ophiuchus' since they would be very interested in hearing about these tidbits.

What nobody knew was that Capricorn knew exactly what was going on with Canes. He never ran away; he stayed home the entire time. Capricorn went into the hidden basement of his home and went into the room. Inside the room with the stench of death laid Canes strapped to a wooden plank and put in the pose of a crucifixion. Canes struggled for breath and yelled out "please uncle, I'm so sorry. Please don't take any more parts of me. I'm so sorry!" Capricorn smirked as he withdrew his carving knife. Canes had gashes all across his body and was naked from the head down.

Canes had been there for weeks and was clearly malnourished. His genitalia were missing as well. Capricorn drew a thin line down his face and near his neck. Canes winced in pain but continued to make eye contact with his uncle. Capricorn whispered "I'm going to make you suffer like she did." Canes' worried expression turned from fear to anger. "You can't do this! I'm the heir to this family! She got what she deserved. She was a lying bitch who needed to suffer. HAHAHAHAHAHAHA," Canes cackled as he grew more and more insane each day. Capricorn sliced another thin slice across his face and then started on his eyes. Capricorn started by pushing slowly and then pushing as hard as he could until he heard Canes' eyes snap and break.

He had gouged out his nephew's eyes and Canes screamed in pain. Next Capricorn cut out his tongue, then ripped his fingernails out. Capricorn then cut off all of his fingers and toes until Canes began to beg for death. Even though he was begging, Capricorn wasn't in any rush. He had healed up Canes' injuries so he wouldn't bleed out. After all that, Capricorn strangled Canes until he had nothing left. Finally, vengeance was his.

Justice For The Ophiuchus

ARCTURUS HAD RECEIVED WORD from one of his contacts about evidence linking the Aquila's to the murder of his wife. The moment he did and verified it he called an emergency meeting. The council all met and the Cepheus Family looked strong despite so many losses. Everyone had heard about what happened to the children and the dad and Capricorn stood stoically in place with his eldest bastard by his side as representatives for the family. Nobody said anything about the change. The council never made mention of these types of things. They were all aware of it but they never spoke out about it out of fear of being disrespectful.

The Aquila's were fuming since one of their best ships had been stolen and their fleet had been completely destroyed. They had other fleets but none were as good as the ones that were lost. The Ophiuchus' had been waiting a very long time for this day. Arcturus had wanted the Aquila's to be held accountable for what they've done and if finally appears that they will finally get what they deserve. Arcturus wanted justice for his wife and it sounds like he would finally have that.

Suddenly, the Aquila's had stood up in fury. Sirius and Ursa raced up to the altar and screamed out into the microphone "we will not stand for this insolence. If you want a war then war is what you will get my old friends." Before anyone could comprehend what, he was saying, there was a large rumbling coming from the outside. Thousand of blue colored ships were coming out and encircling the venue. These were the Aquila's second-best fleet and they were surrounding the entire meeting hall. Taurus and Gemini also stood up and said defiantly "we won't let ourselves be bullied anymore by people like you Cepheus. It's time for us to stand up for our rights." Hundreds of ships in various different colors showed up outside the venue as well and then even more ships. As the council began to delve into chaos everyone realized exactly what was happening. All out war was finally happening once again. And no one was safe this time.

The Humor Of The Serpens Family

Ohidian and Hex started laughing their asses off as they drew their swords. They advanced towards the other council members and slashed at Capricorn and his bastard. Capricorn went down in a whirlpool of blood as his head went flying off his head and landed on his bastard's face. The bastard screamed as Hex took his testicles and stabbed him right in the gut which killed him slowly. The bastard fell to the ground screaming in agony as he slowly bled out. The rest of the council ran away in terror and began to run back to their own ships. The rest of the Families managed to make it back safely to the ships and the waiting rooms were evacuated. The only two casualties were the representatives of the Cepheus Family. The tension in the air was palpable as everyone rushed to get away. The ships fled and everyone began to prepare for war in their own way. No one pursued each other. Yet.

The Serpens were the ones behind blowing up the Aquila's main fleet and they had discovered the evidence linking them to Arcturus wife's murder and the slavery links. They had sent that to the Cepheus Family as an anonymous source since they knew it would get sent to the respective parties right away. They also found the hidden location of the Aquila's nuclear missiles. They weren't able to steal all of them but they were able to make off with about 76. That would be just enough to do whatever they wanted for a long time. The Serpens had no problem using their new found tech to be able to intimidate the other families into backing down and giving them what they wanted. With these missiles they could control the entire universe! It's time for an all-out war to begin as each family races to be the first to both win and gain the ultimate prize: the center of the universe!

The Aquila's vs. The Ophiuchus Family

Sirius realized that many of his nuclear missiles had been stolen and was outraged. The allegations against him and his family were also outrageous and the other families' decisions to fight against them made him want to murder them all. Ursa managed to calm him down with her beauty and grace. Feeling calmer, Sirius had called Arcturus and asked to talk in a neutral location. They decided to talk on a neutral planet that was close to both of their territories. Both Families went in full force to the meeting and they met up on a desert planet with not a lot of vegetation on it. Both Families left their ships with their respective armies.

Both decided to leave their ships on the ground and fight hand to hand. Arcturus led his children into the battle and Sirius and Ursa countered. Both sides which equaled a few thousand soldiers each clashed as both ran towards each other and it was a bloodbath. Soldiers fought against soldiers while Sirius and Arcturus fought with swords. Their swords locked as they thought long and hard about their initial friendship and rivalry. They both hated each other and would take great pleasure in murdering the other. Ursa fought against Arcturus' three children with her two children. They used a mixture of bows and arrows and swords. Both Families were out for blood and wanted to end this charade of a council and friendship. Sirius and Arcturus clashed as they went back and forth. They were like two tornadoes who just kept slashing and slashing against each other.

Both left little knicks and cuts on the other but neither stopped from trying to kill the other. Finally, they each managed to get a decent blow on each other. Arcturus managed to cut off Sirius' right arm and Sirius managed to impale Arcturus's left eye.

Both screamed in pain and fell to the ground as they addressed their wounds. Both tried to stop the bleeding as much as possible on the battlefield while the others kept on fighting around them. It was like both went deaf as all sound just went away and it was just the two of them patching themselves up. They both looked at each other after they had done what they could and they both felt a newfound respect for the other. Both had managed to land a critical injury on the other and both were still alive to tell the tale.

Meanwhile Ursa and her children were fighting for their lives against the others. Ursa thought about how she loathed sharing the same name as the Ursa Family. There wasn't anything she could do about it though at this moment. Scorpius ever the mischief maker was lobbing bombs at Ursa while Libra was using her bow and arrows and Virgo was dueling wielding swords and sword fighting with Altair and Lyra Aquila. Altair was a skilled swordsman and was holding his own against Virgo but couldn't break through her impregnable defense. Finally, Lyra ended up getting impaled with an arrow and fell to the ground dead. Altair screamed in pain and fought back twice-fold. Now Virgo struggled to hold him back as Ursa shrieked and started using her mace and running towards Libra and Scorpius.

Altair managed to get the upper hand and decapitated Virgo while stealing her sword. He held her head aloft and screamed that all would die before him. He joined his mother against Scorpius and Libra but both were outmatched. The bombs flew harmlessly around but none made any contact with the enemy. Finally, Scorpius managed to lob one at Ursa and it blew her legs off. She fell down and began to crawl towards Scorpius in fury. Libra used her arrows and managed to get Altair in the foot before he broke her bow and snapped her neck. He twisted her neck around like a soap dispenser when opening and popped her head off. Blood and gore blew everywhere and covered Scorpius. Scorpius withdrew his sword and met Altair in sword on sword. Their swords clashed as Ursa slowly managed to crawl up behind Scorpius. She withdrew her mace and lobbed it in his back.

Scorpius' mouth instantly filled with blood and his sword dropped harmlessly to the ground. He managed to take a bomb and light it before anyone could do anything. Altair stomped on his head until there was nothing left and then the bomb went off. Altair and Ursa both got caught in the blast and died instantly. Hundreds of soldiers lay dead on the battlefield on both sides and neither side was close to actually winning the day.

Arcturus and Sirius were both aware of the losses they sustained and decided that this had to end. Their family's sacrifices couldn't be for nothing. Arcturus and Sirius dropped their swords and bowed to each other. They decided to settle this like in the old ways. They both raised their heads and raced towards each other. They punched, kicked and grappled as much as they could. Swords clearly wasn't going to solve this so they decided that fists would be the best bet.

Sirius got Arcturus in a headlock but Arcturus managed to reach his hands above Sirius' eyes and gouged out his eyes. Sirius fell back in pain and Arcturus took the opportunity to stomp on his arm and legs. He stomped hard and Sirius' limbs were all broken. He cried out in pain as Arcturus kept on stomping. He kept on stomping until there was nothing left of Sirius and he was barely alive. "That was for my family," Arcturus whispered. He then spit on Sirius' body and rejoined the fray. He fought alongside his soldiers until finally they managed to push back the Aquila's forces. The Ophiuchus had managed to win the battle and they took the rest of their battle into the air with Arcturus leading the charge. He was going to make sure that the Aquila's were finished for good today. Arcturus loaded up the cannons and he fired on the fleeing Aquila's. the Aquila's tried to fight back with their advanced ships but because they were in a tailspin over losing their leaders and so many soldiers they couldn't react fast enough.

Once the fleeing ships were either destroyed or got away Arcturus cheered in happiness. He may have lost an eye and his entire family but he had finally avenged his wife and that of his family who just died today. He took his ships and fired upon the Aquila' planets. He wanted to erase any trace of life from them. He also used gigantic flamethrowers on the lands to destroy anything the cannons missed and didn't stop until each of the planets was an entire pile of rubble. Arcturus didn't care about the innocent people still on the planets, he wanted all traces of the Aquila's to be wiped clean from the universe. He then went to their warehouses and stole their ships before blowing them up to hell.

The Ophiuchus has finally managed to win the day and Arcturus decided to recognize some his bastards and rebuild his family unit. He may even remarry now that his fighting days were going to be behind him soon. He wanted to retire into the sunset and forget about the council for awhile. He knew he might have to fight other Families soon but for now he just wanted to enjoy his victory and the spoils. What he didn't know was that the Aquila fortune was hidden in a secret neutral planet that Arcturus didn't know anything about. Also, many Aquila family members still lived there in safety in case anything like this ever happened. They would recover their losses and then rise up again in the ashes of what once was. They would be back again. And this wasn't the only battle to ever happen during the war. There are other battles between other families that must be documented.

The Delphinus Family vs. the Serpens Family

The Delphinus Family made deals with the Ursa Family in order to help them break free of their bonds from Cepheus. In exchange Delphinus got access to one of the Aquila's prized ships and was able to study and replicate its technology. They also gave a significant amount of diamond cores, other resources, and wealth in exchange for the ship. And as a bonus the Delphinus' even gave the ship to the Ursa Family once they were done studying it. The Ursa's were eternally grateful. Meanwhile, secretly at the same time The Delphinus' had tasked the Serpens Family with blowing up the Aquila harbor and ship depot.

Along with stealing evidence implicating them in slavery and murdering political opponents, they also turned them onto the secret stash of nuclear missiles. The Delphinus had no need for such rudimentary weapons. They would be the strongest family in time and as many families rise and fall the Delphinus would stand above them all and gloat. They would rise from the ashes of another war and create a new and better world. The Serpens fleet began flying towards the Delphinus home planet. They were ready for this however. Even with the nuclear missiles there's nothing that can be done.

The Serpens fleet flies up and begins firing nuclear missiles at the Delphinus Family home planet. The Family hunkered together in their bunker and watched the missiles bounce harmlessly off their forcefield that they had created with diamond cores. Yes, their forcefield made of diamonds combined with other advanced technology is strong enough to deflect a nuclear missile. The Serpens Family isn't known for being quitters however and they keep on firing their cannons and nuclear missiles until they deplete everything. The planet was outfitted with a powerful security system that would activate once firing stops for an extended period of time. The Delphinus activated their machine and suddenly; cannons appeared out of nowhere on the planet and started firing on the oncoming ships.

The Serpens began to flee since they realized that they couldn't win this battle on the home planet. They tried to destroy other planets but they all had the same security system. They were officially at a stalemate and the Serpens ran away with their tails between their legs. The Delphinus stoically celebrated their victory by drinking glasses full of brandy and cheered to their win. The Delphinus' decided to take off their masks for the first time in years and reveal their faces to each other. Each of the Family was happy to see each other beyond their green hair and eyes. They enjoyed their company with each other and decided to enjoy their night to the fullest.

The Ursa Family vs. the Cepheus Family

THESE TWO FAMILIES HAVE been feuding for years in secret. The Cepheus Family have rebuilt themselves with extended family members and the Ursa Family has been gathering all of their soldiers and the other vassals. They also have access to tech from the Delphinus Family which may give them the edge they so desperately need. The two Families decide to meet in a neutral zone and decide to finish this war in a gigantic space battle.

Both sides arm themselves and get ready for a fight. Cepheus has thousands of warships and soldiers at their command and the Ursa Family have access to each of the vassals that were willing to fight back against their oppressors. Each of the ships is equipped with armor diamond plating to protect against cannon fire. The Cepheus have not had time to equip their armor plating to that extent so perhaps that will be the deciding factor of this battle.

The Cepheus Family are outraged by this act of rebellion and are planning on putting everyone down for their insolence. The Ursa Family on the other hand are terrified but determined to win this fight. Leo's in the lead ship with his crew and they are ready for a fight. Each side fires at the same time and many ships get destroyed in the blasts. Leo steers his ship so that he can dodge the cannon fire but it's very difficult. The area is very treacherous and cannon fire is everywhere. Leo tries to head for the Cepheus main ship but its not easy. He figures that if he can get there and just start firing, they can end this battle in one fell swoop. However, it's not going to be that easy. There are ships everywhere protecting the Cepheus Family and they are all eager to put down this rebellion since they will get paid handsomely for it. The battle goes on as both ships try to avoid each other's aerial strikes for many hours. Finally, after many days of fighting Leo finally gets his chance.

He realizes that firing isn't going to accomplish anything since there are too many in his way. Instead, he decided to ram everything in his path. He charged up his ship and rammed forward. He hit everything that he could and that included the Cepheus' Family main ship. He rammed right into and saw the shocked and scared faces of the remaining Cepheus Family. Leo sneered at them as he fired right in their stupid faces and watched their ships blow up. After that the battle became easier and the Ursa Family won the day! They chase the remaining ships away and then head back home. The Cepheus will regroup and become strong again in time but this will be a major loss to their morale. And more importantly; Leo showed that he and his allies are free at last! Now's the time to get ready to head to the center of the universe. There are a lot of preparations to do first.

Journey To The Center Of The Universe

Leo finishes his travel arrangements many months after that fateful battle and begins his trek to the center. It will take him less than a year to get there. He stops by Aries' medical tent and kisses her forehead goodbye. He will come back for her. In the onslaught both of his parents got killed and their ships blew up. He grieved for them and then took his place as head of the Ursa Family. The Delphinus decided to back his bid for the center of the universe in exchange for a favor. Leo agreed and he began his trek. He knew the other families would be gathering the same materials and were making their own bids for the journey so he had to be quick. Leo gathered his crew and materials and began the trek. The way to the center was treacherous. There were blackholes and asteroid belts everywhere.

Leo spent many weeks in space and saw other families trying to beat him to it. He blew them up and moved on. He also blew up any asteroids he saw and avoided and black holes he saw. Leo had nearly found himself in the middle of a blackhole many times but was always able to swerve out of the way just in time. He did admit though, the vastness of space was beautiful and even the blackholes were beautiful in their own unique way. They were dangerous as hell but something about them evoked genuine beauty when gazing upon them. They were something to be feared but also admired and respected in its own way.

After many months it became clear to Leo that he was the only one trying to take a genuine effort in trying to get to the center. He hadn't seen any other family soldiers in months and the most dangerous things he had seen were the asteroids and the blackholes. The trek was beautiful and boring in many ways. Leo wanted to explore the vastness of space but wondered if this was all there is. He also wished he could have seen it with Aries. She still hadn't woken up and her prognosis was really bad. It was feared that she would never wake up.

He really missed her and just wanted her back more than anything. Perhaps the treasure can help her wake up once more. Finally, after nearly a year of traveling Leo finally made it to the center of the universe. He had seen many planets on his way here but nothing could compare to what he saw next. In the middle of space, was a gigantic machine that looks like it had been powered down for millennia. It looked like a tall metal shrine that had two metallic arms that spun on either side. Leo's ship looked like a tiny insect compared to whatever this thing was. Leo landed the ship on the edge of it and docked it. It looked like there was a docking area so that's where he landed. Leo got out and immediately the dust hit his nostrils and invaded his airways. He coughed up a bunch of dust but continued on. He walked through the long-abandoned hallways and saw tons of stairs leading up to the very top. There had to be thousands of stairs. Leo began the trek and after many hours he finally made it to the top. A sense of wonder and euphoria overcame him as he finally made it.

Leo made it to the top and saw a control panel. Before he went there though he saw docks and docks filled with ships. These were the ships of legends and they had eclipsed their current technology by thousands of years. There was also a huge pile of gold coins and diamonds. There were multiple piles of coins and Leo was even richer than before. He went up to the control panel and pushed the big red button. Suddenly, the machine whirred to life and the two metallic arms began spinning. Leo saw a vision of his future. He saw him leading the world into a new golden age and he saw Aries dying from her wounds. He also saw that something dark and sinister was waiting to be called into this world. Something hungry and it would come as soon as Leo gave his consent.

Immediately Leo broke the connection and sweat went down his entire body. He hyperventilated and didn't know what he was supposed to do. There was no way in hell he was going to let that thing get out but he also didn't trust the future of Aries dying. Leo didn't know what he was supposed to do with this information. He decided to get his crew and think about how to proceed. He would tell them everything later once things settled down

Peace Within The Families?

Many years ago, Leo the Just managed to take the center of the universe for himself and created a utopia for him and his compatriots. He forced a peace between each of the remaining families and they all stayed loyal to him. He granted each of them ships, technology and wealth from the center and instead of a council the world became a dictatorship where only Leo was in control. Leo reigned for meany years while his loyal subjects stayed by his side.

He even found love and had children of his own. Unfortunately, the visions came true. He did create a golden age of space travel and peace but Aries did in fact die from her wounds. Her death turned Leo the Just into Leo the Bloody as he enacted bloody justice across those who had wronged him. Many of the original six Families had disappeared and were merged into one entity where Leo had full control and happiness. Still though, he never forgot about the terrifying entity that wanted to devour the entire universe. For a long time, he chose not to think about it, but it would still invade his dreams. He realized that it was aliens that wanted to eat and destroy the entire universe and the more he thought about it, the more he thought that the universe could use a clean slate.

For hundreds of years, he left well enough alone and created an empire based on power and cruelty towards his enemies and peace and love towards those loyal to him. He also provided the banking clan with their favor which was that he would give them a percentage of what he found and provide the information about the aliens which he did. The banking clan was surprised to hear about what happened to say the least but were grateful for the information.

Just before Leo finally passed from the world, he sent his family to the banking clan and they agreed to offer protection towards them. Leo finally pushed the last button and with his dying breath he opened the portal and allowed the aliens to finally come through. They were grateful at his helpfulness and they chose to leave his body where it was on the machine as a sign of respect. Leo died in peace of old age and finally felt at ease with himself that the universe was going to be destroyed and perhaps something new would be created. He would avenge his parents and sister. His sons and wife would stay safe with the banking clan.

Once Leo finally died what was left of the six Families broke apart. A massive civil war erupted in response to the alien attacks and they all wanted a piece of the power. The aliens had been searching for a new home for hundreds of years after eating their last universe. With Leo's intervention they finally were able to alleviate their starvation and could be at peace.

The wars continued for many years as the aliens ravaged the universe. There wasn't much that could stop them in the end. This is a tale of greed and power. Leo started out with good intentions in the beginning, but then it turned to vengeance and then finally genocide. Leo no longer cared about humanity and believed that they had outlived their usefulness. As long as humanity lives, war shall follow. Perhaps the next species shall thrive under better circumstances.

What no one realized was that there was someone who managed to escape the aliens. Someone from the banking clan managed to take a ship and hightail it out of that universe and found their way into another one using stolen technology. The banking clan had disappeared and there was no trace of them by the time the aliens had reached that far into the universe and devoured everything else. After the lone man made his escape, the aliens suddenly convulsed and started dying one by one. The monstrous creatures that had just devoured another universe were felled by a young wizard named Simon who was using the power of the stone given to him by James in his universe to put this universe back to right. Simon used the stone to destroy the aliens and then restarted the universe by creating another big bang and created new life that would eventually grow into humanity once again. Would they do better the second time around? Or would they fall into war once again? What Simon realized was that the aliens were created by someone, someone dangerous who wanted to undo all the good that Simon had tried to do in the world. He needed to return to his universe in order to figure out what was going on.

The lone survivor had heard about the mysterious chronicler flying around the universe in search of stories and finally found Edward and told the tale of the six Families. Edward was shocked but not too surprised. He understood that the cycle of war may never end but he hoped that things would get better now that things had been reset. As Simon attempted to leave, he could feel wrinkles forming on his body and he developed a bad cough. He looked at his wrinkled hands and saw traces of blood on them. Overuse of the stone must be causing this. But he couldn't just stop now, he had to save everyone and redeem himself. Simon used some of his magic to temporarily erase the wrinkles and stop the coughing in order to hide it from his friends. They didn't have to know what was going on. If Simon was going to die then he was going to die on his own terms and only after helping his friends get the peace that they deserve. Simon was afraid though that the threat would be even bigger than he intended. This felt like a genocide of epic proportions and he could feel the echoes of Jeb and Nathaniel in the distance even though they are both dead. Could they be behind this? Read on to find out!

The End!

Preview:

Jeb and Nathaniel seemingly have united and Simon needs help in order to counter them. Can he utilize his friends and allies in order to stop this threat once again? I suppose it's time to bring my ultimate story to light. Everything gets revealed and you shall experience it firsthand!

Schreiber Chronicles Part 4: The Shadows of Redemption.

After hearing the accounts of the lone survivor from the distant future Edward paced around his office as he began to think about what to do next. His next appointment would be an interesting one to be sure. This would be the story to end all stories. That's for sure.

The Shadows of Redemption

Ethan Spadoni

*****

Preface and Acknowledgements:

Hey! It's the author here. I'm nearly done with my series if you're reading this. This has been an amazing journey to go on and I am so grateful to each and every one of you that decided to join me on my quest. When I was a kid, I always dreamed of being an author but never thought I was capable of it. I'd like to thank my mentor Susan and my mom, dad, brother, and friends who never turned their back on me during this whole process. I'd also like to thank my professors and my librarian Trudy who helped me with all of my schooling research and helped me get through my masters when I was too busy to focus on writing. I'd also like to thank my Aunty Cora for believing in me and my Aunties Judy, Janet, and Lynda for supporting me as well. I'd also like to thank my cousins Kyle, Jenna, Kailey, Jillian, and Jeffrey for being there as well for me. But most importantly I'd like to thank everyone that took the time to read this series from start to finish and who chose to believe in this tale despite many of the difficult scenes to get through. I have never tried to end my life but I can understand how difficult life can be and felt that it was important to put many of those types of feelings to paper to demonstrate how important life can be. As is the same with my other books, I may be inspired by many things I have seen and watched but any similarities to other projects are completely unintentional.

It really means a lot to me to be able to publish this for the world to see. The Schreiber Chronicles are nearly complete but there may be more stories to come in the future. Before I sign off, I'd like to add one final note if you will all indulge me for a moment. Whenever things get hard, or if you ever feel like you aren't worth something; just remember that your life does have meaning. It doesn't matter what anyone else says to the contrary, if you can find happiness in something then use that as an anchor and give your life meaning. Whether it's the people around you, your work, or your hobbies; always strive to give your life meaning because that's very important. And never let anyone who doesn't understand you tell you how to live your life. If I listened to the people who thought badly of me, I never would have finished this series to begin with. Thank you all once again for indulging me and allowing me to put my passions into paper for everyone out there. If I ever publish more, I hope to see you all there. If you wish to see learn more about the scholar Edward or have business inquiries, feel free to shoot me an email at the address down below:

espadoni@Lakeheadu.ca

Cheers, Ethan Spadoni

Contents

The First Awakening

A year after the events of **Part 1 Echoes of Dystopia** in a world similar to theirs:

I don't know where I am. I feel like I am completely lost in this world. I feel like nobody cares about me anymore. I feel like I could die and nobody would give a crap. A strong part of me wants to die but there is something holding me back. I don't completely know what that is but I feel like I am not finished here yet. I still have a job to do and whatever that is, I am going to see it through. – Thoughts of an unnamed scholar.

Ugh, ugh, what happened? I tried to get up from the ground but my entire body is in pain. I feel like my body is on fire. I can still move my arms and legs but they feel worn out. I have this sharp pain in my head and I can't seem to open my eyes. I feel that I am locked in the eternal darkness that is my mind. I think I should wait a few moments before I try to move again. After what feels like an eternity the pain begins to slowly decrease and after a few moments, I am able to open my ocean blue eyes. When I finally manage to get them wide open all I can see is the dark grey sky. I sit up and I feel warm but dead air scrape across my face. Something doesn't feel right. Eventually I am able to stand up and my jaw drops at the horrific sight that is laid out before me. My hometown is completely destroyed.

The town of Schreiber, Ontario is in ruins. The environment is barren and desolate. All the trees have been burned down and the grass is dead. All the buildings and houses have crumbled to the ground and are broken. This really is a nice thing to wake up to. I don't even know what happened here. I don't remember much before I woke up. The last thing I remember is that I was out with my friends and then I blacked out, I guess.

I am so confused right now. I need to find some answers. The only thing I do know is who I am. My name is Ezekiel Smith and I am 17 years old. I have somewhat short black hair and I am 6ft tall. I have a clear face and a strong body. That's all I really know at this point. I need to figure out why the town is in this state. Maybe someone can shed some light on this. I am starting to get my strength back so I think I should walk around and see what's what. I don't think things can get any worse than this.

After walking through part of town, I realize that the area has been reshaped. The train tracks have been moved to the other side of town and now there is just flat land going in one direction and the town in the other. I start to walk and I see that some of the houses have been destroyed. Some houses are slightly intact but it's mostly just walls hanging and rubble everywhere. The sky is grey and bleak. The air is somewhat warm and it feels alright. I think it's summer time. I'd say it's probably around August now. The air smells like death and war. After a few minutes I finally managed to walk near the ball park. I don't see much but then a miraculous sight caught my eye. I see a person standing on one of the bases. Every bone in my body is telling me to go to him. I decide to give into my instincts and run down into the park and I yell out to him to try to get his attention. I am running on pure adrenaline. I think that this man might be able to explain what happened here. As I get closer, I see that the man is not what I first thought. As I get closer, I stop dead in my tracks. My heart immediately stopped. The terrifying man had red eyes and dead looking skin. He looks like he should be decomposing in a grave right now. The part that really freaked me out though is that the man had fangs. He smiled in response to me and my fear. The man took a step forward to me and I started to slowly back away. My entire body is cold with fear but I can still move at least. I realize that even if I back away this thing will still come for me so I think I should do the only thing that can be done in this situation. I turn around and I break out into a run. The man followed close behind me and he steadily ran faster and faster as the seconds passed. I ran for so long. It felt like I had run for hours. My body is streaked with sweat. For the first time I truly feel like I am going to die. I want to give up and let myself die but something is keeping me going. I don't know what it is but I know that I can't pass on just yet.

In this moment of fear and terror I feel a rush of hope pass through me. I saw a somewhat sturdy looking tree still standing. I managed to run under it and I kept running. I kept running until I heard a large thump. I turned around and I saw the man had a branch in his chest. I took the opportunity to hide under some rubble I saw nearby. I could just barely see him through the slits of the rubble but I could see enough. The man ripped the branch out of his chest and he slowly got up. He looked around furiously for me but I knew he could never find me. Eventually he sped off in the other direction. I suppose he had given up. I counted back from 60 in order to give enough time for me to calm down. When I finally got to 1, I started to get up but I heard something and I crouched back under the rubble. Has the man come back? Or is this something worse? Both of these questions poured into my mind as my body began to feel nervous again.

After a few moments I saw a wolf dart pass the tree. He has grey fur, pointed ears and yellow eyes. The wolf sniffed around the area. Soon he came close to where I was hiding and it seems like he is going to close in on me. After a few paralyzing moments he gave up and backed off. Then I saw something that I only ever saw in movies. I never thought they were real. The wolf started to glow. It soon started to stand up and it slowly materialized into a man. The man had many scratches and cuts. He has long blond hair and he looks about my age. After a few minutes of looking around he hobbled off in the direction the fanged man went in and I never saw him again. After a few seconds I got up from under the rubble and I looked around until I was sure that no one was around. I had to sit down on some stone and think. My heart is pumping a million miles a minute and my mind is racing. I can't seem to figure out why this is happening. It can't be possible. Vampires and Werewolves don't exist. I can feel tears starting to well up in my eyes. My face has become stricken with tears. This situation is so messed up.

I have to put my head in my hands to calm myself down. I thought long and hard. After a long time of thinking I managed to stop crying and I came to a few conclusions. I decided I am either crazy, dreaming or that this is real and the town has been taken over by Super Naturals. I decided that for now I will go along with this and see where it leads me. I really don't have anything to lose at this point. I think I should first try to see if I can find my family. I think I should check my house on Manitoba street first. I stood up and I started the long trek to my home. As I passed through town I didn't see anyone on the streets. I chose to stick to the shadows for now just to be safe. I feel terrified but I am filled with adrenaline. I could feel the endorphins being released around me. I felt good. Soon I made it to main street but it wasn't what I expected. I saw that the square was filled with Super Naturals. I stayed in the shadows so I can observe what is going on. They are all looking at multiple posters that are plastered against every wall. The posters depict Humans as being weak individuals. They depict that Super Naturals are stronger and more powerful than Humans.

One poster shows a Super Natural putting a Human's head on a stick and another shows a Super Natural ripping out a Human's heart from their chest and a pool of blood surrounds them. This square is full of propaganda. There is even a gigantic TV in the middle of it. The TV soon clicked on as if on cue. What I saw next drove fear into my heart. I saw a shadow appear on the screen. I couldn't tell who it was but I could hear a chilling a voice. The freaky voice said "attention citizens, a new batch of Humans have been captured. They shall be executed tomorrow night in the middle of the town square for all of you to see. Humans are the true enemy. Super Naturals are the true race of this world. I will protect you from any Humans that come into our town. This town belongs to us and soon we shall cleanse it of any Human filth that have infested us." The citizens cheered at this last remark. Many of them even got down and their knees and thanked their leader. Some started to cry out of gratitude.

The New Reality

After witnessing the television flick off my emotions ran wild. I couldn't decide whether I was horrified or just angry at the world. I decided on anger ultimately. I pounded hard on the wall next to me and started to cry silently. These things who I can't even consider calling Citizens are thanking an unknown voice for committing genocide. I think that this is genocide at least. I now know that the Super Naturals have in fact taken over. Eventually I stop pounding and try to avoid the gazes of the creatures who stopped and stared at me. I tried to sneak past all of them but I stopped in my tracks as I saw somewhat intact buildings in front of me. I can't believe the names that are on them. Some said "Human Execution". That particular place has no roof and it is round. I believe it is a coliseum. Others said "Concentration Camps". Another building said "Human Torture and Experimentation". "AH!" said a voice from inside the building. I started to cry silently. Whoever is in there is suffering. Everyone in there must be suffering. I think I need to see what's in there. I snuck in to the building quickly and undetected. The building had a revolting smell. I realize that it must be the smell of death. Must be a lot of Vampires in here. The first couple of rooms didn't have anything in them. They looked completely empty. The third room is where the action is. I see many Humans being dragged into cells and being handcuffed. I also see people being strapped to gurneys and Ghost doctors operating on the people. It seems like there are cells spread apart all around the room and many doors that must have more cells in them as well. There is also a room far ahead called the "operating room". I believe some of the quick procedures are done in front of everyone to see. Some of the people looked horrified and some didn't seem to care. I guess many of them gave up on life a long time ago. Everyone looked awful. Their clothes are ragged and their faces are covered in dirt and scars. Soon I saw a horrifying sight. I saw one of the finished products coming out of one of the experimenting rooms. He didn't even look like a person anymore.

He has crudely shaped fangs in his mouth. His eyes have become blood red and his skin is pale and clammy. This person has become a Super Natural Demon. He sluggishly walked out of the room. He started to look in my direction but he quickly stopped and continued past me and out the door into the empty rooms. I don't think it is safe for me here. I am a taking a big risk even just being in here. I think I should try to leave town. If I can get past the crowd of Super Naturals outside, I should be able to sneak into the shadows and make my way out. Easier said than done or course. I quickly exited the room and I went through the two mysterious empty rooms. I looked out the door and to my luck there weren't any creatures in sight. I checked my watch and it said 4 am. I think the Vampires may have gone into their coffins for now. Daylight should be coming in soon.

When I am positive no one is around, I take off running and I occasionally hide in the darker parts of town. After about 30 minutes of running and hiding I finally make it to the train tracks. I start to run into the empty land. I know that there has to be someone outside of this town; someone who is normal. I race ahead at full speed. I am pumped with adrenaline and for the first time in this bad situation I feel like I can do anything. I take my first few steps over the tracks when something hits me. I fall flat on my back and I can't think straight. I now have a loud ringing in my head and I can barely move. After a few minutes I can feel the pain starting to ease up. The ringing stops and I can move without causing too much pain. I look around but I can't see what hit me. I look straight ahead and I can see the wasteland.

I know that is my goal so I step forward but I can't go any further. There is some invisible force preventing me from moving on. I punch the force and I hit something hard. I see that there is a barrier in front of me. It lit up and then it disappeared. I touch it again and this white grid thing appears and it moves up slightly. It seems like whenever I touch it, it reacts by moving itself up into the sky. I pick up a rock and I hurl it as high as I can. Sadly, though the rock hits the barrier and it comes back down. I try again and again but no matter how high I throw it the same thing keeps happening. This isn't right. From what I read a long time ago this grid could be an electrical force field but when I touch it, I don't feel any electric shock. I don't know how to explain any of this. This shouldn't be happening. I should be able to leave town whenever I want and I shouldn't have to hide around in my own home. I feel angry and completely hopeless. My palms are sweaty and my muscles ache. I can't handle being in this situation. I really want to pound on this grid until my hands break but I know that won't help anything. I need to see how wide this barrier is. Maybe there will be some area that will have a tiny part that I can sneak into and get out of here. I think I should follow the barrier and see where it goes. I begin my trek and I feel hopeful. I see many ruined buildings and new ones in their place.

Some of the houses have been reconstructed into mostly cabins and small houses that act as homes for the Super Natural beings. I see that everyone is inside their home so I don't need to worry about being seen. After a couple hours of running, I have come to the highway. Happily, I realize that part of the barrier is cut off. Some of the highway is free and clear. I start running West of here when I feel the painful surface of the barrier hit my stomach. I see that the barrier is blocking the area. Ironically the barrier started to block me when I reached the sign that said "you are now leaving Schreiber. The town where you can leave whenever you want." I think that sign should be changed since I can no longer leave this town whenever I want. I fell to my knees in despair and sobbed. I didn't know what to do. After wiping my tears, I resolved to find another way out. There had to be something that I could do. I think I should try to run East. The barrier prevents me from going North of the town or South of the town. I guess going East is the only option left so far. It can't hurt to try. Well actually, based on my past encounters of bumping into the barrier it probably could.

What Lies Beyond?

I walk slowly towards the other sign that shows I am leaving Schreiber when I realize that there is no barrier preventing me from leaving. I go to both sides of the highway but I see that the barrier is blocking those sides. I guess the only way I can go is to Terrace Bay. I pick up a stone and I hurl it at the barrier I see that the entire barrier is flashing and I see that I can only go in the direction of Terrace. If this part is unblocked then that must mean there is something there. I think my best option is to see where this takes me. I take a step back and then I break out into a run. My muscles are aching but I don't care; I need to see where this takes me. I run for what feels like hours until I know I need a break. My legs are on fire and my lungs are exploding from exhaustion. I notice a pile of stone and I crawl into it so I can stay out of sight. It doesn't seem like there is anyone around but I can't be too sure. While I'm laying in the pile of rock, I can feel myself beginning to doze off. I know I shouldn't fall asleep but my body is refusing to protest. Resistance is futile so I give into a long and well needed sleep.

Where am I? I don't know what's going on here. The room I'm in is completely shrouded in darkness. I feel hands on my back. Someone is grabbing me. I can hear myself panting loudly when I feel a sharp slap to my face. "Shut up!". Yelled my attacker. I feel so weak right now. I can barely move and I know that this could be the end. The man is pushing me harder down this dark hallway to a slightly open door. I can see a light coming from it. The man puts his hand on the doorknob and yanks it open. Before I can see what is inside, I feel my body leaving this place. I don't what is happening but I fear it isn't good. The next thing I knew I woke up panting beneath my pile of rubble. I didn't realize that I was breathing so loud until I heard a twig snap. I froze and I held my breath. I couldn't see what was going on outside but I smelled something horrifyingly familiar. I could recognize it anywhere. There is a Vampire near me. I dared snag a peak so I pushed aside a stone and I could see that the Vampire had a wound near its heart. I knew that this was the Vampire that chased me earlier.

I put the stone back and I hid under the rocks until I knew it was safe to come out. I could hear it pacing near my shelter and I knew it was closing in. It is only a matter of time before I was found. After a few more minutes I hear the Vampire come closer and closer until I heard a painful cry in the air. I waited for a few more moments until I heard a thump and a crack. I peeked out from my shelter and I saw the Vampire was covered in blood and I could see that it was suffering. I looked around but I didn't see anyone nearby. I crept over to the Vampire but I didn't expect to see vulnerability in his dead eyes. I crept closer and I saw that the Vampire had various scratches and scars all over his body. This thing had been experimented on for what looked like weeks on end. The creature had now noticed me and I began to step back. The Vampire looked me right in the eyes and he said quietly "help me." I thought that entities like Vampires had lost all of their humanity and their souls when they become turned. Perhaps they are just lost souls who are trying to find their way back.

I went over to the man and I cradled him in my arms. I was afraid that me might try to bite me but he didn't. Instead, he grabbed my arm and he sunk his teeth deep into it; so yes, he did bite me. God damn it! I screamed out in pain as I tried to break free from its grasp. The demon bit down harder and harder into my skin until I began to fade. There is so much blood. I can feel my life force being drained from as I laid down to sleep for the very last time. My name is Ezekiel Smith and I have died. I can feel myself floating from my body as I see the Demon sucking on my blood. After a while the Demon had enough and he tossed my body to the side. I know now that I cannot pass on. I am not ready. I feel myself being lowered to the ground as I look upon my mangled body. If I can't get my life back then I will do whatever it takes to figure out what is going on here. I may be a ghost but I am still a man.

I go over to my body and I try to caress it. Of course, it doesn't work but I just wish I knew how to get back in there. As I begin to ponder this troubling predicament I see someone or something coming towards my body. The being appears to be wearing a black cloak with a hood over their face. I tried to get their attention but the being completely disregarded me. The being extended its hand to my body and I saw the hand looked normal and young. The being touched my body and then picked it up. It seemed interested in my body and all I could do was watch it being carried away. I saw that the being was carrying my body back to Schreiber so I followed it there. The being kept to the shadows and then I saw it sneak into the Voyageur. I followed it inside and the being went behind the candy counter. I tried to follow it but it was as if the being had disappeared into thin air. I wonder if there is some sort of trap door that the being went in. Before I try to figure it out, I think that I should look around and see what is what. On the outside the Voyageur looks like it is completely destroyed and only the door is intact and bits of the walls. The inside is exactly the same. The way to the restaurant is completely blocked off by part of the wall that has sunken deep into the ground.

Since I am a ghost, I should be able to walk through here. I start to go to the wall when I bump into it. I try and try again but to no avail. "Why isn't this working?" I say out loud. Before I can even move, I hear a voice coming from the bathrooms. I can't quite hear it but I think it is calling me to them. I decide that I really don't have anything to lose right now so I head to where the voice is coming from. I enter the bathrooms and they seem mostly intact. There are only a few cracks and holes in the walls but it isn't too bad considering the circumstances. I can hear the voice much more clearly now. It's saying "come to me." I look in the first stall I see and in it I see another ghost. This ghost looks much older. He is completely bald and he looks like he has been through a lot. His body looks worn out and he looks tired. I go to the ghost and he says "I'm glad you have come." The ghost left the stall and he raised his hand to beckon for me to come with him. He leaves the bathrooms and he heads outside. I follow him until he goes through the wall into the restaurant. I call out to him by saying "Um, I can't actually go through the walls. I only seem to bump into them." The old ghost said "well why don't you try again. Believe in your abilities and go through the wall." I am about to try it when I hear the old man mutter something very quietly. I think it was something like "stupid kids always needing my help. Why am I always stuck training the new ones." I decided to ignore that comment and I tried one last time to go through the wall.

Who Should I Trust?

I decide to trust in my abilities and suddenly I am able to walk through the wall. I am amazed by my new trick but my excitement is cut short when I see that the Voyageur is completely in ruins. All the tables are on their sides and there are stone and pieces of the wall everywhere. There aren't any holes in the walls which makes me feel like I am completely trapped in here despite me being a ghost. I walk over to the old ghost who is sitting at the only table that is upright. I go to the empty chair across from the man and I sit down. I fall through it the first time but the second time I find I can sit in the chair. I feel like I don't have much of a hold on the human world but I have a faint grasp for now. I don't know how long it will last but I may as well try to make the best of it. I look to the man and he is eyeing me intently.

His eyes look tired but there is something there that shows me he is still strong. We sit in silence for about 5 minutes before he finally breaks the silence by speaking. He said "I haven't seen you around before; and based on your lack of skills I am guessing that you are new. Am I right?" He asks coldly. I say "Yes, I am a new ghost. A Vampire sucked my blood out of me and I couldn't pass on yet. Because of that I am stuck here for now." The man's face begins to darken. I don't know what is going on but I can tell that he has much to tell me. He leans forward and says "I'm sure you have many questions. I will answer them for you if you wish." I begin to feel relieved but I need to remain focused so I know I can cover everything. I clear my throat and ask "What happened here? Why are Humans being captured and executed? Why did the Vampire kill me instead of taking me? Why am I able to sit down in this chair? Who is the shadow that appears on the TV screen on main street? Why can't I leave and why are you still here?" I have to slow down to catch my breath.

Talking for that long makes me a little tired. The man's eyes began to grow colder but he relented and said "I will tell you the story but brace yourself; you are in for a long ride." I nodded in response. Loudly he said "alright then, I shall tell you the story. This began many years ago. On July 25th 2015 to be exact. It was a normal day in this bloody town. I was resting at the home for the elderly when my family came to visit. I was so happy to see them again. Things were going well but then, things quickly turned to shit. I was looking out my window when someone threw a grenade into my building. Me and many other folks were playing games at the time you see. When we saw the grenade come in, we didn't have any time to react. The second it made contact with the window it exploded.

"I was on the far side of the room so I wasn't damaged but I did get knocked over. I had blacked out and I woke up a few seconds later. The entire room was on fire and many of my friends were either scrambling to escape or were slowly being burned alive by the flames. Many of my friends were on the ground burned to death and others had died from the impact. I was the only one of my friends to survive. Or so I thought. I looked to my side and I saw my daughter and my 17-year-old granddaughter near me. Luckily, they were unharmed. I managed to get up and I tried to lead them outside. Before we could make it to the exit a man with fangs and blood red eyes stormed into the place and he sunk his teeth into my daughter. My granddaughter tried to help but I urged her to escape. Luckily, she made it out alive but me and my daughter weren't so lucky. She had died from her wounds and before I could try to help her the Vampire came to me and he bit my neck. He bit it until every last drop of my blood was gone. Before I had died, I saw that there were many creatures destroying the other buildings in town. I saw Werewolves, Ghosts, Aliens, and Demons. I will never forget that day.

"That was the worst conflict in human history I have ever experienced. I soon realized though that I had become a Ghost. I had woken up a couple weeks later and I saw that everything was destroyed. I soon figured out that Super Naturals had taken control of our world. I didn't notice the barrier until I tried to leave. I believe that the leader of the Super Naturals placed that in there so they could keep order within this new society. Things changed quickly. Many of the Humans who had survived were rounded up and taken prisoner by the Demons. The Humans were experimented on so that more Super Naturals could be created. There was a problem with these though. Because they are scientific products of other Super Naturals these creatures are significantly weaker than the originals. They are also somewhat unstable. Because of this the leader forced the newly created beings to remain in Schreiber while the older and much more powerful ones would stay in Terrace Bay. Some of the beings who aren't failures were able to get jobs within the society so they work on experimentation or execution.

"I thought I was safe since I am a Ghost but I realized that even Ghosts are being captured and they can be experimented on for eternity. I saw many of my comrades be captured by Demons and then being sent to the torture rooms. Many of them are still in there. We can't normally die but if we are experimented on long enough then we will become so weak that we fall to pieces and then the pieces disappear forever. I have been caught and experimented on many times but after a certain point they always let me go. I know now that this is to create a false of sense of hope within me before I am recaptured. I haven't been to that retched place in five days. I expect though that I will be caught again. I have given up on trying to fight their forces. They are too powerful and I can't evade them forever. Super Naturals prey on being dominant creatures so that is why humans are always being captured. That Vampire that killed you only killed you because he was weak. Had he been at full strength he would have weakened you and then captured you. The shadow who appears on the screen is the leader of the Super Naturals. No one from this town has ever seen his true face. The reason why we are able to sit is that even though we are ghosts we still maintain a slight foothold to the human realm.

"We are unable to contact with anyone but we can still interact with the world in some ways. The best way to explain this is that we are in the same world as the Humans but we are in a different realm. We cannot hurt another Human but we can interact with some things in order to make ourselves feel alive. After a while you learn to be able to have more control over this ability. Finally, I do not know why I am still here. Perhaps it is because I know my granddaughter is out there somewhere and I want to protect her in any way I can. I do not know if she has survived but I believe she is alive somewhere. She has to be. That is the end of my tale. Do you have any questions or are you alright?" I said to the man, "I only have one more. Do you know who took my body?" The man said "I do not know. I am sorry." he said sincerely. I replied "it is alright. I thank you for your help." I get up to leave when the man grabs my hand. I can see the look of terror in his eyes. He says "There is another way to kill a Ghost. The only other way to kill is to... to...Groan". I see that a creature dressed in dark had grabbed hold of where his heart should be. The creature with ease flung the frail man into a large bag and quickly sealed it shut. I guess this bag must be made of some sort of special material that keeps Ghosts in. The being is literally covered in darkness. He looks a lot like the grim reaper. The being takes off its hood and I see the most horrifying creature I have ever seen. It is a dark being with a long dark tail and red eyes. Its face is the worst. It has one large mouth with sharp teeth and a smaller mouth with razor sharp teeth in it. This thing has two mouths and with them it lets out a long and terrifying roar. I know that I'm about to be finished in a matter of seconds. I stand in terror as the Demon looks me over. If I could piss myself, I probably would have by now; that's how scared I was.

I look back to the wall and I quickly run through it. I run right back to the gift shop because I don't know what else to do. I hide behind the counter but I soon hear the Demon coming into the gift shop as well. That thing is clearly very fast. I can hear it growling quietly and I can tell it senses my presence. After a matter of moments, I can hear the Demon leave the gift shop and I can hear it go through the rubble that blocks the restaurant. I come out from behind the counter and I head out the nearest exit. Outside I can sense other Ghosts nearby. I see that there is a clock hanging outside and I see that it is 7:00 am. I look around and I can now see that Ghosts are starting to slowly appear before me. Every one of them looks defeated and weak. I walk over to one of them but the Ghost sees me and becomes frightened. He quickly disappears into thin air before my very eyes. I look around me but I see that there are no Demons around. I look to all the other Ghosts and they all seem to be afraid of me. I even see Ghost children. I can see the sadness in their eyes and the fear of being caught and experimented on. I see that many of the Ghost children are near someone else like a parent or sibling. I scan them until I see that there is one boy who isn't around anyone. I walk over to the little boy but he notices me before I can reach him. I immediately stop so as not to frighten him. I am ten feet away from him and I raise my hands in order to show that I mean no harm. I see that the boy looks about ten years old. He has short brown hair and a pale face. He has brown eyes as well. I say quietly "hi there." The little boy looked at me but he didn't say anything. I went slightly closer to him but he didn't move. He kept staring at me and I put my hand out to him to show I am not a threat. I say cautiously to him "I want to help you little boy. I am not a danger to you. I will not hurt you." The boy looked me right in the eyes and he said "Please help me. I am all alone here. My parents are gone and I don't know where to go." I could tell the boy was nervous and I can kind of relate to him in a twisted sort of way.

I lost my mother in a car accident when I was fourteen and my dad has never been the same. I felt more alone than ever during that time. I seem to be remembering more of my memories bit by bit. I walk right up to the boy and I kneel to him. I look him in the eyes and I say "I can help you. I don't know what I can do but I promise I will do everything

I can to help you." The boy's eyes lit up and he says "I believe you. I don't know who you are but I feel that I can trust you." I replied "can you tell me what happened to your parents? I know it's hard but it could help me figure out what is going on here." The boy nodded in response and said "it all happened so fast. It was on July 25th, I think. I was playing in the backyard with my brother when I saw this bad man come into the yard. My brother screamed and my parents came out into the yard. The bad man picked up a bottle of something brown and he threw it at our house. The house was on fire and then the bad man grabbed my daddy by his throat. He squeezed it so much that my daddy turned purple. After a few moments the man let go and my father fell to the ground completely dead. My mommy screamed at the top of her lungs and the man stuck his hand in her chest and ripped her heart out. The man quickly bit into my brother and then he fed on me next. I woke up later and I saw everyone was gone. I saw pieces of my family on the ground. I tried to put them back together but they just kept falling apart no matter how much I tried. I then saw the ghosts of my family. I ran to them but this black monster came and squeezed them so much that all three of them came apart. The monster was going to come for me but it left me behind. I guess I was too weak for it and not much of a challenge. I can't go on any longer. I'm sorry but it's just too much." The boy turned away and started crying loudly. I want to help this kid but I don't know how to do it. I tried to think of any solution. Come on brain, give me something. Anytime now. Anything would work. Even one tiny morsel of a shitty idea would be better than this. While I was having a debate in my head over what to do next, I heard a familiar growl. I turned and I saw the same Demon from earlier exiting the gift shop.

The Ghosts that were around all began to scream and port away. I grabbed the little boy and he ported us away as well. I didn't know what had happened until I saw that I was inside my old public school. I quickly thought about how it felt to teleport. It was like every part of my body was being broken apart and being scattered. It then felt like they being put back together in a different place. That may sound like fun but it was awful. It hurt so much. All my muscles are aching so much. I never want to do it again. The little boy said "it hurts at first but after you do it a few times you get used to it. You just have to focus your mind before you teleport and then you can do it easily." I nodded in response to the kid. I saw that I was in my old social studies classroom. Everything was dead.

I saw that cracks outlined the walls and everything was starting to come apart. I saw that some of the desks were overturned and that a dusty smell was in the air. I guess I must've retained a bit of that sense. It never felt so good to be able to smell again. I looked to my partner and he was looking at the old chalkboard. There is an old math problem on here; it looks like it may have been algebra. Many of the numbers are faded though so I can't be too sure. I turned to the boy and I asked him the one question that had been burning in my mind for a long time. I asked "why are the other Ghosts afraid of me?" The boy turned to me and replied softly "you are the chosen one." I couldn't believe what I had just heard. This boy is crazy. I asked him "what do you mean?" The boy turned away and stared into space. He was clearly deep in thought. After a few moments of silence he said "there is a story about the chosen one. Here it is; long ago, an ancient text was found in some ruins outside of town. The leader of our town inspected the ruins and he was able to translate it. The text read 'when the world is plunged into darkness and when the Demons rise the world shall fall into an eternal darkness. It shall last for what feels like an eternity until a powerful warrior shall come to the town and shall vanquish the darkness forever. The world shall be filled with light once more and everyone shall be at peace.' It was soon discovered that there was a second passage on the stone. It read: 'When the world is plunged into darkness and when the Demons rise the world shall fall into darkness. A powerful army will come to fight the demons and a long war shall ensue. The war shall be decided by a powerful warrior passing through the town. The warrior shall aid the Demons in combat and the human armies shall fall. The world will be full of darkness forever and light shall cease to exist.' These are what the ancient texts say. Because no one has seen you around before, you are believed to be the ancient warrior. The question is; who's side are you on?" I was completely shocked. I am speechless.

The boy came to me and said confidently "I am not afraid of you because I believe you are going to fight for the good side. I have a strong feeling about you. I think you are destined to guide us to peace." I said "no way kid. I'm no warrior. I don't even know that the hell is going on here. Find another hero bud. I need to find my body." The boy came up and took my arm and pleaded with me. He said pleadingly "you can't go, I need you. Please stay." I saw that tears are beginning to well up in his eyes. I desperately wanted to help him but I need to figure out why I can't remember everything and then I'll try to help. I said "I will help you but I need to take care of something first." I take my hand from his and I walk through the walls of the school until I am completely outside. The boy followed me and said "you need to help me now. Please." Before I can say anything, I feel the sensation of darkness coming. I turn and I see a Demon coming right for me. I am too terrified to move. I have 5 seconds to figure a way out of this. Just as I feel the cold embrace of the Demon, I feel someone push me out of the way. I got pushed back about 5 feet. I look and I can't believe what just happened. That little boy pushed me out of the way and is now in the clutches of the Demon. Just as the Demon is about to head back the boy yells "do what's right chosen one, I believe in you!" I run to the Demon but he disappears into thin air. "NO!" I keep yelling that out for some time. I can't believe that I let that happen. Just as I am weeping to myself, I feel my world turn to darkness. Someone just put me in a bag. The cold of the bag is suffocating,

I try banging at it but I can't get out. I knew that the Demon must've come back for me. I don't care though. It's time I accept my punishment. I deserve to be operated on for all eternity. This person must've been carrying me for what feels like a millennium. The bag keeps hitting the ground and I keep getting wounded. Man, this is a bad time for my hold on the human world to increase. Damn, I hate being a Ghost. I feel like we are going underground. After a few more steps I see the bag open up and I tumble down into a stone-cold room. The room is completely dark except for multiple torches hanging on the walls. I look directly ahead of me and I see thirteen people in full black cloaks with hoods covering their faces. The person in the middle comes forward and rips off their hood. I see a beautiful dark skinned young woman. She looks about my age. I also see that she has a sword on her back and she says loudly "who are you." I glance behind her and I see my body is crucified on a cross. There are real people still alive. "What the hell is going on here?"

New Friends?

The young woman came closer and drew her sword so that it rested at my neck. "Ill be the one asking questions." She said sharply. I gulped and replied "I'm Ezekiel, Ezekiel Smith. And I take it that you are the one who stole my body and brought it here?" I asked incredulously. The woman nodded, removed the sword and another man came forward. This man took off his hood. He looked about my age or slightly older and was skinny with red hair. He looked strong though. He wielded a magic staff and book and said "Hello Ezekiel, my name is Simon. I've come here to help you. I can return you to your body and I can even have you retain your ghostly abilities while in human form if you would like that." He said softly. I nodded vigorously and he began to chant. I also saw the other hooded members take my body off the cross and lay it on the ground next to me. Simon finished chanting and suddenly I was transported back into my body. I could feel my limbs again and I also feel like I could walk through walls which was awesome. I thanked Simon profusely and he smiled in response. I looked to all of them and asked "Who are you people?" Simon smirked and said "We are the Resistance. And we are here to stop the Super Natural threat. I have found two sites of corruption and if we purify them then we shall be able to free both Towns from this terrible fate. We believe that you are the chosen one to help us through this tough time. Will you help us?" I thought deeply about it.

I was so grateful to get my body back and I felt like I owed them that much. But first I had to know something. "Hang on, why can't I remember anything? I just woke up outside of town." Simon's gaze softened and said "I think I know the answer. Like me, you aren't from this world. This is a parallel world that you stumbled into and when you do it for the first time you lose your memories. It took me many attempts before I got it right. If you wish, I can give you your memories back. That is within my power to do so." "Please," I said quickly. Simon walked forward and placed his hand on my head. I could feel a rush of light pass through and suddenly I could recall everything. Me and my friends were partying on a cruise ship in Mexico when we got attacked by a giant bird. The bird attacked the ship and it caused many of us to go overboard. I tried to save my friends when apparently, I activated a portal a tumbled into it. My best friend Katleyn is back home and I got to get back to her. She and I aren't romantically involved but she's like my sister. I must let her know I'm okay. I remember when I activated the portal, I felt a rush of power as I tried to grab one of my friends from going under the water. It didn't work obviously since only I woke up here.

Maybe if I can help Simon and the others save the Towns then maybe I can go back home. I turned back to Simon and said "Ill help you. My only wish is that once I help you; you help me get back home." I said softly. Simon smiled and agreed to help me. Simon pulled out of his cloak a special looking dagger. The dagger is apparently made of obsidian and is one of the only things that can kill a supernatural creature. Simon made them using the power of his magical stone. Apparently, he made a lot of mistakes in the past and that's why he came to this place in order to gain redemption for his past actions. If I help him then he will use the power of the stone to give me the power to go home all on my own. The young woman stepped forward. "My name is Talia and I will be your instructor. You may have some magic but you clearly know nothing about fighting. I will teach you how to use that dagger without poking your eye out or accidently harming us. There may only be thirteen of us but we are all master warriors and are much stronger than you. We will help you get up to snuff so that we can proudly fight alongside you as we free the two Towns from this threat. Are we clear?" she said icily. I nodded and said "Yes." She nodded and we began our training.

Meanwhile...in Terrace Bay a group of Super Naturals sat around a giant conference table discussing things. The leader of it, an old ancient Vampire by the name of Markos began the meeting. "It appears the Resistance has gained another champion to aid them in their fight. Armos, what intel do you have on this "Warrior"?" Armos an aging Werewolf with a twelve pack gruffly replied "It would appear that one of our scouts tried to capture a new citizen but the Resistance intervened and took him away from us. I don't know much about him but he might be dangerous to our hierarchy." The other leaders agreed. There was a leader of the Demons, the Ghosts, and the Aliens. The five of them were there to go over things with the Vampire at the head of the table. While each member had an equal vote in the council; the Vampires have the final say since they populated the town first and gained the strongest foothold. The Vampire leader then forced an uneasy alliance between the other factions and now they have to work together.

The Vampires also had the largest population along with the Demons since they populated here first and their experiments have turned many humans into their kind. The Aliens and the Ghosts were in the minority and didn't get a lot of respect. The Elder vampire also could read people's thoughts and he could sense that the Alien leader was feeling uneasy. *I don't think we can do this much longer. Eventually the Resistance will rise up and kill us all. Maybe I can get my clan out of town if I can figure out how the damn Vampires put up the barrier in the first place* thought the Alien. The Vampire leader quick as a whip rushed the Alien leader and slammed his head against the table over and over until he was bleeding profusely. Markos then sucked his fangs in nice and deep until the Alien nearly died. Markos stopped and looked at the dumbfounded council members. "This is what happens to those that try to oppose me" he boomed. The others bowed their heads in supplication and the Alien weakly managed to bow as well. He would heal in time but it would take a while.

Markos decided to dismiss the meeting since nothing more could be done at this point. After the other leaders left Markos sat in his chair and sipped a glass of cabernet wine. He was always a big fan of wine and preferred the sophisticated and finer things in life. He sipped as he pondered his plans for world domination after Terrace Bay. The magical stone he had implanted in his heart has kept him immortal and helps to maintain the barrier around the two Towns. So long as that and the other stone in Schreiber don't fall, then nothing shall prevent Markos from getting everything he wants. And once he does then there will be no need for the other faction leaders. A full genocide of every race beyond Vampires will be glorious.

Back at base, me and Talia managed to begin training. The first method we tried was hand to hand which mostly ended up with me getting my ass handed to me. We also trained in the use of swords and stakes in order to get me comfortable with using the obsidian dagger. Both sessions ended with me getting many cuts and bruises but still I felt like I was improving. As time went on, I was able to dodge more of Talia's attacks and was able to even parry a few of them. I even tried using some of my Ghostly abilities in tandem but that just tired me out and left me dazed; which also left me open to many more attacks as punishment by my teacher. We continued though and eventually I was able to even land a few hits on her. After my sessions with her I trained my Ghostly abilities with Simon and learned how to use those abilities in combat. As time went on my endurance improved and I became faster and faster. I think Simon was also using the stone to power me up slightly so I would be more useful in the fight but I didn't care. I was just happy I could keep up with my teachers now.

The other hooded warriors also taught me various things such as advanced fighting techniques and history about the Towns so that I could better understand what we were up against. Finally, Talia taught me how to use the obsidian dagger and eventually I was able to use it effectively by narrowing down where the weak points of the enemies would be. The daggers were enchanted so that anywhere they hit would cause damage but decapitation or a hit to the heart would cause critical damage and instant death. After many weeks of training, we finally felt ready to take the fight to the factories and torture places in Schreiber. If we could liberate those areas then the leaders in Terrace Bay would have a significantly weaker force to use against us. Talia seemed very impressed with my progress and even complimented me on my footwork. "Your footwork's improving and you've got skills with that dagger. I would be proud to fight beside you brother," she said calmly. She took her dagger and sheathed it and then kneeled to me. The others followed suit and I could feel a swell of emotion rise up in my throat as I realized I wasn't alone. I had thirteen powerful brothers and sisters in arms who would help me to survive this and I would do the same for them. I kneeled to them as well in gratitude and promised to fight alongside them in order to free their home.

The room we were in was enchanted by Simon's magic so that we wouldn't be found by any of our enemies but now was the time to move out. We left the base and ended up where I first woke up by the train tracks. I was given my own cloak as well. Apparently, the cloak had special capabilities that would protect me from most wounds and enhanced my speed and strength. I'll take any boost that I can get. We headed out to the town square killing any Super Natural creatures in our wake. My dagger worked perfectly. I faced off against both a Werewolf and a Vampire and managed to slay them both without much trouble. I even found the Vampire who killed me and exploded his heart with my weapon. It was quite enjoyable and gave me a rush of emotion as I finished him off. The Vampire turned to dust as he died and I noticed the wolf also turned to dust as well.

We kept going until we made it to the Town square where everyone was. We ran into each building panting as we went and slayed every hostile creature we could find. We also freed any victims we could and they joined our side. By the time the square was nearly clear we had hundreds of Super Natural creatures on our side who were more than willing to take revenge on their captors. Even some of the Ghosts who hadn't gotten captured aligned with us as well, and I even saw my old friend. He wasn't in much shape to fight but he still refused to lie down and let other people fight his battles for him. Each of the horrific buildings that existed in the town were expunged and cleared out of all threats. The Resistance continued to move forward until they managed to make it to the old Town hall. The Town hall was littered with enchantments but Simon easily countered them with his magic. Simon didn't seem too keen to rely on the stone all that much. I think the more he uses it, the older he'll get so tries not to use it unless it's absolutely essential. With just his own magic he could probably live forever but he seems dedicated to helping as many people as possible.

The enchantments lifted and we all ran into the building. Wiping sweat off my brow I could feel my adrenaline waning and my exhaustion beginning to take root. By the time we made it in there we saw one lone Vampire. He looked pissed. I wanted to say something but then he dashed to Simon and tried to bite him. Simon blocked him with his staff and used the dagger to slash at his fingers. The Vampire lost all of his fingers before regenerating them instantly. The rest of us surrounded him and slashed him everywhere. Eventually Talia managed to stab him right in the heart and he exploded in blood and gore. Apparently when the obsidian dagger hits their hearts, they can sometimes detonate instead of just turning to dust. Simon identified the glowing dark mass that was once the vampire's heart. He used his own magic to neutralize it and suddenly the area began to shake. The barrier around the town was beginning to weaken and any remaining Super Natural enemies collapsed in their tracks. The people weren't instantly brought back to life or cured but this was a very good start. The obvious next step was to go to Terrace Bay in order to purify the rest of the area. But first, we all needed transportation. Talia went out back and saw the Vampire's car was still here. It's essentially a gigantic tank that's really agile.

Retaliation

My jaw dropped at the sight of the monstrosity and my excitement became palpable to the people around me. All of them snickered and laughed good heartedly at my excitement about the moving fortress. There was more than enough for hundreds of people to fit inside so we all climbed in and sped off. The vehicle zoomed off and it felt like I was flying. I huddled in next to Simon and saw his expression as he looked outside at the devastation. His expression seemed to be one of regret but not about this situation. I wonder what happened in his past. I wish I could help him as much as he helped me, but I'm sure I'll find out in time when he's ready to share. The entire trek took about five minutes and then we saw Terrace Bay. The buildings had all been converted into immaculate looking mansions and the surrounding area looked beautiful. It's clear that the more powerful monsters created their homes here and brought their estates here. Lake Superior also seems to be all dried up and in its place is a bunch of condos. I could feel my anger bubbling upwards.

I wanted to scream at the damage these creatures were doing, but I knew we were closer than ever to liberating Terrace Bay. I knew from the information that the others gave was that there were not very many creatures here but they were the oldest and most powerful. They would be a challenge for sure. As soon as we got into town properly there were about fifty Super Natural creatures waiting for us. They definitely look old but strong. We fired upon them with the tank and they all scattered and dodged. We got out of the tank and ran after them. I went after the Werewolf leaders and slashed at them. They parried with their claws and slashed me pretty good across my left arm I nearly lost the dagger in my hand but I kept my cool. If it hadn't been for the training and the previous fighting experience in Schreiber, I would have dropped the dagger for sure. I kept fighting the three Werewolves. They were in their human form but I could see their claws and animal features coming out. They were definitely powerful. But with the cloak and Simon's enhancements they stood no chance.

I twirled the blade in my hand and I threw it at the left Werewolf. It got him right in the heart and he detonated on impact. The impact hit the other two Werewolves and they went flying. I hurriedly grabbed the dagger and ran after the other two. They were dazed but regaining their bearings. I quickly slashed them across their necks and they died instantly. Once they were finished, I could feel that I was covered in their blood and my dagger was covered as well. I assumed the Werewolf leaders were dead until I saw the biggest one I had ever seen. He was in wolf form but he stood twice as tall as me and even wider. I could tell he was the leader and he seemed very upset with me. He rushed me and pounced on me. He bit deep into my chest but I took the opportunity to use the dagger and stab him right through the head. Blood spurted out of him and he fell to the ground dead. He was also on top of me and it took everything I had to push myself out from under him. He was dangerous but not impossible.

I saw the other were fighting against the Aliens so I went after the Demons. The Demons were black creatures that resembled grim reapers and Vampires. They even used scythes as their main weapons. I decided to use my teleporting/ghost abilities in order to help turn the tide. With that combination I was able to teleport and quickly plant my dagger in their chests before disappearing again and targeting another enemy. The Ghosts and the Aliens feel soon after as I learned that the dagger could harm even creatures like them as well. Finally, all that was left were the Vampires. They were clearly the strongest and me, Talia, and Simon decided to attack the leader together. Talia rushed the monster head on while Simon used his magic to try to slow the monster down while I used my teleporting skills to both dodge his attack and try to distract him while attempting to get a hit on him whenever possible.

The fight was agonizing as we each did everything that we could to avoid getting hit by him. The other Vampires attempted to join in when the leader held up his hand and said "No, these are mine to deal with. Kill the others." Our armies fought off the Vampires while we attempted to kill their leader. The leader Markos was strong and it took everything we had in order to just stay alive. Whenever I saw an opening, I went for it but his super speed always allowed him to block all three of us and we were getting winded quickly. Simon tried to use restraining spells on Markos but nothing was working. Eventually Simon switched tactics and decided to use his telekinesis. Simon aimed a concentrated blast at Markos' eyes. Markos smirked and said "Do you really expect that to, AIIIIEEE," he screamed painfully as he grabbed at his eyes. Simon's ability worked and Markos lost his sight. Simon did that again and again on his arms and legs in order to prevent movement. Every limb of Markos exploded until he was nothing but a torso. Me and Talia took the opportunity to slash at him with our obsidian daggers in order to put him down for good. We punctured his chest and he began to die.

Before he did though he coughed out "you really think you defeated me, but you've only just delayed the inevitable. Jeb and Nathaniel are back; and your worlds will all be destroyed hahahahahahahah after their chaos takes root," he uttered out quietly before finally dying. Simon ran up to him to get more answers but Markos was already dead. The corruption in Markos' chest had been destroyed the everyone that had been killed was brought back to life except for the older creatures. My Ghost friends returned to life and hugged me while thanking me for saving them. The barriers around the two Towns had also finally fallen and peace was restored to the area. I went up to Simon and asked "what was Markos talking about?" Simon looked down and said "Jeb was an old enemy of mine. I almost destroyed the world to help him once before I realized my mistakes. I helped to defeat him and I assumed he was gone for good; I never expected him to come back," he said quietly. So, this was the secret Simon was holding onto.

He has immense guilt for helping his old enemy in almost taking over the world. It seems like he realized his mistake in the end though and tried to reverse it. I can tell Simon is a good man with a good heart. I wish I could help him. Simon said quickly "enough about that though, time to help you go home." He used the stone to increase my power and he gave me the instructions on how to actually use and control my abilities. I used my powers and I saw my friends in my world all sadly looking for me with the coast guard. I almost went through right to them but decided I couldn't. I closed the portal and said "no, they can wait. I need to help you first. I can tell you're suffering from your mistakes. I don't care what you did in the past; you saved me and did everything you could to help me. I wish to do the same and help you defeat your old enemy once again. If you will have me that is." Simon hugged me tightly and said "of course you can come my friend. It will be dangerous but we will save the universe together," he said softly. Simon chanted another spell and opened a portal to the place where Jeb and Nathaniel would most likely be. He grabbed my hand and we jumped in together. Before that however, Simon decided that he needed to show me other examples of how we can help the worlds and perhaps find a weak point for our ultimate enemy in order to undo their chaos.

A Tale Of Vengeance:

Meanwhile in another world. Hello, my name is Ethan and I want revenge. I come from a kingdom called Hollow Dark. It's a very dark but beautiful place with dead forests and eternal night across the entire kingdom. We have never seen the sun but we are happy without it. We are neighbours to the eternal sun kingdom of Bright Blaze where they live with eternal sunshine. They also seem happy. We have never been close neighbours but we have never been enemies. I started out as a lowly peasant until I joined the royal guard at 18 and am now 23. I became the youngest captain of the guard and became capable of marrying my childhood love; Princess Eternia. Eternia and I grew up together and I fell in love with her at first sight and she told me it was the same with her and me. When I became a guard captain, I gained a small noble title so I became eligible for marriage.

We were so in love and we were going to be wed in two years time when we turned 25. We were born on the same day and year coincidentally. I admit it felt almost like fate. Anyway, one day I had received a message from her and she sent for me to meet her in the training grounds for the knights. She also trained with us sometimes so that was a place where we were known to meet at times. When I went there it was completely deserted which wasn't unusual during this time of day; it still always made me feel a little nervous when nobody was around. I felt uneasy especially without my gilded armor for being the guard captain but I had my trusty sword at all times so I felt confident I could deal with any major threats that put the Princess' life in danger.

I saw many of my knights come towards me without doing the proper bowing and saluting in greeting which already made me feel off about the whole situation. I decided to push down my unease as they were my subordinates and comrades and went forward to greet them. In response they all pulled out their swords and advanced towards me. Some looked truly shaken about it but others looked either determined or angry at me for some reason. "What is this treason? I'm your guard captain? Stand down men!" I shouted. They didn't listen and they all lunged at me. I disarmed many of them as I didn't want to hurt my own men but they just kept coming and continued to swarm me all at once. I got stabbed, sliced, maimed, and every other adjective you could think of in this situation. I ended up losing my left hand in the process but I kept on fighting until I finally collapsed from my wounds. I coughed up blood as the blood began to pool from every part of my body. I weakly stood up to see the princess and my second in command David looming over me with matching smirks. He had his sword drawn and stabbed me in the throat up to the hilt. As I quickly began to bleed to death he leaned over and kissed Eternia passionately which she returned with equal fervour.

She smiled down and said "oh my love, I've fallen for David instead. He promised to help me take over the blaze kingdom. He's going to be my new guard captain and I will be his queen. And you will be branded as a traitor for attacking the crown princess," she said smugly. David turned back to her and gave her superficial cuts with his sword in order to make it look like she got attacked. I gurgled on my own blood and slowly began to black out...no I can't let it end like this. I forced myself to stand and with my sword I lunged towards David before stabbing him right in the heart. He stared at me in shock as we collapsed to the ground together in a heap of blood and gore as the world faded to black. I had finally died. Beep, beep, beep. I can hear this incessant beeping but I can't place what it is. I feel cold and like I'm floating. I can also hear voices...telling me to wake up. I also feel like there are two people watching over me. I wonder who they could be. Maybe if I can live my life on my own terms, then maybe I won't need vengeance. Maybe I can live in peace somewhere new. Simon glanced at Ezekiel and the two of them went through many other worlds to get to where they wanted to go. "See? Vengeance isn't always the answer," said Simon. Ezekiel nodded in response and smiled thoughtfully at all the people that could be saved with their influence. "Now let's look at Felix Fernandez and try to undo his suffering, shall we?" said Simon thoughtfully.

A Felix Fernandez Story:

Huff, huff, huff. I could feel the air rushing by me as I ran for my life. I had stumbled upon something I never should have discovered and now I'm paying the price for it. If anyone finds this recording, know that I did my best to survive. Apparently, it's a game these people like to play after dark. If I can survive in the woods long enough, they may let me live; or they may end up killing me slower. Who knows anymore? My name is Felix Fernandez; and I'm a dead man. This I know but I don't know how to stop it. Luckily their hearing doesn't seem to be very good so they don't hear me talking into this voice recorder. I can't believe this all started because I wanted to impress my cute coworker and get away from my parents. I managed to find this old abandoned tree house so maybe I can hide out here for the time being. I think the only way I'm going to start feeling better is if I start from the beginning. My tale is nothing tragic or anything awful, I'm just a normal guy who needed space from his parents and didn't know how else to get it. Let me go back a few days in order to really show how fucked up this has gotten.

The First Meeting

It was a day like any other on May 15th 2025; I had another fight with my parents about taking out the garbage. I'm 25 and am trying to make it as a writer. I work for the local newspaper in my hometown of Scranton, Illinois. It doesn't pay much but it does help me get experience and some money in order to make it as an author. I've always loved authors like Stephen King and James Patterson. I graduated from university and I got my masters in English Literature with a minor in Philosophy. Despite my accomplishments I still felt like someone was stalking me at times. I can't explain it honestly. My parents were also proud of me but that soon ended once they realized I wasn't ready to get a job yet. I had been dealing with some PTSD from previous bosses and my masters had not been a pleasant experience. I didn't even want it initially; I only did it so that I could get more time and open more opportunities. I love them but I still feel pushed and pressured by them to move out and live my life alone. I tried doing odd jobs to get more money but none of them turned out to anything. I even once tried selling drugs.

I was successful at first but once my shift was done, I got mugged at gunpoint and barely escaped by the skin of my teeth. I still have a scar down the side of my back from where someone tried to stab me with a rusty knife. I went to the hospital and my parents slapped me hard across the face as they cried. I understood that what I did was wrong, but they didn't understand that their pressure drove me to those actions. I later went to the streets for a few days before they begged me to come back home. Once I returned, they became even more strict and kept telling me to give up on my dream of becoming an author. They wanted me to join my dad at his carpeting business but I refused. I have many scars from their treatment. I once tried to kill myself using my dad's gun, but I was too much of a coward. I never told anyone how bad it got at home. I know everyone would just laugh at me and claim it serves me right since I still live at home like a pathetic and worthless loser. I know I'm just a waste of space to the people around me.

I hid my scars well and the police never arrested me and only let me off with a warning after I told them who my contacts were. It was my buddy Jay and his roommate who started dealing drugs and they wanted to cut me in. Needless to say, I'm not friends with those guys anymore. The stalker always seemed to be looming over me whenever something failed in my life or whenever I did anything good. It just feels like there's a shadow that never leaves me. Maybe it really is someone following me or it's just my own mental issues. I have no idea. I tried to go to the police but they laughed in my face. They told me I had no case for harassment and to leave them alone. I even showed them letters that were sent to me saying that someone loved me but they didn't care. After the stalker incident I felt like no one cared about me anymore.

After that debacle and the drug problems, I felt like I had failed everyone and let them down. As far as my physical appearance, I'm over six foot with short black hair and a lean build. I have bright green eyes and a few freckles across my face. I also have my school ring that represents my masters and I wear it on my right ring finger. I always feel a source of pride whenever I look at it. My coworker Kate was really hot. She had long blue hair and blue eyes. She was about my age and worked at the desk next to me. We never talked much but she was always nice to me. She vented to me once about how she caught wind of this amazing story in our area but she didn't have the time to follow up on it. She asked me if I could take over and she would let me have all the credit. It would be a big boost to my career so I agreed to it right away.

She was supposed to do it herself but she had family problems and she couldn't leave their side during this time so that was why she asked me to take over. The story was about a secretive cult that lived in the forest nearby. If I could find proof of them doing ritualistic activities that would make my career and I could write a book about it. She blushed when I said that I would help her with it and she hugged me really tightly while thanking me profusely. If this turned out to be a success then she would also get a boost in her career for turning me onto it.

The Beginning Of The Journey

I PACKED MY SUPPLIES that night and headed out the next morning. I brought a backpack and had enough food and water to last me a few days with some camping supplies. I drove my old pickup truck to the closest forest entrance and began my trek. Kate had given me a map with coordinates as to where the cult might be hiding out from her research. I also found out that they were friendly and nice during the day but that they changed at night and I should find my own place to sleep if I meet up with them. I searched for many days until I finally made it to their home. The forest was hot and damp but my hat and sunglasses did wonders to keep the worst of it off me. There were also tuns of bugs that I didn't want to think too much about when I slept.

When I found their home, I saw about fifty people dancing in suits and ties around a campfire and roasting a giant hog. I slowly approached them and one of them broke off from their dance to come greet me. He told me his name was Derek and that he and his friends have created a civilization out here. They gave up their corporate jobs in order to commune with nature and eat only what god has given them. He greeted me with a handshake and a hug. I took out my notebook and they were very open to answering all of my questions. They told me that they had been living out here for about twenty years and they were always on the move. They may have lived in a tiny hole in the ground with some tents but it was home to them. Derek told me that they lived underground for most of their time but they come out and above for celebrations and to get food. Derek told me how they hunt for wild animals and they eat bugs and plants in order to survive. They also purify their own water and are happy. I asked if I could see the underground and Derek said no. The area wasn't allowed to outsiders and I accepted that.

We spent the rest of the day talking and he gave me some soup made out of the hog that they roasted. It tasted delicious and we drank homemade alcohol and partied throughout the day. By nightfall I felt good and drunk and decided to head back to my campsite. I camped fairly close to here and was looking forward to getting back. The group bid goodbye to me and I headed back. I wouldn't be telling this story if that was all that happened however. I made it back to my tent and slept for hours.

The True Horrors Begin

I WOKE UP IN the middle of the night still feeling drunk and very groggy. I felt like my stomach wanted to tear itself in two and gush out all of my organs and intestines. I felt very sick and I vomited for what felt like an eternity outside of my tent. It was very dark by now but I decided to head back to Derek's camp and see if he was still awake. In my drunken state I had forgotten that I should avoid the area at night. I trekked back and finally found my way after about fifty minutes. I saw the group was dancing around a giant bonfire again but this time they looked different. Derek was standing on a stump overlooking them and he seemed to be preaching a sermon. Each of the other members began to chant hysterically and I couldn't make out what they were saying. Derek also looked monstrous in the light of the campfire. His eyes had taken on a red sheen and it looked like he had devil horns on his head. I felt myself freeze in terror and I knew that I shouldn't linger. Derek led the rest of the group and they all cut their wrists in harmony as blood gushed out. They looked like they were in ecstasy and moaned in a very disturbing manor. I tried to leave but my feet were frozen to the ground. I also saw that someone was being burnt alive in the bonfire and the people were pouring their blood over him. Once the man finally died the group rushed in and gleefully ate him once the fire was put out. This truly was a monstrous cult.

I regained my courage and decided to run. I ran as fast and as far as I could but I must have made too much noise. I heard screaming and the rest of the cultists began to chase me. Derek in particular seemed very agitated about seeing me and I saw that were all holding machetes. I ran and ran until I managed to find the treehouse, I'm currently holed up in. With all of their chanting they can't seem to hear me whispering into this recorder very well. They ran right past the treehouse with their torches and machetes and went farther North into the woods. However, I can still hear them chanting and screaming. I still feel groggy but I feel like I've sobered up. I do wonder if the soup they gave me was drugged or not. I have no clue but that doesn't matter. It doesn't matter if they are monsters or humans; they are dangerous. I can't remember where my campsite or my truck is and I need to try and survive until morning. I see a hole nearby; maybe I can find refuge in there since I don't trust this treehouse to keep me hidden forever honestly.

I slowly climbed down and jumped into the hole. Luckily the hole wasn't that deep and I didn't injure myself in any way. I picked myself up and saw that the hole extended further beyond my reach. I saw a small torch on the ground and with my lighter I was able to see my way. The hole extended increasingly far to the South of me. A part of me wondered if this was the cult's headquarters or not. I knew that this was going to be dangerous but this would also be the story of a lifetime if I could pull this off. I had a small camera with me and I used it to take pictures of everything I saw. I continued down the path and realized that it was a labyrinth down here. There were torches everywhere so I extinguished mine. There were paintings all around of grotesque rituals and people being devoured by bugs. I didn't fall down very far but it feels like a whole other world down here. This part of the home seems abandoned save for the torches and beds. I still had food and water with me and used it sparingly. I walked into one of the nearby rooms and I threw up at the sight. In front of me was a decapitated skeleton hung and used as a home for rats. The bones were caged and I saw a rat peering out from the ribs. I ran out of the room immediately. I could hear chanting coming towards me so I hid under one of the beds. Two of the cultists came in and they both sat on the bed where I was hiding. They were both men. The two men took out what looked like ceremonial knives and stabbed each other one after the other until the one on the left must have fainted from blood loss. The other one cheered saying that they had won and began to slurp up the blood from the other one.

I could feel the blood pouring down onto me through the bed sheets but I muffled my disgust. I couldn't let him know I was here. Eventually he must have heard though since he jerked up and jumped down to look under the bed. I lunged out and grabbed him by the neck. I found a rock nearby and before he could do anything I smashed it into his head over and over again until he fell to the ground. I continued to hit him even as he begged for mercy but I didn't care. I hit and hit until my bloodlust finally felt quenched and I slid down. I began to laugh maniacally and I took gleeful pictures of the sight before me. HAHAHAHAHA, this was going to be perfect for the article. I decided to take some of the blood and put it all over me. I saw other cultists by the fire had blood all over themselves too so I figured this might help me fit in. I calmed myself down and slowly left the room. I passed by many other cultists and they didn't pay me any mind due to the blood. Each room I entered seemed more and more grotesque as cultists had sex with dead bodies and many drew carvings into each other. Screams of pain and delight echoed throughout the chambers and I shuddered. I forced myself to keep going and for some reason they don't seem to notice me talking into this recorder at all. Maybe they just don't care. I kept the recorder close to me and decided to keep whispering in case they could hear me. I didn't want to agitate them in any way. They still looked monstrous to me and I can't explain why. I walked to another chamber and thankfully this one was deserted. I slid down the wall and decided to sleep. I could feel my exhaustion overtaking me. I went down for a nap and turned my recorder off as I slept.

The Depravity of Humanity.

I awoke sometime later with a start. One of the cultists was rifling through my pockets. He seemed to be the only one around. I took my lighter out of my pocket and I burned his face. He writhed in agony but I continued to push the lighter deeper and deeper into his face until he fell to the ground. I then took my hands and pushed against his neck until he snapped. The snap felt very satisfying in my hands. I took pictures of his burned corpse and I figured I could argue self defense. I turned my recorder back on and continued through. It seemed that it was pretty routine that cultists died so they didn't seem to care much if they found new corpses littering the way. I found a machete on the ground and decided to pick it up for protection. The weight of the machete felt strong and firm in my hand. I gave it a few experimental swings and it felt good. I kept the machete at my side and I began to delve even deeper into the caves.

It feels like an entire city lives down here. I go away from the chanting as best I can in order to try to find an exit but who knows how long I'll be down here. The air feels musty down here and it can be hard to breathe at times. I've seen live animals getting skinned down here and humans being branded with hot knives in order to show ownership. I try to avoid those places as best I can. Some of the cultists even eat each other apparently. This place really is strange.

Light In The Darkness

It's like a whole other world exists down here. I see that the cultists even keep dynamite down here for whatever reason. I decide to examine more of the walls and I can get a clearer picture of their history. Apparently twenty years prior, Derek and a small team found this place and decided to make this place their home. They found magical mushrooms that when ingested seemingly gave them control over nature. These tunnels were created by them apparently but the side effects include that they become monstrous at night and they try to hide themselves away from other people during that time. They do eat plants and animals during the day but at night they hunt for humans when the madness reaches its peak and anyone who trespasses on their lands becomes the next sacrifice. If anyone other than the group ingests the mushrooms and are not properly acclimated will become very groggy as if they are drunk. I did drink some of their soup after all, I wonder if I did get drugged. I still can't tell if these people are just crazy or if they really do have control over the earth. It seems like Derek's the leader and there's a hierarchy below him. Derek and some of his more trusted allies seem to have a mark on their wrists that looks like a mix between a star and a cross. I don't understand the significance but it can't mean anything good. I also notice that there aren't any women in the cult at all, or at least none of them seem to live at camp. I wonder where they are or what the rest of the cult does with them? To be honest, I'm not sure if I even want to know anymore. But that is neither here nor there. The dynamite doesn't seem to have any explanation. I wonder if I should use it to blow up these caves. If I did that then they would be trapped down here and no one could escape. But if I did that then how would I even escape? This place is a labyrinth.

I decide to use my machete to make marks on the walls so I can keep track of my progress. I need to avoid Derek like the plague. He and his lieutenants are the only ones who know I'm not supposed to be here. I also see that there's a bunch of gasoline around the place. If I do happen to run into Derek maybe I should try and end them in order to destroy the cult. Or maybe I should just try to get out of here and send others to come down here and purge them all. I don't know what to do just yet. I decide to just keep moving and keep going. Finally, I see what I hope to be an exit. It's a giant door that looms overhead. It's a faded red color with gold plating around that makes the same shape I've been seeing all over the place. I crouch and slowly advance to the door. I peek inside and see that it isn't an exit, it's a gigantic chamber.

I dart inside and close the door behind me. I creep over and I'm horrified to see corpses splayed all over the place. Both cultists and outsiders like me are scattered all around the room in a huge circle. I throw up at the sight and I quiver in fear. How can people do this to each other? I also see more paintings across the walls. There are depictions of women being raped to death and force-fed cockroaches as punishment for defying the group. Many of the paintings seem to be made out of blood and human skin. At the very edge of the room is a dais with a tome on top of it. I go up to the book and I flip through it. The pages are empty except for more depictions of cult activities. The tome also seems to be made of human skin judging by the consistency of it. I jerk my hands away and the tome falls to the ground with a resounding thud. I flinch and stay completely still for a few moments. After waiting I don't hear anything. Nobody seems to be rushing into the room or anything. The thing I do know for sure though, I need to destroy this cult. What happens to me doesn't matter, I just need to destroy this group and make sure they don't hurt anyone else ever again. If this is where Derek and his group come to pray, I can kill them all in one fell swoop. I just need the gasoline and dynamite. I casually run back and see the cult members still are keen on ignoring me for the time being.

I grab all the gasoline I can carry and head back to the altar. No one even bats an eye at my actions and I pour gasoline all over the floor and that bloody book. I also right the book back on its pedestal and continue to pour. I can hear Derek's chanting getting closer so he might be coming to pray soon. I finish up my work with even greater urgency and rush out of the room. I hide nearby and sure enough, Derek and his group file into the room and slam the door shut. I smile inwardly as I rush back to the dynamite, that I stashed close by. The rest of the cult members seem to be going to bed as they are vacating the area by the red door. I creep over to the door and I open it. I see Derek and his men praying by the corpses and books. I pick the dynamite and after lighting it I lob it as far as I can before closing the door. I hear a resounding boom and the door flies off its hinges hitting me square in the back. The smell of fire is the last thing I feel before losing consciousness.

The Last Stand

I awoke with a start to the smell of fire. My back hurts like hell but I don't seem to have any other injuries. I cough as the smoke infests my lungs and I see the door is wedged into the wall next to me. It must have winged me and flew overhead me. I got extremely lucky. I also must have only been out for a few moments as I can see cult members running around in panic. I feel so much anger towards these despicable people. They deserve what they are getting for sure. I pick up the recorder which miraculously managed to survive the blast and head into the chamber with a machete in my hand. I see that each of the members are dead after being burnt except for Derek. Derek's on the ground crying out in pain as he lies knocked out with the book in his hands and the podium on his back. It's clear his back is broken and he isn't going anywhere anytime soon. I go up to Derek and I pull his head up to me as I crouch onto the ground. I force him look at me as I tell him that I've won.

His eyes widen as I slash his throat open with my machete and I leave him to bleed out. I also take the book he's holding and I force the machete through the pages as the book gets destroyed. I then throw it into the fire and force him to watch as everything he built was destroyed by me. His eyes close for the last time and then for good measure I stomp his head in. He got what he deserved for sure. I pick up the machete I discarded and walk out of the room. I slash at the hamstrings of every cult member I see and they fall to their knees before I kill them. I methodically kill each and every member I see. They were all weak and they look good in red. I see right by the remains of the red door a corpse of someone who doesn't matter anymore. Just another nameless victim of this damn cult. I go over to him and close his eyes out of respect. He deserved better. I flick the blood off my blade and turn to leave. Many of the cultists are burning to death or are in too much panic that they end up running straight into their own machetes or walls and getting crushed to death.

I find my way to an exit and crawl up the ladder and make my way outside. I find a shovel nearby and decide to dig as much as I can to seal up this exit. After many hours I finish and nobody was able to follow me up here. I head back to the campsite and gather up my belongings and head out of there. My black hair's really messy from the ordeal. I pick up my phone and call the police and tip them off to one of the holes I didn't seal up. I drop the recorder and run off into the night.

Where Is Felix?

A MONTH HAS PASSED since the recorder was found and the police investigated the scene. After listening to the recording, it's clear that they are the ramblings of a mad man as he doesn't make any sense. We found the cult and there are many bodies. There are also many bodies buried under the ground with no explanation of how they died. Many of them died from suffocation but others are unknown. A specific body was found crushed by a giant red door. We have no idea who this man is as his teeth have been bashed in and his face has been burned beyond recognition. We dragged him out and decided that he will just be another nameless victim among the bodies. It seems though that many people were able to escape though as there are signs of people digging their way out and beyond the borders of the forest. If they really did have control over the earth then that would be a terrifying thought indeed. Kate's here with me, the deputy police chief of Illinois. She is our liaison with the local paper that was investigating rumors of this cult. She told me that she sent her cute coworker here in order to help her since she had to deal with apartment renovations and couldn't cover this story until much later. I also see that she has a peculiar tattoo on her wrist. It looks like a mix between a star and a cross but I can't be sure. She caught me staring and told me that it was the mark of a family heirloom. I didn't question it and walked away. I wish we could find Felix Fernandez and thank him for his help. We don't condone the murders and he will be charged for them, but at least many of the victims of this cult can rest in peace. This is the deputy police chief singing off.

With a flash the television turned off as a man of unknown origin clambered around his apartment. He muses about how he was able to get out of the cult. Felix really screwed him over by unintentionally bringing him there in the first place. All Connor wanted to do was follow Felix around but then he had to watch him die by the hands of the door.

Connor always loved Felix and even matched his physical appearance to him and even mimicked his voice perfectly. Once Connor was sure that he died he had to make sure that Felix's legacy wasn't tainted. He lived as a nobody and that was how he would die. Connor would take over his identity in time but for now, he would protect that of his love. Felix died alone and Connor only felt hatred towards him for not having his love returned. That pesky cult managed to escape though. I can hear strange rustling from below the floor of my apartment. I wonder if they could be digging upwards in order to get to me. Who knows? Two figures floated above the apartment and one of them used their magic to halt the digging. Simon looked towards Ezekiel and said "we can use magic to help this poor man and avenge the young man who lost his life tragically. How should we do it?" I felt lost in thought until I decided "why don't we resurrect Felix and then erase this man's memories and give him a new life away from all this? We can also use our magic to get rid of the cult or at least put them somewhere where they can't hurt anyone else," I said softly. Simon smiled and nodded. He used the power of the stone in order to make it so. "Now let's look at a tale of vengeance and heartbreak," said Simon. Me and Simon left this universe and went to another one where he could show me what I needed to see.

The Tale Of Jamie And Tony

Have you ever felt your life flash before your eyes? No, just me then. As I lay here dying and my ex-friend is about to perform surgery on my eyes, I can't help but think of how I got in this predicament. My name is Tony and I used to be best friends with a girl named Jamie. She and I were as thick as thieves growing up and that relationship bled into adulthood. We always hung out whenever she or I was back home from our respective universities and we always went on walks and played videogames together. We had lots of fun and she quickly became someone that I could tell everything to. Growing up, I had a normal childhood but I had lots of mental health issues. Mostly anxiety and depression and they didn't help me feel good about myself. Jamie was always there for me and she understood what I was dealing with. She had her own issues and I always did everything I could to help her with hers. We even talked about deeply personal things that nobody else knew about and we were bonded for life...or so I thought.

She had dealt with many negative influences in her life and she had even been stalked in the past. I always was extra careful in order to make sure that I never became one of those people. I was always there for her and I did everything I could not to burden her with my problems. But it got to the point where I was asking her for so many things and I wasn't feeling secure in my friendship with her anymore. She also used to imply that I was like her stalker before immediately backpedaling and telling me I was nothing like them. I began to develop a complex about myself and felt insecure about my friendships and started wondering if I was a burden to them or not. Many of my friends told me I wasn't but some of them did tell me I was or that they never saw me as a friend. That really hurt and Jamie didn't comfort me much in those situations. She said that she actually agreed with what they were saying but wouldn't have said it like that. That hurt more than anything else that my former friends ever told me. After that I swore that I would better myself.

I began to focus more on myself and less on Jamie. Jamie and I still talked but I slowly began to make excuses about why I couldn't hang out as much. She also told me that she didn't want to rely on anyone or have anyone rely on her too heavily as she never liked that. That was always confusing as sometimes when I showed signs of pulling away, she would tell me that I can tell her anything but then when I got comfortable with her; she would give me signs that I shouldn't rely on her as significantly. This contrast became very confusing for me and I decided that I wanted to comfort myself more and not rely on her as much. I started to become more comfortable talking with my parents and I found that after much time alone I started to not doubt my relationships as much. It sometimes felt like a switch was flipped and I wasn't worrying as much about that specific part.

Me and Jamie slowly drifted apart on my end but with her she always kept talking to me even when I said I needed space. I would say that I was going off the grid for a few days or that I needed to destress but she kept on texting me constantly. I initially brushed her off kindly but then it became so much worse. I began to feel constricted and suffocated by her and it felt like she didn't want me to move on with my own life. It felt like she wanted me to be dependent on her but not too dependent or else she would abandon me. It was very hard and the last time she came over to play videogames she stressed me out so much that I began to feel sick. She asked if I was okay but she never took the hint that I wanted her to leave and she kept on rearranging my Legos and ripping my controller out of my hand so she could have a turn playing some stupid game she ruined for me.

I hit my breaking point in time and I told her over text to leave me alone and that she hurt me too deeply. She continued to still try and text me until I finally gave up and blocked her. When I saw her in person, she was really remorseful and fell to her knees begging for my forgiveness. I rejected her and then told her everything she did wrong and how I felt manipulated by her for years and how she always used her struggles as an excuse while trying to pressure me into things like therapy and medication which I was not comfortable with at the time and am still not. I understand that that stuff can be helpful but it's not fair to push that onto me. And if she was so good with her struggles then she wouldn't be skipping out on work constantly for sick days and would be able to do more instead of just bemoaning that she can't do anything she wants while getting to do every single thing she wants. I'm still angry at everything she did to me and how much pain she caused me. When I saw her next in person, she was quite mean to me. She clearly didn't want anything to do with me and I felt the air turn cold. When I came into her bookstore; she kept complaining at how she had to work on her days off and she charged me extra for the books I wanted out of spite. It was unfair but they were books I really wanted so I paid the exorbitant charges and I left. I hadn't seen her since for a long time. I admit, my life without her was extremely hard and difficult.

I spent many nights crying out in despair at the friendship I had gotten rid of and I wanted the good days to come back. I realized though that the good days were long gone with her and that I could have them again with other people. I began to heal slowly and it had been two years since I had seen her last. Despite that though, I think she continued to try and contact me for a long time afterward. I got letters claiming to love me and that I should take her back. I knew it was her but there wasn't much I could do about it as the letters weren't constant or threatening. Once I got a Facebook friend request from someone claiming to be my uncle and I'm certain that it was Jamie in disguise trying to befriend me on my birthday so she could stalk me. I rejected the request and blocked the user after I confirmed that my uncle was not sending me a friend request. She even told people that she was worried about me and that I would hurt myself when I was never in any state to do such a thing. I began to feel frustrated at her attempts to get attention and to bring me back to her. I sent her a strongly worded text to leave me alone after unblocking her and then re-blocking her once again in order to get some peace. There were times I felt someone following me at night but I couldn't prove any of it. In the past she also used to constantly criticize my writing when I never wanted that. I had very specific requests from her when she read my writing but she never adhered to any of them. I don't even think she cared about her family at all. She always talked badly about them and apparently told them to fuck off pretty routinely. She was also a great artist and writer and she even wrote a book.

After the book was finished, she constantly talked to me about it and bragged about the book. It was a big deal and I was proud of her initially, but it wasn't that big of a deal to warrant such a reaction. Even when we weren't friends anymore, she would send me links to how well her book was doing, as if I wanted to see those. She never cared about my time and always asked for favors but never considered that I was in the middle of schoolwork at the time or was busy doing other things. This all culminated in last night. I spent my time drinking with friends and I had told them I thought I had a stalker. They laughed and agreed to comfort me if anything happened again. After many hours and drinks, I left the bar alone and walked home. The next thing I remembered was feeling a strange sense of dread that overtook my entire body. The feeling increased until I suddenly blacked out and hit my head on the pavement with a heavy thud. I woke up to see Jamie fiddling with tools as I laid tied up to a gurney. She took out a scalpel and began to carve out my eyes and scooped them out. The pain I felt was excruciating to say the least as I screamed in pure agony. I felt pure white flashes go across my body as a white-hot ripped throughout my entire body in waves of pain. She slowly pried my eyes out until she finally ripped them out and I was completely blind. She kept muttering about revenge and how much I never appreciated her. She then fed me my eyes and forced me to chew them and swallow them. I was terrified but did as she asked. The eyes were disgusting and I vomited upwards and began to choke on my own puke. She pushed me to my side so I could puke it out and the bile that built up in my throat began to subside after I puked everything up.

She took her scalpel and caressed my cheeks lightly before finally deciding to kill me. Before everything went black, she took a crowbar and smashed it against my head in one swift motion. The impact felt very painful but then there was silence. I thought that I was finally dead and that I could rest in peace. But then I realized I had been moved somewhere else. I don't know where I am but I know that me and Jamie aren't home anymore. I wonder if Jamie joined that digging cult that has been digging across the U.S. I will never know, oh wait. Shit, I can hear her coming back from wherever she went to. I'm totally screwed if she catches me. If there's anyone out there, please help me!

Jamie's response:

So, I don't know how this got posted on here but I need to clear up a few things and then punish Tony for allowing the world to try and take him away from me again. To start, me and Tony were cousins but not by blood. I was adopted and I was in love with him. He and I were so close and I thought he must have loved me too. He always laughed at my antics and always enjoyed my company even if I was breaching his boundaries. I admit I sometimes took things too far when we were together, but I loved him and nobody could ever change that. I dealt with stalkers in the past and I gently told him if he was getting too clingy with me and he took it personally for some reason. I still loved him regardless. Eventually he began to pull away from me and I couldn't have that. I told him over and over that he could come to me with everything while also telling him not to do that. Obviously, that was my way of telling him I loved him but I guess he never got that. Anyway, I tried to talk to him and see if he was okay but he always ignored me or told me he needed space. I even told him I respected his boundaries while texting him but he snapped and told me to leave him alone. I did everything I could to get him to love me but he rejected all of my attempts. When he got sick when we were hanging out one night I asked him if he was okay while stealing his controller so I could play Elden Ring while he retched in the background. I wanted to show him that I loved his favourite game as much as I loved him.

I even played hard to get by charging him extra for a book at my store. I sent him letters constantly to show my affection and I even made a fake account based on my dad in order to wish him a happy birthday until he blocked that account as well. I always gave him unwanted criticism on his writing in order to make it better and I always told him how to play games better so that it would be a better experience for both of us. And I wanted his friends to think of him as a burden so he and I would be alone together. I also wanted him to feel close to only me and that I could abandon him at any moment when in reality I never would. This all culminated into the night I made him mine. I always hated his friends and one night he went out with them to a bar. He decided to walk home while they decided to get a taxi home. The taxi driver never even noticed me cutting his brake lines and causing the three of them to crash in a blaze of glory. They all died and then I pursued my love, Tony. I had been stalking, no following Tony in order to make sure he got home safely. After all, there are lots of crazy people out there and I can't let any of them steal my love from me. I finally found him again and with my crowbar I hit him hard in the head to knock him out.

He was then brought to my warehouse where I wanted to teach him a lesson. I wanted him to only love me so I cut out his eyes in order to show my devotion. He then ate them in order to prove his love for me which he did greedily. He truly loved me. After I whispered my love for him again, I decided to end his suffering with a final blow to the head. He survived but in a vegetative state. I don't know how he managed to recover enough to post this on reddit of all places but I'll deal with him in time. Now, I'm finally living my best life with him by my side. He and I watch tv in my apartment while we wear funny outfits all day long. I spoon feed him the meals I make and while he may not say much, I can see how much he loves me as he and I spend many nights alone in our apartment as I finally got my ultimate wish. He finally loved me and he and I can even have children finally! He will never leave my side again and if the world ever tries to again, I will cut off his limbs so that he may be my doll forever. I love him so much and nobody will ever find us! I will protect him with my life and if he ever falls out of love with me again, I know that it was the fault of the world; nothing I did of course. I think I'll delete this post soon after; I don't want anyone to find out where we are located!

Me and Simon looked at this despicable scene and I felt pity for Tony. He didn't deserve any of this at all. Simon looked to me for guidance. I advised him to lock Jamie up for everything she did and to reform Tony's face and body so he could have his life back. Simon agreed and we set off to another universe.

The Tragic Misadventures Of Mason And John

I don't know where to begin, my name is Mason and I think I'm going crazy. I've been having these really weird dreams but I can't explain any of them. I'm 16 and I've got a best friend Named John. I dream that I live in Medieval times with John as my best friend and boyfriend for some reason even though I'm not gay. He and I got drafted into a magical war with spells and swords and in that dream, I killed my childhood bully when he tried to kill me and John in the barracks. My therapist tells me that maybe I'm dealing with some unresolved feelings towards John and my bully but I don't know for sure. All I know is that I wake up some days with blood on my hands and I can't explain that. Some of my classmates look at me like I'm psychotic and they run away from me. My teachers always give me the highest grades even though I don't do very well in my classes. The only people who treat me normally are my parents, and John. The bully still treats me like crap but that hasn't changed at all which I actually appreciate. I do see that he has more bruises along his face sometimes but I wonder what's going on with him lately. In the end it doesn't matter. It's not my problem. My therapist encouraged me to write this all down so as to get my thoughts in order and to help me work through some of my feelings. I wish the dreams would stop.

I had another dream. I dreamt that I could use flame spells and I burned a soldier on the battlefield. They ended up hurting me pretty badly across my eye. I woke up the next morning with a bad cut across my eye and one of my classmates ended up in the ER for third degree burns across his face. He isn't in any position to speak about what happened to him. I don't know what the hell is happening to me. Did I hurt that poor student? I feel tempted to go check on him but if I did hurt him, I don't know if I can face that. I've tried telling my therapist this stuff but she doesn't believe there's anything wrong with me and my parents are just happy I'm talking to her when needed. I don't know what to do. Nobody seems to believe that I could do anything like this. Either everyone just ignores what's going on or they avoid me like the plague but nobody is telling me anything! I just wish I knew what was happening to me! Will update if anything else happens to me but I don't know if I can keep doing this anymore.

John is dead. I had another dream where I stabbed someone seven times with a sword and the next morning John was found dead in his home stabbed to death with a kitchen knife. He was stabbed seven times. I tried to tell my therapist that I killed my best friend and that I need to be locked up but she wouldn't have it. She told me that I was perfectly fine and that there was nothing wrong with me in any capacity. I finally snapped and took a knife from my kitchen and went to school. I went right up to the bully and stabbed him in the abdomen. It wasn't meant to kill him but it injured him really badly. The police finally got involved and they sent me to a psychiatric institution to be monitored. I told them everything but still the doctors didn't believe me. They agreed to keep me under surveillance for 72 hours but they told me I could go home afterwards. I can't believe any of this! I just want to rot in prison for what I've done. The poor kid that got burned died from his wounds today as well. No statement was given regarding his death. I know that I'm responsible but I can't prove it. I need to kill myself. It's the only way to end this nightmare. As soon as I'm released, I'm going to end my own life and finally be free. I can't take the torment anymore; the voices are so intense and the constant waking up with cuts and blood on my fingers is too much to bear. If anyone finds this, know that I am so sorry. Mom, dad, I wish I was a better son for you guys.

Sincerely, Mason

Breaking News!

Local student Mason Thompson was found dead in his apartment after slashing his own wrists with a kitchen knife and setting himself on fire with a blowtorch. Local citizens mourn the loss of a troubled young man and his parents have requested privacy during this trying time.

Ha, ha-ha, hahahaha. Hi everyone, this is John taking over. I can't believe it worked. My psychology and dream analysis classes really paid off and Mason finally killed himself.

I was the orchestrator of all the events leading to his demise. I spread rumors that he was violent and told the rest of the students to stay away from him. I also blackmailed his teachers into pretending to be afraid of him and giving him the best grades despite being a failing student. I also manipulated his dreams by whispering into his ears at night in order to dream more and have more violent outbursts. I smeared my own blood on his fingertips at night and anyone he dreamed of killing I killed them first. That boy who got burned to death, I broke into his house and messed with his oven so he'd catch on fire the next time he tried to cook something. Everyone blamed it on a blowtorch since I repaired the oven soon after but nobody suspected a thing. Now I can live my life in peace while Mason burns in hell. HAHAHAHAHA. I even faked my own death in order to screw with him further.

Simon took over when he saw my discomfort and decided to destroy John's reputation while bringing Mason back to life and clearing his name. All of these instances happened in less than a second and Simon felt it was important for me to understand the effects we could have on the world and the people in them and to try to undo Jeb and Nathaneil's influence and chaos on the worlds. He also wanted to introduce me to Edward before we met up but he ran off before we could meet.

Worlds Collide

We exited the portal and I saw a world devastated by destruction. I think this is supposed to be Cuba but I can't be sure. I saw a giant humanoid creature who looked to be over fifty feet tall and was purple. It had many faces and looked gooey. It's really hard to describe such a monstrosity but I'll do my best. The figure had two mouths with jagged sharp teeth and terrifyingly large red eyes. The figure looked disfigured in many ways but very strong. The eyes also glowed and the creature had a gigantic laser beam that devastated buildings and ships. It also used its hands to swat away any aircrafts that attempted to get close and its body was increasingly resistant to explosive damage or gun shots. The creature also had a gigantic sword made of blood that devastated anything it slashed against. Clearly this was a world on the brink of destruction and it sounds like this creature has destroyed many other worlds as well according to that Vampire. Simon turned to me and said "we need help. I'm going to go find allies, you make some friends with the locals and see if we can get any aid from them. There's a village nearby, maybe they will offer some aid to you." I nodded and Simon teleported away.

It was just me now. I went to the village and I ran so hard I passed out from exhaustion at the village gates. The last thing I saw was someone reaching over and grabbing me. I woke up in a hut and saw a man making some food. "You're awake, good. I made this for you." He gave me some delicious mushroom soup. The man turned out to be a scholar named Edward who had come here trying to find out information about the creature that's destroying everything. He tried to enlist a hero from his world to come help us but he was busy on an adventure of his own and couldn't spare the manpower. The land he had come from was far away and if we both survived, he wanted me to tell him my side of the story so that he could create a complete historical account of events. I agreed and we became friends. He told me that there were some people hiding out in root cellars nearby that might be able to help. There were twenty of them and they had guns and swords. Edward also told me that the creature really is Jeb and Nathaniel merged into one gigantic creature. After their respective deaths they found each other in death and their mutual hatred bonded them together and this monstrosity was created. Nothing so far has been able to damage them but hopefully something will work.

I went to the root cellar with Edward and officially met and joined this world's Resistance. Our numbers may be small but I believe that together we could make some sort of difference. I spent more time with them training in the use of firearms and I taught them many of my sword techniques. After many weeks of training and hiding out from the creature's blasts; Simon returned with many allies and he introduced them to all of us. There were his friends Christine, Stacy, and James. Then there was Aaron and Darwin. Aaron and Darwin came from the same universe where both were tortured and murdered in their own respective timelines. But Simon managed to intervene and save them both while separating them after Damian was defeated. Simon's friends also looked super happy to see him and I could tell their bond was strong.

There wasn't many of us but I felt even more confident that we could do this now. Edward didn't have any powers available to him in this world but he resolved to fight with us with his special sword that he said a friend gave to him when they went on an adventure together. Edward promised to tell me that tale as well sometime. Simon also told me about how he got everyone to come with him. For Darwin, he was about to be executed by Nathaniel's cronies when Simon intervened and saved him. Darwin was put on ice and in stasis for a hundred years. Darwin also had many deep-seated issues but working with Simon he was able to deal with some of them. Aaron on the other hand wasn't as lucky. Aaron was murdered by Nathaniel's father and Simon secretly merged him and Darwin together in order to effectively fight him off. As for Simon's friends; the moment he asked them for help they eagerly accepted and went with him. They had also forgiven Simon for everything and Simon had redeemed himself. Apparently, Jeb and Nathaniel had only just started destroying universes and were planning on saving the ones with us as the last ones.

Whenever Simon would save a universe, Jeb and Nathaniel would destroy them as soon as he was finished and had left. Simon was devastated when he found that out but he knew that with the power of the stone he could bring them all back even if it killed him. Simon also used the stone to enhance my teleportation power so that I could fly and he enchanted the obsidian dagger into an obsidian sword which suited me better in the long run as I always preferred them. Daggers were easier to wield in the other world but here swords and other weapons were significantly better. Me and the Resistance had spent weeks running between root cellars in order to dodge Jeb and Nathaniel. Now the time had come for us to stand and fight. Edward was given super strength and the Resistance fighters were each given super strength, super speed, and much more powerful versions of their swords and guns to hopefully deal damage against Jeb and Nathaniel from both up close and at a distance. We raced out of the root cellar and confronted the enemy as they aimed their laser at us. We all dodged at the last second and Simon and his friends flew off to meet them head on. I decided to go with them and flew with them while Edward stayed behind and used his sword to shoot laser beams at the monster.

The five of us moved as one and it was as if I had fought alongside these people before. I couldn't explain it but I felt a kinship with them. We flew and the beast slashed at us with his gigantic claws. Apparently, they had also gone by Ricky and many other aliases as they destroyed universes. Their form had also changed depending on the situation. Whatever they went by now, they were going to die. Stacy used her bow and shot many golden arrows into them but they bounced off harmlessly. The air smelt like blood and death and seeing the arrows fail was not looking good. We tried many different attacks and Simon used every magic spell he could think of but nothing worked. Jeb and Nathaniel laughed maniacally as one terrifying entity as our attempts failed and even taunted us by giving us the finger. I decided to fly forward and I dodged many of his attacks. I went to his face and I stabbed him right in his left eye.

The eye exploded and Jeb and Nathaniel howled in agony. I then realized that every attack we laned on him were on either his arms or his body but not his face. I doubled back to the others and they made good use of that information. Stacy repositioned and aimed her arrows at his mouth and the others aimed their melee attacks at his eyes and face. Finally, we were making progress and the creature was bleeding profusely. Both of their eyes were gone and they had no more teeth. The creature eventually lost its footing and fell to their knees as they stared unseeing up towards the sky. The image of the five of us converging on him must have been terrifying to say the least. The other Resistance fighters weren't doing nothing during all of this. They had been shooting him and slashing at his feet in order to find weak points. Some of the fighters got crushed and were killed but most made it out alive. The Resistance fighters had made an agreement with Simon that if they were killed in the line of battle they didn't want to be brought back. They wanted to rest in peace and Simon agreed and consented to their wishes despite it killing him inside. Simon mourned the loss of every person he fought with and every innocent he couldn't protect.

I flew down into Jeb and Nathaniel's mouth and went inside him. His body was long and seemingly endless but I used my sword and cut him open from the inside. I killed the monster and pulled both Jeb and Nathaniel from the beast and brought them into the light. The two fell to the ground in shock as they regained some of their faculties. All of the surviving fighters converged on the two of them and murdered them as a lynch mob. By the time they were done, there was nothing left to bury or burn. The threat of Jeb and Nathaniel had finally been decimated. After that we celebrated by drinking all night before Simon used the power of the stone to bring every universe back to the way it was. Unfortunately, Simon's use of the power had reduced him to atoms and he ceased to exist. He had scattered to the wind from old age and through overuse of the power. The stone also cracked and separated into pieces so small that they looked like grains of sand. The stone couldn't be fixed no matter what we tried. No one cried harder at the funeral than Christine and James. They both missed Simon so much. Me and the others cried as well as we missed our friend. I believe there's a way to bring him back and I won't rest until I do. Edward returned to his office in order to hear our accounts of the story and was more than willing to hear us all out. Edward may have cared about getting our stories to publish but he truly cared about each of us and wanted to honor us with his stories.

As all of this was going on Jeb had actually managed to use the last of his strength to transport his soul into the office of a chronicler and offered to tell his story just before he died. The chronicler agreed and it ended up being Edward. Jeb decided to tell his story from the beginning but of course I didn't know about this at the time. I later found his journals and decided to read them with Edward's permission. I couldn't imagine what Jeb had to say. I decided to read this at Jake's grave since I figured that any words that Jeb had to say should be shared with his dead son. Jake deserved that at least.

The Early Years

For anyone reading this I'm sure that you despise me and the things I did. Especially the things I did to Jake and James. For those who don't know me my name is Dr. Jeb Winter-Fields and I'm a scientist and doctor. I've also been a warlord, zombie king, alien master, and even a soldier. I also had tenure at Lakehead University before James ruined that for me. My tale is long and sordid but overall, I have lived a very accomplished life. I do wish however that I managed to achieve my dream of bringing world peace to everyone. I was born in ancient Egypt and lived during the 1400s BCE. My family lived in extreme poverty while the royals lived with wealth. I used to look at the palaces and rich homes with looks of envy and hatred. I wanted those homes for myself and from a young age I had a taste for power and money. However, despite these shortcomings I always managed to keep my honesty and good-natured politeness. My parents loved me dearly and I them. My mother and father worked the fields and did significant physical labor. They worked eighteen hours a day and barely had time to sleep.

My parents were watched constantly by the elite who would eat fresh grapes in their villas while we barely got enough to survive. My parents saw many workers become shamed and were punished for being poor and not working fast enough. There were also many workers who disappeared and never came back before being replaced with other workers who looked just as broken and sad as the rest of us. I even had to work the fields as well but my parents managed to get me out of that until I was slightly older. Despite these hardships I had friends and I had a childhood. My parents would celebrate every milestone with me that they could and I always received fresh food on my birthday. It was a luxury but my parents always saved and scrimped in order to make it happen every single year.

I loved my parents so much but unfortunately, they weren't able to stay with me forever. Eventually they became very sick. I don't know exactly what destroyed them but their faces became disfigured with boils and puss all over them and they lost the ability to move and function. Eventually they just stopped completely and their eyes became lifeless. I held both of their hands while they died and they lost the ability to speak long before they finally passed. I knew they loved me though and I gave into my grief. I screamed out in agony for many hours as tears streamed down my face. I didn't move for several hours and I cried silently for days. Eventually I had to go back to work so I could eat. I was twelve when they died and then I had to manage the household by myself.

I worked tirelessly in the fields as slave drivers whipped at me to go faster. Luckily, I was never shamed for not working hard enough but the conditions were deplorable. I admit that I wanted to kill myself in order to be reunited with my parents, but I was too afraid to do it. I was afraid that I would be sent to hell. I believed heavily in the gods during my childhood and I prayed to them everyday in order to find relief and to wish for better conditions for my household. When I was sixteen, I had met a travelling swordsman who would travel through town every month in order to teach the royals sword fighting and other methods in order to teach them how to defend themselves. The royals were seen as deities but they were human as well just like the rest of us. It took me a long time before I realized they were mortal just like me. I always hated the royals but the swordsman was a good guy who understood how the world really worked and he took pity on me. He was paid very well for his services and he often gave me extra food and even trained me how to use a sword for free whenever he was in town. I would always meet him in the fields outside of town where no one would be at night and we could train in secret.

I spent two years training with him and eventually I became competent enough to have my own sword. I kept the sword in my house in secret because if the army knew I was skilled with a sword I would have been drafted into the army for sure. They were looking for able bodied men capable of fighting against the other nations. Egypt was very rich and powerful in many ways but they were still at war with many other countries. Egypt also had widespread poverty for the general public and we were ignored except to get out quotas up. After two more years of hiding my swordsman talents I was finally caught training with my master in the fields after dark. Someone had seen me out there and had ratted me out. Me and my master were both arrested. He was let go because of his status as being a protected tutor to the royals. He looked at me with pure pity as I was thrown into prison for training in secret and for hiding my talents.

I spent two more years in prison and I was forced into the army at age twenty-two. I fought in the infantry at first but due to my swordsman talents I was drafted into the elite corps soon after. The military hardened me and I became even more jaded and hateful towards the monarchy. I spent meany years fighting for the royals and I slowly gained their trust. I was soon honored and was given the rank of bodyguard to the Pharoah and his family. I don't want to say who they were but they treated me like garbage. They would spit at me and stomp on my foot in order to see if I would react. I didn't but they kept on trying. On the bright side I got to see my master even more since he stayed at the palace with me and we would chat long into the night on our days off. My pay was better but I was still a slave to the royals. I wanted out and my master felt for me. He got to travel all across the country teaching swordsmanship to the elite and wealthy but I was forced to stay here permanently.

When I turned twenty-six of still being the Pharoah's bodyguard I overheard some very troubling things. I found out that it was in fact my master who had ratted me out in exchange for gold and a brand-new sword made of the finest metals. He also received a golden sword as a bonus for getting me drafted into the army. I think on some level he felt bad for ratting me out but his greed overtook his affection for me. I thought I was like a son to him but apparently not. On my next day off I managed to see him again and we had a long chat. I confronted him about his betrayal and he admitted to everything. He didn't even seem sorry. He was happy I survived but the payout was more than worth it. He also said that he had his own family to look after and that he would do it again every time if given the opportunity. Sweat started to rush down my face as my heart began to beat rapidly.

I didn't even notice what I was doing until I managed to pick up my sword and thrust it into him. He deftly blocked with his sword and threw me to the ground. He held the sword to my neck and whispered that I was finished. He called for the guards and they surrounded us. They grabbed me by the neck and dragged me to prison once again. I was given moldy bread and I ended up having to eat rats and drinking my own piss in order to survive. The guards gave us water but it wasn't fresh and was probably contaminated in some way. More often than not I chose not to drink it. After many years in prison, I managed to craft a crude lockpick and I used it to unlock my doors. I had significant training with the military so I knew exactly how they fight. I cornered one of the guards and managed to choke the life out of him. That was the first time I had killed one of my comrades before but I had to get out of here. I took his sword and ran out of the prison.

There were many guards but I used my advanced training in order to evade them all. I knew that I had to get out of Egypt for the time being. I ran out of the prisons and left the main city behind before making my way to Rome.

Rome was a safe haven for me and I was free to live my life. I rebranded myself as a doctor after going to school in Rome for many years. By the time I was thirty-five I had managed to become a full doctor and was even more experienced with a sword. I even met a beautiful woman who became my wife. A strong part of me wanted to return to Egypt in order to get my revenge but another part of me wanted to enjoy my quiet life in Rome with my wife. We had two children and I loved them dearly. Unfortunately, my wife and children were killed by the same sickness that killed my parents. I had lots of money due to being a doctor but even with my medical knowledge I couldn't save them. I still don't even know what killed them. My wife urged me to live in peace just before she died but my heart was filled with grief and anger towards the world. I soon realized that people from Egypt had come from Rome and infected them. For some reason I seem to be immune from it. I saw three sick people shambling around the town at night so I decided to follow them. I haven't used a sword in a fight to the death in over a decade but I wasn't rusty by any means. I followed the three men and when they were walking in a nearby alley to sleep, I ran up to them and attacked them before they could even think twice. I killed the first one with a stab to the heart and then I decapacitated the second one before thrusting my sword into the final guy's mouth. Blood got everywhere and some of it even got into my mouth. I spit the blood out in his face out of spite.

The look he gave me was one of shock before the life left his eyes. My rage hadn't dissipated even a little and I felt truly hateful for the people of Egypt. It mattered not to me that they were innocent or that them being poor and sick wasn't their fault; the fact that they had invaded my home in Rome was enough to make me go crazy with rage. I was never caught for the murders and my life went on as normal despite my family being dead. I buried them and mourned them privately, but publicly I continued to be a doctor and I researched that infernal disease that claimed every family member I ever had. I also heard that in Rome there existed a sacred spring that could cure any ailment. I looked into it further and realized that it must exist beneath a hidden temple. I traveled all throughout Italy until I finally found it under the water. I swam as deep as I could until I managed to find the temple. My lungs were on fire by the time I was able to re-emerge form the water and into the temple but the results were more than worth it.

I found the temple entrance and I managed to crawl into it easily. I went inside and found that the entire inside was completely separated from the water and that I could breathe easily in there. I had never seen anything so magnificent. I also began to cough and realized I still had sea water in my lungs. After expelling it I began to feel a lot better. I explored the temple and saw that it was filled all sorts of traps like spike walls and areas that would fill with water until you drowned. I barely managed to evade them all but I still felt very out of my element. I also had prayed to many of the Roman gods and realized they were essentially the same as the Egyptian gods, just different names. I don't know which one is true but I do know that if the gods did exist or at least cared about humanity then they wouldn't have made my family suffer so much hardship. They also wouldn't have taken them from me! I hate the gods! What have they done for people like me? Nothing! They have just left me and my family to suffer while the rich and elite get to live their lives free from all of this suffering. I continued to explore the temple and my burning hatred for everything managed to keep me going. I find I'm still coughing but all the sea water has been expelled from me. What was going on? I also began to notice that boils were forming over my face...oh no. I've gotten the same sickness that took my family from me???!!! This is bad. I need to find the mystical spring or else I will surely die here.

When my wife was alive, I spent time traveling in Greece with her as well looking for a cure to that awful disease that ripped my parents away from me. I couldn't find anything but I had a lovely time with my wife before we decided to settle down in Rome and build our family there. Finally, after hours of searching I managed to find the spring. My movement has also become more and more stunted and I fear that the disease is taking my life force away from me. Eventually I dropped to my knees and crawled towards the spring. I begged to any gods that were listening to cure me of my ailment and to help me get revenge on my former master and the people of Egypt. As I collapsed from my illness and the spring water began to enter me, I felt a warm and pleasant feeling spreading through me. I managed to look up and saw that the spring was glowing. The boils on my face began to disappear and my weak limbs began to feel stronger than ever. I stood up and thanked the gods in reverence as tears streamed down my face. I continued to pray when I heard a voice inside of my head.

The voice said that I would become its vessel and that it would give me all that I want in exchange for my mind and soul. Before I could protest black smoke entered my mouth and began to choke me. I fell to my knees in agony as the smoke spread throughout my entire body. I immediately knew what had happened to me as the smoke dissipated. Whatever god answered my prayer granted me a near form of immortality. I instantly felt like I was twenty again and I knew that I aged much slower than the average person. I also had this need to start finding power and gain my revenge. The desires were almost overpowering but I managed to keep them at bay as I left the temple. I still wanted to live my life and take revenge sometime but not right away.

I lived for many years before returning to Egypt and taking revenge on my old master. I found him teaching another acolyte in the same fields where I was first taught and I ran him through before disappearing once again. The acolyte fell to his knees in sadness as his master died from his injuries and died in complete shock at the phantom that managed to best him. The acolyte would be better off now without the poisonous tactics of his master. I took the boy under my wing and he swore revenge against me for killing his master. I told him he was welcome to try. I decided to train him and I shared with him a hint of my power so he could live for many years longer than he should have been able to. I decided not to take revenge on Egypt yet despite the voice urging me to. I ended up settling down in Egypt for many years and had many wives but no children. Having the love of family managed to keep me grounded and I was able to cure many diseases that affected the people of the world but not the one that riddled my body so long ago.

Me and my protégé continued to train and eventually I managed to warp and twist his mind into adoring me and wanting to worship me as his master. He became loyal to me and me alone and he even killed his original family at my orders. His name was Martin. Eventually I had a new wife and I even had a son. His name was Jake and he was the light of my life. However, the voice inside my head warned me to kill him right away. The voice was afraid of him taking my power away from me and killing me. I almost gave in to murder before deciding to leave him be. He was just an infant and didn't deserve to die for that. I left him and his mother in order to find more power in Egypt. I eventually found an ancient army that was loyal to me and me alone and they became my subordinates. Basilisk was a problem right from the beginning but he eventually began to fall in line.

I also heard rumors of the Stone of Legends being in King Tut's possession. I knew that this stone was what my god wanted and urged me to locate it. I showed up as a doctor and managed to persuade the Pharoah in order to let me inside the palace. I had no clue about Rathos until the last second but he became a significant thorn in my side for a long time. He always dissuaded Tut from trusting me completely. Eventually I found my way to the stone and I absorbed what I could before using its magic to teleport away from Tut and Rathos. During Rathos' secret reign Egypt managed to stabilize its instability and Egypt became an even more powerful nation in its own right. I erected my own palace just across the Nile River and declared war on Egypt unless they gave me the stone. I still feared Jake but didn't think much of him. I was quite surprised when he and four of his friends showed up to try and trick me into not getting the stone. I saw through their ruse however and I stole the stone before they could throw it back to Rathos. I used the stone to summon even more of my soldiers and they converged around my palace. Rathos and the five friends left and for over a year they trained with their powers. I used the power of the stone to create even more defenses and summon even more enemies in order to protect myself. On some level I still loved Jake but was more afraid of him stealing my power than anything else.

I never sent any of soldiers over to Rathos and Tut despite the voice in my head almost forcing me into doing that very thing many times. I wanted to destroy their spirit by destroying each of their soldiers when they tried to attack and I wanted to let Jake and his friends have the chance to train. If they really thought they could defeat me then I would give them the chance to do so. They deserved to see why I would later be called Jeb the Immortal Titan. Soon after a year had passed the five friends assaulted my palace and that little wimp Christine stole the stone while I was distracted using it to summon more soldiers in order to overwhelm my enemies. I also saw that Jake was very angry and he had no idea who I really was. Before the fight I manipulated him into killing James' father by accidently pushing him down some stairs. Jake knew that I had done this and swore revenge.

The five used their combined powers and the stone itself to destroy me. They destroyed my body and my spirit but a small part of me had actually managed to merge with the stone just before I perished completely. I decided to cast two final wishes before I would disappear forever. My son had proven to be strong but I still couldn't believe his insolence of actually thinking he could try and kill me. I had given myself over to the voice completely by this time and I wished for each of my enemies to die of heart attacks and for us to be reincarnated throughout the ages. I wanted another chance of finally destroying Jake and his stupid friends.

There have been many other incarnations of me that existed without my memories and they all went onto complete great things despite having significant mental health issues. Not even Rathos was able to keep track of all those incarnations. Finally, I managed to reincarnate into a scientist at Lakehead University and I decided to try and infect many of the faculty and students in order to study the disease that killed everyone I cared about and to see if I could turn them into my thralls. I created my lab in the sub basement underneath the university where I knew I wouldn't be disturbed. Many of them developed boils on their faces but their movement remained intact. Some of them became my thralls but not all of them. I didn't know what else to do but to keep trying. I needed to be able to understand how this disease worked so I could deconstruct it and then use it to destroy my enemies. I spent much time studying the disease but I was never able to replicate it and figure out how it worked.

I instead decided to switch gears and instead solely turn my enemies into thralls. I was so close to turning everyone into my servants but stupid James got reincarnated and him and his cousin Elijah intercepted me and stopped me by throwing my chemicals out the window before I could mix it into the school's furnace and cause the school to explode. My goal was to distribute the liquid in a gaseous form and transform the school into a world of blood and gore. If I could make a big enough splash I could turn everyone into my thralls and make it look like a freak accident. The students and faculty would have been mine for the taking if Elijah and James hadn't intervened! Once they got rid of my chemicals James freed my subjects from their binds while Elijah fought me off with a bow-staff. I fought back and while I was preoccupied James freed the rest of the students and faculty and then engaged me with his sword. I drew my own sword and fought them both at the same time. Even with the powers of the stone, they were no match for me. I had significant sword fighting experience and had gained the power of lightning which I used to my advantage against them. I shot lightning from my fingertips and shot Elijah out the window. I then covered my sword in lightning and engaged James in a one-on-one fight. He was enraged that I managed to incapacitate his friend and cousin but I didn't let him wallow for too long. As he came at me with ferocious strikes I calmly but firmly went on the offensive and we clashed our blades many times together. He kept me on my toes as he lit his sword on fire and our swords came together as one once again. A mix of elements and power that threatened to take out the entire world spread out as the University began to collapse and people ran from their buildings at the apparent earthquake.

James looked at me coldly and said "Why are you doing this? Surely you have enough power with your memories intact and the abilities you gained from the stone?" A part of me wanted to tell James everything but mostly I just smirked and pulled back before firing more lightning at him. He countered with his fire and we kept on battling. The mix of lightning and fire began to singe the world around us and we kept on fighting as we shot our respective elements at each other. I came out of it with burn marks across my face and some burns while James had some nerve damage from my lightning. Elijah was still unconscious but I would make sure to eliminate him in time as well.

James and I both panted and my original plan to enslave the school had failed. After many years the dark voice had completely infected my mind and most of my capacity for love and compassion was gone. I also saw James as the ideal son to me. Jake was strong but James was clearly much stronger and a much better man that I could manipulate into being my pawn. I kept watch over Jake during his early years back in Egypt and I could tell he had severe anger problems. He also had deep insecurities that he could never overcome. Perhaps I could have helped him but my lust for power and revenge overwhelmed me and I couldn't bear to be near my son. James was better than Jake was and understood how to be a man. I don't want to destroy him entirely but perhaps in the next life he and I can become allies. I drop my sword and he does the same. My magic has been completely drained from me but I'm not out of moves yet. I rush towards James and open my mouth deep and wide. I jump onto him and I bite deep into his neck as blood and gore rushed out of him. James screamed in pain and fell to the ground while trying to push me off. I also used some of my magic and inflicted a curse upon his wound. It would never fully heal and he would eventually die. This James had lived for a long time and even had a family of his own. I would hunt them down in time as well.

Eventually he succeeded in forcing me off of him and I was forced back into a wall that fell on me. Jame still had his super strength and Elijah ran over to him and used some magic to teleport them both away. I realized that I would never be able to get my vengeance or accomplish any of my goals at this rate. I knew James was still alive for the time being but I decided that I had to enough to worry about right now. Elijah managed to rescue James before I could free myself from the rubble and lunge out and grab them both. I wanted to strangle them both. I panted as I looked among the carnage our fight had created. Suddenly I could hear a giant rumbling and the ground shook. I fell to the ground as the buildings around began to repair themselves. I also saw that the people who had gotten flattened by the rubble were back to life and going on about their day. Rathos must have used his half of the stone to undo the damage. So, he's watching me even now. His half of the stone wasn't enough to destroy me and he knew it. I smirked and flipped him off. I felt the world shake with anger but nothing could be done. If I wanted to destroy him and remake the world in my image then I would need to learn more about the stone. I could feel a pounding in my head as it began to throb. I grunted in pain and fell to the ground in shock. My beloved god was talking to me again. I could see images of an altar in a distant land that claimed to have the answers I seek. I used my lightning ability to fly up high into the air as the world around me was being repaired and flew to the land. After many hours of flying, I managed to make it to the altar. The altar was dark and craggy and it was a sliver of a tip that reached out into the air. I had no clue what this amazing thing could be but I could tell that the power emanating from it was faint. Even though it was weak I could feel the power that this altar once held and knew it could destroy the world if it was ever brought back to life once more.

I put my hands on the altar and my head began to sweat. I felt my entire body begin to pour out sweat as I felt my body temperature increase exponentially. I tried to take my hands off but they felt as if they were glued to it. I tried even harder but I couldn't escape no matter how hard I tried. My body began to expand and I felt as if I was going to die. I also thought about how for some reason only James had been reincarnated with me. I suppose our conflict was minor in the grand scheme of things. Next time, it would be even greater. My entire being slowly came apart and I could literally feel myself disintegrating. I screamed into the void and a blinding white light enveloped me.

The Death Game Arc

The world turned to black before I woke up to a beautiful woman standing over me. I was no longer at the altar and was within a field of flowers. They were roses and the woman smiled at me as she extended a hand towards me. I groggily grabbed it and she helped me to my feet. As I got a better look at the woman, I saw that she had glistening blonde hair as if she had just gotten out of the water and full lips. She looked to be about thirty and I instantly fell in love.

She continued to smile at me as she explained that I was about to learn exactly what I had been seeking. Her voice was like silk and honey and it felt almost hypnotic. I almost felt like giving up on my desire for vengeance but the voice of my god brought me back to reality and I realized that I had no time for happiness anymore. I had managed to bring my sword with me and I stabbed her straight through her pathetic heart. She looked at me in shock as if she wasn't expecting this turn of events and then she collapsed. She fell towards me but I blocked her with my foot and I kicked her away from me. She would only be getting in the way of my quest for power. I then continued to repeatedly kick at her corpse until I felt satisfied. As the blood dripped from her corpse, I felt my god speaking to me. He said that I had passed the first trial.

He continued to state that my purpose would soon be revealed to me and that she had been sent to test my resolve. I walked through the field of flowers until I saw my son standing before me. He had looked angry and I had seen that he had been bound. He didn't look any older than 19 so it must have been a hallucination. I felt a lump in my throat as I looked down at him before suddenly breaking out in a grin. I raised my sword and began cutting off his hands, then his feet, then his arms, then his genitalia, and finally his eyes. He screamed in pain constantly until I got tired of the screaming and cut out his tongue. I stomped on his head for good measure until he shut up for good. I continued to stomp on his head until there was nothing left but blood and gore. I laughed hysterically at what I had done and felt happy and free for the first time in years. Oh, I should have done this years ago. Me and my son shall never be able to co-exist anymore and I'm okay with that. I devour his blood and smear it all over me as I feel waves and waves of ecstasy flow throughout my entire body.

I spit on his corpse and continue killing every single person in my wake. I see my former wives and I even see my parents bound and gagged. They scream and beg for mercy but my haze of madness overwhelmed me and I went into a rampage. The rampage lasted for many minutes and by the time I was done there were only a few people left.

As soon as I understood the weight of what I had done I broke down and sobbed at the loss of everyone I had ever cared about. I felt a brief hint of regret before I could feel my god intervening again. Suddenly it was as if any regret I had felt was gone in an instant and I continued my rampage. By the time I had finished I felt euphoric. I could feel a tingling sensation between my pants and I felt the most amazing pleasure I had ever felt. I immediately ran behind a tree and released my ecstasy of pleasure and moaned long into the day and night. I ran around each of the bodies and began to lick up their blood and gore once I was finished. It felt like part of me was missing in that moment but as the blood and guts went down my throat, I felt complete. I gulped all of it down greedily and admired my work. The peaceful green field had become red as it was stained with blood. I saw a beacon of darkness that looked as black as night that was beckoning me and roused me from my haze. I spat out the blood from my mouth and headed towards the darkness. The darkness led me to a giant tree with many other people in front of it. There were also many people hung from the tree with nooses around their necks.

I walked towards the tree and felt at peace with what I had saw. I saw that there were about 200 hundred other people standing around the tree and they all looked as clear eyed as I felt. The tree had been glowing with darkness emanating from it but now the glow had begun to dim and light shone from the tree. I shielded my eyes and the field I was once in had been transformed into a giant coliseum. Me and the other people looked around as we heard cheering coming from spectators. Part of the wall of the arena had been destroyed at the top and it reminded me of the Roman Colosseum. I wonder if this was in fact the one and the same arena. As I thought about it, I saw that the tree was gone and, in its place, stood a man with a hood over his face. His cloak was dark purple with gold emblazed on it. He looked to be about 6 feet and he had an air of authority around him. He raised his left hand in the air and he rose high into the sky.

He kept his hood on and stretched both of his arms into the air above his head in a welcoming gesture. His voice boomed and rocked through us as me and many of the others recoiled from the sound. His voice was amazing but eventually my ears began to adjust and I could hear what he was saying perfectly despite him being so far away. "Welcome champions to my world. The world I have created is called Ragnarok and you shall compete in various matches in order to prove yourself worthy of my favor. I am the god Riquarim and you shall bow before me." As one we all bowed before him in reverence. Riquarim smiled to himself and said "now is the time to explain your circumstances. Many of you have come looking for my favor and others may have stumbled here accidently in the search for knowledge or power. I promise you that if you win my tournament, you shall have everything you could wish for and more. I Riquarim am the god of assassins and I shall be presiding over this year's bloodbath. However you managed to find your way here, the important thing is that you have completed your trials and found your way into my domain. For better or worse, you now have the attention of a god. Be wary you don't waste it mortals." I felt a shiver in my spine as I felt the overwhelming power inside of him. He could kill each of us with a thought.

He then continued with his thoughts very calmly. "Now, many of you may not know why you have come here but I will tell you. You shall all compete in a tournament in order to gain a boon from me. This boon can be anything that you wish. All you must do is ask and it shall be yours along with many other rewards and accolades. But be warned, this tournament will be to the death and there can only be one winner. There may be other survivors depending on how the games go but the majority of you will die and I shall reap your souls to either be assassins or be assassinated in my realm of darkness. Do you understand?" All the time he bad been speaking he had been eloquent and calm the entire way through. Not once did he raise his voice or show any hint of emotion. He seemed genuinely happy to welcome us here but I could feel the underlying darkness coming from him. Riquarim was dangerous and was well beyond my power to defeat. I felt paralyzed by fear but I knew that I had to win this tournament.

I and the other competitors nodded our heads in unison and I could tell that we all understood our situation. I could see apprehension amongst many of the others but I also saw genuine terror and despair along with excitement and bloodlust in some of their eyes. This was going to be a very dangerous tournament but I would be ready for it. Riquarim moved his hands and put them back at his sides. He snapped his fingers and a mountain of weapons appeared before us. I could hear him say "my friends, welcome to the tournament and good luck! The first round happens in 2 minutes so you best pick your weapons and fast. Good luck!" He then disappeared in a flash of darkness and we were all left standing before the mountain of weapons. The crowd cheered but I couldn't even focus on that. The only sound I could hear was the sound of my heartbeat and I saw the other challengers looking longingly at the weapons. Eventually they began to stampede towards them and I almost got caught between two giant men with even bigger beards. I don't even know how that was possible honestly. I ran towards the mountain and picked up the first weapon I saw. I couldn't remember the exact name but I believe it was a Spada sword. It may have been a Spada Da Lato but I'm not 100 percent sure.

This was one of many swords I used to train with and was used during the renaissance era. I trained with many swords during my incarnations and I now had memories of each of them. Their experience also transferred into me and I was ready to fight for my life against these insects. I was jostled and jolted but none of that mattered. None of these meatheads could kill me. Riquarim's prize shall be mine. I walked away from the crowd as they begin scavenging for weapons. Many of the other fighters are also wrestling over the weapons and I can tell that many of them are magical in some way. The weapons I mean. I wonder if any of these simpletons have any magic capability. I certainly hope not, that would cause me many problems down the line. As soon as the 2 minutes are up, I see the floor begin to light up. I brace myself as I get sucked in and the other fighters also get sucked in with me.

I woke up in the dark woods with two other challengers in front of me. It's a man and a woman. The woman has a crossbow and the man has two shields in his hands. That's...an odd choice of weaponry. But whatever, who am I to judge? I can hear a voice booming across the land saying that the games had officially begun. The man and woman looked at each other before they began to advance towards me. The woman kept her distance while firing her crossbow at me. I managed to dodge the bolts but the guy with the two shields rammed me from behind. He had been sneaking around me and rammed me with the shields. I fell to the ground and he lifted his now flaming shields into the air and thrust them down in my direction. I managed to roll away just in the nick of time and I drew my thrusting sword and slashed at him. I ended up hitting his shields as he used them to block my sword from advancing.

The Spado sword was good for fencing and getting in between narrow places but with a top-notch defense as this guy had I would never be able to beat him with my sword alone. I had learned lightning from a magical master many years ago and he also taught me many other tricks. I rose to my feet and I sheathed my sword slamming my hand onto the ground. The ground then opened up as the world around us began to shake. The crossbow woman lost her balance and her next few bolts flew wild right past me. The shield user fell to the ground on his ass and yelped when he saw me. He tried to grab his shields but he had lost them in the fray. I conjured up a ball of lightning and fried him. The smell of burning flesh got to me and for a moment I wanted to retch before I composed myself. I spit on his charred corpse but I noticed he was still barely alive. I decided to leave him there for the insects to eat and I advanced on the crossbow woman. She had gotten to her feet and aimed her weapon right at my chest. I re-drew my sword and deflected the first bolt she fired. I walked slowly towards her. The confident smirk on her face had disappeared and now she was full of terror.

She tried to back away and kept firing but I blocked them all. Finally, I got within striking distance and I destroyed her crossbow with one slash of my sword. She fell to her knees in despair and begged me not to kill her. I smiled darkly at her and took my sword and thrust it right in her neck. Blood gushed out everywhere as she struggled to speak. She gurled and choked on her own blood as she fell to the ground in a heap. I made sure the shield user was still watching before I violated her body. By violating her body, I mean I used extreme violence to desecrate her but not in the sexual sense. I maimed her body and I took her head as a trophy. I figured this would come in handy in the future. She was quite striking when she was alive; but in death she just looked disgusting. I had a satchel with me filled with healing items along with food and water so I put her head in it while I scavenged the other two's pockets to see if they had any worthwhile supplies. I also saw that there was a coin marked in red on the ground. This must have been the coin of Riquarim's assassins. I pocketed the coin and left their weapons alone as I wanted nothing to do with them but I did take their waterskins as they could be useful to me.

I saw the shield user glaring at me with hatred in his eyes. He tried to speak but with the burns along his entire body he couldn't speak. He couldn't even cough even though he desperately wanted to. I picked up one of his discarded shields and I decided to use the bottom of it to decapitate him! It took many tries but I finally managed to chop off his head. I also made sure that the man felt agonizing pain in his last moments. I left the head where it was and then I used my magic to raise the ground back up. Other than the bodies it was as if nothing had happened here. I dropped the shield and walked off. It felt so delicious being able to kill my opponent with his own weapon. I also have the ability to conjure up fireballs and summon balls of water in order to toss them or use them to suffocate and drown my enemies. I will use each of these abilities in time but now is not the time.

I walked through the forest as I heard fighting both near and far away. I had no idea how many fighters were still alive and had no way of knowing that. I decided to just keep moving and only fight when I wanted to. I would win this tournament but first I needed to rest. I needed a place to sleep. I kept walking until my limbs began to feel drained from the exertion. The adrenaline from all of the fighting had left me completely exhausted as it left my body. I finally found an old house in the distance and I ran inside. The lights still worked so I turned some of them on and began searching it from top to bottom. After many hours of searching, I concluded that no one else had found this house and I was completely alone. I boarded up the doors and windows so that no one could sneak up on me while I slept and I found a bed to crash in on the second floor. I slept for many hours and I had the happiest sleep of my life. Despite the bloodshed I finally felt like I could relax. I had no dreams and felt well rested after I woke up. I went outside to investigate the house and saw that someone had tried to break down the front door while I was asleep but my defenses held. I decided that I needed to be bolder with my defenses. I used my magic to create a small orb of light that only I could see and used it to create a beacon so I could always find my way back to the house whenever I needed it. I spent some of the day eating food and drinking water from my waterskins. I also saw that the house had a significant amount of canned food and bottled water that would last me for many months.

I spent the rest of the day resting and making adjustments to my sword. I didn't have any armor save for a tunic but I figured my sword combined with my magic would be enough to get me through the tournament. I also had many healing potions that could be used to heal my injuries when needed. So far, I had no significant injuries which would help me a great deal. I left the next day and decided to explore the wilderness. I came across a beautiful spring and immersed myself in the water. There was no one around so I felt at ease to bathe a little. After my shower I left the spring and saw there were two people fighting in the distance.

I decided to sneak up on them and saw that it was two men sword fighting. One was fighting with leather armor and two broadswords while the other one was fighting with a two-handed blade and iron armor. Both had helmets but I couldn't make out either of their faces. I decided to just watch and observe the fight since I didn't necessarily have to engage yet. I figured I would kill the victor. I also made sure to keep an eye on my surroundings to ensure that no one snuck on me but nobody did. Eventually the fight had ended and the one in leather armor managed to pierce a weak point in his opponent and knocked him to the ground. The victor then ripped off his opponent's helmet and fell backwards in shock. I couldn't hear exactly what was being said but apparently the two knew each other. Based on their appearances and similar colored hair I figured they must have been brothers. I grinned in anticipation. The one in leather armor began to fall to his knees while the iron armored guy tried desperately to comfort him. The iron armored one wasn't dead yet, he had just been incapacitated. I snuck up to them both and used my sword to thrust into both of them. I skewered both of them through their eyes and they both fell to the ground dead. My sword began to become damaged so I discarded it and chose to pick up the fallen broadswords. These swords were more my style anyway. Thrusting was for weaklings. I would thrust enough in time to alleviate any boredom.

I tested the two swords out quickly by doing some experimental slashes and they felt perfect in my hands. I took the scabbards and put them on my back as well. I left the two corpses to rot in the sun and went back to my hideout. I started building wooden spikes and put them in front of each of the doors and windows in order to further reinforce my base. There was a hidden hatch that led into the house at the edge of the property line and I used that to sneak in and out of the house. I covered the hatch with shrubbery and wood in order to prevent anyone from finding them. I also put many traps in front of my base in order to catch and kill any unfortunate souls that happened to traipse onto my property in search of blood and glory. I used my time very well. Anyone that fell into my pits of death were taken back into my house for experiments with torture tools and chemicals that were located within the house.

I've lost track of how many people fell into my traps but many did and I gained a lot of research and practical abilities in order to further my original research into the disease that ravaged my family. I was able to turn a few of them into thralls before they died from immolation. For some reason they would always self-destruct and I can't explain it. Whatever. It doesn't matter anymore. All that matters is winning this game at all costs. Everyday I go out into the wilderness in order to get supplies and to kill off any enemies that I see. I've seen many enemies and I always kill them whenever they are distracted or weakened from another fight. I spent many weeks scavenging the woods and killing any stragglers that I saw.

"Hang on, I need a break." I said quickly. The chronicler looked at me quizzically but nodded and put his pen down. He offered me a drink of water and I accepted. I needed a break from telling my story and my mouth was becoming increasingly dry. We talked about random things in the meantime and I could tell that Edward didn't judge me despite the awful things I had done. I think his willingness to hear my story outweighed the fear and hatred that burned his heart. He gestured for me to go on while I could and I agreed.

The Killing Game's Conclusion

After our break I decided to continue. I could feel my life force draining away so I continued my tale. After killing many enemies, I felt myself give into the voice of my god and reveled in it. He loved that I was killing so many people and I could feel his approval skyrocketing every time I did so. There were times I questioned what he actually wanted me to do and if what I was doing was right but every time those doubts creeped in my beloved god would reassure me that I was on the right path and I felt better. There were parts of me that also missed my deceased family and Jake as well. But I know I'm better off without them and they are insignificant compared to what I have become. What my god truly wants is to have the entire world under his control. As a last resort he would wish for the world to be completely destroyed if he couldn't have full control. If he couldn't have full control then nobody should.

After many weeks there were a lot less people running around and the number of competitors began to dwindle. I have heard rumors from the people dying that there is a large group of people getting ready to mount an attack on my stronghold. If that's the case then I'll be ready for them. I hunker down in my house after setting up many more traps and I get ready for the invasion. After many weeks of trying to track them down they finally come to me and I was more than ready to take them down.

They began their march and many of them fell into my traps or what I like to call my pits of despair. There were over a hundred people walking through my pits and many of them fell and broke their legs on the spikes. Others became impaled through the throat and blood gushed up as they tried in vain to free themselves. I also had set up electric fences that looked invisible to the naked eye until the enemy walks through the barriers then it activates. About 10 of them became fried before they managed to short circuit the fence and destroy it. I ran outside wielding my double broadswords and used my lightning to engage them all in combat. I engaged all 80 of them at once with my magic and swords and I fried many of them while impaling the rest. It was a bloodbath and some of them used magic against me as well. I used my fireballs to create walls of fire in order to separate the enemy from me and I used my water balls to drown many of the them by filling their lungs until they couldn't breathe any more. They all died in agony and got what they deserved. I desperately wanted to make these people my thralls but I had no idea how. I was too weak but that would change once I won this fucking tournament.

It was a tried-and-true bloodbath and my swords spun so fast no one could reach me. I incapacitated many enemies before dismembering them and leaving them to then bleed out in my traps. It was glorious indeed. I can still remember the taste of blood in my mouth as I bit into them. Anyway, after the chaos died down, I went over to the stragglers and began cutting their throats. I found the leader of the pack and forced him to look at the corpses of everyone that he had failed by bring them on this mission. No one and I mean no one could beat me with a sword. He whimpered at me not to kill him but I did it anyway. There were no survivors and I was the victor. Riquarim appeared before me and bowed. I bowed in return and then he drew his sword. He said the final test was to fight him in a one-on-one duel. I admit I was excited at the prospect.

Riquarim was one of the ultimate rogues during his lifetime as a human before he ascended to the ranks of the divine. It would be a pleasure to take him down a peg. We clashed our swords against each other and I tried to aim for his head which he swiftly ducked under. He used a sword and a knife combo and used his sword to block both of mine while using his dagger to cut me in various places. He got me in the thigh, my cheek, my legs, and even the left side of my head where my temple was. He only managed to graze them but I knew that the blades had been coated with a potent toxin that would eventually kill me if I didn't end this quickly. I kept on fighting and kept on targeting his face but he kept ducking and dodging. The cuts began to build up quickly and blood pooled out soon after. I slowly started to slow down and thought I was going to die. The fear began to take over me and my throat closed up but I kept on fighting.

As I began to collapse from my wounds Riquarim towered over me and smiled. He said "you fought well, but your time is up." I coughed up blood but then smiled as he raised his sword. His sword came down but just before it reached my head I weaved out of the way and I used my swords to cut off his legs. Riquarim fell to the ground and I lifted my swords and brought them down on his head. Just before I won, he raised his hands as fast as lightning and blocked my swords. He turned up to me and smiled happily. "Well, done," he said cooly. Time stopped and then his wounds instantly healed along with my own. I was lifted gently down to the ground and Riquarim appeared before me. His cloak flapped in the wind and he looked at the bloodshed around us. "My, my, my, you've certainly been busy. All of these lost souls shall be perfect for my trials." I bowed in reverence at his words and I knew that I had done well. "Come now you needn't bow to me. You have passed all of my trials. Now tell me, what is it you seek?" he asked thoughtfully. I raised my head and got to my feet. I said to him "my lord, I wish to become the most powerful man on the planet. I want the ability to raise my enemies into my thralls and to destroy James and his pathetic friends. Please Riquarim, will you help me with this?" I asked quietly. Riquarim smiled and nodded.

The voice in my head seemed to be perfectly happy as well. All of the experience I had been looking for got transferred into me. I learned how to create armies with my abilities and my strength and magic increased tenfold and I was then sent back to my home. Almost as soon as I got there James and Elijah appeared out of nowhere. James looked older already due to my curse and his neck was still slightly bleeding. It would take many years for it to partially heal and he would be long dead before that happened. I readied myself before hearing a voice in my head. It told me that the plans to attain world domination wouldn't be ready quite yet. I needed one more reincarnation in order to perfect the plan. I reluctantly agreed and instead of fighting back I let James and Elijah stab me with their swords. They both looked shocked at my lack of resistance but then I chanted my own spell and was sent away. My consciousness was implanted into a young lad who would grow up to be the next me. He even had my name and would grow up to be a scientist. I would lay asleep for many years as he began his work on trying to perfect the world.

Even though I was asleep I could still influence the world around me. I manipulated him into going down the path of science and wanting to help the world. While he may have grown up the same way regardless, I wanted to ensure that he followed the path I laid out for him. During this time James had initiated his plan in order to clone himself and make sure that the rest of the five would be reincarnated as well. James would be too weak to fight me by the time I had awoken so he wanted to make sure his heir would live. He also raised James as his own son and then left him in order to protect him from me.

As long as the two weren't together I wouldn't be able to find either of them before it was the perfect time. Now comes the next part of my memoir.

The First Death

In a town called Schreiber Ontario was where James' current story began. As many of you know, the Jeb in that incarnation was a scientist who wanted to cure the world of all diseases. He had the best intentions and reminded me of myself from when I first became a doctor. I had manipulated him into making the serum that would change everything. Once he finished it and drank it, I had partially woken up. I was able to share some of my memories to him but he wasn't able to make sense of it at first. It would take a long time for us to merge into one being so I waited patiently. That version of me slowly became manic and then enough of me had been transferred that I could take control. Unfortunately, some of my memories became locked in my mind when we merged and I was unable to recall them for quite a while.

After I had drank the serum, I gained the ability to create zombies and lead them using a hive mind capability. Once I had infected the entire plant I moved into the town. I had a hidden bunker near the plant and I slowly sent out my soldiers in order to locate more of their own. I had poisoned the entire water supply and eventually the entire town had become infected. I was also trying to infect James and his stupid friends but they had an immunity to it unfortunately. That must have been Rathos' intervention but I'm not certain. I no longer cared about trying to cure the initial disease that ravaged my family; I only cared about bringing the world to its knees.

While James had been investigating and his father/clone was in hiding I started assigning my soldiers to analyze these alien eggs that had been found in a crashed alien spaceship from a distant planet. I hoped that we could replicate them and use them to create another army in order to subjugate the rest of the world. I also had a private jet stashed away where I hid the eggs and my soldiers would analyze them in the lab I built there. When James and his stupid friends had found their way into the plant for the first time; I had already moved my soldiers from there but they were still hanging out nearby. Once the fire alarm had been tripped, we could all hear it and I sent my soldiers back to figure out what was going on. They did but they were unable to capture or destroy the friends. I sent some of my zombies into the town in order to find them. I ordered them not to kill them, but to beat the shit out of them. I wanted to test their healing abilities and see if they had gained any of their former powers. I should have been more specific though and ensured that they had captured them as well. Poor Stacy got injured quite severely but she survived. I believe her healing abilities coupled with her love for James kept her alive.

I don't know, but it didn't matter. I sent many zombies to shadow them and I quickly found their base of operations. I could have razed it to the ground with my forces but I decided to wait. I wanted to see if James and Jake had the courage to face me and I was curious to see what plan they could come up with. I began strengthening my zombies with weapons and I created a hierarchy so I didn't have to do everything myself. I often threatened to cut off body parts if they didn't do what I said and that fear worked in my favor. They were obedient and many of them were slaves to me. The aliens had also matured and some of them hatched before going into a deep sleep. Some of the aliens had also died on impact so I kept their desiccated bodies in order to bring them back to life. I was so close to figuring out the right chemical sequence in order to bring them back to life and have them be subservient to me.

It took many days before James was ready to make his move. He had decided to have his friends set up a distraction to lure my forces away from me while he snuck into my fortress and used the cure to free the town from my grasp. I decided to just let him do it and sent a good portion of my zombies to invade the base while the rest did regular menial tasks around my fortress. They were meant go guard it but I had no attachment to my zombies. In the end I could have always made more. I was also working on plans to deploy my serum on a much wider scale through the use of my cannon but those plans would have to wait until either James or I had fallen. I observed him as he went through my fortress and tried desperately not to kill anyone before realizing he had no choice and giving into vengeance. I do admit, it was quite fun watching him suffer.

After he got to my floor, I watched him for a moment before revealing myself to him. My appearance back then was quite sickly looking but very powerful. I do wish I had my sword at the moment but I had left it in my other lab. I taunted James with knowledge about his father but what he didn't realize was I was taunting him about his father back in Egypt. He didn't have to know that quite yet though. After taunting him enough we grappled and fought hard. I wanted to prevent him from using the cure to free everyone but he got the upper hand and kicked me out the window. The shards of glass impaled me and I fell to the ground while bleeding profusely. It took all of my strength to crawl away and heal up and after James activated the cure it got to me as well. I kept some of my powers but the control over my zombies was long gone by now. I had also lost my sickly appearance and I was closer to being human again.

I was very impressed with James' tenacity and decided that I would try to manipulate him into becoming my son and ally. If I could convince him that he was my son then perhaps I could twist his psyche into joining my side and killing his friends. I have no attachment to James or Jake for that matter; but I would be remiss to not take the opportunity of gaining a potential ally for the time being. I decided to leave subtle hints that he was my son by ensuring he found out he was adopted and that Jake already had a well-established family. Technically the old me had Jake and then left him with his aunt and uncle in order to take care of them; but the real me just wanted to torture him even further by giving him a bad home life and to try and turn him against James that much more quickly.

My plan wasn't full proof but I trusted in the will of my god to help me see it through. I hobbled away into the woods and made sure James couldn't see my body anymore. I patched myself up and I even observed their little award ceremony. Jake looked very unhappy after the ceremony and went off on his own. I could tell that he was dealing with his own voices as well and I watched him murder his adoptive parents/aunt and uncle. Jake was still pathetic but at least he was strong enough to do what was necessary at times. Perhaps my god was talking to him as well or perhaps he inherited some of my problems. Who knows? I had a few slaves still helping me even after I lost control of my zombies and they had been working tirelessly on the alien serum as I had requested. I planned on killing the slaves once I was finished with them and that's exactly what I did. They had outlived their usefulness and deserved to be put to my sword.

My moments of doubt happened less and less and I gave myself even more into the voice inside of my head. I stashed a private jet on the outskirts of town and I went there as soon as I could. My slaves had managed to keep the jet hidden from view which helped me greatly. After my slaves were slaughtered like the insects they were I poured the serum onto the desiccated bodies of the aliens and they began to stir. I grabbed their hands and told them how they would love the town of Schreiber once they had recovered. I had labs set up all across the world but my main once was on the outskirts of Arizona in the United

States. The current political climate there was tenuous at best so I was able to bribe the government there in order to let me do whatever I wanted.

Rise Of The Alien Dictatorship

I SPENT SOME TIME caring for the aliens in my care and made sure they received the best help they could get. I may have been evil but I was also a doctor and scientist. I knew exactly what I was doing in that regard. It took me another two months in order to care for them and restore them to their former strength. I also bred the eggs as if they were my own and the aliens looked up to me as if I was their father. I spent some time with them training them and ensuring that they were up to snuff. It took about two months to get everything ready and they built me their technology that was leagues ahead of what I could have come up with.

The most amazing things were that I now had access to hover crafts that could fire different kinds of lasers and fly at incredible speeds. There was other tech as well but this was one of the highlights for me personally. I had set up many comforts of home for me well here. I had a massage chair and a huge living space for me to sleep and watch the Harry Potter movies when I needed a break. There was a small part of me that wanted to leave it to my son and his friends but this was all for me in the end. They didn't deserve anything good for daring to come against me. I even wrote a daily reminder on Jake's photo that someday he and I shall be reunited someday. Perhaps it was out of sentimentality or perhaps it was out of a desire to crush my enemies with as many allies as possible. I will never be sure of that now. Regardless, after two months I was ready to initiate my plan. I also had many tombs marked on a map of Egypt since I didn't know where Rathos' tomb was. That would come later however.

First, I gathered all of my aliens together into their hovercrafts and set off at a brisk pace to Schreiber Ontario. The first thing I ordered them to do was to find them and separate them. I wanted them to be in separate cages for when I was ready to experiment on them and kill them. However, my aliens misunderstood and instead threw them in opposite directions of each other all across the town. It would take forever to track them down. I punished some of my aliens quite severely because of that. Next, I spent a few days enslaving the rest of the town and turning them into my alien slaves. Some were obedient towards me without question but some of them had doubts about our plans. I didn't really care however. All I cared about was how effective they were at getting results and many of them were very successful and were a great use to me for my plans of world domination. I then bombed the friend's hideout and I even saw Elijah poking around. I made sure to finish him by impaling him with a giant piece of wood. He would die in the hideout and it was what he deserved. He seemed very surprised to see me and it felt so amazing to finally get my revenge on him. That was one more threat out of the way. I knew that the original James wouldn't dare come and face me as long as his son was alive so I had to wait until I could deal with him.

Once the town was enslaved, I took the opportunity to take over the rest of the world. I decided to leave Elijah just barely alive for the friends to find. I figured it would be some nice psychological terror for James since they were close once. I explored and bombed many of the tombs on the list except for the last one. I couldn't breach it even with my advanced technology and I realized that I needed the five in order to do it for me. I would wait for them to discover my lab in Arizona and then they would unlock Rathos' coffin for me and find the two halves of the stone as well. The friends eventually found their way back to each other and I had sent out squads of aliens in order to capture them and bring them to me alive. I noticed that they were starting to regain some of their original powers which meant they were starting to remember their past which was perfect for me. I wanted to be able to defeat them once they were at their peak strength since that would be so much more delicious.

Eventually they beat up my squads and found their way to Arizona. Simon's father betrayed me and was able to resist his brainwashing. Whatever, it still worked out in the end. I had abandoned the lab by this point and had vacated to near Egypt in anticipation for their arrival. I could have bombed the lab and killed them all at once but there was the fear that Rathos would simply bring them back to life with the stone. I wanted the stone for myself so I could break this cycle of reincarnation. Edward looked at me surprised and I explained that even though I had created the reincarnation cycle I wanted to be free of it and finally kill those kids once and for all. My god wanted ultimate domination and didn't want any other threats in his way.

I would do whatever I could to give him that. I allowed them to lounge in my private area and Christine had discovered my pictures and saw the inscription I had left about Jake. That wouldn't cause any problems down the line so I decided to let it be. I also saw that they had a fondness for the Harry Potter movies as well. My heart warmed at the thought that we all had something in common. That feeling lasted about all of 20 seconds before my heart turned cold once again. The next day they decided to head to Egypt in order to find what was located at that tomb I circled. They found the correct inscription and were able to gain access. I allowed them to move forward and lay in wait for when they would lead me to the other half. I observed as Rathos told them about my history except for the important parts about my past. He glossed over my swordsmanship training and me communing with my dark god. Ah whatever, it wouldn't matter much in the grand scheme of things. I was insanely proud when Jake beat the shit out of James and left him for dead in that tomb. I wanted to go in just to gloat but I couldn't afford to let them not find the stone for me.

Jake left the tomb in a rage and Simon and Christine left soon after and followed the beacon of light to the other half of the stone. I followed them as well while maintaining close behind them but out of sight. They eventually found the stone and I then ambushed them. I sent my aliens out and attempted to manipulate James when he showed up. I tried to convince him that he was my son but that bitch Christine intervened and revealed that Jake was my son. My plans had been foiled but it didn't matter. I tried to appeal to Jake's nature but he turned on me as well. He used a special gun that he had found in the sands of Egypt and used it against me and my aliens. The five then used the power of the stone to destroy me. Just before I died, I used my strength to hide part of my soul within the stone so I could live on. They really thought that they had beaten me; but they hadn't. I now had access to the stone in a way that no one else did. James used the stone to bring the world back to life and he had no clue I was still in there. The next phase of my plan was about to begin.

Rise Of Medieval And Egyptian Knights

Once the celebrations were over; I used my influence to wish my army back to life but for some reason only my general came back to life. Perhaps I needed to be more specific. He crawled his way out of the sand and his red eyes gleamed as he cracked his knuckles and he felt the satisfaction of coming back to life once again. He rushed into the tomb with his sword drawn and then he wished for me to come back to life. I thought that he was undoubtedly loyal to me and wanted to bring me back but I realized that he was only trying to lull me into a false sense of security and then kill me when I least expected it. Once I was brought back to life, he tried to kill me with his new sword and Rathos as well. Basilisk got a hit on me and slashed open my stomach while Rathos narrowly dodged the ghostly blade as well. Rathos used his power to transport himself and I out of there while Basilisk swiped at nothing but air. He then used the power of the combined stone to bring his army back and declare that I was dead and murdered by humans.

He manipulated them in order gain their loyalty and then led them to Schreiber Ontario on their magical horses. I appeared in the classroom of James' school and saw him and his friends studying while Rathos healed my wounds and explained to them that we were on the same side for the time being. I had no interest in working with them but had decided that I would need their help in order to kill my traitorous general. At this point my beloved god had decided to abandon me for my failures. He said that I would have to handle things on my own for the time being and he wouldn't be intervening for a long time.

In private I later fell to my knees and felt hopeless due to my failures but I didn't let anyone else know about them. Once Basilisk had come to town, he started using the stone in order to make the world fall out of balance like the World of Ruin in Final Fantasy VI. That was always one of my favourite games that I would play in my spare time. Basilisk destroyed the school we were in and then tore the stone in two before throwing it down into a pit he had created. Simon used his telekinesis to bring the stone back to us in pieces and Rathos teleported us back to Egypt. I still wanted to destroy Rathos but I found that my desire for murder had faded since my god left. The voice was no longer pounding in my ears and I felt almost ashamed of my past actions. My god was no longer around to suppress my humanity which wasn't fun. I reluctantly went on the journey with James and his friends in order to go back in time and reunite the pieces of the stone with its brother back in medieval times. We went back in time and I got some amusement out of seeing James' aunt come out of nowhere in order to give him maternal love and affection. And beer, lots of beer. She reminded me of my mother before she passed. The thought almost made me cry but I hid it behind my laughter and joined in with James' friends. After we made it to medieval times we were arrested and locked up until our execution. Only James was able to escape and I got to see Skragg, a distant family member. He was both my ancestor and descendant. It was quite strange to see him honestly.

I didn't feel any love towards him however. He was getting in the way of our mission. I should also mention that during this time I had no intention of trying to steal the stone for myself. I tried to bond with the other members of the group but they wanted nothing to do with me. I don't really blame them. I did so many horrible things and I know that I can never be forgiven. If I were to die in battle that would be one thing but I promised to myself that I would do anything I could to protect Jake and his friends. They deserved better than me but I was all they had. I tried to break us out of our cell but there was nothing I could do. Simon seemed to be the most optimistic and I felt proud of that. Someone had to be optimistic despite all the hardships they went through.

Jake was the one I wanted to work things out with though. I didn't care about James as a son anymore, I only saw him as my son's best friend and I hoped the two of them could work out their issues. Jake needed help and perhaps James could help him down that path. Despite everything I still wanted to be in Jake's life but I felt lost without my god. My humanity was returning to me and I didn't know how to handle that. I missed my parents, and my old family. I wished that I could have helped them. Maybe I could help Jake now though. The very next day James managed to rescue us with his friend Caroline and I felt immensely grateful towards them. James then fought Skragg in single combat and won! I felt so proud of him and saw him as a true warrior. I knew Jake could also become that as well if he had more discipline.

Eventually we made it to a nearby cave where we could hide out and I took the opportunity to make things right with Jake. I chose not to tell him about the dark god since that wasn't an excuse and he didn't have to know my reasons for abandoning him. I told him that he was the light of my life and that I wish I could have stayed in his life. I truly meant it and I still loved my only son. I had lost another child centuries ago and the pain still felt fresh to me. At least I could save Jake now if given the opportunity. Jake refused to forgive me and I later wept. I also decided to talk to James and he said he couldn't forgive me but was glad that we could work together now. I felt happy to hear that and I wanted to make amends with the entire group if possible. After James combined the stone together and we headed back to the present day we saw that Basilisk had taken over the entire world. Humans were forced to push giant wheels with chains around their necks and push them in giant circles. It acted both as a punishment and as a power source for the town. I felt the need to free them but we decided that he had to get rid of Basilisk first. Christine cried at the sight of her town and I wanted to comfort her. She reminded me a lot of myself when I was her age.

I didn't of course and Simon was able to comfort her with his abilities. We decided to try and turn Basilisk's soldiers against him but we weren't able to do so. In the end the plan was to try and sneak in the palace instead. We snuck around each of the guards using Christine's invisibility and we were able to make it to Basilisk when Jake wished that we were all there. We appeared in Basilisk's throne room and did battle with him. Basilisk really wanted to kill Jake and aimed for him specifically. Despite everything that happened I couldn't let him destroy my only living son. I jumped in the way and took the brunt of the hit for Jake. Jake looked devastated at my death. I wished I could have told him that it was okay; that it was my choice to take away his suffering by giving my life. If I could take away his pain then I would. If my death was the only way to end his suffering then I would sacrifice myself in a heartbeat every time. I went to the afterlife and felt at peace. I had finally completed my mission to save my son and his friends.

They then defeated Basilisk and restored peace. The stone also glowed and brought me back to life. I felt like I was 19 again and it felt good to be reunited with my son again. Jake hugged me and embraced me while I embraced him as my son. James had taken the power of the stone and sent it into the heavens in order to protect the earth from outside threats and grant the people of the world a limited amount of magic. Society changed as we knew it and the soldiers became loyal to me once more. I ordered them to stand down and they freed everyone. All the people that were killed had been brought back to life just like me and were able to live normal lives again. Jake considered me his father now and we tried hard to become a family. I had felt complete and was willing to let go of vengeance and the plans of my dark god. We were finally happy...for a time.

After the parties were over and Jake moved in with me permanently my dark god returned to me. I tried to resist his influence but he congratulated me for getting the heroes on my side by sacrificing myself and was now willing to give me another chance. I tried hard to resist and was in agony for many days. My head pounded and my throat felt like it was closing up as I tried to fight back but ultimately, I was powerless. My god had taken control of me again and had repressed my humanity once more. Suddenly it was as if everything I had accomplished was meaningless and all of my pain that I had accepted was coming back as anger. I needed to destroy the world and destroy James and Jake for ever rising up against me. They had to go down and I would rest at nothing to prevent them from getting the advantage over me again. It took many days but my dark god convinced me that the best plan was to turn the group against each other and then destroy the world so we could remake it into our image. I agreed to the plan and all my love for Jake had disappeared. Now was the time for the final act of my triumph.

The End Of Times

I MANAGED TO MANIPULATE my beloved son Jake into siding against James and I even convinced Simon to help by manipulating him as well. It really wasn't that hard at all. Jake always had a complicated relationship with James and Simon already believed that James had betrayed the group in order to have a quick hookup. The key to the plan was Simon since he had contracts with all four of the elemental spirits and could control the elements with his thoughts and magic. I needed him to cast the spell I needed and I needed Jake's brute strength to act as the muscle for the plan. If he couldn't take out James then the plan would fall apart. I needed both of them to act as my pawns in order to make this work.

The plan was that Simon would cause everyone to blackout while he and the rest of his "friends" would undergo trials in order to become stronger and then Simon would bind them and allow Jake to finish James off. Simon wanted each of his friends to get stronger and it would allow me to be able to get strong as well since I could observe and do my own trials as well. Most of my trials involved gaining control over blood and summoning blood swords out of thin air. I could even control the blood inside of another person. Simon made the most potent beer I had ever tasted and I poisoned it with a strong sedative that would allow us to knock them out cold and send everyone to our location at Rathos' tomb. I went to Rathos and took Basilisk's sword and slayed him. He was surprised at my betrayal and crumbled into dust. He got what he deserved. He would finally no longer be watching over my every move and silently judging me.

Once that was complete, we tricked Christine into killing many of her classmates during the trials and then me, Simon, and Jake killed the rest of them and arranged them in a circle around James' chained up body. Once James had been weakened enough during his trial then Jake would finish him off and ensure he stayed dead. Jake was turning into a mini me and I could not be prouder. The ritual was about to begin and the trials were nearly complete. Simon had gained significant strength during his trials as did the rest of his friends and of course myself. I personally don't care about Jake anymore; but I have no problem playing happy family in order to get what I want. And what I want is James' head on a stick and everyone else to fall to despair. After James awoke, I taunted him with my powers and then left Jake to exact his vengeance on him while Simon kept him in place and the others from interfering with Jake's playtime.

It was fun seeing James get murdered so brutally and then seeing Jake play soccer with his decapitated head. The look on Stacy and Christine's faces was priceless. I still laugh at the thought of those pretty faces falling into terror and despair. Back then, they got what they deserved. Anyway, I went along with their plans and even made a side pact with Jake to kill Simon once he outlived his usefulness and keep the spell going. Once Simon initiated the death spell it couldn't be stopped by anyone. I also created a craggy altar in which to place Simon in once we were finished with him. The three of us had our own special dragons summoned by Simon and we each flew away after James's death. We reconvened at the top of Simon's obsidian palace where his throne was at. We decided that we would each fly to our respective territory and lead the troops to the death of everyone in the world. Simon summoned dragons, goblins, giants, other mythical creatures and giant humanoids in order to crush and destroy everyone. From Egypt we sent our soldiers to every corner of the earth in order to destroy as many people as possible. Hearing their bones crunch was intoxicating and it made me want to have a nice big meal afterwards to celebrate. Perhaps I would even eat Jake for dinner but who knew?

Either way, we sent off our respective armies and I lead them throughout my quadrant. Afterwards when I had done enough; I summoned Jake to the pedestal that we had created for Simon. The plan was still for Simon to act as a conduit for the spell and stone but I revealed that I wanted Jake to also act as a conduit so I could absorb his powers. I should also mention that before we initiated Simon's plan I went back in time and went to a parallel universe where the stone still existed and I stole it. That universe fell into ruin but I don't care. It gave me lots of power now and that's all that matters. Me and Jake fought and I remember him and I sparring with swords as I taught him swordsmanship during better times. He had become a good student but still wasn't on my level. I manipulated Jake's body with my blood magic and led him onto the platform. But before I could finish the job, he broke free and lobbed a sword at me. It pierced me through the heart and my body was forcibly taken and put into the altar.

I felt proud of Jake at overcoming me and watched in awe as he took my place as the true main antagonist of the world. My armies became Jake's and he led them against Simon's armies in order to destroy him for good. I wasn't able to see much of what happened next but I am aware of much. I felt proud that Jake had managed to beat me and my consciousness merged with the altar. After Simon died Jake absorbed much of his power but not enough. I still had the bulk of it powered up in my corpse. James somehow managed to come back to my life and my old rival the other James finally died. I felt so happy that another rival had fallen. James and Jake engaged each other in battle and James finally won. He managed to defeat Jake and brutally beat the shit out of him before killing him. Jake got what he deserved.

After James had won all the power collected throughout the fights got sucked into me and I transformed into a powerful dragon to counter them. I lost consciousness during the fight and my dragon form fought against James and the others. Somehow Jake and Simon managed to come back to life briefly and they fought me five on one. I lost my eyes in the fight and I fell to the ground. As the five of them fought me off I boldly declared that they wouldn't see the end of me. They laughed and killed me. My spirit left my body and the world got returned to normal. I saw Jake briefly in the afterlife but my spirit couldn't rest. I couldn't deal with Jake anymore so I abandoned him in the afterlife and went to other worlds in order to regain my power. My dark god finally managed to save me and gave me the ability to shift between realities and to impact other people. He gave me a new body and allowed me to portal jump throughout realms. I finally had the means to impact the world.

Realm Jumper

THE NEXT PLACE I went to was Schreiber Ontario in a new world. The world was similar to mine except that the five friends didn't exist in that world so there were no threats to me and my power. I saw a poor soul named Darwin Fitzgerald who had been abused by his parents. I could have saved him but I chose to let him continue to suffer. He had a cousin named Nathaniel who had potential though. Nathaniel was beating the shit out of Darwin's friend Jared and left him for dead. Nathaniel was then sent to a juvenile detention for many years. He was supposed to spend many more years in prison but I decided to intervene. I posed as his lawyer and got him out on good behaviour and he didn't have to serve the full sentence. When he got out of jail, I met up with him over coffee and we talked things out. I appeared before him as a generous benefactor who was willing to help him get his revenge.

We had many long conversations and I outlined a plan for him to get revenge on Darwin. I would help fund his business venture and give him falsified documents to appear more refined and gentlemanly like. He agreed and we decided the best place to start was Piece for Peace; a small company dedicated to helping amputees. Me and Nathaniel both decided however that we wouldn't be helping amputees in the slightest. That would just be a cover for the real work to begin. I outlined the Stanford Prison Experiment and showed him how it could be replicated in today's society and how to make it marketable to potential investors and willing participants. I gave him the capital needed in order to appear more appealing to the brothers in charge and we began our plan.

Nathaniel would infiltrate the facility and I would help him build and conduct the experiment under the cover of night. He slowly managed to worm his way into their ranks and used his influence to take control of the company. With my guidance he was able to eliminate the competition and get the shareholders on his side. The shareholders along with myself and a few others would become the foundation of a new council that would oversee Nathaniel's experiments. So long as Nathaniel got results then they would keep giving him funding. I also gave him funding in secret so he never had to worry about meeting quotas and could just focus on his revenge.

Nathaniel was the face of the company while I worked behind the scenes in order to help destabilize the world. My dark god was very pleased with my work and helped to suppress my humanity so I could focus solely on the work. The work became my whole life. I dove deeper and deeper into the work hole until there was nothing left but me and the project. I was the architect behind everything and was the reason for Nathaniel's very being. He never would have gotten his revenge if it weren't for me. I also used my influence to ensure he never got into any legal trouble for anything that he did in order to stay on top. Any murders he committed were swept under the rug and nobody was ever the wiser. Nathaniel was great at manipulating people and making them think he was on their side. I however was better at being behind the scenes and striking from the shadows. When Darwin and his classmates were chosen for the experiment and had volunteered, I hid in the shadows while Nathaniel began his torture of them. They may have volunteered but Nathaniel and I perfectly catered our marketing towards them so they would have no choice but to volunteer. I was also the one who came up with the idea of locking memories away and imprinting numbers into the minds to be accessed later. That was all my plan and I decided that Jared should be a guard and help torture Darwin since I figured that psychological mind fuck would give us even better results. Nathaniel agreed and we went forward with the plan. We slowly turned up the pressure on the inmates until they were all having mental breakdowns. The guards however were being tortured in their own way through their dreams and were being subjected to stressful stimuli like genocide in order to formulate more violent tendencies and apathy within them. And the plan worked! The guards became obedient dogs who bowed down to only us and would fuck each other if we ordered them to.

It truly was glorious. But alas, all good things must come to an end I suppose. Darwin eventually got released once the experiment was over and then sent to a mental institution. I helped Nathaniel manipulate Raphael (Darwin's brother) into helping us and helping to torture him. We were working into getting more advanced tech into the hospital so we could have it fully under our control but it took many months before that was possible. The night before we got the last of our tech installed and our control finalized Darwin managed to escape! He escaped into the night and no one knew where to find him. I yelled at Nathaniel for so long for letting this happen and he took it like a champ. He didn't know this but I planned on bringing his father onto the council so the poor man could finally find out what happened to his poor wife and get revenge on his son. I always planned on disposing of Nathaniel and replacing him with his father but alas, that didn't exactly work as intended. Darwin escaped and planned his revenge on Nathaniel. Eventually the two came to blows and after Raphael's death and Jared's injuries, Darwin managed to come out victorious.

Nathaniel was dead and the council was free to take over. They turned Nathaniel into a martyr and the Cult of Nathaneil was born. Damian (Nathaniel's father) became the leader and I found his son's body and gave him the plan to absorb his son's life essence in order to become younger and stronger. Nathaniel was a strong soul and was somehow still alive despite being critically injured. Damian instantly agreed and we moved onto trying to get Darwin killed. We managed to hurt him severely but Simon intervened and saved his life. I wasn't able to locate his body until the very end of Damian's reign but that's neither here nor there.

I may have lost Darwin but I had Damian as a new puppet for me to manipulate. For 100 years I trained him on how to be a capable tyrant and how to attain full control. We adapted the MKUltra Experiment and made it possible in today's standards. With my body no longer aging due to my god's influence; I was there and was able to watch the world grow. Together Damian and I would recreate the world in our image and would be able to get rid of all conflicts and war. There would only be us and us alone.

The Cult Of Nathaniel

Damian was very useful but he lacked a rival to make things interesting. I was hoping to find a successor to Darwin but no one appeared until Aaron Jacobson appeared. Our plan was simple. We would make people work and the people who weren't of age we would kidnap and force them to exact punishments on those who had broken the laws of Nathaniel. They would then have no memory of the event until we allowed them to remember just before their execution. Aaron was used to execute his friend Caroline and then we took him into the factory once he came of age. Somehow though he was able to retain his memories and was able to function in the factory normally. Normally the lives of the people in the factory and their lives outside of it were completely separate but Aaron had managed to keep both together instead of living them separately. He then found Nathaniel's body and Darwin's body also showed up in our hospital. That must have been Simon's doing. I wanted to dispose of him but Damian wanted to keep him there until a new successor showed up. After Aaron discovered our secrets, we knocked him out and Damian absorbed the rest of his son's life essence and essentially became Nathaniel. Darwin and Aaron were eventually merged together and became one being as well.

The two fought together and were able to dethrone Damian and restored balance to their world. After that failure me and my dark god decided to go to another world in order to wreak more havoc. Surely, we would have better luck elsewhere, right? I had to stop and catch my breath and Edward offered me more water which I appreciated. My life force was slowly draining as we talked but I knew I had more than enough for this at least. I needed someone to know the truth and Edward seemed the most capable person of being able to tell my story effectively. I trusted him enough and he seemed to be close to the other people involved in this affair so it made sense he would capture our stories. I decided to ask him one day why he was listening to all of our stories and he said he wanted to compile a history of his homeland and there were many people that were intertwined with that. I understood to a certain extent and decided that since I was the cause of so much suffering then I may as well provide my own perspective on the matter. I plan on telling my entire story from beginning to end before I die. Right now, my body is disintegrating for good after James and his friends and allies killed me but my spirit lives on in this doll while I tell my story. Eventually my soul will disintegrate as well but for now this will have to do.

I've spent so long fighting for my dark god that I almost forgot what it was like to do something just for myself. Edward was asking me whether the corruption was gone but to me it doesn't matter. I know what I did and I have no regrets. Everything I did I thought was right. Well actually that isn't true; I do have many regrets. My god is no longer suppressing my humanity and I do wish I handled things differently with Jake. Slowly the corruption is leaving me fully and I will feel the full weight of everything I did. I'm sure I will have many regrets once that happens. For now, I feel free for the first time in a long time. My god abandoned me when I lost for the final time and that changed me. Right now, it's time to get back to Darwin and Aaron. Simon appeared and agreed to separate them after restoring the world to peace. I decided to move onto another world after Damian's death.

The Kingdom Of Aeccacyre

The next person I targeted was a young man named Gerald. My former protégé Martin had been brainwashed by me and lost many of his memories by my hand. He had been brought to this world in order to cause chaos. He and Martin had been enemies for many years and Martin was easy to manipulate. Martin used to be a politician who would argue for the rights of his people who lived outside the kingdom of Aeccacyre. They lived in a harsh land but were still under the jurisdiction of the main kingdom yet were not given any of the rights and benefits that the people of the main kingdom once had. I had used my magic to convince the gods to bless Martin, Gerald and the princess of the kingdom with amazing powers and to play a game with them. Whoever's champion would win meant that that god or goddess would be that much stronger. They would fight through their champions. It reminded me a lot of my favourite game, but it's been so long I can't recall it. I used my abilities to turn Martin into a giant humanoid creature and stomp over everything. That was what he wanted and he used that power among many others to get his revenge. At first, he merely wanted to use his power to make a point that he and his people should be given the same amount of respect as people from the main kingdom. But after my persuasion that nothing would ever change, he changed tactics and decided to use his power for evil. He was also stuck in a reincarnation cycle just like me and would use that to his advantage to always take revenge. Eventually he tired of the cycle however and wanted to be free from the goddesses. He longed for his freedom and wanted to attain all of the magic and become his own man.

I can respect his ambitions and goals and that's why I wanted to help him. I promised that his people would be saved and would be able to thrive under new management.

He believed me of course and we managed to create many different weapons together. We even took control of the kingdom's weapons and did a full-blown invasion of the kingdom. Gerald nearly died and had to spend time recovering. He spent many years in isolation while he healed and Martin led his invasion against the rest of the world. I advised Martin on where to hit first and how best to rule his new people. There were pockets of people that were still alive but most people were long dead by the time Gerald recovered from his injuries. I felt immense pride that I managed to take out an entire kingdom through the use of a puppet ruler and the dark god inside of me was greatly appeased as well. He was never happy when I failed but was always so happy whenever I succeeded.

I also manipulated Gerald with a time loop and even managed to convince him that he was crazy. I used psychological tactics and images from other universes in order to torment him and make him think he was trapped in a delusion and that he was really a mental patient. Of course, none of this worked but it was fun while it lasted. I even managed to trick him into thinking he killed a bunch of people when he did no such thing. It really was fun tricking him and I have some fond memories of that. But mostly I just feel sadness. Part of me wishes I could do more but another part of me things that what I did was wrong. It's hard not to feel guilty with my humanity coming back. I know I can't be redeemed for what I've done; but I hope that anyone reading this can understand that my intentions weren't always evil. Once upon a time I intended on being a good person and only wanted the best for everyone. But now those dreams are long dead and I've become a shell of who I used to me. I've committed so many crimes but there are some things that I would never do. I even manipulated a young man named Leon into becoming immortal and gave him the push he needed to try and destroy his entire world and undo his descendant's work.

Edward decided to ask me if I ever raped anyone or committed any heinous crimes like sexual assault. That was a fair question and I'm happy to answer in the essence of everything and for the sake of transparency. The truth is, I never raped anyone nor committed any sense of sexual assault on anyone. The only time I ever had sex was with myself and with partners but that was consensual. I may have violated bodies after they were dead but that only included maiming their bodies and propping up the bodies in strange poses to create terror and hatred among the people but I never did anything beyond that. Rape is one of the few things I would never approve of and even if I did my god would never approve of it either. He enjoys brutality but only in the sense of violence and never anything to do with sex. Anyway, Edward and I both figured this was important since I seem to gain sexual pleasure from blood and gore which is true but I would never violate another person or their body in that manner. That's too much even for me when I was at my lowest point.

I also never had sex with my god or anyone else in any capacity. The only other people I had sex with were my wives but that was it. And it was consensual on both ends. I also don't think I could ever hurt an animal. I always loved animals when I was a kid and still do. They are some of the creatures that I would never hurt if I can avoid it. Animals are better than humans in many ways. Especially cats. Cats are great creatures and they deserve the best. I'm pretty sure Jake had a cat. I hope James takes good care of her.

Anyway, enough of that. Time to move onto the rest of the tale. Gerald managed to gain his strength back and despite me holding him in a time loop he managed to find allies to aid him in his cause. I had advised Martin on how to manipulate Derek and turn him into a pawn to be used against Gerald. Derek's story was tragic since he wasn't able to figure out how to break free of his trauma until Gerald managed to help him. Every evil person that was involved in every plot had been manipulated by me in order to gain control over them. Eventually Gerald managed to get through to them and turned them onto his side. He and Martin decided to leave their kingdom behind to let it heal on its own. In truth, I believed that was the best idea for peace but my god wasn't happy with that. I also wasn't completely happy with that if I was being completely honest. He wasn't happy that I wasn't taking a more direct route in taking over these universes and I decided that he was right.

The Final Chapter

I NEEDED TO HAVE a much firmer hand so I decided to travel all across the multiverse and absorb everything in it. I killed various versions of James and his friends and I even found Nathaniel's spirit and the two of us merged into the creature known as Ricky Jacobson. We became a giant purple humanoid that would stomp and absorb everyone in our path. At that point we were at our strongest and I had given up on reincarnation and decided to go all out with my skills and I let my anger do the talking. Nathaniel and I had merged and I shared his desire for world domination as well. Both of our desires were one and the same and that was to exterminate all human life. My god didn't even have to intervene anymore. I was so lost in the haze of bloodshed that I was entirely on my own. Those actions are mine and mine alone. Sometimes I would even host a talk show named *Ricky Jacobson Presents* and would talk about the current events and then I would absorb the studio audience and everyone else left in the universe.

I really was obsessed with that back then. I wanted to put on a show for people just before they died and many of them seemed to enjoy it. I even got renewed for a second season. It's a shame that no one will ever get to see more content. Anyway, that was fun and Nathaniel enjoyed the showmanship that went along with it so he was very much on board with the talk show. He and I shared the same desires and body but our minds were somewhat separate while also merged together if that makes sense. We could think independently in some cases but most of the time our thoughts were merged and anything one felt the other felt as well. We weren't two distinct beings in any capacity; we were one entity and, in a way, I felt happy during that time.

I got lost in the haze of murder and showmanship that I forgot about all of my problems. I think on some level I wanted to be defeated despite the dark god suppressing my humanity. The thought of everything makes me sick now and I have many regrets.

I know that I'll be going to hell or some other afterlife once this is all over and I accept that. Edward jotted down some more notes and looked up at me as if waiting for me to continue. I very much like Edward. He's a good guy and I can tell he has the best interests of everyone at heart. I wish I could have heard more about his adventures but perhaps I will in another life. For now, though, I'm done with reincarnation. When I die, I plan on dying for real. Okay, after James and his allies confronted me for the last time I tried to destroy them with my new abilities but they beat me fair and square. I accept my fate and agree that it was well deserved. I lived a long and eventful life. It may not have been a good life but I did finally manage to figure out what the disease was that took my parents away. I can rest easy knowing that I finally figured out what it was and how to cure it. I sent that information to James so he and the others could cure the world of it in time. I know that I'll never see my family again but I hope they can learn to be happy. They deserve that at the very least.

Okay, I've had enough. I can feel my body beginning to shimmer away into dust. Edward looks at me with an almost sympathetic look and says "I'm sorry you couldn't make it up to Jake." I smile and say, "It's okay. He deserves to be at peace and I accept that. Please watch over the rest of his friends for me, will you? They deserve to be happy as well." Edward nodded happily and he closed his tome. This was the end of our tale and I feel satisfied of how everything came together. I feel the weight of everything that has happened and I want to cry. Edward hands me a tissue as I blow my nose. I really do feel sad about everything. I wish I could have told Jake what he really meant to me and I wish that I could have saved him from himself. I had the opportunity but chose not to go for it. That will always be my biggest regret. If I could do it again, I would have raised Jake like the man he deserved to be. Goodbye, everyone and thank you. This is the end and I hope you can forgive me for my part. I'm sorry Jake for everything. You deserved better than a worthless father like me.

Doctor Jeb's body slumped down on in his seat for the last time and Edward couldn't help but shed some tears for him. Dr. Jeb was an enemy but he was still human in the very end. Edward wished he could have done more for the man but he felt good knowing that he can chronicle his final wishes. Jeb's body was now an empty shell and Edward buried it in a special grave out of respect. After everything he deserved to rest in peace.

Epilogue:

Three Years Later

After that, I Ezekiel decided to go back to my home world and reunite with my friends. I told them all what happened and then after a happy reunion I told them I was leaving. Before I did though I chose to read Dr. Jeb's book to Jake's grave so that we could all learn the truth. I cried after reading it and I felt the wind turn from cold to a nice warm breeze. I think that means that Jake was at peace with his father's actions. I'm glad I could help him get some closure in the end.

Afterwards I decided to go with James and the others in order to bring Simon back. Darwin even came with us and we all became really close. Darwin eventually made peace with his actions and reunited with his friends and family and was able to clear his name along with becoming like brothers with Aaron after their separation. The rest of the group went their separate ways after that and I'm planning on reuniting with them soon. "And what about Simon?" a nearby voice asked. "Ah I almost forgot. We were able to bring him back and he promised not to overuse the stone's power anymore. We got to live in peace and now I make my home traveling with Simon and checking in on the universes. And what about you? What have you been up to lately our favourite scholar?" I asked jokingly. Edward put his quill down and laughed softly. He had been interviewing each of us for our account. He even got Nathaniel's and Dr. Jeb's accounts before they died. Edward smiled and said "I've been compiling each of your accounts and I believe I've finally completed it. The entire account will be multiple volumes and sold to the public. I've become quite a wealthy man with my book deals but I spend my time at the museum doing my life's work. I'm finally happy and I'm glad to see that you're happy as well."

Me and Edward shook hands and I left his office. I teleported back to Simon and he and I continued our adventures as I bid Edward goodbye.

Edward sat back at his desk after escorting Ezekiel outside. He took a moment to reflect on all of his adventures and everything he had accomplished throughout his early twenties. Many people told him that his work was boring but the money in his account and the scars he gained from his travels begged to differ. He had made many close friends such as James, Ezekiel, Darwin, Simon, Aaron, Stacy, and Christine. Edward considered these people his new family and even considered introducing them to his actual blood family. Edward never got to utilize his powers much on his adventures but that was okay. His days spent training helped him to master his powers quite quickly. Maybe he will write a tale about those experiences but that's for another day. Overall, Edward was quite content with his life and as he finished adding finishing touches to his stories he closed the book. He felt satisfied that he had completed another book to his name. It may not have been as long as he liked, but it was important to him and that's what matters. He took a breath of stale air from the museum and left his writing desk. He closed up the museum for the night and went home to spend time with his family and take a break from all of the adventures he had been on.

Edward never told anyone other than his family, but he considered ending his life and felt that he was worthless. He was only good at the museum stuff even though it didn't pay much initially and he thought that he wouldn't amount to anything. He felt that his life was the only valuable thing he would be able to give but that was wrong. Finding the secret journal changed everything and his true writing talents came to light for the world to see. He also thought that he didn't have any friends and that he was a loser to everyone but he proved that he was more capable than anyone else he had ever known. Edward always remained humble and was just happy to be living a life that fulfilled him and having a family that loved him. Maybe he'll write more tales, or maybe he will retire and settle into contentment with his family. Who knows what the future holds? But isn't that the beauty of life; it may be hard, it may be awful, but there is always something exciting hiding behind the next door. And perhaps, the next chapter will be even more exciting than the previous ones.

The End?

In a distant afterlife far away, there was a scientist who looked to be quite young at about 19 and walked closer to a young man who appeared to be around his age. No one would be able to tell but these two were father and son. The older man looked happy but heartbroken to see his son again. He cried and apologized for everything he had done and the son listened stoically without making any moves towards him. After the older man finished crying the younger man ran up to him as it to slap him. The older man braced himself but wasn't ready for the embrace that he received. The older man stared dumbfounded at his son as he stared down at him and was crying deeply. The young man opened his eyes with tears streaming and said "I forgive you dad, for everything." The older man cried as well and they embraced happily as father and son. They would spend the rest of their days rebuilding their relationship and the young man even got to meet his half sibling and got to see his grandparents. Everyone was finally at peace...for ten years. Another story was about to begin.

Bonus Chapters!

A New Adventure

Nine years after the events of the fourth book:

This is a story about Edward and Darwin going across the world in order to find eight historical artifacts in order to locate the lost city of Cliburg. These eight artifacts are of varying sizes and are able to unlock the ancient city of Cliburg and locate hidden riches. The story opens with Edward in his office in Schreiber Ontario in the main universe. James had just left his office after chatting with him for a while and Edward goes back to his books and writings. He's always wanted to go off on an adventure of his own but never had the opportunity. His trials with Leon and Elias mostly involved training and going around the worlds for fun but Edward never felt like writing those tales down. He wanted to go on a real adventure with his friends and feel like he'd contributed to the world. True he managed to help get rid of Jeb and Nathaniel and he compiled every one else's adventures into a series of books to sell but Edward still didn't feel satisfied with himself. After James had left, he got a letter from Simon. Simon sometimes used his magical hawk in order to send messages back and forth and Edward always appreciated seeing the furry little creature. The hawk was brown with magic shimmering off him as he glowed. The little hawk was just a baby and he dropped off the letter that was clutched in his teeth before he disappeared back into the void and back to Simon.

The letter read Dear Edward, I need your help in Egypt. There is a grand discovery that has been uncovered by Rathos' tomb. I wish I could be there in person but I have other matters to attend to. Please come post haste and you shall have the adventure of your life if you wish. Signed Simon. "A great discovery!" yelped Edward as he read the letter multiple times over. This just might be the adventure he's been looking for. Darwin came into his office looking sad right at that moment and perked up when he saw Edward's smiling and shocked face. "What's going on buddy? Another telegram from Simon I presume?" Edward looked at Darwin and replied "Yeah! Simon wants my help on a grand adventure! I got to pack and get ready. But what's up with you? You seem down my friend?" Darwin looked down and shuffled his feet together as he attempted to hide his nerves. "I got dumped man; she dumped me for another guy. I get it but it really hurts you know?" said Darwin sadly. Edward nodded and hugged him tight. Darwin and Edward had become close friends since their last adventure together in beating back Jeb and Nathaniel. After what happened, Darwin felt best talking with Aaron, James, and Edward himself.

"I understand friend, don't worry though; it'll be okay. Would you want to come with me on my adventure to Egypt? I'm sure Aaron can look after the museum in your absence for a little while. It also might help you take your mind off things." Edward said reassuringly. Darwin eventually left the embrace and nodded vigorously. Edward and Darwin didn't look much different from ten years ago. Darwin still had his green eyes and light brown hair. Edward still has red hair and still looks like a scholar despite also looking like he could be a model in certain circles. He lost the freckles on his face and he's gained a lot of muscle mass. Darwin also gained a lot of muscle and Edward is now just under 6 ft which is the same as Darwin. The two looked slightly older but due to the magic powering Schreiber and Edward's own immortality the two don't look much older than twenty-five. The two age much slower than most humans and are more than capable of living forever if they wished to. The magic of Schreiber has no effect on Edward but Darwin has also been blessed with immortality from both Simon powering him up and the magic of the town.

Edward packed his things into a satchel and Darwin ran back home to tell Aaron the good news and to pack. Darwin had been teaching Aaron the ropes on how to run the museum and he finally believed that Aaron was ready to look after it by himself for the foreseeable future. Darwin packed all the essentials like clothes, food and water, and his sword. His beautiful sword that he used against Nathaniel many times in the past was still just as shiny as it was when he first saw it. Due to Simon's power up and his years of training he was very skilled with swordsmanship and was stronger than most humans. He was still far from being able to beat James in a fight but he was still stronger than most. His magic enhanced his strength and allowed him to and allowed him to imprint scary images onto other people's minds. It was a rare form of telepathy that Simon helped him to learn and master.

He packed the blade up carefully just in case and headed back to Edward's office. Edward on the other hand packed up his essentials which included food, water, writing tools, and some books along with a change of clothes. Edward also packed both of his swords carefully as well for the journey ahead. He had gotten them from Elias and Leon. Leon passed on his sword before he died permanently and Elias had no need for his weapon anymore. The swords could shoot out beams of light and when used together they could create a powerful magical shield of energy around the user that would protect them from harm. Edward could control the elements to a certain extent and had some super strength but the bulk of his abilities came in his writings. With his skills he could read an entire book in a single second if he wanted to and could use his telekinesis to cause heart attacks. It was a very rare and dangerous ability that Simon taught him to utilize if he were ever in extreme danger. Edward didn't like to use it but he couldn't deny that it was a very useful ability to have in his pocket. Edward was also able to use portals to jump to different worlds and was also given the power of flight. Darwin also had the power of flight as well and the two often flew around the world together when bored.

Once Darwin returned to Edward's office Edward greeted him with his packed satchel and the two jumped into a portal into Egypt. Edward and Darwin made it to Egypt instantaneously and headed to Rathos' tomb. After James's adventure and Rathos passing on to be reunited with his family; the tomb had become open to the public and became a tourist attraction. Everyone awed at the sight of a new tomb being discovered and recently; there had been evidence of something new being uncovered under his tomb. Edward and Darwin walked the streets of Egypt until making it to the tomb where they met with the curator of the area. A short plump man with a long white beard named Gamal greeted them both at the entrance to the tomb. "Greetings travelers, Simon informed me of your arrival. Please follow me into the tomb and I shall explain to you that we have found," he said happily. Edward and Darwin bowed to him as he bowed and then he led them forwards into the tomb. As soon as they entered the air became dry and hard to breathe in. Darwin nearly choked many times while Edward just calmly breathed in through his nose and out his mouth. The dry air didn't bother him since he was used to going on archaeological digs and such. Gamal led the two past Rathos' coffin and through a secret passage that led downwards.

"As you can see" said Gamal without a pause. "History is very important to the people of Egypt. And to me as well. Once we started poking around the tomb, we found this secret passage along with many new tablets depicting ancient art and hieroglyphics."

Gamal pointed to the hieroglyphics on the walls and showed off the tablets that had been put on display. "However, we have found something even more precious. We believe that we have found the remains of the legendary city Cliburg. The city was lost to time many centuries ago but we believe we have found the entrance to it. We need eight keys in order to unlock it however and that is where you two come in." He said happily. Gamal pointed out various things on their walk and Edward and Darwin looked at each other with interest.

Finally, they walked towards a pedestal that held eight slots of varying sizes and shapes. It resembled some sort of coffin. Gamal gestured to the pedestal and explained "the city of Cliburg was known for having streets of gold and for being home to the rich and powerful people of Egypt. Sadly, the city disappeared with no explanation many centuries ago and no one has been able to find any traces of it. Until recently that is. When I was exploring these ruins, I found this pedestal and the runes imbued on it are reminiscent of the ancient texts talking about the legendary city. If we were to find the eight lost historical artifacts it's believed that the city will unlock its doors and give us access inside. Will you two help me find the eight artifacts? If so, I can promise you twenty-million dollars in Canadian currency for your trouble." He said excitedly. Darwin and Edward looked at each other and both had the same excited expression on their faces. They nodded to each other and Edward turned to the curator and said "we'll do it!" Gamal clapped his hands together excitedly and brought forth an ancient looking map of the world. He pointed to where the first artifact was. "The first artifact is locked within the temple of the ancients in Greece. If you head there and locate the temple then you'll be able to find the first artifact. It looks like an ancient looking crown. Once you find it return it here so that we can safeguard the object and it shall lead you to the next one through the use of the old magic."

Edward and Darwin both nodded and they began to pore over the map together. It was a map of the world and the first spot circled was Greece. The two of them asked Gamal many more questions about logistics and where to find the temple once they made it into Greece. Gamal explained that there would be a guide found at the Temple of Poseidon. Edward used his magic to create a portal and he and Darwin entered through it and made it to the center of Greece. They walked the streets and eventually made it to the cliff where the Temple of Poseidon was located. The air felt fresh and exhilarating and Edward could feel the history of the place as he walked. Darwin also felt the history and enjoyed being there with his friend Edward. The two were quite close and were like brothers in many cases. The two went towards the temple where they saw a beautiful woman waiting on the steps looking bored. As soon as she saw them, she perked up and said "Heya, I'm your guide for the day. Shall I take you to the temple of the ancients?" She asked brightly. Darwin felt entranced by this woman and went forward. "Yes please, but first what's your name? Mine's Darwin and this is Edward," he said as he pointed to Edward. The woman had long brown hair, looked about their age, and looked like she was cosplaying as Indiana Jones with the hat and whip and all. She smiled even wider in a beautiful way and tipped her hat. "Nice to meetcha Darwin and Edward, my name's Hailey." She looked at Edward with respect but she smiled entrancingly as she looked Darwin up and down. Darwin blushed and looked away while Edward chuckled to himself slightly.

Edward came closer and said "where is the temple of the ancients Hailey? Me and my compatriot are ready to head there." Hailey nodded at Edward and said "right this way fellas." Her bright smile never leaving her face. Hailey led them both through the Temple of Poseidon and to a small obelisk at the edge of the cliff. "Only us treasure hunters know about the significance of this obelisk you, see? The true temple of the Ancients is hidden beneath the Temple of Poseidon. It requires a special chant in order to open the way to the temple and luckily, I know the chant by heart." Hailey bowed her head to the obelisk and chanted. Darwin and Edward couldn't hear what she was saying but the words sounded ancient and in a language they couldn't recognize. She seemed to be whispering to herself and neither of the two could pick up on what she was saying. After thinking that this might be a wash a resounding crash echoed from the obelisk as lightning hit it straight on and shattered the object. A bright blue light in the shape of a circle opened up and Hailey began walking through it.

Edward and Darwin quickly hurried to catch up with her and they whooshed through the portal. It felt different than Edward's usual portal jumping. This felt older, and colder like he was utilizing something older than his magic. He couldn't place it for sure though. After a few minutes their bodies reformed and they looked at what appeared to be the past. The Temple of Poseidon looked built again and not in ruins like it appears in Modern Day and the entrance appeared to be sealed. Hailey smirked at the entrance and chanted again softly. The door opened with a click and the doors extended inwards. Hailey started to head inside while gesturing for Edward and Darwin to follow. They did of course and they ended up in a beautiful temple that looked like it was made of water. This was a temple to the god Poseidon and it made sense that the god's magic would make it appear as if it was made of water. The Temple of Ancients must be beyond the Temple of Poseidon. The temple smelled of the sea and Darwin felt comforted by it. He always enjoyed being near the water and felt at ease here. Hailey led them through many rooms until they came across an entrance to a temple that looked darkened. A swirling purple vortex seemed to be coming from the depths. Hailey strode up confidently and said "this is the true way to the Temple of Ancients. You boys aren't scared, are ya?" She asked playfully. Edward chuckled while Darwin tried to make himself look tough. Edward smiled and said "we will be fine. Lead the way." Hailey nodded and winked at Darwin before heading inside the portal. Edward and Darwin walked up together and jumped inside as well.

The Temple of the Ancients

GOING THROUGH THE VORTEX felt like being swallowed up by something and then being spat back out again. Need less to say it wasn't a pleasant feeling. Edward and Darwin exited the vortex to see Hailey standing confidently admiring the view ahead. The temple ahead looked enchanting and beautiful. It was a beautiful black and white temple that looked ancient and intact. It looked so gorgeous that Darwin couldn't help but stare in shock. Hailey noticed him staring and said "beautiful huh? This is my favourite part of this job. Getting to explore new places and see amazing things." Hailey sighed wistfully and Darwin spoke up. "I never got to go out much, and part of me feels scared yet I feel fulfilled. I can't explain why that is. Perhaps it can't be explained." Darwin paused for a moment as Hailey and Edward looked at him expectantly. "Maybe, it's because that while I got to read about the world, I never got to experience it. But right now, I'm going on a grand adventure with one of my best friends. I wonder if it could be pride. Heh, I'm sorry guys. I must sound so pathetic, don't I?" Darwin said ashamed. Darwin began to put himself down until Edward came up to him and gently tapped his shoulder. "Hey man, I get it. It's the same for me. You're not pathetic, you've struggled with issues but you've been able to combat them with strength that I have admired for so long. I've told other people's stories yet I never got to tell my own. I never felt my stories were worth anything. But I feel strong because you're here with me and we can do this together." Darwin smiled at his friend and Hailey lightly punched Darwin in the shoulder as a way to show support and Darwin blushed.

Hailey looked deep in thought. She turned to Darwin and said "I have my own issues that I'm working through. Never feel ashamed of being scared or feeling inadequate.

You're stronger than you think fella." Darwin blushed even harder and Hailey chuckled at his reaction. Darwin was falling more and more in love with this woman. Perhaps he could tell her how he felt sometime but right now they had a job to do. He didn't know that she felt the same about him. The three continued onto the temple and saw how marvelous it was. On the inside there were crystal goblets all around the room and torches and candelabras lit the way. The floor and walls were made of marble and Darwin could see part of his reflection. He didn't look half bad.

Hailey continued to lead them inside until she suddenly stopped and said "over there, that's where the crown should be." Edward and Darwin looked ahead and they saw a beautiful golden crown in the distance. It sat on a lone pedestal not far from their current position. The air smelled of cleanliness for some reason and Edward could feel the history coming from this place. This place had so many stories Edward figured. Darwin slowly walked up to the pedestal and picked up the crown. He expected there to be some sort of trap getting triggered or something to happen but there was nothing. Hailey came up to Darwin and said "good job fella. You got it!" Hailey giggled and laughed happily while Darwin felt even more entranced with her. Hailey led them out of the temple and they went back through the portal. After they returned to Greece it was nightfall. Edward decided to portal back to Egypt to drop off the crown while Darwin decided to escort Hailey back to her hotel before flying back there as well. Edward waved goodbye and headed off. Darwin escorted her back and before he left, she gently grabbed his arm. Hey Darwin, would you want to spend the night with me?" She said softly. There was no hint of seduction in her voice this time. But there was a hint of nervousness. Darwin replied "yes". Hailey beamed and she gently led the way into her room. They started kissing passionately and Darwin began to feel himself taking off his clothes while she did the same. They spent many hours kissing and going further before Hailey finally fell asleep. Darwin kissed her forehead and headed back to Egypt. He couldn't stay the night no matter how much he wanted and Hailey understood that. She was a world-renowned treasure hunter and her life was on the road. She wasn't in the mood for a long-term relationship and neither was Darwin.

After many hours of flying and feeling the rush of wind in his hair Darwin made it back to Egypt while Edward was in the middle of discussing things with Gamal. "Hey man, welcome back." Said Edward. Darwin nodded in Edward's direction and sat near Gamal. Gamal had placed the crown into one of the eight pedestals and it began to glow. Edward and Darwin quickly clutched their heads as bright light began to overtake their vision.

Blood gushed out of their noses as they fell to the ground. Gamal didn't seem concerned however and just continued to sit in peace. Suddenly a picture began to materialize in their minds. Edward and Darwin saw pictures of a lake and they saw a gauntlet at the bottom of it. They realized that the next relic was found at the bottom of Lake Superior! They would need a boat captain to get them to the specific spot so they could dive down and retrieve it but that shouldn't be a problem. Gamal stared at them and said "It'll get easier my friends. The more artifacts you find the more attuned you'll be to their magic." Edward and Darwin nodded and decided to get some sleep in one of the many hotels in Egypt since they didn't want to portal back home since it was so late at night. Edward and Darwin crashed at the finest hotel at the courtesy of Gamal's generosity. They slept like babies at the hotel and felt completely refreshed the next morning.

The Dangers of Lake Superior

Back in Canada, Edward and Darwin searched Lake Superior on the Canadian side of the border with a fisherman named David Lengyel. He was a master fisherman and a close friend of Darwin's. He was a lean man with a big temper and an even bigger heart. He would do anything for the people he cared about. David looked towards Darwin and said "you sure you want to do this?" Darwin nodded and David said "Alright then, let's get this done. For the record, you're a good man Darwin. Always have been. And Edward, I can't wait to read your next book. I always loved your stories." Edward choked up a little and so did Darwin. David reminded them of family members that they had lost so it meant everything to hear that from him. They scanned the lake until Edward and Darwin found the spot where they saw their vision. The two of them jumped off the boat and flew down in the lake. They used their magic to be able to manipulate the water and air particles so they could breathe underwater. They both went down and traversed the clear waters and kept going deeper and deeper until they saw the gauntlet submerged in some dirt. Edward grabbed it from the dirt and pulled when they heard a deafening roar coming from the depths of the water.

Edward almost lost his grip on the gauntlet but managed to keep it together and Darwin helped him pull it up. The sound caused blood to come from their ears but they ignored the painful sensation for the time being. They had other things to worry about right now. There was a distant rumbling and Edward and Darwin flew back upwards as fast as they could. They made it back to the boat safely and David had asked "what the hell is going on?" Before Edward or Darwin could elaborate a gigantic creature the size of multiple houses appeared from the water and looked down at them. The creature looked like the Loch Ness monster of legend. "Isn't that thing supposed to be in Scotland?" Asked Darwin. Edward wanted to respond but he had to focus on the mounting creature in front of him.

David looked at the creature and said "Woah Nelly, that looks like a gigantic son of a bitch. How about we get out of here before it eats us." He tried to turn the boat around but the creature's gigantic tail rose up on the other side as if to block their way. They were surrounded. The only way forward was to fight. Edward drew his two swords and summoned beams of light from them and fired them at the creature's head. It looked a lot like the Loch Ness monster from legend but still appeared quite different. It had a long slender body and had two gigantic mouths; one inside of the smaller one and the teeth looked wickedly sharp. The creature also had red glowing eyes. Clearly this was some sort of hybrid of the monster and something else. Darwin felt terrified and could barely move. He knew he had to act but he was paralyzed by fear. Edward was facing off against the creature by using light blasts but it wasn't doing much damage beyond blinding the monster. Darwin finally breathed in deep and felt a surge of confidence swelling up inside of him. He could do this.

Darwin breathed in and out and then flew upwards before he could think twice about anything. He needed to save his friends. Darwin flew towards the creature's mouths and slashed at their teeth. He managed to catch a tooth and rip it out of its mouth but that was all he could get before the monster howled in pain and tried to devour Darwin. Edward was still firing blasts of light at the creature while it tried to reorient itself. Darwin took the opportunity to go deep into the creature's mouth and use his sword to cut him up from the inside. He flew inside his mouth while Edward yelled out "DARWIN!" He began firing even more bolts and used his flight and swords to slash at his abdomen to try and get Darwin out. After sliding through the creature's mouth and stomach Darwin used his sword and cut himself out through his back and exploded outside in an explosion of blood and gore. Darwin was covered everywhere but he didn't care. Edward was also covered in blood but continued to hack into the abdomen until he heard Darwin flying next to him. Edward stopped and embraced his friend. The creature howled in pain from being slashed from both ends and slowly began to drift back into the water. The creature had died and the Loch Ness monster was no more. Edward and Darwin went back to David Lengyel and he congratulated them both on defeating the monster. "Woah Nelly, congrats boys. You managed to slay that creature before my very eyes, I'm so proud of you boys!" He embraced them both and they happily hugged him back. He was like a father to them and they truly wanted to make him proud. After the embrace Edward and Darwin went to get cleaned up before heading back to Egypt where Gamal was waiting for them. He slept in the tomb day and night while waiting for them to return. He was really dedicated to his work. Gamal placed the gauntlet on the coffin as well. Edward and Darwin had another vision and this time they saw a beautiful sword thrust inside of a volcano. It was encased in magical properties so it wouldn't be disturbed by the lava. The volcano appeared to be in a gigantic forest somewhere. It appeared to be a place where dinosaurs roamed and even had their own little society.

Edward and Darwin would have to be careful regardless and they decided to head there straight away. After getting some much-needed rest of course and replenishing their supplies. Edward always needed new books to read and he needed more ink and paper in order to properly catalogue all of these adventures. After getting some rest and supplies Edward used his magic to teleport them to the magical land of dinosaurs where the volcano would be.

Land of the Dinosaurs and Other Relics

EDWARD AND DARWIN APPEARED in the middle of a huge forest and the air smelled so hot that it invaded their nostrils and made them want to throw up. Edward sweat so profusely that he was afraid he would need a change of clothes before too long. Darwin however was sweating but not as bad. After the Prison Experiment he was used to unexpected things like an increase of temperature. The white room could go from very hot to very cold in an instant so this didn't feel too bad to him. The thought of that place still gave him chills despite the heat but there was nothing that could be done now. Nathaniel was long dead. The duo decided that it would be best if they could get to the volcano without accidently pissing off the dinosaur population. They had no idea if the dinosaurs would be hostile or not and were wary of accidently upsetting them by invading their sacred spaces. The two of them wandered through the forest until they saw a little village. They saw gigantic dinosaurs but they didn't expect to see them doing what they were doing.

There they saw a Tyrannosaurus Rex having tea and scones with a pterodactyl while discussing the nice weather. There were other dinosaurs discussing philosophy and some were playing YUGIOH and Magic the Gathering. These dinosaurs seemed very intelligent but the two had a mission to go on. They didn't want to have to fight anyone if they could avoid it and they didn't trust themselves to talk things out and avoid an international incident. Edward and Darwin snuck through the village and eventually made it to a path that led to the volcano. The burning heat became even more unbearable the closer they got to the volcano but that didn't deter them. Edward ended up changing his clothes more than once while Darwin only changed his clothes once.

The two found a path into the volcano and went inside there. Inside the heat became even worse but there was nothing they could do about it. They kept on chugging water bottles to try and quell the heat but it didn't help much. The heat just kept getting worse and worse. Edward tried casting a spell to cool their body temperatures and that seemed to help immensely. Edward and Darwin would walk comfortably now. They followed the path of blazing heat until they managed to make it to what they assumed was the final chamber. The duo opened the door and saw the sword encased in magical ice in the center of the room and treasure was spilling everywhere from mountains of treasure. What they saw beyond was a gigantic dragon looking over them; and he didn't appear to be too interested in conversation. The door slammed shut and the dragon roared before breathing fire down on them. Edward and Darwin ducked and ran out of the way while trying to find an opening. Edward used his swords to turn them into ice and shot ice crystals at the dragon. They seemed to help but not much. Darwin on the other hand ran up its body and tried to slash at it. His slashes were effective but they also caught the dragon's attention and the fire kept getting closer to him before he could make it to the dragon's head. Edward tried using the ice as a shield to block him and Darwin from the onslaught and tried running up the dragon's body from the other side.

Edward made it to the dragon's head this time and used his ice swords to stab into the dragon's deep neck. The aim was true and the dragon howled in pain. Eventually after enough slashing the dragon soon fell dead. Edward took as much treasure as he could for historical significance and they left the volcano. As soon as the two of them left the volcano they were met with the dinosaurs from the village. The lead dinosaur the T-Rex came up to them and bellowed out "did you defeat our sacred dragon, and plunder his treasure?!" Darwin and Edward nodded ashamedly and the T-Rex said "I see. Thank you, brave heroes! He was terrorizing us for generations and we couldn't escape his cruelty. But you saved us. Hooray for the heroes!" Edward and Darwin felt honored by the dinosaurs and ate up the praise they were given. Edward learned about their history while Darwin played chess with some of the younger dinosaurs and they all partied late into the night. After the celebrations Edward and Darwin took the sword still encased in ice and returned to Egypt. After returning Edward used his magic to de-spell the ice and Gamal placed the sword in its proper place on the coffin. Edward and Darwin felt the familiar sensation in their heads and they saw the next item on the docket.

The next artifact was a necklace worn by the King of a far away land. Edward recognized this king from his books. He was known for being a brute who would murder his wives for looking at him wrong and for speaking to him at times. This man was an awful person and should not be the leader of an entire nation. Edward used his portal skills to teleport him and Edward to the kingdom and they ended up near the castle. The castle town was bustling and the guards were on high alert. Edward and Darwin decided to find a place to stay for the day in order to wait until nightfall and try to sneak in. Edward could do many amazing things with his powers but his portal abilities were limited. He could only portal to places he has seen or heard of but not to specific parts of that world. He can get close but not right to their objective. It was a pain but he did what he could with his abilities.

Darwin found a gambling hall and they decided to hang out there for a few hours. Darwin won on some bets and flirted with some of the waitresses and they flirted back. Edward won briefly but lost more than he wanted to admit. Ah well, he didn't care much for money anyway. Sure, it was nice but he had everything he needed on him. He also knew his family was nice and safe so he was happy about that. After many hours it was time to try and infiltrate the castle. Darwin had also gotten some information from the locals. Apparently, the castle was a lot laxer at night and there weren't as many guards. There was also a secret area through the gardens that would lead them to the inside of the castle. Edward and Darwin would make great use of this information.

The two of them left the hall and went to the castle. They went to the side where there weren't as many guards and they snuck across the wall with their flight abilities and then they snuck through the paths and went right to where the gardens were. The air inside the hall had been filled with liquor and sweat but out here the air felt fresh and the smell of flowers permeated their sense. It was truly nice. The pair kept moving forward until they managed to make it to where the secret entrance was and they hopped in and got inside the castle. The two of them snuck through the castle and avoided as many guards as they could until they finally made it to the king's room. They crept in and saw the king was sleeping. They snuck over to him and gently took the necklace from his neck. The king awoke with a start and Edward and Darwin flew out the window before they could be seen and flew away from the kingdom. Once they were sure it was safe they portaled away and headed back to Egypt.

They panted when they got back and were scared and tired from nearly being caught by the king. They gave the necklace to Gamal and he of course put it on the coffin. Edward and Darwin felt a bad headache come on but blood wasn't gushing from their noses this time. They were becoming used to this kind of magic. The vision they saw was one of heartbreak. They had to find a lost helm that had been buried in a graveyard in Egypt? This helm was actually really close to where they were. Edward and Darwin had permission from Gamal to desecrate the gravesite and they went to see the gravesite of Elijah Daniels. His tombstone read: Here lies Elijah Daniels, a great and honourable man. Beloved father, son and uncle. There was a sword that was lain beside the grave. Perhaps he was a warrior or a soldier of some kind.

Edward and Darwin dug deep into the earth until they found his casket. They pulled the casket up and found he was wearing it. Edward carefully touched the help and pried it off the man's skull. The help came off easily and the body wasn't disturbed in any capacity. Edward and Darwin said some prayers for Elijah and then they re-buried the body back where it belonged. The corpse was put back to rest and Edward and Darwin headed back to the tomb. They did the same thing again and gave the helm to Gamal. Gamal placed it atop the coffin and then the two of them felt the familiar sensation of their visions. The next place they saw materializing was a hedge maze. At the center of the hedge maze was a goblet filled with amber. That was the next place to go to. Edward and Darwin decided to get some sleep first and then the next morning they headed out to find the hedge maze.

The Secrets of the Hedge Maze

Edward and Darwin reached the hedge maze in record time and found out that it was located in Madrid Spain. They hired a guide to help them get there since it was off the beaten path. Edward spoke some Spanish and was able to communicate with the man. The guide left them to their own devices once he led them to the secret maze and went back to his business. Edward used an orb of light to guide them through the maze. Inside they saw shadow creatures which Edward was able to stave off with the orbs of light and his beams of light from his swords. The shadow creatures threatened to possess the two friends but Edward and Darwin fought them off. The shadow creatures were humanoid entities that died horrifically and wanted revenge on the human population. They didn't care if the humans involved were innocent; they just wanted them all to die. It was meant to be a true genocide.

However, there were so few shadow creatures that at best they could only kill a few humans at a time and were contained to very specific places like this hedge maze. They couldn't leave the maze no matter what they did and had to rely on people coming in which no one did because it was closed to the public for being too boring. I know, right. Anyway, no one knew the truth about what was actually going on which helped Edward and Darwin greatly. After navigating the maze for some time; they finally made it to the goblet of amber. It was made of amber and it also contained amber inside it as well. Anyway, Edward slowly picked it up and suddenly there were tons of shadow creatures coming from everywhere at once. Edward summoned his balls of light and Darwin drew his sword and enchanted it with light in order to attack any that got close to the either of them. Edward handled range and Darwin handled melee and hand to hand. They suited each other's styles perfectly.

After a long fight and many cuts and bruises on both of them finally managed to pull off the win. Edward panted while Darwin sat down and caught his breath. After a while the two felt a bit better and decided to take the goblet and go. Theye teleported back to Egypt and Gamal put it on the coffin once again. This time the pain they felt was twice as intense. Darwin fell and hit his head on the ground hard while Edward banged his foot into the wall. The two of them saw an abandoned mental hospital or asylum in Italy. Twin daggers could be found there. The place was rumored to be haunted and Edward knew all about that place. It was protected by the local Mafia and they needed their permission to be able to even get inside. Edward and Darwin decided that was the next best course of action. They got some rest and then went to Italy in order to get some answers.

The Horrors of the Italian Mafia

Darwin managed to buy his way into getting a meeting with the mafia. After his experiences with Nathaniel, he was in a dark place and dealt with many unsavory characters. Some of those contacts lived in Italy so he used ever favor he was owed in order to get a meeting with the mafia. Edward was curious to see how Darwin would handle himself so he decided to follow his lead. Darwin clutched a box with him and refused to tell Edward what it was. They went into the meeting and they a bunch of mobsters sitting around playing poker and one of them was sitting on a throne in the far back. He was clearly the leader. He was the oldest and was smoking a cigar. "Well, well, well. Who comes knocking at my door at this hour? I heard about you two. What do you want and why should I help you?" He sneered at the two of them. Darwin approached and said "sir, I have something that might interest you. But first, what we desire is to be granted access into the haunted asylum on your property and have a guide as well. We wish to find something in there that had historical significance to our quest." The Mafia leader thought about it then burst out laughing. "Why the hell would we care about historical significance? That place has bad mojo there. I'd rather soon see it burned down then send one of my guys in there with you. Why the hell shouldn't I kill you right here and right now?" He bellowed. "Well, that's because I have something that would interest you. Open up the box," Darwin said. Darwin handed the box to the leader's aide who passed it to him.

The leader opened the box and saw three severed heads. These were heads of the three biggest mafia families in Italy. How in the hell had Darwin managed to this you ask? With his bare hands and his sword. Darwin never liked the mafia but he understood that to get results he needed to produce trust. Trust would go a long way into getting what they wanted. Edward looked horrified at the sight but he understood why Darwin had done what he did. These were criminals he had killed and wouldn't judge him too harshly for doing what he had done. The leader stopped laughing and took on a serious face. "You managed to get rid of all of my rivals in who knows how long. I admit I'm impressed. You wanted a guide you said, fine. Antonio, lead them into the asylum tonight. And if they try anything kill them both. You got that?" He asked incredulously. A lean young man nodded and pulled out his twin pistols. Clearly, he meant business.

Edward and Darwin were instructed to come back later that night and would be guided to the asylum properly. The two of them decided to do some sight seeing while they waited and Darwin opened up a bit about his past with Edward. Edward understood where he was coming from and only wanted to help. Once the appointed hour came about the two of them headed back to the headquarters. Antonio guided them into the asylum and they all went together. The inside was completely deserted. There were gurneys overturned and beds left in the hallways. The air smelt of death and blood. There were bloodstains all across the way and everything seemed quiet. Too quiet. The kind of quiet that haunts your very bones. Suddenly a loud scream came from out of nowhere. Antonio didn't appear fazed but Edward and Darwin nearly jumped out of their pants. This place really was terrifying. Antonio guided them throughout the asylum and the three of them fought off any ghosts that appeared in their path. Antonio's guns were filled with special powder that allowed them to harm ghosts. He was definitely prepared for this.

They continued on until they got separated. Antonio just disappeared from view and Edward and Darwin couldn't find him. Suddenly they peered into a room and saw him staring into a mirror. He dropped his guns and seemed to be in a trance. He wasn't saying anything but he was shaking. He turned to look at the two and he looked terrified. His eyes were bloodshot and blood was leaking from his mouth. His hands were also covered with blood. What the hell happened to him? Antonio picked up a carving knife and brought it to his throat. Before Edward or Darwin could intervene, he plunged it deep into his throat and kept on cutting while screaming for the pain to stop. Something must have truly terrified him. Darwin looked into the mirror after Antonio fell down to the ground dead and the screams stopped. Antonio gurgled on his own blood and then died forever. Not peacefully, and not quickly. But painfully and slowly. Darwin stared into the mirror and saw Nathaniel staring back at him!

Darwin raised his sword to try to shatter the mirror but he couldn't move. He was paralyzed by fear. Nathaniel smirked and said "Hey Darwin, good to see you. I think I'll drag you with me to hell where I can torture you for eternity and we can have so much fun. Maybe I'll take your balls as a trophy before I kill you and maybe I'll cut out your tongue. What do you think Darwin? What kind of playtime should we do first?" He asked while laughing cruelly. Darwin got flashbacks of all the torture and felt terrified of Nathaniel. He took his sword and began to point it towards himself. This was the only way to end the suffering. Darwin was prepared to do it when Edward stepped in front of him and disarmed him. Edward shook him out of it with a spell and suddenly Darwin regained some of his faculties. "What the hell happened Edward? I thought I saw Nathaniel and I guess I wanted to kill myself or something." Darwin looked cautiously at their dead guide and realized the same thing must have happened to him. "Thanks for saving me," he said sincerely. Edward smiled in response and gave him a fist bump.

The two of them looked at Antonio and knew that they were going to be blamed for this. They searched every floor together and found the twin daggers on the top floor. Edward used his magic to portal them out of there but not before using his magic to set the entire place on fire. They could never come back to Italy while the mafia was around and no one needed to know what really happened here. They would make it look like all three of them died in the fire. The smell of fire and smoke invaded their nostrils just before they teleported out of there. There was something beautiful and purifying about fire isn't there?

The City of Cliburg

Edward and Damian made it back to Egypt and Gamal placed the last piece onto the coffin. The entire coffin glowed in response and a gigantic door appeared in the middle of the room. Gamal cried happily and kissed the floor as it slowly rose above and then it opened. The door to Cliburg was finally here. The three of them went in and saw that there truly was a city made of gold. There also didn't appear to be anyone around. Perhaps they all died off when the city disappeared or perhaps, they were frozen in time somewhere. Who knows? All that Edward knew was that he wanted to explore every inch of the city from top to bottom. Darwin was still traumatized however but he still wanted to come in as well. They would take some time exploring the city and then would return home. What they didn't know was that there was something evil brewing back at home.

The Beginning of a New Story

One Year Later

The year is 2026 and James and Stacy are living in Schreiber happily. It's been a year since Edward and Darwin left to locate the city of Cliburg. The magic that blessed Terrace Bay has also made its way to Schreiber and the people there have also been blessed with immortality. It's been a decade since the calamity of Jeb and Nathaniel. Jake, Jeb and Nathaniel have long been put to rest and the world is at peace finally. James and Stacy are married and they have a beautiful young daughter named Lenore. Lenore looks exactly like her parents and James and Stacy look the exact same as they did nearly ten years ago. James still retains his black hair and green eyes along with his strong build. Stacy also retains her long brown hair and blue eyes as well. The two are very happy together and Simon and Christine sometimes come and visit as well. Christine has been living in New York with her new boyfriend while revitalizing the strategy guide industry and making it big there. Physical copies of strategy guides are now being released once again with the same quality that they used to have and Christine is at the forefront of it.

After Simon disappeared into atoms the rest of the group decided to go on a journey to save him. It took James and his friends many months but they managed to find an alternate version of the stone once again and used it to bring Simon back. Simon promised not to be self sacrificing anymore but he still promised to watch over the world and be its guardian for whenever anyone needed him. James trusted him with the stone fully once again. Once Simon left, he would reappear occasionally and they would all grab lunch or get a drink or something. They were all finally at peace. Leon managed to alleviate his curse with the help of Elias and he finally passed on from this world. Elias read the eulogy and everyone was moved to tears by his words. Elias decided to stay in Terrace Bay with his family and got along well with James. Darwin continued to run the Schreiber Rail Museum and Aaron had been promoted to his second in command. Edward visited occasionally but his home was in Linia.

He had a family there and would go back frequently in order to be with them and to run the museum and archives there. Edward still looked the same and was given immortality from Elias and Leon. Edward's immorality was much stronger than everyone else's immortality however. He could die but only on his terms and he never aged. James on the other hand aged very slowly along with Stacy, Christine, and Elias. Simon also had the power of immortality but it was augmented by the power of the stone of legends.

This story begins ten years after Nathaniel and Jeb were finally put to rest. James is enjoying time with his wife Stacy and kisses her goodbye before heading to work as a philosophy teacher. He teaches at Lakehead and uses his magic to fly there everyday in order to teach his class. Stacy on the other hand decided to start her own business and it's been very successful. Lenore goes to school and gets to meet many other kids her age as well. Lenore is only nine but she's much wiser than the other kids. People like James and Stacy are able to age very slowly due to the blessings of the stone and they are unaffected by the blessings put on the towns. They will live thousand years of years if they wish to and they can heal quickly even though they are still capable of dying. Lenore has inherited some of her parent's magic but her powers and aging will not develop and slow respectively until she becomes an adult. Darwin, Ezekiel, and Aaron however are blessed by the magic of the town so they will not age any further unless they leave the towns. Ezekiel decided to stick around Schreiber to enjoy his immortality while continuing to train. He even opened a studio to teach people how to defend themselves with wooden blades. Ezekiel is really happy here as well. Everyone from each of the adventures either lives in Schreiber, are close by, or visit often enough that everyone is one big gigantic family. These people have gone through hell and back and their bond is stronger than ever. James sometimes goes to Jake's grave in order to speak to him.

He understands that the two could never live in the same world together but he still misses him. "I miss you everyday brother," whispered James to himself. The grave held no response but it was believed that Jake would watch over them and was proud of the man James had become. Jake reunited in heaven with his father Jeb and the two of them made peace with each other. They embraced each other as father and son and the two managed to move on from their pasts. Jake let go of his hatred for James and felt at ease with the way things had gone between them. Everything was finally perfect for everyone involved. That is...until one of them turned traitor.

The Unknown Variable

What no one knew was that Ezekiel had been studying magic in secret. Ezekiel had been using his time in order to enhance his own abilities. He also had a secret group that had been growing in numbers everyday. By day his dojo was a safe place to train and spar under the guidance of masters. During the night however, the dojo transformed into a meeting place for the occult. After reading Jeb's journal at Jake's grave Ezekiel felt close to Jeb in a way that he never felt close to anyone before. Not the Jeb that found peace and was good, but the Jeb that was corrupted by power and wanted to end all life. Ezekiel began gathering up tons of followers in order to remake the world in his image. In a way, he wanted to bring Jeb back. But in reality, he wanted to absorb the power and intelligence of the former master.

Ezekiel had been studying magic in secret by sneaking into Simon's workshop whenever he wasn't around in order to learn all of his secrets and how to bring someone back from the dead. Ezekiel realized that he couldn't bring Jeb back the way he is now, but perhaps a version of him could be brought here and killed. Ezekiel took his followers beneath the dojo and began the ritual. Ezekiel had been corrupted from reading Jeb's journal even though that wasn't the intention. Remnants of the dark god emanated from the journal and have been absorbed into Ezekiel. Ezekiel and his followers chanted for many hours beneath the dojo until the sun began to rise the next day. Ezekiel's forehead began to sweat as he continued to chant and eventually his followers began to bleed from their eyes. Others clutched their throats as they began to choke on their own blood. Some of the followers grabbed their ears and fell to the ground screaming as their ears began to bleed as well. Ezekiel urged them to continue chanting until they all fell to the ground dead in puddles of their own blood.

Some of the bodies twitched as they tried in vain to escape but they all died soon enough. Ezekiel walked through the blood as he grinned in anticipation. He grabbed his ceremonial knife and cut his palms in order to get the rest of the required blood for the ritual. The combined essence in the air opened a portal and Ezekiel bowed in supplication as he waited. Soon enough a man walked through the portal. It was a monstrous version of Jeb. He still looked humanoid except that instead of speaking he growled and his eyes looked more like a beast than any man's. His eyes were light green this time around and there was only darkness found within his eyes. Ezekiel continued to bow as he readied his obsidian knife. He said to the beast "hello my master, I've summoned you from the multiverse in order to serve my purposes. It's time for you to die!" he yelled briskly as he lunged towards Jeb.

Jeb saw the attack coming and swiped his claws in front of him to protect himself. Jeb swung his claws and slashed Ezekiel in the chest and tossed him across the room. Ezekiel lay on the ground bleeding as Jeb made his escape. Ezekiel felt like he had failed but then realized that maybe this plan could still work. This Jeb was clearly unstable and wanted vengeance against anyone who came across his way. Perhaps James would suffer still. Ezekiel chuckled to himself as the light left his eyes and he choked on his blood. Simon happened to be nearby and used his magic to heal Ezekiel. He hadn't understood the situation; he believed that Ezekiel and his friends were victims of the monster that got released. Simon hadn't been using the power of the stone anymore except when absolutely necessary. Simon's healing magic was enough to bring one or more people back to life at once without using the power of the stone. Once Ezekiel was stabilized Simon left the dojo in order to see where the beast went. Simon's work was never done.

Meanwhile, James was up late training in the middle of the night when he saw a monstrous beast coming towards him. James drew his sword and thrust it towards the beast. The sword collided with the beast and black blood gushed out of it. James was shocked to see the face of Jeb in this monstrous form. James planted his feet on the ground and thrust his sword even further until the sword broke through Jeb's skin and went out the other side. Jeb growled in pain and uttered the words "James! You will pay for what you did to me! You and Jake turned me into this and I shall use this new form to eliminate you forever!" He screeched and he swiped at James once again. James caught the claw with his right hand and crushed Jeb's claws in his hand. Jeb howled in pain and tried in vain to use his other claw to swipe at James. James went back and forth with him and he managed to pull his sword out of Jeb and continued to slash at him with each one hitting its mark. James also used his time to learn fencing and thrust his blade into every weak point of Jeb that he could find until finally Jeb fell to the ground and lay dying. Jeb tried to speak but all that came out were growls. James took his sword and pushed it down into Jeb's skull. Jeb's skull split open like a pinata and blood and bone went everywhere. James ended up covered in it and he managed to survive all that without getting a scratch on him. James ended up collapsing from the exertion. Lenore and Stacy came running out and saw the blood and gore everywhere. Stacy covered Lenore's eyes and ushered her back inside before checking on James. She held him and kissed him until he managed to wake and kiss her back. He said "I'm fine hon, don't worry. I don't know what that beast was but the threat is over now my love." Stacy looked at her husband lovingly and the two of them went back inside to comfort Lenore who thought her daddy was hurt.

James went into the shower and washed off all the black blood that covered his entire body. He didn't feel right though. The black blood seeped into him as it washed away and he slowly began to feel sick while in the shower. As he left the shower he ran to the toilet and retched in there for what felt like hours. Stacy came in to check on him soon after putting Lenore back to bed and was horrified to see black blood oozing out from him as he lay on the floor by the toilet. James wasn't breathing and Stacy pushed on his chest hard in order to try and revive him. After many attempts of resuscitation, she finally managed to get him to wake up. James awoke with a start and Stacy embraced him. James still had black blood and puke all over him but Stacy didn't care. She kissed him all over and he hugged and kissed her back. "Don't scare me like that again James," she said sharply. James nodded and Stacy seemed satisfied. James explained what happened and Stacy looked very concerned. "I think we should get Simon to look you over," she said calmly. James nodded and replied "I think you're right my love as always." Stacy hugged him again and they cleaned each other up and headed to bed.

The Sickness

Simon healed Ezekiel and his followers and soon after Ezekiel had forgotten what he was doing. His followers also seemed to have been in a haze and they couldn't recall anything from the last while. Ezekiel felt horrified when he realized that he had released Jeb from another dimension and sent him to wreak havoc on the world. He bowed in supplication and apologized constantly. Everyone eventually forgave him and they moved on. Simon was able to heal all of the corruption from each of them. James however wasn't so lucky. When Simon was examining him with magic in his workshop James felt very violated and it felt like he was getting a magical colonoscopy all throughout his body. His entire body hurt like hell even though he was drugged out and he wondered if Simon was some kind of sadist. Eventually the examination was over as Simon used his magic to scan James all over and finally came to conclusion of what was going on. "James, you've been infected with a strange virus that I can't cure. I don't believe even the stone can cure it. It's the type of sickness that has infected your soul. Once it reaches your heart it will eventually kill you," Simon said softly but clinically. James felt horrified but kept calm and kept his composure. "How long do I have old friend?" Asked James cautiously.

Simon looked at the readings and said "You probably have a couple hundred years, but you won't be able to use your magic reliably anymore. It will spiral out of control and it may backfire on you." Simon began crying at this point. James was his best friend and like a big brother to him. He tried to stay calm and professional but this was his best friend. How could he not feel anything for him. James stood up and hugged his friend. "Thank you, Simon. I appreciate your help in this. Is there anything I can do to either cure myself or slow it down?" Simon wiped his tears and said through them "there might be something, but it's risky. You'd have to go to the dark world of Nocturnia. There exists an herb called Darkwood that might be able to help you but I can't guarantee it." James released him and said "I think I need to speak to my family about this," he said quietly. Simon nodded and led him back outside.

James's family was waiting for him outside and they hugged him gratefully. James released them and said solemnly "there's something you need to know." James took his wife and daughter home and then explained everything to them. The conversation was raw and emotional but Stacy and Lenore listened intently as James said everything he needed to say before he started crying. Lenore began to cry and she ran to her daddy and hugged him. "Don't cry daddy, we will do everything to help you. Right momma?" Stacy looked at them both through tears and said "yes of course Lenore. We will do everything to help Daddy." James hugged his family close and felt grateful to them for everything. They grabbed dinner and then went to bed soon after. James tossed and turned all night as he had nightmares of his powers backfiring and spiraling out of control as they hurt the people he cared about. One of his most vivid nightmares was him holding his daughter close to him as she died from third degree burns. James awoke with a start and he could still smell the charred flesh of his daughter and he could still feel her charred corpse as he tried to will her back to life.

Stacy woke up as well and comforted him. She knew exactly what he was dreaming about judging by the look on his face and she consoled him. She knew that he was worried about hurting them even though she knew that he wouldn't. Or that even if he did it wouldn't be intentional. They held each other close and Stacy knew that she had to do something to help him. The next day she went to Simon's workshop where he was stationed for the foreseeable future and asked him straight up what they could do about the herb Darkwood. Simon sighed and tried to explain that the place would be treacherous and that magic was blocked there so Simon's abilities would essentially be useless there. James would have his super strength there but that's about it. No elemental powers, no magical weapons, no nothing. James would be entirely on his own and no one knew what existed in that place. It was very dangerous since no one could accurately create a map of the place without getting killed. The herb existed and was found there in multiple springs but those are the only records of where the herb could be found.

Stacy thought long and hard about this. Nocturnia was a place that James couldn't go but perhaps she could. She was an expert with her bow and her agility and strength were more powerful than most other humans. Stacy pitched the idea but Simon rejected it. The mists surrounding Nocturnia made it very lethal to anyone who approached it and even if you could approach the area, you never knew what was going to be found there. Stacy eventually relented and left his office in a huff. She understood his concerns but she still wanted to do everything she could to save her husband. Stacy also knew that Simon felt the same and felt awful for having to warn her of the risks. Darwin and Edward had been on their own adventure as well and they had just come back recently. They were horrified when they learned about what happened to James and Edward began going through all of his research in order to find anything related to Nocturnia and how to survive there.

His research came up with nothing except for one obscure note found in an even more obscure text. Allegedly, there was a special amulet that could allow you safe passage into Nocturnia. The amulet was found in a cave near Nocturnia and could be used to ensure safety through the mist. James decided that he would go and Stacy agreed to go with him. She needed to watch over her husband and Edward decided to come as well. His knowledge of history and geography would allow them to find the cave more easily. Together the three of them packed up and got ready to advance. Edward wouldn't be able to use his magic but he had enough fighting abilities to be able to hold his own with his swords. James took a powerful sword that he had forged himself with him and Stacy took her most powerful non magical bow with her as well. The three spent the night discussing plans while Lenore was left in the care of Simon and Darwin was put back to work at the Museum.

The Journey Ahead

The night before James felt himself tossing and turning throughout the night. He knew that he should have stayed home but he couldn't in good conscience let Stacy and Edward go off and do this alone. He trusted Stacy and Edward so it wasn't reasons of jealousy. He just felt like he had to do something and didn't want to just stay home and do nothing while his body slowly deteriorated. He hadn't told anyone about this but for a while he had been feeling useless as of late. He's grateful for the peace don't get him wrong, but he sometimes felt that without an enemy to fight that he was useless. He knew that he should tell Stacy about it but he didn't want to worry her. This was his fight and he didn't want to get anyone else involved if they could avoid it. Him getting sick just made it that much worse. He wondered if he had the same disease his father/maker had. This version seems to be a more extreme version of that strain since James himself was supposed to have an immunity after inheriting his father's abilities and powers. He still missed his dad, and his cousin Elijah.

He still had his adoptive parents and he loved them dearly but it wasn't the same. He also had his Aunty Janice who constantly supplied him and Stacy with alcohol and doted on Lenore whenever she wasn't travelling around the world. He still couldn't explain how she managed to find him everywhere he went and how she even found him back in time. Ah, good times. James and Christine were still close as ever. He didn't have any romantic feelings for her and the feeling was mutual but they were still best friends. Stacy wasn't jealous since she was also still best friends with her and they understood each other. James wanted to prove himself to Stacy even though he knew in his heart that he didn't have to. His anxiety and depression were making it really hard to let go of the past. He missed Jake despite their differences. He didn't want him back but he wanted the person he used to believe he was back.

Right now, James just had to get some sleep. He could figure out his problems later. He loved teaching and they gave him life and he loved his family of course. But he didn't know how to be there for his family when he struggled to make himself happy. He needed to be better not just for them but also for himself. He deserved better.

Stacy saw James tossing and turning and she felt for him. She knew about some of his struggles because she could sense what he was dealing with whenever he went to visit Jake's grave. He missed his friend and he felt useless without someone to fight against. All Stacy wanted was for James to be happy and she knew that he loved her and Lenore 100%. That was never in doubt. She just wanted him to be happy for his sake and she knew that while the two of them made him happy; she knew it wasn't enough. He deserved to be happy and she knew he could be. She wished he would let her in but she understood why he didn't. He didn't want to worry her. She turned back to her side and went back to sleep once he seemed to settle down. She always fell asleep really easily while James had insomnia.

The next morning Stacy and James got up at the same time and headed out. They hugged Lenore goodbye and headed to Edward's office. He set up a teleportation portal that would get them close to the cave and they they'd have to travel the rest of the way on foot. Edward went in first and then James and Stacy grabbed each other's hands and walked through together. Once they left, the portal closed and the office was empty once again. James felt the whoosh of teleportation and it felt like his body was being torn apart and then rebuilt slowly atom by atom. When the three of them emerged in a dark forest James threw up black blood and began coughing on the ground. Stacy comforted him as he coughed his lungs out. After a while he stopped and grabbed Stacy's hand gently to lift him up. He wiped black blood off his face as Edward and Stacy looked at him concerningly. "Don't worry, I'm okay. Just not used to the effects of teleportation after so long." The two nodded cautiously and they looked at their surroundings.

There were dark craggy trees all around and the air smelled like death. The wind blasted past them and the harsh wind felt like paper cuts on their skin. There were strange looking animals like desiccated deer walking around with moss growing out of their eyes and mouths. Clearly whatever lived here was undead. The animals shuffled around awkwardly and their limbs jerked in unnatural ways as they tried to get to wherever they were going.

Edward looked both fascinated and startled by the creatures. Clearly, he had never seen such entities before. James and Stacy looked at each other and then drew their weapons.

They needed to be on guard just in case. Edward drew his swords as well but it was unnecessary. The creatures shuffled off without giving them a second glance. Perhaps the creatures would leave them alone so long as they weren't bothered. The three of them sheathed their weapons and moved on. They slowly walked through the dark forest and James didn't even have to throw up once during their entire trek. The three kept on walking and walking while stopping to take a breath every once in a while. After countless hours of walking and brushing bush and branches to the side they finally made it to the cave.

Edward's navigational skills had been accurate. Before he was a historian, he studied geography and he understood bow the landscape worked. History was his true passion but he loved geography as a side hobby. Writing was also one of his passions in case anyone decided to forget that. Edward had done as much research as he could on the cave before he got there but he didn't know much. All accounts of the cave suggested that the amulet was hidden deep beneath the visitor's worst memories and impulses. The amulet was supposedly easy to locate but the manifestations of darkness made it that much harder for people to find it and bring it out. Those who didn't die or kill themselves due to the hallucinations barely ran out of there with their lives and they were never the same again. There's a reason why this place and Nocturnia were never explored properly. Both places are considered to be death traps. The air smelled cold and moldy. The smell of moss also filled the air and the three companions shivered involuntarily. This was going to be tough.

James took Stacy's nervous hands and massaged them gently. She turned to look at him and he said softly "It's going to be okay my love. We've been through much worse situations. We can do this together." Stacy nodded and said "I love you, James." James nodded back and kissed her. "I love you too," he said happily. The two touched their foreheads together quickly and then they let go. Still holding hands however, they entered the cave however and Edward led the way. The moment the three of them entered the air felt instantly hot and it felt like they were on fire. There were no flames however and despite the pain no damage seemed to be happening. They kept on walking along until they all slowly began to fall unconscious. James saw the amulet in the distance and tired to reach out his hand before giving into sleep.

Nightmares

James awoke alone in the cave and there was no amulet in sight. He kept looking around but there was no one else near him. The exit had also been sealed up and he couldn't leave. "Stacy! Edward! Where are you guys!" yelled James at the top of his lungs. He needed to know where his wife and friend were. He pounded on the stone walls until his fingers began to bleed. He still retained his superior healing abilities and despite his super strength he couldn't break through. His hands recovered quickly as if it never happened and James fell to his knees in despair and began to cry. He had failed everyone. There was nothing else he could do. James had to talk to someone. He decided to meditate since he didn't have anything else he could do. The rest of the cave was deserted. He sat cross legged and began to breathe inwards. After what felt like forever, he saw his true father materialize in front of him. James was a clone raised by him but they still treated each other as father and son.

He was long dead but he could still communicate with his family like this. "Hello my son", said older James. He looked the same as the day he died and James broke out in tears that much more. James held his head in his hands and said "I'm so pathetic. I'm sorry dad. I failed you; I failed everyone. I became sick and I can't do anything right. I'll never be the man you were father." Older James looked at him with pity and sadness before his eyes hardened. "You're not wrong my son. You are not me; but you shouldn't strive to be like me either. You and I may be the same person in some cases, but you are your own man. I wanted to tell you that. You have just as much right to be your own person as I did. You haven't failed anyone. I have failed many times in my life, but I have no regrets anymore. I've struggled with the same things you have at times and passing on my power to you allowed me to move on from my past. I am so proud of you and you have accomplished much more than I ever have." James looked up at his father and his eyes were now that of a kind father. James broke down crying once again at his father's words. He never thought his dad had felt these things as well. James wiped his tears and saw his father smiling down at him. James began to feel at peace but he still had questions. "Dad, where are we?" Do you know where we are?" Older James looked around and said confusedly "I'm afraid I don't know my son. But I know you will find your way out. The wisdom I offer is this, try not to punish yourself over things you can't control or for things that you wished you did differently. The past is not your burden; it is just an opportunity to grow and surpass yourself in greater ways than you ever thought possible. Learn to forgive yourself my son, and not let the world crush you with its weight." Older James said this as he began to disappear.

James took some time to breathe before coming out of his meditation trance. He steeled himself and when he opened his eyes, he saw a door had appeared where one hadn't been prior. James slowed his breath and began the walk forward. James slowly entered the door and he saw someone standing at the far edge of the room. Their back was to him so he couldn't see their face in the darkness. James did catch a sliver of blonde hair though and the presence that they were giving off was quite familiar. James stepped closer when the door slammed shut behind him. James turned around ands aw that the door was indeed shut. "Hahahahahahaha", said a voice from behind him. James whirled around and saw the person was still not facing him. "Well, well, well, James. What took you so long old friend?" he said sharply. James' heart dropped in his chest and it began to race non-stop. No. It couldn't be. The figure came closer and James realized who it was. It was Jake. His oldest and former best friend. Jake smirked. "You seem surprised buddy? What, weren't you expecting to see one of your oldest friends here man?" James stood there shell shocked. Jake moved his limbs jerkily and James realized that he still had significant injuries from their last fight. This couldn't be real. Jake stretched out and popped his muscles. It felt good to him and they made a satisfying crack.

Jake looked on at James and said "I seem to still be injured after our last fight. My eyesight has recovered somewhat but my muscles still hurt. They constantly hurt and it's all because of you!" Jake boomed and James recoiled. He also saw where he had cut into Jake's neck and the hole where his heart got stabbed. Jake looked rough and he also looked almost skeletal and rotten. James could tell though that this version of Jake would still be incredibly strong and hard to defeat. And because he's undead, he might not go down easily. James readied his sword and began his battle stance. Jake smirked through rotted teeth and growled in agreement. This was going to be an interesting fight. James ran forward and Jake rushed forward as well with surprising speed of that of an undead. James slashed but Jake deftly ducked and bit into James. "This is revenge for all that you did to me and my body buddy," Jake whispered before biting James' ear off. James screamed in pain and flung Jake off of him. Jake smiled and ate James's ear. James clutched the place where his left ear used to be and lunged forward once again.

Jake ducked out of the way but this time James saw it coming. He outmanoeuvered Jake and plunged the sword deep into his heart and impaling him into the cave wall. Jake struggled to free himself but blood began to fall from his mouth. "Ha, you've got me again brother. Groan. You've passed my friend." Jake smiled sincerely and morphed into that of his younger and healthy self. James looked on in shock and dropped the sword onto the ground. Jake smiled and pulled the sword out of his heart before handing it to James. James took it and Jake looked sad for a moment. "Look man, I'm sorry for everything. I never wanted to hurt you but this place corrupts everyone who enters. I had to test you in order to see if you were willing to put me down again. You aren't useless James. You just need to find a purpose for yourself. That's what your twenties are about man. I'm proud to call you my oldest friend and I hope you can find peace in yourself once again. You're still a force to be reckoned with and anyone who gets in your way will have a hell of a time putting you in the ground. You'll figure things out man, things just take time." Jake walked over to James and put his hand on his head. James's ear grew back instantly and Jake started to disappear into dust. "For what it's worth man, I miss you too and I'm proud of the guy you've become." Jake disappeared into dust fully and James fell down onto the ground. He cried so hard but he felt lighter than he had ever been. Suddenly his illness didn't seem to be as heavy as it used to be. Perhaps he could do this. Maybe he didn't have to prove himself to anyone anymore. He just had to find something that made him happy.

The walls fell apart and suddenly James was back in the room with the others. He woke up and saw Stacy and Edward laying on the ground still. They had been knocked unconscious. James realized that they must have been dealing with what he had been dealing with so he decided to wait for them to wake up. He drew his swords and took on a guardian position beside them. He would watch over them for as long as it took.

Worst Case Scenarios

James ran out of the cave as fast as he could. He had Stacy and Edward in his arms and he began running as fast as he could back to where they initially ended up in the first place. Edward was still conscious but Stacy wasn't. Edward was weakly guiding James back to where they came from and he was also chanting something under his breath. After many hours of running, they finally made it back to where they showed up and a portal materialized in front of them. Edward finally fell unconscious as James jumped through with everyone intact. The three of them fell onto the floor and tumbled all around the office. Edward hit his head hard on his deck but still wouldn't wake up. James tried in vain to wake Stacy up but nothing he did worked. Eventually he called for Simon and he came running. Simon stabilized Edward and Stacy in his workshop and began his work. James went home and had to explain to Lenore what happened. She cried in James's arms and he consoled her. He didn't know if it was going to be okay or not. He still had the amulet in his hands, but it felt worthless to him if some of the people he cared about dying trying to save him.

James felt worthless but he knew he had to have faith in Simon. If anyone could save them it would be him. James waited for countless hours and paced around the room. Lenore waited with him until Simon came outside. Simon hugged Lenore tight and hugged James. "I managed to stabilize them both, but I can't wake them up. Even the power of the stone isn't enough to help them. I don't know what the problem is. It seems like something similar to what happened to you also affected them but in a different way," Simon said sadly. James kept his composure for his daughter and he decided to take her home. Simon went with them and promised to watch over them for as long as was necessary. After two weeks of waiting Simon came to tell James some good news but he found James passed out in his bathtub and black blood covered every part of him. At first Simon thought that he had cut himself to death but then realized that he had threw up so much blood that it came pouring out of every single one of his orifices. Simon kneeled in front of James to check his pulse and saw that he was still alive but barely. The disease had advanced to his heart much quicker than he thought. Simon took him back to his workshop and did everything he could to stabilize him as well.

Edward had woken up briefly and told Simon that the cure for them was in Nocturnia. It was the same herb. Darkwood would save them. Edward then passed out once again. All three of them had now fallen into comas. Clearly that cave had a negative effect on each of them. Simon used his magic to slow the disease down as much as he could but there wasn't much he could do. At this rate, they each only had about a hundred years left to live if they didn't wake up. Simon wanted to cry but he chose not to. He had to think logically about this. Someone had to go to Nocturnia in order to save the three of them. James till had the amulet and he had given it to Lenore in order to keep it safe. He didn't trust anyone else more than her. Simon considered calling back Christine from New York but her magical abilities would be almost useless in Nocturnia. And even if she could go it would be too dangerous for her to go alone. Simon wanted to go but he had to stay here and keep watch over his friends. He could call Darwin and Aaron but Darwin was still recovering psychologically from their last adventure and Aaron was too young and inexperienced for this type of trip. What could he do?

While he was ruminating over what to do Lenore came in. She held the amulet in her hands and looked down at her parents. "They aren't waking up, are they? Mommy and daddy." She said sadly. She briefly broke down in tears before regaining her faculties. Adults never cried even though they actually did a lot. James and Stacy always taught Lenore that it was okay to show her emotions even if it was difficult. They were both very understanding and they loved her so much. Lenore appreciated that but she wanted to be strong for her parents. Simon always forgot that she was nine years old because of how mature she was. Sometimes she acted her age but not always. He really felt sorry for her but there was nothing he could do. Lenore turned to Simon and with a determined look said, "let me go. I know I'm not old enough or strong enough to help but please. Train me to become strong like mommy and daddy and then I'll go off and save them. Please Uncle Simon, help me." Lenore started crying once again at his feet and he realized that he didn't have any other option. "Okay, Lenore. Honey, I'll help you become strong. It won't be easy but I'll start you off easy to help you get into it okay?" Lenore nodded and wiped away her tears as she sniffled and snot began to come out of her nose.

Simon hugged her once again and he led her back outside. Lenore caught a glimpse of herself in the outside fountain's reflection. She looked so young with her dark black hair tied up into a small ponytail. Her eyes were a mix of blue and green and they looked striking on her. Lenore vowed to be strong for her parents and decided to train as much as she could and become powerful. Simon could still remotely watch over the others so he could be away from the workshop for small periods of time but not in the long term. Lenore went to Darwin and Ezekiel and they both agreed to train her. Darwin was still messed up after his last adventure but he felt well enough for this at least. Darwin agreed to teach her swordsmanship and Ezekiel agreed to train her with other weapons while Simon taught her how to manipulate magic and use her innate powers.

Thirteen Years Later

Lenore had spent over a decade honing her powers and this is what has occurred. James, Stacy, and Edward were still in comas and hadn't woken up at all. Lenore felt pangs in her chest whenever she went to go see them but she stayed strong to help her family. Lenore had bloomed into quite a powerful nine-teen year old. Her blue and green eyes were even more striking than before and her skills were stronger than James and Stacy were at her age. Her dark black hair had had gone long and she kept it in a long ponytail in order to honor her parents. She never changed her look and only wanted them back. She became skilled in swordsmanship and could also use spears with ease. She was also a master archer and she had gained her parents' super strength, agility, and endurance. She inherited the abilities of both of her parents and she could manipulate magic as well. Her favourite ability was to summon fire from her fingertips.

Lenore spent many years training and she finally felt ready. The amulet burned in her hand but she felt calm and collected. Simon teleported her to the border of Nocturnia and she got out after hugging her teacher's goodbye. She was ready to finally save her parents. She entered the portal and appeared outside of Nocturnia. The mist felt lethal to the touch but the amulet protected her. She tried to use her flame magic but the fire fizzled out before she could do anything. Magic was clearly out here. Her strength however didn't seem to be affected as she punched as hard as she could into a tree and it cracked before falling over. Lenore had her bow slung on her back and she drew her short sword. Her preference was to use either a short sword or spear and she had both on her. She walked through the mist and could barely see anything. The mist even threated to choke her but she managed to keep her wits about her. The amulet burned even brighter on her neck as she advanced through the mist but she kept her cool. At first it was barely a whisper of heat but now it was burning into her flesh. She considered tossing the infernal thing aside but decided it was better to keep it on for the time being.

She used the pain in order to find her way through the border. After what felt like an eternity of going through the area she managed to finally make it into Nocturnia's mist less areas. The area looked almost beautiful. Whereas she could barely see anything through the misty areas; now she could see everything. The central castle looked very imposing up ahead and see could see there were springs scattered throughout the world. She knew that she'd have to be careful in order to avoid everything. She didn't want to have to fight if she didn't have to. Lenore did a bit of exploring and found a graveyard. She went over to it and see saw faded inscriptions of people her family knew. Perhaps these were an alternate version of her parent's friends. She went to the one that said Jake and whispered "please give me strength uncle Jake." She knew about the history between her parents and Jake but her dad still talked fondly of Jake at times. Lenore didn't know what to believe. She knew that while her mom missed Jake the world was better off without him. That was harsh but probably true. Lenore felt the air turn cold and suddenly zombies began to crawl out of the ground. They dug their way out from the ground and they advanced on her with large red eyes. Lenore took her spear and lunged outwards just as she was trained to do. She managed to decapitate a few of them before suddenly becoming swarmed by them. She knew that their scratches wouldn't do anything but if they bit her then it could be lethal.

She kept on fighting and fighting until her injuries began to pile up. She had scratches all over her legs and arms but she kept on going even as she began to run out of breath. She wasn't used to fighting for this long and her endurance was strong but fighting for real with it was a different battle entirely. Just as she was about to go down and get bitten, she saw something move in her peripheral vision. There was a hooded figure in a dark cloak who ran past her and used daggers to decapitate the zombies in swift motions and cut their throats entirely. After two minutes each of the zombies were laying on the ground and no longer moving. Lenore stared at her saviour and said "thank you, but who are you?" The figure wiped the blood off his daggers and turned to face her. They came closer and took off their hood. It was a guy who looked about her age. He had dark black hair with hints of blonde and brown circulating throughout. "My name is Cole; I was sent here to find you. My mom sent me. She knew your parents as well," he said quickly. He pulled out a faded picture and Lenore saw that it was of her parents with Simon, Christine, and Jake. The picture was worn and faded but she could clearly see her parent's smiling faces. This must have been before they became immortal; when they were just normal kids having fun.

I looked at his red eyes and I remembered that Aunty Christine also had red eyes and I could see the resemblance instantly. He was Christine's son no doubt. And he was hot. She almost lost control of herself before she regained her composure. "Thanks again Cole, how did you get here and find me?" Cole took out an amulet that looked identical to mine and explained that he had been sent here at the same time I was but he got lost and couldn't find his way back in time. That's why he found me later than he intended. Lenore forgave him and they moved on. The two decided to travel to the nearby springs and see if they could find out what was going on. Suddenly Lenore and Cole felt a cold rush of wind coming from the graveyard. They turned and saw a spirit emerging from the graveyard. The spirit began to take shape and out came the smiling face of Jake. Jake turned to them and said "Hey kids, it's good to see you both." Cole drew his daggers but Lenore raised a hand and signaled for him not to. "Uncle Jake, is that really you?" She said cautiously. Jake bowed and said, "yeah kid it's me. In the flesh." He said sagely. Lenore hesitantly walked up to him and hugged him deeply. She knew that he was scum and that he did so many horrible things but he was still family to James once and she missed her family so much. She cried in his arms as she hugged him and he hugged her back tightly.

After she released him, Jake knelt down towards her and said "I'm sorry kid for everything I did to your parents back in the day. I'm here to help now, I hope you can forgive me or at least accept my help." Jake looked genuinely sorrowful and Lenore decided to forgive him at least for the time being. She needed help to find the herb and perhaps having another set of hands could be beneficial. But first, there was a burning question she had to ask. "How are you back?" Jake looked thoughtful and said "this place affects the world in a strange way. I heard you calling to me and I decided that you were worthy of my help. Any kin of James are worthy of my help and I want to make things right from the person I was so long ago. Even though the two were about the same age Jake seemed much older and wiser compared to her. Lenore led Jake back to where Cole was. Cole said "be careful, I don't trust him yet." Lenore nodded in his direction and the three of them moved on.

Nocturnia and its Dangers

The three of them walked onwards and checked out the nearest spring first. Lenore felt in awe of the beauty of the spring and was happy to have finally found it. Jake looked at her amused and could tell that she was James and Stacy's daughter. Cole glared daggers at Jake. Jake may have changed but he heard the stories from his mom about who Jake was as a person. He would never forgive him for what he did to his mom's friends. She may have forgiven him but he never would. Lenore had seen a picture of the herb from Edward's books but she couldn't find it in the spring no matter where she looked. They were a few other springs nearby so they decided to check them out as well. After many hours of searching, they hadn't found any herbs. Lenore was just about to give up when she saw something glinting in the distance. She saw what looked like a baby kitten cowering near the spring. The kitten's glowing eyes were beautiful and she was a calico cat. Lenore slowly went closer to the kitten as it slowly tried to cower. "Hey, it's okay little one. I'm not a threat to you. I love animals. Can I help you? Please, let me help you, my friend." Lenore said softly. The kitten slowly began to regain its courage and she slowly went over to where Lenore was. Once the kitten was in petting distance Lenore gently extended her hand out and the kitten butted her head against her hand. Lenore happily petted the little kitten and the kitten purred happily. "I'm going to call you Sophie. My friend Darwin had a cat named Sophie and you remind me of how he described her. Is that okay?" Lenore asked quietly. The kitten seemed to nod in agreement and Lenore hugged the cat lightly to her chest. Sophie had a bit of ragdoll in her so she was happy to be held like a baby. Jake and Cole came over to where the two were and they both agreed the kitten was really cute. Sophie purred against Cole and Jake as well and seemed happy to be with them all.

Sophie also seemed to be in good health despite being in the cold all alone for who knows how long. She led them along the path to where several Darkwood crops have been harvested and destroyed. Lenore fell to despair at the sight of them. "What happened?" She asked through tears. Cole comforted her and Jake looked on towards the crops. "Looks like someone didn't want us getting those herbs. But who would do such a thing?" Jake mused to himself. Sophie perked up and pointed in the direction of the gigantic castle looming ahead in the darkness. Lenore stopped crying and said "that must be where we need to go then." Cole nodded and Jake grunted in agreement. He didn't want them to be put in any more danger than necessary but he would do anything he could to protect them. Jake had lots of regrets in his life. He regretted his part in helping Dr. Jeb take over the world and for killing James and Simon. His anger got the better of him. He was foolish enough to chase his pride back then and let his anger get the better of him. He knows better now. Jake made amends with his father Dr. Jeb in the afterlife and he felt like he and James were on better terms for the time being. Jake knew that he would probably never see James again and that's okay. James didn't need to see him again in order for things to be made right. Jake would even give his life to protect James's child.

Lenore didn't know how to feel about Jake. She wanted to trust him but it was difficult after everything he had done. She decided for the time being she needed him and was grateful for the help. As the three (and Sophie) got closer to the castle the air began to feel suffocating and the darkness swirled around them like a vortex. They continued to make progress despite each of them having to stop and cough every so often. This place really was corrupting. The three of them kept continuing on until they saw the great drawbridge looming up ahead. There didn't seem to another way inside. Jake went up to it and punched hard into the wood. The wood and metal bent with a loud screech and Jake continued to pummel it until there was a big enough hole for them to go through. There was no point in being subtle for what they needed. Jake may have mellowed out but he still had his temper in some cases and he still wanted to get things done as quickly as possible. Cole shook his head and walked ahead while Lenore and Sophie followed.

Lenore had wondered why she had never met Cole before. Cole explained that they had never met because Christine wanted to train him in secret in order to protect him. She didn't want to get him caught up in everything until he was ready. Simon also had a son who he protected fiercely. Simon's son was a mage just like his father and was incredibly powerful. Lenore and Cole inherited their powers from their parents so they didn't get their powers from the stone directly. The Stone of Legends could be dangerous so it was best not to be used unless it was absolutely necessary. The four walked inside and were greeted by a large lobby in which there were stairs leading upstairs and many branching rooms from the ground floor. There were torches and candelabras hanging overhead. The air smelled of wine and wealth. Suddenly the air swirled around them and something began to materialize. Cole stepped up protectively to defend Lenore while she readied her bow. Jake stood off to the side with his fists at the ready. He didn't have his sword anymore but that was okay. He could still use his fists when needed. Sophie scampered behind Lenore and hissed at the air. She was getting ready to swat at it if necessary. She really is a cute kitten. They all shielded their eyes with their arms until the dark air stopped circulating. In its place appeared a regal looking man with a blood red cape and shining black armor covering his torso and legs. The top of his head was exposed but he didn't seem concerned. He seemed like a warrior king from legends. The kind who would fight on the front lines with his people. The man stared in the direction of the four and bowed his head deeply. "Welcome to my castle my friends. While I wish you wouldn't have destroyed the drawbridge, I can understand your haste to meet someone as amazing as me. My name is Lord Issac and I am your humble servant in these lands. Now what can I do for you on this fateful day?" The man appeared to be friendly enough but his eyes held a sinister glint in them. This man couldn't be trusted. At least not one hundred percent. They needed to be careful and they all knew it. Lemore sheathed her weapon and went towards him.

His threatening aura increased tenfold the closer she got to him and she felt his darkness threatening to overtake her. She pushed through it and got as close to him as she possibly could. She bowed to him and said "my lord Issac. Can you help us find Darkwood? We need it to save some friends of ours." Issac thought to himself. "But of course you can have some of my stock. But you will have to beat me first in combat. I warn you though, if you kill me then this realm shall cease to exist and you shall be turned into nothing. If you wish to risk that then by all means; make my day." He said cockily. Lenore drew her bow while Cole drew his daggers. Jake readied his fists and even Sophie extended her claws despite being scared shitless. Issac extended his right hand into the air and snapped his fingers. "But of course, you'll have to deal with my servants first. Ta-ta," he said confidently. Suddenly from all corners of the room zombies began slowly shuffling their way towards them through every open door imaginable. They were surrounded. What were they going to do?

Castle Nocturnia

Undead corpses from all over the area were pouring into the castle lobby and the four of them had no clue what to do. Lenore readied her bow and started firing her arrows in every direction imaginable. She managed to catch most of them in the head so they went down pretty easily. Cole ran around with his daggers and whipped them around as he became a tornado of death. Jake ran towards every creature in his path and punched them in the head. Their heads exploded in an explosion of gore and death and Jake happily started laughing at the carnage. He truly loved violence. Lenore was glad that Jake was on their side. The zombies just kept coming and coming but the four of them kept on fighting. Sophie also proved to be a ruthless fighter in her own right. She bit them on their legs and sometimes even jumped on their backs and bit deep into their heads. Sophie was adorable but very deadly when she wanted to be. Sophie also seemed to grow more lithe and agile while she was fighting. The four kept on fighting until their sweat began to cover their eyes and blind them. Lenore missed her next shot due to that and she had to grab her short sword quickly and decapitate one that was advancing quickly on her. Cole didn't see the lone zombie that was coming towards him until Jake ran behind him and punched the zombie out of the way. Cole realized just how close he was to getting devoured and said quickly "thanks man." Jake turned to him with a hardened look and replied "don't mention it. Now let's win this fight." Cole nodded and the four began to become rejuvenated for the fight ahead. Eventually the tide began to turn and the number of undead creatures began to die down. By the time it was all over Lenore, Jake and Cole were all covered in blood and gore. Sophie however managed to stay mostly clean but still chose to clean herself when she had the opportunity.

Jake didn't seem bothered by the blood and ogre on his face but he wiped it off as best he could regardless. The three of them lay on the ground back-to-back panting. That was a tough fight and there was no way they should have been able to survive that. Lenore spat out the blood and the pieces of brain that she got in her mouth. She ended up ingesting some of the gore and had to vomit it out. Cole comforted her while she did by holding her hair back and striking her shoulders. Cole may have been gruff and tough to read at times but he really did care about his companions. He was even starting to care for Jake after seeing him prove his worth in battle and saving his life when it counted.

The three got up and Sophie trotted over to them after cleaning herself up. Lenore looked rough. Her hair was in mats but she still looked tough. Cole looked gruff as ever but appeared ready to go another round. Jake knelt down and gave her a little pat and she rubbed up against him as well. Jake really loved cats. The four decided that their next move was to explore so they left the lobby and went into another room. They thought they saw Issac heading in there just before he disappeared so they figured it would be a good place to start. They headed into the room and saw that there was nothing in the room. There were no furniture and no artwork. The room was completely barren and empty. They looked around but couldn't find anything of use. Jake tried punching the walls of the room but nothing happened. The boards didn't even creak. Magic wasn't allowed in this realm but perhaps Issac had magic of his own that he could manipulate. This was his world after all and no one had been able to explore this world in great detail at all. No one even knew how long the world existed for. They left the room after a while of fruitless searching and continued on. The four decided to head upstairs next and they saw a reading room where Issac was sitting down and reading a book by the fire.

He looked up as they approached. "Ah my friends, you have found me at long last. If you wish to have the Darkwood you can. It's in the garden just out there. Go ahead, you've proven yourselves." Issac waved his land lazily towards the door to his left and a garden appeared outside of it. Issac went back to his reading and seemed to forget they were even there. Sophie growled and hissed but Issac had no reaction whatsoever to it. Lenore went up to the door and started to open it when Jake grabbed her arm. "Wait, I don't trust this. Something ain't right here." Issac turned away from his book and said "how perceptive of you. I figured you'd be dumb enough to fall for my illusion but perhaps not." Issac snapped his fingers and the door disappeared completely and in its place was a giant pit of lava. Lenore jerked away from it as quick as she could and glared at Issac. Issac carefully put his bookmark back in his book and put his book to the side. "Well, I suppose we have to do this the hard way. You couldn't just be agreeable and lay and down die now could you." Issac got up from his leather chair and cracked his knuckles as he stretched and let his muscles stretch with a satisfying pop.

Issac turned to face them and said "time to die." He snapped his fingers again and his appearance changed. What was once a handsome young-looking man now appeared to be skeletal and decrepit. Despite that there was an abundance of power emanating off of him. He was a lich king. For those who don't know what a lich king is; it's someone who managed to escape the shackles of time and death and made them immortal. In place of regular immortality however they are skeletal and undead. They do not require sustenance to survive and never get tired. Some may require blood but not Issac. He's a particularly powerful lich. He uses a sword and his claws as his main weapons.

Issac screeched and ran towards the group. Sophie jumped out of the way and swatted at his feet. Issac dodged them and tried to kick her but Sophie evaded the blow. Jake tried to punch his head in but Issac blocked his attempt with his claws and scratched Jake's hand badly. Jake grabbed his bloody hand and was pushed back against the wall. Lenore fought him as well bur he blocked her and Cole's weapons with one of his own. Jake came back into the fray after a moment and managed to punch Issac in the chest. His skeletal chest creaked but remained intact. Issac retaliated and slashed Cole across the chest and sent him flying across the room. Cole fell to the ground and hit a bookcase books went flying everywhere and a few of them hit him on the head. Cole was dazed but used his innate abilities to try and patch himself up. He needed to heal himself so he could get back in the fight. He inherited his mom's healing abilities and her rogue abilities. He couldn't turn invisible here but he was faster than most humans. As he was healing himself using potions to speed up the process, he saw a special book that looked old and worn. It turned out to be a journal. Cole decided that while he was waiting to heal, he would read through the journal to see if he could find any insight into Issac's abilities and weaknesses.

Flipping through the journal while the fight was going on was tough but Issac managed to do so while observing and making sure Jake and Lenore were still okay. They were, so he kept on reading. The journal was long and boring but essentially Issac turned himself into an Elder Lich King and used his abilities to create this realm many years ago. He also used his abilities to cancel out any magic other than his own in order to better protect himself since he was vulnerable to magic. Cole managed to find one other weakness however. There was a special book that was bound in blood and human skin. If that book were to be destroyed then Issac would be vulnerable to all types of attacks. Cole quickly began scanning through every book while Issac was distracted holding off Jake and Lenore. Eventually after much searching Cole found the book. It was a blood red book and he could see and feel that the pages were made of human skin. Cole wasn't sure if this book was made of Issac's skin or if it was made of other people's skin. Cole also was aware that when a Lich was made it was possible that many people had to be killed in order for the treatment to be successful.

Cole was disgusted. He took his dagger out and stabbed it downward into the book itself. The aim was true and the dagger slid through like butter. Issac recoiled in pain but it wasn't enough. Cole then took the book and tossed it into the fire. Issac tried to use telekinesis in order to bring the book back to him but Cole was too quick. Cole forced it into the fire and even burned his hand in the process. It hurt like hell but it was enough to make the difference in the fight. Issac's magic was disappearing and he was now vulnerable. Jake grabbed Issac's skeletal throat and squeezed while Cole and Lenore used their weapons in order to pierce his heart and then decapitate him. Issac's head popped off like a toothpaste lid and slid into the fireplace. Issac's screams lasted long into the night as his body dissolved into dust. A new door opened up and it appeared that the Darkwood was actually in there this time. Lenore rushed towards the garden and found the herbs. She knew what they looked like after seeing them in Edward's books.

She scooped them up and placed them into jars that she could use to carry them out with. She stuffed the jars into her bag and suddenly the entire realm began to collapse in on itself. Issac wasn't lying when he said that the realm was tied to him. The entire building began to collapse and magic seemed to be going haywire. Lenore tired to summon her fire and found that she could but that it went off in the wrong direction. The magic ban was gone but magic was now unpredictable. Fucking great. Lenore decided to stop using fire magic and she ran to Cole and Jake and they ran outside the castle. They kept on running and they realized that they didn't have way out of here. They decided that maybe Simon was watching over them and could conjure a portal if they get out of range of the castle.

They ran for what felt like hours until they made it back to where they started. Sophie was still with them and was panting as well. Suddenly a portal opened up a young red-haired man poked his head out. "Hey over here, my dad Simon sent me to help you guys out. Come on!" He gestured with his hands and the four decided that they had to trust him. Cole jumped in and Sophie leaped in after him. Lenore was just about to leap in when Jake pulled her back. "Her kid, I'm sorry but I can't go back with you. I don't belong in that world with you. This realm is falling apart and I belong here. I was sent here to help you and I did just that. I belong in the afterlife with my father. Tell James I'm sorry for everything and that I wish I could have done more." Said Jake sadly. Lenore hugged him and said "I'm going to miss you uncle Jake." "I'm gonna miss you too kid. Now go, your friends need you." Jake patted her on the back and she jumped in after them. Jake stared at the landscape as it got destroyed and felt at peace. His life was in the afterlife with Dr. Jeb and his family. He's done enough in this world. Now Jake can move on without any regrets. Jake welcomed the abyss of darkness and woke back up with his family once again. He was excited to tell them about his newest adventure.

Home

Lenore made it through the portal and ended up back in Simon's workshop with Cole and Sophie. Simon's son piped up and said "hey guys, nice to meet you all. My name is Mason and I can do magic like my father. I couldn't help much while the magic ban was ongoing but I figured I could at least help you get home." He said quickly. Cole gripped his hand and said "thanks mate, you saved us all." Lenore came forward and said "thank you so much. Where's your dad?" Sophie butted her head against all three of them. "Wait, where's Jake?" Asked Cole. Lenore explained the story and Cole's face fell. He really was starting to care for Jake and didn't like that he didn't make it. Mason pointed with his finger across the room and Simon was overseeing James, Stacy, and Edward. Lenore ran up to him and exclaimed "Uncle Simon, I brought back the Darkwood. Can you use it to help my parents?" Simon turned towards her and embraced her. "Yes, my child, I can help you. Thank you, son for helping out Cole and Lenore," he said sincerely. Mason beamed and looked embarrassed at the praise but happy nonetheless.

Simon worked around the clock to make the cure out of the Darkwood herbs and help his friends. It took two weeks but the cure was finally finished. Simon wiped sweat from his brow and then injected the cure into James first, then Stacy, and finally Edward. After two minutes of waiting, they all finally woke up. James groggily woke up and said "hey Simon, what happened old friend?" Before James could ask anything, else Simon rushed forward and hugged him tight. "I missed you big brother. It's been thirteen long years man. I'm so glad you're back." Said Simon through tears. "Really, it's been that long? Wait, where's Lenore? Is she okay?" James asked frantically and began to look from left to right until Simon gently pushed him back down. "See for yourself," said Simon with a genuine smile on his face. James and Stacy looked where Simon was pointing and they saw Lenore standing nervously off to the side. "Hey mom, hey dad. I know you might not recognize me but I'm your daughter. I missed you guys so much." James uttered through tears "Lenore? You've grown up so much. And you're the one who saved us aren't you? I'm so proud of you." He said happily. Stacy covered her face with her hands as she tried to stop the tears coming from flowing but she was so happy to see her daughter. Lenore rushed over to them both and hugged them as tight as she could. Edward also got up and asked Lenore for everything that happened so he could alter the history books.

Lenore happily told them everything about what happened and they were so proud of her. Cole came over and gave her a hug as well and Sophie jumped up on James's lap and purred happily in his arms. James patted her as he listened to Lenore's tale. He then explained that after he had awoken from his trance in the cave Stacy and Edward had seen countless horrors and were infected with a similar virus that got to him. Being in that cave accelerated his illness much faster than intended and that was why everyone was injured by the time they got home. He was so grateful to Lenore and the others for saving them. He was also told about Jake and how he helped. James finally began to let go of his demons and was grateful to Jake for helping them. James decided to stop living in the past and focus on the future and be the best father and husband that he could be. If the world was ever in danger again then he would step up once again but was happy that the world had more heroes now.

Epilogue:

This is the end of the tale. Lenore, Mason, and Cole decided to train together in Schreiber before travelling the world. They wanted to see the world and explore everything that there was to offer. Lenore spent her time training with James and Stacy. James, Stacy, and Edward were officially cured of the virus that was infecting them and were healthy again. They could now live for as long as they wanted and would live long and meaningful lives. Lenore was happy spending her days with her parents and her friends. Sophie was also blessed by the town so she was immortal as well which made everyone happy. Edward was happy learning everything he could about Nocturnia and about lord Issac. Edward was happy rewriting the history books and Darwin had recovered from is psychological trauma and was back in action and better than ever. Everyone was living in peace and were genuinely optimistic about the future. Our heroes live on in peace and they agree to always remain close. I suppose there isn't much more to say so I shall end it with this. Going on a new journey can be hard or doing something new is difficult but it's important to move forward. Even if you misstep, that's okay. It's important to always try to move forward because that's the only way to achieve your goals and see what's behind that next door. There's always something new waiting for you behind that door.

Final Thoughts

Final Thoughts:

Hey everyone! It's the author again. I want to thank everyone for deciding to come on this journey with me. I hope this book finds you well and that you enjoyed this final volume of the Schreiber Chronicles series. I have some other works in progress and I'm excited to show you them all once they are finished. It may be quite a while before they come to fruition but I hope you'll be patient. Cheers everyone! I just wanted to clear up some things before I sign off. The way I wrote it was that Talia and the old ghost who lost his granddaughter are related. Talia is his granddaughter that managed to get away. As for Jeb's ending, when I was writing his perspective, I wanted to write him as a tragic figure who wanted to do good at the end of the way and wanted to make things right. That's why I decided to give him the ending he deserved with Jake at the very end even though I don't name names during that scene. I also wanted to give Jake another chance to shine by helping out the next generation of heroes. I hope you all enjoyed this collection as much as I enjoyed writing it.

Regardless, I feel proud of being able to finally publish this book in its entirety. For now, I must say that this is the end of the Schreiber Chronicles. For the time being I have other stories I'd love to write first so perhaps I will focus on those. These stories have been my labor of love that I have loved for the last fifteen or so years. My very first story with James and his friends was my first love for my stories and ending their stories in this way feels like the best way to move forward and say goodbye to them. I will still be around and writing for many years but I am taking a moment to breathe. I hope everyone who reads this has peace in their lives and is able to conquer any demons that are holding them back from unleashing their true potential. This is good bye for now but I wish you all well.

Talk to you later,

Cheers,

Ethan Spadoni

www.ingramcontent.com/pod-product-compliance
Lightning Source LLC
LaVergne TN
LVHW041051080826
845145LV00007B/1533

* 9 7 8 1 0 6 9 8 5 0 1 9 5 *